CITY OF ANGELS
CITY OF RAIN
BY
E.D. HAYMAKER

I WISH TO EXTEND SPECIAL THANKS TO ALL THOSE WHO READ THIS NOVEL IN PARTS AND PIECES, AND SAW ME THROUGH TO THE END.

FOR
STACY ANNE

GIVEN ENOUGH TIME,
AND LUCK
WE MIGHT COME
TO UNDERSTAND
HOW IT ALL BEGINS
AND HOW IT ALL ENDS.

PROLOGUE

THE PARTY!' That's how the women, more often than not, had referred to the unveiling of Martin Osborne Newton's latest gift to the City of Angels. *"I've just been out shopping for the party,"* they would say. *"You do know about the party, don't you? I received my invitation yesterday. You haven't? Well, don't worry darling, I'm sure yours will arrive tomorrow. Mine came by personal messenger. He was the cutest young man! He made me all liquid inside, if you know what I mean. He had these beautiful blue eyes and thick dark curls and pouty lips. My God! When he said my name, I almost fainted! And that was before he slipped the gold envelope into my hand. The party! I'm going to the party!"* On and on and on they would go.

The men had tended to react in one of three ways: the more confident had gazed smugly at the young man, knowing full well that their moment had arrived; the less confident had tensed at the shoulders and neck as if a cold chill had run through their loins; the truly frightened had turned a ghostly shade of gray while their eyes had defocused into that realm that filled with the nightmares of self-doubt and the longing to turn back and retrace their steps along the winding trail of time.

Simply by looking into their eyes, Albro Swift had sensed unerringly how each person had been about to react before he had handed over those envelopes.

CHAPTER 1

"IT was no party," Albro Swift spoke half out loud, as he watched orange flames curl around the dry branches piled in the campfire. His friend, Roger Ranger, sat next to him, but Albro had withdrawn so far that he might well have been speaking to himself in another place and time.

At least it was unlike any party he'd ever known, he started to say, but only mouthed the words, his lips trembling in the shifting firelight. His and Roger's lives had been short on parties.

He recalled how they had once stumbled into a party on a desolate stretch of beach somewhere along the coast of Baja California. How old had they been, fifteen, sixteen? They had been drawn to the light of a raging bonfire not by curiosity, but by outright starvation. They hadn't had a decent meal in nearly two weeks and had consumed the last of their water the day before. They had brought the leaking row boat in through the surf late in the day and they had approached the crowd not knowing what they were about to get themselves into. They only knew that that their stomachs were beyond empty and their tongues had begun to swell.

That scene slid into a vague memory of a birthday party. He must have been five. It was hardly a memory at all, only the shape of a cake with burning candles and the blurred faces of an old man and woman as if he were looking back in time through a cracked lens. Flames, was that what brought these memories back?

1

A party for him and Roger had meant splitting a pack of Twinkies and a carton of chocolate milk outside a 7-Eleven before thumbing a ride to the next town. A party had meant sitting at a table in a church basement with a plate of hot food at Christmas or maybe Thanksgiving, the smell of urine and dried vomit mixing with the steaming fragrance of turkey and gravy.

"It was no party," Albro said again, louder now, his eyes lighted by the flames, but still more to himself than to anyone else. "It was my one chance to change everything." And in fact, it had changed everything, but not in any way that he would have imagined even in his wildest dreams. "That night, I thought..." Albro started, and then let his voice trail off. What had he thought? Only a few weeks had passed and already he'd begun to think of that time as another life, a life that had been lived by another person. Who was that person? Even more puzzling, who was he now?

Albro Swift sat in silence and stared into the campfire. He struggled to pull the thick robe closer. The movement caused the wound between his shoulder blades to scream in pain and he felt an ooze of blood trickle down his back. His hand went automatically to his chest in search of the gold medallion, and then he remembered that it no longer hung there. He fought back the rising nausea, and sipped a muddy narcotic tea concocted of leaves and roots and strong enough to knock down a horse, but for him only dulled the brightest outlines of the pain. He forced his mind to think of something other than the gash that could have killed him if Roger hadn't been there, so he thought about the party. That party, that night, all seemed so long ago. Had it been only a few weeks, or had it been a few millennia? Time had become so twisted and folded in upon itself that the simple concept of a single day, not to mention whole weeks, seemed to no longer have any real meaning.

The fire had begun to burn low. Roger threw on another log, and a fountain of sparks rose into the sky. Albro watched them as they drifted higher and higher until each one became a star. "A star?" his lips mouthed in a silent whisper. Yes, he had been a star, a blazing star in that brightest of constellations where celebrities and millionaires and

2

politicians and gangsters all shine with a kind of glittering light that blinds them to any other reality, where dazzling women draped in diamonds and satin gowns and powerful men dressed in silk tuxedos engage one another in sexual combat with the merest of glances, where the weak are consumed by the fires of lust and avarice and are reduced to ashes, and where the strong grow ever brighter, ever more lustrous, in the way that angels grow ever more radiant as they gaze upon the face of God.

The party had been like a perfectly set stage, or a lavish and opulent scene from a movie. He had played the leading role in a 'rags to riches' drama in which the hero overcomes seemingly insurmountable odds to inherit a mountain of dough and marry the woman of his dreams. He hadn't had an inkling that just off stage fate had been laughing wildly, howling like a raving banshee at his gullibility. It would be easy to think of the whole event as having been an illusion had he not been so immersed within it. He had been an indivisible part of it. For without him, there would have been no reason for any of this to have happened.

Those invitations, he thought! How could he have been so stupid! Martin Osborne Newton had asked him to hand deliver each one of them, which meant that five hundred individuals had read his face, had taken the measure of his mind, had appraised his mettle. How could he have known the significance of that? He had trusted the man completely and had fallen head over heels in love with his daughter. At least, that was what a distant corner of his memory was telling him. Had it actually happened that way?

He stared into the flames and tried to remember. He could feel himself slipping back toward that remarkable night. He could feel himself sitting in that comfortable chair of hand-carved wood. He let his mind find its own way and he began to hear music that drifted down from somewhere overhead. Waiters appeared and disappeared in perfect harmony with the diners. Silverware clinked, glass tinkled, laughter flitted about the table no more obtrusive than a flutter of birds in a spring garden. His right hand rested on the smooth fabric of the tablecloth and he rolled the stem of a champagne flute between his thumb and fingers. His left hand rested on the thigh of the woman next to him. She had

3

shifted slightly to accommodate his touch as his fingers traveled slowly over the surface of her skin like explorers wandering aimlessly in a land of fabled treasures.

To his right sat an even more beautiful woman whose fingers traced random designs on the back of his hand, and who dipped her head toward his and whispered what she had planned for him when they next met.

Ah, but the real prize, Monique Olivia Newton, the daughter of the richest man in the world, the woman he had fallen deeply in love with and would soon be married to, sat directly across from him. So much had happened in such a short period of time that he was having trouble believing it was all true.

He closed his eyes and smiled and breathed in a mixed bouquet of exotic perfumes and the rich aromas of rare meats and expensive wines and held the air in his lungs, wanting to keep it there, to extract the wealth of fragrances and send them out to the extreme limits of his body. He began to muse to himself in a melancholy way, about how he had spent the better part of his life adrift, rather like a shipwrecked sailor struggling to survive on a raft in shark-infested waters, and how suddenly, when all hope had seemed lost, he had been tossed upon the shores of a paradise island.

He had deserved it, hadn't he? Hadn't he paid his dues in a hard-scrabble life in which bad luck and hard times had pursued him as unrelentingly as a pack of wild dogs pursues a wounded deer? Yes, he thought to himself, his luck had finally changed. To be sitting here, at this table, with these people, on this particular night was proof beyond a shadow of doubt that his life was on a new and glorious path. What had begun as a purely chance meeting, had blossomed into the equal of winning the lottery, discovering Aladdin's lamp, and being blessed with his own fairy godmother all rolled into one. And as if to banish the old adage that warned if things seemed too good to be true they probably weren't, he opened his eyes and exhaled slowly. It was all still there.

He sat midway along the length of a table that spanned nearly the whole extent of the great hall of the newly completed Martin Osborne

Newton Asian Art Museum (already referred to as the MONAAM). The floors appeared to float in concentric rings as they climbed one above the other, creating a vast space that seemed to suggest that Martin's Osborne Newton's influence might border on the infinite. One hundred feet to his left and one hundred feet to his right were seated the *chosen*, for every last one of them had been carefully and deliberately chosen, and no amount of begging, pleading, bribing or threatening would have made a whit of difference when it came down to whose name would appear on the gilt-edged invitations.

Albro Swift knew this for a fact, because he had been the one who had fielded the barrage of incoming requests for inclusion, and it was he, who had in most cases, delivered the truly sympathetic but firm reply of, 'I am so sorry.' Only those women of such heartbreaking beauty who had persisted, who had appealed to him in person, who had offered all that they could in exchange for a mere consideration to be included in what everyone knew to be the most important cultural event in the City of Angels' long and albeit sordid history, did Albro Swift extend a personal apology for circumstances beyond his control. In those few, but extraordinary cases, he had arranged a subsequent meeting at one of the luxurious hotels down on Wilshire and always ordered in advance fresh flowers and chilled champagne.

Women who wanted something badly, Albro Swift believed, always made the most fervent lovers. And although there was nothing he could do to get them an invitation, he at least left them feeling that they had done everything they possibly could.

For those who had been granted an invitation, it was like receiving a guaranteed place in heaven (or hell, depending on Newton's plans), no matter the extent of past or future good works (or sins), because each name had been personally chosen by Martin Osborne Newton himself, who now sat directly across from Albro Swift. (Newton had been declared by People magazine as having the most recognizable visage in the world.) One might have thought the place of importance would have been at either end of the span, but no, Martin Osborne Newton was at the center of his realm and defined its gravitational center in the way that a galaxy defines its center by drawing in stars to form its central bulge.

In contrast, Doctor Felix Krupp, the museum's curator, a thin and wrinkled old man with a pronounced hump between his shoulder blades that forced his neck forward so that his face was always tilted upwards as if in eternal supplication, sat at one end of the table, nearly hidden in the shadow of the floors above. Krupp had insisted on giving Albro a guided tour of the exhibit just the night before when he'd had countless things to attend to in preparation for this event. It had been well past eleven when Krupp had shown up unannounced at his office just as Albro had been about to leave.

He had been the only one remaining on the darkened floor and was startled by the sudden appearance of the odd looking man who wore a dark overcoat buttoned to the neck and a black wide-brimmed hat pulled down across his forehead which made it difficult, if not impossible, to see the man's eyes.

At first he mistook Krupp for a derelict who had somehow made it past the security guards, and he was about to pick up the phone and alert them when the little man doubled over in a spasm of coughing. His whole body shook and rattled as he staggered blindly into the wall. Albro Swift caught him by his bony shoulders and held him up. Eventually Krupp cleared his throat with a wet and rasping groan, and deposited a gobbet of yellowish phlegm on a discolored rag he'd pulled from his pocket, and wiped his thin, purplish lips. He then removed his hat and in a high-pitched voice said, "My name is Doctor Felix Krupp. I thought you might like to see *my* museum before the hordes begin their invasion. I have a car waiting in the street."

Albro Swift looked down into the upturned face that rose no higher than the middle of his chest. The eyes were a watery pale green and his nose was long and hooked downward, with a gray pearl of snot hanging from its pointy end. Dark tufts of hair poked from each nostril as well as from both ears. The few strands of hair that still sprouted from his spotted scalp were plastered in place by a greasy film of sweat. Albro looked beyond Krupp down the dimly lit and empty hallway. Usually

6

anyone connected with Martin Osborne Newton had a least one escort and sometimes half a dozen who most often posed as associates, but it was common knowledge they were highly trained bodyguards. Here was this gnome of a man completely alone. That fact by itself gave Albro an uneasy feeling. The man's accent bothered him as well; vaguely German, vaguely Russian, but something else was in there, far back in the throat, a guttural, almost gagging reflex that seem to catch at every other word. In addition, Albro had caught Krupp's use of the word 'my' in regards to the museum. Perhaps, it was fair for him to feel it was his creation. After all, Krupp was the curator. Nevertheless it caused a slight stirring in the hairs on the back of his neck, and a tingling of the skin of his chest where a small gold coin, his good luck charm, rested.

Albro was sure that anything Doctor Felix Krupp had to show him was all very interesting, but he'd seen most of it, and had even procured some of the pieces. Admittedly though, what irked him most was the prospect of missing the card game that he was due to attend in little more than an hour. He'd been having a fantastic run of luck lately and had been making steady progress paying down his gambling debts. On the other hand, there was no indication his run of luck was anywhere near its end and there would be ample opportunity in the coming weeks to get well ahead. Besides, it wouldn't hurt to have a preview of what was in store for the deniens of the great city by the sea.

Once they reached the street level, Krupp motioned Albro Swift toward the long, dark vehicle parked at the curb. The walkway was deserted, but the boulevard was clogged with traffic. He had not yet lived in the city long enough to become totally accustomed to the fact that nobody walked unless it was an absolute necessity.

The driver, a burly eastern European type with a shaved head and hairy hands stood next to the open door of the limo. When Albro stooped to enter, he felt a hand on his back, a not so subtle reminder as to who was in charge. As he settled into the back of Krupp's car, the sense of unease that had prickled the hairs on the back of his neck, began traveling down the length of his spine and came to rest in the sensitive flesh of his loins. It was the same uneasy feeling that he sometimes felt at the card table when he would notice that something had changed, and he would look around at the faces and try to determine whose breathing had abruptly changed, or whose heart had skipped a beat, or whose sweat had taken on a hint of sourness. He'd learned long ago that drawing the right cards was only a small, although important part, of winning. Just as important was being aware of the other players' habits and behaviors. Even on nights when luck treated him as petulantly as a jealous lover might, he could manage to come out ahead if he could focus his senses and maintain a high level of concentration.

Only at those rare times in which luck abandoned him completely and his senses provided an unending flow of false readings would he begin a slow and inexorable losing streak, and like a man who suddenly finds that he has stepped into quicksand, the harder he struggled, the faster he would sink. It would seem to make perfect sense that at first hint of his changing luck, he would simply walk away from the table, his pride a bit tarnished, but with his bankroll still intact, to admit that well, yes, he was a bit tired and maybe a little rest would do him good, to profess his shortcomings to the circle of players and withdraw. But to do so, would have at least one immediate effect. He would lose his seat and would have to wait for someone else to give up a place, which may only take a matter of hours, or it could be days, or even weeks, and he would be forced to bide his time at lower stakes tables in other, more dangerous places in the city. He wouldn't even consider on-line poker, which in his mind amounted to no more than a parlor game for punters. He might as well slouch down to the local senior center for an afternoon of bingo with the wrinkled widows and pasty old gents. Even worse than this prospect, however, was the loss of face that would inevitably occur in the presence of some of the most powerful and wealthy individuals he would ever likely encounter. He had worked hard to get where he was and he knew that no matter how skillfully he might play, his place at the table could only be held by the force of his daring confidence. He thought of himself as a Player amongst Players. As a Player, he was accepted as a worthy opponent. The amount of money involved didn't matter to a Player. Ten thousand dollars more or less for a few hours of play wouldn't cause a

Player to blink an eye. It was the winning and the losing that mattered. Albro Swift cared not to give up his place at a Player's table until he had exhausted all of his resources, which he had come perilously close to doing only months before.

The driver pulled away from the curb and maneuvered the big car into the flow of traffic, glided through the green lights of two intersections and then swung west onto the wide arching roadway that rose above the maze of streets and swept in a great curve through the center of the city. They left the inner sanctum of skyscrapers and drove through mile after mile of densely packed sub-divisions that squatted in a false sense of security behind low concrete block walls. The highway passed factories and foundries and assembly plants arranged like boxes on a grid that spread north and south and dissolved into a yellowish glow. The whole mess spread a hundred miles to the north and south and a hundred miles east until it finally ran out of sustenance at the edge of the desert.

The freeway hooked to the south, but before that they dropped off and turned onto the coast road. Albro caught glimpses of the surf lit by the powerful nightlights of the beach-front residents, who like their urban cohorts, seemed fearful of anything that suggested darkness. The driver continued north for a few miles and then turned onto a newly completed road that carried them in broad and sweeping curves up into the hills. Streetlights marked side roads where grand residences sat behind screens of pine and oak, protected by high walls of iron and stone and electronic monitors. As they climbed, the estates became fewer and larger and less visible until finally any sign of habitation was completely hidden from view and they drove on in complete darkness save for the blue-white glare of the car's headlamps slicing into the blackness ahead. At last, they rounded a steep curve onto the summit where the museum stood like a ten-story glass and steel monolith lighted from within by a pale green light. As if by prearranged instruction, the driver slowed. He made a complete circuit of the building, while Krupp, with his face pressed against the glass, stared in complete rapture at the glowing sight.

Albro Swift was surprised by his own reaction, for he too found himself in a kind of rapturous trance, captured by the eerie sense that he was witnessing an apparition of gigantic proportions. Beyond them to the south a sea of sparkling lights filled a basin rimmed by the blackness of the actual ocean. It was as if a monstrous net had been spread and it was slowly closing upon a vast school of tiny fish, which were just beginning to sense the danger and were lighting up in a luminescence of fear.

The site appeared to be completely deserted, although he assumed guards stood just out of sight within the shadows of the trees at the perimeter of the cleared area. As the car came back around to the entrance, Krupp rapped his knuckles on the glass partition and the driver brought the limo to a halt precisely in line with the main doorways, got out, and opened Krupp's door.

Krupp leaned toward Albro Swift and said, "Tomorrow at this time there will be more than a thousand individuals inside these walls. Most will have no interest whatsoever in what this building contains. As I am sure you are aware, they will be in attendance to satisfy their prurient desires and to further their own petty self-interests. What they and the twenty million inhabitants of this city do not realize," he uttered in a tone of absolute distaste, and then paused, as if to distance him from those millions. "What they do not realize," he repeated, biting off each word as it left his lips, "is that the world they see and touch and hear and smell is only a small fragment of what truly exists. The proof of that is held within these walls."

Krupp turned abruptly and scooted out of the car. Albro Swift sat, puzzled by what Krupp had just said. Had it simply been the rant of someone who spent far too little time in the sunlight or had Krupp lobbed some message to him that he'd failed to catch? He looked up to see the driver showing yellowed teeth in a twisted smile and offering him his hand.

For the next four hours, starting in the grand entrance hall and ending on the uppermost level, Albro followed the hobbling figure of Doctor Felix Krupp and listened, between fits of coughing in which it seemed he was attempting to bring up the lining of his lungs, as the curator described in minute detail the significance of the collected pieces. Sometime around 4 a.m. Krupp motioned him into an elevator and they descended into the bowels of the structure. He followed Krupp through a maze of corridors until they ended at what appeared to be a blank wall. Krupp produced a keypad from his pocket and punched in a code. The wall parted down a seam that Albro hadn't noticed. They walked to another doorway where Krupp stopped and fussed with the collar of his shirt. He pulled a long, cylindrical key that had no teeth and was attached to a silver chain. Krupp inserted the key into small a hole above the door's handle and twisted it. The door opened outward with an audible wheeze of air and they entered a darkened room with just enough light to reveal the shape of a tall glass case. There was no telling how big the room really was. It felt a bit like being in a cave where all sense of proportion becomes lost in the surrounding darkness. There was just enough light entering from the adjoining room to reveal that the case was empty. Krupp closed the door and the room was plunged into absolute blackness.

By now, Albro Swift had had about all the carved jade, painted vases and terracotta warriors he could handle for one night. In addition, there had been one whole level of primitive art, and not the kind of scary masks and such that came out of Africa. These items had come out of the vastness of China and the great sub-continent to the south and were depictions of humans in every animal form imaginable. Primitive art had never done much for Albro. In fact, it tended to give him the creeps. He'd take a Monet or a Renoir any day. Yeah, yeah, he knew those people had some kind of connection with the natural world that modern man had exchanged for electric lights and indoor plumbing. All in all, though, it seemed like a good trade.

Not that the experience of seeing the museum in its entirety hadn't been valuable. He'd soaked up more than just a few facts which he could put to good use the following night when the place would exhibit no shortage of beautiful women to impress, but he was looking forward to a few hours sleep before starting what was going to be a very long and busy day. He was getting concerned about the time and was about to say as

11

much, when he heard Krupp's fingers scratching at the wall. Albro heard the snick of a switch, and suddenly multi-colored beams of light issued from the upper corners of the cabinet and converged to form a figure of amazing reality within the glass walls of the cabinet.

It was as if a creature of his worst nightmare had jumped out of the shadows. Had Albro not been somewhat prepared, having just viewed a whole menagerie of imaginary creatures, he might have run. As it was, he flinched and took a few steps backward just to put some distance between himself and the creature behind the glass. Like the others he had seen earlier, it was a least partly human. It was about his height and it had feet and legs and arms and hands, a torso with a head, but that's where the resemblance ended. It was heavily muscled, not the bubble-like muscles you see popping out of bodybuilders. These muscles were long and sinewy, more like steel cables banded together and covered by a sheath of skin. The toes and fingers ended in claws that curved slightly inwards and appeared to have a razor thin edge on the inner curve. It was male, and the sculptor had not stinted on that part of the anatomy either. Above all else, it had been the face that held Albro's attention. The eyes were large and cat-like in their shape; the forehead slanted back, the nose flattened, with its nostrils elongated. Deep shadows pooled below sharply angled cheek bones. The lips curled slightly under and the jaws parted just enough to reveal immense fangs. The figure's hair was pulled tightly and knotted at the back of the head. A long braid hung down its back.

Albro guessed that he was looking at a hologram, but this was no ordinary image. A whole slew of Martin Osborne Newton's electronic wizards must have refined the technology down to the point where imagery crossed into reality. Except for a slight shimmer when he shifted his gaze, the image looked as solid as anything he'd seen upstairs.

But the thing that made the figure with all its intricate details even more amazing was that it appeared to have been carved from a single massive slab of pale, flesh-colored stone. Was it jade? The light made what appeared to be stone glow from within, and for a moment, Albro had the uncanny feeling that he was looking at a living being that had been turned to stone. He walked around the case several times looking at it from all angles. As extraordinary as the workmanship was, the melding of the human and animal features were repellant. He looked at Krupp who stared back at him with a look of cold appraisal. He realized that Krupp had been studying his reaction to the image in the glass case. He suddenly knew that this was the purpose of their outing, the thing that Krupp had wanted to show him. The rest of the museum was window dressing for the dim witted public. This was Krupp's real prize. As to why Krupp wanted him to see it, he had no idea.

"Do you know what you are looking at?" Krupp asked.

He thought about Krupp's question. Of course, his first question was where Krupp had stashed the real object. He knew a thing or two about Asian antiquities, mostly from the standpoint of their value on the black market and what it would cost to transport an item from point A to point B which not only included the initial price but all of the bribes that would be required. Trying to move artifacts was always a tricky business and often dangerous. He'd once come perilously close to winding up in a Myanmar jail. As for the academic side of things, he'd never had much time, or inclination, to devote himself to any kind of formal study.

Again, Albro slowly walked around the case. As he moved, the image seemed to shift ever so slightly. He decided that was a trick of the lighting. Yet, when he stood perfectly still he almost sensed that the object was anticipating what he might do next.

One thing he knew with a certainty he felt deep within his bones was that it was something special. Was it old? He hadn't been able to tell. It seemed too pristine. He'd not seen a chip, or scratch anywhere on its smooth surface. Was the image a true representation of the object, or had it been altered, Photo-Shopped in some way, like they always did to those models in magazines to make them look flawless? Anything seemingly perfect always made him suspicious. Whatever its age, whoever had carved the original was a true master. He said, "It looks to me like someone's worst nightmare."

Krupp didn't smile. "I'm sure you noticed the claws. Imagine each one is as sharp as a honed razor. The structure of the muscles suggests immense strength. See how the line of the jaw drops slightly away from the mouth? And the bulge where the muscles attach the jaw to the lower half of the skull? That would allow the jaws to open sufficiently wide to allow the fangs to grasp a large amount of flesh and close with bone-crushing force. The size of the eyes makes me think this creature hunted at night, or perhaps during twilight. Imagine, a pack of these creatures stalking their prey, slowly encircling it and then charging in for the kill. If you were the prey, Mr. Swift, it would be your worst nightmare. But it would be over in a matter of seconds."

Krupp made it sound as if the image within the glass case had actually existed as a living creature. The thing was so lifelike that Albro supposed if you looked at it long enough you might begin to believe that it had lurked somewhere in the ancient past. Maybe there had been a creature which had sprouted on some evolutionary branch. Perhaps its image had become locked in the chemical matrix of one of our tree climbing ancestors. Fortunately for humans, that particular branch had withered ages ago. But if this was the point of dragging him all the way out here, so what? His growing consternation must have shown on his face.

There was a discernible note of irritation in Krupp's voice when he asked, "Mr. Swift, you have not asked me about the braid that hangs down its back. Considering the brutal nature of the figure, it is curious, don't you agree?"

Albro looked at it again. Krupp was absolutely right. The creature was the personification of brutality. Everything about the figure suggested a depiction of unbridled savagery except for the braided hair, which struck him as odd. It reminded him of how Chinese warriors tied their hair. Its length was supposed to be some kind of indication of the warrior's strength. It was as if the artist had become frightened by his own creation and had attempted to tame it with a gesture of human vanity. For a moment Albro was seduced into believing that perhaps he was not looking at a wild beast, but rather the beastly nature of man. Then he caught himself. The thing was pure evil.

"I'm assuming this image is a reproduction of a genuine sculpture," he said to Krupp. Why else would Krupp go to all the bother? "So where's the 'Real McCoy'?"

"You assume correctly, Mr. Swift," Krupp said, "and that is a very good question. Before I answer it, I want to beg your indulgence for a few moments longer. For you to understand the significance of what you are seeing, I must tell you a story. How much do you know about the Mongol invasion of China?"

"I know a little." Albro answered. He had tried to make the most of his intermittent attendance in the public school system, but to say that he was a scholar of any stripe would have been a stretch well beyond the elasticity of truth. It wasn't that he'd been a slow learner; just the opposite was true. The real problem had been a lack of continuity. He'd spent a good deal more time either on the road or locked up in juvenile detention. But wherever he'd been, he'd always been drawn to books, which was where his real education had come from. Public libraries had often provided a warm a dry place to while away an afternoon reading Zane Grey westerns. The JD Halls always had a meager collection of books, mostly crap novels that even the thrift-stores couldn't sell. But sometimes a real treasure poked out from a sagging shelf: a Dickens, a Conrad, or better yet, a John D. MacDonald. And he would read it front to back over and over, squeezing every last nuance from its pages until he'd done his time and was booted back out onto the street.

He said to Krupp, "The Mongol Empire ran roughly from the 13th through the 14th centuries and was the largest empire in the history of the world." Where he'd picked up that scrap of knowledge, he couldn't say. It might even have come from the back of a cereal box.

A faint smile crossed Krupp's lips. "Very good," he said. "How, in your opinion, did they accomplish that?"

Albro thought for a moment. "I'd have to say it was their leaders. Starting with Genghis Khan, they were smart, ruthless and never took 'no' for an answer."

Krupp nodded in agreement, obviously pleased with Albro's response. "If you were a royal prince locked behind your city walls, and a

15

Mongol warlord with ten thousand troops demanded your surrender, what would you have done?"

Albro wondered where Krupp was taking this. He was more than ready to get to his apartment and crawl into bed. Nevertheless, he considered Krupp's question. There was no real answer. It wouldn't have mattered what the prince would have done. The prince's fate and the fate of everyone else within the city walls had already been determined. "I would have prepared myself for death."

"Exactly," Krupp said, obviously pleased with Albro' answer. "But what if someone had told you that you need not die, that you could save your city and all its inhabitants?"

"How could anyone stand up to the Mongols?" Albro asked.

"By being transformed," Krupp uttered, spreading his hands as if revealing the most wondrous event since the Resurrection.

"Into what," Albro asked.

Krupp turned and pointed to the figure within the glass case. "*The Jade Prince*," he said.

Those three words were the last thing Albro had expected to hear, and they rocked him backwards. In a place and time long past, those three words had resided in his thoughts like a thorn lodged in the palm of his hand. Those three meaningless words scrawled on a scrap of rough paper and left by whomever had abandoned him as an infant, had tormented him day and night until like the paper itself, they had become brittle and faded but still resided in a dark corner of his memory. How could Krupp know about his past? It had to be a coincidence, yet he couldn't quite bring himself to believe that it was. He listened with a renewed sense of attention as Krupp spoke.

The story that Krupp went on to tell could have been plucked from any number of ancient texts. Albro knew about recurring themes in myths and legends, the origins of which had become lost in the depths of time. He'd heard those themes time and again from Homer to Virgil to Lao Tzu, to the Brothers Grimm, to Tolkien. You could go on and on. In this particular case, a Chinese prince rules an opulent city which has been carved from a mountain of jade. Its inhabitants live in regal splendor.

They're undoubtedly the envy of everyone else and eventually the inevitable happens. Mongols get wind of the wealth that lies therein and lay siege to the city. The prince, having foolishly gone into battle is captured. The leader of the attacking army informs the prince that he will be tortured unless he orders his city to surrender. He refuses. For several days, his cries of agony are heard behind the walls of the city. The inhabitants huddle in terror, but their prince had told them that under no circumstances were they to surrender. Amongst the citizens is an alchemist who declares that he can save the prince and the city, but in order to do so, he requires the blood of a tiger. It just so happens, the prince keeps a pet tiger. The animal is sacrificed, and the alchemist mixes secret ingredients with the tiger's blood. Dressed as a monk, he carries a vial of the mixture into the enemy camp where guards seize him and drag him before their leader. The prince is there and obviously close to death. The alchemist convinces the Mongol leader that he can revive the prince, asserting that another hour of his cries will cause his followers to give up. The Mongol leader, knowing how tedious a siege tends to become, agrees to the alchemist's offer. After all, what does he have to lose? If the prince dies, he'll simply lop the head from the alchemist and get on with business. The Mongol leader, along with his most fierce warriors gather into a tight circle as the alchemist administers the tiger's blood to the dying prince.

In the meantime, the inhabitants of the city are certain that dawn will bring their deaths. They wait in desperate fear that this dawn will be their last. Then, from out of the black of night, come the terrible roar of a tiger and the screams of dying men. When at last the sun rises, the view across the plain surrounding the city is one of total annihilation. The Mongol army has been torn to pieces. Naturally, the prince and the alchemist are nowhere to be found. And, naturally enough, word soon begins to spread of a warrior with the face of a tiger who roams the countryside saving villages from all sorts of bad guys. The Mongol empire falters and then etcetera, etcetera, etcetera.

True to form in this kind of scenario, the hero has been given the gift of immortality and becomes known as the *Jade Prince*. He becomes a

17

kind of Chinese super-hero who by day walks as a man and by night takes on the form of a tiger. Along with his sidekick, the alchemist, they perform countless good deeds for the poor. This goes on until he meets a beautiful woman, (surprise, surprise), whom he falls deeply in love with. Unfortunately, she is the daughter of the evil emperor, who knows an opportunity when he sees one. He will allow their marriage only if the *Jade Prince* agrees to join the emperor in his plan to conquer the world. Of course, he refuses. The *Jade Prince* along with the alchemist, grab the princess and race across China, pursued by the emperor's massive army. Eventually they are cornered in the *Jade Prince's* mountain hideout. The emperor demands his surrender. If he does not, the princess will most certainly die in the ensuing battle. To make a long story short, the *Jade Prince* agrees to give himself up. When the emperor enters the mountain enclave he finds that he has been tricked. The Jade Prince has been turned to stone. His daughter and the alchemist are nowhere to be found. Presumably, they have disappeared into the cavernous depths of the mountain. The evil emperor, though, is determined to have the last laugh. He orders the stone statue to be destroyed. But just then, a massive earthquake occurs. When the dust settles, not a trace remains of the emperor and his army. Even the mountain itself is unrecognizable. The *Jade Prince* is but a memory.

Which just goes to show you, Albro thought, what falling in love can do to the unwary. Albro smiled at Krupp.

Krupp pursed his purple lips and glared at him. "You don't believe a word I have said, do you."

Albro stifled a yawn. For a moment there he'd actually thought that Krupp might shed some light on one of the little mysteries of his past. "Nice story," he said. And then and not caring to hide the disappointment in his voice, added, "I've heard it all before. Maybe not this variation, but you know what I mean. It makes for a great fantasy, but..."

"It is not a fantasy!" Krupp burst out. "You know nothing. You don't know how long I searched for the *Jade Prince*, what sacrifices I made, how I suffered." He balled up his little fists and shook them in

Albro's face "I share this with you, and you accuse me of believing in a fantasy!"

Krupp's face turned an alarming shade of dark red, his eyes bulged and he lurched forward on his stubby legs. He would have fallen flat on his face had not Albro caught him.

"Take it easy. I didn't mean anything by that. Hey, it's a great looking piece of art. People are going to love it. You have every right to be proud. Too bad it's just a hologram." To soften the obvious blow Albro had delivered to the little man he said," You were going to tell me about the actual piece."

Krupp, who had gathered his strength for another tirade, looked as if he'd been doused with a bucket of ice-water. His eyes became slits.

Albro said. "To make a hologram you need photographs. At least that's how they did it in the old days. I suppose it could now be done with some sort of scanner and computers, but the image looks too real even for digital animation."

Albro realized that he was starting to think of the image as a real object. How had that happened? One minute he knows it's a fantasy and the next he's thinking it really exists. He told himself to slow down. He hadn't given the object's authenticity any real thought. And anyway, what did 'authentic' really mean in this case? That the myth of the *Jade Prince* was somehow true and his calcified remains lay hidden under a billion tons of stone? But there was something more to the image in the glass case than a mere stone sculpture. There was an immediacy to it that did not come from creating a three dimensional object from drawings or photographs or even one's imagination. One need only stand before Michael Angelo's works to understand that true art flows from living flesh. He looked closely at the image. He wasn't ready to start believing Krupp's fairy tale, but he was beginning to feel a tingle of possibilities. He said to Krupp," My guess is that someone was pretty close to a similar sculpture at one time

"Yes, very close indeed," Krupp said with more than just a little anger in his voice.

"So What happened?"

19

"Lost!" Krupp hissed the single syllable.

Ah, Albro thought, it's always the big one that gets away. It wasn't surprising. Antiquities dealers would steal from their own grandmothers. He suppressed another yawn. "There's no need to get all worked up. Something like that is eventually going to turn up, and when it does, Newton can buy it for his collection."

At that instant, Krupp took on the appearance of a rabbit who suddenly finds himself on open ground with no burrow to scamper into. He struggled, unable to decide what to say. Finally he said, "This is not just a piece of art. This is the *Jade Prince I'm talking about!*"

Albro had been ready to agree to anything just so he could get out of there, when something in Krupp's eyes stopped him. He felt an odd tugging on a string that was tied to his past. Could there be something in this? "What do you mean?" he asked.

"*I mean exactly what I said! I am referring to the Jade Prince, once living flesh, now stone!*" Krupp emphasized each word as if he were speaking to a stubborn child.

"You can't be serious," Albro said.

"Believe me, Mr. Swift. I am very serious. I have never been more serious about anything in my entire life. Now do you realize why I have brought you here? Why I need your help? Why *you* need *my* help?"

Albro looked at Krupp and then at the image that stood serenely in its case. *The Jade Prince,* those three words from out of his past, had taken on the monstrous form before him. Was this what that long ago message had meant? No, it had to be a coincidence. In an infinite universe, coincidences happened all the time. One simply wasn't sufficiently aware to recognize them for what they were. Albro knew that the human mind will knock itself out making connections where none exist, more often than not to simply bring a bit of peace and quiet to the noisy chaos of life.

He studied the monster's face. Had he missed something at first glance? Were there lines of familiarity below the eyes, around the mouth? Krupp had made a connection to him and this object. What did *he* have to do with this thing behind the glass? Why did he need Krupp's help? Either Krupp was totally crackers, or something weird was going on here, but he had to admit that he still didn't have clue as to what Krupp wanted. Whatever it was it had definitely worked the little gnome into a state.

"You were going to tell me how you acquired this," Albro reminded him.

Krupp hesitated before answering. He seemed at odds with the implications of giving up that information, while at the same time fearing that he'd made a blunder by offering it in the first place. "I found it in a Buddhist temple in a nearly inaccessible region of Tibet."

Albro had never heard of anything remotely like this turning up in Tibet. He asked Krupp, "How did the monks happen to have it?"

"They were excavating to enlarge a dormitory. They came upon a sealed chamber. The walls were covered in beautiful paintings that depicted the life of the *Jade Prince* and his beloved princess."

That was plausible enough, Albro had thought. All great finds, it seemed, were the result of pure accident. But that had raised another question. He asked, "And you, Krupp, how did you find out about it?"

"I have contacts," Krupp said vaguely and left it at that.

"In Tibet," Albro said, somewhat surprised. The Chinese had pretty tight control of the country.

"I have contacts all over the world, and yes, I have contacts in Tibet," Krupp said in an irritable tone as if Albro had questioned his status as a world-known scientist. And then as if realizing how querulous he had sounded he softened his tone. "I had long been interested in the area. There is evidence of villages having been buried by massive earthquakes of armies having been destroyed. It is an area known for its labyrinth of caves."

"So you think this is where the *Jade Prince* was cornered?"

"I don't think that, Mr. Swift, I know that for a fact," Krupp stated firmly.

Albro had sighed inwardly. 'Facts' were about as substantial as smoke rings. He asked, "When did all this happen? And how did you get in and out of the country? You can push around the Tibetans, but I doubt

21

the Chinese would let you cart off anything without a fuss. It's hard to keep a discovery like this secret. Word always gets out."

"I made the discovery less than a year ago," Krupp said. "I tried to convince the monks to remove the statue to a safe place in Lhasa. Their monastery was in terrible disrepair. It could have crumbled at any moment and damage to the sculpture would have been an unimaginable loss. They refused to allow me to move it. As it turned out, my concerns were prescient. There was a horrible earthquake. The temple and all of those within were buried in a landslide. Fortunately I was in Lhasa at the time."

"I see," Albro said, "just like in the story." His remark may have been flippant, but his mind started working fast. Sure, Tibet was earthquake prone. The Indian sub-continent was still muscling its way into the heart of Asia and was forcing the Himalayas ever higher, but what were the odds of an earthquake occurring? Maybe not all that long, he'd decided. But what were the odds of an earthquake at just the right moment? It wasn't likely unless someone had planned one. With anything this valuable there were always competing interests. If anyone had wanted to stop Krupp, explosives could have the same effect as an earthquake. Snatch the dingus and then destroy the monastery and all of its occupants. Treasure hunters have few scruples when it comes to human life.

"No, you do not see," Krupp paused, wringing his hands before going on. "The Chinese intervened. I could not return to the site, but I had reliable informants. They told me an army of workers dug through the rubble. It took weeks. There were many bodies. No one in the temple survived."

"What about your statue?" Albro asked.

"Nowhere to be found, not even a shard," Krupp said. "Fortunately, the monks had allowed me to take measurements and photographs. This image is beautiful, but it pales in comparison to the real *Jade Prince*. And now I need your help to recover it."

"I'm flattered, Krupp, but I think this is way out of my league. If the Chinese government is involved you can forget about recovering your statue."

"But they did not find it. It was gone. There is something more," Krupp said and then lowered his voice to a whisper. "She was seen."

"Who was seen?" Albro asked.

"The princess, she was seen in the village!" Krupp uttered, failing to hold back the exasperation in his voice.

"C'mon, Krupp, that was a long time ago. Maybe she did get away, but you know how these legends take on a life of their own. People hate to see a story end."

"No, no, no, you don't understand!" Krupp pulled at his stringy hair and paced back and forth. "I'm not talking about then, I'm talking about now! The princess was seen just weeks before I arrived. I heard it from the villagers. The monks refused to answer my questions about her. I persisted and finally one individual told me that she had come to the monastery, and she was recognized from the paintings in the chamber. Of course, I didn't believe it then. What a fool I was!" Krupp paused and looked around as if the walls might have ears. He lowered his voice. "But then, after the earthquake, when the Chinese excavated the site, do you know what they found?"

"Do you want me to guess?" Albro asked. He'd really just about had enough of this. He was again falling asleep on his feet. If Krupp didn't get to the point soon, he'd have to call time.

Not waiting for Albro, Krupp whispered, "*The Chinese found a tunnel!*"

The pieces of Krupp's puzzle were finally starting to fall into place. Albro said, "So you're telling me, the princess scouted out the monastery and then hung around until the opportune moment arrived and then snatched the statue."

"Yes! She came back for him!" Krupp said emphatically.

"He *Jade Prince*," Albro said.

"Yes."

23

"Let me get this straight," Albro said. "The princes tucked a 600lb chunk of stone under one arm and disappeared down a tunnel. That's why the Chinese authorities didn't find the statue, and that's why all you've got is this hologram."

"Yes, yes, yes!" Krupp exclaimed as if it were all as plain as the hooked nose on his face.

"I suppose the next thing you're going to tell me is that the two of them were seen leaving town on a bus."

Krupp stood stock still. "How did you know that?"

Albro opened his mouth and realizing that he was at a loss for words, closed it. He stared at Krupp. It was clear the guy was nuts. He thought of asking Krupp where the princess had been for the last seven hundred years, but decided he'd had enough. He started to speak, but Krupp stopped him.

"Don't you see? She brought him back to life!" Krupp shouted at him. His eyes were blazing and a dribble of foam was coursing down his chin.

Albro tried rubbing the sleep out of his eyes. This was getting out hand, and he had to do something to end it. "Look," he said. "I would like to help you, but this really isn't my area of expertise. I'm really not the man you need." He'd thought of adding that what the Doctor really needed was a good psychiatrist.

Krupp went to the base of the glass case and pushed a button. The four glass sides of the case slid silently into a recess in the base of the cabinet. The image seemed to take on a new intensity. Krupp looked at him quizzically. "Do you feel anything?"

As a matter of fact, he did. He felt a slight buzzing that began under the good luck charm that hung around his neck and rose in a warm glow up his spine and settled between his ears. He blinked.

"Step closer," Krupp said.

Albro took a step. The buzzing spread down his back. The feeling was pleasant, like a gentle massage. It made him think of being on a beach in Thailand with one of those cute young girls with her sarong and bottle of oil.

24

"Closer," Krupp intoned.

Albro took another step. He came as close to the image as he could get without interfering with the light beams. The buzzing, still barely perceptible moved out into his arms and legs. The effect was mildly hypnotic and he wondered what Krupp was doing to create it. It made him almost giddy. He grinned and started to turn toward Krupp but then he'd realized that he couldn't take his eyes off the image. He stood there all abuzz with a silly grin on his face.

"Would you like to reach out and touch it?" Krupp asked softly.

That was exactly what he wanted to do. He hadn't realized it until Krupp had said it, but it was true, he wanted to do that more than anything else in the world.

"Go ahead, touch it," Krupp said.

Albro raised his hand. He fully expected his hand to pass through the image, but it stopped. The image had suddenly become solid, but not solid like stone, it had the warmth and suppleness of flesh. He pulled back suddenly, as if he'd received an electric shock.

Out of the corner of his eye he saw Krupp push the button and the glass walls ascended, the light beams flickered out and the image disappeared. He put his hand to his good luck charm and abruptly, the buzzing stopped. A shiver ran through his body and he shook himself.

"How do you feel?" Krupp asked.

Albro didn't know how he felt. One instant he had been immersed in a sense of euphoria and then it was as if his mind had played cruel joke on him. "What did you do?"

"It was not I," Krupp said. "It was the *Jade Prince*. To put it simply, the two of you are compatible."

"Come again?" Albro asked. The euphoria had already begun to dissipate. He began to feel a slight let down, a growing hollowness. He wouldn't have minded another hit of whatever Krupp had given him, but then he came to grips with that thought and suddenly became suspicious. Had Krupp slipped him something? It had felt good. No, it had felt better than good. It had felt dangerously good. He'd seen opium users laid out with that glazed look in their eyes, and cocaine addicts ablaze with

25

incredible highs. Once any of them started down that otherworldly road, few of them ever found their way home.

"What I mean to say," Krupp said carefully, "is that you have the right temperament. I have been searching for that person, and now I have found you. You will be my assistant and together we will find the Jade Prince."

"You want me to be your assistant?" Albro asked. That was the last thing he wanted to consider, but he'd a feeling that his gig with Newton was about over. After the flurry of activity over the invitations had ended, there really hadn't been much to do. Nobody in the vast array of offices surrounding his own seemed to know what to do with him. His calls to the HR department had gone unanswered, so he'd fiddled away his time doing crosswords and reading cheap crime novels. His paycheck rested in the center of his desk every Friday morning, which was all that really mattered. The job had been a real cash-cow and he would continue milking it for all it was worth, but he knew that sooner, or later, the paycheck would be replaced with a pink slip. On the other hand, maybe this was what Newton had been grooming him for. He'd never considered being Newton's son-in-law was going to be a free ride. He didn't care for Krupp, and would have to watch him all the time, but he'd worked with worse scoundrels.

"I would be willing to pay you quite well," Krupp said.

Well, well, Albro thought. Now they were getting somewhere. But Krupp had answered a little too quickly, as if he had been anticipating his agreeing all along. Albro realized he was one step behind and he needed to get out in front of this.

"How much?" he'd asked.

"Half a million dollars," Krupp said immediately.

What could Krupp be willing to pay that kind of cash for? Although the sum startled him, Albro kept his face relaxed, his voice flat. "That could be a start," he said.

"Of course there would be more to follow," Krupp added hurriedly. "But we would have to keep our relationship confidential."

The e it was! Albro could have kicked himself for not seeing it before. It was the proverbial 'elephant in the room' that everyone's always too istracted to see. Suddenly things began to make sense. He said, "Mr. N wton doesn't know that we're here, does he."

Kru p staggered backwards. A look of panic flashed into his eyes. Albro could have jumped on Krupp's chest and the effect would have been no les dramatic. He thought Krupp was going to stop breathing. It was as if a n invisible hand had clamped around his throat and was squeezing th e life out of him. He stumbled to the wall and slumped to the floor. Albro rushed to loosen his collar. Krupp's eyes rolled back into his skull. Albro smacked him hard on both cheeks. Krupp spluttered and coughed.

"Yo must not tell him," Krupp managed to wheeze. His eyes clamped shu t as he struggled for breath.

"Te him what?"

"Th t..." Krupp's face twisted into a grotesque mask of agony. He was giving e very sign of getting ready to check out of this world and into the next.

"Te him what?" Albro had him by the lapels and was ready to boost him i to a fireman's lift. He wondered if he could get him to the elevator be ore he expired. And even if he could how long would it take 911 to respo nd?

"Th t I asked you," Krupp struggled to say and then finally had coughed ou in a final spasm before he collapsed into unconsciousness, *"to find the ade Prince!"*

Kru p had begun breathing ragged, shallow breaths by the time Albro had h m inside the limo. Except for an occasional groan, Krupp didn't utte another word until they had pulled up outside Albro's apartment b uilding.

"I've made a terrible mistake. You will forget everything about tonight, wo 't you?" Krupp pleaded. He looked as limp and forlorn as a discarded ra g doll.

"Su e," Albro said. He'd decided that everything Krupp had said was pure no nsense, but what else could he do but placate the poor devil?

During the long ride back to his apartment Albro tried looking at Krupp's last request from every angle, but he couldn't make any sense out of it. It bothered him that Krupp had pulled on a thread that might connect in some way to his own past. It was clear, though, that Krupp's mental engine wasn't hitting on all cylinders. Had the poor sod taken a sharp turn into dementia alley, or had he been wandering around in those narrow confines for a while? Either way, Krupp would have to find his own way out. He had more immediate needs to attend to.

"And you won't say anything to Martin, will you?" Krupp clutched his wrist and forearm with both hands and Albro needed to pry him lose.

"Don't worry," he said, trying to reassure Krupp. "It's all between you and me. It will be our secret."

Krupp breathed a sigh of relief. "Thank you. I knew that I could trust you."

And that had been the last he'd seen of Krupp until they'd literally bumped into one another while Albro was maneuvering a tall and lithesome brunette in a glittering green dress with very thin straps toward her place at the table. The beautiful woman had looked upon the stooped figure with an unforgiving combination of disgust and revulsion and Albro Swift had felt a touch of pity rise into his chest as Krupp sputtered an apology and hurriedly backed away.

Albro now caught Krupp looking at him closely and returned the look with a smile, which he realized later, must have seemed to Krupp as a very condescending gesture.

Albro Swift took another sip of champagne and let the bubbles tickle the surface of his tongue before swallowing. The alcohol was giving him a pleasant buzz. Ordinarily he avoided the stuff, but tonight was one of those occasions that required one to follow the rules of engagement. He nodded to the man who sat on Martin Osborne Newton's left, an action-hero movie star (and quite possibly the runner-up in the most recognizable contest); with the wife whose face looked as if it had been assembled by Picasso. The movie star smiled his toothy smile and said something to his wife who looked at Albro and showed her teeth as well. Everyone, he thought, was showing as many teeth as possible tonight.

Albro remembered a nature show he'd watched a long time ago in which a troop of baboons had made much the same display when greeting one another.

On own the table, seated to one side or the other, were those closest to Martin Osborne Newton. The chief executives of the various divisions of the Martin Osborne Newton Company, otherwise referred to as 'The Company', the largest privately held entity in the world, (His daddy always had a dislike for corporations which encouraged interference by shareholders and snooping by the government.), were seated with their wives or current paramours. The logos, MONERGY, MONTRONICS, MONCOMP, MONAV, MONSHIP, MONPHARM AND MONGENE, (Energy, Electronics, Computing, Aviation, Shipping, Pharmacology, and the latest of his endeavors, Genetics), had been displayed in discreet gold lettering on the wall that listed the names of the donors who had helped make the museum possible. This was definitely the inner circle, where the faces glowed with self-assured confidence and the conversation hummed like a low and sweet melody.

Albro saw the Vice-President of the country speaking with the husband of the state's most powerful senator. The Senator, herself, was trying to appear relaxed, but was clearly unsure of the political consequences of any perceived relationship with Martin Osborne Newton, but she, like all of the politicians present were like moths drawn to a flame, only in this case the flame was the glow of a wealth beyond measure that burned with a far greater intensity than any real fire, and would destroy just as effectively anyone who approached too closely.

The Chinese ambassador sat with a ravishing beauty. She was recognized as a world-renown expert in Asian artifacts, and was also rumored to be an agent of the Chinese intelligence services. A hint of recognition crossed her cool demeanor when their eyes met. He recalled that she had presented the same expression when he had handed her the invitation. Across from them was seated a Russian billionaire, an ex-KGB general who had acquired his wealth through the dispersal of surplus Soviet military equipment, and was said to be the man behind Putin's rise to power.

Farther down the table sat the executives of his lesser holdings and overseas operations. Beyond them were interspersed members of the clergy of several different, and some might assert competing, denominations, of whom some were accompanied by women, and others who extolled a thinly veiled celibacy. Albro suspected a few of them would leave the gathering with newly formed liaisons of a decidedly non-ecclesiastical nature.

There were a few members of the local underworld who operated their little empires like the barons of fiefdoms granted to them as reward for their loyalty to their King.

At the distant ends of the tables were placed those individuals for whom Newton had no immediate need but who, in some way, served him with either their talents or their personal philosophies. There sat the Eskimo hunting guide whom Martin Osborne Newton hired each winter to hunt polar bear in the arctic. His shifting eyes scanned the crowd as if assessing each individual's weakness. More than once, his eyes rested upon Albro Swift before moving on. Near the Eskimo sat a woman so sunken in age that she had to be carried in and supported with pillows. The old woman, so far as Albro could tell, had neither moved nor spoken the entire evening, nor had she touched her food. Rumor had it that she was a seer, and Newton never made an important decision without consulting her first. A rumor so blatant in its falsity that Albro suspected there had to be some truth in it.

There too, at the far ends of the table, were those few persons who once had been members of the inner circle, but who now had been shunted like useless machinery to the fringe; a warning to any who might consider himself indispensible.

Amongst them all, scattered like sequins for added sparkle, were the movie stars, the artists, the professional athletes who seemed to be a requirement of any bash in the City of Angels.

Albro Swift had an excellent memory and remembered the name of each face. Some had tolerated his presence only long enough to receive their invitation while others had implored him to remain with them for as long as he liked as if he were a long lost and beloved relation.

The task had taken him nearly two months to complete, and while on the surface he had appeared to be no more than a well-dressed postman, he had come think of himself as Martin Osborne Newton's emissary.

Albro tried to take in the total spectacle. Ten floors holding some of the greatest treasures on earth rose above them. Bright lights from high overhead shown down onto the table and reflected off the crystal goblets and made the eyes of the women sparkle like stars and the eyes of the men shine like cold moonlight. He looked up. All around, on pedestals, in glass cases, hanging on the walls and suspended from almost invisible wires, all arranged to catch and hold the eyes of the beholder was the largest collection of Asian art anywhere in the world. It was dazzling not only to the eye, but to the mind as well.

Even more dazzling than this, Albro thought as he lowered his gaze, was the young woman who sat to the right of Martin Osborne Newton. Monique Olivia Newton was the daughter of the multibillionaire/inventor/entrepreneur/philanthropist who had cut short her career as a fashion-model-turned-movie-star to become her father's executive assistant. Her blonde hair flowed like liquid gold across her shoulders and her deep green eyes caught the light like jewel-cut emeralds. The beautiful women who flanked Albro were barely noticed by anyone other than him. They were like two candles that had been placed next to a search light; they were hopelessly caught in the glare of the other woman's beauty. Incredible as it seemed, she had fallen in love with him and they were going to be married. But there was still time, he reminded himself, to enjoy the pleasures of the single life, before the encumbrances of fidelity kicked in.

Albro turned to the woman whose thigh he had been exploring for the past minute. Her face was turned slightly away as she spoke to the man next to her. The skin of her neck was white and smooth and her red hair was pulled back and held in place by a band of diamonds. The brilliant stones cascaded down her neck, curved like a stream of light across her collar-bones and descended across her full breasts. He squeezed her leg and saw the muscles along her jaw tighten. She caught his hand between her thighs and held it there. Message sent, received and acknowledged; time and place to be arranged. Yes sir! His luck had not only changed, he was now on a long, and seemingly unending roll. He extracted his hand and gave her a gentle pat before bringing it back to the table. He squeezed the hand of the woman on his right and was about to propose that they meet on one of the upper levels later in the evening when Martin Osborne Newton pushed himself back from the table and stood.

A sudden applause broke out and he stood there patiently accepting the warm admiration of his guests. He was a tall man with a heavy chest and muscular arms, a tanned face set with blue-gray eyes. His brow was broad and shadowed his eyes slightly, lending them an intensity that grabbed onto and held one's attention. His nose was long and somewhat blunt, and the taper of his jaw line rounded to more of a point than most men and its length provided room for a larger than normal mouth. The whole effect was unarguably wolfish. His iron-gray hair was long and swept back and he had the habit of running his broad hand through it in the manner of a west Texas rancher.

His father, a direct descendent of Sir Isaac himself, (At least that was the official storyline, and there was little doubt that the genetics could be produced to prove it if anyone had dared to question Martin Osborne Newton on the matter.), had actually been a rancher until oil had been discovered on the land. His mother had given birth to the genius son right there in the ranch house, it being more than a hundred twenty miles to the nearest hospital, and they continued living on the ranch as the oil revenue piled up in the banks of Texas first and then later in New York and California. Home schooled until the age of fourteen, young Martin had gone directly to Princeton where he received his first advanced degree in mathematics before he was sixteen. More degrees at more universities became a matter of routine. When he turned twenty-one, his mother had suggested a change of pace, and encouraged him to serve his country. It was while on duty as a young officer in Army Intelligence in Bangkok during the Vietnam conflict that Martin Osborne Newton had discovered Asian art and antiquities and had begun collecting.

After the war and his discharge from the army, he assumed control of the family's fortune. While keeping a large portion of the wealth in cash, he made major investments in electronics and computer development. In a few years he had transformed a sizable fortune into an exceedingly large fortune, and in another few years had quietly become one of the wealthiest and most powerful men in the world. His latest venture had been into the field of genetics. Never one to dabble, Martin Osborne Newton had poured billions into the field, funding research at major universities around the world and as the knowledge of the various genomes had begun to accumulate he had begun to assert his vision of a great industrial complex to consolidate that knowledge into usable and ultimately marketable products. Some described the science of genetics as the next great revolution and Martin Osborne Newton was at the head of it. Some even called him the savior of the planet. No one was surprised when the billions he invested, began returning in astounding multiples. It was the Martin Osborne Newton *touch,* in which everything dull was turned to gold.

Martin Osborne Newton raised his broad hands to quiet the crowd. "First," he said in a voice that was a rich mixture of baritone refinement and west Texas drawl with just enough gravelly undertones to give it weight and authority, "I would like to thank y'all for attending this little party. It's truly an honor to have y'all here. Many of you have worked alongside me these past ten years to make this magnificent museum a reality. Within these walls are some of the greatest treasures ever created by man, and I want to thank you for your efforts.

"Moreover, each of you here tonight has in some way played a role in making the Martin Osborne Newton Company the world's most successful enterprise and therefore in some way has helped me to realize my dream of creating this museum. I thank you." He paused for the polite round of applause to fade. "Then there is my lovely daughter, my right hand gal, who has devoted herself not only to this demanding project, but to the company as a whole, and whom I cannot thank enough."

Newton turned and looked down at his daughter who smiled her famous silver-screen smile to the great pleasure and applause of the guests.

"However," Martin Osborne Newton drawled and waited for the applause to subside, "there is one individual here tonight who not only has shown intelligence and creativity in the face of many challenges, but who has proven himself to be of inestimable value in bringing together the objects that you see around you here."

At this point, Albro turned to Krupp. He was surprised to see the curator who was about to be presented to the appreciative crowd sink into his seat with a completely vacant look upon his face. Albro heard Newton's words as the big man continued, but they refused to make any kind of sense.

"I have the pleasure," Newton stated, "of presenting to you an amazing young man whom I know you all recognize, but I doubt you really know much about. A young man who has overcome the obscurity of his birth, and who one day will take his rightful place among the great personages of civilization."

Puzzled, Albro began looking around at the faces, wondering who Newton was talking about. And then it dawned on him that everyone's eyes were upon him.

"What's more," Newton continued, "I am doubly pleased to announce the engagement of my daughter, Monique, to this amazing young man. Ladies and gentlemen, I take great pleasure," and here Newton paused and looked directly at Albro, "in presenting to you, Albro Marshal Swift."

With that, Martin Osborne Newton raised his glass of champagne, as did the guests. He drank and then the others drank, and then applause filled the great hall.

Albro rose on wobbly legs and nervously smoothed the slight wrinkles at the sides of his tuxedo. The vast space of the room seemed to spin slowly on a slightly tilted axis as if his previous life had been suddenly knocked off kilter. For a moment, his eyes refused to focus, and then he found that he was looking at Newton's daughter and she was looking at him in a way that she had never looked at him, and suddenly his world righted and locked itself firmly in place. He flashed a smile to the faces that were all turned toward him. The applause was exuberant and carried on for what seemed like an exquisite eternity. Finally it began to lessen, and eventually a hushed silence descended upon the gathering.

"There is a man," Albro began, "who has extended his hand to help and guide me, whose generosity is exceeded only by his business acumen, whose love of great art is exceeded only by his love for his beautiful daughter. He is a man who has treated me like a son and to whom I humbly offer my respect, my admiration and my loyalty. I think all of you know that I speak of Martin Osborne Newton. "To you, sir."

Albro raised his glass and watched as all the glasses in the room were raised and found to his great surprise and even greater pleasure that Monique Olivia Newton had not turned to face her father. Rather, she had turned those dazzling green eyes directly at him.

"In less than a month," Albro said, "Monique and I will be joined in marriage. I haven't the words to tell you how much this woman has changed my life, but I can say that I love her more than life itself."

At this point a large tear flowed down Albro's cheek and plopped into the champagne that he held over his heart. Monique raised her hand and wiped tears from her own eyes. The strength went out of Albro's legs and he settled back into his chair.

CHAPTER 2

THE applause was still ringing in Albro Swift's ears when the chauffeur pulled up at the entrance of the Newton's Beverly Hills mansion. He accompanied Monique and her father to the open door where a dour looking old coot in a butler's outfit stood. Albro shook Martin Osborne Newton's strong hand, and kissed Monique on her cheek, lingering half a beat, breathing in the fragrance of her body. Being that close to her made his mind swirl with possibilities. He wanted to take Monique in his arms and smother her with kisses, but not with her father standing right there. Hell, maybe that's what Newton expected. That speech Newton had given sure made it sound as if he could do anything his heart desired. Albro took a step back and watched the two of them enter the mansion. The butler cast him a dismissive glance and closed the door.

"Shall I take you home, sir?" Charles, the white-haired chauffeur was standing at his elbow. Albro had not heard him climb the stairs. The sound of the man's voice startled him out of his reverie, and he turned and looked upon the kind, grandfatherly face. Albro guessed him to be somewhere in his early seventies, but knew that he was no one to trifle with. He had been a colonel in the Army's elite Special Forces division and had participated in many missions to neutralize undesirables around the world. Albro had accompanied him to a shooting range one afternoon and had been shocked as well as awed, as old Charlie had fired round after round from various hand guns and rifles at moving targets with deadly accu acy. Albro reasoned there was a veritable arsenal within easy reach of the driver's seat just in case the need arose.

"Su ," Albro answered.

Cha es eased them down the long drive and pulled expertly back onto the str et.

"Ca for a drink, sir?"

Alb considered the question. He had a long night ahead of him and he nee ed to be sharp. The champagne he'd drunk earlier was still buzzing arc nd his brain stem, but a drink just seemed so appropriate. Wasn't tha exactly what the ultra-rich did behind the smoked glass of their limou nes? But what did they prefer, scotch, bourbon, brandy? He'd never eveloped a taste for any of it. Mostly it tasted like gasoline and made H n want to puke, even the so-called good stuff. But now, his life was cha ging and he was going to have to learn to like it.

"Br idy, if you have it," Albro said, thinking that might be the most innocu ous of the poisonous liquids.

"I a afraid there is only Cognac, sir. A Tesseron, Lot 29. Will that do?"

Alb had no idea what a Tesseron was, but figured it had to be good. "That my favorite." He said. And it would be from now on, he thought. C arles flipped a switch and a door opened in the rear of the front seat t reveal a dimly lit cavity. Within was a crystal decanter and snifter. Al o poured himself a good measure. He sipped the amber liquid. His yes watered and the flush of hot vapors made him sneeze. Then the a oholic warmth swelled out through his chest into his arms and legs an mixed with the haze of champagne. He sat back into the lush comfo of the leather seat. He relaxed and thought of Monique Olivia New on. He knew that she was in love with him, but the announcem nt of their engagement had changed something in her feelings for im. He could feel a certainty that he hadn't felt before. He sensed that she had finally seen that deep down he was truly someone worthy of h r attention, that he was someone she could spend the rest of her life wit He thought of the day when their paths had crossed and how, in the pan of six short months, everything in his life had changed.

37

On that day in June, he had risen before dawn, a desperate act in itself, but desperate times had called for desperate measures. The import business he'd launched with his gambling profits and a small bank loan in a well-intentioned effort to become an honest and legitimate business man, had proven to be an excellent cover for his somewhat less than legitimate business of smuggling ancient artifacts from the Far East. He'd tramped around those countries during the nineties when it was still possible to survive on next to nothing, and he'd had made a lot of contacts, some good and some not so good. He'd learned to balance the savvy business skills of the Hong Kong Chinese against the entrepreneurial spirit of Burmese pirates. The experience, although harrowing, had been priceless in terms of its potential for future business dealings.

It was an elegantly simple operation. He located wholesalers who wished to have a product manufactured. He put them in touch with factories in Malaysia, Indonesia, Thailand, Taiwan, mainland China, any place that could produce a product of reasonably good quality cheaply. He would get the whole process rolling and then oversee its delivery. Hidden within the random container load of the kind of crap consumers never seemed to get enough of, would be one or two or sometimes a dozen carefully packed boxes of rare and extremely valuable object d'art. While custom officials were busily confiscating heroine, their beagles and spaniels had yet to learn to sniff out a set of fine Ming Dynasty porcelain.

Unfortunately, the business had foundered on a recent labor dispute. Who could have foreseen what had begun as a sympathetic gesture by local dock workers in support of reforming child labor laws in Malaysia, would have blown itself into a major trade dispute? West coast stevedores, whose traditional concerns had amounted to the steady encroachment of automation and containerization, had suddenly taken it upon themselves to champion the causes of young Malaysian factory workers. At least he and others like him were giving those kids a productive way to spend their days. Did any of those dock workers know what it was like for a ten year old to spend his days roaming the streets of Kuala Lumpur? No. Did they care how many almost legitimate businesses they ruined No! No! No! But no amount of ranting was going to save him. Children were resilient! No one knew that better than himself.

The real tragedy was that a container load of raincoats he'd arranged to be produced in one of those factories had been sitting for months behind a chain-link fence while his shipping agent was screaming to be paid, his bank was ready to foreclose on his meager assets, and his wholesalers were cancelling orders because no one wanted raincoats in the middle of June. Far worse, however, was the opportunity seized by the US Customs agents to methodically and thoroughly search containers that would have otherwise passed through their hands unchecked. Within his container, in a specially marked box, was a beautifully carved jade dagger which had been owned by a Chinese emperor of the fifth century B.C. The dagger had more recently rested in an ornate display case in the library of a Hong Kong billionaire. It had taken a good deal of time and nearly all of his resources to get the object out of the library and into the container in Malaysia and then to get the container into the United States. He'd done the job entirely on spec and had, as yet, not even dared to locate a buyer. It was only a matter of time before the customs agents found it, and then they would find him.

In the meantime, he had fallen two months behind in his rent and had to resort to playing cards not simply for recreation, but as a way to make ends meet. It was something he'd always done when times were lean, and when he was lucky he could do quite well. He had borrowed two hundred dollars from a waitress he'd been dating and had used it to work his way up from the nickel and dime tables to a high stakes game. There had been at least ten grand on the table when his luck had decided to take a vacation. He'd been knocked off his chair by a queen-high sequence of diamonds when he'd been holding a random set of hearts, a very good hand in itself, but not good enough. The odds of a flush meeting a straight-flush in the same game were ridiculously high, but nevertheless it had happened and it had been a tremendous blow not only to his bank roll, but to his self-confidence as well. That was when someone had mentioned the name of Salvatore Goldstein, and bad times had become very bad times.

Sal Goldstein was a loan shark, and Albro knew that loan sharks by their very nature preyed on the vulnerable. In the same thought, Albro also reasoned that just because someone is flat broke doesn't necessarily mean he's vulnerable. What Albro leaned later was that Sal Goldstein was an astute observer of human behavior.

He'd sat Albro down and explained it all carefully. "It's like this, Albro. I understand well the extent that people will go to fool themselves into believing they are in control. In fact, the success of my business could be predicated on that single observation."

He likened it to a person who puts one foot into quicksand. A normal person would pull his foot back and get the hell out of there. It was simply amazing, though, the number of people who stick the other foot in and then start looking around for someone to pull them out. All Sal had to do was wait and watch, and when the time came, toss the sinking individual a life line. Of course, that life line was actually a loan with a very high interest rate attached. The business had not made him wealthy, but he had a nice home in Huntington Beach and another in Palm Springs. He loved going to Vegas. He took his wife, Mitzi, and they would take in a show. Then he'd let her do a little gambling. When the mood struck him, he would leave Mitzi at home and hire a beautiful woman to hang on his arm. He never gambled himself, but he loved to watch. He loved to see that look of anticipation on people's faces. He loved that look of triumph when they won. But what he loved most was the look of abject terror when a loser finally realized that his luck had run out, that he was broke beyond broke, that he was in shit deeper than he ever thought possible. It was a look that reaffirmed everything he believed about humanity.

Sal thought of himself as a conservative investor and always made a careful assessment of perceived risk versus potential return. Word gets around in the gambling community and Goldstein knew of Albro's situation. He'd heard of the young man's often remarkable runs of luck and was confident that Albro Swift would bounce back, and when he did he wanted to be in a position to reap some of the profits. More importantly though, was the fact that the young gambler had become 'connected' and was able to sit in on some very high-stakes games, which was not without its own risks, but Salvatore Goldstein had a strong sense of what might be gained by such associations. "Besides," he'd said to Albro reassuringly, "I like you. I really do."

Goldstein had seen right away the thing that made Albro Swift truly vulnerable. It was the recent winning streak itself. It was as obvious as his boyish good looks. He saw that Albro's heart told him his high-stakes loss was a minor setback, an insignificant anomaly, and he was still on a roll. Sal knew that the boy's mind was telling him to go back to the nickel and dime tables and bide his time. There, he would at least make enough to pay rent. If Sal had learned learn one thing and one thing only in life, it was that a man's heart would lead him into peril every time he listened to it. Goldstein had decided that somebody needed to teach the boy a lesson. It had pained him to think of hurting the boy, but in the end he would be doing him a favor. Besides, kids were resilient.

Sure enough, when Goldstein offered to help him through his difficult period, Albro found his heart crowding up into his throat and before he knew what he'd done, he'd agreed to Sal's terms and had a bundle of very expensive money in his pocket. The terms were ten percent per week on the outstanding balance. As a generous incentive, Goldstein had waived the first week's interest. In Albro Swift's view it was an offer of free money, and he would be a fool to turn it down.

The first twenty-five grand had disappeared in two nights. It took three nights of winning, losing, winning, losing, winning, losing, losing, losing, to eat up the next twenty-five grand. In five days, he'd burned through fifty thousand dollars of Sal Goldstein's money. By the end of the following week, Mr. Goldstein would expect a payment of five thousand dollars to cover the interest.

Here the feeling of desperation Albro Swift was feeling as he had waited in the early morning dampness in the alleyway behind his apartment building. He'd had only one hope. If he could get to the container under the cover of darkness, unload it with the help of his friend, Roger, and get the raincoats to his wholesaler who had agreed to take them at a steep discount, he could at least stave off his legitimate creditors and make the first payment to Sal Goldstein. Even more important, was to get his hands on the jade dagger, whose value in the underground antiquities market, far exceeded his total indebtedness.

Roger had arrived on his bicycle with a backpack slung over his shoulder a little after 1a.m. "All set?" he asked.

Albro looked at his long time friend and instantly regretted that he'd asked him to get involved. Roger was the most innocent person he'd ever known. Tall and gangly with loose-jointed limbs and shoulder length hair which he kept tied behind his head in a long pony tail. He had known him since they were twelve years old. They had met in a juvenile detention center and he'd been looking after him ever since.

"Where's your helmet?" Albro asked. "How many times have I told you, that you have to wear your helmet?"

"I like to feel the wind in my hair, especially at night," Roger answered.

"And then what," Albro countered. "You get hit by a car, and you spend the rest of your life as a vegetable. I have too much to worry about. I can't be worried about you ending up as a vegetable."

"Sorry," Roger said. "I promise I'll wear my helmet."

"Good. Now help me with this trailer." Albro had wanted to rent a truck, but he hadn't had enough money. He'd cajoled and wheedled the local U-Haul dealer into renting him a sixteen-foot trailer overnight for twenty bucks. The agent had dropped it off and would be waiting to pick it up at eight o'clock that same morning. He planned to pull it with an aging Fiat convertible which he'd won in a card game. The car was little more than a scattering of paint spots held together by a lacework of rust riding on four bald tires, but it had a surprisingly strong engine

Roger looked at the trailer and then at the small convertible. "You're pulling this trailer with that car? No way! You don't even have a trailer hitch."

"Look, Roger, I don't have much choice. I asked for a truck and this is what I got." He had slipped the rental agent a fiver for the use of a bumper hitch. He pointed out the hitch which lay on the pavement at the rear of the vehicle. "I've got everything we need. You can make it work, can't you?"

Roger rummaged in his backpack for a headlamp and then bent to one knee and grasped the heavy steel contraption with both hands and examined its workings. He then ran his hands along the underside of the Fiat's narrow bumpers. Then he pulled out a set of wrenches from his pack and set to work.

Albro stood silently as Roger worked. He had to admit that he didn't have an ounce of mechanical aptitude. Within minutes Roger had the hitch in place and the trailer locked onto it. The rear of the car sagged ominously.

"Okay," Albro said. "I knew you could do it. Let's go."

"Wait," Roger said. "We need to hook up the lights."

"There's no time for that. Besides, the car has lights," Albro said.

They climbed in and Albro started the engine. It coughed and sputtered as he ground the starter and finally the engine caught and settled into a hesitant idle. Albro let out the clutch and the car and trailer slowly moved forward. The empty trailer made the little convertible sway and buck as they drove the surface streets out to the San Pedro dockyards where Albro handed the gate keeper, a loser he knew from the nickel and dime tables, a hundred he'd been hoarding. The gate keeper gave them a map with the approximate location of his container and a pair of bolt cutters to snip the lock, and then he slid open the gate and waved them through.

It took longer than expected to locate the container within the maze of steel boxes stacked four high. Fortunately, the one they needed to open was at the bottom of one of those stacks and hidden from view down a long narrow corridor. Roger cut the lock and within two hours, they had the trailer as well as the back seat and trunk of the car packed with the shipment of raincoats. The jade dagger, which Albro hoped and prayed would be his salvation, was stashed safely beneath the driver's seat.

As they climbed back into the car, the eastern sky was showing the first signs of light. A cool, fresh breeze blew in from the ocean. Albro

43

revved the engine and let out the clutch. A screaming sound came from somewhere forward of the gearshift and foul smelling blue smoke enveloped the car. He pushed in the clutch and let it out slowly this time and after a few seconds the car began to creep forward.

At the approach to the freeway, Albro caught the green light and pressed the accelerator to the floor and heaved a sigh of relief as they shot down the ramp. A thousand raincoats at fifty bucks apiece wholesale, minus what he owed the shipper, minus what he owed the bank, minus a few miscellaneous expenditures left him with almost twenty thousand dollars. Five thousand to Goldstein at the end of the week and more than enough remained to get into a high-stakes game and recoup his loses. That would allow him time to find a buyer for the jade dagger. He couldn't quite believe that he'd actually started to worry about how he was going to survive the coming weeks. True, his life had just experienced a minor upheaval, but things were falling back into place, or so it seemed until Roger began shouting.

"Ahead!" Roger shouted above the scream of the engine. "Look at what's ahead!"

In the far distance was the sunrise. Streaks of thin, ragged clouds burned a dozen shades of pink and orange, and from their midst burst a brilliant sword of white light that stabbed Albro in both eyes. He fumbled along the dash for his sunglasses. Ahead of them, against the dazzling light of dawn, Albro could distinguish a black mass of cars seemingly on fire with the glow of red tail-lights. He grasped the wheel and stood on the brake pedal with both feet until every muscle in his body cried out in agony.

Roger braced himself with both hands. "We're going to hit!" he cried.

The tires screamed and the car fish-tailed wildly as if whipped by some gigantic beast. Albro bore down on the brake pedal with every last ounce of strength he possessed. The little convertible seemed to be propelled inexorably forward by an unstoppable force from behind, but amazingly the car began to slow and finally came to a halt just inches from the car in front.

"Good work, Albro," Roger said and they both took one long breath before the truck hit them.

In addition to its own mess, the accident precipitated several minor fender-benders on both sides of the freeway, tying up traffic for several hours in both directions. The aerial news cameras of six different helicopters caught the ensuing chaos and had zeroed in on a crowd of drivers who had momentarily abandoned their cars and were seen gathering up raincoats of various colors, styles and sizes. The whole scene had been featured on all the morning news casts. Although the accident did not make the national news, a picture of the mangled Fiat convertible and trailer along with the caption, *'Two men survive unharmed…,'* appeared on page three of the evening edition of the L.A. Times. The story went on to detail how *'the two men had broken into a container at the San Pedro docks and had attempted to transport over one thousand imported raincoats in a stolen U-Haul trailer. The trailer's lights had not been functioning, which, authorities stated, had contributed to the accident. The driver of the truck, also unharmed, told the CHP, "I had no idea they were stopped." The two men are currently being held in the L.A. County jail, pending arraignment on charges of burglary, grand theft, and negligent driving.'*

By the time the late-night news rolled around, the main component of the story had been reduced to a fist fight that had broken out between a very large black female and an Asian male who had laid hands on the same hot pink, hip-length coat. As the sun had risen the following day, the people of Los Angeles had forgotten it entirely. Everyone, that is, besides Albro Swift and his good friend Roger Ranger and the jailer who opened the door to their cell.

"Okay, boys, it's time to roll out," he called. He was a short, thin man with skin the color of polished walnut. He looked at them. "Hey, you two are the ones in that accident yesterday. It was all over the news. How the two of you got out alive is beyond me. You've got one special guardian angel, and that's a fact." He shook his head and clicked his tongue. "Come along with me. You're out of here."

45

Albro rolled on his side and pushed himself to a sitting position. He was stiff and sore in every place imaginable. He put his elbows on his knees and placed his face in his hands. Roger was in the middle of the cell seated in a lotus position, his back straight as a board his hands resting delicately on his bent legs, his palms turned upward and his thumbs just touching his middle fingers. His eyes were closed and his breathing all but imperceptible. Albro assumed that his friend had been in that position for hours.

The jailer eyed him suspiciously. He asked Albro "Is he all right?"

Albro looked up. "Sure, he's fine. He's meditating."

The jailer had stooped and had peered into Roger's serene face. "Can he hear us?"

"Maybe, maybe not," Albro answered. "It depends on which plane of consciousness his mind happens to be floating on at this moment." Albro pushed himself to his feet and shuffled over to his friend and tapped him on the shoulder. "Roger," he whispered.

The jailer stepped back, his eyes completely captivated by the scene. Slowly, Roger's breathing began to deepen. His eye lids fluttered briefly and then popped open. His limbs unfolded like a gigantic stick-legged insect and he rose to his feet. He looked entirely refreshed, in stark contrast to Albro's haggard appearance.

"Hey Albro, what's up?" Roger asked pleasantly, seemingly oblivious to their surroundings.

Albro answered, "Must be time for our arraignment. We're criminals, remember?" Albro pulled at the lapels of his orange jumpsuit. "But don't worry. I'm getting you out of here."

"Nope," the jailer said. "No arraignment. As soon as you change into your street clothes, you'll be on your way. Like I said, you've got a guardian angel looking out for you. Follow me."

They followed the jailer down the gray-walled cell block, through two steel doors and then down another gray hallway to an elevator. The jailer led them to a room where they changed out of the orange coveralls. The last stop was a counter where they were given their personal belongings. "Sign here," the officer said and pushed a clipboard at them.

The officer pointed to the door behind them and said, "Go through that door. Take the elevator. Follow the exit signs. Have a nice day."

"You have a nice day too," Roger said and smiled at the officer. The officer stared back with a blank expression.

"Have a nice day," Albro muttered barely under his breath. He put his arm around Roger's shoulders and turned him toward the door. "Have a nice day," he repeated. "My business is down the toilet. My car is demolished. I'm broke. Who knows how many lawsuits will be slapped on me before the day is over. And if I don't have five grand for Goldstein by the end of the week, I'll have broken bones too." He hoped beyond hope that the jade dagger was still safe and sound beneath the driver's seat of his car. The first order of business would be to find out where the car had been taken. And then get something to eat, but he had no money. He had spent the absolute last of his cash.

He didn't have a single friend that he hadn't tapped to the limit in terms of money and favors. Everyone had begun avoiding him weeks ago; everyone, that is, except Roger, loyal Roger. His only friend in the world, and now he'd let him down too, in addition to almost getting him killed. *What had he been thinking?* He kept his arm around Roger as they rode the elevator down to the exit. He was about to ask Roger to forgive him for all the grief he'd caused him over the years when the elevator came to a jolting stop and the doors rattled open.

A small man in a trim, blue business suit stood before them. He looked at Albro and then Roger with professional, but courteous eyes behind wire rimmed glasses. He held a briefcase in his left hand and his right hand hung relaxed at his side.

"Lawyer," Albro whispered to Roger. "Keep going." Albro started to take a step and then stopped cold. Next to the man in the suit was the most beautiful woman he had ever seen. She was more beautiful than all the sunrises and sunsets lovers had swooned over for a thousand years. Throw in the moon and the stars and you still wouldn't rival the radiant glow from her deep, emerald eyes. Her hair had the color of Troy on fire. Her lips were rubies come to life. The fragrance that came from her body was more delicate than that of the first violets of spring. She wore a dress of white silky material that suggested, rather than revealed the smooth, yet strong body that lay beneath.

Albro stood, flat-footed, open mouthed, stunned by her incredible beauty, while from somewhere far off he heard someone speaking to him. It was the little man. The little man was saying his name. Albro tore his gaze from the woman to the man who now had his hand out and was beckoning them to come out of the elevator.

"Please, you must exit the elevator. Otherwise, I fear you will draw attention," the little man said.

Draw attention? Fear that he and Roger would draw attention? The little man was standing next to a woman who could bring a presidential motorcade to a screeching halt by stepping off the curb, and he was worried about Roger and him drawing attention? If he was not so depressed, he would have burst out laughing.

Albro took Roger by the arm and brushed past the two of them. "Sorry," he said.

"Wait," the man called after them. "It's about that accident."

It was starting already, Albro thought. He stopped abruptly and raised his hand. "You'll have to speak with my lawyers," he said. Wasn't that what everyone said when the word 'accident' entered the conservation? But he might as well have said, 'You'll have to speak to my barber' for all the good it would do him. He neither had a passel of lawyers, nor the money to hire even one. He noticed then that the beautiful woman was looking at him attentively.

"Mr. Swift, please," the little man said, trying to keep his voice down. "We're hoping to avoid litigation. I represent an interested party who wishes to compensate you for your losses."

"What did you say?" Albro asked. The little man in the blue suit came up to them, and the beautiful woman stepped closer as well. Albro noticed that a small crowd of onlookers had formed in the lobby. A worn-looking woman with dirty gray hair and swollen feet that threatened to burst from her torn shoes forced her way to the front. She clutched two bulging shopping bags, and a little dog held in the crook of her elbow began yapping loudly.

"Ga d!" the bag lady exclaimed. "It's Monique Newton!" A murmur of greement rippled through the crowd. "Could I have your autograph? She asked and began digging through her bag for paper and pencil.

Mo que Newton? Albro looked again at the beautiful woman. It was, and n t on a movie screen, or the cover of some supermarket tabloid, in t e flesh. Although her career as a movie star had been short lived, her m vies had been blockbusters, which added all the more to the mystery sur ounding her withdrawal from the industry. But what did all of that ma er? She was the daughter of billionaire financier Martin Osborne Ne vton. How had he not recognized her the moment he had seen her? I e watched as she smiled at the old woman and then casually walked ove to her and signed her name on the scrap of paper the woman held out to her with trembling hands. She then signed her autograph several mor times as the crowd closed in around her.

The nan in blue pressed in close to him and spoke in a low voice, "Mr. Swift, e would like very much to avoid a scene. Could we impose upon you ai d Mr. Ranger to accompany us to my office?"

In t e limousine, they sat facing one another, the man in blue and Monique N wton in the deep-set leather seats, and Albro and Roger on the smaller ut no less plush seats that faced them. The man in blue set the briefca he'd been carrying on his knees and popped the latches. Inside on a ed of black velvet rested the finely carved jade dagger that had once belonged to a Chinese emperor. The man in blue said, "I believe, Mr. Swift, this belongs to you."

Albr Swift had looked from the jade dagger into the face of Monique N wton and in that instant he'd realized that he was, after all, about to ha e a nice day.

CHAPTER 3

"MAY I help you inside, Mr. Swift?" The chauffeur gently shook Albro. He had nodded off somewhere south of Compton. He pushed himself off the seat and climbed out of the car and stood, a bit unsteadily, on his feet. He was still seeing green circles from the explosion of flashes as the photographers had jostled each other to get photos of him with Newton and his daughter and countless other celebs who had wanted to mark the moment.

"Where are we, Charles?" Albro asked.

"We have arrived at your home, sir. Let me help you up to your apartment," the chauffeur offered.

"No, I'm fine. Really, I just fell asleep." Albro rubbed his face and stretched his arms. "Thanks for the ride."

Albro took a deep breath of the cool, damp air. "How long did I sleep?"

"Almost an hour, sir," Charles said.

"Thanks. And thanks again for the ride. Good night, Charles."

"Good night, to you sir," Charles said. He nodded slightly, touching his hand to the brim of his cap and got back behind the wheel. Albro watched as the limo pulled away, looking like a giant black cat leaping into the darkness. He squeezed his eyes shut and shook himself hard. He was not accustomed to drinking. In fact, he had discovered early on in his life that far from relaxing, alcohol served only to fog his concentration and arouse in him a heightened sense of false confidence, which was a very bad combination, particularly when he had work to do.

He guessed that it was sometime around 2 a.m. His watch, a knock-off Rolex that he'd kept as a souvenir when Martin Osborne Newton had bought out and reorganized his import business, had stopped working. Still, it looked good on his wrist and that was important since he was now vice-president in charge of Market Evaluation and Procurement for Newton Swift Trans Global Imports which meant he had an office and secretary, but other than deliver five hundred invitations, there hadn't as yet been a whole lot of 'evaluation and procurement'.

In a carefully orchestrated announcement to the news media, the jade dagger had been returned to the Beijing government, its rightful owner, which made Albro Swift a minor hero. He could forget all about trying to negotiate deals on the black market. No collector in the world had deeper pockets than Martin Osborne Newton. In addition, those same deep pockets would surely make the whole process a good deal easier than it had ever been, but as yet, he'd done little more than fly to Hong Kong half-dozen times, pick up a package, and after a few days of recreation, fly home. That whole business of delivering those invitations had been a puzzling assignment as well. It had seemed a poor use of his skills, but he'd happily accepted the salary of six thousand per week that the lawyer in the blue suit had proposed. That covered the interest payments to Goldstein and he'd leveraged the balance at the card tables to meet day to day expenses. The real plus was that he'd been taken into the Newton fold. There had been dinner parties at Newton's mansion, flights to London, Singapore, Delhi. Everywhere he went he had been treated as if he was a member of Newton's inner circle, and Monique had fallen madly in love with him. Evidently he'd done something right and as a result, he felt that his star had definitely ascended high into the firmament of Newton's realm.

The salary, although extravagant by most measures, had done barely more than allow him to keep his head above water, and the job itself had cut into the time available to ply his luck at the card tables. Now that the museum was up and running, he was looking forward to devoting more time to paying down his debt to Sal Goldstein. (He'd written off Doctor Krupp's offer. The good doctor was an obvious nut-case.) One good night was all he needed to wipe the slate clean. He'd been reluctant to mention anything to Newton's lawyer about his indebtedness to a loan shark. It just didn't seem to be the sort of thing one included in his curriculum vitae. The real issue, of course, was his overwhelming desire to impress Monique. Given her reaction tonight, perhaps he'd finally accomplished just that. The last thing he wanted was for her to discover that he was connected in any way to the underbelly of a loan shark, and so he felt an added pressure to terminate his relationship with Sal Goldstein. He always played his best, he reminded himself as he climbed the stairs to his apartment, when the pressure was greatest. If he hurried, he could still get a seat at one of the card games that would just be starting at the Shanghai Club down in Chinatown. He had a roll of hundreds hidden in the drain pipe of his kitchen sink. As soon as he got inside, he'd call a cab, retrieve the hundreds, change out of his tux into something less conspicuous and be on his way.

The apartment building was one of those that had gone up all over Los Angeles in the mid-sixties with the main wing facing the street and with two shorter wings attached to form a 'U' shape, with a swimming pool not much bigger than a soup bowl planted between the wings. Graffiti was splashed on the walls and some of the windows were patched with plywood. His apartment had two bedrooms and he and Roger had lived there for two years along with a parakeet named Butch who had flown into the apartment one summer day a year ago and made himself at home. A pepper tree hung its ragged branches at their end of the building and screened some of the light and noise that intruded from the street. Tonight, it also hid the presence of a long, dark sedan parked at the curb.

Perhaps, it was the alcohol, or maybe he was still overcome by the shear spectacle and emotional drama of the evening, but Albro Swift was already in his apartment before he realized that the lock had been expertly jimmied. Someone behind him switched on the light. Salvatore Goldstein, looking perfectly at home, sat on the worn sofa. The low angle light from the corner lamp served only to emphasize his massive girth and turn his swarthy visage into a rather comical version of a Buddha in heavy, horn-rimmed glasses. The effect, Albro knew, was only illusory. Comedy was not Salvatore Goldstein's long suit. He was holding an open paperback in his lap. Albro angled his gaze, but he couldn't tell what book it was. He kept a small library, maybe a dozen volumes, favorites he could read time and again. The one saving grace of the juvenile detention centers he'd bounced in and out of during his adolescent years was that most of them had libraries, which was undoubtedly based on the misconceived notion that great literature would have a positive impact on delinquent behavior. Good books had never kept him out of trouble, but at least the books had provided a distraction in an otherwise dismal environment, and he'd subsequently developed an interest in old books. Every town he found himself in he would seek out the used bookstores and prowl their musty smelling stacks. He preferred hardbacks. There was a sense of permanence to a hardback. The book that Goldstein held was a paperback. He wondered where it had come from.

Albro turned and looked at the man behind him. He was short and compact and stood with his legs apart, his hands hanging loosely at his sides. He had a two-day growth of beard on his square and sullen face. Another man sat at the kitchen bar which separated the living room from the sink and range. He was taller, but just as heavily built as the other man. His head was shaved and he wore an expensive looking, calf-length leather coat. The hundreds that he'd been looking forward to were spread out on the counter.

"Your sink wasn't draining so good, so I fixed it for you," he said. He grinned and Albro could see that his teeth had been repaired with gold-rimmed porcelain. Albro had heard that Sal Goldstein's brother was a dentist, and from the look of the man's mouth probably a good one. Butch, Roger's parakeet, was perched on the man's shoulder and he bobbed his head as if to confirm what the man had just said. "By the way, I think your birdie likes me. I've been teaching him some new words. Listen. Say, fucking hell'".

"Ucking Ell!" Butch repeated on cue and then bobbed and weaved on the man's shoulder obviously pleased with himself.

"Come in and sit down, Al," Goldstein said by way of greeting. He closed the book and laid it next to him on the faded cushion. He removed his reading glasses and slipped them into the inner pocket of his jacket. "We've been waiting all evening for you. No harm done. It gave me a chance to catch up on my reading." He tapped the book next to him. "You remind me in some ways of the hero in this story."

"Hero," Albro repeated nervously, trying desperately to understand where Sal was going with this. He had far worse things to think about than the hero in a cheap paperback novel.

"Sometime we'll have a discussion on the literary merits of myths and legends and how they seem to have found a new home in the Fantasy/Adventure novel."

"What?" Sal was sounding like a high school English teacher. Albro tried to imagine Sal in a corduroy jacket with leather patches on the elbows shuffling in front of a smeared blackboard lecturing thirty bored students. No, it could never happen, not in a million different versions of the universe. Sal was a cold-blooded crook, and that's all he would ever be. But what could possibly have come over him? What had Sal been reading?

Albro could just make out the title and the upside down image on the cover. There were flames and what looked like people running for their lives. He puzzled out the title: *The Jade Prince*. His heart jumped, and the awful image of the creature in Krupp's glass case leapt into his mind. He tried to hide his reaction, but from the piercing look in Goldstein's eyes, he knew that he was doing a poor job of it.

Sal motioned for Albro to sit in the kitchen chair that had been positioned directly across from his place on the sofa. "You know Mr. Bozeman and Mr. Hopkins." He moved his head an inch toward the two men but didn't take his eyes from Albro's.

"Hello Jimmy, hello Hoppy," Albro said as he sat in the chair, trying desperately to keep his voice steady.

"Ello Immy. Ello Oppy," Butch repeated.

"Jimmy, put the bird back in its cage," Goldstein said.

"Sure, boss." Jimmy Bozeman gently closed a gigantic hand around the parakeet and carefully slipped him into his cage. "Be a nice birdie and keep your beak shut. The boss don't like any interruptin' when he's talkin'."

A prickling of sweat had begun to form inside Albro's tuxedo. Hoppy Hopkins closed the door and remained standing with his back to it. Jimmy Bozeman stood leaning against the bar with his arms folded. They'd both been in and out of prison for various small-time offenses over the years, but had finally settled into steady employment with Goldstein. A funny thing about Hoppy was that his nickname had nothing to do with name 'Hopkins', rather it came from his uncontrollable tendency to bounce on the balls of his feet whenever he became excited. He also knew that Hoppy had recently got married and bought a house. It seemed to Albro that the American Dream called out to everyone, even the low-life of the world. Hoppy reached over and flipped on the overhead light and bounced a little as he did so. That was not a good sign, Albro thought.

Sal Goldstein sat with his legs spread apart and his trousers pulled up. Albro could see an inch of veiny, white skin above his dark socks. He wore a mustard colored suit that was shiny at the cuffs and elbows over a rumpled gold shirt with tiny green diamonds in it. His dark green tie was loosened. His skin had taken on a shiny, oily gloss. You could tell that he'd been fat as a child and then fat as an adult, but in the past few years his fat had been in retreat and now remained in a bastion of girth around his middle. His legs and arms were now as skinny as bean poles and he carried around a special cushion upon which to sit. His gray, thinning eyebrows and his sunken and sallow cheeks and red-rimmed eyes gave him an unhealthy appearance. Albro came to the sudden realization that Goldstein was sick. He was getting a strong reading. A *reading*, as Albro referred to these revelations, would spontaneously pop into his head. They were completely beyond his control. He couldn't force them, no matter how hard he tried, and he'd learned to accept them when they came along. And neither did a reading carry much detail. Just now, something was telling him that Sal Goldstein didn't have long to live. Well, anyone could look at the poor man and give that assessment. But Albro had the overpowering sense that Goldstein was being threatened from something outside himself. God only knew how many people would like to see Goldstein in the grave, hence the presence of two body-guards where ever he went. The feeling was so strong, that Albro actually felt a pang of sympathy rise in his chest and then immediately dismissed it. Feeling sympathy for Goldstein was as sensible as feeling sympathy for an injured great white shark.

"When you didn't show up at my office today, I began to worry about you," Goldstein said looking intently at Albro.

"I meant to bring my payment, but with everything happening, it completely slipped my mind," Albro said. It was a lame excuse, he knew, but right now all he wanted to do was buy some time.

"I understand. May I offer my congratulations on the success of your new career, and more importantly, on the news of your engagement to one of the richest women in the world. I'm happy to know that you're moving up in the world. I have great hopes for you. I might even say, *of mythical proportions*." Sal Goldstein said wistfully and laid his hand on the book at his side.

Albro glanced at the money on the counter. It would only cover half the interest on his loan. He'd hoped to make up the rest before morning. "How did you know about our engagement?"

Sal waved his hand dismissively. "I have eyes and ears all over this town. Besides, good news travels fast. I'm very happy for you and your future bride. Forgive me if I don't attend the wedding." He then paused and shifted painfully on his cushion. "You know, Albro, I ordinarily don't pay personal visits to my clients. Normally, I leave that to one of my account representatives. A visit from either Mr. Hopkins or Mr. Bozeman is usually sufficient to convince a recalcitrant debtor to not fall behind on his obligations.

"But you are a special case, Albro. To tell you the truth, I've come to think of you as a son, an errant son you may be, but a son nonetheless. When a son doesn't follow his father's wishes, the father is obliged to pay attention to his son's problems. Otherwise, the father is remiss in meeting his responsibilities and the son may lose all respect. Do you understand that's why I am here?"

"Actually, Mr. Goldstein, I'm having a little trouble following you," Albro said. He had begun to experience a tightness that began in his groin and had moved up through his stomach and chest and now had ended in what felt like a huge hand gripping his throat. His breath, when he could get one, came in short gasps.

A look of dismay folded Salvatore Goldstein's face into a series of deep creases. "Let me make myself clear. You came to me because you needed help. Your business was failing and you were down on your luck. I happened to believe that you're a young man of talent who needed a helping hand. If you thought it was an easy thing for me to come up with fifty thousand dollars, think again. I put myself at substantial financial risk to help you out. All I expect in return is for you to help me to meet my obligations."

"I've been on time with my payments every week," Albro interjected. There was an undeniable note of panic in his voice.

"I'm talking now, so don't interrupt!" A touch of color had come into Goldstein's sallow cheeks. He leaned forward and continued, "As I was saying, I have my obligations and one of them is to teach you the lesson of responsibility."

Goldstein paused and in that moment of silence Albro sensed the lesson that had been mentioned was going to affect him in a bad way. He felt now, just like he had in his last year of school when he'd sat before the vice-principal listening to all the reasons why he needed to be punished for an untimely remark regarding what John Donne might have thought of the view of his English teacher's gartered stockings when she'd reached high on the chalk board while writing out the last two lines of the poem *The Good Morrow*.

The remark had started a classmate laughing and the two of them had laughed uncontrollably until in frustration, the teacher had sent the two of them to the vice-principal. Albro had unwisely attempted to engage the vice-principle in a discussion of 17th century poetry and theology and how they related to modern cultural norms. Albro had succeeded only in pointing out the depths of the older man's ignorance. The punishment for unruly behavior in the classroom had been three whacks with a two foot long paddle of heavy plastic with holes drilled in it to prevent a cushion of air from softening the impact for each of them and a week's suspension for Albro for having embarrassed the VP in front of another student. The teacher had later apologized, and she had even shed a couple of big tears. She had insisted that he had left her no option. She'd had to maintain discipline in her classroom. But then, she had pulled him into the coat closet and had allowed Albro the pleasure of slipping the garter snaps from the tops of her stockings, an experience that had more than made up for the sting of the paddle. Albro still remembered the look of surprise in her eyes at how adept he had been.

Sal Goldstein said, "When a client doesn't pay, I have his arms broken. It's nothing personal. Jimmy found twenty-six hundred-dollar bills which covers half your interest plus a little extra. That means I have only one of your arms broken. Or," and here he paused, as if to choose his words carefully, "you help me find something."

The adrenalin pumping through Albro Swift's arteries had begun to diffuse into his muscles giving him a jumpy, jangly feeling. Goldstein's last statement hadn't made total sense. His brain felt like it was taking a break while his muscles were struggling to come to some sort of decision regarding the advantages of fight versus flight, neither of which had even a remote possibility of success under the present circumstances.

"What?" Albro looked into Goldstein's face where, for an instance, he saw something that seemed a good deal more threatening than the prospect of having his arm broken.

"Tell me where I can find the *Jade Prince*. Better yet, you find it and bring it to me, and release it. Do that and I'll forget about the fifty thousand? Plus, I will pay you one million dollars."

The Jade Prince? There it was again, twice in as many days. Three, if you counted the book at Goldstein's side. Sure, it was something out of his obscure past, but how could three words on a scrap of paper suddenly become front and center to Krupp and Goldstein, two people

58

who could e no more different if one had been imagined by Charles Dickens and the other by Ray Bradbury. What was going on? Even if the Jade Prince eally existed, why was Sal interested in an ancient Chinese artifact? H d Sal taken up amateur archeology?   That was an alarming idea. Neve heless, the mention of the million did have a calming effect on his nerve . Something was going on here that required some clear and precise thir ing. He recalled the look on the good Doctor's face when Krupp had 10own him the high-tech image. The slightly crazed, slightly reverential aze that had coated the man's eyes was genuine. There was nothing cra ed about Goldstein's eyes, but the cold, calculating and entirely ser us gaze was just as genuine. But why Goldstein? He could see Krupp's nterest, but what would Salvatore Goldstein know about the existence o such an object? It didn't make any sense.

"I ca 1't," Albro said.

"Tw million," Goldstein said.

Wh t the hell was going on here?   "If you mean the fancy hologram t at's locked in a vault in Martin Osborne Newton's new museum, yc I can forget it. There's no way I can steal that for you. There has to be at east a dozen layers of security. It would take…"

"Wl at are you talking about?" Goldstein shouted. His watery eyes narrov ed to two dark slits. "What use do I have for a hologram?" He picked u) the book and thumbed through it until he found what he wanted. H held the book open with one hand and stabbed a finger at the figure o the page. "This is what I want."

Albr) looked at the picture. Rendered in precise brushstrokes in that sparse but elegant style that had become the defining hallmark Chinese pai tings for over two thousand years was an image of the figure he had seer staring out at him from within the glass case.

"Ma / I see that?" he asked Goldstein.

"Jin ny," Goldstein said. Jimmy Bozeman took the book and handed it to Albro.

Albr) tried to calm the tremor in his hand as he reached for the book. It w s one of those small, but thick paperbacks whose printing dives into t e center forcing the reader to continually break the glued

59

binding in order to pry out the story. He studied the illustration. It looked to be the same object that Krupp had showed him. He looked at the cover. Across the top was emblazoned the title, gold letters on a red background: *The Jade Prince*. Across the bottom was the name, A. M. Swift. In between was a surging mob of naked people who looked as though they were escaping from Hell. It couldn't have been any more lurid. He looked again at the author's name, and then looked at Goldstein.

"Is this some kind of joke?"

"You never told me you were a writer," Goldstein said.

Albro looked inside the front cover where someone had written, 'To Roger, my best and most loyal friend.' And someone had signed it with his signature. It looked enough like his hand writing to be the real thing. Was this Roger's doing, or had he, somewhere in the night, slipped down the rabbit hole into Goldstein's Wonderland? Or maybe he'd taken the short route to Never-Never Land. He wiped the sweat that had begun to stream into his eyes

"Where did you get this?" he asked Goldstein.

"From your bookshelf," Sal answered. "Are you denying that you wrote this?" he demanded.

"Sorry, I've never seen this book."

"That's your signature. I compared it to the notes you signed!"

Albro looked again at the dedication. *Someone* had written it, but it hadn't been him. It looked genuine, but it wasn't that difficult to forge a signature. The question was, why? There had to be a logical explanation. It just wasn't coming to him at the moment. He needed to ask Roger about it, but it was just as well that he wasn't here right now.

"Sorry Sal, but like I said, I've never seen this book. And as far as your *Jade Prince*, I can't help you."

"You can. You know all about the *Jade Prince*. You wrote that book!" Goldstein shouted and half rose off the sofa. "You are the one who can find it! You are the only one who can release it!" The veins had popped out on his forehead and he'd raised his clenched fist. He dropped back, breathing hard.

The e it was again, exactly what Krupp had said, that he could 'find it', 'th : he could release it'. Did they really think he had the inside track on thi thing? Coming from Krupp he could pass it off as the wacky imaginings f a total nutcase. But Sal Goldstein was no nutcase. He was cold, calcul ing and while not entirely sane, he was nobody's fool. In addition, he ould smell money like a shark smells blood.

"Ta e it easy Sal. I don't want you having a coronary on my sofa. If it's any cc solation to you, I would help you if I could. The truth is that I don't know hat you're talking about."

"Yo do!" Goldstein shot back.

"Wl am I not getting through to him?" Albro asked of Jimmy and Hoppy. hey stared back at him with noncommittal stares. "Look Sal, if you want o buy the thing you can ask Newton, but I really doubt that you can con e up with the cash. By the way, who's really behind this?"

Gol stein ignored the question, and then asked his own. "How much did M Newton offer you to find the *Jade Prince*?"

"M tin? Nothing. Zip. Nada. Zilch. The topic hasn't even come up. And if ou want me to hazard a guess, I'd say that just like I do, he knows that 's a fantasy, but that didn't stop that nutty professor Krupp from offerir me half a million. By the way, do you mind telling me what this 'release business is all about? It sounds fishy to me."

Sal oked coldly at Albro.

"Th was a pun, Sal. Catch and release, get it?"

Gol stein studied him for a long moment, but didn't crack a smile. "You know actly what I am talking about. The book proves it."

"An what exactly is it that I'm supposed to know?"

"Yo know how to bring the Jade Prince back to life!"

Alb burst out laughing. "Now I see what's going on. This is all an elaborat hoax. Someone got you, Sal. Someone's pulled a good one on you. I w uldn't think that you, of all people, would fall for something like that."

Gol stein's eyes turned to two orbs of black ice. "If you think that I am so stu d to, as you put it, 'fall for something', think again. I am no fool." He g red at Albro until he got his temper under control. "Perhaps now is not the time. In the morning, we will revisit this topic. In the mean time, I will think on what you have said."

"Do that," Albro said. "And remember, I'm just a lousy business man and a mediocre gambler who happens to be down on his luck at the moment. But I do have my pride, and I always make good on my debts." Albro passed the book to Jimmy Bozeman who handed it to his boss.

Goldstein laid the book at his side and brought his pudgy fingers together across the bulge of his stomach. His dark, bushy eyebrows had formed a line parallel with the line of his pursed lips. Albro could see that he was clearly disappointed in his response. Albro swallowed hard. He'd regretted from day one having borrowed money from Goldstein, but there it was, a foolish decision. He could add it to a long list of bad decisions. He'd contemplated coming clean to Newton's lawyer about the debt. Newton was so rich that he'd no more miss fifty thousand dollars than he would a set of misplaced cufflinks. He'd finally come to the conclusion that he couldn't do it out of a simple matter of pride and also the fear that if Monique found out he associated with loan sharks, she might call off the wedding. "I have my pride too," Goldstein said. "Mr. Bozeman and Mr. Hopkins have their pride as well."

Albro looked at Jimmy and Hoppy and they nodded in solemn agreement.

"Pride is a good thing," Goldstein went on, "but in your case I think it is misdirected. There are many examples of individuals holding steadfast to the image of their own pride in the face of imminent danger. It always seems to end badly for them." He glanced down at the thick volume and tapped it with his index finger. "Ah well, it seems we never learn from the tragedy of others." He sighed deeply and pinched the bridge of his nose and closed his eyes for a moment. When he opened them he said, "It's getting late. We will discuss the issue of the *Jade Prince* tomorrow. Jimmy?"

Jimmy Bozeman pushed himself off the counter and removed his coat and laid it across the back of the sofa. He went across to the small bookshelf that stood in the corner and pulled out two handfuls of books and made two stacks on the kitchen counter, rearranging them twice to make them equally high and leaving about twelve inches between the stacks.

"You want to take off your tux, Al? They'll have to cut away the sleeve at the hospital and that's just more expense for you."

"Thanks Jimmy," Albro said. "I can't say how much I appreciate your thoughtfulness."

He shrugged his muscular shoulders and said, "Don't mention it. Now if you'll just lay your arm across these books I can make a nice clean break."

Albro was grateful his knees didn't try to buckle when he stood. He took off his jacket and removed the cummerbund from around his waist and stripped off his tie and shirt leaving the suspenders to dangle around his hips. His undershirt was soaked with sweat. Hoppy pulled a nasty looking pistol from the waistband of his pants and leveled it at him. He was now into a regular rhythm, something between a samba and a mambo, Albro guessed.

"I know you're a cooperative guy at heart," Hoppy said. "It's just that sometimes people panic and can't help themselves and try to run. Seeing a gun always makes them stay put."

Jimmy hefted a steel rod that was about two feet long and an inch in diameter. He'd wrapped one end with cloth tape to provide a good grip. "Right or left, makes no difference to me," he said.

The statement struck Albro as funny and a nervous chuckle rattled in his throat.

"What's so funny?" Jimmy asked.

"Oh, it's just the thought that I have a choice. I'm left-handed, you know. You don't know how much grief that has given me over the years. Maybe there's some sort of justice in letting you break the left one."

"Sounds a bit like cuttin' off your nose to spite your face, but if that's the way you want it, go right ahead," Jimmy said and made a sweeping motion with the rod that seemed to convey a grand sense of accommodation.

Albro realized the foolishness of such a decision and placed his right arm on the books. If he was going to have only one working arm, it made sense to make it a useful one. Jimmy spread his feet and took aim by touching the end of the rod to Albro's forearm approximately midway between his elbow and wrist. The steel was surprisingly warm. Albro had imagined it was going to be icy cold.

"Jimmy," Goldstein said. "Remember, we just want to break the bone. You know that I consider a compound fracture to be cruel and unusual punishment."

"Right," Jimmy agreed.

Albro turned to Goldstein who had risen to his feet. A look of genuine sadness and disappointment was set in the deep lines of his face. He heard Jimmy take a sharp breath and from the corner of his eye, saw him raise the bar over his head, but before he could bring it down, a phone rang.

"Hold it," Goldstein said. He looked around and then picked up Albro's jacket and found the phone. "Excuse me," he said and shuffled into the bedroom and turned on the bedside lamp.

Albro's heart was slamming so loudly in his ears that he couldn't make out what Goldstein was saying. He looked at Jimmy and Hoppy who both stood relaxed waiting for their boss to return. After a few very long minutes, Goldstein came back into the living room and placed a hand on Albro's shoulder.

"I have sad news for you. That was a lady calling from Seattle. She says that she's been trying to reach you since yesterday afternoon. You should check your messages. It's about your father. He was found two days ago."

"My father?" Albro asked and wavered slightly under the weight of Goldstein's hand. "Someone found my father?"

"Yes. Unfortunately, he was dead when they found him."

Albro's vision blurred and he thought he might faint. "How...? I mean why... Who...? The questions floated in his head but couldn't seem to find the necessary momentum to complete themselves.

"It must be a shock," Goldstein said. "I feel great sympathy for you. I loved my own father and a day doesn't pass that I don't miss him. I wrote down a number. I said you were going to be occupied for the rest of the night by a very important matter and that you would call first thing in the morning." He paused and squeezed Albro's upper arm lightly. "You have my deepest condolences."

Albro looked into Sal Goldstein's avuncular countenance and didn't notice the signal he gave to Jimmy, but he heard the crack, like a pencil snapping in a tiled room and he felt a nearly simultaneous pain shoot through his entire body.

CHAPTER 4

THE bedside phone rang in the home of Frank Giddes, who was nearing the end of a long, loyal and fruitless career with the Central Intelligence Agency of the United States of America. He was fully awake before the first ring had ended and before the phone rang another three times, he had noted that the time was 3:15, had turned on the bedside lamp, and had reached for a pad and pen. He had trained himself long ago to be fully prepared to respond when important calls came through. His personal calls were routed to an answering service so that he would not be awakened unnecessarily.

He picked up the phone and spoke crisply and clearly, "Giddes."

"Potter, here," the voice at the other end informed him. Potter was a junior intelligence officer. He had taken a degree in computer science from Northwestern, but had a penchant for history. Giddes also had an interest in history and had struck up a friendship with his younger colleague. Giddes headed up a department whose sole task was to manage the history of certain less than successful operations whose more significant, and perhaps ruinous, details had been quietly and carefully kept from public scrutiny. These were cases which the Agency, for all intents and purposes, would have preferred to bury deeper than a Virginia coal mine. Nevertheless, unexpected and undesirable information did, on occasion, rise to the surface. Managing those histories was a mundane and methodical job requiring an individual whose personal characteristics meshed wit the day to day routine of collecting and collating massive amounts of ata in hopes of extracting that little nugget of gold

Pot r's job was to monitor data from computers that kept track of phone tr ffic, news media, public records and surveillance cameras all across the c untry and to a lesser degree the rest of the developed world, looking for ey words and phrases, or images that in some way might relate to th aforementioned cases. Now and then a name popped up in the monito ng program whose electronic eyes and ears never rested. Potter wou shunt them along to Giddes' department and for the most part they t nded, after careful investigation, to be examples of pure coincidence Potter had a hunch that this one was going to be different. His monito ng program had snared a name from the ether and had highlighted in red, which meant that he was to notify Giddes, and only Giddes, imn ediately; no matter what the hour might be.

"Go head," Giddes said calmly into the phone.

"I t nk we got something that might interest you." Potter said. "Does the n me Thomas Crane mean anything to you?"

Gid es, who had been poised to write, suddenly froze. The name meant a gr at deal to him. He would not have replied to Potter had he not been bsolutely certain his phone line was secure. Without answering t e question directly, he said, "What's the context?"

Pot r answered, "Seattle, recently deceased, and classified as a 'John Doe'. An alert came through when the name came up in regards to a routine quest by their medical examiner's office for finger-print identificatio from the national data base."

The monitoring systems were set up to raise red flags but not to impede any requests, which in itself might attract attention. Giddes asked, "Hav they received a response?"

"Ha g on a minute," Potter replied.

Gid es could hear the muted tap of keys as Potter searched for information In all likelihood Potter was hacking into the medical examiner's omputers. The minutes that passed seemed very long and he realized tha he was gripping the phone much too hard. He relaxed and took in a de p breath.

"Time of death was approximately 0100 local time, 10 December. Two days ago, sir. The request for prints went through on Friday at 1630. At the pace these requests are processed, it'll be two, maybe three working days which puts them close to Christmas, and that could be another delay. Things tend to back up over there during the holiday season."

Giddes did not tell Potter what the medical examiner's office would do once they discovered their 'John Doe' was Thomas Crane. He knew that Potter, if he had not already, would research the name and realize that he had found the tip of an immense iceberg. The story would be on every news source in the country, and that was something Giddes could not allow. He thought carefully before asking the next question. He had Potter working in this capacity because he knew he could trust him, but he'd also developed a fondness for him too, and he didn't want to make matters any more complicated than they already were. But then again, it was probably already too late for such considerations. "What was the cause of death?" he asked.

"According to the medical examiner," Potter answered, "Crane seems to have died from stab wounds." Potter scanned the report and then accessed photos from the pathology report. "Christ!" he blurted before he could stop himself.

"What is it?" Giddes asked.

Potter had to swallow hard before answering. "Photos," he said, trying to sound calm. "This guy was cut up pretty badly."

"Copy the files," Giddes said. "I also want to know every detail of the police investigation."

"Yes sir," Potter confirmed. That would take some time. He'd already discovered that the record system of city and county was not centralized which meant he would have to hack into different departments. It was nothing he couldn't do. It would just take time. He said to Giddes, "There are a couple more things you should know about."

"What?" Giddes asked. He looked at the bedside clock and the relentless sweep of its second hand.

"Fir :, the FRS has made a match with the name," Potter said. FRS referred to ne *facial recognition software* they were using to scour the massive am unt of visual data recorded at thousands locations around the world. A camera outside the Chinese Consulate in San Francisco caught Thor as Crane a week ago it seems."

"WI at do you mean, a week ago?" Giddes spoke quietly into the phone's mo thpiece as he rose slowly to his feet. He wanted to shout, but kept his v ice calm. "Why didn't the information come through immediatel ?" Giddes knew the system wasn't infallible. Unless the image was narp and clear it could generate a hundred possible matches and therefc e would be considered a low priority until a specific search was made.

"Th t happens, sir. When the name came through, I made a general sea h of all monitoring systems and there it was."

"Ok y," Giddes said. His mind began racing through the possibilities of why, and how, Thomas Crane had returned. He asked Potter, "WI t else have you got? Was any report filed by our contact at the Consula ?

"Nc hing that I can access at the moment, sir," Potter said.

Gid es thought about that. Retrieval of data was akin to dipping a net into t e vast digital ocean. All it required was the right kind of net and the kr wledge of knowing where to dip. On the other hand, encryption /as becoming ever more sophisticated and the cracking of convoluted ata streams ever more time consuming. He missed the old days of ha d written messages passed from one clandestine hand to another in s me remote location. However vulnerable the courier might be, one cou always limit the points of access. Nowadays all it took was a laptop and phone line and the entire world was at your disposal. "What about airpo t surveillance, customs and immigration? Do you have any other accou ts of his movements?"

"Nc hing yet, but I'll keep looking. How far should I go back?"

Giddes tho ght for a moment. The case involving Thomas Crane had been a nea disaster for the Agency: two agents dead, several more compromis to the point of rendering them worthless, a dozen members of the Army's elite special forces unit, an unknown number of support personnel and four world-renown scientists lost and presumed dead while involved in an ultra-top-secret project in a mountainous jungle in Southeast Asia. It had taken place during the final collapse of America's effort to fight a losing war, and the agent in charge of the operation had been a young, but very capable man by the name of Frank Giddes. A story like that would have been ruinous had the press gotten hold of it. The official version that had been leaked to the press had been bad enough. The President had fed the Agency to the lions of a Congressional subcommittee investigating the incident. The result of which, required the head of the Agency to throw a great deal of political meat to those lions. While Giddes' career had not ended, it had, in effect, been pushed into a small corner and there he had stayed. It was an incident the Agency had been more than happy to let die away, and he was certain now they would have little interest in opening old wounds. Nevertheless, the Agency had a tradition of tying up loose threads and the fate of the two missing agents, not to mention all of the others, still remained a mystery. This loose thread needed to be tied up quickly and quietly. After all, Thomas Crane had been declared dead thirty-five years ago.

"Search all relevant data bases back to June 14, 1970," Giddes said. The date was as fresh in his mind as if it had occurred yesterday. "Find out everything you can. Put it all on a disk and scrub your files, thoroughly. Leave no tracks. Do you understand?"

"Yes sir," Potter said. He could hear the strain in Giddes' voice. The name, Thomas Crane, had certainly set off some powerful alarms in his boss's head. He'd typed the name into a simple Google search and had come up with only one hit, a paper authored back in 1969 in the American Journal of Particle Physics. If the guy was important enough to be on Giddes' 'list' there should be a whole lot more information floating around out there, unless, of course, they'd tried to reduce the man's life to the smallest speck possible, which prompted the question, why?

"You said there were a couple of things," Giddes said interrupting Potter's thoughts.

"Yes n," he swiveled his seat around to another screen. "The print request produced another hit. There's no doubt about Crane. The folks in Seattle have your man. They just don't know it yet. It's just odd that another positive identification could be produced from the same set of prints. It happens when they have just a fragment of a print, but not with a complete set. I'm sure it's an anomaly."

"What's the name?" Giddes asked.

"Allo Marshal Swift," Potter said. "It's from an arrest record with the city Los Angeles police department. In addition, it appears the subject was a ward of the State of Washington. Juvenile records aren't the easiest to access. The older ones were never digitized. Do you want me to look into it?"

"Forget it. Concentrate on Crane," Giddes said, agreeing with Potter that the system had thrown them a red herring. Then he stopped. He reminded himself that he had focused too tightly on Crane once before and had missed entirely the bigger picture. "Wait," he said to Potter. "Go ahead and give me whatever information you can find on... What did you say the name was?"

"Allo Marshal Swift," Potter answered.

"Yes," Giddes said. The name meant nothing to him, but on the off chance that it was somehow tied to Crane, he would need to know what the connection amounted to. "Stay there until I arrive and don't speak to anyone about this," he added.

"Yes sir," Potter said. He waited until the line went dead and then went to work.

Giddes held the phone in his hand and stared at it while gathering his thoughts. The image of the scorched patch of earth loomed large in his memory and threatened to crowd out the more immediate need to get moving. He could hear the pounding of the helicopter blades and feel the rocking of the army gunship as they hovered over the scene of total devastation where only hours before an orderly compound of buildings and tents had once stood. If it had been an explosion, one would have expected to see torn and shredded bits of the structures blown by the shock wave into the surrounding jungle, but there had been nothing.

71

Everything had vanished, including Thomas Crane. It was a memory that remained as vivid in the intervening thirty-five years as the day he had seen it.

Giddes pulled himself out of the memory. He punched a number into the phone. A woman's voice answered on the first ring, "Yes?"

Giddes knew that what he was about to do was an act of treason, but he'd gotten over any sense of guilt long ago. He considered it payback for what the Agency had done to him, how they had side-lined him when he'd been destined for far greater things. Giddes said, "Wake the Old Man."

The Old Man was not part of the Agency, and Giddes had never been certain what he was part of. He only knew that the Old Man had offered something far more meaningful than false praise and a meager pension after thirty years of dogged service.

"This better be important," the woman replied. "Do you realize what time it is?"

"Are you suggesting that I call back later?" Giddes let some of the urgency he was feeling spill into his voice. "Are you sure that's what you want me to tell the Old Man when he demands to know why he was not awakened?"

There was a brief pause before the woman said, "Please, hold."

Giddes waited several minutes before the Old Man's voice, cool and measured, without a trace of sleep, came through the phone. "What is it?"

"We have a situation," Giddes said.

"Oh?"

"Thomas Crane," Giddes said. There was a lengthy silence during which Giddes thought he could hear a muffled conversation in the background, but it could easily have been his imagination.

"I'll expect you later in the morning," the old man said to him. Giddes waited for the dial tone to return and then he placed the phone back in its cradle.

CHAPTER 5

SALVATORE GOLDSTEIN and his two thugs were kind enough to drop Albro at L.A. General where he sat watching the casualties from the Los Angeles nightlife being wheeled into the emergency room. The throbbing pain in his right forearm kept him suspended somewhere between unconsciousness and hysteria. A nurse had given him an icepack, and a nice looking receptionist kept sending sympathetic glances in his direction, but neither did little to relieve the painful depression he'd sunk into. The news that his father had, at long last, been found should have brought a feeling of elation. Instead, he assumed it be another false alarm. He had spent years trying to find his parents. He'd followed one false lead after another until he'd finally given up in despair. He'd finally faced up to the fact that neither his father, nor his mother would ever be found. And now, out of the blue, news had come, saying that his father had been found. He dreaded making the phone call that would lead to the inevitable case of mistaken identity and the ensuing reassurances that it was just a matter of time before his parents would be located. No one ever disappeared without a trace. At least that's what every investigator he'd hired to find them said. But then they'd all hit the same blank wall. He winced at the thought of tens of thousands of dollars he'd spent over the years, and not one scrap of information had ever tuned up. He pulled the piece of paper Goldstein had given him and looked at the number. What had Goldstein said? He'd said something about his father having been located, but that he was

73

dead. That was a new twist! What was that old saying? A fool and his money are soon parted? It didn't matter what this was going to cost him, because he had no money. It was time, he decided, to accept the fact that his birth parents had not wanted to be found. It was time to get over it, he told himself.

He balled up the paper and was ready to toss it when he caught the security guard glaring at him. He stuffed it back into his pocket and slumped down in his chair. He was a foundling, and that simple fact had shaped his life more than anything else. Dead or alive, someone claiming to be his father wouldn't change the past, but maybe it could change the future, a future which at this moment held out the prospect of more broken bones. What if the old man had some money and made a confession on his death bed and left his entire estate to the son he'd abandoned all those years ago. He'd held on to similar fantasies growing up in foster homes. A favorite was one in which he'd been born the illegitimate son of a man about to inherit vast wealth, whose beautiful mistress, his mother, had died in childbirth. His father, forced to abandon his son over fears of losing his inheritance, had shortly thereafter regretted his mistake and had been searching for him ever since. Some night, there would be a knock at the door and there he would be, standing tall and he would lift his son into his strong arms and carry him away from whatever squalid home he was in at the time.

That was pure fantasy, but what if this time it were real. There could be something to it, maybe even enough to get Goldstein off his back. Albro looked up and saw the receptionist looking in his direction. He smiled weakly at her. Her shoulders dropped an inch and pulled slightly inward as her lips came together in a slight pucker of sympathy. He was about to pull the phone number out of his pocket when an orderly, pushing a wheelchair, called out his name.

He went first to X-ray where a technician took several pictures of his arm and then he was wheeled to an exam room. In a few minutes, a tired looking doctor in a white coat arrived and slapped the gray and white transparencies on a viewing panel. The doctor, an immigrant from the churning mass of humanity south of the Himalayas, with a long black

74

braid hanging down her back and dark circles under her eyes from having been up all night, checked the name on the x-rays. "Swift, Albro?" she asked. Her voice had the distinctive lilt of upper class, highly educated India, with a no-nonsense edge to it.

"That's me," Albro answered

"Date of birth?" the doctor asked.

That question always gave him a painful jolt. He had no actual date of birth only a given date, which was along story in itself.

Albro said, "December 12, 1976."

"You're certain of that?" the doctor asked."

"Is there a problem?" Albro asked. He was ready to get this over with and go home to bed. The previous night had been short and this day seemed already long.

"No problem," the doctor said. "I've got to make certain they've given me the right x-rays. You wouldn't believe the mix-ups we have here. Do you know what today's date is?"

What was this? Would the next question be to name the current president? He was here to get his arm set, not to be tested for brain function. He started to say a date and then stopped. What was the date? He knew it was getting near the middle of December because there were Christmas lights, and Christmas trees and garlands and ribbons everywhere He happened to be under a lot of stress at the moment. Could he really be expected to come up with the exact date? He looked at the doctor whose dark, unpainted lips waited expectantly in a slightly downturned frown. Then it dawned on him.

The doctor said, "You don't even know that it's your birthday?" She shook her head and let out a derisive sigh. "Let me have a look at your arm."

It was his birthday, at least the day he always considered to be his birthday, and it was getting off to a great start. Perhaps later, to prolong the fun, he could manage to get his foot run over by a bus. She lifted his arm and placed it on the narrow support she had swung over to him. He winced as she touched the darkening bruise on the surface of his forearm.

As she examined his arm she said, "Today is twelve, twelve, two thousand and twelve. You're thirty-six. That's three times twelve. Divide 12 into 1976 and you get 164 with a repeating line of sixes that trails off into infinity, as if the number was searching for wholeness."

"I suppose you're going to tell me there's some special meaning in my birthday?" He remembered seeing a newsstand tabloid proclaiming the world would be ending in a couple of weeks, a prediction the Mayans had made thousands of years ago. Somebody, somewhere, was always predicting the end of the world, and a good part of the world's population was ready to believe it. Given the miserable hand that most people had been dealt, he couldn't say he blamed them for being gullible. He just hoped that the doctor who was about to fix his arm wasn't the sort to believe in such things. Then again, if one did believe that the world was about to end, it might intensify one's desires. She did have a dark and alluring beauty. Her red lipstick made him think of…. She interrupted his thoughts.

"No," she said, "it's just an interesting pattern. Both my mother and father were mathematicians. I grew up fascinated by numbers." She sighted down his arm. She asked, "How did this happen?"

"I fell on some stairs," Albro answered. He was still dressed in the trousers of his tuxedo and Jimmy Bozeman had stretched the suspenders back over his shoulders.

"Nice clean break," she said.

"Too much champagne," Albro added.

"I see," the doctor said. "The bruising is very intense." She touched the spot where the steel rod had made contact. Albro flinched with pain.

"That must be where I hit the step," Albro said as the pain in his arm spiked and then settled back into its dull, throbbing ache. Albro could feel a rising pressure from his stomach into his chest. He clenched his jaws tightly. His face had begun to feel moist and the room was threatening to twist out of shape.

"Were you going up or down?" the doctor asked as she continued to palpate Albro's arm, creating ever increasing waves of pain.

76

"Okay, Doc. You win," Albro said gasping for breath. "The truth is that a Jewish loan shark who thinks of himself as my surrogate father had it done by one of his goons because I was late on my loan payment. Other people have their cars repossessed. I get my arm broken, but I was lucky because I had half my payment. Otherwise, you'd be setting both arms."

The doctor looked at him coldly. "That's very funny Mr. Swift. Relax. I'll be back in a few minutes." She turned and left him. He noticed that she was wearing expensive looking heels. Not much for bedside manner, Albro thought, but at least she had nice looking calves.

A nurse shot him with something that put a hazy glow on everything and reduced the pain to a distant ache. Albro was then vaguely aware of the doctor straightening his arm and wrapping it with plaster gauze. When she was finished she said to Albro, "This needs to stay on for approximately four weeks. Your regular physician can remove it and tell you if the bone has healed properly. Try to keep it dry. Put it in a plastic bag when you shower. Do you understand?"

"Keep it dry for four weeks," Albro repeated, a bit groggy.

"I'm going to write you a prescription for the pain. You're going to be fine. No driving or operating machinery. And be careful on those stairs. Okay?"

"Sure, Doc," Albro said, "careful on the stairs."

She turned and then stopped to face him. "And one more thing," she said, allowing the barest hint of a smile to part her lips, "Happy birthday."

The next thing Albro knew he was standing outside the hospital in the bright sunshine with a sheaf of paperwork clutched in his hand. The air was cool with a hint of ocean fragrance overlaying the metallic stink of auto exhaust that seemed to permeate everything in Los Angeles. The pain killers were beginning to wear off and his arm had begun to throb. Jimmy Bozeman had stuffed one of the hundreds into his pocket and he was pondering his options when the pretty receptionist drove up in a red Civic.

"Would you like a ride?" she called out.

"Thanks," Albro answered, "but I live in Compton. I'm sure that's out of your way."

"No problem, it's not far from where I live," she said and jumped out of the car and helped Albro off the curb and into the seat next to hers and carefully stretched the seatbelt across his lap. They were ahead of the crest of commuters and sailed along to his apartment. She helped Albro up the stairs where, for an awkward moment she watched him fumble with his key and then took it from him and opened the door and led him to the bedroom. She gently slipped off his suspenders and then worked his undershirt over his head and pulled off his shoes and lowered his trousers. Evidently, she'd made up her mind earlier because she didn't hesitate about slipping her fingers beneath the waistband of his shorts, steered him to the bed, and crawled in next to him.

She had stopped to fill his prescription and had given him two of the tiny white pills while still in the car and now he felt like he was floating in a warm sea. He felt himself being lifted and lowered in ever increasing waves until he was lifted one last time and was sent rushing onto to a warm and quiet shore.

Sometime later in the morning, he felt the covers being pulled up and tucked under his chin, but he couldn't rise out of his drug induced slumber to open his eyes. He heard light footsteps and a door close, and then he was lost in a deep sleep of fitful dreams.

CHAPTER 6

FRANK GIDDES wheeled his government sedan into the parking garage.   The expressway had been snarled by an overturned semi-truck and trailer that had skidded on the snow covered roadway before rolling onto its side and blocking all three lanes.   He'd been forced onto a winding detour that had not yet been plowed.   The trip had taken nearly three quarters of an hour when ordinarily he could have done it in seventeen minutes.   Fortunately, it was not yet four a.m. and the morning commute wouldn't begin to clog the arterials for another hour.   His cardkey allowed him entry through the afterhours entrance. Cameras monitored his presence and a guard would log him into a computer before allowing him to proceed through the locked gate to the elevators.   The morning shift wouldn't start until seven which meant he would likely encounter no one else. Giddes handed his badge to the sleepy looking guard.

"Still snowing?" the guard asked as he examined Giddes identification.

"Still snowing," Giddes answered.

"You have a good day, Mr. Giddes."

Giddes acknowledged the sentiment with a nod. He got in the elevator and rode it down three floors to Potter's level. Potter's office was a room roughly eight by twelve with a U-shaped desk upon which sat four computer screens. Potter was twenty-three, the same age Giddes had been when he'd been recruited by the Agency. Although Giddes disapproved of the younger man's habit of dressing in blue-jeans, running shoes and T-shirt, he'd been impressed by Potter's sharp mind and attention to detail. And although their career aspirations couldn't have been more different, (Giddes had never wanted a career outside the Agency, whereas Potter's goal was to work a year or two before pursuing his doctoral degree.), they'd nevertheless developed a friendly working relationship.

Giddes entered without knocking. Potter had the overhead lights turned low and loud music with a strong Latin beat came from speakers hidden somewhere in the semi-darkness. Potter reached out and flicked a switch and the music died.

"Tito Puente," Giddes said. "Nineteen-sixty, I'd guess." John Kennedy had been the new president. He'd voted for Nixon because he'd been skeptical that Kennedy had the guts to stand up to the Russians. Even before Castro there was plenty he hadn't liked about Cubans, but he'd always enjoyed their music.

"Miami. Nineteen fifty-nine. You have a good ear, Mr. Giddes," Potter said. He touched the keyboard and a disc popped out of one of the machines. "Everything's on this," he said and held out a square plastic case to Giddes.

"No tracks?" Giddes asked.

"Not a trace. Anything new that comes through on Crane will be routed directly to you.

"Good," Giddes said. He slipped the case into his side pocket. "Do you have plans for the holidays?"

"As soon as my shift ends, I'll be going up to Pittsburgh and spend Christmas with my folks. I thought I would take Route 50, and maybe do some climbing today if the conditions are right. The Alleghenies are not what I would call mountains, but they're the closest thing we have around here. How about you?" Potter asked.

"I'm afraid I'll be busy," Giddes said and turned to leave.

"Anyway, have a Merry Christmas," Potter said.

"Thank you," Giddes said, "and Merry Christmas to you and your family." He left the room and rode the elevator up and let himself into his office. He took the laptop from his briefcase and inserted the disk that Potter had given him into the computer. Potter had organized the information in a series of numbered files. The first, labeled SF624 contained the original stills pulled from the surveillance camera. Six photos, taken one second apart, showed a tall man in a dark coat walking against a dimly lit background. One photo had managed to capture the man's face in three-quarter profile. One could well imagine that something had caught the man's attention and caused him to turn. Giddes moved the cursor to the man's face, clicked on the image to enlarge it, and studied the now somewhat blurred image for several minutes.

He then moved to the next file which contained the processed images from the Facial Recognition software. The image that came up was remarkable for its improvement in sharpness and clarity. Once again, he studied the image. Anyone else might have been hard pressed to make a definitive statement as to whether or not it was actually Thomas Crane. A man could change a lot in thirty-five years. Giddes, though, had no doubt about the identity of the man in the photo.

He closed the window and then opened a file from the hard drive which contained Crane's official dossier. He searched it until he found the photo he wanted and then brought up the surveillance photo and placed the two side by side, the older man on the left and the younger man on the right. The FRS had estimated an accuracy of eighty-seven percent. He would put it at ninety-nine point nine.

He quickly scanned the fingerprint report and then went on to the information that Potter had managed to get from the medical examiner: Caucasian male, graying hair, blue eyes, six feet two inches, one hundred fifty pounds, obvious emaciation. Identifying marks: heavy scar tissue of unknown origin from base of neck to buttocks. Cause of death: severe blood loss due to deep cuts to torso and legs. Giddes read through the report and then studied the photos. He could see why Potter had been shocked. Giddes also noted that none of the wounds had pierced a vital organ which suggested that Crane had endured a slow and painful death. He stared long and hard at the photos that showed the back of the victim.

The scarring was obviously old. Giddes was no expert, but he had the impression that he was looking at someone who had been flayed alive and had survived the ordeal.

Giddes closed the file. He was pleased to see that Potter had managed to get into the police report. He clicked on that file and began reading through the report. Officers had responded to an anonymous 911 call and had found the victim, still breathing, in an alleyway. A trail of blood led to an abandoned warehouse a few blocks away where it was determined the victim had been present. The victim died at the scene. No incriminating evidence had, as yet, been found. The case had been officially classed as a homicide. There were photos of the body as well as the supposed crime scene which proved to be even more gruesome than those of the medical examiner.

Giddes sat back and thought. The two reports provided enough information to make it clear to Giddes that Thomas Crane had been tortured. The methods had been crude which suggested time might well have been the overriding consideration. There were cleaner, more precise ways of extracting information. Then again, perhaps there was more to this than simply a need for information. He was about to close down the computer when he saw the file labeled, Albro Marshal Swift. He glanced at his watch. This was something that could wait, he surmised, and then a voice at the back of his mind told him otherwise. He opened the file. The first image that came up was so startling, that he flinched backward away from the screen. It was the photo of a good-looking young man with a beautiful blonde-haired woman. His first reaction was to assume that Potter had placed the photo in the wrong file, until he noted the date in the upper corner of the image. It was an image taken from the December 1st issue of the *Los Angeles Times*. He read through the brief article that described the near completion of a museum. He quickly scanned the other images in the file. He realized then, that they had a very serious problem.

Giddes picked up the phone, punched in a number and waited. When the other end picked up he said, "Newton is involved in this."

"Martin." It was the Old Man's voice and not sounding at all surprised.

"Yes," Giddes said and went on to explain how the request for fingerprint identification had produced another name besides Thomas Crane's.

"We will need to be extremely careful," the Old Man said. "You know what you have to do."

Giddes paused, thinking. He said, "Of course." He listened as the line went dead, ejected the disk from the laptop, placed it carefully in its protective case, folded down the screen and placed the computer in his briefcase. He took one last look around the office, knowing this would be the last time he would see it, and then turned out the lights.

The snow had stopped by the time Potter's shift had ended. It had been an interesting night for a change. Giddes was definitely an odd duck, but that fact too, helped to break up the routine of keeping an eye on the names and numbers as they scrolled down the screens. Whatever it was about Thomas Crane, it had certainly grabbed his boss's attention. He'd noted the sharp intake of breath at the other end of the phone line and then the slight agitation in Giddes voice before he'd gotten it under control. He had a good ear for such things, but it was just a job and none of his concern. In six months he'd be at Northwestern working on his graduate degree.

Potter maneuvered his aging Volvo, the worn tires catching and spinning on the snowy parking lot, still nearly empty even though the day shift was supposedly underway. He assumed that the highways were a mess and workers would be trickling in all morning, or not showing up at all. The task of guarding the nation's security would have to be put on hold until the streets were cleared. He slid through the exit points and onto the boulevard that bypassed the expressway. The sun was starting to peek through from the east and the stark beauty of the bare oak trees, each branch covered in a sleeve of white made him smile. It was Friday and the start of his Christmas holiday and he was planning to make the trip up to the New Hampshire mountains a week of camping and ice-climbing, and then spend Christmas in Philly with his parents. His gear was all stowed in the back. He slipped a Miles Davis tape into the player and settled into the slow, grooving beat of *All Blue*.

He crossed the Shenandoah River and near Berryville, pulled off for gas and purchased a double tall Americano and a couple of bran muffins and then caught Route 50 that would carry him west and north. The two lane road was covered with snow and the tires gave a satisfying crunching sound as the stalwart old Volvo made its way up the gentle incline. The car had belonged to his parents who had passed it onto him when he'd left for college. He'd actually learned to drive in it, his father next to him and patiently coaching him through the confusion of clutch and gears, expressway merging, and the dreaded act of parallel parking. He was due at his parent's house on Christmas Eve, which was twelve days away. He would camp a few nights then drop in on some old friends. He reminded himself that he still needed to buy some gifts. He relaxed, luxuriating in the thought of the leisurely days ahead. Occasionally, the old car would fishtail a bit and then he would deftly steer into the rotation just as his father had taught him to do in the empty mall parking lot, and the car would obediently straighten out. He knew that soon, before the road began to climb into the mountains, he would have to pull over and put on the chains. He'd travelled Route 50 before which, like so many of the older roads, followed the winding course of a river that cut its way down through the hills and was little used now that a new expressway had gone through. He knew there was a turnout not far ahead, just as the road crossed the river.

The road made a wide sweeping curve, which for a short distance actually turned the road east just before crossing the river and then swung west again. The sky had cleared and the sun was dazzling and momentarily blinding as it reflected off the snow-covered landscape, and as Potter reached for his sunglasses, a vehicle pulled onto the roadway from his right. He hit the brakes, his quick reactions getting the better of him, and in the millisecond it took for him to realize this and get his foot off the brake, the rear of the old Volvo had already passed the point of no return. He might have avoided the collision had he simply steered slightly to the left. He hit the vehicle with only a glancing blow, and he had time to fully appreciate the effect of time dilation just as it was portrayed in the movies, everything moving in a silent ballet of slow motion, his car spinning, the unsmiling face of the driver behind the wheel, the sparkle of ice crystals in the cold air, before he went crashing through the bridge railing. The old Volvo landed on its roof and broke through the ice and settled quickly to the rocky bottom.

The other vehicle paused, its exhaust forming a cloud of vapor which caught the sunbeams in a playful embrace, before moving off slowly to the east. The driver suspected that the left headlight was smashed. There would be the tell-tale sprinkling of glass on the snow, the paint scrape on the bumper, and when the local deputies discovered the stolen sedan later in the day abandoned at the entrance to a side road up ahead, it would give them the missing piece of evidence to stitch together the last seconds of the young man's life whose body would be found still strapped inside the car when they pulled it from the river.

Frank Giddes brought his sedan up the long, curving tree-lined drive to the front of the house. It was a modest home, single story with a red brick facade, covered porch and a two car garage joined to the house by a breezeway. It was the site that was impressive. The house stood on a low knoll above a small lake with successive rows of snow covered hills rising one upon the other into the distance, and not another house in sight. A wisp of smoke rose from the chimney and he was greeted with the comforting scent of wood smoke when he opened the car door. A path had been shoveled to the entry and he was thankful for that, not having had time to go back to his home for overshoes. An older man in a gray cardigan stood in the doorway. He extended a gloved hand to Giddes. Giddes knew that if he hesitated even for an instant the Old Man would take note. He silently cursed himself for never having been able to overcome the revulsion he always felt when grasping the Old Man's hand. Nevertheless he extended his own hand and looked the Old Man square in the eyes. When the Old Man let go of his hand, Giddes resisted the urge to wipe it on his trouser leg. Together they walked into the living room where a fire blazed in the fireplace.

"Coffee?" the older man asked.

"Please," Giddes answered. He breathed in deeply and gathered his thoughts as he studied his host. The older man filled two cups from an insulated carafe. The 'Old Man', as everyone referred to him when not in his presence, and 'sir' while in his company, wore in addition to his sweater and gloves, a pair of flannel slacks, a plaid shirt and a well worn pair of loafers. He could have been anyone's grandfather, a quiet, soft-spoken gentleman of exquisite manners. That demeanor, Giddes knew, had lulled many an unsuspecting victim into a complacent state of mind; most of whom had not lived beyond the recognition of their mistake. Giddes knew things about the Old Man that gave him a distinct advantage in dealing with him. Perhaps, that was why after thirty-five years, he was still among the living. The Old Man needed him. As powerful as the Old Man was, he still needed someone like himself to do the necessary legwork when the need arose, as it had now.

"How are the roads?" the Old Man asked.

"Treacherous, to say the least," Giddes replied without a hint of irony in his voice, "and more snow on the way." He removed the laptop from his briefcase and inserted the disk. He gave a brief outline of the morning's events and then began opening the files. After about twenty minutes he ejected the disk.

The Old Man was silent and stood looking into the fire. After a few long moments he spoke, "Who else knows of this?"

"If we know, then certainly Marlowe knows as well."

The Old Man clinched his jaw and his loose hands momentarily curled into fists. He wished to hell that he'd killed John Marlowe years ago when he'd had the chance, but he had needed him then and it was not beyond the realm of possibility that he would need him in the future. John Marlowe had been a close friend and confidant of Crane, and he knew the workings of Crane's mind better than anyone. "We don't know that he is directly involved," the Old Man said.

Giddes was about to argue that point, but he held his comments. For now, Marlowe was the Old Man's problem. He said, "We cannot be absolutely certain about anything at this time. The people in Seattle will remain in the dark for a few more days. That should give us time to trace Crane's movements. Eventually it's going to hit the media."

"Can't you stop it?"

"I've put a hold on releasing Crane's fingerprints. The medical examiner's request will simply turn up negative. I'm sure they will accept that. It happens all the time. But there are other ways of identifying a body."

"Who could do that?" the Old Man demanded.

"Next of kin, a friend, or an old colleague, are just a few ways. We could spend weeks tracing his movements and still not discover everywhere he's been and everyone he's met with," Giddes said.

The Old Man seemed to brood on the possibilities that existed for a man who had literally disappeared off the face of the earth. Changing the subject for the moment, he asked, "What's the status of the surveillance record?"

"Still intact," Giddes answered, "but all notations of the FRS have been deleted. Officially, the Agency is unaware that Thomas Crane has surfaced."

"What about the technician who spotted him?"

"Taken care of," Giddes said. He felt his chest tighten slightly at the unfortunate need to deal with Potter.

"You're certain?"

"I took care of it personally. The fewer involved in this, the better, wouldn't you say?" It was an impertinent thing to say, but Giddes did not care to have his own abilities questioned. Potter had posed a negligible risk, but a risk nonetheless. The fact that he had liked the young man had never given him pause.

The Old Man looked at Giddes and said, "You have no doubts that Thomas Crane had returned and is now dead?"

"None," Giddes said.

"And we can safely assume why he returned," the Old Man said.

"Yes and no," Giddes said.

"What do you mean?" the Old Man asked. There was a sharp edge to his voice. Giddes knew that he expected this to be taken care of simply and efficiently with no unnecessary complications.

"There is something else that you need to see. This photograph was taken two weeks ago. It was featured in the society section of the *Los Angeles Times*." Giddes said and slipped another disc into the computer. He brought up the picture of Albro Swift and Monique Osborne Newton.

The Old man's demeanor instantly became clouded with rage. "Who is that?" he shouted while stabbing a finger at the screen.

"This is a photograph of Monique Olivia Newton..."

"I know who she is! Tell me who that is with her!"

"His name is Albro Marshal Swift," Giddes said.

"Why was I not told of this?" The Old Man's voice had dropped to a reasonable level, but his rage continued to grow.

"We somehow missed it when it was published..." Giddes started to reply.

"That's not my point, and you know it!" The Old Man interrupted as he slammed his fist on the table. The image blinked off. Giddes hit several keys and it reappeared, but the Old Man didn't bother to look at it.

I can only assume that Martin felt it was in his best interest to not inform us," Giddes said. He did not bother to hide the smugness he felt in being able to say what he had just said. "You will remember that I told you Martin would sooner or later cause us trouble."

"Yes, and it was your job to see that he did not." The Old Man glared at Giddes.

"In many respects, Martin has always been beyond our control. You've said as much on many occasions, but there's no use arguing about that now. I think we're looking at the answer to your question as to why Crane returned. The question is what do you want me to do about it?" Giddes gestured toward the image on the computer screen.

The Old Man drew a calming breath. "Assuming Crane knew where he could find..." The Old Man paused and returned his gaze to the computer screen and studied the face of the young man. "What did you say his name is?"

"Albro Marshal Swift," Giddes answered.

"Assuming," the Old Man continued, "that Crane knew where to find him, is there any evidence that he made contact?"

"Nothing, but that is not to say they did not meet. If not, what was Crane waiting for, the right opportunity? Perhaps, Crane had no intention of seeing him," Giddes said.

"Wouldn't you try to see your child after that many years?" the Old Man asked.

"If you can call him that," Giddes said.

"For lack of a better word," the Old Man said.

"He's an adult," Giddes said, and quickly realized that he was mincing words. "To think that we've been trying to find Crane all this time, and his child, as you wish to refer to him, has been right under our noses."

"If you are going to hide something," the Old Man said, "the best place is always in plain sight. Do you think the young man knows who he is?"

"All I have to go on at this time are the photographs on this disk. I've studied them closely. A lot can be learned by the look in someone's eyes. There exists a complete lack of innocence in that woman's eyes. She definitely knows who she is. She has known since she was a child. I believe the young man to be completely unaware. How long that will remain the case I can't say. Not much longer would be my guess."

"Then the sooner we act, the better," the Old Man said. "Kill him. By the end of the day, Albro Marshal Swift will no longer pose a problem to us."

"And if he possesses a medallion? Giddes asked.

"All the more reason to eliminate him," the Old Man answered. "Kill him and bring me the medallion."

"Killing him could be a difficult task. As you know, the medallion will do everything in its power to protect him."

"Don't tell me what I know!" the Old Man exploded. The veins at his temples stood out like small, green snakes. "Your job is to do as I say!"

Giddes waited before he spoke, giving the Old Man time to cool down. He'd seen what could happen when the Old Man was pushed too hard. When he considered if safe he said, "Allowing him to live could be to our advantage."

"In what way?" The Old Man's voice rose again, but the angry edge was tempered by a hint of doubt.

"Crane undoubtedly has an understanding of events that none of us has been able to achieve."

"Had," the Old Man said. "He's dead."

"That's precisely the reason we should let the young man live, at least for the time being. Don't you think Crane made some sort of arrangement to pass that knowledge to his son? Don't you think that is the real reason he returned?"

"That may very well be the case," the Old Man said, "but we can't afford to take that chance. Crane made a mockery of us once before, and I'm sure he planned to do so again. I do not doubt that Crane believed he possessed knowledge that could change everything. Whether he passed that knowledge to someone is of no consequence. Only Crane could have used that knowledge, and he is dead."

"I still think that killing Albro Marshal Swift would be a mistake. At present, we have a small advantage. This young man is not aware of us. We can easily find him. He might even agree to work with us. You always asserted that Crane would never destroy the key that unlocks it all."

"That was then, this is now. Thomas Crane is no more!" There was genuine vehemence in the Old Man's voice. "We are very close and there is no evidence that anything more than a few more days' time is required."

"Are you completely certain of that?" Giddes asked. "Until we are successful, there will always be an element of doubt. What if that young man is crucial to the completion your plans? If Martin should get to him first, you may lose an opportunity as yet unknown to us. You made a crucial mist ke in assuming Martin's interests coincided with our own. In my opinion, here is far too much at stake," Giddes said. He had never so strongly or o directly confronted the Old Man. Perhaps, he had not fully understood his role in all of this until earlier in the day when he had forced youn g Potter off the bridge. It was not the first time he had committed nurder and would not be the last, but this time had been different. was as if a door had opened, however briefly, and had allowed him a glimpse of what eternal damnation really meant.

The Old Man's face grew suddenly dark. "Are you questioning my judgment? f Thomas Crane returned, then it is almost certain that others are here as vell. Who do you think killed him? Have you asked yourself that questic n?"

Gid es avoided the Old Man's glare. No, he had not considered the prospe of having to deal with any allies or, for that matter, any enemies wh o might have followed Crane. The Old Man, of course, was right. If any one were able to use Albro Marshal Swift, the result could be disastrous. le looked into the dying embers of the fireplace and regained his compos re before he spoke, "What about the Chinese?" he asked.

"I'v already spoken with our contact at the Consulate," the Old Man said, h s voice was once again calm. "Using a false identity, Crane applied for nd received a tourist visa for travel between August fifteenth and Septem er twenty-first. He travelled first to Hong Kong. From there, no one seer s to know what happened to him."

The ignificance of what the Old Man had just stated was not lost on Giddes. nose five weeks coincided with the discovery in Tibet and the earthquake hat had buried everything under a million tons of rock when the mounta n had collapsed. There was overwhelming seismic evidence to explain t e disaster, but looking back at it now, Giddes couldn't help but assume that Crane had somehow been responsible, that he had drawn them into a trap in the same way that a terrorist draws his victims to the scen of a bomb blast and then detonates his real weapon, killing countless n ore. The Old Man had declared the site to be genuine. According 1 him, there were twelve such sites, the only surviving remnants o a future civilization.

91

Giddes had presumed the whole idea that a physical piece of the future buried in the deep past to be preposterous, a concept defying the laws of physics. 'Future', by its very definition, precluded its own existence. How could a thousand years of reality fold itself back in time? Giddes would not have believed such a thing could happen had he not seen with his own eyes the ruins filled with crumbling machinery and the terrifying creatures carved in the stone walls. Of the two sites that had been found, both had been destroyed, (the first most definitely by Crane, and the second quite possibly as well). Of the other ten, no one knew where they were located or even if they still existed.

The Old Man claimed that the sites had been doorways into other realities governed by unique dimensions, which had allowed their makers to behave like gods. How ruins could be artifacts from the future, the Old Man had not bothered to explain, other than to say the people who had built that civilization possessed knowledge only God had previously known. Each of those portals, the Old Man claimed, marked the site of a great city that had existed in its own, independent reality, yet linked to the other great cities. Those links, narrow fields of space-time embedded in the invisible dark matter of the universe, passed through a central metropolis built on a monumental scale, where the present coexisted with the past and the future.

Giddes had imagined a Ferris wheel like contraption with twelve gondolas connected to a central hub, and when he had mentioned this, the Old Man had smiled indulgently, as a great intellectual might smile at the musings of a child. To describe the array of portals as points on a great wheel and their connection as spokes, the Old Man had said, would be like describing the human mind as nothing more than a collection of neurons. 'Mind' was the result of the continuous interaction of the vast array of neurons, and likewise, the continuous interaction of those twelve cities, allowed their inhabitants to experience 'the totality of existence'.

The cities might have been destroyed, but the lines that connected them, the Old Man insisted, still existed. They need find only one portal and the pathway would lead them to the *Jade Prince*.

Tibet. Even that bumbling idiot, Krupp, the Old Man's so-called 'expert', had not been able to contain his excitement, and in the few precious weeks they had to examine the ruins, they had discovered tantalizing clues regarding the location of another of the great cities, constructed in a far off future, that most assuredly now lay in ruins, buried in the Mongolian desert, hidden away, literally, beneath the sands of time. Was that ruined city another portal, or the center of those converging pathways? Would the Old Man find the center of all existence? Frankly, Giddes had his doubts. The Chinese were excavating that site at a feverish pace. As yet, they had discovered nothing but seam after layered seam of coal as they dug deeper and deeper into the earth. The site was huge, covering roughly a square mile and until now, the Old Man had not been perturbed by the slow progress.

Giddes brought his mind back to the moment. There was no evidence that Crane had returned through the Tibetan site. The machines had all but turned to dust. That fact alone gave Giddes his greatest concern. The Old Man was certain that the other ten sites, if found, would be in the same ruinous state. If that were true, Crane had accomplished something that even the Old Man asserted was beyond the realm of all possibilities. Did Crane know of a site outside of the twelve portals? Perhaps, there had been a back door known to only a few. And why not? If those people were so smart, wouldn't they have built in some sort of fail-safe mechanism? Maybe he was being stubbornly pragmatic, but if the Old Man's efforts to find the *Jade Prince* failed, that 'back door' would be their last chance of success. He thought of pointing that out to the Old Man, that maybe they should put some effort into finding it, but that would call into question the Old Man's abilities to carry out his plan and Giddes knew that he had pushed the Old Man as far as he dared. He did not care to bear the brunt of the Old Man's rage.

Still he had a nagging hunch that Crane had been bent on preventing the Old Man from finding the *Jade Prince*. The questions that loomed over him now was who had killed Crane and why? Had Marlowe killed him? Had Martin Osborne Newton played a role? Had Crane, himself, in some perverse act of self immolation arranged his own death?

It seemed impossible that Crane could have set anything in motion that could stop them, but to be absolutely certain of that, they needed to know the answers to these questions.

"Even with a false identity, how could he have avoided detection?" Giddes asked the Old Man.

"He undoubtedly had some help."

"Who?" Giddes asked.

"As yet we do not know. Most likely it was someone in a highly placed position of internal security. We must be very careful not to bring undue attention to the Chinese."

"Are you so sure it was not they who were helping him?" Giddes had never trusted the Chinese to do anything other than serve their own best interests.

"If so, I doubt very much that they would have allowed him to slip from their grasp."

"Do you think Crane found the Tibetan ruins?"

"Perhaps, but perhaps he wasn't searching for it," The Old Man answered. "Perhaps, he knew its location. We don't know, but we should assume that he was at least in the area."

"If the *Jade Prince* had been there, do you think he meant to destroy it?" Giddes asked.

"That is a question I am expecting you to find the answer to," the Old Man said.

"Then I will need to speak with the son," Giddes said looking straight at the Old Man. He had not meant it to sound as if he were issuing an ultimatum. No one issued ultimatums to the Old Man, and much to Giddes relief, there was not the flash of anger he had expected.

The Old Man said, "Very well, you have forty-eight hours. As a safeguard, I will alert our agents in the field. Albro Marshal Swift will be under constant observation. If at any moment he is deemed to be a threat, he will be eliminated. I will take no unnecessary risks. We will not have another setback. Do you understand?"

Giddes felt the muscles in his jaw tighten. The Old Man had never made an outright accusation, but he never let an opportunity pass to insinuate that Giddes' shortcomings as a field agent had allowed the initial incident to occur. That might well have been the case, but he was not alone in having been lulled into a kind of complacency by Thomas Crane's acumen and unbridled arrogance. Crane had been given far too much authority, and it was the Old Man who had been responsible for that. Giddes relaxed. He had made his point and he had gained some time. 'Time', he thought to himself and almost allowed an insouciant smile to cross his lip. It was time, after all, that hovered at the center of all their efforts. It could very well be that time, that phantasm of the collective dimensions that would, in the end, make fools of all of them. But there was no turning back. He momentarily mused as to how the scientists who witnessed the explosion of the first atomic bomb must have felt, and how undoubtedly some of them must have wished that they could put the genie back in the bottle. He tried to imagine the calamity that had caused time to fold back on itself, dragging an entire civilization with it. He was thankful, that for now, this genie was still in its bottle, but it wouldn't be for long.

"Yes," Giddes said calmly. "I understand completely." For the next hour they discussed various points of what Giddes would need to accomplish.

Frank Giddes sat back and relaxed as the Gulfstream lifted off at a steep angle and banked to the left. He looked down at the dark ribbon of the Potomac as it cut through the sea of lights and then it all quickly faded as the jet shot upward into the thick cloud cover. It had been a long wait, but now things were in motion. The Old Man had finally given in and agreed to his plan. He really had no other choice. There were too many questions that needed answers, not the least of which was how Crane had managed his return. Obviously the *Jade Prince* was the reason for his return. Hadn't that always been Thomas Crane's goal, to understand it, to control it to possess it? There was no secret more closely guarded in the history of the world, and yet the bitter irony was that it was probably the least understood. Thomas Crane had been at the center of its discovery, and it was he who had begun calling it the *Jade Prince*, and would speak of the phenomenon as if it were a living, sentient being. He had even made the assertion at one point that the *Jade Prince* could destroy them all if it chose to do so. And it was he, along with all those other members of the project, who had died at that site. At least, that had been their working assumption for the past thirty-five years. Then a letter had surfaced written by Thomas Crane to a colleague at Cambridge in which he described the location of a second site and claimed to have knowledge of a third. They had found the second site which was located high on the Tibetan Plateau where their search had ended in near disaster. They had painstakingly excavated the site with the cooperation of the Chinese, and had come to a complete and disastrous end when the mountain they had burrowed into had collapsed. They had found the information they had sought, which had led them to the ruins of the city deep in the Mongolian desert, but their efforts had yet to show any results. Nevertheless, the Old Man was adamant in his belief that they were very near the end of their search. The *Jade Prince*, he kept repeating, would be found any day.

If Crane hadn't died all those years ago, then what had been the fate of the others? Perhaps they were all still alive. Perhaps, the *Jade Prince* had allowed them passage into a world beyond this one which the Old Man often alluded to. That brought him back to the question of how Crane had returned. There was no indication that he had returned via the site in Tibet. Two known sites, both in ruins, and both had been destroyed. If anything were found at the Mongolian site, it too, would be in ruin.

Giddes returned again to the possibility that another portal existed somewhere, not one of the great cities, but something smaller, easily overlooked, to be used as an escape hatch, a lifeboat, a trap door that opened into a hidden tunnel. The Old man had never ruled out such a possibility and now, it occurred to Giddes, that it was a distinct option. And if something like that existed, the Old Man would know about it. Giddes wondered what else the Old Man might be holding back. But more importantly, it brought up the question who else besides Crane and the Old Man would know of its existence.

As soon as the seatbelt light went off, he folded down the desk in front him and opened up his computer and typed in the name Albro Marshal Swift, and began reviewing all that was known about the young man. The public record did not contain the kind of detail he had hoped for, and unfortunately an extensive investigation could take days, time that they didn't have. He would have very much liked to interview anyone familiar with his early childhood as well as his more recent friends and work mates. The official record had a way of glossing over, or worse, completely ignoring the subtle details that revealed a person's true self. Nevertheless, there was enough information to bolster his initial reaction to the photo from the newspaper. There was little doubt in his mind that Martin and his cohorts would have done their homework. There would be little that they did not know about Albro Marshal Swift.

Probing the life of Martin Osborne Newton was another matter entirely. Here, it was not a case of too little information, but one of having too much. Google alone registered more than two million entries under the man's name. Notoriety, Giddes realized, was a perfect way to maintain one's privacy. Anyone on the outside could easily be overwhelmed and blinded by that much information, while those on the inside operated with impunity. Fortunately, Giddes was not limited to looking from the outside. The Old Man had made an uneasy peace with Newton. He had, in fact, made it possible for Newton to flourish. Cooperation toward a mutual goal had been the ostensible reason for their liaison. That cooperation appeared to have ended. Soon the masquerade would end as well. After an hour, Giddes closed down the computer and began making phone calls.

Satisfied that he had done all that he could at forty thousand feet, he reopened his computer and entered the name Monique Olivia Newton. The image that appeared was of professional quality. The pose, the lighting, the make-up, her hair, were all perfect. It was undoubtedly a photo released during her time as an actress and showed her extraordinary beauty in a classical Hollywood fashion, artificial yet so convincingly real.   Giddes studied her eyes.   They were large, nearly almond shaped and a very dark green.   They were eyes, Giddes decided, that hid more than they revealed.   They were the eyes of a woman who was totally aware of who she was, and not one to be fooled by the ephemeral world of fashion and fame.   They were the eyes of a woman who knew a great deal more than she let on.   He could see how one could easily be seduced by those eyes into believing that anything was possible.   And then a less obvious, more ominous conclusion began to form in his mind.   It was not Martin that they needed to worry about.   His hubris was matched only by his ambitions.   One would assure his place in history and the other, in the end, would prove to be his undoing.   She, on the other hand, could very well out-maneuver all of them.   She was going to be trouble.   He could feel it deep inside his bones, and killing her was not an option.   The Old Man had explained that very clearly to him.   As of now, he did not know how he would deal with her, but he would find a way.   He was confident of that.   All he knew with certainty at the moment was that he would have to be very careful.

He switched off the machine and put it away.   He glanced at his watch.   There was still an hour before the plane began its descent into the Los Angeles basin.   He tilted his chair back and closed his eyes.   A long night was still ahead.

CHAPTER 7

A pounding at the door woke Albro Swift from his troubled dream. This time, it was the dream of the burning city. It was a dream that came to him in various forms. Sometimes he was running through deserted streets. Sometimes he was lost in an abandoned house. Sometimes he saw the city over his shoulder, far in the distance. The common element, the feature that seemed to tie them all together, was that he was forever running. From what, or toward what, he never knew. What's more, the dreams never came on slowly. There was no lead up to the action. It was like being thrown from a dark and silent room into the fully fledged chaos of real life, and then just as suddenly he was awake, and more often than not, drenched in sweat. Lately, the dreams had been coming more frequently, their duration lasting longer and their realism, well, becoming more real, if that was even possible. Maybe, he thought, he should see a shrink. Then he dismissed the notion. He'd been cornered by psychiatrists, psychologists and every stripe and color of social worker while in juvenile detention. He considered them barely a step above palm readers, tarot dealers and psychics. As far as he was concerned, you could lump them all together in a circus side-show.

He rolled onto his back, heaving for air. The weight of the cast dragged him back onto his side. He tried to ignore the pain and looked at the rumpled folds of the sheet, unsure of what had startled him from the dream. He closed his eyes, wanting only to crawl back into the warm cocoon of sleep, when the pounding came again.

99

He then remembered what Goldstein had said about 'revisiting their conversation' of the previous night. Where did Goldstein learn to talk like that? Had he gone to some kind of finishing schools for thugs? It was probably Jimmy or Hoppy and they would haul him down to Goldstein's office, and start in on him. He'd need to come up with some sort of story, because Goldstein wasn't the kind of person to let go of something once he set his teeth in it. But right now, he just wanted to find a nice quiet hole and crawl in and hide for a week. He closed his eyes and as soon as he did the pounding came again.

He sat up and looked around. The pretty receptionist was gone and if not for her lingering fragrance on the pillow, he would have dismissed her as just another dream fragment. Deep pain thudded from inside the plaster cast and his head felt like it had been stuffed with wet cotton. He rolled off the bed and got to his feet and found his shorts. With a great deal of difficulty he managed to pull them on with only one hand. He cradled his broken arm against his chest and padded to the door.

Through the peep-hole he could distinguish two figures in loud shirts and sports coats. They had to be cops. What did they want? He opened the door and the man in front held out an identification badge and said, "Detective Miller, LAPD. This is detective Blum," he said without taking his eyes off Albro. "We're looking for Albro Marshal Swift."

Albro thought for a moment that maybe he was still dreaming. He felt limp and deflated from the alcohol, the pain killers and the too few hours of sleep. He shaded his eyes from the morning sun and looked at the two men. They looked to be in their late thirties, early forties, crew cut, clean shaved and tanned. Miller was slightly shorter than Blum. Otherwise they appeared to have been cast from the same mold.

"Are you Albro Swift?" The man asked again, leaning forward to look into Albro Swift's face.

"Yes. Sorry, I'm not quite awake. I spent most of the night in the hospital," Albro answered and raised the plaster cast

"Is that right," the detective said and glanced at the proffered arm. "Mr. Swift, may we come in? We'd like to talk to you."

Albro led them into the apartment. "Mind if I get a robe?" he asked.

The lead cop jerked his head toward his partner who followed Albro into the bedroom. He got his left arm through the sleeve of his robe and shrugged it over his shoulders. He went back into the living room and lifted the cover off Butch's cage and opened the door.

"Ucking Ell," Butch squawked. He was obviously unhappy about being confined in his cage all morning.

"You're free. Stretch your wings and fly away," Albro told him. Butch eyed Albro with a silent glare and then appraised the two agents and unlike the friendliness he'd displayed with Goldstein's thugs, decided to remain on his perch. "Suit yourself," Albro told him and sat on the sofa.

The two detectives stood in front of him. Miller said in that manner policemen have which makes it difficult to tell if they're making a statement or asking a question, "Last night you met with a Mr. Salvatore Goldstein."

All the possible answers from flatly denying that he had ever heard of Goldstein, to confessing to the fifty thousand dollar debt raced through Albro's mind. He wondered if he should give any answer. Why were they here? Weren't they supposed to read him his rights? The thoughts that raced through his mind must have registered on his face.

"Relax, Mr. Swift. We know all about your relationship with Goldstein," Miller said, "and why and how you got your arm broken. We've been following Goldstein's activities for some time. As a matter of fact, the FBI were about to arrest him on racketeering charges, but when they get to his office this morning, nobody's there and all his records have been cleaned out. Then we get a call from the Sheriff out in San Bernardino saying they found Goldstein along with a Mr. Bozeman and a Mr. Hopkins both of whom I believe you're acquainted with. All three were dead. They were outside Goldstein's car which leads us to believe it was some sort of prearranged meeting."

"Ucking Ell!" Butch exclaimed, and they all turned to look at him.

'Fucking Hell' was right, Albro thought. Sure, Goldstein was a small-time racketeer and both Jimmy and Hoppy were thugs who had inflicted a good deal of pain and misery on the likes of himself, but they didn't deserve to be killed, did they?

"So now we got the FBI," Detective Miller continued, "the San Bernardino county Sheriff's department and the LAPD involved. It's a major fuck-fest."

"And you think that I had something to do with having Goldstein knocked off?

"Not directly," Miller answered. "We've accounted for your whereabouts. We've even talked to the young lady who brought you home from the hospital. After your meeting with Goldstein, did you speak with anyone other than the hospital staff?"

"No."

"No phone calls?"

"No."

"Do you mean to say that you didn't call anyone about your predicament? How were you planning to get home?"

"At the time, it seemed to be the least of my concerns," Albro admitted.

"You know a Mr. Roger Ranger. Can you tell us where to find him?"

What could they possibly want with Roger, Albro wondered? Roger wouldn't hurt a fly. In fact, he would take great pains to capture any that got trapped against the windows and release them alive. Albro had recently set him up in his own apartment, thinking it was time to get Roger out on his own. Thus far, it had been a difficult transition. More often than not, he'd wake up to find that Roger had spent the night on the floor of his living room. "He has his own place," Albro said.

"We've checked it. It looked as if he hasn't been around for a while," Miller said pointedly.

Albro felt a pang of guilt and shame. He'd been so involved with Newton's new museum that he'd neglected to check in on his friend, and it was worrisome too, that Roger hadn't been around here.

"He likes taking trips on his bicycle. He could be just about anywhere," Albro said. "What makes you think Roger is mixed up in this?"

"Like you, Mr. Swift, he's a person of interest," Miller said. Then, as casually as if he were asking Albro to comment on the weather, he said, "Tell us about your relationship with Martin Osborne Newton."

Albro took a deep breath. He needed to think, but feared hesitating too long and looking guilty. The last thing he wanted was to give the cops an excuse to spill the beans to Newton about his involvement with Goldstein. He slowly let out his breath and said, "We're business partners. Why?"

"Tell me this, Mr. Swift. Why does a multi-billionaire, one of the richest, if not the richest man in the world, take up with a person like you?"

"I would like to think," Albro ventured, "that Mr. Newton saw something special to be gained by my expertise."

"Right," Miller said, his voice blatant with disbelief, "but what exactly is your expertise?"

"I facilitate the shipment of goods from the Far East," Albro said and regretted immediately the tentative sounding manner in which it had come out.   He said more forcefully, "I connect wholesalers with manufacturers."

"Which provided you the perfect front for smuggling illegal artifacts into the country," Miller said. "Don't look so surprised, Mr. Swift. We've done our homework. We know all about you. The part I don't get is why Newton needs you. Christ, the man makes Bill Gates look like a pauper."

"To be honest with you, Detective, I don't see how my relationship with Martin Osborne Newton has anything to do with Sal Goldstein. As a matter of fact, Monique Martin, Mr. Martin's daughter and I are engaged to be married. So you might say our relationship is one of family," Albro said.

"Yeah, it's all over the morning papers, congratulations. Did Newton or any of his associates know about your debt to Goldstein?"

Well there it was. He was feeling about as optimistic as a gravedigger nearing the bottom of his own grave. He said, "Maybe. If anyone knew, it wasn't because I told them."

"Wouldn't it have been an easy matter for Newton to pay off Goldstein?"

"You just told me that Martin Osborne Newton is the richest man in the world," Albro countered.

"But what if Goldstein had gone to him and demanded a good deal more money just to keep your name out of the news. You know how the gossip columns love that sort of thing," Miller said and then turned to his partner. "Hey Blum, I just thought of something. We could give out that news ourselves."

Albro considered what the detective had just said. Sal Goldstein would never have gone to Newton. Sal was a sleaze-bag, but not a blackmailer. The part about Miller spilling the news regarding his association with Goldstein was an obvious bluff. He'd learned a thing or two playing high-stakes poker. They were trying to play with an empty hand, and were doing an amateurish job of it.

Albro smiled and said, "I'll make you a deal. You tell me what you have besides wild speculation that connects Martin Osborne Newton to Salvatore Goldstein, and I'll tell you who I think killed him and his two thugs."

Detective Miller opened his mouth and then closed it, and then seemed to consider his next move. Albro said, "Just to show you what a good citizen I am, I'll tell you anyway. You know as well as I do that Goldstein had a long list of clients, and each one of them had a good reason to wish him dead. It's very likely one of them decided to retire a debt, and then disposed of Goldstein's records in order to avoid any embarrassing inquiries by the Feds."

Miller seemed to chew on that for a few moments and then said, "There's some truth in what you say. You might, after all, be off the hook, which would make a tidy ending to your problems. There are a couple of possibilities that I don't think you've considered."

"Oh " Albro asked warily. He'd just begun to feel that he was beginning to get the upper hand with Miller.

"Somebody wanted Goldstein's business. In the parlance of the financial world it's called a hostile takeover. It's like when someone buys up enough outstanding shares to become a majority shareholder. No big deal, it happens all the time. Granted, the methods employed by whoever took over Sal's business were a bit crude. My point is, within a week or two you'll receive a notice informing you of the change. If that's the case, you're still on the hook for that fifty-grand, and it's just a matter of time before they reel you in."

Albro considered the implications of that possibility for a moment and then asked, "What's the other possibility?"

Miller said, "The other possibility is that Goldstein got wind of something much bigger, something a small-time loan shark had no business sticking his nose into. Do you have any idea what that might be?"

Albro Swift struggled to keep from reacting in even the slightest way. He kept his eyes fixed on the detective's, his hands and his feet still, his breathing normal, his mouth in place, his heart rate a cool fifty beats per minute all those little tricks he'd learned years ago to maintain the bland façade known as 'poker face'. Nevertheless, he could not control that atavistic response whose stimulus begins somewhere in the limbic region of the brain and triggers the tiny hairs at the base of the neck to rise up and start dancing around. "No," he said calmly.

"Mr Swift, do I understand correctly that you've traveled extensively in the Far East?" Miller asked. He moved over to the sofa and sat on the padded arm.

"That depends on what you mean by extensive," Albro answered being careful to keep his voice level.

"And you have something of a reputation for being able to deliver rare artifacts," Miller continued. Not waiting for Albro to comment, he said, "You recently discovered a rather valuable item which you turned over to the Chinese government. The news article I read stated that you found it in , 'small out-of-the way antique shop,' and didn't realize its

105

true value until you had it back here. I would have thought that a man in your financial position would attempt to sell something like that."

"Look," Albro said, "My interest in Asian artifacts is strictly that of an amateur. It's a hobby, something to fill the time between business meetings. That dagger was a lucky find. That sort of thing happens once in a lifetime. Even I didn't know what I had until Mr. Newton saw it. As it turned out, that item had been stolen from a museum vault in Beijing some years ago. How it turned up in an antique shop is anybody's guess. Mr. Newton suggested, and I agreed that it should be returned to the Chinese people, who were its rightful owner."

"And what did you get in return?" Detective Miller asked.

"Nothing other than the satisfaction that I'd done the right thing," Albro said.

"That must have hurt," Miller said.

The detective's tone was anything but sympathetic. Albro had the feeling that Miller was steadily and inexorably herding him into a corner. Was he referring to his broken arm, or to the fact that he'd gone to great expense to get that dagger only to give it away? He decided there was only one truthful response. "Yes," he admitted. "It did hurt, and it still does."

"I guess that means you're still alive," Miller said, and smiled. He rose from the sofa and nodded to his partner and started for the door, but then stopped and turned to Albro. "I almost forgot," he said. "The Sheriff found a slip of paper in Goldstein's pocket." He handed it to Albro.

Albro took the paper. On it was written the words, '*The Jade Prince*' and under that, his own name underlined twice. There was a dark brown stain along its edge that could have been blood. He suppressed an urge to swallow and abruptly halted his diaphragm from sucking in a breath of badly needed air. He waited a moment to steady his hand, but it was a beat too long and he knew that Miller was thinking, '*Gotcha!*' Albro handed back the scrap of paper.

"Does that mean anything to you?" Miller asked, and grinned widely.

"It's a character in an old Chinese myth," Albro said.

"Is that so," Miller said. "Does he happen to carry a knife?"

"Only during the day," Albro answered.

"And at night?" Miller asked.

"At night he doesn't need to. He turns into a creature that has fangs and long claws," Albro said. "It's a story," he added.

"Uh huh," Miller said smiling. "Did I mention how Goldstein and his two associates died?"

"No," Albro said. He swallowed hard. He had a bad feeling that Miller was going to tell him something he didn't want to hear. He thought of the brown stain on the note.

"They looked as if they'd been ripped apart," Miller said, "all three of them. It was impossible to tell if there was even a struggle. Whatever happened, it happened fast. Think of someone being thrown into a spinning blade. It left a real mess from the way the Sheriff described it body parts everywhere." Miller withdrew his wallet from inside his jacket and pulled out a card and laid it on the counter. "If you learn anything about this *'Jade Prince'*, or anything else that might pertain to Salvatore Goldstein's murder, give me a call."

Miller left, and Blum followed. Before closing the door Blum, who had not spoken a word turned and said, "Have a nice day, Mr. Swift."

CHAPTER 8

ALBRO leaned his head against the door. His thoughts raced as he listened to the heavy footsteps of the two detectives as they slowly retreated down the outside corridor. He had to do something, but what? Run? Like in the dreams? He felt panic begin to coalesce around his heart and begin to rise inexorably into his throat. He forcibly choked it back down only to have it rise again, this time stronger, choking off his breath. There had to be a rational explanation for what was going on. But how could there possibly be a rational explanation for murder? Reason consisted of ordered facts, logical, and therefore predictable outcomes governed by the laws of probability. Right? But murder was a result not of reason, but of chaos, and chaos was complete and utter disorder, the infinitude of absolute hopelessness, the unimaginable realm of pre-primordial darkness.

Albro face turned a lovely shade of purple and gradually to a sour yellowish green and he began to slump down the face of the door. He slipped toward a darkened recess at the back of his mind, sliding slowly into ever diminishing space, and there, he saw the *Jade Prince* beckon him forward with a low sweep of his sword. All strength left his body and he pitched forward, his broken arm folding under him and taking the full weight of his fall. A sharp pain shot from his forearm into his brain. He rolled onto his back. Butch fluttered in panicky circles above his face crying out, "Arning! Arning! Arning!" like a space robot with a speech problem.

Albro pulled himself up and staggered to the sofa. Butch followed him still sounding his alarm.

"I'm all right," Albro attempted to shout at him, but it came out in a ragged whisper. He cleared his throat and tried again. "You can relax. I'm okay."

But Butch made one last circle around Albro's head and settled on the arm of the sofa and eyed Albro with guarded skepticism.

"I almost fainted," Albro said. "It must be the pain medication."

Butch ruffled his feathers as if he didn't entirely agree, but for the moment he would let it pass.

"What," Albro said to the little bird. "You think it's something else?" His arm hurt like hell, so maybe the pain killers had worn off hours ago, but he wasn't going to give Butch the satisfaction of saying so.

"Roger, Roger," Butch said, and stared pointedly at Albro.

"I know," replied Albro. "We have to find him." But as he said it he knew there was something else he needed to do, but he couldn't remember what it was. His mind felt like someone had thrown sand in the gears.

"Call, Call," Butch said.

The memory of the previous evening hit Albro and played out in his mind; the call from Seattle, the news about his father, the phone number Sal had given him. He reached for his trousers and searched the pockets until he found it. He found his phone where Sal had left it on his bedside table. He punched in the numbers and then hesitated before pushing the dial button. What if was all a hoax? Even worse, what if was true? Could he live with what he might find out? Some things were better left undisturbed.

"Uc ng Ell!" Butch called out from the other room. "Call, Call."

"Alright," Albro called back. "I'm calling!" He pushed the call button and waited.

After three rings a voice informed him he had reached the law offices of Lee, Wong and Ho. The voice informed him that Ms Wong was not available, and requested that he leave his name, number and purpose

of his call. He started to do so when a call came into his phone. "Hello,"
he said.

A woman's voice said, "Listen carefully."

"Who is this?" Albro asked. He could hear what sounded like
traffic in the background.

"I'm an attorney representing your father. You have a seat
reserved on United, flight 362 departing LAX at 5:20 tonight, arriving
Seattle at 7:40. Your confirmation code is QPS372. I will meet you at the
gate."

"Who...," he started to say, but the call had ended. He found a
pen and wrote the information on his cast. He checked received calls and
punched the number, and counted out a dozen rings before he hung up.
He tried again, and this time got a recording telling him that number was
no longer in service. He sat for a moment looking at his open phone,
more than a little dazed. He closed it and as soon as he did so it rang,
which served to rattle even more his already jangled nerves. He looked at
the number, and wondered if it was the 'someone' whom Detective Miller
had said would be contacting him about the fifty-thousand. No, he
decided, that sort of contact wouldn't take place over the phone. He
would be coming home late at night and there would be a black sedan
parked at the curb, or he'd be walking down the sidewalk and suddenly
there would be two men on each side of him, one with a gun pressed
against his ribs. He flipped open the phone. "Hello," he said softly.

"Albro, darling," a woman's husky voice crooned to him.

He recognized the voice immediately. "Monique," he said.

"Is everything all right?" she asked.

"Uh, sure," he said, "I'm fine." She must have heard the anxiety
in his voice. "I mean, I'm fine now."

"What do you mean, you're fine now?" she asked, her beautiful
voice full of concern.

"I had an accident," he said, and then he found himself telling her
how he'd received a call the night before informing him that his father
had died and how he had suddenly lost strength in his legs and how he
had foolishly stuck out his arm to break his fall and how it had snapped

and how he'd spent the night in the emergency department at L.A. General, and then went on to tell her that he needed to catch a flight that evening. Granted, it was a leap of faith, but the flight information had to be connected with the news of his father.

"Oh Albro, why didn't you call me from the hospital?"

"I knew that you were sleeping. Besides, there was nothing you could have done."

"You poor baby," she cooed. Albro loved it when she cooed. Albro had never heard Monique coo to anyone else, even in her movies. More often than not, she gave out crisp and precise orders. "And your father, how terrible," she said. "Had he been ill?"

"I don't know many details yet," he answered. He now regretted mentioning anything about his father. The last thing he wanted to do was to have to start explaining his past to Monique.

"I'm coming with you," she said. "I'll call and arrange to have one of the company planes take us."

"No please, Monique. I think this is something I need to do on my own."

"Albro, are you sure?"

"Yes I'll only be gone a few days."

"Then I'll drive you to the airport."

His mind began to race. For six months he'd been trying to project a sophisticated lifestyle. What would Monique Olivia Newton think of him if she saw the dump that he lived in? "That's not necessary. I'll call a cab. You don't need to drive all the way out here. Traffic is terrible."

"But darling," Monique said to him, "I'm just a few blocks away."

"You know where I live?" he said weakly.

"Albro, darling, do you think I would marry a stranger?" She laughed her incredibly sexy, deep-throated laugh. "Sweetheart, I know everything about you."

Albro was still sitting on the bed fumbling with his bottle of pain killers when Monique Olivia Newton swirled into his apartment. It had been one of those southern California Decembers that the rest of the

111

country can only dream about. The weather had been sunny and warm and today was no exception. She was wearing red heels and a full white dress with red polka dots held up by two thin straps across the perfect skin of her shoulders. She looked as young and innocent and fresh as a high school prom queen. She wrapped her arms around him and pressed his face against her perfumed bosom.

"You must let me come with you," she said as she stroked the back of his head.

Albro sat back and tried to catch his breath. Here he was on the edge of his bed with one of the most beautiful and richest women in the world and she was begging him to allow her to be with him, and he was finding it hard to breathe! Hadn't he fantasized over this very moment a hundred times? He told himself to get a grip on his nerves. Even so, he had the uncanny feeling that events had already spun beyond his control. He gulped in air and said, "I'll be fine, Monique. I would love for you to come, but I think you should stay. I know that you still have so much to prepare for the public opening of the museum. Your father needs you here."

"Oh, Albro, you're right. Father would be furious if I abandoned him now, but this is *your* time of need and I do want to help you," Monique said, and looked into Albro's eyes and touched her hand to his cast.

The way she looked at him, actually brought tears to his eyes. What was wrong with him? His emotions had suddenly jumped on a careening rollercoaster. Women had never made him react this way. Was this the onset of grief over his dead father, or the fact that he'd never known his father? He'd really never grieved over anything in his life. He didn't know what it was supposed to feel like. He feared that he must look like one of those crying snots on Dr. Phil. He could just hear that comforting drawl giving him permission to let it all out and then the stinging admonition that he needed to face his past like a man. He looked away and blinked hard and wiped away the tears with his free hand. "Thank you, Monique. It means a lot to me that you want to help. I have to pack. You could help me with that."

Albro got himself dressed while Monique haphazardly stuffed a few clothes into an overnight bag. He took Butch over to his neighbor, Harold, a retiree from Wisconsin who had moved out west to give his aging bones some relief from the frigid winters.

"Don't you worry none," he said to Albro and then looked past him through the open door of his apartment at Monique who was standing in profile and applying lipstick while looking into a compact mirror. Albro saw a look of shocked surprise shake the old man's ordinarily calm demeanor.

Albro looked back at Monique and said half-jokingly, "My ride to the airport," but Harold had pulled back quickly and closed his door. Albro shrugged. Usually Harold would try to engage him in an unending conversation, stringing one subject to another like a chain smoker going through a pack of *Camels*.

He returned to his apartment. He needed to leave Roger a note. He was more than a little worried about Roger. When Roger didn't spend the night, he would show up just about the time Albro woke, which was rarely before ten o'clock, and here it was almost two in the afternoon. Roger refused to carry a cell phone, something about microwaves interfering with brain functions. Albro wrote down his flight information and a short note saying he had to check out a lead regarding his father. He didn't want to mention anything about the possibility that he might actually have been found. He placed it within a Spiderman comic and laid it face down on the kitchen counter. Roger would be sure to open it up when he came in for a bowl of cereal.

"Ready," Albro said to Monique.

She carried his overnight bag and tossed it onto the backseat of her cream-colored *Rolls* convertible. They climbed into the big car and she gunned it forward and merged across four lanes of traffic without once touching the brake and swung onto the freeway on-ramp and into the flow of traffic. She had tied her hair in place with a red silk scarf and with her sunglasses she looked every bit like Grace Kelly playing the part of the billionaire's daughter that she was. He marveled at the way she handled the car. He then noticed that she had missed the airport exit.

"The airport's back that way," he said, turning and pointing in the opposite direction.

"There's something I want to show you first," she said as she changed lanes onto a freeway that would carry them north and away from the city. "It's a surprise, Albro, and it won't take long. Sit back and rest."

They sped north and then turned off the freeway onto a road that wound up into the Santa Monica Mountains. She slowed and turned off onto a narrower, steeper road that ended at a high steel gate. She pressed a button under the steering column and the gate swung open. The road continued to climb through green hillsides covered with oaks, then opened onto a cleared knoll of a couple of acres of green grass and flowers. A house of white stucco and glass stood at the edge of the hillside where it dropped steeply into a canyon. In the distance, Albro could see the blue line of the Pacific.

They got out of the car. Albro was a little unsteady on his feet. The winding road had left him feeling dizzy and the bright sunlight hurt his eyes. "What's this?" he asked.

"Happy Birthday, Albro," Monique said and swept out her arms to encompass the scene. "We intended to surprise you Christmas morning, but now with you needing to leave, I thought why wait? You like it, don't you?"

"This is for me?" Albro asked. He looked around, keeping a hand on the fender of the *Rolls* to steady himself. He was getting a clearer understanding of how Dorothy must have felt when she woke up in that strange corner of her subconscious.

"Yes, a small 'thank you' from Father for doing such a fabulous job with the museum. Come inside," Monique said and led Albro by the hand across the brick courtyard complete with fountain and hanging baskets of flowers of every color imaginable and into a spacious room with windows that looked out in all directions. He knew the city was out there somewhere beyond the last hill, but it was nowhere to be seen.

"What about my apartment, my things?" Albro asked.

"Albro, you worry about the silliest things!" she said in mild admonishment. "I cancelled your lease, and arranged for everything to be taken away."

"Everything? What about Butch?"

"I wouldn't dream of leaving your cute little bird behind. We'll build him an entire aviary and he'll have all the little female parakeets he could ever desire."

Albro suddenly remembered Roger. Monique must have seen the look of concern cross his face. She said, "Don't worry about your friend, Roger. There's a caretaker's cottage just below the hill, behind those trees. He can live there, and we'll still have our privacy."

"We?" Albro asked.

"Albro," she said with a mock pout of her lips. "Aren't you forgetting something?" Monique asked and smiled coyly at him. She pulled him close and touched her nose to his.

"Oh yeah," he stammered. "We're soon going to be married."

"You're such a tease," she exclaimed and pushed him gently away. She threw her head back and spread her arms and twirled around the room like a ballerina. She came to a stop in front of him. "You like it, don't you?" she asked. Not waiting for an answer, she said, "Albro, your past is behind you now. You're starting a new life." She giggled and swiveled away from him and disappeared through an arched doorway.

"It's beautiful, but isn't it a bit far from everything?" he called after her. How did she expect him to live out here? He didn't even own a car. He followed her into the house and heard the far off sound of running water. The place had the smell of new paint and that unmistakable feeling of having never been lived in.

Monique reappeared, sticking her head around the corner of a doorway. "You're not going to *live* here," she said, and once again disappeared leaving Albro to stare into the expanse of his 'new life'. That was what she had said, wasn't it? The pain killers were wearing off and the pain in his arm was returning with a vengeance. He dug into his pockets and thankfully found the bottle of pills. He pried off the top and tilted the bottle into his mouth.

115

"Albro, darling, come here," Monique called to him.

He found his way through a labyrinth of corridors to a tiled bathroom larger than the entire apartment that evidently was no longer his. Monique Olivia Newton's head stuck above the foam of a bubble filled tub. She smiled at him and the pain in his arm was suddenly very far away.

She washed his hair and then his fingers and toes and then the rest of him all the time mindful of the need to keep his cast dry. She toweled him off and then led him to a bedroom with mirrors on three sides and a mirror over a bed the size of a tennis court and a wall of windows that looked out to an infinite blue horizon.

Monique Olivia Newton made love as if she had been trained in a boxing ring. Twice Albro cried out when his arm got caught in an awkward position, but she continued to drive relentlessly for the knockout until finally it came and they both lay in a sweaty heap, their lungs heaving for oxygen.

Albro flew in comfort that evening out of the purple twilight of the L.A. basin. He had given his flight information to Monique who had called her personal assistant who in turn had arranged to have Albro's cramped economy class seat upgraded to VIP first class, which assured that the adjoining seat would be vacant. They were of course late, but Monique simply called to have the plane held until they arrived. Before boarding, she gave him a long, lingering kiss and stuffed a wad of cash into the pocket of his jacket. Albro promised that he would call her as soon as he checked into a hotel.

When the seatbelt light went off, the stewardess asked him if he would care for a drink, and he asked for cold milk which she brought in genuine crystal, no plastic for VIP passengers. He popped another two pain killers and sat back and gazed at the sea of colored lights below. He tilted back his seat and closed his eyes. The muffled roar of the engines gradually became more distant and in a few minutes he was dreaming, and in the dream he opened a worn paperback and began to read.

It is not long before he is dreaming and in the dream he is an infant lying in a cradle woven of willow branches, and looking up at the dark silhouette of a man. From far back in the recesses of his mind he hears a voice speak to him. "On the day that you were born, the winds ceased and the dust settled from the sky." He watches the tall, wide figure that looms over him with a hand that hovers flat against the blue sky. "The sun," the voice continues, "burst through the clouds of dust like a host of fiery angels on a golden chariot pulled by a stallion of immense brightness." The hand sweeps back and reveals a dazzling sun and he is momentarily blinded. He squeezes his eyes shut and flails his stubby arms and tiny fists in a vain attempt to make the sun go away. "But then," the voice exhales sadly, "the winds once again lifted the earth into the sky and your mother was lost."

"What?" Albro said out loud. He blinked and sat up, startled by the sound of his own voice. The dream hung at the edge of his memory before dropping into oblivion. There had been something familiar about the shape of the silhouetted figure. He tried to bring it back and had almost succeeded when it vanished completely. A man in a dark suit who sat across the aisle gave him a curious stare and then returned to his laptop. Albro wondered how long he had been asleep. Someone had covered him with a blanket. He rubbed his eyes and looked out of the window. In the moonlight he could see the spine of snow-covered peaks. He pressed his face to the glass and shielded the interior light with his one good hand. The mountains' flanks were smooth with fresh snow. The world down there looked pure and serene. It was a place, he thought, where the follies of man were kept in check by the forces of nature. A man could lose himself in that wilderness, or could have a century ago, he decided. He would have hunted and fished for his own food, would have built a cabin with an axe, would have sat by a campfire every night watching the gleam of the stars in the overhanging blackness. He was startled by the vividness of the image that came to his mind and he shivered involuntarily feeling the imagined chill of a cold wind on his back. He thought of a time when he'd been barely older than thirteen and hitchhiking across the Rocky Mountains in August wearing only T-shirt and

117

jeans when he'd been caught by a freakish blizzard and might have died had not someone stopped for him. He remembered how at first the cold had been cutting, but then after just a short time, the cold had actually become soothing. He had thought it was his father who had half carried, half dragged him to the open door of the old pick-up, but that had been a fantasy cooked up by his brain as it was getting ready to shut down for good. It had turned out to be an old rancher on his way to Reno who had slapped him back to consciousness and force-fed him a thermos full of hot coffee laced with whiskey.

Since then he'd avoided anything that even resembled a wilderness, and his father had remained a fantasy. And now, was it really possible that his father had come looking for him? How had he known where to find him? How had he even known his name? After all, his was a made up name, the junction of two streets on the tattered, southern edge of Seattle. Had his father been there always, like a shadowy figure in the background of his life? The enormity of the questions depressed him. Albro wondered if having a dead father was any better than having none at all. "Why did you leave me?" he said half out loud.

"Pardon me?" the stewardess asked as she leaned over him smiling. There was a slight lilt of Scandinavian accent in her voice.

"Sorry," he replied, "I was thinking out loud."

"It's time to fasten your seatbelt," she said and smiled sweetly.

She moved off to the other passengers and Albro struggled to fasten his seatbelt with one hand. Then she was back in a few minutes. "Is everything all right?" she asked. Albro pointed to his broken arm. "Here," she said, "let me help you with that."

As she eased herself crosswise into the empty seat, her skirt rose up on her long, slender legs. She reached around him and as she did so her blouse tightened around the shape of her full breasts. She found the two ends of the belt and clicked them together across his middle. She then gave a gentle tug to cinch up the slack and then tested it by curling her fingers between the buckle and his stomach.

"Not too tight?" she asked. Albro thought she smelled faintly of wildflowers and dry grass. Her sandy brown hair was cut short and swung forward in two soft curves that framed her face in an aura of soft light. "I'll see that you get some help with your bags," she said. She touched his hand. The plane bounced and shuddered as they slowed over the city and her hand closed around his. "We'll be landing in a few minutes. Would you mind if I sit here?"

It was past midnight as they rode through the City of Rain, the name Albro had long ago given to the city of his birth. He peered through the rain streaked window and remembered how the damp and dreary days of winter in Seattle could seem never ending. He shivered and slid his hand unconsciously across the seat until it met Elsa's warm thigh. Elsa, (She had introduced herself as the plane touched down.), had found him standing and searching disconsolately the empty waiting area outside the gate.

"I guess I've been stood up," he had said to her. And she had suggested they share a cab.

As they traveled through the dark and rainy night he told her how he had received a phone call the night before with the news of his father's death.

"I am so sorry," she said. She held his hand in both of hers. Her hands were large and warm and she alternately squeezed his fingers and stroked the tops of his knuckles.

"And your arm," she asked, "when did that happen?"

"Almost immediately after I got the news about my father, I went for a walk to clear my mind," Albro said and paused for a moment. "I witnessed a mugging, a woman being attacked by two young men. I shouted and when they took off with her handbag, I rather foolishly went running after them. When I overtook them, I leapt for the bag and came down hard on my arm. It was quite dark." It was a mild untruth, Albro admitted to himself. He couldn't tell Elsa what had really happened. There was a time and place for the truth, and seldom did those circumstances come together. If he had learned one thing in his short life, it was that truth was a rare and powerful commodity and to be used only when absolutely necessary. Most people, he knew, were really not interested in the truth. They would rather hear things that reinforced

119

their own sense of goodness about the world, and why upset them unnecessarily? Life was hard enough the way it was without adding a lot of depressing details that you couldn't do anything about anyway.

"My goodness," Elsa said. "You're lucky they didn't turn on you."

"Yes, I suppose I am," Albro said.

They rode in silence and Albro could sense that Elsa was working herself toward some sort of decision. The cab pulled to a stop in front of a cluster of townhomes. She turned to Albro and in the blue aura of the street light Albro could see that Elsa's eyes were full of concerned innocence. "It's such an awful time to go looking for a hotel room," she said. "My roommate is out of town and I'm sure she wouldn't mind if I let you use her room. That is, if you would like to."

Albro reached awkwardly for his empty billfold, but Elsa was already passing money to the cab driver, who carried their bags to the front door. Pine trees were planted around the front of the building and dim lights glowed along the walkway. A light rain fell and after the warmth of the cab and Elsa's closeness, the cold and damp air quickly chilled him. Elsa opened the door and flicked on the lights and adjusted them down to a comfortable glow. She then crossed over the thick carpet to the fireplace and turned a valve and pushed a button and blue and yellow flames filled the opening.

"Sit here and get warm," she said. "I'll fix us a snack. I'm always famished after a flight."

She took off her coat and draped it over his shoulders and went into the kitchen. He listened to the opening and closing of the refrigerator, the faucet running and the heels of her shoes clicking on the hard flooring like some kind of domestic metronome. The living room was small, but cozy with two leather sofas and a low, glass-top table. A few pieces of art hung on the walls. Stereo speakers stood in opposite corners. There was no traffic outside, and no sounds from the neighbors. An occasional gust of wind blew rain against the windows. Albro sighed heavily just as Elsa returned with a tray piled high with crackers and cheese and olives and smoked salmon. She set the tray down and went back into the kitchen and returned with two wine glasses and a bottle of wine. She tepped out of her shoes and sat on the carpet, demurely tucking her gs against her body and smoothing her skirt.

"Sit ere," she told Albro and patted the space next to her.

Albr turned to Elsa and saw the flames of the fire reflected in her eyes.

CHAPTER 9

FRANK GIDDES stepped down from the plane onto the tarmac. He breathed in the air and wrinkled his nose. Although he was fifty miles from the core of Los Angeles, he could smell the warm, oily scent that the city always seemed to exude. A car was waiting for him and he climbed in and tapped his phone and spoke the address of his destination. A map came up and he studied it briefly and started the engine. He'd had a good sleep and then a light breakfast. Although it was 3 am, he felt refreshed and fully awake. Twenty-four hours had passed since he'd been awakened with the news that Thomas Crane had returned. He let the engine idle and watched as a tank truck pulled up and two men got out and began refueling the plane. Satisfied that his orders to have the plane ready to fly were being carried out, he put the car in gear and found the freeway.

He made good time traveling from one freeway to another, to still another following the directions he had in his mind and finally dropping down to street level, near the city center. He found the luxury high-rise condominium he was looking for and entered the parking garage by punching a five digit code into a keypad that stood next to an unmanned kiosk. He was able to use the same code to enter the elevator. He rode the elevator to the fiftieth floor where he got off and walked to the end of the corridor to another elevator and punched in a different code. This elevator would open directly into the penthouse apartment which occupied the entire top floor. It had not been particularly difficult obtaining the codes which allowed him to pass freely through the building's security systems. His government security clearance allowed him to use the over-ride codes that the local fire department used to enter private apartment complexes in the event of an emergency. The fire department might not consider this an emergency, but he did. The doors opened and he entered the semi-darkened apartment. He had not called ahead to notify the occupant of his arrival. He wanted this to be a surprise visit.

He paused a moment to listen. Only the whisper of the ventilation system disturbed the otherwise silent space. The glow of the city came through a wall of glass and lighted the room enough to allow him make out the general arrangement of the place. A sunken living room, large enough to hold his entire D.C. apartment, lay straight ahead. The kitchen and dining area opened onto the living room like a stage set. One hallway ran to his right and another to his left. Scattered throughout the space were tall, slender display cases which held shadowy shapes and figures, any one of which was probably worth more than a year of his salary. He stepped quietly down the left hallway, casually searching each room as he went. Finding no one, he retraced his steps and then more cautiously entered the right hand hallway. There were two doors and the first was a rather expansive powder room. The other, partly open, would be the master suite. He looked in. He could see the bed clearly and the shape of the person who lay on his back drawing in deep and even breaths. Frank Giddes withdrew the gun from his coat pocket and screwed in the silencer and then crossed to the bed. He lowered the gun and worked the barrel into the man's mouth.

Doctor Heinrich Krupp took in a sharp breath, gagging as he struggled against the cold steel. His eyes bulged with fear, when he saw the dark figure standing over him. He pushed up but that only forced the object in his mouth farther down his throat. He moaned wildly as his arms flailed and his legs jerked spasmodically.

"There, there," the figure said to him as if he were a child in need of comforting. "I don't want to kill you. I simply want to ask you some questions. I'm going to remove this gun from your throat. If you scream, I will pull the trigger. Do you understand?"

Krupp recognized the voice immediately. He tried to calm his old heart, whose paper thin walls felt as if they were tearing themselves to pieces. He struggled to hold still and managed a guttural sound, which he hoped to God, conveyed that he meant 'yes', that he would do whatever the man asked. He felt the barrel of the gun slowly retract. When it was out, he rolled over and vomited up bile from his empty stomach.

Giddes looked around and located the switch for the bedside lamp and turned it on. He pulled a chair close to the bed and sat. When Krupp finished heaving, he rolled back onto the pillows and wiped his mouth and nose with the sheet. His face had gone a sickly shade of gray and his eyes were bloodshot and watery, his puffy lower lip trembled. Giddes had one leg crossed over the other with the gun resting comfortably in his lap.

Krupp groaned as he struggled to push himself up against the pillow, trying to get as far from the end of the gun as he could get. "I've done nothing wrong," he whined plaintively. "Why are you here?"

Giddes ignored the question. He said, "It's quite a nice place you have here, Felix. You appear to be very comfortable.

"It is all because of Martin. All of this belongs to him," Krupp sputtered. He shivered out of fear and pulled up the sheet to cover his silk pajamas.

"Ah," said Giddes, "How is Martin? It's been a long time since I've spoken with him.

"He is well," Krupp said and shuddered as if he had a severe chill

"And Monique," Giddes said, "I assume that you see her often."

"Yes," Krupp answered. The panic in his eyes that had begun to subside intensified at the mention of her name.

"And Thomas," Giddes said, "when did you last see our old friend Thomas?"

"Crane?" The word had leapt from Krupp's mouth before he could stop it. He looked at the gun and then at Giddes. "It has been more than thirty-five years since I have seen Thomas Crane."

Giddes raised the gun and looked at Krupp as a school master might look at an errant student. He said, "I did not come all this way to fuck around with you, Felix. If you tell me another lie, I will shoot you. Now tell me the truth."

Krupp stared at the gun. He knew that Frank Giddes would feel no more remorse over killing him than he would over swatting a mosquito. Amongst other insidious talents, Giddes was an expert in the art of killing. He knew that his death would be neither swift nor painless. Giddes may have aged over the years, but he was no less capable. "Three nights ago," he said quickly. "I was here, dining alone and suddenly he was sitting across the table from me. He came out of nowhere."

Giddes raised the gun and leaned forward and placed it against Krupp's ankle bone. He looked at Krupp's face that had contorted itself into a mask of panic and fear. Three nights previous Thomas Crane had been found bleeding to death in a rain soaked alleyway. "I'm afraid that's not possible Felix."

"I can't explain it!" he shouted in a hoarse whisper. "He was here, I swear to you. I thought he was an apparition, a ghost. I thought that I had drunk too much wine and it had affected my senses."

Giddes pulled back the gun an inch. "Tell me about it," he said.

"He spoke to me. He told me that he had come for the *Jade Prince*."

"Yes," Giddes said patiently and tapped the barrel of the gun on Krupp's ankle bone, "go on."

"He said that he intended to return it to its rightful owners," Krupp said.

"Rightful owners," Giddes said with a hint of amusement in his voice. "I don't suppose he gave a hint as to who that might be?"

"The Mongi," Krupp answered, which caused Giddes to raise an eyebrow. "Please, you must believe me," Krupp said in a panic, "I asked why and he ignored my question. He warned me that we should not try to stop him."

"Or else he would do what?"

125

"He said there was nothing we, or anyone else, could do to stop him."

Giddes paused, thinking. Should he tell Krupp that Crane was dead? That he'd purportedly been killed the very night that he'd appeared before Krupp? He couldn't see any advantage in keeping that from Krupp. "Thomas Crane is dead. His body was found early on the morning of the 10th, three nights ago. So you see, Felix, what you've been me telling hasn't made a whole lot of sense."

"What? Are you certain?"

"That he's actually dead?"

"You don't know what he might be capable of."

Giddes had to admit that Krupp had a point. Whether or not he believed anything the little worm had said really didn't matter. It was always what you didn't know that inevitably caused you the most trouble. "What else did he say?"

"He said nothing more. He vanished."

"How could he just vanish? You let him into your apartment and then you let him out."

"No! It was not like that! You must believe me! I didn't even move!" Krupp was sputtering like a hysterical old woman.

"Calm down, Felix. You told Martin?"

"Of course, I told Martin."

"But you didn't tell me. The old man is going to be very disappointed when he hears this. We had an agreement, Felix. You were to keep me informed."

"I pleaded with Martin, but he ordered me to remain silent."

"You waited," Giddes said.

"Yes," Krupp said. "Martin said he had something that Crane wanted. It would simply be a matter of waiting for Crane to come to us."

"And he did so," Giddes said.

"Yes. They met"

"Where?"

"How should I know? Martin tells me only what he wishes me to know."

"Where was Monique? Was she with Martin?"

"I don't know. Maybe she was with him, maybe not. She was not here. That is all I know."

"What happened at that meeting?"

"I don't know. Martin will not talk about it. All I know is that he was shaken. I have never seen Martin shaken. Something must have happened to leave Martin that way. And there is something else."

"What?" Giddes asked.

"Something has changed between Martin and Monique. There exists...," and here Krupp faltered as if searching for the right word. He put his hand to his lips and looked up at the ceiling. "She has a look of estrangement in her eyes," he concluded in an oddly satisfied way, as if he were pleased about the idea of something coming between Martin and Monique.

Giddes considered that for a moment and then asked, "Do you think they killed Crane?"

"Martin wanted to kill him. You know that. You also know that he has neither the skill nor the strength," Krupp said. "But with *her* present, Crane might have made a mistake."

Giddes didn't consider that to be likely. Thomas Crane wasn't the sort of person to make mistakes. If in fact he had agreed to meet with Martin and Monique then it was with a specific purpose in mind, and he would have been prepared. He needed to know what had gone on at that meeting.

"Then you are not convinced they killed him," Giddes said. Giddes did not let Krupp see the anger that was building within him. It had been the Old Man's idea to trust Martin. Giddes had been against it from the very beginning. Although Martin possessed a formidable intelligence, not to mention his immense wealth and influence, he had his own agenda, and Giddes had never trusted him to act in a rational manner. Because of Martin, they had now lost the opportunity to take Crane alive.

"On the contrary, I'm not convinced that Thomas Crane is dead."

"You doubt the validity of my information?"

127

"All I am saying is that I would need to examine the body myself before making a determination. You and your people have a bad habit of reacting before you know all of the facts."

Krupp had managed to regain some of his Teutonic superiority and it irritated Giddes. He sat back and was silent for a moment. He needed more information and Krupp was not providing much. He decided to change his tact. He asked in mild, off handed way, "How long have you known about Albro Marshal Swift?"

"Swift? Who is Albro Marshal Swift?"

Giddes was on Krupp before he could even flinch, pinning his bony arms beneath his knees. He placed the muzzle of the gun into the corner of Krupp's left eye. Krupp lay rigid as a board, not even daring to take a breath.

"I swear to Christ, Felix. I ought to blow out your fucking brains right now."

"I thought he was another of Monique's young men! I swear I didn't know until just two days ago who he really is!" Krupp wheezed and struggled for breath. Giddes kept his weight on him until his face began to turn an alarming shade of purple, and then he eased himself off the bed. He stood looking down as Krupp struggled to get some air in his lungs.

"Let me guess," Giddes said, "you were going to call in the morning to tell me."

Between rasping gasps for air, Krupp said, "I had my suspicions. How was I to know? Our paths seldom crossed. She saw to that. You must believe me," Krupp pleaded.

"Then I take it something happened to allay your doubts."

"Yes. I managed to get him alone with me. I showed him an image of the stone creature we found in the ruins. It told him it was the *Jade Prince*."

"You did what?" Giddes shouted. He could not believe what he was hearing.

"It was just a hologram! I assure you, nothing serious happened!"

"But what if something had happened?"

"There are safeguards."

"Yes but we don't know that they will actually work. You're a careless piece of shit, Felix. You've become too much of a risk." Giddes raised the gun and tightened his finger on the trigger.

"Don't!" Krupp wailed and held up his hands as if they had a chance of blocking the bullets.

"Why shouldn't I kill you?"

"It was not until last night when I heard Martin speak at the reception that I knew with certainty."

"Know what?"

"That Albro Swift is the one we've been waiting for."

Giddes glanced at his watch. He would like to know everything that Martin had said, but that would have to wait. Daylight had begun to seep beneath the bedroom shades. He had wasted enough time already. "How can you be so certain?"

"He is," Krupp began and then seem to grope for invisible words with his small, delicate hands. "He is a rather curious version of the father."

"What do you mean by, 'curious'?"

"He is not perfect. As you know, they sometimes made mistakes. Imagine, if you will," Krupp went on, "all of Crane's ability to survive, yet none of the moral superiority that has caused us so much trouble. Combine that with how should I say, Ms Newton's unique abilities. In short, she has found him to be easily manipulated." He went on to tell Giddes about how Monique had found Albro Swift. "It was quite by accident. It was almost as if he had come looking for us," Krupp concluded.

Giddes considered Krupp's last statement. There could very well be more truth in it than either of them wanted to admit, not to mention the ensuing complications that would inevitably arise, if Monique chose to act upon her own. She had the ability to draw men to her. Not only had she pulled in the father, she had undoubtedly pulled in the son as well.

"How much does he know?"

"He knows very little, if anything at all. He believes the *Jade Prince* to be a mythical artifact. He senses that he is somehow connected, but he has no idea how, or why. I offered him a half million dollars to find it for me. He seemed skeptical, but he did not deny that he wouldn't try. He is highly motivated by money."

"What of himself?" Giddes asked. "Does he know where he comes from?"

Krupp smiled. "He knows himself to be a foundling. It is unlikely that he knows anything about his parentage, let alone the Mongi, and even if he did discover something, he would not believe it."

"You seem very confident of that," Giddes said.

You may think that I am simply a collector of artifacts of long dead civilizations, but in doing so, I have learned a great deal about human behavior. Human beings believe only what they want to believe. When they do not find what they wish to believe in, they imagine it into existence. It is a trait that has led to the downfall of countless civilizations, and in the end, I fear, will lead to our extinction."

"I hope that you don't forget, Doctor, that is exactly what we are trying to prevent," Giddes said.

CHAPTER 10

ALBRO turned his head and focused his eyes on the window. H was wide awake, yet he had the feeling of a great fatigue lurking som where in is body. He tried to remember if he had slept. Gray light came hrough the blinds. He'd heard a door close somewhere outside anc footsteps coming down a stairway, the slam of a car door, the sound (an engine starting, and the sound of the car receding over wet paveme it. Elsa lay on her side facing him with one arm draped over his chest a d her leg slung over his. She had shown him into the roommate'; bedroom, had pulled down the sheet, and had opened the door to the athroom and turned on a nightlight. She had then said good night and h d gone to her own room. Sometime in the night, Albro had rolled onto is injured arm. He had cried out in pain, and Elsa had come running in t see what was wrong.

"Ar you ill?" she had asked and had sat on the edge of the bed and had pla ed her hand on his forehead. She had placed two of the painkillers on hi tongue and had touched the cool rim of a water glass to his lips. Then er hand, as if following a plan of its own, had caressed his cheek and t en his chest and had traveled in descending circles to below his stomach where it set in motion a series of events that had ended with Elsa snoring softly in Albro's ear, and Albro lying wide awake. He had lain the last hou before dawn staring up at the dark ceiling trying to grasp the reality of ha ing, at long last found his father, or rather, his father having found him. fter thirty-six years, what were the odds of that sort of thing happening? Add to it, the fact that the man who claimed to be his father was dead, and the odds began to look about as promising as winning a bet that the sun wouldn't rise on Christmas day. It had to be some sort of mix-up, or worse, somebody's idea of a prank. Why hadn't anyone met him at the airport? How ironic, he thought, to have been lured back to the city of his ostensible birth on the pretext of discovering who his father might have been, on the anniversary of very day that he'd been found. He tried to put all of these thoughts out of his mind, but he could not. His mind kept returning to the questions that had plagued him all of his life: Was it possible that after all this time, he would find out who he really was, and why he'd been abandoned shortly after birth? Did he have family? Could there be brothers and sisters and aunts and uncles and cousins, everything that a foundling should have, but never knew about? What about his mother? Was she alive somewhere?

He thought about his 'official history' that had been handed to him by an office clerk after he had turned eighteen and was declared to no longer be a ward of the state of Washington. The plain manila envelope had contained a document titled: *Washington State Department of Health, Public Health Statistics Section, Certificate of Live Birth*. It had been embossed with the official seal of the state in the lower right-hand corner. In the *place of birth* section had been written the word, *UNKNOWN*. In the *date of birth* section had been written *December 12, 1976, APPROXIMATE*. In the section for *Father* as well as the section for *Mother* had been written in the same bold cursive handwriting, *UNKOWN*. So much for statistics, Albro had thought. There was his name, of course, but that had come years after his actual birth, and the date the document had been signed, *12-12-1982*. There was one other section entitled, *INFORMANT*, and filled in with the name, *ANNA SAWYER*.

"That's it?" Albro asked the clerk

"You're welcome to petition the court for access to your complete file," the clerk said before turning to the person next in line

That was just great. The document he held in his hands didn't tell him squat. He remembered just fine the succession of foster homes, being locked up in juvenile detention, and counselors who had questioned him with furrowed brows and had scribbled onto yellow pads while their mouths twisted into expressions of concern. As far as getting his records from the State, thanks, but no thanks. He looked again at the name, Anna Sawyer.

Finding her turned out to be as easy as looking up the name in the Seattle phone book. He dialed the number, and when the pleasant voice confirmed the line as the Sawyer residence, he introduced himself and asked her if she was the Anna Sawyer who had signed his birth certificate and if so, could she tell him anything about the first years of his life. The line had went quiet for what seemed like a long time and then she gave him her address and told him the bus number that would get him there. A small, white-haired, black woman met him at the door and welcomed him inside and fed him a big slice of chocolate cake and then took him into her office where she spread out a collection of newspaper articles on a side table. As he looked at them, she began telling him the story, as best as she knew it, of the first four years of his life.

According to Anna Sawyer, who had been the original caseworker assigned to his case, he had been found early one morning, hours before dawn by a janitor who was cleaning up the mess from the night before at a drinking establishment called the Terminal Bar and Grill which was located in an old business district that was caught between the north end of the Boeing Aircraft plant and the spreading grid of factories and foundries and warehouses at the southern extreme of the Seattle city limits. The place was called Georgetown, which had nothing in common with its namesake in the area outside of D.C. It was a neighborhood of crumbling brick buildings and railroad tracks. It was a place where the fragrance of jet fuel lingered on warm summer evenings and arsenic and lead settled peacefully into the rich alluvial soil. It was a place where folks who couldn't afford anything better found a place to live.

The janitor had found him swaddled in strips of a soft woolen material, lying on the hard wooden seat of the phone booth in the back corner of the tavern next to the men's room. Next to the baby lay what looked to be a small scroll of paper bit of rough twine. The janitor, a slow moving, slow thinking man, whose name, ironically enough was Swift, was the descendent of a pioneer important enough to have had a street named after him. He was old and his hair had gone white longer ago than he could remember and his joints creaked and popped from bone spurs and arthritis, but his eyes were clear and sharp. He untied the scroll of paper and set it aside and lifted the baby in his strong, gentle hands, and gazed at the little figure and realized that he was the witness of a miracle. Unfortunately, as often happens with miracles, he misinterpreted its true significance.

The old man saw the infant child as the answer to the prayer that he and his wife had offered up to God each night of the fifty years of their marriage. The prayer asked that they be blessed with a child, preferably a baby boy.

The old man, recalling this detail, quickly and carefully unwound the strips of cloth. Sure enough, as if in confirmation from God Himself, there was the little snub of a penis. The baby cooed and kicked his tiny feet and released an arcing stream of warm urine into the old man's face. Nothing in all his seventy years had ever made the old man happier. He quickly pulled a large handkerchief from his pocket and dabbed the baby dry and wiped his face. He then saw something else. A small, gold coin about the size of a dime hung from the infant's neck by a slender, silver chain. The old man touched the coin with his finger, and suddenly, inexplicably, he felt the need to hurry. He rewrapped the cloths as best he could and tucked the small bundle inside his coat. He was nearly to the door when he remembered the scroll of paper. He went back for it and slipped it into his pocket and hurried home.

A light snow fell and the streets were deserted. Nevertheless, he kept to the shadows and paused twice in doorways when he felt the unnerving sensation that eyes were watching him, and listened intently for footsteps. Satisfied that no one was following, he continued on until, with great relief, he reached the small house that he and his wife shared.

The old man's wife was so overcome with joy upon sight of the child that she fell to her knees and with her eyes closed tightly and her hands clasped together gave thanks to God who had seen fit, if somewhat belatedly, to answer their prayers. The old woman took the baby in her arms and snuggled him against her ample bosom. And she, being the real thinker in the family, dictated to her husband a long list of items they would need immediately. There were diapers to buy, bottles and formula and nipples. And not the old style nipple, but the new kind that more closely resembled a mother's natural shape. The old man reddened at the thought. How would he know the shape of a woman's nipple? He had glimpsed his wife's breasts only once early on in their marriage when he'd stumbled into their bedroom one morning while she was pulling up her brassiere and slipping her snow white arms through the straps. She had always been more than willing to offer him her favors, had in fact shown a real eagerness in the early years of their marriage, but only under the covers of their bed in a darkened room, while wearing a long cotton nightgown which she pulled up only far enough to make things possible. And afterwards, she had insisted that he go into the bathroom and wash himself and put on pajamas before returning to bed. His hand had ventured once, and only once, to the full and soft flesh of her breast, and had barely brushed the hard little bump at the end when she had become rigid and cold as stone and tears had flowed down her cheeks until the pillow was soaked and she had whimpered, 'no, no, no,' over and over. Such were the mysteries of women, he had concluded, and he had learned to keep his more ardent impulses in check.

But the old woman didn't give her husband time to think about things that had happened so long ago. She handed him a used envelope and pencil and instructed him to write as she dictated her list of items until he had filled both sides. He had never earned much money. His work had always been of a menial nature. Nevertheless, soon after they were married, they had begun to set aside a little money each month for the hoped-for baby. And even though they had long ago given up on the idea of ever conceiving a child, the habit of saving had endured. She had taken in sewing and sometimes laundry and for many years had cleaned the houses of the wives of engineers and executives from the airplane factory and the little money she had earned also went into the savings accounts. The woman found the bundles of small, faded blue bankbooks.

She held the baby in the cradle of her left arm and flipped through the latest little book. When she came to the last page, she scrutinized the figures. She had long ago learned the power of compounding interest. The balance read one hundred one thousand, sixteen dollars and forty seven cents. She carefully entered the number into a calculator and multiplied it by twelve. Her sharp intake of breath caused her husband to lay a hand on her shoulder and lean forward to look at the numbers on the tiny screen. The digits coincided with the day's date. He felt his wife begin to tremble

"It is a sign," she whispered, "but we must be careful." She instructed her husband to go across town to do the shopping where the selection was better, but also, and she did not tell this to her husband because a tiny seed of fear had already sprouted in her heart, he needed to buy the items where no one knew him. If anyone found out about the gift that God had given them, they might try to take their baby away.

It was then, that the old man remembered the small scroll, and produced it from his pocket and told his wife how it had lain to the baby. Maybe it was something they should have a look at, he suggested, and laid it on the kitchen table next to the pile of bankbooks. His wife looked at the object and then looked quickly away. He wanted to ask her about the gold coin. He looked at the back of his wife's head and knew that when he returned from his errands, the small scroll and the gold coin would be nowhere in sight and that the two of them would never speak of them. He turned toward the door, but then turned back again to see his wife holding the baby in her arms and singing softly. His heart suddenly filled with fear and he wanted there and then to call the authorities, but the words caught in his throat and his eyes filled with tears. If he had waited only a few moments until his mind and his eyes had cleared, he surely would have taken the sensible course and they would have avoided all the pain and turmoil that fell upon them years later.

The old couple raised the baby boy in their small home and he grew from an infant to a toddler, to a little boy with dark curls, bright blue eyes and perfect white teeth. He was slender and agile and extremely bright. All that time, they called him 'our baby', 'our boy', 'our dumpling', 'our sweet ake', 'our miracle', and a host of other affectionate names. He learned o call them mama and papa, and they were all very happy. Their neigh orhood had once had many homes, but the factories and warehouses and new streets had gobbled most of them until theirs was the only or e that remained on their street. And while there was no socializing f r the old couple, neither were there any prying questions from nosy n ighbors.

One day, the old couple took their 'handsome little man', as they now called eir miracle child because he was five years old, across town to a small c y park. The old man pushed his son on the swings and the old woman gave her son scraps of bread to feed the ducks that swam about in a ater filled ring of concrete. One could not find parents who were more roud or more loving of their child. As they strolled back to the bus sto with their boy between them, they passed by a school yard. On the othe side of the tall fence, children ran after each other shouting playful taun s and gathered in small groups playing school yard games.

The old couple paused, thinking the same thoughts, as old married cou les often do. Together they thought that someday their son would go to school. He would get a fine education and perhaps become an enginee or a doctor, or perhaps even a professor. They turned to each other nd smiled. The old woman smoothed the boy's jacket and brushed th sand from his trousers and licked the corner of her handkerchie and wiped a smudge of dirt from his cheek. She combed his hair neatly and reminded him to stand up straight. They found the entrance to he school, asked directions to the principal's office and were soon sitting comfortably in padded chairs facing a smartly dressed young woman bel nd a polished wooden desk. Their handsome little man sat behind ther on a bench next to the door. The nice receptionist had given him a pictur book and he was casually leafing through it.

The principal asked in a very polite manner how she could be of help and th old couple told her that someday their little boy would be an engineer, o a doctor, or maybe even a professor. Their voices rang and their eyes one with the pride they felt in their hearts. The principal looked at t e old couple and then leaned to one side and lowered her glasses to get a clear look at the little boy who had closed the book and sat quietly with his hands folded in his lap. She pulled out a form and squared it in the middle of her desk and asked the old couple for the boy's name.

Immediately, the old woman realized their mistake. They had been so filled with pride, that they had not seen the trap that had been laid for them. Panic seized her. Her frail hand reached out for her husband's sleeve. Her soft lips trembled, but she could not speak the name the well dressed lady had asked for, because there was none. They had been so filled with love and had felt so close to the little boy that they had never felt the need to give him a name. After all, they had called each other 'mama' and 'papa' for so long that to speak each others' names would have made them feel like awkward strangers meeting for the first time and it had felt completely natural to call their little boy simply, 'son'. The old man half turned in his chair to look at their child. The boy smiled and the old man suddenly felt too weak to stand. He knew that they should leave, should never have come here in the first place, but now it was too late. He started to rise from his chair, but the strength had gone out of his legs. The principal, who was now leaning forward and whose face had taken on the hint of a frown, was once again asking for the boy's name. And then, the inevitable question came. It was the question that they had buried far back in their minds. The question that neither of them had dared to speak, but knew in their heart of hearts existed and would someday be asked

A puzzled look came into the principal's eyes. She was, in fact, a kind and caring woman and had she known the impact of the question she would not have asked it in such a casual manner. She was accustomed to dealing with grandparents, many of whom were immigrants with a poor grasp of English, who cared for their grandchildren while the parents worked, sometimes two or more jobs which left them little time to spend with their children. In other cases, grandparents had taken on the complete task of raising the children when the parents had lost custody due to alcohol or drugs or violence and neglect. It was a tough neighborhood, but she welcomed the challenges and felt that she was doing some good. Since she was not getting the child's name she moved on to the next question on the form and asked for the parents' names and added that she would need the boy's birth certificate.

Tears began rolling down the old woman's cheeks. The old man sat silent, staring into his hands that lay upturned in his lap.

The principal, who had begun to sense that something was wrong, picked up the phone and punched in the extension of the school's social worker.

After that, the questions rained down upon them like a cold, wet winter storm and by the end of the day they had told their story to so many people that they had begun to grow weary and confused. They were held, pending charges, while local and then national records were searched in hopes of identifying the child. The boy was given over to foster care and the old man and old woman were eventually charged with kidnapping and held on half-million dollar bonds. Their lawyers were able to convince the judge that they were unlikely to flee and posed no threat to the community and got their bail reduced to one hundred thousand apiece.

The trauma of arrest and the time spent behind bars had taken a terrible toll upon the old couple, not to mention the story itself which caused them both a great deal of shame as it was splashed across newspapers and TV news shows coast to coast. The nest egg, so carefully husbanded over the years was soon eaten up by medical and legal fees. In the end, they were acquitted of all charges. The child's parents were never located, but even so, the old couple now penniless, were deemed unfit to assume custody of the little boy. In addition, their health had become so frail, that they had to be moved into a nursing home.

The long neglected task of giving the boy a name fell to his assigned caseworker, an overworked black woman two weeks from retirement who had poured herself into her job over the last forty years and now looked forward to the serenity of her home and her church. She had considered briefly taking the cute little boy and raising him herself. Unlike almost all of the children she dealt with, he was well behaved and

139

seemed to have been endowed with an unquenchable sense of self-confidence and happiness. But she was old, she reminded herself, and it was time for her to live at a much slower pace. So, as her last professional act, she vowed to give the boy a name and find him a good home.

She thought long and hard about this name. A child needed a good strong name, particularly a male child who might have a difficult time ahead of him. On all of his documentation he had been referred to as the Swift child. She had interviewed the old couple during their last days at the little house on Albro Street, and had felt a good deal of sympathy for them. They had clearly loved the baby boy and had done a wonderful job caring for him. It just did not seem right and fair that their lives should have been ruined by a system that was supposed to respect and nurture its citizens. She had to admit, though, that things turned out that way more often than not.

She her husband, Marshal, had brought six children into the world, all girls, and they were all grown up and college educated and two of them were married with children of their own. Her husband, had he lived to see them mature into accomplished young adults, would have burst with pride, but he had died from a heart attack when only forty-eight and she had raised their children on her own. She had loved her husband dearly and at times missed him so much it made her ache inside. She smiled at the memory of how he sometimes held her face in his big brown hands and kissed her. His hands had been capable hands, gentle hands. She sometimes wished that she had given birth to a boy child so as to bestow his name, as a way of honoring the man he was. It was a good name, a family name handed down from his great-grandfather, a freed slave and the first black man to settle in the area.

She wrote the name *Swift*, which had been the name of the old couple who had found him, and the name of the street in front of their home. She then wrote *Albro*, which was the name of the cross street. The names of the two streets, Albro Place and Swift Avenue, near the home where the boy had spent his first five years would at least give him a place, an actual grounding that no one could take from him. She then wrote the name again, this time she inserted the name, *Marshal*, and liked the look of it. She said it out loud a few times, testing the feel of it in her mouth and decided it would do nicely.   She made the formal application to the State of Washington for an official birth certificate and then, as if to make it so in the eyes of God, saw to it that he was baptized amidst a great deal of singing and praising of the Lord.

She then found Albro a foster home with a well-to-do family of four. A pretty stay-at-home mother and her pediatrician husband unable to have children of their own had already adopted two young children, a boy and a girl, close in age to Albro, and who wished for one more. All had progressed well during a six-month trial period and the stage was set to begin the paper work for adoption. But fate, who can never seem to leave well enough alone, placed the family, sans Albro who was lying safe in a hospital bed recovering from an appendectomy, square in the path of a drunk driver who had lost his job at the airplane factory and had spent his final day of life downing schooners at the *Terminal Bar and Grill.*

"I was already retired by then," Anna Sawyer told him. "You had been turned over to another caseworker. It was ten years before I was to hear your name again."

Albro thought for a moment. What Mrs. Sawyer had just told him might have sounded like a load of sentimental crap except for one small fact. He had heard a similar version of it once before. Maybe what she had said was all true, but it wasn't the same as having an actual memory. But how much did anyone really remember of those early years. He shrugged his shoulders and said, "That was when I left the Ranch. You found out about that?"

"The police contacted me and told me what you had done. They considered you dangerous." Anna Sawyer allowed the barest hint of smile to part her lips. "They thought you might come here. Do you mind telling me what happened?"

Albro finished off the cake while collecting his thoughts and then he told Anna Marshal what had happened.

Following the loss of the dentist and his family, a succession of foster homes were interspersed with sometimes short and sometimes long stints alone on the streets, until Albro, at the age of fifteen, found himself a resident of the notorious Olympic Boy's Ranch, a juvenile detention center outside a small rural community in the southwest corner of the state, not far from the ocean. It was a hopeful name that some well-meaning person had given the place. The word 'Ranch' wanted to invoke a rustic lodge of hand-hewn pine logs and grand, stone fireplaces with the sweet scent of wood smoke permeating every pore of the place, with bunk houses and barns and corrals all set amid the vista of spreading grasslands with the sparkling grandeur of the Olympic Mountains in the distance. In actuality, it was a collection of squat concrete block buildings connected with barred breezeways surrounded by tall chain-link fences topped by coils of razor wire. The interior seemed to alternate between bone-chilling dampness and suffocating heat, and the smell of disinfectant barely covered the underlying scents of urine and sweat and fear.

There, recalcitrant boys were encouraged to become responsible young men through the judicious application of fresh air and exercise, class room instruction, medical care, counseling and the occasional beating and rape. It was here that Albro met his friend Roger.

Sensing that danger lay in wait, Albro began planning his escape the day he arrived. He asked for a job washing dishes. He knew that working in the kitchen would provide him with the best meals and would give him the best contacts with the outside world. He learned the layout of the place by slipping quietly though its maze of corridors late at night and by studying the routines of the staff. During one of these forays, he heard labored breathing and muffled whimpers coming from behind a closed door just off the main room of the infirmary. He listened with his ear pressed against the door. He carefully tested the knob and finding it locked, retreated to a shadowy corner to wait. It wasn't long before Albro saw the night nurse, a middle-aged man with a finely trimmed mustache, open the door and lead a tall, slender boy whose face was flushed with fever and from whose nose ran a tickle of blood. The boy climbed into one of the beds and pulled the covers over his head, and the night nurse settled at a desk where a low light burned. He lit a cigarette and opened a paperback book. Albro studied the satisfied smile on the man's face for a long while before he silently slipped away to his room.

A few days later, Albro saw the boy sitting alone in the cafeteria picking at his tray of food. Albro set his tray on the table opposite the boy and slid onto the bench and told the boy that he was leaving early the next morning and if he wanted to, he could come along. Food deliveries came early every Friday morning. Meat came on one truck and produce came on another. The two drivers would have a smoke together and shoot the breeze before leaving the facility. Albro chose the produce truck with its roll up door and simple latch. The easy part was getting in the truck when no one was watching. The difficult part was getting out without being seen. They would just have to take their chances at the driver's next stop, where ever that might be, and hope that they could slip away unseen. To prevent the door's latch from locking them inside, Albro wedged a stick into the mechanism. He was betting the driver wouldn't see it. He and Roger were sitting behind a pallet of lettuce when the door came down.

Albro felt the truck swing to the right as it left the Ranch and gather speed. They were heading into town, and that was just what he wanted. There was something he needed to do before heading south. He had told Roger about his plan to get out of the cold, damp weather and go someplace warm like California, or maybe even Mexico. But he hadn't told Roger what he needed to do first. He liked Roger, but he hadn't known him long enough to know how he might react to breaking the law. Escaping from the Ranch was one thing. The worst that could happen was that they would be returned and would have to spend some time locked up in their rooms and would lose most, if not all, of the so-called 'privileges' for a few weeks. The authorities were bound to come down much harder on them if they were caught for breaking and entering and assault with intent to kill. Albro relaxed and enjoyed the ride, which lasted no more than twenty minutes.

The felt the truck slow, turn and then shift into reverse and slowly move backwards before stopping abruptly with a hard jolt as the driver hit the loading dock and shut off the engine. Albro held his finger to his lips. They listened as the driver's door open and close, and then the sound of boots crunching gravel. Albro gripped Roger's arm and

143

whispered, "Wait." They listened as the footsteps receded. Albro got up and put his ear against the metal door. He then lay on his side and lifted the door a few inches. He could make out a concrete loading dock and got a whiff of bacon and maple syrup. His stomach growled. They had arrived at a café and the driver had gone inside for coffee and probably a donut before unloading his delivery. Neither he nor Roger had had any breakfast, but that could wait. He eased the door up and rolled out of the truck and motioned for Roger to follow. It was a Monday morning and still early, but two boys on foot might arouse suspicions. So, they avoided the front windows of the café and skirted around back to the next block before walking the short distance into town

Albro found the street he wanted and then the house number. He had found the address in the rolodex file on the desk of the Ranch administrator's secretary while she had been away to the ladies room. He walked straight to the back door and looked around. There were several potted plants on a wood deck. They only needed to tip up three of them before they found the spare key. Albro wondered why some people even bothered to lock their houses. He opened the door and then replaced the key. Albro instructed Roger to keep a lookout while he searched the house. They really didn't need a lookout, but Albro had a feeling that Roger was the type who did best when given a specific job. The night nurse wouldn't be off shift for another hour, and even though he didn't know exactly what he was looking for, he would know it when he found it. The house was small, a living room, a kitchen, two bedrooms, one set up as an office, and a bathroom. He discovered what he was looking for in the bedroom. After that, they waited.

They sat in the semi-darkness of the bedroom closet and talked until they heard the car pull into the driveway and then they were quiet as they listened to the car door open and close and then the door to the kitchen open and the footsteps through the house to the bathroom. The sound of running water started, and then the sound of the morning news from the little radio that was plugged into the wall socket above the sink and sat on the vanity top next to the tub. After a while, the water stopped and they heard the sound of splashing and a deep and leisurely sigh. The night nurse had more than once told the boys in the infirmary that this was his second favorite activity.

What Albro had found was a pair of handcuffs and a blindfold in the bottom drawer of the nightstand. He rose from the floor of the closet and he and Roger went into the bathroom. There is nothing quite so vulnerable, Albro had told Roger, as a naked man in his bath. Albro ordered the man to stand and hold still while Roger held the little radio which was now playing a popular song from sometime in the middle of the century over the tub full of foamy white bubbles. Albro locked one cuff on the night nurse's left wrist and then ran the other end between the man's legs and locked the other cuff on his right wrist. He then ordered him to sit, which he did with a great deal of difficulty and splashing. He then tied the blindfold around the man's eyes. The night nurse had begun to curse viciously until he felt the string that Albro tied around his neck. Albro advised the night nurse not to move because the other end of the string was tied to the little radio which now sat on the narrow window sill directly above the tub. Albro turned up the volume so any cries for help wouldn't be heard from the street.

Albro's plan was to place a call to the local police some time the following day. By the time they arrived, the night nurse should be well into the first stages of hypothermia. He probably wouldn't know his own name. The police would naturally assume that the night nurse had been the victim of a vicious crime. To make certain they knew who the real victims were, Albro laid out on the vanity top the photo prints that he'd found in the shoebox at the back of the closet. He'd recognized only two of the boys in the photos so they most likely had been taken over a long period of time.

They found cereal and milk and sat at the kitchen table and had their breakfast. Albro found peanut butter and jelly and made sandwiches to take along. He warned Roger that it might be a while before their next meal. There were twenty-seven dollars in the night nurse's wallet. Albro took the twenty and the five and folded them neatly and pushed them into his pocket. A thief, he explained to Roger, would take all of it. They were perfectly capable of making their way in the world and needn't resort to outright thievery. Also, they needed to get out of town without being noticed. By now, Albro knew, their absence from the Ranch had been noted and most likely the local authorities had been notified.

"We need to borrow his car," Albro said. He knew it was risky, but so far they'd had luck on their side. "Can you drive?" he asked Roger, and saw his new friend smile for the first time. Much later, when Roger had begun speaking again, Albro would learn that Roger had grown up on a farm in North Dakota and had been driving since the age of eight. Albro had no real reason to believe that they'd get any farther than the edge of town, on other hand, he had the sense that this was all meant to happen. It wasn't like seeing into the future, rather it was a feeling that events had always been pulling him forward, and it would be unthinkable to start resisting them now. He picked up the bundle of keys that lay on the kitchen counter and tossed them to Roger. The night nurse had already begun to babble by the time they left.

Albro stopped and took a swallow of milk. Anna Sawyer looked at the empty plate and then pushed herself up from the table and went into the kitchen and came back with the cake. She cut another slice and set it front of Albro.

"Thanks," he said. "I don't think I've ever had cake like this. I mean to say, ma'am, it's very good."

"You eat all you want, son," Anna Sawyer said. "That man went to prison, you know. They closed down that wretched place. You caused quite a stir. A few higher-ups lost their jobs. Even the governor was called on the carpet. They were looking for you, but you seemed to have disappeared off the face of the earth. And then it all died away. Where did you go?"

Albro swallowed a few more bites of cake than then continued his story.

A day later and five hundred miles south, Albro woke to the mixed fragrances of wood smoke and of food cooking. Roger had eased the car onto a side road the night before as the engine had coughed and sputtered as it had sucked the last remaining drops of gas from the tank. They hadn't known exactly where they were, only that they were somewhere in the mountains of southern Oregon, and in the pitch blackness of the night, they had curled up on the car seats and had gone to sleep.

Albro stood at the rear of the car and relieved himself. Roger still slept. Roger's eyes had gone bloodshot red from the fatigue of driving a straight ten hours and had fallen dead asleep as soon as then engine had quit. Albro looked around and breathed in the fresh, crisp air. Evergreens towered over him and the undergrowth was thick with ferns and plants with broad and spreading leaves. He walked out to the main road and saw that they had pulled in across from a campground, and where surely breakfast must be waiting for them. He would go back and wake Roger, but there was something he needed to do first. They had passed a small gas station a quarter mile back down the road and he had noted the light above a pay phone. He needed to place the call that would bring the police to the night nurse's rescue. In all likelihood, the authorities wouldn't put much effort into finding them, unless the night nurse had panicked and had pulled the radio into the tub. The night nurse wouldn't be great loss to humanity, nevertheless justice would have to be served, and the police wouldn't rest until the two of them were behind bars. A judge would go light on Roger, but Albro envisioned little mercy for himself. Considering all that, Albro still felt that he had done the right thing and would do it again if he had to, and so it was with a light step and a clear conscience that he made the trip to and from the pay phone.

They strolled through the campground, their hands stuffed into their pockets and their shoulders hunched against the cold. Although it was June, the sun had not yet warmed the thin, damp mountain air. Campers sat around smoking campfires sometimes nodding, sometimes waving as the two boys passed by. Albro returned their greetings with a wave or a cheery hello. They were nearing the end of the loop with their stomachs growling audibly when Albro saw what appeared to be the figure of an old man coalescing from a pillar of smoke. He stopped cold in his tracks and grabbed Roger's arm and pointed to the apparition. They stared as the figure seemed to float a few feet above the ground. Then, as suddenly as the tenuous image had appeared, a freshening breeze swept away the smoke and beyond them stood a stooped and wizened oriental man firmly planted to the ground.

The old man coughed and wheezed and pulled a large red bandana from the pocket of his worn khaki pants and wiped his tearing eyes. "This wood is wet," he shouted over his shoulder toward an old canvas-style tent. To the left was an old, but well-kept pick-up truck. "It makes too much smoke and not enough flame!" He removed the fedora from his head and bent over the campfire ring and fanned the smoking logs.

"You there," he called out to Albro and Roger, "find some dry wood and bring it me, if you would, please!"

Albro looked around, and seeing no one else near them pointed to himself questioningly. The old man nodded and smiled encouragingly. The camp was next to a river which had provided the heavy dew that coated everything. The camp had long since been cleared of downed wood, but Albro remembered that just across the highway where they had stashed the car, the ground had been dry. He motioned for Roger to follow, and in a short time retuned, each with an armload of dry twigs and branches.

"Excellent," the old man exclaimed. He placed a few of the twigs on the smoking fire and fanned it with his hat. Within moments, bright orange flames jumped between the smoking logs. Albro and Roger turned to go. "Wait," the old man said, "you must stay and have breakfast with us." He placed a battered kettle and a large, blackened pot on the grate above the flames. "Tea and congee will be ready shortly. Please sit, won't you?" He motioned toward the rounds of firewood he had turned on end and had positioned in a half circle on the upwind side of the fire.

"Allow me to introduce myself. I am Chan Sai Lo," the old man said, and extended his hand.

Albro took the man's hand and was surprised by the strength of his grip. Albro had to consider now whether to use his own name or one of the aliases he had used in the past. 'Allen Sanders' was the name he most used. It was close enough to his real name that he could easily use it in the way that he might use a coat or hat if the weather required. But this time there was the problem of Roger and he'd sensed early on that it would be asking too much to expect him to assume a false identity. He was barely coping the way it was and he didn't want to add to his burden. And besides he always had a good sense of whom he could trust and whom he couldn't and he was getting a positive reading from the old oriental man. "Albro," he said. "And this is my friend, Roger."

Roger kept his hands at his side and glance nervously in the direction of the highway. "He's shy around strangers," Albro said.

"He is not the only one," the old man said. "Mei Ling," he shouted toward the tent. "We have guests. Please come out and meet them."

The tent flap opened and a diminutive girl emerged and walked over to where they sat. She was dressed in powder blue pants and white shirt, spotless white tennis shoes and pink sweater. Her long, shining black hair was pulled back into a pony-tail that hung to the middle of her back. She came to where they sat and stood with her eyes pointed toward the ground.

"May I present my granddaughter, Mei Ling," the old man said, smiling broadly. "Mei Ling, this is Albro and his friend Roger. They were so kind as to bring us dry firewood. Please say hello to them."

"Hello," the little girl said without looking up.

"Hi," Albro said. The little girl responded by digging the toe of her shoe into the soil.

"Mei Ling and I are on our way to the high peaks. She might not look it, but she is a very accomplished climber. She is very strong for her size. She climbed her first mountain at the age of seven. And you boys, where are you going?"

Albro had not come up with any plan beyond breakfast. He said, "South. We're going to California. San Francisco."

"Ah," the old man said, "a fine city. There are many Chinese there, and some of the finest restaurants. You have chosen a perfect time of year to travel."

At this point, the kettle boiled over into the fire with a loud hissing. The old man hurried over and pulled it back from the flames and found the tin of tea and dumped a measure into the boiling water. "Cups and bowls, Mei Ling" the old man said.

The congee was a thick porridge of rice and chicken and eggs and green vegetables. That, along with the strong green tea warmed them and filled them. As they ate, the old man informed them how, during the latter half of the nineteenth century, thousands of Chinese laborers had come to America to build the railroads and to mine the silver and gold. Few of them earned more than enough to feed themselves and most had left the countless small towns and had either settled in the large coastal cities or had returned to China. His own father had been one of those immigrants who had had the good fortune to have been educated in a missionary school in Nanjing and spoke perfect English. After working in the mines, his father had become a successful merchant and was able to send all twelve of his children to universities. Chan Sai Lo had become a physician. Retired now for ten years, he was devoted to his grandchild, Mei Ling. He spoke freely, as if telling his life story had long ago become a ritual to be performed with everyone he met.

Albro was thankful that the old man did not ask him or Roger any questions regarding their pasts, not that Albro hadn't the talent to spin out a past, as normal and unassuming as the next person, when the occasion called for it. Right now, though, he was ready to get going. He stood up from the picnic table. He could hear traffic picking up on the highway. They really should be putting some distance between themselves and the car they had abandoned. It wouldn't be long before a sheriff's deputy found it and the first place he'd begin asking questions would be at the campground.

"I can see that you are anxious to be on your way," the old man said. "Unfortunately, you are going south and we are continuing east. If you would indulge me for only a few more minutes, I would be truly grateful. Please sit," he said to Albro.

Albro sat, wondering what the old man wanted. Chan Sai Lo sat opposite him, and from a leather case that he pulled from inside his jacket, withdrew a slender, silver needle. "My mother," he began, "came from a small village near the headwaters of the Yangtze River, high in the mountains of the Himalayan plateau. My father, after having made his fortune in America had journeyed into those mountains in search of a mysterious object he had heard about since he was a child. He did not find his object, but he did find a teller of fortunes in a remote village. She read his palm and informed him that he was destined to meet a beautiful maiden in that very village, fall in love with her and marry her, which indeed happened! Little did he know that the young maiden in question was the fortuneteller's daughter, and it was not the first time that she had told that same fortune to an unsuspecting traveler, having had four daughters which to find husbands for. I cannot speak for the others, but in my father's case, he fell in love the moment he set eyes upon the young woman. From her mother she had learned the science of reading palms, and she passed the knowledge onto me. I must admit, though, that for me it is little more than hobby, something to entertain my own fanciful thoughts as I sink into old age. I have noticed that you are left handed. My I see your right hand please?"

Albro felt an odd flutter in his stomach and a slight chill run down his back as he extended his hand across the rough timbers of the table top. He could sense Roger standing behind him. Mei Ling climbed up next to her grandfather, crouching in her knees and resting her elbows on the table. The old man looked at Albro's palm and then reached for a pair of reading glasses. "My eyes are not what they used to be," he said as he adjusted the glasses. "Ah, that is much better. Now, let us see where you have come from and where you are going."

Albro looked up at Anna Sawyer. "He knew all about me. Not all the details that you just gave me, but he was able to tell me the general outline of my life. He said that someday I would return to the place of my beginning. He said there was something waiting for me there."

Anna Sawyer looked at him and then reached into her apron pocket. She extended her hand and opened her long, dark fingers. In her palm lay a small packet of folded paper tied with twine. "This might be what you are looking for," she said.

Albro took the packet and held it for a long minute. He slipped off the string and unfolded it. In the packet was small, gold coin the size of a dime, strung with a fine silver chain. On one side of the coin was a rabbit, and on the other side were twelve marks as one might find on a clock face, and at the center, what appeared to be a strand of frayed rope. Later when he examined the coin with a magnifying glass he would discover that those twelve marks were actually twelve different intricate designs. But at that moment, all he could do was to look at Anna Sawyer. "Do you know what this means?"

Anna Sawyer shook her head. "I am sorry, but I have never looked at it. Something always told me that it was not for my eyes."

Albro looked again at what he held and saw that there were three words written on the paper. He lay the little gold rabbit aside and examined the words. The odd thing was that they were not without meaning, but for the life of him, he could not say what meaning they held. It was like hearing three notes played on the piano that made no sense on their own, but nevertheless created a resonance that reverberated deep within ones memory. He passed it back to Anna Sawyer.

She lifted the pair of reading glasses that hung around her neck and positioned them low on her nose. She slowly said the words half out loud and with an air of puzzlement in her voice, *"the Jade Prince."*

CHAPTER 11

A BRO let the memory evaporate. He lifted aside the blanket and carefully rolled onto his side and raised himself to a sitting position. H arm throbbed and for a moment little black circles danced in his vision. ie pushed himself off the bed and went into the bathroom. He sat on ie toilet and looked at the bathtub and for an instant the image of th night nurse, naked and hairy came to him as clearly as if the man were t ere. The man had survived his ordeal. The fact that the man had served me had provided a certain satisfaction. But that really hadn't been the er ling because the night nurse, once released from prison, had vanished. F was out there somewhere, older and meaner and, in Albro's imagination still preying on the helpless. He squeezed his eyes shut making the ision go away. He put the past out of his mind and tried to concentrate on the present.

Albi went to the sink and splashed cold water on his face. He looked at hi disheveled hair, the two-day growth of beard, the dark rings that had be un to form under his eyes. Was this the face of his father? The questio left him feeling hollow inside, and the thought crossed his mind that h should forget this whole endeavor and catch the next flight back to Lo Angeles. After all, what exactly was he to do now? The promised c ntact had not met him at the airport, and the number he had been given vas no longer in service. His only option was to go to the police and 3k..., ask what, if could he please look at a dead man? He didn't have a name to give them, nor did even have a description. He

153

hung his head and stared at the water slipping into the drain.   A soft knock came at the door

"Albro, are you all right?" Elsa called to him. "Would you like some coffee?"

His nakedness suddenly made him feel awkward and embarrassed. He grabbed a towel and held it from his waist and opened the door a few inches. Elsa had put on a fluffy white robe. She held a steaming mug of coffee.

"I was alarmed when I woke and you were not there," she said and handed him the mug.   "How is your arm?   Can I help you get dressed?' Her face was full of concern.

"Thanks, but I think I can manage," Albro said.

"Good," she said. "I'll make us breakfast."

Albro took two of the pain-killers and washed them down with the hot coffee. He rubbed his eyes. Maybe what he needed was to get a hotel room and try to get some sleep. By the time he had struggled into his clothes, the pain had abated from his arm and the coffee had revived him.

Albro was swallowing the last bites from a pile of scrambled eggs as he finished his tale of woe to Elsa who sat across from him in her small, but tidy kitchen. Gray light came through the filmy curtains and did little to lighten Albro's mood. Suddenly he felt a pang of guilt over what had happened in the night. "About last night," he began and then stopped, unsure of what to say next. He had never apologized for sex. In his mind, he had never had any reason to do so. It had always been something that he had taken advantage of when the opportunity had presented itself. It was like coming across a hundred dollar bill being blown your way by the wind. Of course, he would grab it and spend it without a second thought as to who might have lost it.

Elsa reached out and touched his hand. "That was my doing. I am the one who should apologize. Do you have someone special at home?"

The image of Monique and all her radiant beauty came to Albro. Was she someone special? Without a doubt, she was. But was she *his* special someone?   In reality, Albro couldn't imagine Monique ever belonging to anyone. She had gushed about the love that existed between them, but for the life of him, he could not understand why she had agreed to marry him. Granted, love made people irrational and impulsive, but those were two traits Monique never displayed. So really, it was just a matter of time before Monique reassessed their engagement. He could hear her laughing voice in his mind, "Oh, Albro, you silly boy. You really didn't think I was serious..."

Albro considered Elsa's question. An afternoon's romp between silk sheets didn't exactly presage living happily ever after in marital bliss. As for the concept of 'home', a tiny apartment in a squalid part of town hardly qualified for the prize. The closest thing to a real home had occurred so far back in his life that it was nothing more than a few disconnected vignettes of foggy images which seemed to have lodged in various places of his brain and would pop into his thoughts when he least expected them.

"No," Albro sighed, "there's no one."

"Then perhaps someday you will find your special someone. In the meantime, there must be something you can do to find out about your father. You really don't think this is some sort of joke, do you? That would be a very terrible thing to do." She tapped her painted nails on the table top and pulled her lips into a kind of concentrated grimace. "I have an idea," she said. "Give me that phone number. Maybe I can find out if there is an address for it."

Albro proffered his cast and she jotted down the number on a pad. She went into the next room to use the phone and returned in a few minutes, and handed Albro a piece of paper with an address "I have a friend who works for the phone company. She rang the number, but as you said, the phone is out of service. Maybe the phone is simply unplugged. She couldn't say. You will go find out, won't you? I would go with you, but I have a flight I must prepare for."

Albro looked at the address.

"Do you know where that is?" Elsa asked.

It had been a long time since Albro had been in Seattle, and he couldn't say that he knew the city as he once had, but he did know the approximate location of this address. He looked up into Elsa's blue eyes. "Yes," he said. "It's in Chinatown."

"That's not far away, fifteen minutes at most. I will call a cab for you. I think you're going to find out something about your father. Aren't you excited?" Her mood was ebullient to say the least. While not exactly excited, Albro did feel a spark of hope. Perhaps, he would find out something.

"I'm flying to London, and will be gone two days. You must call me and let me know how things turn out," Elsa said. She had pressed a card into his hand with her number written on it. Her eyes were filled with tears. "Do be careful, Albro." She clasped his face in her hands and kissed him and the cab pulled away.

He gave the driver the address. He looked out of the rain streaked windows of the cab at the on again, off again city of his childhood. It didn't seem to have changed much in the twelve years since he'd last been here, unless perhaps, it was wetter and grayer. He had not thought to bring an overcoat and the thin material of his sports coat offered little warmth. He had his left arm through the sleeve and the right side draped over his shoulder. He huddled on the seat with his broken arm pressed against his chest trying not to shiver. He asked the cabbie to turn up the heat.

"It's already like Katmandu on a summer day in here," the driver shouted back at him.

"I'm cold," Albro said.

"Where're you from?" The driver glanced at Albro in the rearview mirror. There was something familiar in the dark eyes. Not that it was surprising. It seemed like every cab driver in the country came from somewhere on the vast Asian subcontinent.

"Los Angeles."

"Ah, yes. They call it City of Angels, am I right?"

The question created an odd resonance in Albro's mind, the phrase repeating in peaks and valleys and he was struck by the incongruity of its meaning. There were no angels that he knew of in that city, except, perhaps, fallen angels.

The driver did not wait for Albro's confirmation. He said, "One day Los Angeles will turn to dust. It is written." He passed to Albro a paperback book. "Take it, with my compliments. My wife tells me this book is full of evil and that I must take it from our home, otherwise she will not stay. I tell her that it is only a story. She tells me that she will not stay another day and begins packing her clothes. Okay, okay, I tell her. It is gone. Women are such strange creatures, don't you think?"

"Albro looked at the cover. Its title, *The Jade Prince,* was printed in a Cyrillic style in red letters on a black background across the top half of the cover. The lower half showed the crumbling ruins of city half-buried in a desert wasteland. Below the title was the author's name, Albro Marshal Swift. He experienced a sudden lurch of déjà-vu. It looked similar to the book that Sal Goldstein had showed him, but the cover was different. He turned to the back. The end paper had been torn from it. The last page was now partially obscured by a reddish brown stain. Was it blood? Was it Sal Goldstein's blood? It could not be the same book. That wasn't possible. He turned to the front. Someone had written: *For Isaiah, Walter, Nancy and the Mongi People. May they live in peace where the cool waters flow.   Albro Marshal Swift.*

Albro stared in disbelief at the words in what appeared to be his hand writing. Who were these people to whom he'd dedicated a book that he hadn't written? "You read this?" Albro asked.

"Cover to cover," the cabbie answered with a note of pride in his voice. And then as if to justify what might be considered a poor use of his time he said "In the time between fares, I read to improve my English."

Albro flipped to the first page and read the first line: *'None of them had understood the why or the how. They had only understood the need. The Jade Prince must not be released, no matter the cost.'*

Albro dropped the book. He looked at the cabbie's eyes. "Where did you get this?"

"It is good, yes?"

Albro leaned forward and grasped the cabbie by the collar. "Where did you get this book?"

"Take it easy! Are you trying to get us killed? You know I could have you arrested for assault."

Albro released the driver. He sat back and tried to calm his breathing. "I'm sorry," he said. "It's just that..." He stopped. It was just what? He looked at the driver who now had a wary look in his eyes. Albro took a deep breath and blew it out. He needed to watch himself. Something was going on and he had no idea what it was. "I'm sorry," he said again. "This book has my name on the cover. Can you tell me where you found it?"

The cabbie's eyes brightened. "You are the author? Are you famous?"

"No," I'm not the author," Albro replied, "and I'm not famous. Can you just tell me how this book came into your possession?"

"Someone left it in my cab. People leave all sorts of things. Their minds are always where they are going, not where they are. If the items are of any value I take them to the office. I kept the book. Nobody ever calls asking about a lost book."

"Do you remember who the fare was?" Albro asked.

The cabbie thought for a moment. "I'm not sure that I remember."

Albro pulled out the wad of cash that Monique had given him and peeled off a hundred and handed it up to the driver. "Would this help your memory?"

The cabbie took the bill and looked at it and stuffed it into shirt pocket. "It was four days ago. It was very late, and I was ready to be home in my bed. It was raining hard and I see this man waving me down. I almost passed him by, but I felt sorry for the poor bugger and stopped. He wanted me to take him to Chinatown. That was on my way home, so I say fine, get in. He was old. He looked, as they say, like he'd been through the wars. I figured him to be a bum and he would stiff me for the fare, but he paid."

"Where did you drop him?" Albro asked. His heart was beating hard.

The cabbie pulled to the curb and turned to Albro. "You're here," he said.

"Where did you drop that man? Please, I need to know," Albro said.

"You're here. I dropped him right here at this same address you gave me."

Albro craned his neck looking out and upward through the side window and then past the slapping wipers through the windshield. The cabbie had angled into the curb on a steep side street in Chinatown. "You're certain this is the same place?" Albro asked.

"Yes of course. Two men were waiting for him. They went up those stairs."

"What did they look like?"

"I don't know. It was dark. One was short and the other was tall. That's all I can say. Do you want to get out, or go somewhere else?"

Albro thought for a moment. "Go down two more blocks and turn right," he told the driver.

"This is not the address you asked for?"

"It is, but I've change my mind. Do you know a place called the Hun Lo Society?"

"The secret gambling club?" the cabbie asked. "Everybody knows about that place. A man was murdered there, in the alley. And two more men found dead in the gambling club above the noodle factory. A bloody business, if you ask me."

The news set Albro back in his seat. The Hun Lo Society had been a well respected, if illegal gambling club where a man could go and spend a quiet evening playing Mah Jong, chess, and on Friday and Saturday nights, poker. It had been located above the Hun Lo noodle factory where Albro had worked one summer. He'd received his introduction to the various forms of poker from the aging Chinese men who frequented the place. It was also where he'd picked up most of the Mandarin he could speak. "When did it happen?" Albro asked.

"Three nights ago," the cabbie answered.

"Take me there," he told the driver. Albro sat back and considered what the cabbie had told him. Could the murdered man have been his father? The derelict and homeless frequented the dark alleys. It was not that uncommon to find a rain-soaked body when the sun came up.

The driver pulled ahead and wound his way through the pedestrian filled streets and past double and triple parked vehicles and nosed the cab into an alley and stopped.

Albro let the book slip from his hand and handed the cabbie another hundred. "Thanks," he said, and got out of the cab and walked down the alley to a door marked **Hun Lo Co**. Large green dumpsters flanked the door. Strands of police tape lay twisted in a trickle of dirty water that coursed its way among the red-brick pavers. He knocked twice and waited. After a few moments an elderly Chinese woman opened the door a crack and was stopped by a heavy chain. A single dark eye looked at him.

"I want to see Auntie Lo. Tell her Albro Swift wants to speak with her."

The door closed. A few minutes passed and the door again opened a crack and then closed. He could hear the metallic rustle of the chain. The door opened and a diminutive figure stood in the doorway. The three steps up from the alley put her eyes on the same level as his. She looked to be in her eighties, but she had always looked that old, so Albro really had no idea what her actual age might be. Her white hair was pulled back and braided into a long strand that hung down her back. She wore an apron over a faded plaid work shirt that hung below the waist of her dark cotton pants, and on her feet were a pair of blue and white nylon and leather running shoes. Her small hands were dusted with flour. She pushed up her glasses and looked at him. From within he could hear the hum and clatter of machinery and voices shouting at one another in Chinese.

"Albro?" she asked and stared in disbelief.

"Auntie Lo," he answered.

She turned and shouted to the others and in a moment a dozen people were in the alley slapping him on the back and then pushing him into the building. They guided him down a narrow corridor, past the noodle making machinery into a small room that smelled strongly of garlic and oil and fried pork and fish that served as both office and cafeteria. They sat Albro down at the head of the table and someone hurried into the kitchen and brought back a steaming plate of noodles and vegetables and meat.

Everyone stood silently as he deftly lifted a mouthful with the chopsticks and chewed thoughtfully. He swallowed and took a sip of tea that had been placed at his elbow. "Delicious. Just as I remember," he said, and the room erupted in a barrage of questions.

"I'm here only for the day. There has been a report about my birth parents. This time it is my father who may have been found," he said, and the room suddenly fell silent. Those around him exchanged furtive glances with each other.

Auntie Lo stood up and said to them, "Back to work. Albro and I will talk."

The others filed quietly out of the room and closed the door. Auntie Lo studied Albro closely as he set the chopsticks next to his plate of unfinished noodles. "You know that a man was found just outside. We were told not speak about it."

"Do you think it was my…," Albro found that he could not bring himself to finish the sentence.

"I do not know. I never knew your father." Auntie Lo glanced nervously toward the door.

Albro wondered who would silence her and the others. He hesitated, not wanting to press her. He said, "I received a call from a lawyer, someone from Lee, Wong and Ho, who informed me my father had been found and that he was dead. I was on my way there when I decided to come here first. Do you know of them?" He watched as Auntie Lo visibly relaxed.

"Mr. Lee and Mr. Wong were both very good attorneys. Mr. Wong helped my husband to start this business."

161

"I take it they're no longer practicing."

"Mr. Lee and Mr. Wong are dead," Auntie Lo said matter-of-factly. "Mr. Ho lives in a retirement home. I sometimes take him a plate of noodles and we talk about the old days. Did you know that Mr. Ho and I came from the same village in China?"

"No, I didn't. So who took over the business?"

"Mr. Wong's youngest daughter manages the office."

"Is she good?"

"Oh yes, and she's still very young looking. She had many men ask her to marry, but she refused."

"I see," Albro said and considered that 'young looking' to Auntie Lo was anybody under the age of sixty-five. "Auntie Lo, I heard from someone about what happened at a meeting of the Hun Lo Society."

"Yes, it was very terrible. The Hun Lo Society used to be a very nice place. Nobody ever got hurt. If a man was losing too much of his pay and couldn't feed his family he was told to go home and stay there." Auntie Lo looked down at her hands. "My husband liked to gamble, but he got old and careless. After he died I found out that he had lost everything, including the noodle factory to a man named Chang Wu."

Albro's chest tightened. He had narrowly avoided crossing paths with Chang Wu once before while having a fantastic fun of luck in one of Wu's Kowloon casinos. Wu controlled an empire of gambling, drugs and human trafficking. What was he doing here? Was he attempting to corner the noodle market one small factory at a time? It didn't make sense.

Auntie Lo said, "Soon there was gambling every night at the Hun Lo Society, and prostitutes coming and going all the time. I became so ashamed, but there was nothing I could do. Last week, a man came into the Hun Lo Society. His face was covered. Only his eyes were visible. He killed two men right there in front of the others. The police closed down the Hun Lo Society."

"Did they catch the killer?"

"No. Some say he was one of Chang Wu's own men. Others say he was one of Chang Wu's rivals. Nobody knows for sure."

"Why did he kill them? Did they try to put up a fight?"

"No. All I know is that the men who were murdered were from China," Auntie Lo said and looked toward the door where the workers had gone. And then in a voice barely above a whisper she said, "They were asking about you. They wanted to know if anyone knew where you came from. Albro, are you in some kind of trouble?"

What kind of trouble could he be in? Sure, some of his deals in the artifact trade had been somewhat less than legal, and a few had been a whole lot less than legal. He had once narrowly escaped being thrown into a Myanmar prison, but never was there anything that came close to requiring murder to settle the score. He just was not in that league. If anyone had needed to know where he came from, there was always the public record. Go to the library and look it up. The local newspapers had run stories for a week. It was all there, about how he'd been found in a phone booth in a bar and how the old couple had kept him and had told no one for nearly five years.

He side-stepped Auntie Lo's question and asked her, "Did the men who were murdered say why they wanted to know where I came from?"

Auntie Lo's eyes shifted again to the door. She came close to Albro and touched the finger tips of one hand to his heart. "No one knows, but I saw something that night. I cook meals, noodles with meat and gravy, for the card players. I can make a little extra money that way. I served one of the men who died. I came from behind and I saw it at the base of his neck."

"What did you see?"

Auntie Lo looked again toward the door and then traced a design of two intertwined strands on the polished surface of the table top. Albro looked at it. There was an instant familiarity to its symmetry, and his hand went to his chest. "What does it mean?" he asked.

At that moment a door opened and a blocky Chinese man in a dark suit and shiny black shoes entered the room. He stopped and stood as solid as a two hundred pound sack of rice. His face was molded into a brooding frown. He glanced at Auntie Lo and then fixed his gaze on Albro.

163

Auntie Lo quickly smeared the design with a swipe of her hand, and stepped forward placing herself between them.

"Who are you?" the man asked, not taking his eyes from Albro.

Auntie Lo answered, "He is a flour salesman. He says that he can do better than our supplier. I told him we are happy with our flour. I was just showing him out." Auntie Lo took Albro by the sleeve and gave him a tug toward the door.

The big man took half a step toward Albro. "Wait," he said, "Who let you in?"

Albro stuck his hand out and said, "Allen Saunders, American Mills. The door was open." The man ignored his outstretched hand. Albro could see the wheels turning behind the dark eyes rimmed in red. He was not ready to buy Auntie Lo's story, but he also didn't know what to make of Albro with his overnight bag and broken arm. He was standing and staring at him just like those rhinos Albro had seen on the nature programs that Roger was always watching. The big animals were invariably stopped cold by anything new in their environment and whose attack was always preceded by a few moments of indecision. Albro dropped his hand and picked up his bag. "I'd be happy to show you some samples of our products," he said and displayed his most salesman-like smile.

The man curled his hands into loose fists. He lowered his right shoulder and took another step forward.

We have been using the same flour for fifty years. That is why our noodles are always the best. Isn't that so," Auntie Lo said as she took another step and directly faced the man. "Isn't that so," she repeated like an aged schoolmarm admonishing a student for behaving badly.

The man gave a reluctant shrug and relaxed his fists, "I guess so," he said.

She turned to Albro. "Go to Chang Foods. They use cheap flour in their noodles. Maybe you will have better luck there. I will give you the address." She pulled a scrap of paper and the stub of a pencil from her apron. She turned her back to hulking man and hastily wrote. She folded the paper tightly and pressed it into Albro's hand and bowed slightly. "You must excuse me. It is time to go back to work."

Albro did not waste the opportunity. "Thanks for your time," he said. He let Auntie Lo show him to the door. The sack of rice followed a few steps behind. Auntie Lo leaned close and whispered, "Go now, and be careful."

CHAPTER 12

ALBRO stood in the alley. Rain fell steadily. He struggled to unfold the paper by gripping it with his teeth and working it with his good hand. On it was a hastily drawn rendition of the design Auntie Lo had drawn on the counter and below it the words, *The Jade Prince*. Rain drops hit the paper and soaked into it making the ink run. Albro crumpled the paper and pushed it into his pocket and walked back out to the street.

He paused, looking in both directions. He caught himself scrutinizing everyone on the street. What was he doing? Did he really believe that someone was after him? No one approached. No one even looked at him. Everyone was going about his or her business, and the world was still spinning normally on its axis. The only thing important at the moment was the fact that he was getting soaked. He put his head down and walked to the corner and then headed up the hill to the offices of Lee, Wong and Ho. His plan was simple. Meet with the dowager Wong, (He had begun to think of her as such after Auntie Lo had described her reluctance to marry.), get a quick assessment of her claim that his father had been found, and if he were truly his old-man, get an estimate of any estate that might fall his way, sign whatever papers needed to be signed, and then get out of town. He didn't think he could bear viewing the body, or dealing with burial arrangements. Anyway, wasn't that what estate lawyers were paid to do?

As he approached, he saw two men standing in the sheltered entrance of the old office building with their shoulders hunched against the cold and damp. They wore heavy wool robes that were brown and of a thick weave. They looked to be monks, refugees from some mountain monastery, or maybe they were just another pair of homeless bums passing the time until the local shelter opened. Albro started to climb the stairs and kept his eyes on the steps to avoid eye contact.

"Blessed is he with a charitable heart," the smaller one said and held out his hand. The other one, a hulking black man pulled back his hood. He had bulging cheeks and tiny ears that hugged his large, round head. Thin, spiky whiskers stuck out from his face. That, and his massive bulk, combined to give him the distinct appearance of a walrus standing upright on two legs. He leaned toward Albro, his hands clasped behind his back and smiled, as if somehow that might reassure him of their sincerity. Albro reached into his pocket and felt the pad of money that Monique had given him and closed his hand tightly around it. He avoided looking into the big man's eyes and brushed past them. Before he could enter, the smaller one called after him, "He that sees, yet does not feel, shall be condemned to blindness."

It wasn't so much the words, but the sound of the voice, as if the man were speaking to him from within Albro's own brain that stopped Albro and caused him to turn around. He looked at the little man who was shivering in his wet robe. He could discern the points of the man's bony shoulders. He looked as frail as a dried twig. The other man, by comparison was a brute with huge arms and shoulders and legs as solid looking as tree-trunks. He stood with his feet apart in splayed out boots. Bent forward like that, with his hands loose at his sides and his bullish head lowered, he gave the impression that he was not accustomed to taking 'no' for an answer. Albro, who was half-way up the narrow entrance with the closed doors at his back and unseen from the street, suddenly felt cornered.

The little man must have sensed the effect his companion was having and pressed his advantage. "Is it not written," he asked, *thirst and ye shall drink, hunger and ye shall sup?*" He stuck out a scrawny hand, fingers twitching from the cold.

167

Right, Albro thought. Don't produce cash and ye shall have a knife at your throat! Albro knew men like these, homeless derelicts living on the street, sleeping in doorways, or camped in the jungle-like green strips between the freeways. One thing he'd learned from his own experiences of living on the streets was to never let them get close enough to grab him. Albro slowly teased a bill from the others and held it out to the little man who examined it carefully, pointing out the image of Benjamin Franklin to his partner who nodded approvingly, and then slipped it into a slit in his robe. He withdrew his hand and held out a small card.

Albro took the card from the man's bony fingers. Printed in a Cyrillic style were the words:

SEEK AND YE SHALL FIND

Albro looked up. Within the shadow of the hood Albro could just make out two beady eyes which locked on his and held him for a moment, and then the two of them were gone.

Albro gulped a breath and backed up the stairway and pushed his way into the building through an old style bronze frame and glass door. The door groaned on its spring hinges and closed with a rattle of glass and clanking metal. The lobby was dimly lit and had a floor paved with white and black hexagonal tiles chipped and worn by ages of shuffling soles, and smelled strongly of mildew and urine. He peered thought the dirty glass front of a reader board until he found the name of N. Wong, Attorney. The office was located on the third floor. A hand written sign on the elevator advised him to take the stairs.

The third floor hallway was lighted by a single hanging globe and was quiet. In fact, the whole building seemed to be deserted. He found the darkened door marked **Lee, Ho and Wong Attorneys at Law** and tried the latch. The door swung open. A tall window at the far end of the room let in enough harsh gray-blue light of a street lamp to reveal a narrow space that had literally been turned upside down and inside out. He felt around on the wall and located the light switch. A surviving bulb in a twisted and dangling overhead fixture lighted a room in complete ruin. Files had been emptied onto the floor. Desks had been overturned and pulled apart. Padding had been ripped from the chairs. The carpet had been pulled up and great, gaping holes had been punched into the plaster and lath.

Albro worked his way around the debris and into an adjoining room only to find a repeat of the former scene. It was obvious that whoever had been there, had not found what they were looking for and had vented their frustration on the space itself. He was about to retreat when something caught his eye. A glass-front case that had once held law books lay scattered on the floor, the thick volumes piled in heaps. The backing of the case had been torn free and lay at the other end of the room. Whoever had ripped it apart must have had immense strength. Albro squatted and cleared away the debris until he was able to free what turned out to be a guilt-framed photograph of three young Chinese men dressed in dark suits, and standing on the street below. Albro clearly recognized the alcove and the stairs which looked much brighter and cleaner than they did now. There was a look of pride on the men's faces. It was easy to guess that he was looking at Lee, Wong and Ho soon after they had set up shop. He was about to toss the ruined photo back on the heap of debris when he noticed something in the background. There were two faces looking out from a third floor window. Albro shook the lose shards of glass from the frame and held it up to the light to get a better look. Did he know those faces? No, it was just a trick of the lighting, he told himself, and his paranoid state of mind. The mind was wired to seek out the familiar, to see patterns where only random shadows existed. What he really needed was a magnifying glass. He cast a glance about as if he might have a chance of finding one in the chaos that surrounded him.

A voice called out from the other room. Albro held perfectly still and listened. He could hear the crunch of footsteps moving through the rubble. He bent the frame against his body and pulled the photograph free and hastily folded it and stuffed it in the side pocket of his bag, and then looked around for a weapon. He reached for a splintered chair leg and then peered through the doorway at a man who was standing in the middle of the other room. He was dressed in an expensive dark brown suit. His overcoat was draped over his arm and he held his hat in his hand. He had the ruddy complexion of a redhead, but his thinning hair had gone to a dull gray. He gave Albro a cursory glance as if he had fully expected to find him there, and then went on to more closely examine the room, his eyes moving from broken object to broken object until he had taken in fully the destruction. Only then did he return his gaze to Albro.

"Crude, but thorough," he said. The accent was British and his voice had the polish and precision of someone who thought carefully before speaking. "Well, we can't talk hear. They could be watching the building. You best come along. I have a car waiting."

Albro hesitated. "They?" he asked. "You know who did this?"

The man ignored his question and said, "Unless, of course, you'd rather be here when they come back. I doubt that chair leg will do you much good in a fight."

Albro shifted his eyes to the sorry excuse for a weapon that he still meekly brandished and then back to the stranger. What with his broken arm, he wasn't likely to instill fear in any attacker. Still, why should he put trust in a complete stranger?

"It really is in your best interest not to linger here," the man said evenly.

The man had a point, Albro had to admit. He said, "But that doesn't explain why I should go with you. I don't even know you. For all I know, you might have done this."

"That's true," the man said, "but it's hardly my style. As to why you should accompany me, I have some information regarding your father that might prove useful to you."

Albro considered that. He was having no luck at all with N. Wong. He looked around at the destruction. She might even be dead. At the moment, he decided, he didn't have many options. He dropped the chair leg and followed the man down the stairs and into the street.

It was barely five in the evening and what light had come into the sky that day was already gone. The rain was coming down harder and the wipers on the car that idled at the curb slapped it away enough for him to see an Asian man behind the wheel. The man in brown opened the curb-side door and motioned Albro in and then went around and let himself into the other side. The driver pulled away and the car shuddered over the cobbled street and then descended on down into the center of Chinatown. They circled around the crowded streets and the driver pulled up to a restaurant.

"An hour should be sufficient," the man in brown spoke to his driver. And then to Albro, "We'll have a bite to eat and some hot tea."

Albro, who by now was feeling a bit dazed, followed the man inside. The man looked around and said, "This is not perfect, but it will have to do. He spoke to the maitre'd who took them to a table that provided them a clear view of the entrance and exits. A waiter brought menus and tea. The man in brown filled the two cups, sipped his own and grimaced.

"At least, it's hot. I'm afraid all the years I spent in Hong Kong spoiled me for fine tea. It doesn't bode well for the food, but I'm absolutely famished. I've never been able to eat on a plane. It seems I need both feet on the ground. Mind if I order for the two of us?"

The waiter came, and after a short, but animated discussion with Marlowe who spoke in perfectly inflected Mandarin, the waiter wrote something on his pad and disappeared.

"We're in luck. The fish is fresh and the chef is from an establishment that I have frequented in Macao. Allow me to introduce myself. My name is John Marlowe." He reached into his pocket and withdrew a small silver case, opened it and handed a gilt-edged card across the table. Albro looked at the name and the phone number below it. "You can reach me anytime at that number."

"Why would I want to reach you? I don't even know you. Your name means nothing to me. What were you doing there, in that office? Were you following me?"

"I was not following you. Our meeting was fortuitous, but purely coincidental. I went there because I knew that was where your father would have gone."

171

"My father..." Albro repeated. He shook his head. I don't have a father, he thought. I've never had a father, a birth-mother, sure, because I'm here, and she undoubtedly had a lover..., but a father...?" The word caught in his mind. There seemed to be nothing real to connect it to.

"Yes, well, I'm sure all of this has come pretty much as a shock to you," Marlowe said.

"Shock," Albro blurted out. "This whole thing is someone's bad joke. I get a call from someone who claims to represent my father. She's supposed to meet me at the airport and doesn't show, and when I get to her office it's been pulled inside out. And by the way, I don't believe in coincidences."

"Your father didn't either. He had a profound belief in causality. Once the universe was set in motion, he once said to me, nothing could stop its inevitable outcome. There was very little room for randomness in Thomas Crane's world. Please accept my deepest sympathy for your loss."

"What makes you think that I'm the offspring of this man?" Albro's mind was beginning to swim. The restaurant was hot, and the cacophony of voices and rattling plates was making it difficult to concentrate. "What was his name?"

"To answer your first question, simply listening to your word choice, reminds me of your father. How often does one hear the term *'offspring'*? It comes from Old English, you know. Your father was very fond of Old English. To answer your second question, his name was Thomas Crane. Let me simply say that I have access to a great deal of information, some of it factual, some of it circumstantial. Security agencies all around the world gather information. I don't need to tell you that we live in a time of intense paranoia; everyone spying on everyone else. They've become quite blatant about. You might not believe it, but there are those who try to monitor such things in an effort to prevent misunderstandings, some of which can prove to be quite disastrous. I am one of those individuals. Your image came up as a remarkably close match with the image of a man seen entering the Chinese Consulate in San Francisco. Your fingerprints, as well, appear to be nearly identical. That could be a glitch in the software, but it's curious nonetheless. The only logical conclusion at this point is that the two of you are very closely related. A simple DNA test would be the final proof. For now, let us assume that Thomas Crane is your father.

"How do you know all of this?"

"The initial match was made by someone in your government. Frank Giddes is his name, a nasty piece of work, I must say. As I said, I try to keep track of such things, particularly when they pertain to someone of special interest. In addition, I've traced the phone call to your cell and the outgoing call you made, both of which correspond to the phone line in the office you and I just visited, and that leads me to believe that your father instructed Ms. Wong to call you in the event of his death."

"And that office, you think this Frank Giddes did that?"

"I can't say."

"You can't say, or you don't know?"

"I honestly don't know, but I hope to find out soon."

"If my father knew where I was, why didn't he contact me? What's going on?"

"A great deal, I'm afraid," Marlowe said gravely. "Most of which, I am not certain of at the moment. For instance, why has Ms Wong not reported the vandalism of her office? If the police knew of it, I suspect they would be questioning the both of us at this very moment. As for your father, my guess is that to have contacted you would have put you in more danger than you are already in. Do you carry a gun?"

"No I don't carry a gun. I've never even held a gun."

Marlowe seemed to mull this over. "Just as well, I suppose. You'll probably live longer. Who searched Ms. Wong's office? I have no idea. Nor do I know of her whereabouts. I would like to question her. Let us hope that she was not on the premises when the wreckers arrived, and that she has the good sense to keep herself hidden. I suspect that she will attempt to contact you soon."

Albi was about to ask Marlowe exactly what his interest in all of this was, when the waiter arrived with a cart loaded with steaming plates of food.

"Ah," Marlowe said, "let us eat. I will talk and you will listen."

Marlowe dished up food for both of them. He took a mouthful, chewed appreciatively and then continued.

"Your father, God rest his soul, was a man of extraordinary talents. I met him my final year at Cambridge, 1968. He had come over as a Fulbright Scholar studying high-energy physics, nothing I could understand, of course. I haven't the mind for mathematics. International relations had always been my interest. We met in a pub and hit it off. He was a year younger than I, but he already had two advanced degrees in his field, whereas I was struggling to complete my basics. He knew his literature as well as philosophy and history. There didn't seem to be a language that he couldn't pick-up. We had an Arab fellow in our group who had him speaking Farsi after only two pints of bitter. Where he found the time to study those subjects was beyond me. He had an intensity that some found off-putting, but most of us found exhilarating, particularly the young women. He seldom went back to his flat alone.

"He suddenly went missing. After a fortnight, he showed up at our local pub looking a good deal worse for wear. He said that he had been holed up at the British Museum. He said that he had gotten special permission to study some ancient Chinese texts and artifacts. How he managed that I never knew. Evidently he knew somebody who knew somebody who gave him access to areas that are ordinarily restricted to specialists in their field, and that's only after a lengthy application and review process. The British are very protective of their treasures, and even more so when a foreigner expresses interest in them. Something to do with our inflated sense of self-importance, I'm afraid.

"Months passed before I saw him again. He had a worn and disheveled look about him, and at the time, I assumed he'd been bearing down on his studies. I suggested he take a break and join me for a pint. He seemed literally torn between that idea and whatever was preoccupying his mind. As we drank, he relaxed just enough to relate to me that he had not been studying, that he had not even been at Cambridge. He had spent the intervening months inside mainland China. I assumed he had received the blessing from your state department, no

174

mean feat, given the relationship between your government and the Maoists. O, he might have developed a relationship with one of your security agencies; nothing official, mind you, rather a quid pro quo. They wouldn't interfere, in the hopes that he might prove useful at some future date.

"Whatever happened there had changed him. The intellectual fires had gone out and had been replaced with a fire of a different sort. It was more the look of a raging fever. He claimed to have found evidence for the existence of a mythical object called the *Jade Prince*, and had been very close t finding it, but circumstances, which he refused to describe, had prevented him. Coincidentally, I had some familiarity with the eponymous legends and asked him if his sought after object was the source of those legends. He told me there was no doubt in his mind that the source of those legends was based upon actual events. I assumed, naively so, that the object's intrinsic value lay in its archaeological significance

"Two years would pass before I saw him again and then, as it turned out, or the last time. It was in Hong Kong. I had been recruited by a major financial institution and I was a junior officer. Our government was hosting a group of scientists from around the world, your father among them, who had gathered in Hong Kong to present their latest discoveries in the field of high energy particle physics. I was in attendance on behalf of a group of investors who liked keeping their fingers on the pulse of advancements in the sciences. The gathering took place at our embassy and was the typical non-diplomatic affair: cocktails and hors d'oeuvres and everyone engaged in pleasant conversation. Yet, due to the importance of the guests, and given the tensions between your country and the Soviets, after all, the North Vietnamese would never have been able to mount a war without the flow of Soviet arms through Haiphong harbor. But even more worrisome was the intense fear the Chinese felt over that proxy war on its southern border between the two nuclear super-powers. Therefore, the security detail was on full alert.

"An argument broke out in the center of the main reception hall where everyone had gathered. By the time I got there, it was all over.

175

One man was standing, another lay sprawled on the floor unconscious. The man standing was your father. I'm not sure that he even recognized me. Our security chaps were about to take your father away when an American interceded. That man was Frank Giddes. The man on the floor soon regained consciousness, but nevertheless had to be carried from the room." Marlowe drained his cup of tea and then seemed to contemplate the residue before continuing.

"Not long after that, Thomas Crane disappeared, along with several others, from a site in northern Laos on June 14, 1970. You can check any major newspaper archive to verify that. The reports will tell you that he was part of an archaeological expedition who perished in a helicopter crash. Due to the utter devastation of the crash site, and the rugged, mountainous terrain, none of the bodies were recovered. What the news stories don't mention was that in addition to the eight passengers on the helicopter more than fifty others on the ground perished as well. Satellite photos showed only scorched earth. Vientiane was under the thumb of the Americans. They allowed in only a small group of investigators. I was not one of them, but I did see the official report before it was sanitized for public consumption. In an area roughly the size of a football field, where once had been several portable buildings and tents, nothing remained. Not a piece of metal, glass, splinter of wood, or bone fragment was found after extensive sifting of the soil. Even the soil itself was absolutely devoid of life. It had been sterilized to a depth of twelve feet.

"There were rumors, of course. Any incident on that scale is bound to cause rumors. Some claimed it was a small nuclear explosion, but there was no sign of radiation. Others speculated that it was some kind of bio-agent that literally consumed everything, but any metabolic process leaves behind some telltale sign. Then there were those who were convinced that whatever they had discovered there was not of this world. Those in charge of the investigation were encouraged to expound on their theory and then they were unceremoniously labeled as crackpots. The supermarket tabloids had a heyday with the story. It was, as it turned out, an excellent way to pass off the incident as just another product of someone's over wrought imagination.

"Your government, who had been running the operation, denied all knowledge, which was easy to do since no evidence existed that any operation had been conducted. The soldiers who had been present were simply added to the long list of those missing in action, and the civilians were said to have died during a humanitarian mission to war victims. Every attempt had been made, it was claimed, to recover the bodies, but the area had been deemed too dangerous, and they could not justify further loss of life. What a group of scientists was doing on a humanitarian mission was never full explained. They had become the unfortunate casualties of war. The story died a quiet death, and was forgotten."

Albro pushed back his untouched plate. He had listened attentively to Marlowe's story, and didn't believe half of what he'd heard. The man was just too slick, too polished, too urbane, to take at face value. 'Charlatan' might be a better way to describe him. He'd known a sleight of hand artist, a real master at his trade, who was nothing alongside this guy. He'd missed something during Marlowe's monologue, a turn of phrase, a fleeting mannerism that didn't quite fit, or maybe it was just that damned British accent that exuded a miasmic aura of confidence. Whatever it was it had put his nervous system on full alert.

Albro said, "So what you're telling me is that Thomas Crane managed not only to escape the disaster, but to father a child, bring him to this city and then disappear again for thirty-three years before returning here to die. And let me guess, somehow the *Jade Prince*, whatever it might be, is at the center of all of this."

Marlowe took a last bite of steamed fish and chewed thoughtfully. He laid his chopsticks across his empty plate.

"Yes, everything you just said is correct. But understand this. I am not the only one who has made that connection. I'm sure there are those who will have a keen interest in uncovering the true cause of that disaster. Then again, perhaps they know its cause and are intent upon keeping it a secret. The Chinese, as well as the Russians, recognize that

177

something of immense power was unleashed that day and their efforts to discover its source have not ended."

The waiter came and left a fresh pot of tea.

Speaking of great mysteries, Albro thought to himself, and was about to pull the photo from his bag when he stopped. Suddenly, everything was telling him not to trust Marlowe. Marlowe had walked all around the real issue being careful not to step on it.

Marlowe asked, "What is it?"

"Let's set aside the questions about Thomas Crane for the moment, and assume that the *Jade Prince* is something more than just a chunk of stone. If governments are as interested as you say, then whoever finds it could be in a position to make a bundle. What's your interest in it?"

Marlowe looked around the room and then he poured himself more tea and surveyed the remaining food, teased out a tidbit of pork from the surrounding eggplant and chewed it slowly. He then caught the waiter's attention and made a sign that he was ready for the bill.

"There was a time," he said at last, "back there at Cambridge, if anyone had asked me if I knew Thomas Crane well I would have answered, yes, without hesitation. It's interesting, isn't it, how we can fool ourselves into believing certain things. Were we friends? I thought so at the time, but in reality we were not. Perhaps, we would have been, had our passions been more aligned. I realize now he was a man of closely guarded secrets, but he was a man worthy of respect, and I shall always regard him so."

"That was very nice," Albro said. "Now answer my question." He thought he saw a fleeting look of surprise pass through Marlowe's cool facade.

Marlowe looked at Albro and said gravely, "Very well. Whoever releases the *Jade Prince* could realize knowledge and wealth beyond his wildest dreams. Bear in mind also, there are those who will do everything within their power to prevent its release. Think of me as a kind of broker between those two opposing parties.

"If you need to reach me, you can call that number and leave a message. Until Ms. Wong surfaces, I'm afraid there's not much I can do for you. I wish I could stay, and speak further, but I have some things I must attend to, and then a flight to catch later in the evening." He rose from the table. "No, no. Don't get up. You've barely touched your food."

He looked down at Albro. "There is one more thing. That man I spoke of, the one Thomas Crane knocked unconscious."

"What about him?" Albro asked.

"His name was Martin Osborne Newton." Marlowe then turned and left, pausing at the front counter where he chatted briefly with the woman behind the register, handed her a few bills, bowed his head slightly and then disappeared through the front door.

CHAPTER13

MARTIN   OSBORNE   NEWTON

stood at the window of his lavishly appointed office at the top floor of MON Tower and looked northward across the expanse of the Los Angeles basin toward the mountains which wore a cap of fresh snow. Rain had swept in from the Pacific the night before and the air was sparklingly clean, a rarity since the middle of the century when automobiles swarmed in like invading locusts. The scene was in stark contrast to Newton's mood. He turned to look at Doctor Felix Krupp who had sunk deep into a black leather armchair and whose lip trembled like a toddler who knows he has misbehaved and is going to be punished for it.

"Where is he now?" Newton asked trying to keep his voice even. The only clue to the rage that was boiling inside him was the slight tick that jerked the muscles along the right side of his jaw.

Krupp, confused by the question, looked in panic to Monique who sat languidly on the matching sofa, her long legs bent and spread comfortably apart with her stiletto heels resting on the polished surface of the ornate rosewood table between them. The table was early Ming and would easily bring a quarter million at auction. She had let her skirt slip to her upper thighs. Her gaze was cool and calculating. She was never one to let rage get in the way of business. For her, rage was something to be anticipated and enjoyed to the fullest, on par with a well orchestrated act of coitus. Krupp had just told them about Frank Giddes's nocturnal visit. Krupp's lips were still puffy from the trauma of the gun barrel. The Monique had stated flatly that Albro Swift was gone from his residence a d no one seemed to know of his whereabouts. Thus, the confusion a to whom Newton was asking about.

Kru p decided his best option was to straddle the fence and hope that he didn t fall off. He said in a quavering voice, "Giddes will find Swift. Find one an I'm sure you will find the other."

"An where might that be, Doctor?" Newton flexed his fists and paced behi d his desk. He had come close to murdering Krupp a few minutes ear er and Monique had stopped him with a single word.

"Ma tin," she had said in that soft, but admonishing tone that she knew woul make him want to shove the words back down her throat if only he had the courage to do so. The belittling act had only served to intensify his age.

Kru p whined in response, "I told Giddes that you had met Crane in Seattle. le knows that Crane is dead. I didn't have to tell him that. You made a ness of things there."

"I n de a mess of things?" Newton exploded. "You betrayed us, you fucking nonkey! You've been spying on us for Giddes!"

"W needed to know what he and the Old Man were up to," Krupp coun ered trying his best to offer up a reasonable argument, but knowing ful well there was nothing he could say to placate Martin. His only hope not receiving the beating of his life was to keep Martin talking until Monique decided to intervene.

"An just when were you going to tell us about them?" Newton shouted int Krupp's face.

Kru p shrank as far back as the cushion behind him allowed. He decided to sk a little impertinence. He said, "You wouldn't have known what to do ad I told you. You're a fool, in over your head in things you don't under tand."

Nev ton lunged at Krupp and with one hand picked him up by the throat and eld him at eye level. The veins in his neck bulged like fully charged fire hoses. "I could throw you through that window, and you would have seventy-five floors to think about what you just said, but I think it wou d please me more to watch you suffocate."

181

Krupp kicked his dangling feet and clawed at the single hand that held him aloft. His eyes bulged as if they would explode, and his tongue protruded through a foaming wreath of saliva.

Monique waited until Krupp's thrashing began to subside and his face had turned a deep purple.

"Put him down, Martin. We're going to need him. If you kill him, it will just make things more difficult for us later." She had not even flinched at Newton's display of savagery.

Newton, who had not begun to breathe hard, dropped Doctor Felix Krupp back into his chair. Krupp gasped and made various horrible noises as he struggled to regain his breath. Martin pulled out the creases on his sleeves and smoothed back the lock of hair that had fallen into his eyes. He went to the small but well stocked bar that occupied a corner of the room and poured a generous serving of whiskey and drank it down.

Mark my words. I'm going to kill the bastard before this is all over."

"You must remember, Martin," Monique said as she rose from the sofa and walked past Krupp ignoring his retching and gurgling and came to where Newton stood. She ran the tip of her fingernail from his temple to the corner of his mouth. "As much as you dislike the good Doctor, we are in this together, and we won't succeed in releasing the Jade Prince, if we don't get along."

"I can get along, goddamn it, if I know whom I can trust. That piss-ant weasel was working behind our backs. If he had a way to do it, he would join up with the Old Man and cut us out of the loop."

"But he can't," Monique said. "That's not possible, and that's just the point. He needs us as much as we need him."

"How can we trust him?"

"I think he understands now what will happen if he tries to keep something from us. Am I correct Felix?"

Krupp groaned and rolled to an upright position. He managed to grunt and nod his head.

"Good. We need to make plans. I want to be ready to intercept our young hero when the time comes."

CHAPTER 14

FRANK GIDDES leaned casually against the wall
of the waiting area and looked through large plate glass windows into the
exam room. The hard-edged florescent lights against the wall of stainless
steel and white tile created an impression of an environment drained of
life, which seemed appropriate, given what the place was.   Even the
technician, who at first had balked at showing him the body at this hour of
the morning looked as if he'd gone through a severe blood-letting. The
harsh lights washed out any color that might have been in the man's skin.
Giddes had produced a federal identification and had described the John
Doe in question.   The technician had grudgingly agreed to pull the body
from its refrigerated drawer.

The technician lit a cigarette. "Helps with the smell," he said and
went into the adjoining room.

Giddes watched as the technician shuffled from one drawer to the
next checking the tags. He could hear the quiet hum of the ventilation
system as it worked to keep the smells of disinfectant and viscera to a
tolerable level. The thought struck him that few odors were as persistent
as that of death. At last the technician found the right drawer and gave
Giddes a wave. The technician pulled off the cover. Giddes considered
himself to be totally inured to the site of death.   Yet, he took an
involuntary half-step backwards. It was not the huge cut down the thorax
to the pubic bone which had been grossly stitched, that had shocked him.
That was the normal autopsy procedure. What had stunned him was the

array of cuts and slashes across his entire body, starting at the tops of the feet and going all the way to the forehead.

"Do you know him?" the technician asked. "It might help explain why he died if we knew who he is." The technician folded his arms and shifted his weight back onto his heels. He really hadn't expected an answer and wasn't surprised when the man ignored his question.

Giddes forced himself to make a studied examination of the body. The dead man had a head of long white hair, and even drained of blood the skin had a tawny color as if the man had spent a great deal of time in the sun. He could tell that the chest, arms and legs had been well muscled at one time, but something had caused them to waste away. Even so, there still existed an intense vigor in the lifeless blue eyes that stared openly at the ceiling. Time had changed him, but it was Crane, alright. Giddes had waited a long time for this moment and was surprised that he felt a tinge of regret that Crane was dead. If anything, he should be feeling relief that Thomas Crane no longer posed a threat.

"Surprisingly," the technician said, bringing Giddes out of his thoughts, "none of these cuts was deep enough to cause death. Even collectively, these cuts weren't so severe to make him bleed to death. See those abrasions across the chest, on his legs and wrists?" He pointed with the cigarette held between two fingers. "It's my guess he was tied to a chair and tortured. My old man was in a special-forces unit in 'Nam, back in the seventies. He used to tell us kids stories of how they would do this sort of thing to the gooks. They used razor blades. When they were finished playing with them they'd pop them through the ear."

The technician cocked his finger and placed it next to the dead man's head and made a soft popping sound through his lips. "My dad scared the living shit out of everyone but me. I guess that's maybe why I ended up working in a place like this."

"So you're saying he was shot?" Giddes asked.

"You see, that's the funny thing, no gun shot, no deep punctures with, say, an ice-pick, or a needle. You might assume that his heart gave out from the stress of being tortured, but that's not the case. His heart was fine. The toxicology report, as far as we can tell, shows no foreign substances in his blood. What do you make of this?" the technician asked. He grasped the dead man's left arm and twisted it to reveal the inner surface. On it was an odd looking scar that appeared to be two strands of a rope twisted together and spanned the middle third of the forearm.

Giddes looked at the scar. If he had needed a definitive mark of identification this would have been it. He knew the scar, had seen it once before, but not on Crane. The Old Man had told him its significance. At the time, he'd been unable to believe what he'd been told, but later he'd come to the conclusion that eventually time made believers out of all of us.

The technician waited for a response and when he got none he said, "There's something else you should see. Here," he said and pulled a pair of rubber gloves from his pocket and handed them to Giddes, "help me roll the body."

Together they turned the body. The technician took a long draw in his cigarette and grimaced as he pulled the dead man's hair away from the base of his neck. "I've seen a lot of shit, but never anything like that."

Giddes looked at the body. From the base of the neck to the top of the buttocks the skin, if you could call it that, had the ugly, marled look of scar tissue.

"What caused that?" Giddes asked. He had a good guess as to the answer to his own question, but he was curious to know what the technician thought.

"I've been asking myself that same question," the technician answered.

"And what do you think?" Giddes asked.

The technician drew on his cigarette and held it for a moment looking at the dead man's back. He blew out a cloud of smoke and said, "At first I thought it was the result of third degree burns. I've seen a lot of that, especially among street people they bring in. The get drunk and fall on their camp fires, or somebody decides to settle a grudge with a can of gasoline and a match. But look how delineated the scarring is."

185

Giddes saw how the scarring was sharply outlined across the backs of the upper arms, around the base of the neck and down the man's sides to the straight line across the man's lower back.

"Burns always leave an uneven edge," the technician continued. "I'd have to say that he was flayed. My guess is that his skin was peeled like a grape by someone who knew what he was doing. It must have hurt like a motherfucker. Hard to imagine how the son of a bitch survived it, but you can see that the scarring is old."

Giddes stared a long time at Thomas Crane's back. He wondered why someone would go to the trouble of removing the skin off a man's back. Why not kill him and be done with it? Had it been the perpetrator's intent to torture Crane? Or had there been another reason? Perhaps, the intent had been to send a message to someone else.

"There's one more thing," the technician said. "Maybe it's important, maybe not. He lifted the dead man's left arm away from the body. "He suffered a wound in his side years ago. It was deep and the stitching was crude. It looks as though the stitches tore through before the wound had a chance to heal. Somebody had it in for this bastard and not just lately."

Giddes looked at the scar and silently catalogued it along with the rest of the gruesome details.

The technician asked, "Have you seen enough?"

"I have," Giddes said, "but you still have not told me the cause of death."

"The M.E. put it down as severe trauma," the technician answered. "You can interpret that as you like. Satisfied?"

Giddes stood motionless his eyes on the eyes of the dead man. He then reached into his pocket and counted out three hundreds and handed them to the technician. "I wasn't here. Understood?"

"Right," the technician answered. He scooped up the bills and stuffed them into his shirt pocket. "Help me roll him back," he said.

CHAPTER 15

THE sky had grown dark by the time Albro had stepped back onto the street. It was the start of the rush hour and the sidewalk and street were crowded. The air had grown colder, and the wind had picked up, whipping the rain into visible curtains. A few of the shop keepers had made half hearted attempts at Christmas displays, lights strung haphazardly and a Santa and sleigh minus his reindeers, a dusty looking snowman abandoned amid a clutter of cheap cookware. The shopkeepers seemed to have accepted the fact that no one in his right mind goes Christmas shopping in Chinatown.

Albro instantly regretted not calling a cab. He considered going back into the restaurant to make the call, but where was he going? He clutched his open jacket and bent his head to the weather. At the next corner, he hailed a cab which sped past in a cloud of spray. By the time one stopped for him, the rain had soaked through to his skin and he was shivering.

"Cold night, eh? Where do you want to go?" the cabbie asked. He could see the man's dark eyes in the rearview mirror. He was the same driver who had brought him into Chinatown. What were the odds...? Maybe the driver had been watching and waiting for him. He considered getting out and flagging another cab.

Was he being watched? Was someone after him? The image of the ransacked law office was stuck in his mind, and the mysterious John Marlowe had only served to heighten a growing sense of paranoia.

Paranoia? Whoa, slow down, he told himself. Get a grip. The smack of the wipers in time to wailing Indian music brought him back to reality.

"If you want to just sit here, that's fine too," the driver said. "The meter's running. It's all the same to me."

Albro looked up. Maybe he should find a hotel room and sort things out. Contact the authorities. And tell them what? Or, maybe he should go back to Los Angeles. Monique and his new life were waiting for him there. What he really needed to do was clear his mind, and there was only one thing that was guaranteed to do that. He leaned forward and spoke to the driver. "I know there must be a card room nearby." He pulled out the money Monique had given him and peeled off another hundred and showed it to the driver. "This is yours if you can find it."

The cabbie pulled out from the curb and made a U-turn, went four blocks and pulled into the lot of a convenience store. "This is my brother-in-law's business. Wait here, please."

He was gone only a minute and when he returned he was smiling broadly. "Okay, boss. We're in business." Out of the lot he turned right and sped south for about ten minutes before slowing and then turned into a crowded parking lot. Red and blue neon flashed and a dull, heavy beat emanated from the windowless building like a throbbing heart.

"Tell the man at the bar what you're looking for," the cabbie said.

Albro handed him the hundred plus a twenty to cover the fare. He opened the door and got out. He was feeling better already. He walked over to the entrance where a man the size of a refrigerator stood with his legs apart and his hands clasped behind his back. He wore a black leather jacket and Santa cap. Nice touch, Albro thought. Everyone seemed to be in the Christmas spirit. Albro started past him when the man reached out with a hand the size of a catcher's mitt and stopped him. Albro came to just below the man's chin.

"That'll be ten for the cover," the man said.

Albro placed a ten in the man's hand and he stepped aside. Albro pushed open the door and he was hit by the full force of the music. A red glow infused the room punctuated by a flashing strobe that lighted the form of a woman naked of everything but high heels and long, dangling earrings. She was prancing and gyrating on a stage to the pulse of the pounding beat. The stage was surrounded by men, their heads barely above the level of the stage and their jaws hanging half open. The strobe gave the woman a kind of herky-jerky motion that made the whole room undulate in a way that made Albro feel slightly seasick. He looked away and crossed to the bar.

"We don't serve alcohol, so don't ask," the barman. Albro noticed that he paid no attention to the woman on the stage. He'd seen it all, Albro was certain, a thousand times over. The thrill was long gone.

"Coffee," Albro said.

The barman brought a cup of black liquid. "Ten dollars," he said.

"Must be good," Albro commented. He laid a ten on the bar.

The barman rang up the sale and placed the bill in the register drawer. He turned back to Albro. "Table dances are fifty. Lap dances are a hundred. The private rooms are two hundred and up."

"Seems a little high," Albro said.

The barman gave a slight shrug. "It's the weekend."

Albro looked around the room. His eyes had adjusted to the gloom and he could see tables where women stepped in place in a kind of desultory dance. Around the perimeter were curved booths. Here and there a man sat with his arms at his sides and his legs spread wide, his head tilted back slightly and his eyes locked on the naked torso of the woman astride his lap. Albro watched as a stunning black woman with heavy breasts and long legs led a chubby, pasty looking man through a red velvet curtain. By the end of the night most of the men would be stripped of their paychecks and hung out to dry like so much wet laundry.

"I'm sure they're worth every dollar," Albro told the barman, "but I'm looking for the card room."

The barman stared at him until Albro placed a ten on the bar. The barman continued to stare. Albro put a hundred on top of it. The barman lifted the bills and folded them and placed them in his shirt pocket. "Wait here," he said and went through a door at the end of the bar.

The music ended and a new song started immediately. This one was a slow, bluesy number and an excited murmur came from the men

189

around the stage. Albro turned to see what was causing the stir. The strobe had been extinguished and a single, blue tinted spot lighted the stage and in it stood a tall, slender woman in black heels and dark stockings. She had her back to the men. The blue light made her skin shine in other-worldly white. Her hair was black and cut short, short as a man might wear it. Her arms were wrapped around her nearly shapeless torso and even from a distance Albro could see that her hands were extraordinarily large and her long fingers ended in dark pointed nails. As her arms unfolded he could see the muscles ripple beneath the skin. The men had fallen silent. They seemed mesmerized by what they were seeing. Suddenly the music accelerated into a fast beat and she was at them like a tiger thrusting against the bars of its cage. A few of the men, taken by surprise, stumbled backwards and then the mood changed as if a switch had been flipped.

The men began whooping and hollering and elbowing each other out of the way. They all wanted to press themselves against the stage. The dancer seemed to be everywhere at once. She was working hard to the music, and her small breasts glistened in a sheen of sweat that appeared first on her shoulders and then across her back and belly. The men were proffering bills they had folded with a sharp crease along their lengths. The dancer would swing her leg over them and lower her shaved pubis and snatch the bills from their hands. She would then step back, tease them mercilessly and then thrust herself at them again, staying tantalizingly just out of reach, driving them into a heated frenzy. The trick was a real crowd pleaser and by the end of the song, she had a wad of bills in both hands.

The barman reappeared and even he was caught by the scene on the stage. He stopped in midstride seeming to forget everything else. As the song ended, the barman blinked hard and wiped his mouth with the back of his hand. He turned to Albro and instructed him to go past the men's room through second door on the right to the end of the hallway.

Albro followed the route and was met by a thickset Chinese who told him to lift his arms. He looked at the cast, shrugged and then patted Albro from his armpits to his ankles. He dug through the overnight bag.

Without turning, he knocked twice on the door behind him. The door opened a crack and the guard uttered something unintelligible. The door closed momentarily while chains rattled and then it opened and Albro stepped in.

It was a typical backroom operation. There were six tables with five chairs each. Five of them were fully occupied at the moment. The sixth had an open seat. A cashier sat behind a thick Plexiglas window. She too was Chinese. She was wearing one of those tight silk dresses with the standup collar and heavy makeup and a gold ring with a diamond the size of a wren's egg. A cigarette stuck in a long, black holder burned in the ashtray next to her. For five hundred dollars, she informed him, he could buy a place at the table and play as long as he cared to. If he left the room, his seat would be available for someone else. If he required, there was a toilet behind the only other door in the room.

"Why all the security?" he asked."

"Chang Wu does not like trouble," she answered.

The name brought to mind what Auntie Lo had told him. He handed her five bills and bought another fifteen hundred in chips with the remaining bills that Monique had stuffed into his pocket.

"We keep ten percent when you cash in."

"The house always wins," Albro said.

"Maybe you would like to quit while you're ahead," she told him.

"Thanks, for the advice, but I'm feeling lucky."

"They all say that." She lifted the cigarette and placed it delicately between her lips. She kept her eyes on his and pulled heavily on her cigarette and exhaled slowly through her nostrils letting the smoke wreathe her face in a blue cloud.

Albro stepped over to the table with the empty seat. The other players, a florid looking man heavy and balding whose tie hung in a lose knot, a middle-aged middle-management type who nervously pulled at his wedding band, a confident-looking Korean who sat back in his chair with his short fingers serenely interlaced across his stomach, a tall skinny fellow with the tired eyes of a truck driver and a gray-faced kid with long hair whose eyes kept jumping from one player to the next, all looked as if

191

they were once a week regulars. They were the kind of card players who worked all week at mundane jobs for the momentary thrill that being in control of their own destiny gave them, even if that perception of control was completely illusory. They were not professionals. Albro allowed himself a tinge of guilt for what he was about to do to them, and sat down.

The Keeper, an elderly Chinese in gray work clothes and closely cropped hair who had been walking casually about the room, unwrapped a new deck and set it in the middle of the table and then retired to his chair next to the door. The florid man picked up the deck, shuffled it awkwardly and allowed Albro the cut. Over the course of the next nine hours Albro Swift did not rise from his seat.

When it came his time to shuffle and deal, Albro pointed to his cast and passed the deck to the man on his left. The first time it caused a minor stir as the other players looked at one another for agreement. Eyebrows lifted, shoulders shrugged and then play resumed.

Players came and went all night. He let each new-comer take a substantial number of his chips and then he would take them all back. At two o'clock, the music in the next room died away and Albro got the sense that the tables were about to settle down to some serious play. A man entered the room and the Keeper announced that the night was set, that is, no one else would be admitted. The man who had just entered had narrow shoulders and sinewy neck. He wore dark slacks, a black silk shirt and a black Nehru-style jacket that been custom tailored to fit his long torso. His thick black hair was oiled and combed in waves and his skin was deeply tanned. Albro watched the man's eyes coolly survey the room. Albro's table was down one player. The man stepped casually to the table and pulled out a chair. He gave a curt nod before sitting and let his dark eyes take in the other three players and the value of chips on the table. Only then did he allow his eyes to meet Albro's in a mirthless sign of recognition, conveying clearly, 'Ah, yes, the young and careless fool. We meet again.'

He smiled at Albro and reached for the deck. With very fast hands, he shuffled, waited for the cut and then dealt smoothly around the table.

At his point, Albro reckoned that he had accumulated somewhere in the neighborhood of sixty thousand dollars. The thought of cashing his chips and leaving had been foremost in his mind until he had seen the man step into the room. He had recognized him immediately, and had no trouble remembering exactly when and where it had been. Seven years before in a hotel room in Bangkok he'd played recklessly all night, yet luck had been with him until the man in black had sat down and had taken every Bhatt he'd had in his possession, a wry smile always on his lips. Afterward, Albro had learned that the man, Alexi Ruslonov, was an ex-KGB official who had made a fortune in Afghanistan offering guns to the various warlords in exchange for heroin which he sold to the Russian troops. He had then expanded his business interests to the Far East. What were the odds, Albro asked himself, of running into Ruslonov here. What were the odds...?

The man smiled now, closed mouth, with just the merest upturning at the corners of his narrow lips, as he won the hand. He raked in the pile of chips. Albro blinked. He'd just played the hand and had no memory of what had taken place. There had been close to ten thousand dollars on the table, and a good part of it had been his. He needed to focus his mind on the here and now.

Albro dealt the next hand, and again, the man in black succeeded in besting every man at the table. After two hours, Albro was down by half of what he'd had when Roslonov had sat down. There was something wrong, not with the cards, but with himself. He was letting Ruslonov read him as easily as he might read the morning newspaper, and there didn't seem to be anything he could do about it. The Russian bastard was going to break every man at the table, and he knew it.

At four o'clock it was down to the two of them. The other three had pushed back their chairs but had not risen. They were staying to watch the crushing blow that would soon be delivered. Ruslonov had steadily and incrementally increased his bets until he was now raising a thousand dollars with each round. At five o'clock Albro called the Russian's last raise and laid out four Jacks and the Queen of Spades. Ruslonov looked at the cards, looked at Albro and then folded his own hand into the deck.

"It is late," the Russian remarked with an air of boredom in his voice. "Would you care to cut the deck for what now sits on the table? Winner takes all."

Albro looked at Alexi Ruslonov and tried not to look at the pile of chips that lay before him. He had bet his last dollar and had won back a tidy sum, but it was nothing in comparison to the small mountain that Ruslonov had carelessly mounded up. He had played consistently well all night, but the Russian had played better. He had a troubled feeling that the Russian had folded a better hand in a calculated ploy to test his nerve with this one last grand temptation. He should have seen it coming. He felt his face grow hot. It had not been about the money or for that matter the winning. The real pleasure for Alexi Ruslonov was, just as it had been in Bangkok, the pleasure of forcing the other players to give themselves away, to show them to be the weak and vulnerable individuals that they were.

"I will allow you to shuffle the cards," Ruslonov offered, and held out the deck. He nodded toward Albro's cast. "Take your time."

Albro took the deck. He lifted the deck and began a one handed shuffle and then stopped. He suddenly had an over-riding sense that to change the order of the deck would be like changing the order of the universe. He laid the deck on the felt and pushed it to the middle of the table. The Keeper, who had not slept all night and had been close to drifting off, got up and stood close to the table with his arms folded and his eyes suddenly alert. The other players looked at the chips on the table and knew there was well over a hundred thousand there and knew also they were not likely to see such a thing as this again. It would be something they would tell over and over as their gambling habits sucked them into that bottomless pit of impoverished misery.

"After you," Albro said.

"As you wish," Ruslonov said with an obliging tilt of his head that seemed to suggest that if Albro wished to become an impoverished fool, then far be it that he would be the one to stand in his way. The Russian grasped the deck near its midpoint and lifted and turned his hand upward. The Keeper grunted knowingly at the sight of the King of Hearts.

Albro touched his thumb and fingers along either side of the remaining cards and caught Ruslonov smiling at him. And then an odd thing happened. Time stopped, just like it does in the movies. Was he dreaming? It wasn't the painkillers. They had worn off hours ago and his arm was killing him. He looked around at the faces frozen in various stages of anticipation. He sensed that he could have gotten out of his seat and walked around the room without breaking the spell. He glanced at the cashier who had been caught in the act of plucking a bit of tobacco off the tip of her tongue. It was as if the smoky room had become a tiny microcosm of the universe and God had called a time out. Is this what Moses had experienced on that mountain top? There was no burning bush, but the deck of cards did seem to be trying to tell him something. If he'd cared to, he could have sorted through it for a card that would beat the King, but then he knew that wasn't necessary.

Albro blinked and time resumed. His heart was calm. He lifted his hand slightly and flipped up the very top card.

The Russian's smile froze and his eyes grew cold as he looked upon the Ace of Diamonds.

He said. "Someday, Mr. Swift, we shall play again, for higher stakes. Now you will excuse me."

Ruslonov crossed the room, the soles of his shoes clicking sharply on the hard linoleum and exited the room. The others stood silently looking at Albro Swift until the gray haired Chinese ordered them to leave. "It's all over. Go home."

They filed out, a tired troupe of losers. When the last of them were gone, the old Chinese turned to Albro and said, "You sit. Chang Wu wishes to speak to you." And then he left.

The cashier had made quick work of counting the chips and had left a very large stack of banded hundred dollar bills on the table. The cashier had deducted the house cut and now there was something just over a hundred thousand dollars and he wondered if Chang Wu was going to allow him to leave with it. He waited and listened for footfalls. He thought briefly of trying the outer door, but admitted the place was probably guarded like a fortress.

At last, the door opened to a Chinese man elegantly dressed in a dark blue suit with a stripe so fine as to be barely visible, a dark blue silk tie and a shirt so white as to be dazzling. His hair, pure silver with no hint of gray or black was combed back from his pronounced forehead to the nape of his neck. His eyes were narrow and hooded and black and shiny as onyx, and his lips were set in a business like line. The two men who flanked him were also Chinese and broad as battle ships and judging from the bulges in their sports coats, as heavily armed.

Albro stood and the silver-haired man extended a hand as delicate and smooth as a young boy's, and spoke in a soft, almost feminine voice. "Mr. Albro Swift, I am Chang Wu. Please excuse the inconvenience of making you wait. Let us sit. Would you care for tea, and perhaps, something to eat? You must be hungry after such a long night. Chang Wu had yet to even glance at the stack of money that sat within inches of his hand.

Albro was, in fact, hungry. A shot of caffeine wouldn't hurt. "That sounds great," he said.

Chang Wu snapped his fingers and one of the bodyguards stuck his head through the doorway and spoke to someone on the other side. Within seconds a tray with a pot and two cups and a plate of freshly steamed buns was brought in and set between them. Chang Wu poured the tea.

"Please, Mr. Swift, while they are warm," Chang Wu said and motioned with a subtle gesture toward the plate of buns. He sipped at his tea then said, "I understand that you met with Mr. Marlowe before coming here. He is an interesting man, is he not?"

Albro slowed his chewing. Chang Wu undoubtedly had spies all over the city so he wasn't surprised that he'd been informed of his whereabouts. The question was, why? He had a suspicion that Chang

Wu's question was a round-about way of informing him that to not be forthright with his answer would be to incur Wu's dissatisfaction. "I can't say I really know the man. We just met last evening."

"I, on the other hand, do know him," Chang Wu said and then deftly changed the subject. "And like you, Mr. Swift, he is a man who takes great risks. Your win was most stunning." His head gave a barely perceptible nod toward the pile of cash. "You are now a wealthy man."

"By my standards, sure, but I doubt yours."

"Nevertheless, you must visit my establishment again soon."

"I'd love to, but I'm actually in town on other matters."

"Your father," Wu said and bowed his head. "I you offer my condolence "

'Your father,' the words resounded in Albro's mind. Wu had said the words without a hint of doubt or speculation. Everyone seemed to be so certain. It made him want to prove them wrong. "That's still an assumption. I'm still waiting for the facts."

"Ah, you must be referring to the elusive Ms. Wong."

"So, you know about her too."

"Yes, I know all about Ms. Wong, and your father, Thomas Crane."

"What do you mean, you know all about them?"

A period of silence ensued in which Chang Wu appeared to study Albro Swift as if he were plumbing the depths of his soul. Something similar had happened to Albro when the old Chinese doctor had read his palm and had outlined with phenomenal accuracy the intimate details of his life; things a stranger could not possibly have known. At first, the experience had astounded him, but later he had passed it off as some kind of stage trick. Still, he had never been able to come up with a rational explanation as to how it had been done.

At last, Chang Wu cleared his throat. "Mr. Swift, I have no reason to doubt that Thomas Crane was your father. His death has brought me a great sadness, as well as a great inconvenience. Not only was our friendship far from over, a business arrangement has been left incomplete.

197

"What kind of business arrangement?"

Chang Wu hesitated a moment and then chose his words carefully. "Your father came to see me, quite unexpectedly. I had not expected to ever see him again."

"Then you knew him before he disappeared?"

"Yes, but that is not material at this time. He came to me because he needed to enter Mainland China without attracting the attention of the authorities. I agreed to assist him."

"But not without a fee," Albro said.

"Our arrangement was more complicated than that."

"So? What does that have to do with me?" Albro's eyes went to the stacks of hundreds. How did the saying go, something about, 'the sins of the father being visited upon the child?' It looked as if Chang Wu was here to collect and he probably wasn't in a mind to offer the easy payment plan.

"Do not worry, Mr. Swift. It is not money that interests me. It is something far more important."

"Oh, and what might that be?" Albro was on his second steamed bun.

"When do you plan to release the *Jade Prince*?"

Albro nearly choked before he managed to swallow the mouthful of dough and sweet pork. He washed it down with several gulps of tea. "You're making two assumptions: one, that I know where this thing you and everyone else call the *Jade Prince* is located, and two, that I know what the hell you're talking about when you say that I know how to 'release it'."

Chang Wu hesitated before speaking. "You said, 'everyone else'. Who are you referring to?"

Albro held up his casted arm and wiggled his fingers and then counted off, "First there was Krupp, then Goldstein, who happens to be dead along with his two dimwit thugs." Albro looked up at Chang Wu's two bodyguards. "No offense. Then, there was Auntie Lo, Marlowe, and now you. I can probably count the 'elusive' Ms. Wong as well. If there is a connection between those names, I don't know what it is."

"Your father," Chang Wu said, "is the connection. He did not contact you."

Albro started to argue the point about his alleged father, and then decided it was useless. "No."

Chang Wu brought the tips of his fingers together in a prayer-like pose and closed his eyes and took several deep breaths before speaking. "That is a disappointment," he said.

"Sorry."

Chang Wu waved a hand. "If that is the hand we are dealt, then that is the hand we must play."

"We?" Albro asked, not really liking where this conversation was leading.

"Like a rope of many strands, our lives are intertwined," Chang Wu said.

Being tied to Chang Wu in any way wasn't an image that Albro was entirely comfortable with. "Like I've told everyone else," Albro said, "count me out. I'm not interested in playing your game."

"You may find that you have no choice," Chang Wu said.

"Yes, well, all the same. You can count me out." Albro pushed back his chair and stood. "I brought an overnight bag with me. Has anybody seen it?"

Chang Wu gave a slight sideways motion of his head and one of the bodyguards fetched the bag and placed it on the table. Albro worked open the zipper and began loading the cash.

Chang Wu stood. The fabric of his suit fell smoothly into place. "You need a hotel. I keep a suite at the Hilton for my special guests. It is yours if you wish. My driver will take you. You need not worry; your privacy will be respected. It is the least I can do to assure your safety."

"Thanks," Albro said. "You're very generous, but I'm accustomed to watching out for myself. Besides, I think I can afford to pay my way." He hefted the bag. "I'll call a cab."

"Surely, not at this hour," Chang Wu said

"I'm feeling lucky," Albro said, and started for the door.

199

A shadow crossed Chang Wu's face. "If I may, I have one last thing to say to you."

"What's that?"

"Your father was a resourceful man. Let us hope the son is likewise," Chang Wu said and gave a short bow. One of the bodyguards opened the door for Albro and motioned for him to leave.

CHAPTER 16

A BRO SWIFT waited in the half-light of the gray and drizzly lawn. In his left hand he held the over-night bag whose bottom was now lined with packets of hundred dollar bills, and scanned the street or his cab. A winning night should have left him feeling blissful, particularly one as profitable as he'd just experienced, but he had a nagging, unsettled feeling that drawing that Ace of Diamonds had not been entirely of his own doing. In the past, when he'd drawn the card he'd needed, he'd never known with any real certainty that it was going to happen. There was no telling about the capricious nature of luck; either it was with him, or it wasn't. Tonight something entirely new had happened. It was as if he'd already lived the moment and it was his memory that had guided him. But what had really happened; what about that whole sense of time having stopped? Had that really happened? The more he thought about it, the more implausible it all seemed. He wanted to blame it on fatigue. His body ached for an opportunity to curl up in a warm, dry corner. He'd had but a few hours of fitful sleep in the last two days and yet his mind was wide awake. He thought back to that moment when he was about to split the deck and then he remembered something odd had occurred. He'd actually felt the presence of…, of what? It hadn't been a thought or an idea, or even a hunch. He'd heard no voice. He'd felt no cold draft on his neck. No, it had been more of an intense urge. It had been more like the need to take a breath after having swum from a great depth A *directive,* yes that was it, one that had suddenly appeared in his mind that had said, *"Take the top card!"*   And even if he had wanted to disregard the thought, he wasn't sure that he could have.

It was the same sensation that gripped him now, as a cab pulled into the empty parking lot. He started toward it and then abruptly changed his mind and waved it on. The driver glared at him and then sped back onto the street. Albro stood there wondering what had come over him. He turned and looked over his right shoulder. Someone stood in the side door of the strip joint. The figure was tall and slender and made no pretense of trying to hide. In the grey, half light he recognized the dancer he had watched the previous evening. Her face was in shadow, but there was no mistaking the shape of her shoulders and her long legs. He saw a slight movement as she brought up her hand and then the orange glow of a cigarette. He had the uncanny feeling that she was watching him and waiting for him to come to her. Then he was startled by the blare of a horn. He turned and saw another cab wheel around the corner and drive past.   He watched the driver stop at the next intersection, execute a U-turn and come back to where he stood. Albro turned back to the figure in the doorway, but she had disappeared.

The cabbie rolled down a window and shouted at him, "Hey, I knew it was you."

Albro looked at the cabbie. He was the same driver, the Nepalese, who had driven him to China Town and later had brought him to the gambling club. What were the odds...? Zero to none, he decided. It couldn't be a random event. But right now he didn't care. He was cold and wet and beginning to shiver uncontrollably. He opened the door and got in.

The cabbie turned and smiled broadly, and then his smile died away. "You look terrible," he said. "Are you all right?"

Did he look bad, Albro wondered? He ran his hand over his face and through his wet hair. He felt greasy. He needed a bath and a place to sleep. He looked again at the empty doorway and wondered if the woman had gone inside. Not likely, he decided. The place was certain to be locked and would probably remain so until the lunch crowd started showing up.

"Where do you want to go?" The cabbie asked.

"I saw someone. Drive around back of the building," Albro said.

"What do you want to do that for? Are you looking for one of those sexy ladies? I sometimes take them home. Believe me when I say they never look as good in the daylight. They all want to talk about how difficult their lives are. Mostly about how the fathers of their children left them and how badly they are treated by their boyfriends."

"Stop yammering," Albro said.

"Okay, okay," the cabbie said. He put the car in gear and slowly circled the building.

Albro peered through the rain at the chain-link fence that separated the parking lot from the railroad tracks. A row of dumpsters flanked the empty doorway. A large, black Mercedes, presumably Wu's, was the only car in the otherwise deserted lot.

"You see? Just as I told you, there's no one here. They all went home hours ago."

The cabbie was right. The woman had gone. She must have gone back inside. So what if she had been watching him? What did it matter?

The cabbie interrupted his thoughts, "Where do you want to go, a hotel?"

Yes, a hotel. That sounded right: hot bath, soft bed, room service. But then, there it was again. He was intent upon one thing and then suddenly without any contemplation he changed course. "Lakeview Cemetery," he said.

"You mean the one where Bruce Lee is buried?" The cabbie asked.

"Before my time," Albro answered. The famed Kung Fu star had died a few years before Albro was born. "But yes, that's the place."

"You got it boss. I'll have you there in a jiffy. You sit back and relax.

Why go there, Albro wondered. What did he expect to find? You can't bring back the dead, he told himself. And the dead didn't care one way or another whether the living remembered them or not. He considered that for a moment. Perhaps, they did care, in as much as they existed in the chemical matrix of memory, his, and the memories of

203

countless others. The cab surged forward and the tires hit a deep pothole. The cabbie jerked the wheel swearing something in his native tongue. Albro looked down and there, between his feet was the paperback. He reached for it and in the gray light of dawn opened it to a random page and began to read.

The cab lurched and suddenly I'm thinking of that morning with the old Chinese and his silver needle probing the lines my palm, tracing out not only my past, but my future. No, I'm not just thinking about it. I'm actually there, facing the old man, the dripping evergreens forming a gauzy backdrop, the smell off wood smoke strong in my nostrils. I feel a tingling sensation as the old Chinese traces the needle across my palm, and then the tingling becomes a burning that begins creeping up the length of my arm. A point comes when I can no longer stand it and I jerk my hand away. The old man gives me a silent stare and I break the silence with a nervous laugh. He says an awkward good-bye and I'm relieved when Roger and I are back on the road.

It is a beautiful morning and a light breeze pushes us along until we come to a highway that leads to the coast. Roger has yet to speak a word. That doesn't worry me much. I haven't felt like talking much after having had my palm read. It has left me feeling unsettled and slightly edgy, like I've had way too much coffee to drink. Besides, Roger will talk when he's ready. He always does, and when it comes, it will come in a flood.

Right now, I'm thankful for Roger's silence. I need to think about what we're going to do to evade the authorities who will be on our trail in pretty short order. I turn to face the traffic and walk backward with my thumb held high.

Roger does the same. We walk this way, Roger occasionally stumbling. I see that my friend can't quite get the hang of the quick backward glance that gives me all the information I need to steer deftly around rocks and potholes. Less than ten minutes passes before a camper-van slows, hesitates, speeds up and then pulls sharply to the side of the road.

"Come on," I say to Roger, and we sprint toward the waiting van.

204

It's always a risky thing to approach a vehicle from behind. I know this from experience. You can't always tell what kind of crazy is waiting up there ready to throw a half-empty bottle in your face or swing the door out and catch you full in the chest and knock the wind out of you, or simply punch the gas and squeal away in a spray of gravel. The lessons of the past prompt me to swing wide of the rear corner of the van and to hold out my arm to keep Roger from blundering forward.

The face that greets us is a welcome combination of concern and outgoing generosity with a bit of grandmotherly admonition thrown in for good measure. Her hair, mostly gray with a few lingering streaks of sandy blonde that had been cut in a kind of no-nonsense pageboy, frames her sparkling blue eyes and her cheeks have a fresh air and sunshine glow to them. She leans forward with both hands on the door frame.

I study her hands and heave a sigh of relief. I look to the woman behind the wheel who is wearing a blue flannel shirt and a tractor cap and has a somewhat harder look in her face. While not exactly anger, it is more a look of frustration, as if once again, she has lost the argument over whose decision it had been to stop.

I lean close to Roger's ear and whisper, "lesbians. It's okay."

"You boys missed your bus? Need a ride to school?" The woman asks. She speaks with a slight southern drawl, clear and precise and to the point. West Texas, I guess. I'd crossed that broiling landscape once and had been glad to put it behind me. There had been a kind of haunting malevolence in how the wind and sun had never let up in their unrelenting mission to kill everything in sight.

"No ma'am," I answer her. I smile my best smile. "School's out for the summer." It is the first week in June and I have no idea what kind of schedule the local schools are on, but it seems to me plausible enough.

Everything is going along swell until the woman leans forward, locks her eyes on mine, and exclaims, "Well, lucky you, and such a fine day!"

Her voice creates a kind of tickling sensation behind my eyes that travels up under the top of my skull and suddenly I am looking at myself and Roger and I know things about her that I have no right to know. She is *a retired school teacher and has had a long career in the public schools with the last ten years of her career in an alternative high school. She has known immediately that the I was lying, but there must have been something compelling about the sincere look in my face and even more so the look of jumpy nervousness in the eyes of my companion that has urged her to let the my answer ride, at least for the time being. She's been endowed with a major bullshit detector and ordinarily does not tolerate liars or cheats or bigots and has often been reminded by her partner, who is a retired math teacher, that she needn't be so brutally confrontational, particularly in social settings where people's feelings were going to get hurt.*

The tickling stops as suddenly as it had begun and I am back seeing the world through my own eyes. I have the feeling of having just stepped off a merry-go-round. I look at Roger and then back at the woman. My mind has suddenly gone blank, like some sort of over-ride in the electrical circuitry of my brain has tripped. I look up into the sky and see a few fluffy white clouds floating there, and then I hear a low whirring sound as my neurons come back on-line.

"Yes, ma'am, it is a fine day," I reply casually as if nothing out of the ordinary has just occurred. I begin to wonder how long this is going to go on. Usually the question is: 'Want a lift?' or 'Looking for a ride?' as if there is any doubt why someone with his thumb stuck out is walking backward alongside the road. The people with any real sense simply ask, 'Where're you headed?' I hear the other woman clear her throat and the woman who is looking down at me reaches around without taking her eyes off mine and places her hand on the other woman's hand which is gripping the steering wheel. My left hand twitches involuntarily as I feel the rough skin on the woman's knuckles.

I tense and then relax because at that point I know that a decision had been made and that an offer of a ride will soon be forthcoming.

The woman says, "We're on our way to California. If there is some place not too far off our route, we would be glad to take you there."

"Actually," I say, thinking that it would be a good idea to put as much distance as possible between us and the authorities back in

Washington State, "I have an aunt in Yreka. She wrote to me and said that I could come anytime. Do you know where that is?"

The woman behind the wheel gives a groan that means she knows the consequences of transporting underage individuals, not to mention possible fugitives from the law, across state lines.

The woman at the window says, "Yes, I do know where that is." I know that she has heard the bullshit alarm in her mind go off again, but it is a mild warning and, after making note of it, turns it off. "We had not planned to drive that far today, but if you don't mind spending a night with us, we could drop you there tomorrow."

I see the woman behind the wheel drop her head and shake it slowly.

"That would be fine with us," I say and step closer to the window and extend my hand. "My name's Albro Swift and this is Roger Ranger."

The woman opens the door and steps down. "Please to meet you. My name is Jackie Barnes. My friend is Ruth Olson." I accept her hand and I'm surprised by the firmness of her grip.

"Let's see if we can't make room for the two of you. There's a table at the rear with cushions around it. I think you'll be comfortable. There aren't any seatbelts, but if you don't tell the State Police, we won't either," she says and smiles what I take to be a somewhat conspiratorial smile and opens the side door and the two of us climb in.

By ten o'clock that night we're somewhere in the mountains that rumple the landscape between Oregon and California. A wall of dark trees guards our backs and a campfire warms our faces. Jackie Barnes has extracted the major highlights of both our lives. And just as I had predicted, once Roger had got started, his story has come out in a deluge ending with him sobbing and hiccupping in Jackie's lap. The circumstances surrounding our escape from the Ranch and what to do about Robert Damien has caused a great deal of debate between Ruth and Jackie. In the end, Ruth's sensible arguments have won out over Jackie's vehement sense of justice. If the man had become desperate enough, he might have panicked and ended up fried to a crisp, a fate Jackie has contended was far too lenient, but one which Ruth has assured her would only serve to *needlessly complicate the two boy's fate. It is finally agreed that at first light, a phone call will be placed to discreetly inquire about the man's condition.*

The next morning, I wake up as Jackie Barnes opens the door of the camper-van and steps out. I reckon that dawn is still an hour away, but already the fainter stars have begun to disappear. I and Roger are in sleeping bags under some trees not far from the van. I'd listened closely the night before when Jackie had told Ruth that she was going into town on foot because it was her favorite time of day and that it would take her at least two hours and not to worry if she woke and found her gone. They had decided that he and Roger should stay with them for at least a few days, but then Jackie had said the part about being gone for two hours, and now I know why. She is giving them the chance to accept their offer, or respectfully decline.

I can manage life on the road just fine, but Roger, I know, needs something more stable. I should leave him with Ruth and Jackie and slip away on my own. I get up and pull on my shoes and jacket and go to the edge of the trees and relieve myself. I shiver in the cold air. I have shivered before in the cold morning air and I know that a half-hour of walking will warm me. We are close to the California border and not too far from the Interstate. That part about an aunt in Yreka hasn't fooled Jackie Barnes. I'd seen that in her face as soon as it had left my mouth. But she hasn't called me on it. Why not? Maybe she and Ruth Olson are good people, but what choice do they have but to eventually turn us over to the authorities?

I look back over to where Roger lies sound asleep. Life is going to be tough on Roger. There is no doubt in my mind about that. I think of waking him, but then I decide not to. I pull up the collar on my thin jacket and stuff my hands in my pockets and turn my back on my friend.

The light is changing from gray-black of night to the first pearl-essence of dawn when the rubber soles of my worn tennis shoes begin slapping the blacktop. My stomach growls with hunger and I tighten up the muscles around my ribs and try to ignore it. Yet, the hollow feeling persists. The road winds down hill in wide, gentle curves and the occasional vehicle speeds past me. It isn't long before it is fully light and I can see the town, if one could call it that, just a café and post office and a decaying motel, and the lone figure of Jackie Barnes walking in my direction. When we meet face to face, I say to her, "Who are you, really?"

"Hey! Wake up."

The voice startled Albro. He opened his eyes to the chipped paint of the cab's door frame. His head was pressed against the window and saliva had dribbled down his chin. He still gripped the open book in his hands. He sat up and wiped away the spit. "I was reading and I must have nodded off."

"Ah, that book. What do you think?"

Albro felt dazed by the question. Had he read anything, or had he fallen instantly asleep. He looked at the open page, but the small print refused to come into focus. He squeezed his eyes and asked, "Where are we?"

"Cemetery, just like you asked."

Albro looked at the black, wrought iron gate, and the graveyard beyond. How had he gotten here? He'd just been...where? He'd been dreaming. He closed his eyes and took a deep breath. He reached into his bag and pulled a bill from one of the bundles. The cabbie started to make change. "Keep it," Albro said and rubbed the kink out of his neck.

"Thank you very much," the cabbie said. "Anything I can help you with? You want me to stay?"

"No. And thanks, I'll be fine. Oh, and thanks for the ride."

"My pleasure, I'm sure."

Albro got out of the cab and walked past the heavy iron gates into the cemetery. As cemeteries go, it was relatively small with the markers laid out in neat rows. A few of the markers were on a grand scale, but most were modest, the names and dates chiseled in polished granite or marble. In the far corner was the wall of cremation niches. The grass was thick and the ground soggy and by the time he got there his shoes were soaked through. He scanned the names until he came to the two he was looking for: Jacqueline Barnes and Ruth Olson. He put his hand out and traced the carved lettering of their names. They had perished while driving through a mountain pass in a rain storm. A boulder the size of a house, loosened by the torrent had rolled down the mountainside onto their camper-van, crushing it in the way a passing truck might flatten a soda can. They had simply been at the wrong place at the right time. What were the odds of a rock hanging in place for eons of time letting go at just the right moment. Granted, the mountain had been disturbed by the building of a four-lane freeway and slides were inevitable, but how could Jackie and Ruth have been at that exact spot at that exact moment when the rock dropped. If they had just been a second sooner on their journey they would have passed unharmed. Albro tried to fathom all of the events that must have occurred in their lives to have brought them to that sudden end, and he knew that the intersection of his life with theirs was one of those events. Had it been the deciding factor that had refused to be mitigated, even in the smallest way, even to alter their lives by a single second?

He and Roger had been with them for six months. It was the only time that either of them had had the experience of a real family. They'd had their own rooms and dinner on the table every night, new clothes and someone to watch them in the school play. Ruth and Jackie had been just like real parents with their incessant questions: Where's your homework? Where're you going? When're you coming home? What's her name? Who told you that? You did what? It never ended, just as it shouldn't. But it had, in one random blow. Two old Lesbos, not exactly minding their own business, but trying to do something good in the world, and they had paid a terrible price for it.

Jackie and Ruth had been discussing adoption, but nothing had been formalized. Their brothers and sisters divided up the estate and showed no interest in taking on two teenage boys. And that was that. Still being minors, they had once again become wards of the State.

Rain was starting again. He trudged back to the entrance where the cabbie was still parked. He jumped out when he saw Albro approach.

"I decided to stay, just in case. That man, I said to myself, is going to need a hotel. Am I right?"

"You're right," Albro said.

"I knew it! Where to, boss?"

"What's a nice hotel in this town? And stop calling me boss. My name is Albro Swift."

The cabbie's eyes grew large. "You're the one who wrote that book!"

"No I'm not the one. It's just some sort of crazy coincidence. Since we keep running in to each other, you might as well tell me your name."

"I am Ajaya Singh, at your service."

"Singh is a Hindu name, isn't it? I thought you said you were from Nepal."

"My father came from India. He managed a hotel in Katmandu."

"Hotel," Albro repeated and felt a wave of fatigue wash over him. "I need to find one before I fall asleep on my feet."

"Well now, let me see. There is the Hilton."

"No," Albro had almost shouted the word. "Sorry," he said.

"No problem. There are many others, the Four Seasons, the Hyatt, and Mayflower Park, to mention a few. The Marriott is very nice. You can fish from your window."

"I don't think I need to do that." Albro thought for a moment. He needed someplace safe. He asked the cabbie, "Where does the President stay when he comes to town?"

"The President? Do you mean Mr. Obama?"

"He's the one."

"I'm not sure that he has ever stayed in this city. I think he stays only long enough to collect money from the rich people and then he's off. But if he were to stay, it would surely be the Olympic."

"Are there plenty of people around?"

"Oh man, yeah, especially this time of year."

"Good. Take me there."

"You got it, boss."

The ride downtown took less than fifteen minutes. Albro offered another hundred to the cabbie.

"No, no. This one's on me. Will you be staying long? I will be happy to take you anywhere you need to go. Just call this number." He handed Albro a scrap of paper on which he'd carefully written a number.

Everyone seemed to be eager to give him a phone number. "Thanks. I'll keep you in mind." In mind for what, he thought dejectedly. He had no plan. Except for the money, the whole trip had been a waste of time. He should quit while he was ahead. The words to a once popular song floated into his thoughts, *'Know when to hold 'em and when to fold 'em.'* That sounded like good advice. He was getting too old for this kind of life. It seemed as though he'd been running all of his life. Running from what? A past he could never remake?

It was time to settle down, he told himself. He was suddenly tired of hustling his way from one crisis to the next. What did he have to show for it? He had passed well into his thirties. The next thing he knew, he would be turning forty. He wasn't a kid anymore. He'd heard somewhere that forty was the new thirty. Did that make thirty the new twenty, and twenty the new ten? Look what happened to the 'Young Generation', the Boomers who swore they would stay *'forever young'*. They were dropping like flies on a frosty day from strokes and heart attacks and cancer, and the rest were skating on ever thinning ice while dementia waited impatiently for them to stop playing around like a bunch of kids on spring break. Most importantly, and for the first time in his life, he now had a bright future waiting for him with the daughter of the richest man in the world. Well, maybe he was jumping to conclusions about a long term future with Monique. Celebrity marriages tended to have a shelf life slightly longer than a chicken sandwich. She had certainly displayed passion. Any fool could see that, but was there also love?

Rich people really didn't need to fall in love, he reminded himself. They already had everything that love could provide. They simply wanted to live life to its fullest, with no cares and worries to get in the way. That was exactly what he was ready for. Didn't that make the two of them a perfect match? And here he was in this God-forsaken backwater of a city with its incessant rain chasing a ghost. What was he thinking?

The again, what if he could settle once and for all the question of who he was and where he had come from? When might another chance like this come around? After all, he was here. Another night couldn't hurt. Maybe the mysterious Ms. Wong would surface. Besides, he needed a shower and a good sleep.

"I can reach you at this number?" Albro asked the cabbie.

"Day or night, I am at your service," Singh answered.

"I'll need a ride to the airport tomorrow. I'll call you when I know my flight plans."

"I'll be waiting for your call. And don't forget that book."

Albro hesitated, and then slipped the volume into the side pocket of his bag. He got out of the cab and went into the hotel. It could have been any fine hotel anywhere in the world. Everything was bright and cheery, everyone well dressed and intent upon making their little sphere of existence the center of the universe. A gigantic evergreen stood in the center of the atrium festooned with a zillion tiny white lights. The beautiful young woman at the reception desk nearly blinded him with her smile.

"Good morning, sir. How may I help you?" Her eyes gave him a once over and her smile dimmed.

"A room for the night," Albro said. Christmas music drifted down from somewhere overhead like recycled snowflakes.

She shifted her eyes to her computer screen. "Ordinarily check-in is at 3:00 p.m. Do you have a reservation?"

"Yes. Allen Saunders." The name came out automatically, as if all of those intervening years had not occurred and he was a twelve year old living by his wits.

The pretty girl keyed in his name and studied the screen. A slight frown creased her otherwise perfectly smooth brow. She pursed her lips, and shook her head slowly. She turned to him and said, "I'm afraid we don't have you in the system."

"Any room will do."

"This is a very busy time of year for us, but let me see what we have." She flicked her dark polished nails across the keys. "All of our regular rooms are taken, but we do have an executive suite available."

"I'll take it."

She cleared her throat. "You might prefer something more modest. We have an arrangement with the other hotels. I'm sure that I can find you a less expensive room."

"How much is the executive suite?"

She dropped her voice. "The rate is twelve hundred per night. We accept all major credit cards."

Albro was sure that he could bargain her down, but it didn't seem worth the effort. He reached into his bag and pulled out a stack of bills. He counted out twelve of them.

The receptionist's eyebrows came up in two suspicious arcs. "We require a security deposit of five hundred dollars for all cash transactions."

Albro counted out another five bills.

"Mr. Saunders, I'll need to see a photo ID."

Albro counted out two more bills and slid them to her. "Will that do? My hair was longer when that picture was taken."

She looked at the two portraits of Benjamin Franklin and then glanced left and right. "That works for me." She gave him a printed receipt for his payment and deposit and handed him a room key. "My name is Brandy. If there is anything I can personally attend to, you can call this desk. I'll be here until the shift change and I have no plans for the evening." She smiled.

Albro looked at her. She was leaning slightly forward showing off more than a hint of young, firm cleavage. She had caught her tongue and held it between her teeth. He felt a stirring in his loins, like an old dog who picks up a passing scent, cocks his head and then settles back down. He *was* tired, but nothing that a few hours of sleep wouldn't solve. "Come wake me when you're finished. Room..." He fumbled with the card key.

"Oh I know which room," she said and coyly tapped her nails on the counter

Albi dropped his bag beside the bed and did not bother turning back the covers. He collapsed on his back. The weight of the cast on his chest made breathing difficult. He tried shifting his arm to the side, but it began to throb. He turned onto his side, but that made it worse. He sat up and groped for his bag and dug into it for the bottle of pain pills. He remembered then that he'd left them next to the sink in Elsa's bathroom. He cursed himself for being so careless and then cursed Goldstein and his two thugs, but the memory of their deaths cut him short. A horrifying image came to him of Goldstein raising his hands only to have them cut leanly off at the wrists and blood spurting like twin fountains into the air. A wave of nausea rolled over him and he stumbled into the bathroom and bent over the sink, his eyes squeezed shut and his body shaking, until the image passed. When he dared to open his eyes he looked up to see his own sallow face. He could see flecks of gray in the four days growth of beard that shadowed his sunken jaws. Dark circles ringed his eyes. He ran cold water and splashed it on his face. His arm throbbed.

He slumped back on the bed and wondered if room service could bring him something for the pain. Surely anyone in the executive suite had benefit beyond aspirin and Tylenol. It was then he saw the corner of the paperback that he'd stuffed into the side pocket of his bag. He pulled it out and with it came the old photo he'd taken from the ruined law office. He turned on the bedside lamp. He scrutinized the image of the man and woman looking out from the window. He took it to the bathroom and attempted to use the thick bottom of the water glass as a magnifier, but that succeeded only in blurring the already grainy image.

He went back into the main room and picked up the book. The cover had gone back to the picture of the burning city. His memory had to be playing tricks on him, but he hadn't the energy, or the will to ponder why. He stared at the cover and had the odd sense that he understood the fear that was painted on the peoples' faces. He placed his finger tip on his name that was printed across the lower half of the cover. He found it amusing that someone else had his same name. That really wasn't so extraordinary. He'd used his alias Allen Saunders for that very reason. Pick any phone book in any major city. There would be at least one Allen Saunders, and usually more than one. He opened the book and checked the copyright date. It said *Copyright 2035 Albro Marshal Swift.* That was an odd place for a printing error, he thought.

He looked again at the dedication. This had to be Roger's doing. He was clever that way. Good old Roger. He could have you believing even the most outrageous things. The problem was that he was such a sweet guy, not a mean bone in his body, you *wanted* to believe him. Right now he and Butch were probably cracking up over this one while they shared a bowl of popcorn in front of a really bad sci-fi movie. Albro felt a wave of home-sickness fill his chest. Here it was almost Christmas and he had left Roger. At least he had Butch for company. He made a mental note to find a great gift for him in the morning. He would find something for Butch too. Maybe he could find an old Caruso recording. Butch loved opera and was particularly fond of Caruso.

He pushed his back against the pillows and stretched out his legs and opened the book to the first page and the words came into his mind as if in a whisper.

No one in the City of Rain knew the why or the how. They only understood the need. The Jade Prince must not be released, no matter the cost. They all felt the same prescient foreboding, a collective consciousness rooted deep within their very being that told them the Jade Prince must forever be sealed within stone. To release the Jade Prince would be to open a chasm of darkness beyond which nothing lay. There would be no laughter, no sorrow, no song, no prayer, and no hope. It would be as if time itself had never opened for them, as if they had never been.

His eyelids sagged and Albro forgot about the pain in his arm. The weight of fatigue began to grow, and he let the book drop from his hand. His eyelids closed and he relaxed as the weight pushed him down into a deep and unconscious sleep.

CHAPTER 17

CHANG WU looked at the man who sat opposite him. This was a development he had not fully expected, at least not at this time. He had known that sooner or later Giddes would seek him out. After all, Frank Giddes had resources at his disposal that he did not. On the other hand, he had resources of his own that were unique to his position. He did not feel threatened or intimidated by Giddes' presence. On the contrary, he welcomed this opportunity, and he reminded himself that Frank Giddes need not be his adversary.

Wu studied the deep lines that cut both sides of Giddes' mouth, the sagging skin around his neck, hair the color of lead. There was weakness in Giddes' body, but not in his mind. Wu could see that in the sharp glint in Giddes' eyes. Giddes had the eyes of an aged predator. Yes, Giddes had aged, but hadn't they all? At least those who had escaped the devastation all those years ago had aged. For those who had disappeared who could say? Death was a mystery. Was the soul, or spirit, or whatever you wanted to call it, beholden in any way to the rule of time? Did the soul exist beyond the dreadful boundary, and if so, did it have a memory of its past life, or lives? Or did the soul simply vanish into the slime of the dissolved body to be absorbed into the earth, gone forever. The answers to those questions and a thousand like them were all locked within the mystery of creation. To open that, all one needed was the right key, and what then? Cheating death was the least of his considerations. Chang Wu let his musings slip from his thoughts and brought his full attention to Frank Giddes.

"Mr. Giddes, I was about to have my morning tea." Chang Wu tilted his head toward the steaming cup of liquid next to his hand, but did not take his eyes from Giddes'. "I will have a cup brought to you. Or do you prefer coffee?"

"Thanks, but I've had mine," Giddes said dismissively, knowing full well that he was insulting Wu's sense of hospitality by turning down the offer. He wanted Wu to have no doubts upon whose ground this conversation was about to take place. Wu absorbed Giddes slight with a momentary flare of his nostrils. He said, equably, "You are an early riser. The sun has barely risen and yet you look refreshed. You must sleep well." Wu absorbed Giddes slight with a momentary flare of his nostrils. He said, equably, "You are an early riser. The sun has barely risen and yet you look refreshed. You must sleep well."

After leaving the city morgue, Giddes had checked into a hotel and had managed a solid two hours sleep before taking a scalding shower and shaving his silvery stubble. He had then sat alone in the hotel dining room with his coffee and two poached eggs. He had wanted to make certain he was wide awake when he faced Wu.

"One could say the same for you, Chang." They were by no means on a first name basis, and so Giddes had deliberately used it as a means to set the tone of their exchange. He gave Wu a hard look taking in the man's smooth features, his silver hair, the precise cut of his suit, the gold band set with an emerald the size of a small frog on the middle finger of his right hand. He then lighted a cigarette and blew the smoke at a point above Wu's head. He knew that Wu hated cigarette smoke, which was a rare trait among the Chinese he knew, and he did it to put Wu in his place. They might be seated on the top floor of a fifty story office building that Wu owned, along with a dozen others more or less like this one, scattered in the cities that defined the broad arc of the Pacific, but Giddes still thought of him as the common street thug he'd found thirty years ago in a Hong Kong slum. And that was a puzzle. Why did a multi-millionaire like Wu keep the dirt of prostitution, drugs and gambling under his fingernails, and why Seattle with its squeaky clean demeanor sitting like a forlorn child on the edge of modern civility and culture. Undoubtedly Wu considered a place of opportunity, not dissimilar to the early Europeans who had traded trinkets with the natives for the treasured rights of land and trees and fish, and the gold and silver that had washed out of the mountains. The only difference now was that the natives had been replaced by avaricious entrepreneurs who seem to be no less naïve than their nineteenth century predecessors, and made easy targets for Wu's prescient sense of how genuine wealth was created. More likely though, there was a more compelling reason that accounted for Wu's presence here: a meeting that had been prearranged years ago.

Wu cleared his throat, doing his best to ignore the smoke that now encircled his head, and said, "Ah, if only that were true, Mr. Giddes. Sleep seems to be the one thing that age has robbed from me." Wu lifted his cup and brought it to his narrowly parted lips.

Wu might have added, Giddes thought, '*and what has age robbed from you, Frank Giddes?*' 'Only my life', he could have answered, but he hadn't come here to bandy words with Chang Wu. He'd come for information and to enlist Wu's assistance, as distasteful as that was. If Wu refused it was bound to make matters more difficult, but not impossible. Besides, it would give him the excuse he'd been waiting for all these years and have him killed. No, he thought, he would do it himself, as a little payback for Wu sticking his nose where it had never belonged.

Wu had been there at the site, the day before it had been destroyed. The news had come to Giddes from an Army captain, a liaison to ARVN Command. The captain had told Giddes how some hotshot ARVN colonel had flown into the site on a Huey gunship. ARVN brass, Giddes had known, loved flitting around the provinces dropping in anywhere they'd have little chance of coming face to face with the Viet Cong.

It had taken him a week to track down the South Vietnamese colonel. He'd driven him to the outskirts of Saigon to an abandoned shrimp farm. He'd tied his hands behind his back and turned him over the edge into an empty concrete holding tank. He'd then driven back into

Saigon and waited two days before returning. By then, the colonel was ready to talk. Giddes had been convinced that Crane had requested the meeting with the ARVN colonel. How else would the colonel have known about the super-secret site? As it turned out, the colonel had simply gone up for a sight-seeing jaunt for the purpose of logging in a few hours of 'air combat' to fatten his monthly paycheck that was being underwritten by US taxpayers. It was just the colonel's bad luck that he'd spotted the clearing in the jungle with the tents and plywood structures that was not marked on any military maps. Giddes could just see the fucking prima donna jumping from his Huey gunship and strutting across the dusty landing pad in his shiny boots and pressed khakis and demanding to see the officer in charge. Naturally, he'd been rebuffed which had compelled the naïve colonel to raise a stink back at ARVN Command. If he'd kept his mount shut, Giddes would never have found out about him. Some people just couldn't help turning bad luck into worse luck.

Giddes would have shot the colonel there and then for wasting his time were it not for the fact that the colonel had been the last known individual to have visited the site. Eventually though, he'd had to shoot the South Vietnamese colonel in both kneecaps before he'd reached the conclusion that that the poor man had in no way been connected to Thomas Crane. But, as it turned out, the colonel had one precious bit of information to give up. The colonel had mentioned how a young Chinese boy had run into the tent where he'd been sitting for several hours under armed guard. The boy had had a brief exchange with the guard and then he'd left.

At the time, the incident hadn't registered in Giddes mind. He'd given up on the colonel and had placed the muzzle of his gun in the slight hollow between the colonel's nose and eye and had pulled the trigger. It wasn't until days later that the question occurred to Giddes: What was a Chinese boy doing in the camp? Giddes had then started with the refugee camps nearest to the site. The NGO's tried their best to keep records of who entered the camps, but the Viet Cong had been on the move and had overrun several camps, burned any structures to the ground and had driven the refugee's back out into the countryside. Nevertheless, Giddes had met a French doctor who had described a young Chinese boy who spoke broken English whose back had been badly burned. The boy had been airlifted to the airbase hospital at Da Nang. The medi-vac helicopter had never made it to Da Nang. Days later, its remains had been spotted on a barren hillside. Giddes had gone in with a squad of Army Rangers where they had found the bodies of the pilot and co-pilot and the remains of three individuals who had been transported out of the refugee camp, but no sign of the Chinese boy.

Giddes had been convinced that the boy was the last living soul to have seen Crane before whatever happened had made the place as barren and sterile as a lifeless desert. He'd monitored immigration records around the world until he had come across the description he'd been looking for. It had taken time to find him, but it had been well worth the effort. And then Giddes had labored many more years to solve the mystery of that day, and now he was close. Given enough time, Giddes knew, all things were revealed. Only now, time was in short supply.

Giddes brought his thoughts back to Wu. He said, "Speaking of thievery, how's business these days? I understand the banks are starting to put the squeeze on their creditors. Real estate seems to have lost its luster, and a lot of deals are coming under close scrutiny. There's a lot of shit lying around and it's my guess the bankers will have their noses rubbed in it.

"It will be an uncomfortable situation for many," Wu said, referring to what the media had begun calling the Great Recession. Wu considered a quaint term that was intended to raise the level of anxiety among the laboring masses. An anxious individual was a distracted individual; an individual who was easily manipulated.

"But not for you," Giddes retorted.

"It helps to be patient, as well as cautious."

"And being in the right place, at the right time, with the means to act never hurts," Giddes added.

"As you say," Wu agreed.

"Which brings us to the point, doesn't it." Giddes saw Wu's eyes tighten, an almost imperceptible movement that he would have missed

221

had he blinked. It was the second sign that he'd breached Wu's defenses, and where there was a crack there would soon be a chasm. He relaxed.

"What point are you referring to, Mr. Giddes? " Wu asked, feigning a look of puzzlement. "I'm afraid that I do not follow you."

"You know, Chang," Giddes drawled, "the whole point of living." He paused, letting that statement sink in. He then continued, "When we first met you were a street rat and I was an inexperienced agent, tenacious, but as naïve as they come. Was it fate that brought us together? Who's to say? What's intriguing is that our lives continued to cross, but never really connected until now. And now that we have, I have a feeling that we've become inseparable. Most people live their lives like travelers groping through a fog. But we're not like that, are we Chang?   For you and I, the fog cleared a long time ago. We've known exactly the path to follow, and here we are, standing together at the threshold of our destiny. Am I right?"

Wu tapped two beats on the desk top with his heavy ring. "You are proposing a partnership of some sort?"

"Well, no," Giddes said and smiled in an almost embarrassed way and looked at the glowing tip of his cigarette. He took a deep pull making the cigarette burn brightly and then he let the smoke drift lazily out of his mouth. "What I'm proposing is that if you do exactly as I say, you will continue to live and prosper in a way that pales in comparison to what you have already experienced."

Wu studied Giddes. He did not need to ask the obvious question. He already knew the answer. If he said no, he would simply become an obstacle in Giddes path; an obstacle that would have to be removed. And it was not a question of trust, an arrangement he'd never relied on in any serious dealings. It was always question of who had the advantage. The advantage lay, Wu knew, in being at least one step ahead of everyone else, and at the moment, he knew that he was several steps ahead of Giddes.

"I assume," Wu said, "that you are referring to the *Jade Prince*."

Giddes leaned back and crossed his legs. "The *Jade Prince* is just the beginning, Chang. It's just the beginning."

Wu llowed a slight smile to part his lips. "How can I be of help?"

CHAPTER 18

ALBRO enters a crowded room, darkened to give that false sense of privacy, that insular feeling of remote intimacy which is alluring and at the same time, repulsive. He's in a club, he can tell that much. There is a bar that is dimly lit. The bartender, his back turned, moves in languid steps and reaches. Glasses clink, voices rumble. Those around him are male. He knows this not by their shapes, but by their smells, rangy, musky, animal smells, the smells of a zoo, or worse, the smells of the circus where he had spent a summer mucking out cages. He feels a tingling in his groin.

Music starts up and thuds against his half-conscious brain like a sand-filled sock. He takes a step, and the room begins to rotate, and he catches the edge of the bar. He takes a deep breath and fights down a wave of bile that is climbing in his throat. He needs some air, and heads for the door, but he has forgotten where it is. He looks around in a panic for a green exit sign. That is a law, isn't it? Exit signs? In case there is a fire? His heart is pounding. He feels that he might cry out. Then his eye catches the flicker of blue, as a spot lights a tight circle on the stage and he turns, along with everyone else, to the female figure that steps out from between black curtains and into the light.

She is tall and slender and she stands with her shoulders slumped and her head bowed, her face hidden behind a cascade of dark, tangled hair that reaches to her waist. Her arms cross her chest, her large hands grip her shoulders as if she is holding something within herself that she *might not be able to control once released. Her long, painted nails glint like darks claws in the harsh, blue light. Her skin sparkles with a spray of glitter. She wears a black fish-net body suit and tall, spiky heels that only emphasize her already towering height. She seems at least seven feet tall. Is that some sort of trick? The light is doing funny things to his eyes. Everything is jumping in and out of focus, making him feel like he's on some sort of carnival ride.*

The music dies and he feels a sudden deceleration, and for a long moment the room falls into an absolute silence as if every breath were being held for what is about to come, and when it does come, the band erupts into a mind-warping explosion of sound. Strobes start flashing and the figure on the stage begins to slowly unfold her arms, sweeping back her hair to reveal the taught muscles of her torso, her breasts, barely hidden beneath their filmy covering, and then he sees her face. She stares at him and then suddenly her head jerks backward and her spine bends at an impossible angle. Her arms shake uncontrollably and she collapses, her legs kicking out, her heels pounding, her head thumping against the stage floor.

Albino woke with a sudden gasp for breath. He was on his back with his broken arm twisted under him and shooting with pain. He cried out and rolled on his side and swung his feet off the bed. He cradled his arm against his chest until the pain subsided. His shirt was soaked with sweat. A dim light shone through from the half open door of the bathroom, casting the room in unfamiliar shapes and shadows. At first, he thought that he was still in the dream. His mind reeled with the harsh beat of the music, and the image of the woman's face. It had been the face of a woman, but there had been something more to it, as if she had been wearing a partial mask, something feline. But it hadn't been a mask, because it was the eyes that had been most startling. Their shape and color were more cat-like than anything make-up could accomplish. He shuddered when he remembered how the eyes had bored into his own. What had happened to her? He concentrated on the memory and had almost brought it back when his phone rang, and the dream vanished like smoke in a puff of wind.

225

He dug his phone from his jacket pocket. "Hello?' he said weakly.

"Albro, darling, where are you?" "Monique?"

"Thank God you're all right. I've been worried sick. When you didn't answer your phone, I thought something had happened to you."

"You've been trying to call me?"

"Yes! I was afraid that something terrible had happened to you."

"I fell asleep. I was having this strange dream about..."

"Where are you? We've been looking all over the city for you."

"You're here? You're in Seattle?"

"Yes! After the police came, we realized that you were in danger, and we've been trying to find you."

"The police," Albro wondered out loud. It had to have been about Goldstein. "Monique, it's not what you think. I had nothing to do with what happened to Sal Goldstein and his two thugs."

"What are you saying?"

"Trust me Monique, I can explain everything."

"Albro, darling, there's no need to explain. We know everything now, and we can help you. Tell me where you are." The urgency in her voice made him look to the door of his room. Had he remembered to throw the dead-bolt? He needed to tell Monique where he was and for a moment he drew a blank, and then he saw the pad of stationery on the low table next to the bed. He read the name out to her.

"Stay there," she instructed. "You'll be safe. Whatever you do, don't leave and don't open the door to anyone until we get there. Do you understand?"

He hesitated a moment. Monique sounded genuinely concerned, but underneath that concern he detected a note of cold fear. She was a trained actress and could probably convey any of a hundred different emotions, but he didn't get the sense that she was acting. Was she being coerced? Was she, in a subtle way trying to warn him? Were they communicating with each other in that extraordinary way of true lovers? But then he felt an odd sense of suspicion about what she'd said creep into his thoughts, and right on the heels of that thought was an undeniable feeling of panic. He looked at the four walls of the small room and suddenly it felt more like a trap than a place of refuge.

"Allo?" she asked, jarring him out of his thoughts.

"What?" He was startled by the sound of his own voice.

"Stay calm. We'll be there in five minutes."

"Monique...," he paused a moment. There was a question nagging at the back of his mind, and finally it burst through. "Who is with you?" He listened for an answer, but the line had gone dead.

He rolled to his feet and began pacing the short distance between the bed and the door. Should he obey what Monique had told him, stay put and don't open the door? Or should he obey what he was certain he had heard in the tone of her voice? What kind of danger could he really be in? Goldstein was dead. At least that was what he'd been told, but either Monique had not seemed to know about him, or had not cared. He stopped at the door and peered through the peephole. The fisheye view of the hallway was empty. Unable to make a decision, he turned, bit his lip and dejectedly thrust his free hand into his jacket pocket and was about to take another step when he felt the crumpled ball of paper, and remembered the encounter at the entrance to law office of Lee, Ho and Wong. He smoothed out the note. The numbers had become smeared, but he could still read them. Without really thinking, he pulled out his phone and dialed the number. The ring had barely a chance to sound before it was answered.

"WHERE THE FUCK HAVE YOU BEEN?!!" A voice shouted at him.

Albo jerked the phone from his ear. The response had nearly deafened him. He brought the phone back to his ear. He could hear traffic noise and indistinct voices in the background. He asked, "Who is this?"

"YOU LITTLE SHIT!" The voice shouted again.

It was a woman's voice. She sounded like the same woman who had brought him on this wild goose chase. There were other voices in the background that seemed to be trying to calm her. Good luck, he thought. From the anger in her voice, he guessed they had their work cut out. "Is this Ms. Wong?" he ventured. He heard her draw a deep breath and was

227

ready for another blast when the voice came back to him with an icy edge of control.

"If you want to know who your father was, be at the corner of Sixth and University in two minutes."

"Wait! I can't..."

"Time is running out! Be there!"

"I can't leave my room!" he said into the phone, but there was no one listening. He stared at his phone, thinking that he should leave a note for Monique until he saw the minute advance, and then without another thought, he reached for his bag, flung open the door, and swept his gaze up and down the corridor. He heard the elevator ding, and then, without looking back, sprinted for the stairs.

CHAPTER 19

A**LBRO SWIFT** ducked into the sheltered entry of a boutique gift shop. The overhang protected him from the worst of the wind and rain, but his cast was getting wet and it had begun to dissolve, leaving a white smear of plaster down the front of his slacks. He clutched his bag to chest trying without much success at keeping the wind from cutting through his thin shirt. His teeth had already begun to chatter as he scanned the traffic filled street not knowing what, or who to look for. He wished that he'd chosen shelter at a men's store. He could have gone inside for an overcoat. He had enough cash to buy an entire wardrobe, but it was just his luck that it was a store filled with trinkets from China. It was the sort of junk that was all glittery and shiny and totally worthless, except maybe to pack rats.

Looking at all of it was a sour reminder of his failed business. What a waste of time that had been. What had he been thinking? That he could actually hustle his way into the heart of American consumerism? Well, yes, that was exactly what he'd thought. And he'd come so close. But close didn't count in this world. You had to hit the bull's eye, and be satisfied with counting pennies. And then do it over and over again. It was a hustle, but it wasn't his kind of hustle. Nothing in his life had ever been as tedious as his attempts at being legitimate. The planning, the paperwork, the schmoozing, had nearly driven him to tears. Maybe the Buffets and Waltons of the world could get a rush thinking about numbers on spreadsheets, but for him there was nothing like the feel of cash in his pocket. He'd never found delayed gratification to be an appealing lifestyle. Besides, there was something about the shady deal, the gamble, the challenge of living on the edge that had always excited him, that had always given him a kind of self assurance, a feeling of fulfillment. But... But what, he asked himself. Why had he tried so hard to be something he wasn't? Had he been looking for security, respect, even happiness? They were all stupid concepts, he told himself. Collectively, they made about as much sense as watching a dog chase its tail. Sure, it was amusing to watch, but really, how much fun was the dog having?

So what was he doing now, if he wasn't chasing his own tail? Monique must be up in his room worried sick about him. He could be feeling her hot hands on his chest and her lips pressed against his own. He hadn't really liked how she had tried to jam her tongue down his throat, but right about now it didn't sound half bad. He could probably get used to it, and maybe even learn to enjoy it on occasion. So what was he doing out here freezing to death? Did he really believe that something good was going to come of this? Did he really have a chance of finding out about his father? Never before in his life had he felt pulled in such opposite directions.

He turned from the window. Christmas lights were hung in the trees that lined the sidewalk, and shoppers laden with bags of gifts hurried in and out of stores. A few glanced at him and then just at quickly averted their eyes, and steered their children away. Did he look that bad? His open sports coat flapped in the wind. He couldn't hold it tight and hang onto his bag at the same time. In addition to his chattering teeth, he'd begun to shiver. If something didn't happen in the next thirty seconds, he decided, he would go back to the hotel.

An irregular movement caught his eye half a block away. A vehicle was forcing its way into the unyielding stream of cars. A cacophony of horn blowing had erupted and above it all, Albro could hear the roaring strain on an engine laboring, it seemed, to keep itself in check, and then suddenly a battered Land Cruiser lumbered onto the sidewalk in front of him and skidded to a halt. A woman screamed and clutched frantically a her two children. The rear door swung open and a voice shouted at m, "JUMP IN!"

Alb hesitated. He looked left and right. This could not be happening t him.

"GE IN THE FUCKING TRUCK!" The same voice commanded him.

He ove in and the vehicle accelerated at the same time, throwing him into the tailgate.

"AR WE BEING FOLLOWED?" The driver shouted at him.

Alb struggled to his knees and wiped the fog off the back glass. All he coul make out was a lurching array of headlights as he was bounced ba k and forth as the driver wove through traffic. And then he saw it, a da blue sedan seeming to match their every move, only it was much faster and more nimble.

"Is i a dark blue sedan?" Albro shouted back.

"Sh !" the voice hissed.

Alb looked to the front and saw the top of a head just above the seat back. /as a child driving? The vehicle skidded and swerved sharply to the left. lbro was slammed against the opposite wheel well and then rolled merc essly to the rear as they again accelerated. He could hear the screech of res and the blowing of horns and then suddenly he was thrown forv ard as the driver braked to a stop and threw the truck into reverse. Th y spun and then charged forward bounding over a curb and then slamm ng hard onto pavement before picking up speed.

The shot down a narrow alley. Albro pawed his way through a jumble of b gs and sharp objects. He grasped the top edge of the seat and was able to ull himself up and roll himself over in time to see two figures blocking th end of the alley and waving frantically. The driver stood on the brake p dal and threw Albro against the dashboard. The rear of the truck starte coming around and he could feel the tires starting to skip and chatter ver the rough pavement. The driver fought the wheel and kept them f om rolling over, and brought them to a halt, just inches from the two fig res, a large one and a small one, dressed in long, brown, monkish ro es with drawn hoods. They came around to the passenger side and the smaller one got in first and the larger one squeezed his bulk inside.

The driver immediately hit the accelerator, turned at the next corner and hurled them down a cobbled incline. The truck rattled and banged and they were going fast when they reached the bottom. Albro was huddled on the floor when they hit the raised traffic divider snapping off the caution sign as if it were toothpick. He felt the truck lift into the air and then come crashing onto the freeway onramp. In a moment, they popped up into a crush of fast-moving, rush hour traffic. The Land Cruiser's engine screamed and the heavy tires hummed as the driver brought the big vehicle up through the gears to freeway speed. He planted his feet against the floor and pushed himself into the seat and finally got a chance to look at the driver. There was a vague familiarity to her, but in the faint glow of the dash lights, he could not bring to mind where he might have met her. She was a diminutive woman dressed in hiking boots, leggings and wool sweater. She had her half of the seat pulled up against the large steering wheel and she sat on a thick cushion which allowed her to just see over the dash. Her hair was pulled back into a long braid and her dark eyes stared with intense concentration onto the roadway.

"Do you see them?" she called to the rear.

The little man who had stationed himself at the rear window wiped his sleeve across the glass and peered intently into the darkness. After several minutes, he crawled toward the front and hung his hands over the seat. "That was very good driving," he said. His voice was both low and raspy, as if maybe he'd been kicked in the throat at one time. He had an odd accent, maybe Arabic, and Albro had heard it before. It was the same man who had taken his hundred and handed him the phone number. "You lost them." He looked ahead, and then asked, "How long will it take us?"

"Two hours, maybe longer depending on the weather," the woman answered without turning her head from the road. The traffic was heavy, but moving fast and all the spray thrown up from the roadway made seeing difficult.

"Does that mean I can get some sleep?" It was the big fellow in the back. His voice had the same odd accent and was about four octaves lower than his companion's. He had shoved what looked to be a large backpack against the rear gate and had stretched out with his shoulders against the back and his hands intertwined behind his head. The light was dim, but Albro could swear the man was smiling at him.

"Yes Walter, get some rest," the smaller man said and within seconds the other was snoring loudly.

So far, everyone seemed to be doing their best to ignore him, Albro thought. Neither the driver, nor the little man had even given him a glance. Wasn't he supposed to be the guest of honor at this meeting?

"Well," said Albro, "now that things seem to have settled down, how about a round of introductions? I'm Albro Marshall Swift."

A stony silence greeted him. "Maybe you'd prefer a game of Twenty Questions. I'll start. *WHO ARE YOU PEOPLE AND WHERE ARE WE GOING?* That's two questions, by the way."

The woman behind the wheel gave him a quick and obviously angry look. She said, "How dare you take that tone with me! I've spent the last two days trying to keep you and the three of us alive, while you've been fuckin around town like you don't have a care in the world!" She turned her gaze long enough to drill him with her black eyes and swerve across two lanes onto the shoulder. She jerked the vehicle back onto the road and stared out into the darkness.

"Please," cautioned the small man, and then he turned to Albro. "You must excuse us. We've all been under a tremendous strain. We are very near exhaustion."

The man kept his face hidden within the hood of the cassock.

"We have already met," he continued, "but allow me to introduce myself. I am Brother Isaiah. My companion, whom you've met as well, is Brother Walter. Under the circumstances, we should dispense with titles. You may simply call us Isaiah and Walter. And this, of course, is Ms Nancy Wong, Attorney at Law."

And with the name, came back the memory. "You mean, *the Nancy Wong?*" The last time he had been this close to Nancy Wong (aka

233

Mei Ling Wong) had been eighteen years previous on the night of their senior prom, when she, the skinny (some would say wispy, others might say sinewy), gawky, (doe-eyed?), braces-filled mouth, (at least she had smiled with closed lips for the portrait), had been his date. All might have turned out well had it not come out, before the night was over, that the only reason he had asked her to accompany him when he'd had the pick of any number of physically precocious young girls, was that he owed a substantial gambling debt to Nancy Wong's older cousin, Freddie, who had offered to write it off if he would take her to the dance. The evening had not turned out well. She had seen Freddie and Albro exchanging looks and had gone straight to the heart of the matter like a mongoose after a snake. She had attacked both her cousin and Albro with her tiny fists and sharp teeth and had to be pulled off, and physically restrained. He still had a small white arc at the top of his left ear where she had hung on until, Mr. Swenson, the gym teacher, had managed to pry open her jaws. He remembered seeing his own blood streaming down her chin. A few classmates thought "Carrie" would make a nice nick name for her, until she had beat the shit out of them. After that, everyone had thought it best to forget the whole thing. Obviously, she had not forgotten and time had not assuaged the pain, not to mention, soften her temper. And now, here she was. What were the odds...?

"Ms Wong, to you," she said pointedly to Albro. This time she did not take her eyes off the road.

"Yes, well, perhaps we will become more familiar once we can rest," offered Brother Isaiah.

"Don't bet on it," Nancy Wong stated and set her lips in a thin, narrow line.

"In the meantime, Mr. Swift, may I suggest we wait to answer your questions until we reach our destination."

"And where is that?" Albro asked.

"Miss Wong is taking us to a place she feels will offer us a degree of safety while we decide what to do next."

"Keep us safe from what, or from whom?" Albro asked.

"As said, it is best to wait," the little man repeated. "I know you feel as though you have been abducted, but trust me, we would not have resorted to such measures had it not been necessary. Now, I too, feel the need for sleep. It has been many days since I have closed my eyes for more than a few moments." He dropped back, pulled the hood closed and withdrew his arms into the sleeves of his robe. He then curled up into a ball on the truck's hard floor.

Albi looked ahead into the darkness. Big slushy raindrops were hitting the windshield and then suddenly it was snow, and they were tunneling through a blizzard of white flakes. Patchy, icy mounds appeared alongside them, which soon became an unbroken line, and then a solid low wall of snow and ice that grew taller with each mile. The roadway, too, soon became an unbroken ribbon of white and still, Nancy Wong did not let up on the accelerator. Occasionally, the big truck wanted to slip to either the left or right and she would feather the gas slightly, give a minute correction to the wheel, and the truck, like an obedient animal, would respond and straighten out and continue charging forward.

Albi wanted to speak, but he feared that any distraction might send them skidding into a snow bank. So, he kept silent and watched the shadowy white landscape fly past them. At one point, gigantic icicles illuminated by the headlights, loomed out of the darkness like a fairy castle turned upside down, and then it was gone just as quickly as it had appeared. He didn't like to be cold and he'd made it a habit to steer clear of any mountains. He much preferred warmer climates where a man wouldn't die simply because he forgot where he left his hat. And now, here he was with mountains all around and he was being carried deep within their frozen realm by an angry woman who had managed to foster an adolescent slight well into adulthood, along with two religious zealots riding shotgun. *And he had placed them in danger?*

Nancy Wong. Of all the lawyers in all the cities, why Nancy Wong? He remembered the little girl and her palm-reading grandfather, and then years later when he'd returned to Seattle, there she had been in the same school, a year below him. At the time, he really hadn't given the coincidence a thought. After all, he'd barely known her. He'd known her cousin until he'd gotten himself killed over a turf battle between rival gangs, and except for that one fateful date he'd had nothing to do with her. So, why would she know anything about his father, and why all the intrigue? It seemed like everywhere he turned someone was telling him his life was in danger. Even Monique had warned him. And don't forget that character, Marlowe. What was it he had said? That he would be better off without a gun; that he might live longer? Were they all vying for the *Jade Prince*? Sure, Sal had had his arm broken and Sal and Jimmy and Hoppy had come to a bad end, but that was just the cost of doing business, wasn't it? So far, he hadn't seen any sign of this so called 'danger'.

They approached what looked to be a ski village, the powerful mercury lights giving the night a city-like glow, and for a moment Albro became hopeful that they would stop within the boundaries of the known world, but Nancy Wong didn't even give the scene a glance. She continued to hurtle them forward into the night. Albro eventually succumbed to the hum of the tires, the blasting warmth of the heater and the mesmerizing snowflakes, and fell into a fitful slumber.

Nancy Wong gave an inward sigh of relief as they crested the pass. Her greatest worry had been the prospect of the blizzard forcing its closure before they had made it through. She knew that soon it would be closed, and that fact gave her an added sense of security. She had thought of the cabin as soon as she had opened her office the day before and had been faced with the scene of devastation. She had given her apartment barely more than a passing thought; it would be, she knew, in the same state. She hadn't gone into the office. One look had been enough to convince her that she needed to move quickly. She hadn't even considered going back to her apartment. Everything she needed was already packed in the Land Cruiser which she kept parked on anonymous side street in a neighborhood north of town.

She hadn't panicked, and although her heart was racing, she had breathed in deeply and closed the door. She had long ago learned to master her fears and to think clearly under pressure. She did not worry about the condition, nor was she concerned about the contents of the office. That part of her life was over. She knew that she would not be going back. Ever.

She had walked calmly to her car. She had driven around the block until she was certain that the big, blue sedan that she had seen earlier was following her. She had driven into the heaviest downtown traffic and waited until the blue sedan was trapped behind a row of cars at a signal and then she had slipped into a parking garage. She had climbed the stairs two at a time and then had walked quickly through the crowded department store to the opposite side of the building, exited and hopped on a bus. She had sat in the Land Cruiser that night and all through the next day. She had just about given up hope, when Albro had finally called.

She had barely ventured out when they had been on her tail. Had they known all along where she had been hiding and had simply been waiting for her to move? It had been a huge risk leading them right to their quarry but now, she thought, let them try to follow her. It gave her a kind of perverse pleasure knowing that, at least for the time being, she held the advantage. She was in her element. Her grandfather had been a mountaineer, rare in the Chinese-American community where seldom, it seemed, anyone ventured beyond the confines of family and profession. He had taught her how to deal with the hazards of ice and snow, and more importantly, one's own fears.

She had accompanied him to the summits of all the major peaks on the North American continent, and then she had gone on to climb the highest peaks on the remaining continents. Her major advantage, to the surprise of her male counterparts, was that pound for pound she was half-again as strong as the strongest among them. Although she was small, she was concentrated.

She had forged a workable division between the law practice she had inherited from her uncles, and the rarefied atmosphere of world-class climbing. She had seen no need to marry. Besides, there had never been time for it. Occasionally she would have an affair with a climber, but never on an expedition. She had seen too many hotshot guides let their dicks do their thinking, and then end up killing themselves or their clients.

If overtures were made in her directions, she would politely decline, but leave the door open for a later time. Her aunt might accuse her of becoming an old maid, but she was satisfied with the life she had made for herself.

That is, until a year ago, when the haggard looking man had come unannounced into her office. He was lean, with a face deeply lined and darkened by too much time in the sun. He had that look in his eyes that she had seen in climbers after a particularly demanding and exhausting assent, and an intensity that hinted of vistas beyond the sight of most men. Her first thought was that he was like herself, an alpinist. She could only guess his age, late forties, early fifties, and was taken aback when he showed her the documents that proved him to be nearly seventy, and she had learned that he did not exhibit the frailties of a man of his age. But that was not until months later.

He had introduced himself as Thomas Crane. He needed a lawyer, he had said, to draw up the necessary documents to pass on his estate to his single heir, a child he had given up soon after his birth; a routine task for her. There was a caveat. His heir, now a grown man, was not to be informed of his father's existence until after his death. Only gradually had she learned why.

The rear lights of a slow-moving semi jumped at her from the blur of snow flakes, and startled her out of her thoughts. She reminded herself to concentrate on the driving. Because if she fucked this up, and if what Thomas Crane had told her was true, and she believed that it was, then they could all just kiss this world good-bye.

So, here she was, heading deep into her snowy mountains at break neck speed with the two strangers, who were very strange indeed, and with someone from deep within her past, and feeling a kind of perverse thrill. Before her meeting with Thomas Crane, her life had fallen into a predictable routine: awake at four-thirty, strong tea and run five miles, shower and eight hours at the office, two hours at the gym and a light dinner, and another two hours of work in her pajamas and then to bed. Somewhere along the way, she had lost her enthusiasm for climbing. Was it simply that she had accomplished so much at such an early age?

Or was it the inevitable creep of middle-age and its cautionary plea that had come upon her? Thirty-six, and already she had been firmly set in the rut to retirement. And then Thomas Crane had walked through her office door, seemingly from nowhere, and into her world. Or, to be more precise, he had pulled her forcefully into his.

Her grandfather, she knew, would have seen it quite differently. He would have pointed out, in all seriousness, that it had been her destiny, set down in a time long before she had been born. He would have pointed to the lines in his palm and then to the lines in her own as proof, and told her that she could no more direct her life than she could direct the motions of the planets and the stars. He had reminded her time and again that life moved through her and all living things, and not the other way around. She wished now that he were here to help her understand what was happening. But then, if what Thomas Crane had told her was true, her grandfather was not far away.

She glanced at the sleeping figure next to her, and felt the emotional turmoil begin to rise from the pit of her stomach. She forced it down abruptly. She needed to keep a clear head, and it was going to be a difficult task knowing what she knew.

They were nearing their turnoff. All of the road signs were whited out, but she knew the road so well that she had no problem picking out the narrow, half-hidden gap in the snow bank. Once on the secondary road she slowed to a stop and got out and locked the front hubs into four-wheel drive. She kicked the snow, gauging its depth and grip. She guessed that the county had plowed it early in the day and it had been piling up ever since. There was nearly a foot on it now and she was worried the truck would lose its traction before they got within hiking distance of the cabin. When she got back inside, she shifted into the low range, revved the engine, and let the clutch out slowly.

Albin, who had awakened to the surreal scene of a figure moving about in the swirl of white flakes illuminated by the headlights, felt that he was must be stuck in another of his wild dreams, or perhaps one of those dreams within a dream in which he would awaken to what a first he took to be consciousness, but soon became a nightmarish parody of

239

reality. A rush of cold air forced him fully awake. Nancy Wong was pulling herself into the driver's seat.

"Are we there?" he asked.

"A few more miles," she answered and eased the truck forward.

"There's a road out there?" Albro asked, straining to see more than swirling snow.

"Believe it or not, I've been driving this road since I was fifteen. My grandfather made it a point to teach me how to drive it in the worst weather," she answered. Getting off the freeway had calmed her. Driving at high speed over the icy pavement had been nerve wracking. This was relaxing by comparison. The truck still wanted to slew and would have given most people white knuckles, but she felt completely at ease, knowing exactly what the big truck could and could not do.

"I was just thinking," Albro said, "if it was really necessary to come all this way."

"We're almost there," she said.

"What I mean is that maybe you're over reaching. Maybe the break-in was coincidental. It happens all the time."

She considered this for a moment, ran the evidence through her mind, and said, "No."

"Are you sure about that? There must be…"

"Yes, I'm sure," she said, cutting him off.

"You don't really know…"

"That's just it," she said forcefully. "I do know. I know a good deal more than you. I wish that I didn't, but there it is." She said this with a finality that even Albro could understand. For now, the conversation was over.

The big man in the rear of the truck rolled over with a groan and pulled himself to his hands and knees and crawled to the front. He gazed through the windshield. "Hey, Izzy, wake up." He shook the smaller man gently with his huge hands. "Look, it's beautiful."

The little man stirred and opened his eyes and sat upright and rubbed his face. He pulled back his hood a fraction and looked into the night.

"It's snow, Walter," he said and then to Nancy and Albro, "He has never seen snow."

"Snow," Walter repeated slowly with a sense of wonderment in his deep voice. "Is it alive?"

"No," Isaiah said. "It's rain that has frozen into crystals. It's cold, Walter, very cold."

"Is this where you live, Miss Nancy?" Walter asked in a hushed voice.

"No live," Nancy said. "I visit when I have the time. The cabin belonged to my grandparents. Now it's mine. It's a special place."

"You're lucky. Izzy, maybe someday when the troubles are over, we could find a place like this. Do you think we could?"

"Yes, Walter, when the troubles are over," Brother Isaiah replied with more than a hint of weariness in his voice. "In the meantime, we must fulfill our duty to keep Albro Swift safe."

"Don't you worry, Mr. Albro. Nothing bad is going to happen to you. We're going to protect you. We won't fail you like we failed your …"

"That will do for now Walter," Isaiah interrupted. "Watch the snow."

A look of momentary confusion crossed Walter's face and then he settled his chin on the back of the seat and gazed at the snow. Albro was about to ask what they had meant by 'the troubles', and why he needed their protection when the truck bounced hard and the tires began to spin.

"Shit!" Nancy Wong uttered half under her breath. "That's as far as we can go. We'll have to walk from here."

"Walk? Out there? You can't be serious. It's a blizzard," Albro said.

"It's not a blizzard," Nancy stated. "It's snowing heavily, but there's no wind. The cabin isn't far. I have an extra pair of snowshoes." She got out and went around and opened the back.

Walter rolled off the tailgate, and dove into a deep drift. He emerged in an explosion of ice crystals. "Come on, Izzy! This is wonderful!'

241

Brother Isaiah, who was standing knee deep in the powdery snow, was shivering. Albro, who had tried stepping in Nancy Wong's tracks to avoid loading his shoes with snow, had joined them. They were all being covered very quickly by the falling snow.

Nancy Wong had strapped on a headlamp and handed one to Albro. She then pulled out a heavy parka and handed it to him and then placed a pair of snowshoes at his feet. "Step into the bindings, and I'll strap you in." She turned to the others. "I'll lead him to the cabin and then I'll bring the snowshoes back to you."

"That won't be necessary," Brother Isaiah replied. "Walter, come over here."

Walter lumbered over to them. His large feet gave him a definite advantage. Despite his enormous weight, he sank only half way to his knees. The smaller man climbed on his back.

"You're sure about this?" Nancy Wong asked, shining her lamp on the pair.

"Don't worry, he's very strong," Isaiah answered.

"Stay close. If you have any problems, be sure to call out." She swung a heavy pack onto her shoulders, turned and headed into the darkness.

On his second step, Albro fell, face first. He floundered onto his back coughing and spitting snow. Walter reached down and plucked him up onto his feet with one hand.

Nancy Wong turned back to him. "Keep the ends of the snowshoes up, and try to shuffle through the snow."

All Albro could see was the dim glow of her headlamp. He tried keeping upright, but invariably something would snag the tip of the ungainly shoes and throw him off balance. His cast was too large to fit through the sleeve of the parka, and he struggled to keep it closed against the snow with his one good hand. In the short time it took to get to the cabin, he lost his headlamp and lost track of the number of times he felt the huge hands grasp him and set him on his feet. All feeling had gone out of his hands and feet and a trickle of cold sweat had begun coursing down his back.

He was very near exhaustion when, at last, they came to the cabin. Snow had drifted nearly to the eaves of the broad, overhanging roof which kept the snow from the doorway. Nancy Wong was already inside and she had lighted a gas lamp and had a fire going in a large iron stove. He fumbled with the snowshoe straps but his fingers would not do what he asked of them. Nancy Wong bent and undid them for him. He attempted to thank her, but all that came out of his mouth was a stuttering, "ukukukukuku…"

"Go stand by the stove. I'm going back to the truck for the supplies," she said and went back out into the night.

Albro stood next to the heat and slowly the feeling came back into his extremities. The odd couple joined him. The big one stooped to enter the doorway and deposited his companion.

"Go assist Ms Wong, please," the smaller one said. His glasses had fogged and he pulled them off and wiped them with the hem of his hassock. He pulled the hood close about his head and moved to the fire and stood with his head bent and his hands out to the warmth.

Albro looked around. The room was maybe sixteen feet square. There were four bunks made of peeled logs against one wall. Against the next wall was the wood stove with mullioned windows to either side and shuddered from the outside. Two easy chairs flanked the stove. The next wall allowed space for a simple kitchen with a sink, a refrigerator and small gas range. It was all paneled in amber-colored knotty pine. The ceiling, held up by rough-cut timbers rose to a low peak. Cozy, Albro thought. He wondered where the toilet was and had a bad feeling that it would require dogsled and guide to reach safely. By the time Nancy Wong and Walter returned, (she wearing a backpack almost as large as herself and he loaded with stuff sacks), the room had begun to warm up.

Albro shrugged off the parka. His damp slacks and sports coat began to steam. His Italian hand-sewns were sodden. At least, he had a dry pair of socks in his bag with the money. His heart lurched when he realized that he had left his bag in the truck, and then he saw it sticking out of the pile of gear the big man had dropped. He went over and pulled it out and hefted it. He wanted to check its contents to be sure that it was

243

all still there, but he didn't trust the three pairs of eyes that seemed to be watching his every move.

"Don't worry," Nancy Wong said. "It's all there."

She had dropped her heavy pack and was filling a kettle with water from a plastic jug. She set the kettle on the range and struck a match and adjusted the flame. She set out mugs on the table. She pulled out a pot and set another burner ablaze and then looked through the cupboard pulling out cans which she opened and emptied into the pot.

Albro watched her fuss about the small space. She had definitely grown into a good looking woman. She didn't have the drop dead beauty of Monique Osborn Newton, but she could improve her looks with a little make-up, something to accentuate the shape of her eyes and to enhance to color of her lips. She had a wholesome look about her, the glow of someone in good health, like the pictures of those women in the running-shoe ads. He imagined her with tiny beads of sweat on her upper lip. Suddenly aware of his appraising gaze, she turned momentarily in his direction meeting his eyes for the first time and looked long and hard at him. He smiled and dipped his head slightly. He'd learned a long time ago that women could not resist that move. No matter how hard they tried, they could not resist smiling back at him. But Nancy Wong didn't smile before turning back to the stove. Nevertheless, he felt certain that she was beginning to thaw.

Albro cleared his throat. "I think it's time somebody told me why we've driven four hours through a snowstorm to this quaint, little hideaway. Did you or did you not find my father?" He'd spoken to Nancy Wong's back since she seemed to be the one in charge, but it was the little man who spoke first.

"Yes, we found your father, but there are things you should know first," he said. He pulled his hood back. It was the first time that Albro really had a good look at him. Under the harsh glare of the gas lamp he could see that something was wrong with the man's face. His skin had a gray pallor. A thin beard clung to his sunken cheeks. His dark, beady eyes behind the wire-rim glasses were rimmed with red. His thin lips formed a narrow slit above a nonexistent chin. His nose was just a nub of flesh, made purple by the cold air. The hair grew back away from the face and two pointy ears were stuck higher on his head than they should be. The man had what seemed to be the face of a rat overlaid on what might have been human. The effect was startling and Albro took an involuntary step backwards and fell into one of the easy chairs.

"Walter," said the little man, "please come over here. I want you to show Mr Swift your hands and feet."

Walter had found one of those crystal spheres filled with liquid and flakes that act like snow. He'd been totally absorbed with turning it over and over, letting the fake snow settle on the little cottage and trees. He carefully returned it to its shelf and shuffled over to where Albro sat. The man was immense. He looked like what might have resulted if Andre the Giant had been stranded on a desert island with only a female walrus for a companion. His skin was dark and leathery and he showed big, blocky teeth as his bulbous lips and puffed out cheeks spread into a broad smile.

Walter did as was asked and held out his hands for Albro to examine. They were a foot across from thumb to little finger, and between them were webs of flesh. The same was true of his feet. They were more like flippers than true human appendages.

"Thank you, Walter," the little man said. "You may go back to your toy."

Walter eagerly retrieved the glass ball and settled onto the floor. Nancy Wong had turned and was now watching them.

"I am sorry," Brother Isaiah said to Albro. "Our appearance must come as a shock to you."

CHAPTER 20

HE had to be dreaming, and this had to be the part where from far back in his brain came the voice that told him to wrap things up because things were just getting a little too weird for one night, but no such voice was waking him. He looked across to where Nancy Wong stood with her arms crossed. Did she actually have a look of amusement on her face? Well, forget her. Forget the freak show. He was getting out of there now. Then he remembered where he was. They had him. No phone, no 911. No street, no sidewalk. Nothing but snow and ice for a hundred miles. No one to hear his cries for help. How had he been so utterly stupid to get himself trapped like this?

"Calm down, Albro." It was Nancy Wong who finally broke the silence. "No one is going to hurt you, at least, not tonight. I can't guarantee what's going to happen tomorrow, or the next day, but tonight we're all safe."

"That's all very sweet for you, Nancy, but who are these freaks?"

Nancy Wong pushed herself off the counter, and started for him with balled up fists. "Albro Swift! If I didn't promise your father…"

"What about my father?" Albro shouted at her. "What do you know about him?"

"Your father is dead! They killed him!" Nancy shouted back at him. Tears brimmed in her eyes. "Isaiah and Walter risked their lives to protect him, and now they're risking their lives to protect you."

"These two? You've got to be kidding! They look like they belong in a zoo," Albro said sarcastically.

"Damn you, Albro Swift! You…"

"Tell me about my father! Who killed him?"

Nancy threw up her hands and glared at the ceiling. She said, "I should never have agreed to this. You're still the arrogant, immature little bastard you always were!"

"*I haven't changed*? You're as cold hearted as ever. Everyone called you t e *Ice-Queen*. Did you know that?"

"Don't call me that!" Nancy Wong clenched her fists and took a step forward.

"Ha ! The truth makes you angry!"

"Trust me, you don't want to see me angry," Nancy Wong said quietly. She relaxed her shoulders and shifted her weight to the balls of her feet.

Albro was about to say something about what he imagined her love-life to consist of, but then he thought better of it. A very cold look had come into Nancy Wong's eyes that made the term *Ice-Queen* seem like an endearment. He took a step back and made a quick glance toward the wood stove where an iron poker leaned against the wall. She had read his intentions and a smile creased the corners of her mouth. "Go ahead," she said. "Reach for it."

Albro froze. She was probably some kind of Kung Fu Ninja warrior for all he knew. He already had one broken arm. He didn't need another. "Take it easy, Nancy. I was kidding."

"You weren't kidding," she said. "I knew they called me that. And you know what? I rather enjoyed it then, but not now."

"Okay, okay, I'm sorry," Albro said. He held up his hand as a sign of peace.

"Thank you. I know you don't mean it, but thank you anyway," Nancy Wong said. "Isaiah and Walter are not freaks. They're human beings. Apologize to them."

Albro looked at the rat man who had been watching them with rapt interest and then the big fellow who hadn't looked up from his toy.

247

"I'm sorry," he said. "I didn't mean anything by what I said. I was just surprised, that's all."

The little man held up his hands. "Please," he said firmly. "We take no offense. Believe me when I say that we have endured far worse." He turned to Nancy Wong, "Besides, he is, as yet, innocent."

"Innocent! That's a laugh. I think it's a fair assumption he lost his innocence a long time ago," Nancy said.

"At least I never had to go begging for it," Albro said smiling lewdly at Nancy Wong.

"You little fucker..."

"I'm sorry," Brother Isaiah said quickly. "Perhaps that was a poor choice of words. I meant to suggest that there is much he does not know." He looked at Albro. "We will tell you about your father, but first, let me tell you who we are. Nothing else will have any meaning for you if you do not understand who we are."

Both Albro and Nancy opened their mouths, but the little man closed his eyes and brought his hands together as if to pray. It was a subtle, but powerful move that caught them both by surprise and caused them each to pause and take a breath. Nancy Wong glared at Albro and then turned back to the kitchen.

"Thank you," Brother Isaiah said in a quiet voice. He said to Albro, "I can only tell you the truth. What you chose to believe is up to you. We are known by many names, but we refer to ourselves as the Mongi. The others, the Purim, call us *malforms*, or simply, *mal*. As you might guess, the Purim are not like us. Like your people, they are blessed with God's purity of form. We, alas, carry the burden of God's curse against humanity. At least, that is how the Purim see us. So, yes, you are perfectly right to call us 'freaks', because from your perspective, that is what we are.

"But the differences between us, and the Purim, run far deeper than mere appearance, and have their roots, the Scriptures tell us, in the time of the second coming of the Christ. It is a story that would take days for me to tell, but the Scriptures are clear in their message. Those who accepted the Christ figure as the emissary of God were allowed to retain the purity of God's image. Those who rejected the Messiah were forced from God's embrace just as Adam and Eve were banished from their sacred garden, and were condemned to wear their shame, forever to be marked by the sign of the beast.

"I offer you this by illustration only. It is, of course, nonsense. I say that not only as a follower of the one true God, but as a man of higher learning.   would be wonderful if history could be reduced to a few simple acts of a disgruntled God. Nevertheless, it is the accepted truth, not only for the Purim, but for many of the Mongi as well. To defy that truth, is to subject oneself to a sentence of death.

"I can see from the look on your face that I have raised more questions than I have answered. There is much more to tell you, but I see that Miss Wong has prepared our meal."

Nancy Wong had set out bowls and filled them with steaming soup and had placed a box of crackers in the middle of the table. The smell of the soup had filled the small space and Albro realized that he was famished.   He'd not had a decent meal since he had sat with Auntie Lo and her co-workers. Had that been little more than twenty-four hours ago? He couldn't quite remember the last good night of sleep he'd had. True, he'd managed to grab an hour here and there, but each time he'd been plunged into one of those crazy dreams that had left him feeling drained and exhausted. He pulled himself out of the chair and sat at the table opposite Nancy Wong.   Albro observed that the chairs were woefully undersized for Walter's bulk. The big man had pulled it aside and had settled onto his knees.

"Walter, would you like to ask the blessing of this meal?" Brother Isaiah asked.

Walter brought his huge hands together and placed them on the edge of the table and bowed his head and closed his eyes. He moved his lips silently as if to rehearse what he was about to say and then said slowly, "Dear God, He who loves all the peoples of the earth, bless this food we are about to eat, and bless Miss Nancy, who prepared it for us, and bless all of the friends we left behind, and bless especially good Mr. Albro, and keep him safe from harm. Amen."

"Was that good, Izzy?"

"That was fine, Walter.

Walter scooped up the bowl, which looked like a teacup in his massive hands and tipped its contents into his open mouth. When it was empty he set it carefully on the table. "Ahhh," Walter said drawing out the syllable into a long and satisfied appraisal of the soup. "This is very nice soup, Miss Nancy."

"Would you like another serving?" she asked.

"Oh, yes! I mean," Walter answered turning to his companion. "If it pleases Miss Nancy, may I have another bowl?"

"Only if there is enough," Brother Isaiah answered.

"Is there more, Miss Nancy?"

"Yes. We have a good supply of soup."

"Miss Nancy says there is a good supply of soup."

"Yes, Walter, I heard her. You may have more, only this time please use your spoon."

"Oh. My spoon. I was so hungry and the soup smelled so good, I forgot. I won't forget again."

Albro was half listening to the simple-minded interchange. There was something the little guy had said earlier that was bouncing around inside his brain. He dipped his spoon into the soup and he got it nearly to his lips when he stopped cold. The rat man had said something about the second coming of Christ. He'd made it sound like old news, a done deal, a fete acompli. As far as he knew, and he knew a surprising amount about Biblical fact and fiction thanks to a three-month stint with the Reverend C. Dobson Powel and his wife, Louisa May and the holy-rolling congregation of the Calvary Pentecostal Church of Christ, there hadn't been a replay of the original Event.

It had been the Reverend's mission to take in young boys from the local juvenile detention center and rehabilitate them through an intense indoctrination in the tenants of the Christian faith, and he had required Albro to study the Good Book assiduously day and night. This regimen, the Reverend had contended, would serve Albro well in the coming yea s, for God had a plan for him and he needed to be ready for the day whe n He chose to reveal it.

Afte the blessing of each meal, the Reverend C. Dobson Powel would quiz iim and the number of correct answers equated directly to the amount of food Louisa May would be allowed to place on his plate; the Reverei d being a firm believer that hunger was a great motivator. Unfortunate y, the more astute Albro became with Biblical knowledge, the more d ficult became the questions. It would have been obvious to anyone lool ng on that a contest of wills had begun to take shape, and it was only a atter of time until things came to a show down, which it had one Sunday norning.

Albi) had been studying Paul's epistle to the Romans all week. He had cor mitted to memory all sixteen chapters and God only knew how many \ rses. He'd always had a good memory, but he hadn't known just how go d it was until he'd been put to the test. Unfortunately he'd been distra ed by a dog-eared copy of the Maltese Falcon which he'd discovered the free bin outside a used bookstore, and what with his brain still g owing, he'd gotten Hammett's prose mixed up with Paul's rant against he fun-loving Romans, and he'd averaged only about .500 on the quizzes or the week. The result was that he'd barely held his own in his quest fo calories, and hunger had begun to gnaw at him. He'd stayed up most of Saturday night pouring over the text, reciting chapter and verse, until e knew it from front to back.

Sun ay morning came and the Reverend had his *Nine Pounder*, the huge lea her bound King James Bible that he claimed had been carried across the ains by his great-great grandfather in a covered wagon. He was clean s aven and his jet black hair was well oiled and combed back into a high, rown-like affair. After a long and beseeching prayer in which the Reverei I C. Dobson Powel asked God to, among other things, take pity on the inful minded orphan before Him, the Reverend dug into his breakfast w ile Albro was left to look on.

Lou a May had set a plate of steaming, butter-dripping hotcakes with a ring f glistening, plump sausages arrayed around the edge of the plate, and a all glass of milk before him. He tried not to look at the plate of food, but the more he tried to ignore it, the more his mouth flowed with saliva, and the louder his empty stomach growled. At last, the Reverend finished his plate and opened the great volume to the New Testament chapter of Romans. He pulled his wire-rims from his inside pocket, hooked them behind his large ears, and adjusted them low on his long nose. The gilt-edge pages had made a crackling noise as he flicked them back and forth. He traced down the pages with his white, bony fingers. At long last, he seemed to have come to a conclusion and looked up. Louisa May, who had stood through all this in her gingham apron with her thin body pressed against the kitchen counter and wringing the ragged gray dish cloth until it was wound into a nervous knot, did not make a sound. Help of any kind from her quarter was strictly forbidden.

Albro took a deep breath and let it out slowly. He felt like a rookie waiting for his first pitch from a seasoned pro. The Reverend C. Dobson Powel brought his fingertips together and then pressed his palms together to form a steeple. He tilted his face to the ceiling and then he looked directly at Albro. But when the pitch came, it was like nothing Albro had expected. It was like one of those pitches that seem to come out of nowhere. You see the wind-up and then the next thing you know the ball is whizzing waist high across the plate, and all you can do is stand there and blink in disbelief.

"Young man," Powel said with an edge sharper in his voice than the long butcher's knife that Louisa May used to slice off strips of bacon from the huge slab she brought home from the market. "Do you experience sexual urges?" He'd pronounced the word sexual with that slurred x into s way that quasi-intellectuals do when they believe they have conquered their baser feelings.

Louisa May gave out a sharp cry and the Reverend silenced her with his raised hand.

Albro knew better than to be taken in by such pompous displays, but what could he do? He was hungry. Then again, what could he say? Of course, he felt urges. He felt urges every waking moment. Plus he felt urges every time he closed his eyes. Nearly every morning his last dream ended in an explosion that loaded his underpants. He then had to stuff them in the laundry. They'd always reappear clean and neatly folded in his dresser drawer. Louisa May had never said a word, but he'd been unable to look her in the eye. Was this all about dirty laundry? He knew that he should say something, but he sat there, dumb-faced. Strike one!

With out waiting for an answer the Reverend pitched another question. Do you touch yourself down there?" the Reverend asked pointing his long nose in the direction of Albro's crotch.

Touch himself? He'd done a whole lot more than simply touch himself. He was amazed his member was still attached after all the yanking and pulling he'd done to it, and he wasn't the only one. The neighbor girl had been more than willing to lend a hand. Albro shifted uncomfortably in his chair. Had Louisa May ratted him out? He gave a tentative nod.

The Reverend turned and shot a withering glare at his wife. "I told you," he declared, "and yet you doubted me!"

Albro glanced up at Louisa May and tried to convey some sense of gratitude for her support.

"Look at me, young man!" Powel slapped the flat of his hand on the table and made the plates jump. "Do you know about homosexuality?" The Reverend C. Dobson Powel demanded, and then without waiting for an answer, he shouted, "How is it you know? Have you had a personal experience? Don't lie to me. I've been told what goes on amongst you wretched boys while you're locked up in those filthy detention centers."

"No sir, not me, personally," he answered, looking directly at old Powel. He heard Louisa May give a sigh of relief, which made that answer the equivalent of a foul-tip that had gone careening up into the crowds. This was not the kind of questioning Albro had been anticipating. The Reverend had always asked for a recitation of a particular verse, or perhaps a list of the players in some obscure Biblical drama. It was clear the Reverend had upped the ante. Albro looked at his breakfast. The steam had dissipated from the hotcakes, and the butter had begun to congeal. The sausages had gone cold and now looked about as appetizing as a ring of dog turds. Powel's questions had been leading up to

253

something. He had to think fast. An old ball player had once told him that the only way you get a clean hit is when you know exactly what's coming at you. You needed to reach into the mind of the pitcher and feel what was there. At the time, it had sounded pretty far-fetched. Nobody could read minds, or could they? Nevertheless, he'd begun trying it out, but all he'd ever gotten was a kind of low-level static. You had to work at it, the old duffer had told him. 'Nothing ever comes without hard work', he'd told Albro.

He looked into the Reverend's black eyes and then he pressed his weight against what seemed like a door to the man's thoughts. Suddenly the door was yanked open and he literally stumbled in. But instead of touching the Reverend's thoughts, it was like grabbing the bare ends of a live 240 volt wire. The next thing he knew, he was sitting back in his chair, his arms and hands going spastic and his lower half paralyzed. He very nearly blacked out.

The Reverend C. Dobson Powel smiled and then he delivered the pitch he'd been holding back. "Tell me, young man, what would St. Paul think of your urges? You don't have to go into the nasty details, but you do need to support your points with chapter and verse."

The words had come at him like a wobbling slow-ball. He couldn't decide if he should hold back, or step into it. What he wanted to do was smack the question straight down The Reverend C. Dobson Powel's throat. He wanted to speak, but something had happened to the circuits between his brain and his mouth. He tried harder, but what came out sounded like a cat trying to cough up a hair ball.

"Having difficulty, are we?" asked Powel? "Is guilt preventing you from speaking?"

He got his thoughts lined up and tried again, and blurted out, "GOD'S PECKER!"

Albro gulped a breath. What had he said? Somehow his thoughts had slewed off onto a side road. The Reverend C. Dobson Powel wouldn't have been anymore insulted if Albro had stood on the breakfast table and pissed in his plate. He turned a terrible shade of yellowish red and started to rise out of his chair.

What Albro meant to say was that St. Paul would probably tell him to give his urges a rest and try to think about God instead. In a nutshell, that was what old Paul had told the Romans. But Albro, just like the Romans had found that easier said than done. He wanted to explain it all to Powell He had the whole book of Romans clamoring to get out of his mouth, but after that first attempt, he was afraid of what he might say.

"WHAT DID YOU SAY?" Powell bellowed.

The spasms finally subsided and Albro found that his feet were working. He jumped out of his chair.

The Reverend C. Dobson Powel lunged across the table with outstretch hands, but before he could grab Albro by the throat, Albro snatched his cold breakfast and bolted through the door.

The first thing Monday morning, the Reverend had hauled Albro and his meager belongings back to the CPS officer. "Keep him!" Powel had told the counselor. And that had been that. He had learned, though, to be very careful about poking into people's thoughts. That had been the one and only time he'd tried to enter anyone's mind. He'd learned his lesson. From then on, he learned to be satisfied with what he could get from the outside.

In addition, something else had jumped into his mind from out of that far away past. There was something in Paul's preaching to the Romans that came back to him now from that far away time. It was something about *'changing the incorruptible God'*...something, something... *'into an image made like to birds, and four footed beasts'*..., *'and creeping things'*..., *'to dishonor their own bodies'*..., *'worship the creature more than the Creator...'*

Albro looked up. The three of them seemed to be watching him closely, and he felt the hair of the back of his neck began to rise. He turned to the rat man.

"What did you mean about the second coming of Christ?"

"That happened long ago. The scriptures say..."

"I know all about the first event, the blessed Virgin, the water into wine, walking on water, etc, etc. Maybe I've been out of touch the last few weeks, but as far as I know, there's been no second round."

"'Second round'?" the little man asked looking puzzled.

"The Four Horsemen, reign of the Anti-Christ, world-wide chaos until the triumphant return of the Boy Wonder and his thousand year reign. There are plenty of nuts out there who predict that it's coming down any day. It's the sort of thing Fox News would have been all over, but as far as I know, it hasn't happened."

"You are quite right, in a very strict sense. But in another sense, it has all happened, just as you described. It is still in your future, while it is far in our past."

"How..."

"I'm sorry, but I cannot tell you how. I can only tell you what is. I will try to explain. Walter and I belong to this world, this exact same world that you think of as yours. The only difference is that the shape of our worlds has been altered slightly to allow us to be in the same time. Our world is this world, just as this world is the same world that you experienced yesterday and you will experience tomorrow, the only difference is that the shape of it all has changed slightly. Your mind senses that change in shape and perceives it as a shift in time."

"Oh, sure, I get it," Albro said, "You're time travelers. H. G. Wells. They load you in some sort of contraption, spin the dials and POW!"

"No. We have traveled nowhere. In fact, I was born not far from here. Time is not a roadway that can be traversed. It is the un-crossable chasm, the un-breachable wall. We are here because..." And here the little man faltered as if he had become lost in the translation from one language to another.

"They are here, because of you. It is your existence that brought them here." It was Nancy Wong who had spoken.

"Precisely," agree the rat man, and smiled at Albro as if all had been made perfectly understandable.

"Like maybe I dreamed you up and guided you through the ether."

"Yes something like that…" the rat man agreed.

Albro smacked the side of his head. "Well I'm glad we cleared up that little misunderstanding. I thought this was all real. All I need to do is wake up and POOF, you're gone."

"I'm afraid it won't be that easy," Brother Isaiah said and glanced uneasily at Nancy Wong.

"Sure it is," Albro countered. "This is just a very bizarre dream and all I have to do is wake up."

"Albro," Nancy Wong said in a very calm and very level voice. "You are not dreaming. You're wide awake and so are we. I can't explain all of this to you because I don't understand most of it myself. For now, you're just going to have to accept it. Try to understand that every event in your life has been tied to every event in ours. That is why we are all here." She paused, took a breath, and then said, "There is a very important reason all of this is happening, and I think you know what it is."

Albro closed his eyes. Any second now, he told himself, he was going to wake up in his own bed, in own apartment, and Butch was going to start yammering, and Roger was going to come through the door with his bicycle over his shoulder and… . "Okay," he said to Nancy, 'just for the sake of argument, let's assume that the three of you are here because I brought you here. I don't know what that means, but for the moment let's just say it's true. Now, to satisfy my own curiosity, tell me why *I* am here?"

This time it was Walter who spoke, "That's easy, Mr. Albro. You're going to help us find the *Jade Prince*."

CHAPTER 21

EXCEPT for the crackling fire, the room had grown very quiet, as if all other sounds had been absorbed by the expectant air that had suddenly filled the small space.

Albro drummed the fingers of his left hand on the table, and thought about what Walter had said. He'd heard the part about the *Jade Prince*, and he had to admit that he'd half expected it. It seemed like every time he tried to dodge the subject, it was thrown right back in his face, but what did it have to do with him? But that was *the question*, wasn't it? Hadn't that always been *the question*? After all, that had been the only clue surrounding his birth. Whoever had placed him in that phone booth on that hard wooden seat could have written any number of things that would have been more helpful, like maybe the names and addresses of his parents, and the reason they had abandoned him. Even a name would have been nice. How difficult was a name? He'd spent the first four years of his life without a name! And then, to top things off, he'd been bestowed with a name that had been plucked off a road sign!

Stop it, he told himself. Like Ruth Olson had said, 'There's no use crying about the past…', but then Jackie Barnes had countered, 'For heaven's sake, Ruth, the past is the only thing you *should* cry about. You can't cry over a future you've never experienced, and if you spent your time crying over the present you'd have no hope of getting anything done'.

He'd dismissed a long time ago any notion that those three words, *'the Jade Prince'*, held any significance. He'd taken those three words and turned them every which way possible to no avail. If the Chinese myth held any clue to his past he'd never discovered it. He'd never found anyone who had given it more than a passing interest until those early morning hours three days previous when Krupp had taken him deep into the bowels of Martin's new museum, and now everyone seemed to think it was the *Holy Grail*. Why the sudden interest? And what did it have to do with the appearance of someone who claimed to be his father? From his own experience, he knew that treasure hunters were a secretive, half-crazed lot whose demeanor bordered the fine line between paranoia and schizophrenia. Good luck, he thought, trying to get a straight answer out of any of them.

He had the uneasy feeling, though, that this was something more than a treasure hunt. He thought about those characters in the Maltese Falcon. Were they still out there somewhere searching for their elusive black bird? Or, had they, along with Hammett, been stopped permanently. In the game of treasure hunting, there tended to be only one winner, and a lot of dead bodies left on the game board, which made a person wonder: Was it ever a question of the rewards out-weighing the risks, or was it something that resided deeper in the psyche that compelled one to take those enormous risks? Homer had tried to answer it, and so had Shakespeare, along with countless other literary greats and hacks. They all cited the well worn motivators of avarice and greed and lust. You could pretty well throw in the rest of the seven deadly sins and add good ol' hubris for good measure, he thought. And then, to make matters worse, when you didn't win they tried to tell you there was more to winning than coming in first. Hah! Try offering up that idea to the likes of Ulysses, Alexander, or Indiana Jones. Those boys would tell you that winning was what it was all about, the shear exhilaration of winning. The prizes that followed were just the icing on the cake. Albro would go even further and claim that winning was what *life* was all about. There was just no percentage in being a loser.

"You're going to help us, aren't you?" Walter asked.

259

The rumble of Walter's voice jarred him out of his thoughts. He looked around at the expectant faces. He thought about the *Jade Prince*. Did such an artifact really exist? Maybe. Could he really find it? Maybe. Could it be worth a lot of money? Maybe. Could it be sold? Maybe. Albro knew that any uncertainty tended to be compounded by any other. Risk was an exponential process. Eliminating any one risk didn't significantly reduce the overall odds of success. But the obverse was also true. If the risk was already astronomically high, additional risk barely counted. If you flipped a coin and it came up heads ninety-nine times, the odds were still two to one that it would come up tails on the hundredth toss.

"I can try," Albro said, knowing full well there were far too many unanswered questions to even contemplate a plan of action. He would have to go slow, and feel his way. There was no way of knowing just what these three were up to.

Walter turned to his companion. "I knew that he would help us."

"Whoa, big guy, slow down," Albro said quickly. "Don't get so excited. I said I could try, but first I need some answers."

"Yes, you deserve some answers. What would you like to know?" Brother Isaiah spoke. An obvious note of relief had come into his voice as if they had cleared a major hurdle.

"Two questions," Albro said. "Number one: Why should I believe anything the three of you say?"

"Who else can you believe?" Nancy Wong challenged.

"You would be surprised who I can ask for help," Albro said confidently thinking of Newton and his beautiful daughter. The smart thing to do, he decided, would be to call Monique first thing in the morning and arrange a meeting with her father. If anyone could get to the bottom of this, Martin Osborne Newton could. Then again, was it really worth embarrassing himself with some far-fetched tale? No, he decided. If he was going to further his relationship with Monique, he would have to come to Martin with some hard evidence.

Nancy Wong exchanged a nervous glance with her two cohorts. "You had better be certain whom you can trust," she said.

"That was my exact thought, Nancy," Albro replied.

"Miss Wong, if I may answer his question," Brother Isaiah said. "You have an item from your past. Something you have carried with you for many years. It was given to you when... how does one say it? Ah, I remember now, 'when you came of age'. I my time and place, we say 'when a child steps from his parent's shadow'. You have kept this item from all eyes including your good friend, Roger. Yes, I know about Roger. I know many things about you that would surprise you, but there is only one thing that might convince you to trust me. Miss Nancy, would you kindly supply me with a writing instrument and a scrap of paper."

Albro had a sudden sense of apprehension. Who was this rat man? How did he know about Roger? Did he have spies who had been watching him day and night? What else did he know?

Nancy Wong went to one of the kitchen drawers and came back with a magic marker and a tablet of lined paper. "I'm sorry," she said, "that's the best I can do."

"That will suffice, thank you," Brother Isaiah said. He removed the cap from the marker and made a few practice strokes and then he wrote something. He tore the page from the pad and folded it once and handed it to Albro.

Albro took the paper and opened it. What he saw startled him, but it was in no way convincing. On the page, the rat man had written the words, *the Jade Prince*. He felt a stirring in his chest and his hand unconsciously went to the gold coin under his shirt.

"That is some kind of proof?" Albro asked.

"Compare that, if you will, to what you have in your possession."

Albro hesitated and then with some reluctance, took his wallet from the inside pocket of his limp and wrinkled sports coat. He laid the wallet on the table, and awkwardly with his one good hand, carefully removed a folded piece of paper. It was the scrap of paper that Anna Marshall had given him. The years had left it fragile and it had all but come apart along the creases. He painstakingly unfolded it, and laid it next to what the rat man had written. He compared the two and felt a tingle along his spine.

"Now lay one on top of the other," the rat man said. "Hold them up to the light."

Albro did as instructed. What he saw made him swallow hard. Given the difference in the writing utensils, he saw that one over laid the other almost exactly.

"You see," said the rat man, "it was I who wrote the original. There was more to the message, but you were torn from my grasp at the last instant." From within the folds of his hassock he withdrew a small leather purse. He opened it and took from it a piece of paper. "You should find that the two ends match."

Albro read the words and then fitted the two scraps of paper. He felt a flutter in the pit of his stomach. It was the same feeling he got when he held in his hands an aged object that had miraculously found its way out of the past unscathed, or when he knew, that he held a winning hand of cards. It was a feeling that told him to step very carefully, because appearances are not always what they seem, and this time the feeling was about a thousand times more intense than usual. His breath literally caught in his throat. He didn't dare lift his hand from the two pieces of paper because he knew it would shake uncontrollably.

"Well?" Nancy Wong asked. "What does it say?"

Albro Swift's heart was pounding so hard that he didn't hear her. He just sat there staring at the words.

"Albro?" Nancy Wong asked. When she didn't get a response, she got up and came around behind him and looked over his shoulder.

The completed message read: *Protect him, for He is the One who will find the Jade Prince.*

Nancy Wong touched Albro's shoulder, and he jumped out of his chair. "Take a deep breath," she said.

Albro pulled in a shaky breath. The room was spinning, as if he were at the center of a merry-go-round.

"Another," Nancy Wong said, "and let it out slowly."

Albro breathed in.

"Do you feel sick? Do you need to get to the sink?" Nancy Wong asked.

Albio raised his hand. "I'm okay," he said weakly. He took another breath and the room slowly came to a halt. "I'm just a little dizzy."

"You jumped up from your chair too quickly, that's all," Nancy Wong said. She handed him a plastic water bottle. "Drink this, you'll feel better in a few minutes."

Albio drank down the water and waited for his mind to clear. He looked down at the message. He looked down into the dark eyes of the rat man. "What's this supposed to mean?" he asked.

"It means you are the One."

"I am the one what?"

Walter said. "You are the *One* who will find the *Jade Prince* and deliver us from the Purim. You will lead us from the desert into the land of milk and honey. It is written."

"There is something more," Isaiah said. "Before she handed you to me, your mother took from around her neck a gold medallion and placed it around your neck. On it is the emblem of a creature that no longer exists on our time, but it is a creature that stills looks down upon us from the face of the moon. The image is silver on gold, an appropriate trinket for a child, and yet you never removed it from around your neck, not even when you bathe, not even when you have joined yourself to your female companions. I'm sure they all found its luster irresistible. Can you explain to me why?"

How could the rat man possibly know what he had around his neck? Maybe the little coin with the embossed rabbit resembled something that came out of box of Cracker-Jacks, but it was some small link to his past, and he'd come to regard it as his good luck charm. For anyone who has ever placed a bet, the origin of luck and how to be favored by its whimsical disposition was one of the great mysteries of the universe. Almost every gambler of at least average competence carried a good luck charm. Usually it was an animal part; a rabbit's foot, a monkey's paw, the penis bone from a wolf, were all things he'd seen revered for their talismanic powers. Some people carried clay frogs, or a lucky penny. Almost any object you could imagine could be imbued with

263

the elusive magic that conveyed luck to its owner. For Albro though, having the gold coin close to his skin had simply been a means to focus his thoughts, like repeating a mantra.   At least that was what he'd always told himself. And sure, he'd often seen the shining disk reflected in the eyes of his lovers. In fact, Monique had taken a keen interest in it while sitting astride his hips. Albro realized that the conversation was getting off track. What business was his personal life to this rat-looking character?

"Okay," Albro said, "you know a few details about my personal life that any half-way competent person could find out. But that doesn't begin to convince me that I should believe your story.   And as far as that quip about the land of milk and honey…"

Without saying a word the rat man reached his boney fingers around his neck and tugged at a braided string. He pulled forth a gold coin seemingly identical to his own and held it out. It caught the harsh light of the gas lamp like the mesmerizing metronome of a hypnotist's pocket watch.

Albro's breath suddenly caught in his throat and he felt the floor shift under him. A momentary vision of dry, dusty hills and an ocher sky materialize before him. He stumbled forward and the little man caught him.

"Albro!" Nancy Wong called out and rushed forward.

Albro pushed himself away from the rat man. He held up his hand while his vision cleared. The hallucination must have been some symptom of withdrawal from the pain killers. He steadied himself against the armchair. "I'm all right," he said. Suddenly, his mind was extraordinarily clear.

"Take it," the rat man said. "Examine it closely."

Albro reached out a shaking hand and grasped the proffered coin. An immediate warmth coursed down his arm to his chest where his own coin hung. He looked closely at both sides of the coin. On the one side were the minute markings that he could not make out clearly, but he guessed them to be the same as his own. On the reverse side a different image was presented. It was the unmistakable figure of a rat.

"W ter," the rat man said. "Please give to him the medallion that you have."

Wal er stepped forward and retrieved the tiny object that he, too, wore benea h his robe. As Albro grasped the second coin he felt another surge of en rgy bloom inside his chest. His heart rate quickened. He could feel h s face begin to flush. A faint sensation of pins and needles was growin in his finger tips. He looked at the second coin and saw that the one sid was the same as the others, but its opposite face bore the image of an x.

"M Wong," the rat man said. "Give him the object that your grandfather gave to you."

Nar y Wong stepped to Albro and looked at him as if she were weighing th level of trust she could put in a climbing rope whose anchors she had no set herself. A look of doubt crossed her face for an instant. She then s pped her hand beneath her sweater and tossed the gold medallion in o the air. Albro caught the coin by its necklace of gold, and although he had not touched the coin, its energy ran up the gold string and conduc ed through him like an electric charge. He thought, for a moment, th t the top of his head might come off. With tremendous effort he fo used his eyes the coin and saw the feline shape of a tiger. It was then t t the coins receded down a long dark tunnel and the floor gave way b eath his feet.

Son one pushed him. Had it been on purpose? He turned to see a hulking f ure stagger away into the shadows. The air is thick with cigarette si oke and carries the heavy odor of alcohol, sweat and the sickly sweet dor of vomit. For a moment he can't remember why he has come to thi place. An odd memory of snow and darkness flashes into his mind and en he sees the stage, its lights turned low and a few silhouetted gures milling about. Suddenly he knows where he is and why he has com . He approaches the bar. The bartender is bent, washing glasses, his hin shoulders hunched over his work, his stringy hair falling into his fac but not enough to hide the long line of the man's jaw, the blunt nose.

265

"Last call was thirty minutes ago," the man says without looking up.

"I was hoping you could help me find someone," Albro says.

"You're asking the wrong joe," the bartender says with a surly edge to his rough voice. "I'm no pimp."

Albro reaches over the bar and grabs the man by the lose folds of his shirt and pulls him forward. The man is forced off balance; his feet splay out behind him. He has to plunge his hands deep into the sink in order to steady himself.

"Hey! What the fuck..."

Albro pulls the man closer and stares into his yellow eyes. "I was here last night. A woman collapsed on stage. Where did they take her?"

"How the fuck would I know that?" The man splutters and attempts to pull away, but he can't get his feet under him.

Albro grips the man harder. "Tell me her name," he says.

"Dewclaws," the man said. "Her name is Melody Dewclaws. But that's just a stage name."

Albro releases the man. He asks, "Where can I find her?"

The man stands back and swipes a hairy forearm across his face. He grins savagely. His tongue plays across his sharpened teeth like a pink snake. "Find her?" he asks with a guttural laugh. "She's gone, man. You'll never fucking find her."

Albro shuddered. An acrid smell filled his nostrils. He sneezed and looked around. He was slumped in a chair. Nancy Wong stood over him holding a small brown bottle of smelling salts.

"What happened?" he asked.

"You fainted," Nancy Wong said. "Walter caught you before you hit the floor."

Albro remembered that he had been holding the three medallions. His hand went instinctively to his chest. "Where are they?" he asked.

"The medallions?" the rat man asked. "For now, it is best that they be kept separate. They are the first four to be gathered together. After so much time apart, they are awkward, mistrustful of each other. Eventually, all twelve must come together."

"Twelve?" Albro asked. His mind was still floundering between the hazy recollections of the dream he'd fallen into. What had been the woman's name? The last part was 'Dewclaws', but he couldn't quite remember the first name. It seemed to hang at the edge of his memory like a misty ghost. And why did the name seem to be connected to something the rat man had said? It was all just too weird. As to why he had fainted his arm was hurting like hell and he was dog-tired or maybe Nancy had slipped something into his soup. He thought of how Sam Spade had fallen for the fat man's ruse of conviviality and had tossed down two drug-laced whiskeys. And then once he was out cold, that lousy kid had kicked him in the head. Albro forced himself back to the present.

"Yes the twelve sacred signs shall be gathered as foretold in the book of Aram," the rat man said.

Albro thought about the four figures on the gold coins. The rat, the ox, the tiger and his own, a rabbit and realized what they were adding up to. He said, "The other eight wouldn't be dragon, snake, horse, goat, monkey, rooster, dog and pig, would they?"

"Yes of course," the rat man said. "They are the..."

"Yeah," Albro interrupted him. "You told me, the twelve sacred signs. Look, I don't mean to question your religious beliefs. You're free to believe whatever you want, but I've never put much stock in astrology, Chinese or otherwise."

Albro thought back upon what the rat man had told him, and before that, what the walrus looking man had said. There was something else he should remember, but he couldn't quite grasp it. "Look," Albro said to the man, "I think somewhere along the way you got your wires crossed. I'm not some kind of modern day Moses. The United Nations are the people you want to talk to. They deal with all sorts of humanitarian issues. The *Jade Prince* is a myth, a story. Maybe it has a basis in fact. I don't know. Some people seem to think so. If you think it's an ancient artifact, we can talk about that."

The rat man stood up and pointed to the papers. "Look! They fit perfectly! Why do you think you have carried your half all of these years? How do you explain that?"

Albro looked again at the two scraps of paper. They looked as though they could have been joined at one time, but so what. It wouldn't be that hard to fake, he thought. As to why he'd carried around that little piece of paper all of these, he didn't know. He couldn't even verify its authenticity. He'd taken Anna Marshal's word regarding its provenance, but that was beside the point. He knew a ruse when he saw one.

"Nice trick," He said. "You almost had me convinced. When did you get a look at my half? Did Nancy pick it from my pocket while I was floundering in the snow?"

"Are you calling me a thief?" Nancy Wong asked.

"Not at all," Albro said. "You're not a thief. You're a con. You're not exactly an artist, but you show some potential. With a little more practice you might do well, but I wouldn't quit my day job just yet."

Nancy Wong threw up her hands and said to Isaiah, "I told you he wouldn't believe you."

Brother Isaiah seemed unperturbed. "As I said before, I can only speak the truth. What he chooses to believe is entirely up to him. The Mongi have a saying: 'You can offer water to a thirsty Purim and he will believe it to be poison'. For now, it does not matter. The Almighty has His plan and all shall be revealed in its own time. In the end, we all become believers. In the mean time, we must address matters at hand. You said that you had two questions. I have done my best to answer your first one."

Albro was taken aback by the rat man's cool response. He'd rolled over without a fight. Usually when someone is caught in a lie he'll try any number of ways to convince you otherwise, which made him think that either the lie wasn't worth the effort, or there was some truth in it. He had a hunch that it was a little of both. Plus, Albro sensed that the rat man was holding back something. Maybe he was telling the truth, but it wasn't the whole truth.

"It's clear I can't trust the three of you," Albro said.

Nancy Wong started to speak, but the rat man stopped her. "Let him speak," he said.

"As I was saying, I can't trust you, but that doesn't mean I can't work with you. Maybe I can help you find your *Jade Prince*, but you aren't the only ones who are after it. I've been offered a lot of money to find it."

"By whom?" Nancy Wong demanded.

"Right now, that doesn't matter. My question is if I find the *Jade Prince* for you, what's in it for me?"

"What if I tell you," the rat man said soberly, "the fate of the world hangs in the balance."

"Then I would say to you that would be worth a lot of cash."

"We have no money. Both Walter and I have taken a vow of poverty."

"What about your order, your church? Don't they have a chest full of gold, silver, precious gems?"

"No. We subsist on our small plot of land. The soil is poor. There is not enough water. Even if our Order did possess such a treasure, I cannot speak for them."

"What about Miss Wong? Lawyers make a pretty good living. Maybe there's been a family inheritance she's been sitting on."

Nancy Wong took a step forward. She said, "You are the most disgusting, despicable, degenerate..."

"Thanks, Nancy." Albro cut her off. "I'll take that as a 'no'. So, where does that leave us? I can't trust you and you're broke. That doesn't make for much of a partnership."

"You have money," Nancy Wong said. Her eyes went to Albro's bag.

"True," Albro said. That could be a start. I could begin making discreet inquiries, a thousand bucks here, a thousand bucks there. Information is never free. And if we did get a lead then there would be travel expenses, lodging. We might need trucks, equipment, and

269

protection. That hundred grand wouldn't begin to cover the costs. Unless, of course..." Albro let his voice trail off.

"Unless, of course, what?" Nancy Wong shouted.

"You know where it is," Albro said calmly.

Albro watched Nancy Wong's face. There was a glint in her eyes that hadn't been there before. She looked away and started gathering up the dishes. She took them to the sink and then filled a kettle and put it on the gas ring.

Albro said to the rat man, "Am I going to have to wait for her to finish the dishes before I get an answer?"

"We don't exactly know where the *Jade Prince* is," he answered.

"What do you mean by that?" Albro asked.

"There is a kind of map," the rat man said and looked to Nancy Wong.

"What do you mean, 'a kind of map'? Albro asked.

"Your father," Nancy Wong said, "left us a map. You would trust your father, wouldn't you?"

"Short of a DNA test, I don't think you can prove you've found my father."

"That would take weeks," Nancy Wong said.

"Well then, let me see the map," Albro said.

"We don't have it," the rat man said.

"But you know where it is," Albro said.

"Not exactly," the rat man said. "But we know how to find it."

Albro shook his head. "Why do I get the feeling that we're talking in circles?"

Nancy Wong came back to the table. She stood with her feet apart and her arms crossed. "To get the map, we have to go to Hong Kong."

"Then go get it. What are you waiting for?"

"We can't," Nancy Wong said. "Only one person can get the map."

Albro rolled his eyes to the ceiling. How long was this going to go on? "Okay," he said. "Who can get the map?"

"Yo ," Nancy Wong said. "You're the only one who can get the map. That's why your life is in such danger."

CHAPTER 22

"A MAN," Nancy Wong said, "came to me nearly a year ago. He was tall, late middle-age, thin. Actually, gaunt is a better word. He looked like someone who had just returned home from an arduous journey. He reminded me of climbers who come down from an attempt on a summit during which a member of the expedition has died. He had that hollowed-out look in his eyes that comes after witnessing tragedy and then living with it for the rest of his life. He had a vague familiarity about him and at first I thought he might have been a member of an expedition I had been on. He said his name was Thomas Crane. No one I had known."

Nancy Wong paused. She opened the iron door on the wood stove and fed in another log. Tendrils of smoke curled upward and evaporated like ghosts looking for hiding places in the cracks and crevices of the ceiling boards. They had moved from the table to a semi-circle around the wood stove. Outside, the temperature had dropped a few more degrees and the snow continued in an unrelenting effort to prevent them from ever returning to the city. Walter had joyfully plowed a path to the outhouse and they had all taken a turn on the icy seat.

Albro had agreed to at least listen to What Nancy Wong had to say. Their assertion that somehow he could provide them with a treasure map that would lead them to the *Jade Prince* was, to say the least, laughable. No, it wasn't laughable, because he hadn't laughed. It was utter and complete nonsense. Did they think he was completely naïve?

He knew every underhanded trick in the world, because either those same tricks had been used against him, or he had employed them as a means to satisfy his own ends. Few knew better than he the old adage, 'a fool and his money are soon parted', because he'd played the part of the fool too many times in his short life. And what was that story of the two monks coming from the far off future? Did they really expect him to believe that? Sure, he'd lived in L.A. for a few years, but not enough years to believe in half-human, half-animal creatures from the future. A good make-up artist could have you believing anything!

The were the worst bunch of amateur cons he'd ever seen, and he'd told them so, which had invoked another temper tantrum from Nancy. They'd had another round of name calling, which had put a real damper on the evening's festivities. Once she'd settled down, Albro had very politely asked her to tell him what she could about the man who claimed to be his father. What the hell, he thought, what else were they going to do to pass the time. Given the tense atmosphere in the little space, charades was probably out of the question. He'd let her sulk for awhile before asking again. Women could be such a pain.

"He said that he wanted to locate his son," Nancy Wong continued, "whom he had not seen since a few days after his birth, more than thirty-five years before. I advised him that there were agencies better suited for that kind of task and suggested he would undoubtedly have a better chance of success if he contacted one of them. He was adamant, though, that I be the one to help him. I told him that it might very well cost him more in the long run, and he assured me that money was no object. Rather, discretion was what he desired most. Furthermore, there could be legal problems to deal with, and he would require my advice."

Albro, who had slumped in his chair and whose eyes had begun to droop, suddenly perked up. Had he heard correctly? Had the man said that money was no object? He pushed himself up and forced himself to concentrate on what Nancy Wong was saying.

"He had no name, no hospital, and no adoption agency. Nor would he give me the name of the mother. All he had was a place and an

273

approximate date. That wasn't much to go on, but as it turned out, it was easy to pick up your trail. An afternoon in the basement of the city library scrolling through old micro-fiche newspapers was all it took. You were quite the young celebrity for a few days. I'm just curious, do you remember much about that time? I mean about the old couple and being separated from them?"

Albro shifted uncomfortably under Nancy Wong's questions. He didn't like talking about that time, let alone share he feelings about it with strangers. Remembering the old couple always brought an odd stirring in his chest. He only had the haziest of memories of them, yet he held a sense deep down that the time with them had been the only safe and secure time of his life.

"I remember a little, not much actually," he said.

"Huh," Nancy Wong said. Albro saw that she was about to comment on his terse reply, and then had decided not to. Was it because she, too, had grown up without her parents, and felt some commiseration with him? He doubted that. More likely, he suspected, she was holding back some juicy tidbit that she could use against him at a later time.

"Of course by then," Nancy Wong continued, "I knew who you were, at least it was a name I was quite familiar with, and I became even more intrigued as to why your father had chosen me, of all people, to find you. Do you recall our first meeting? My grandfather always called me by my Chinese name, Mei Ling. He was a very kind and sweet man. Do you remember how he read your future in your palm? I can still see your young face, the frightened look in your eyes, as if you'd turned a blind corner and found the bogey-man standing in your path. After that, I thought nothing more of that chance meeting, until several years later when you suddenly showed up mid-term at my school. Even then, I didn't realize the true significance of your appearances in my life. It wasn't until I was sitting there in the basement of the library that I began to see the connection. My grandfather had told me that one day a stranger would walk into my life and my life would be forever changed. I naively assumed that he was referring to a future husband who would sweep me off my feet and carry me across the threshold of marital bliss. It's funny, isn't it how we can get things so wrong.

"Anyway, when you left school you seemed to drop off the radar. Your friend Roger disappeared too. Was he with you?"

"Most of the time," Albro said.

"Where did you go?" Nancy Wong asked.

"Lots of places," Albro said.

"How did you survive? You were just teenagers."

Albro shrugged. "You learn fast when you're living on the streets. Sometimes people helped us. Sometimes we helped ourselves to what was there, if you know what I mean."

"I found your arrest records, if that's what you mean."

"I was a juvenile. You would've had to have a court order to look at those records."

"I have a friend who arranged to let me have a peek. You weren't such a bad kid. Believe me, there are far worse than you out there."

"I thought this was supposed to be about the man you say was my father," Albro said.

"Sorry, I just thought you might be interested in knowing what I found out about you. There really isn't much more. In San Diego two boys fitting your descriptions were seen walking onto sailboat that was subsequently stolen. The boat was later found caught on a reef south of Acapulco. The dinghy was missing, and so were the two boys."

"We made it to tip of Baja," Albro said.

"And then?"

"I met someone who took me under his wing," Albro said.

"That someone taught you to play cards?"

"I already knew how to play cards. He taught me how to win."

"He also got you started smuggling artifacts?"

"That was just a side line. We spent a lot of time in the resort towns. The stuff was everywhere. The jungles down there are full of that kind of stuff. The poor Indians have to make a living somehow."

"But then you went to the Far-East."

"Things got a little hot in Mexico. Besides, Asians love to gamble. Plus, they're convinced they have to save face. It's a ruinous combination. No offense to you."

"None taken," Nancy Wong said. "Gambling has never interested me. One is required to leave too much to chance. I like being in control."

"Really. I hadn't noticed," Albro retorted and was a little disappointed when she didn't take the bait. He said, "Some say that chance is what gives life its spice."

"And yet you tried to give up gambling and start your own business."

"It was just a momentary lapse of sanity. I recovered quickly," Albro said dryly.

"It seems to me more like the classic case of jumping from the frying pan back into the fire."

"Let's just say that I wasn't about to be anybody's meal."

"Do you ever wonder how you've managed to survive?"

"Yes, by living by my wits," Albro answered.

"Living by your wits," Nancy Wong repeated. "That's good. That's real good. You wouldn't have survived a day without the help of others. And have you ever noticed how many of them ended up dead?"

"What are you talking about?" Albro shifted uneasily in his chair.

"Let me refresh your memory," Nancy Wong said. "The old couple who found you? Dead. Ruth Olsen and Jackie Barnes? Dead. Sal Goldstein along with his two henchmen? Dead. And they're just the ones I found out about. I'm sure there are others."

"Are you blaming me for their deaths?"

"I'm saying they were drawn to you. They couldn't have helped themselves even if they had wanted to."

"Sal Goldstein had my arm broken. Am I supposed to feel sympathy for him? Besides, given half a chance he would have stolen your *Jade Prince*."

"Yes, I know," Nancy Wong agreed, but with no hint of concession in her voice. "He was that kind of man."

"You knew him?" Albro asked.

"We knew about him. We knew what he was capable of."

Albro thought for a moment about the last time he had seen Goldstein. He looked at Nancy and said, "The phone call that was supposed to be for me. It was you. You knew that Sal would answer it, didn't you?"

"Yes," Nancy Wong answered, not shifting her eyes.

"You knew that Sal was going to break my arm. You could have stopped him but you didn't," Albro said angrily.

"Goldstein was there. I doubt there was anything I could have said to stop him," Nancy Wong said. "Besides, we needed a diversion. They were getting close. We knew that you would be safe at a hospital."

"Who was getting close? What are you talking about?"

"Albro, there are those who have always been trying to get to you."

"And so you let Goldstein break my arm. I can't believe what I'm hearing!"

"Don't be so dramatic," Nancy Wong said unsympathetically. "This isn't some high school play. You should be thankful. You're alive and your arm will heal."

"Thanks a lot for the broken arm."

"It's better than being dead."

"Tell that to Sal Goldstein."

"His time was short. You must have sensed that."

"Yes, but..."

Nancy Wong did not allow him to finish. She said forcefully, "They died for something far greater than their own lives. They died saving you. Think about that."

Albro started to speak, but he found he had no way to respond to what Nancy Wong had just said. She'd delivered her last statement as if she were summing up the case against him to a jury of his peers. He wanted to shout 'Objection!', but he knew that he would be over-ruled. There was always more than one way to look at things. There were dozens, maybe hundreds of angles to view a given situation, and every one gave a different perspective.

After a few moments Nancy Wong said, "He tried to help, you know."

"Who?" Albro asked, pulling himself out of his thoughts. "What do you mean?"

"Your father," Nancy Wong answered. "He gave the money to Sal Goldstein who then loaned it to you."

"What are saying? That Sal Goldstein was working for you?"

"No. Sal Goldstein was never working for us. He was on his own. You brought him into your life, and he did what he had to do."

"He broke my arm!"

"He knew that he was going to die that night. Jimmy and Hoppy knew as well. They fought bravely and died saving *you*."

Albro tried thinking about it, but nothing made sense. It was like suddenly being told that hot was actually cold, and up was down, and you'd had it wrong your whole life. He thought about the grisly scene painted by the L.A. cops. His heart skipped a couple of beats. "Where's Roger?'

"He's safe. He's with Harold, your neighbor."

"Harold? He's one of your spies?"

Nancy Wong's eyes flickered toward the rat man and then back to Albro. "Albro, once we found you we couldn't afford to lose you."

"Can you at least tell me where they are?"

"I can't say."

"You can't because you don't know, or because he doesn't want you to tell me?" Albro said pointing to the rat man.

"I honestly don't know. It's been weeks since I've spoken with Harold. The plan was for Harold to take Roger somewhere to keep him out of this. We can only hope that he accomplished that. We knew that you would not want to endanger Roger. We've tried to limit any one person's knowledge of the plan to a minimum in the event that any of us were found out. Your father was the only one who knew everything. But I'm getting ahead of myself.

"As I said, once we had your name I was able to trace you through the public records to your current residence. I told your father that I would cont... ...t you and, with your permission, arrange for a DNA test and begin the p... ...erwork to establish his parentage. He asked me if he would need that t... file a will with you as his sole heir. I told him that he was free to leave his ...state to whomever he wished and that it would be the heir's responsibili... to pay the government any inheritance tax. In that case, he told me, a ...st would not be necessary. He seemed to have no doubts that you w... e his son. I had to admit, that even from the rather grainy newsprint p... otos, the resemblance was very strong.

"He... nade me swear that I would neither contact you, nor would I tell anyone about him. I informed him that I was bound to such an agreement... nly in as much as he was not involved in any illegal activities. He neither... ffirmed not denied the legality of his activities, but simply agreed to m... caveat."

"I d... not see him again for several weeks. He arrived at my office early one e... ning unannounced. I rarely work at my office in the evening and so it w... just by chance that I happened to have work that couldn't wait until m... rning. Nevertheless, I had the uncanny feeling that he knew I would be... here. He said that his presence was purely a social call and would I be... nterested in joining him for dinner. I found myself readily agreeing. H... s appearance was much improved. He wore a nice suit and the deeper... nes in his face had filled in. He looked rested and relaxed.

"It... as a very enjoyable evening. I don't get out much and it was a pleasant c... ange from my usual routines. I hadn't realized at the time, and it wasn... until the next day when I found myself scouring my mind for every detai... of our time together, that he had talked very little about himself. He... ad deftly steered the conversation around to me. It had been, if you will, a very covert interview. At the conclusion of which, he asked if I w... ld be willing to accompany him on a trip to San Francisco. It was to be a... usiness trip, he stressed, separate accommodations, and he would pay... hatever fee I felt appropriate. We were to be gone for five days at mo... . He had hired a car and would be leaving first thing in the morning.

"Bu... why not fly? I had asked him. He said there were stops along the way tha... he needed to make. That did not sound convincing to me, but I didn't press him on the matter. I think because I had already begun to suspect that he wanted to avoid drawing any attention to himself. My schedule was full, but nothing I couldn't put off for a few days. I asked him, that if this were truly a business trip, what was to be my role? He said that he wanted me to assist him with a research project. What kind of project, I asked, and he said there would be plenty of time during the drive to fill me in on the details. More importantly, he told me, he wanted a reliable witness. Of what, I asked? He said that he could not tell me, because he did not know with any real certainty himself. Then for whom, I asked? 'For my son', he answered without hesitation.

"Ordinarily, I would have dismissed such a proposal by a near total stranger. Believe me, I am not the kind of person who drops everything on the spur of the moment to go running off into the unknown, but that was exactly what I felt compelled to do. My experience as an alpine climber had taught me the necessity to plan for every conceivable problem that could possibly arise and there I was, with my mind full of questions and doubts, and knowing full well that I had already made my decision to accompany him. I admit this as a means of convincing you of the confidence I had in Thomas Crane, but also the imperative I had begun to feel. You will no doubt try to dismiss my state of mind as the infatuation of a lonely woman for a handsome man. It was nothing like that.

"That was our first trip to San Francisco's Chinatown, and we made another trip several months later. In between, we traveled to an old mining camp in Oregon, to a small and all but abandoned town in the mountains of New Mexico, and far into the interior of British Columbia, and finally to a mountain town in Idaho.

"After that..."

"Stop," Albro said, interrupting her. "Why were you going to those places? What we're you doing?"

Nancy Wong began to speak then hesitated. Albro saw her eyes glance to the rat man as if to ask permission to answer his question. The rat man's face remained passive, obviously leaving it up to her discretion to answer him.

"These were all places where Chinese immigrant laborers came to work. They cut roads through the mountains and laid rails for the steam locomotives. They built logging camps. They dug deep into the earth and hauled out the gold and silver. Many of them died from injuries and disease."

"That's interesting history, Nancy, but what were you and Crane looking for? Albro asked.

"It was the mines that Crane was interested in. Crane had a letter written in Chinese by one of the laborers to his family back in China. In the letter the man had described an incident that had occurred in a gold mine. He had not mentioned the specific location of the mine, but he had given several hints and clues. It was obvious that he had not wanted just anyone knowing its location. It took several tries before we found it in central Idaho. It was a mine that had been worked from the 1890's until 1950. They had followed of vein of gold five miles into the mountain and more than a mile deep. When the vein finally played out, the mine was closed down and the main shaft was sealed. But mines from that era often had auxiliary shafts. We went around to the nearest towns and asked the locals if there was anyone left who might know something about the early days of the mine. No one could tell us much other than that the mine had been plagued with a history of cave-ins. The cost of extracting the precious metal had been heavy in terms of lives lost. We were about to give up when someone suggested we check at the veterans home in Spokane.

We found someone whose father had been a supervisor in that same mine. Not only did he remember an incident about a group of Chinese laborers who had been buried when a side shaft had collapsed, he had a newspaper clipping describing the event, dated June 21, 1907. The mine owners had made the decision not to dig them out and so that part of the mine had remained forever closed off. But a curious thing happened. His father made a trip to a neighboring town. There, he saw one of the Chinese who was presumed to have died in the cave-in. His father knew immediately what that meant. There had to be a way out of that side shaft, and at least one of those Chinese laborers had escaped

281

death. But why had he not told anyone? In his father's mind, there could be only one answer. The Chinese laborer had discovered a new vein of gold and would eventually return to it.

"His father began watching the man who had taken employment in a laundry. He became obsessed with the man's movements. After several months, the Chinese laborer made his move. His father followed the man who was heavily laden with ropes and tools deep into the mountains. After days of trekking, he watched as the Chinese laborer literally disappeared. He had been standing looking at the ground, and then in the blink of an eye, he was gone.

"His father, who had been observing from across a deep gully, rushed forward only to find the space previously occupied by the Chinaman was completely empty. He had followed the man's passage up the loose scree of the slope onto a smooth granite outcrop. He searched in vain for hours and was about to give up when he saw the rope cleverly hidden beneath fresh cut branches and the opening in the rock that had been likewise disguised. He cleared away the debris and examined the small, irregular shaped hole that was barely large enough for a small boy to squeeze through. He peered down into it and thought for an instant that he saw a flicker of light, a miner's lamp, perhaps, and then nothing but blackness. He could enlarge the hole with dynamite, but he'd brought none. Besides, that might cause the shaft to collapse. Nor had he brought adequate supplies for an extended trip. He could not sit and wait for the Chinaman to emerge. He had eaten his last dry biscuit the day before. The only recourse was to disguise the site, as the Chinaman had done, and return another day."

Nancy Wong paused and looked at Albro. "The man we spoke to in that nursing home was very old. I have never been in the presence of such an aged individual. The nurse who brought us to his room informed us that he was one hundred and twelve years old. She must have seen the doubt in my eyes, because she showed us the man's birth certificate. The man was bedridden, but alert. As the story flowed out of him though, he seemed to diminish in size, to shrink back against the pillows, as if the only thing that was keeping him alive was the need to tell us this tale."

Albro stifled a yawn. "This is all very interesting Nancy, but I don't see what this has to do with anything."

"If you don't want to hear the rest, take your bag of money and leave. You're free to go," Nancy Wong said curtly and flicked her head sharply toward the door.

Albro thought of the blizzard raging outside and sighed audibly. He resisted the urge to roll his eyes, and slumped down farther into his chair. "I'm all ears," he said.

Nancy Wong paused for a long moment to get her feelings under control. Then she continued, "The man told us how his father had returned home in an agitated state. A heated argument erupted between his father and his mother. The man we spoke to was only seven years old at the time, but he remembered the wild, fevered glow in his father's eyes. His father loaded a pack with lamps and ropes and food, and then, taking his son in tow, returned to the place where he had seen the Chinese laborer disappear into the ground.

"They walked all that day and well into the long summer evening. The boy had never gone so far into the mountains. That night while sitting at a campfire he told us how his father told him that they would soon be rich beyond their wildest dreams. At daybreak, they journeyed on until at last they came to the hidden opening in the mountain. They pulled up the rope left by the Chinaman. His father fashioned a harness and then instructed his son on how to use the headlamp he strapped around the boy's head. He told the boy how the gold might appear as luminous slivers in snowy veins of quartz, or how it might sparkle like fairy dust scattered on the face of the dark granite. Above all, he was not to be afraid. After reaching the bottom and having a look around, his father would haul him out. His father had made it sound as if a descent into a crack in the earth was no more dangerous than excursion to the city park. He told us how his father kissed him on the head and then lowered him into the shaft.

"The father eased his son down until he felt the taught rope go slack. He felt one tug and then nothing more. He pulled on the rope and it rose loosely. He shouted down into the dark hole for his son, but there

283

was no answer. By his reckoning, he had paid out more than a thousand feet of rope, and knew that his son could not hear his shouts, nevertheless he continued calling until he grew hoarse.   Panic seized him and he began attacking the solid granite around the opening with a heavy steel pick. Sparks flew until the steel shattered. He battered the stone with a sledge-hammer until he had no strength left in his arms and still the solid rock only yielded thin fragments. For all of his effort he had not succeeded in enlarging the opening.

"The father sat through the night, half-mad with fear that his only child lay injured somewhere in the dark. At first light, he knew that he would have to go for help. He knew that to save his son, he would have to give up his dream of wealth.

"His father ran home never stopping for rest. Nearly at the point of exhaustion, he burst through the door of their home. There, he found his wife sitting with an old man with long white hair and beard before the hearth. Ignoring the old man, he fell on his knees and confessed to his wife what he had done to their son and how they must organize a rescue team immediately.

"His wife gave him a cold stare and then informed him that their son was not lost, that he had walked into the house early that morning, that he was sitting right there with them."

"Hold on, Nancy," Albro said. "You're telling me that old man is actually their seven year old son?"

"Yes," Nancy Wong said.

"But..."

"I know what you're thinking. The same thoughts went through my head when I heard this story. How could a seven year old boy become an old man in a single night?   And furthermore, if he were already an old man in 1907, how could he still be alive in 2012? The fact is, that boy died in 1936."

"Nancy, facts get mixed up and twisted over time, especially with old people. Don't tell me you believed him," Albro said.

"We found the grave marker with the son's name on it. Yes, the man had twisted the truth. It was the only way that he could live all of those years knowing what he had done to his son. We had, in fact, been listening to the father. The nurse had shown us his birth certificate. His son had told him to tell no one about that entrance into the earth and that he was to never go there, yet he was to never forget its location," Nancy Wong said, her voice rising, and her little hands clenched into fists.

"Okay, okay," Albro said. "Take it easy. So you figured out that the old geezer was not the son, but was actually the father."

"Yes, and he told us where to find the hidden entrance to the mine because that was other part of his son's instructions, that someday two strangers, an older man with long white hair and a younger Chinese woman, would arrive and ask about that place, and it would be imperative that they be told of its location."

"And you went there," Albro said obligingly. It was a crack-pot story, Albro knew, but he'd decided the best policy was to play along. If he let Nancy Wong ramble on, maybe she would wind down and he could talk some sense into her.

"Yes," Nancy Wong said, taking a deep breath. "He drew us a map. It was crude, but accurate enough that we found the place without too much difficulty. It was just as he had described. We could still see the marks in the granite where he had attempted to enlarge the hole. A large coil of rotted hemp rope lay at the base of a tree.

"I could fit into the opening, but Crane could not. We determined that the shaft expanded just below the surface. Crane had brought along explosives which he placed around the opening. He worked as if he had done that sort of thing before. The explosion was actually quite small, but it served the purpose of creating an opening large enough for either of us to enter.

"I had never gone into a cave, but Thomas Crane was well experienced. My skills as a climber translated well for the purpose of descent. We had brought along ropes and harnesses and battery powered lights. It was the absolute darkness and the fear that our lights would fail that was most difficult to bear. The descent took hours as we worked our way from one ledge to another until eventually we reached the bottom. By my reckoning we had descended over a thousand feet.

285

We dropped into an immense chamber. If not for our ropes, it would have been possible, but by no means easy to descend. Therefore, we concluded it had been possible for someone to climb out of there

"We explored the chamber and found that one end had been blocked by a rock fall. We found a lone, skeletal hand reaching out from under the rock. Had we found the final resting place of those lost Chinese laborers? We couldn't say, but it was easy to imagine them running through the darkness and being buried an instant before they might have escaped. All but one, that is. One of them must have been a step ahead of the others. We found two sets of footprints on the sandy floor. Presumably one set belonged to the lone survivor of the work gang and the other, much smaller was that of the boy who had been lowered down by his father. We followed their tracks to a low opening that was just large enough for us to squeeze through. With no space to turn around, we pushed ourselves forward on our stomachs, shoving our packs ahead of us for what seemed like hours. At one point, I nearly lost it. Crane was somewhere ahead of me when my light faltered. Have you ever experienced claustrophobia in total darkness? I literally felt the rock pushing down on me. I panicked and began screaming. Fortunately, Crane heard my cries. He talked to me and calmed me down and we were able to proceed.

"Finally, the walls began to recede and we were able to crawl on our hands and knees and then to walk. The tracks were there, one set smaller and smooth, and the other larger with a deeper imprint. What we could not understand, though, was why they pointed in only one direction. Neither of them had returned along that route."

"All right, so there must have been another way out," Albro said.

"Yes, but not one that you would imagine. We attempted to keep track of our position, but our compass refused to hold steady. It would point in one direction and then slowly rotate to another. All we could do was to follow the path that seemed to be leading us deeper into the mountain. We came at last to what we thought was another chamber, larger than the one we had descended into, much larger. Our lights could not penetrate to the surrounding walls. Their beams were simply swallowed by the darkness. We saw flecks of what we thought were some kind of bioluminescence. We did not realize what we were looking at until we switched off our lights. As our eyes adjusted to the darkness, those flecks of light became stars, a whole night sky filled with stars."

"So," Albro said, "you found another way out."

"Yes," Nancy Wong answered. "We had found another way out, but not to the outside world where we had been a few hours earlier. We had descended a mile deep, and maybe five miles into the mountain, and we had found what Thomas Crane had been looking for. We could feel a light breeze and smell the fragrance of dried grass. The stars gave enough light for us to make out the shapes of hills in the distance, and behind them we could see a domed glow, the kind a sizeable city creates."

"What did you do?" Albro asked.

"We did the only thing that seemed reasonable at the time. We waited for the sunrise. I rested, but I couldn't sleep. I spent the hours lying on my back studying the stars. My grandfather had taught me the constellations when I was a child. He had told me something that had always been puzzling to me until then. He had said that if I ever doubted my place in the universe I need only look up into the night sky and in those stars I would get my bearings. The patterns of these stars were subtly different. I could make out the familiar outlines that I had always known, but they were elongated in some instances and contracted in others. I mentioned this to Crane who lay silent for a long time before answering. I had thought that maybe he had fallen asleep. He said that we had come a relatively short distance, but we had traveled a vast amount of time. He then asked that I forgive him, for there would be no retracing our steps. The only way back would be to move forward.

"It was true. When dawn came, we found our backs to a solid wall of rock."

Albro smiled and shook his head. "You found yourself in the future and the only way home was to go forward? Nancy you're not making any sense."

"Just hear me out."

"Sure, Nancy, but I don't see the point," Albro said.

"You will, just listen. I'm almost finished." Nancy Wong paused and collected her thoughts. "When dawn came, we crossed to the east into the rising sun and threaded our way through a pass in the distant hills. We came to a point where we could look out to a dry valley that was enclosed by another range of mountains farther east and stretched both north and south for as far as one could see. In the center of this valley was a vast, modern city surrounded by a black wall. I could make out the shapes of tall buildings that reflected the sunlight off glass walls. I could see lakes and rivers and green forests and farmlands. Outside the walls I could see elevated highways leading away from the city like the spokes of a great wheel, and below the highways the scene could not have been more different. A dusty brown ring, miles deep surrounded the black walls like a ring of filth left by a dried up pond. At first, I did not know what I was seeing and then the truth dawned on me that I was looking at city of vastly greater proportions than the walled entity, teeming with millions of lives.

"We descended a winding path and by nightfall we approached the first mud houses. Thomas Crane spoke with the resident of one of those houses and arranged for us to sleep in a barn-like structure. The following day we avoided the main highways and walked along dusty, rutted tracks. We had lost sight of the distant wall in the way that one loses sight of a mountain the closer one approaches, and then as we crested a low rise it was there, a giant monolith, as oppressive as it was black.

"It was not until mid-afternoon that we reached the outskirts of the slums. I say slums because that is the only word I have to describe the conditions. One might have called it a ghetto, but it lacked the organization that is typical of a ghetto. The streets were chaotic, twisting and turning back on themselves, or ending abruptly at the base of the wall. The streets were dirt and in places open sewers ran between the crumbling houses. The stench was terrible. Above all else, it was the wall, rising above us like an ever present shadow that seemed to define the place. From a distance it had appeared smooth, as devoid of features as polished granite. But when we came close, I saw that the wall had slight undulations in its surface, and when I touched it, I found that it was not hard and smooth. It had a texture like shark's skin and I felt it move beneath my fingers. Crane must have seen the shock in my face, because he then explained that it was safe to touch the wall, but to leave one's hand on its surface for too long would result in being consumed by it. It was alive, but slow moving, like a coral reef and thousands of years old.

"And then there were the people who crowded the streets. This place was the city of the Mongi. I have to admit, that like you I was shocked when I first saw them, but they were kind and helpful to us. Perhaps it was because everyone seemed to know Crane, but I had the distinct feeling that they would have treated us the same had we been complete strangers. They guided Crane where he needed to go, and to help him find whom he was looking for.

"This place, Albro...," Here Nancy Wong paused and closed her eyes as if to recall the place as vividly as she might. "They called this place *The City of Rain*. At the time, I did not understand. It looked as if it had been centuries since rain had fallen."

Albro, who had begun to feel the effects of the hot meal and the warmth of the fire and had begun to drift off into a state of waking sleep, suddenly sat up straight. Either Nancy Wong had not noticed his startled response, or she had been expecting it. She did not register his reaction on her face, and continued speaking.

"They led us through what can only be described as a labyrinth of streets. I soon became completely lost. One street looked the same as another. Soon, I could not distinguish one mud hovel from the next. We came to a wooden door that led us into a courtyard that was surprisingly beautiful. There was a small fountain and flowers growing in small pots. We crossed directly to another door and were let into the house. It was there that I met Isaiah and Walter. Also present were the Chinese laborer and the boy whom Crane had been seeking.

"I know that what I am about to tell you will be difficult for you to understand, but you must trust me. They were the ones we had followed out of the mine. I know what you are thinking. How could we possibly be in the company of someone who had died more than seventy-five years ago? What I learned then is that time is the creator of all and the destroyer of all. Crane had to get the two of them back to their own time, otherwise everything would change. Had he not been successful we would not be here at this moment, because I would not be here. Albro, the Chinese laborer that I speak of is the same man that my grandfather told you about, the one who came to America and made his fortune. He was my great grandfather. If he had become stranded out there in the future, he would never have been recognized as having survived the cave-in, and he would never have piqued the curiosity of that inquisitive miner and we would never have been lead to the location of that hidden entry into the mine. I would never have been born. I hope this helps you see how the future governs the past, and shapes the present.

"How were they returned? The Mongi have a rare and powerful gift. They are able to minutely change the shape of reality. The shift is so small as to be imperceptible, but over time its effect becomes magnified. You have no doubt heard of the 'Butterfly Effect'—how the single flap of a butterfly's wing can produce a hurricane half-way around the world. Now imagine an incident of magnitudes less in its initial force and resulting in an outcome many orders of magnitude greater at its outcome. To compensate for that change, time itself will shift in order to maintain the balance between the future and the past. Otherwise, the entire universe would collapse upon itself. That is how the two men were returned to their time and I and Thomas Crane, along with Isaiah and Walter, to this time.

"But, there was a price to be paid. Someone had to assume the accumulation of years, absorb the wrinkle in the fabric of space-time, as Thomas Crane described it. He was a sweet boy, innocent of all he had stumbled into. But the universe cares nothing about innocence. It only cares about its damned balance, its own fucking tranquility. The boy paid the price for all of us, and for all I know, continues to do so in some pinched-off bubble of time.

"After that, I didn't see Crane for more than six months. I was awakened late one night by a pounding at my door. It was him. His clothes were torn and blood-soaked. He had suffered several deep wounds. He remained conscious long enough to order me not to call for help. I did what I could to stop the bleeding, but he was dying before my eyes. I knew of someone, a Doctor Yuan, who had been a physician in China and still worked at treating the old people who do not believe in modern medicine. Auntie Lo gave her two small rooms, a place to live and see her patients. I called Auntie Lo and an hour later the three of us started work on him. We needed to cut away his clothes, and I nearly fainted at the sight. Auntie Lo pulled me away and told me there was blood outside my door and along the covered walkway and told me to go wash it away. 'Quickly', she said, and pushed me toward the door.

"As I knelt with my scrub brush, I was thankful I had been given the mundane task. I could wash away blood, but I could never wash away the sight of his body. Thankfully it was raining hard so whatever trail of blood he had left in the street would be washed away by the time daylight brought people out of their homes. I stood for a few moments and let the cold rain hit me in the face before I returned back inside. Auntie Lo and Doctor Yuan had bound his wounds and had washed the blood from his body. We carried him into the guest room and laid him on the bed. He had lost a great deal of blood, and his face was as white as the sheets. His breathing was shallow. He belonged in the intensive care of a hospital, but that was impossible.

"Doctor Yuan left a bottle of dark medicine from which, if he regained consciousness, he must drink. If he survived the next few hours, then perhaps, he would live. I pulled a chair next to him and sat. Sometime around dawn, I must have drifted off. When I awoke, he was gone. I ran into the street, but there was no sign of him. The bottle of medicine lay in the grass, empty. I was frantic. I drove around in circles looking for him. It should have been impossible for him to even walk. I was certain that he could not have gone far. It was soon going to be light.

"I drove to Auntie Lo's noodle factory to get help. There was a crowd in the alley. I could hear sirens approaching. I pushed my way through. Someone had found a blanket to cover him. I knelt beside him and he opened his eyes. I told him that an ambulance was on its way. He moved his eyes in such a way that told me to go. When I didn't leave, he moved his lips. I leaned close. The sirens were now only a block away. He whispered to me and then he died."

Nancy Wong paused. She stared into her folded hands for a long moment, and when she looked up at Albro there were tears in her eyes. "What he said was for you. He asked that you would forgive him."

"Forgive him for what? I never knew him," Albro said.

"He spoke once of his regret for having abandoned you. He said that he wished there had been some other way."

"Once," Albro said.

"He wasn't the kind of man to dwell on things he could not change. Besides, I think he was referring to something else in his request for forgiveness. I think he was asking that you forgive him for what was yet to happen."

"As if he knew the future," Albro said flippantly.

"As if events had been set in motion by a future that neither he, nor anyone, could change," Nancy Wong said.

CHAPTER 23

"IT'S nothing more than a fable, a legend, a myth!" Albro Swift said. He was pacing the short space of open floor of the tiny cabin, and waving the worn paperback that had been given to him by the cab driver. Once again, the truce between him and Nancy Wong had degenerated to a shouting match. His hair had fallen into his eyes and he looked like a disheveled sidewalk preacher haranguing three passersby who had momentarily stopped to listen. Nancy Wong's description of Thomas Crane had served only to create more questions and doubts in Albro's mind. Who killed Crane? They didn't know. Why was he killed? They could only guess. What was Crane's plan? None of them knew beyond getting to Hong Kong and finding the map. How were they getting to Hong Kong? They didn't know, or they weren't telling. When he'd asked about Marlowe, they'd suddenly clammed up.

"The *Jade Prince* is nothing more than a fairy tale!" Albro said again and tossed the book into the open door of the wood stove.

"Your father brought that for you! It's your book! You wrote it!" Nancy Wong shouted at him. "It was to help you understand!"

"I've never written a book," Albro said. "Can't you get that through your head?" The argument had erupted when Albro had laughed in Nancy Wong's face over the verity of her story of time travel to the land of the Mongi. Albro had then taken the book from his bag and demanded an explanation for its existence.

"Not yet, you haven't," Nancy Wong said.

293

"If I've yet to write it, then I haven't written it!" Albro said.

"You're twisting my words," Nancy Wong said.

"I'm twisting words? None of what anything you have said has made any sense. You've got the wrong guy, Nancy. I've got a life to live."

"Your father believed the *Jade Prince* to be more important than his life," Nancy Wong said.

Albro shook his head. "I wish you wouldn't refer to that man as my father."

"But he was!" Nancy Wong insisted.

"You have no proof. So what if he knew where and when I had been abandoned. As you said, it was public knowledge."

"You look like him, only younger."

"Okay, show me his picture."

"I don't have one."

"Great. How about *his* public record? Driver's license? Social Security number? Birth certificate? Tell me, if you can, just who was this Thomas Crane? The mysterious Marlowe, whom everyone seems to know but no one wants to talk about, claims that Thomas Crane went to Oxford. Did you check there? I imagine they keep pretty good tabs on their graduates."

Nancy Wong sat silently in her chair with her chin raised in a defiant pose. Then she dropped her eyes. When she spoke, it was with an uncharacteristic meekness. "There is no record of Thomas Crane. I did a very thorough search."

"Well now, the truth finally comes out. Just to show you that I'm willing to give you the benefit of the doubt, let's go to your home tomorrow. From the way you described it, there must be a blood stain somewhere. We can run a DNA test."

"There was no trace of him," Nancy Wong said, her eyes downcast.

Albro asked, "And then later, when they came and tore the place apart, what were they looking for?"

"I don't know."

"All right, let's visit the city morgue. You can identify the body. Tell them you're Crane's lawyer and you require a DNA sample."

"I told you, there isn't time. Besides, it's too dangerous."

"Okay Nancy, do you want to know what I think? I think the simple answer is that Thomas Crane was mixed up with a bad crowd. You knew nothing about him. He was someone who finally paid some attention to you and you fell for him and you bonked your pretty little head on the way down."

If Albro Swift had blinked, he would have not seen her leap from the chair. As it was, he saw her fly at him, more cat than human, but he missed the blur of movement from his left. Somehow, Walter had intercepted Nancy Wong, and carried her kicking and screaming, and placed her gently on the top bunk.

"Thanks, Wally. For a big guy, you're pretty fast on your feet." Albro paused. He looked at Nancy Wong. Her nostrils flared and she was breathing hard and her eyes were focused on his. She seemed totally oblivious that Walter was patting her lightly on her shoulder as if to calm an angry child.

"As I was saying, maybe you've been the victim of an elaborate shakedown. Someone set you up and then pulled the rug out from under you. I can only guess what they were after, your bank account, client information? You'll probably find out as soon as you get back into town. Let the cops investigate who's behind this. Right now, you're in shock and imagining all sorts of terrible things."

"Don't patronize me."

"Okay, that was a cheap shot. I apologize. Now you apologize to me."

"For what?" The question came out of Nancy Wong's mouth in a low, guttural snarl that made even Walter's calm demeanor falter for a moment.

"For leading me," Albro said levelly, "to believe that you had found my father when you had absolutely no evidence. You risked my life bringing me here. I have pretty good grounds to charge you with fraud and abduction. Plus, you've cost me a lot of money. Just look at my suit, it's ruined. And my shoes! They're Italian leather! I could file major claims against you. As a lawyer, you should know that."

"If money is what you're worried about, I'll cover your expenses and compensate you for any inconvenience I've caused you. I'm sure you're anxious to get back to your affair with Ms Newton." Nancy Wong's snarl had moderated to cold contempt.

"What business is that of yours?"

Nancy Wong said, "You probably think she's still waiting for you at your hotel."

"How did you know she would be there?" He pulled his phone from his pocket.

"Don't bother. There's no coverage here. I listened to your messages as I drove. You were sleeping. 'Albro, where are you? I'm in your room. Call me right now.'" Nancy Wong mimicked Monique's voice. "She sounded disappointed in you. You shouldn't run out on women like Monique Olivia Newton. Women like her have ways of punishing men who behave badly. I also checked your call log. You placed fourteen calls to her in the last two days. They all went unanswered. Doesn't that tell you something?"

"She's very busy."

"I'm sure that she is, but she must have a phone with her at all times. Perhaps, she doesn't want to be interrupted."

"What's that supposed to mean?"

"Maybe you're not high on her list of priorities."

True, it was something that had been bothering him. Was that the real reason he'd decided to meet with Nancy Wong, a kind of lover's tit-for-tat? No, there had been that outside chance that he would find out something about his father. He knew that Monique would understand when he had a chance to explain everything to her. "Monique and I are very serious," Albro said.

"Give me a break!" Nancy Wong said. "Do you know how ridiculous that sounds coming out of your mouth? If you would start thinking with your brain instead of your dick you might realize the trouble you've gotten yourself into."

"If I may interrupt," said the rat man. "Walter, please return Miss Wong to the floor."

Walter lifted Nancy Wong and set her back on the floor.

"Thank you, Walter," she said.

"I didn't hurt you, did I, Miss Nancy?"

"No, you were very gentle," she assured him.

"It's my job to protect Mister Albro. His father saved my life. He saved Izzy's life, too. That was my fault. I wasn't careful. We swore that we would protect Mr. Thomas. We tried so hard, but we failed him. We can't fail Mister Albro. We just can't."

"I know, Walter. I know." She stood on her tip toes and kissed the tip of his chin. "I wasn't going to hurt him. I just wanted to teach him some manners." She shot Albro an intense glare and then returned to her chair next to the stove.

"Mr. Swift," said the rat man, "forgive me. I know that it is late, and although the night is long, time is short. Daylight is not far away. There is still much to tell you and we must also rest. I admit that we have no evidence to prove beyond a shadow of doubt that Thomas Crane was your father. He was certain of it and I had no reason to question his word. I think he realized the he could never be a genuine father to you. The time for that has passed, and so I will henceforth refer to him by his name only.

"Thomas Crane had one purpose, and that was to recover the *Jade Prince*. I say recover, because at one time it had been in his possession. Once he recovered it, he would return it to the Mongi. With it, the Mongi have a chance for survival, and therefore the world may go on. You notice I do not say 'my world', or 'your world'. Such distinctions are meaningless. Each moment that we experience is connected to all other moments by an infinite number of threads. Your life, my life, every motion of every object are spun together and joined by more threads and woven into a fabric that is all time, all things; past, present and future are all of one piece. If the *Jade Prince* should fall into the hands of anyone other than the Mongi, the world will be subject to a fate beyond comprehension. Time is the sacred garment that clothes the body of all

297

existence. The *Jade Prince* gives one the power to not only touch the fabric of existence, but to reshape it, rend it, even destroy it entirely.

"Do you know that the skin is the most sensitive part of the body? The skin is our intimate connection to the world and at the same time, it protects us from it. It is the wall that forms the sacred vessel that is the body, and on it is written the story of our lives. Look at the palms your hands. The lines tell a story, your story. Those lines are the ends of the threads that bind you to all things.

"Do you believe in destiny, the preordained course of events that one is powerless to alter? I once thought that I, and only I, determined my fate. Why? Because I believed that the past formed the future. In reality it is just as easy to believe that the future determines the past. Whatever happens in this moment has been determined by events in its future. You, Albro Marshal Swift, owe your existence to what has already happened in a place and time far, far from here. And everything in that far off time owes its existence to you. You *will* help us find the *Jade Prince* and return it to the Mongi. It has already been written."

He took the iron poker and opened the wood stove. He shielded his face from the intense heat of the coals. He probed with the poker and then pulled out the book onto the stone hearth. A few coals came with it. The rat man brushed them back toward the opening. He picked up the book and blew off a rime of ashes. It appeared to be totally unburned. He held it out to Albro, who shrank back not believing what he was seeing.

"Take it," the rat man said. "It's barely warm."

Albro took it and riffled the pages. He smelled it. It didn't smell of smoke. It had the funky smell of an old paper-back that might have sat in a used bookstore for years. He looked at the rat man.

"You're wondering why it did not burn," the rat man said.

"It must be some kind of special fire-proof material," Albro said.

The rat man smiled and shook his head. "No, it is ordinary paper. It didn't burn because it is not of this time. It doesn't exist here in the same way the fire exists. Therefore it cannot be destroyed by fire. Are you beginning to understand?"

"No, I can't say that I am," Albro said. He thought for a moment. "You say this book is from the future. You also said that you and Walter are from the future. Let me see you put your hand in the fire."

"Don't!" Nancy Wong cried.

The rat man's face became blank and he thrust his hand into the flames. There came an instant crackling as the hair on his hand singed into stinking curls.

"Hey!" Albro shouted. He grabbed the little man by the shoulders and pulled him away from the stove.

The hair on the rat man's hand had shrunk into tiny black specks. The room stank with the acrid smell of burnt hair. Nancy rushed outside and brought back a handful of snow and wrapped it around Isaiah's scorched hand.

"Look what you've done," she said scornfully to Albro, "as if we didn't have enough trouble!"

"I didn't do anything," Albro said. "He said he wouldn't burn."

"He said nothing of the sort!"

"But..." Albro said.

"I am not harmed," Brother Isaiah said. "I am only missing a little hair." A puddle had begun to form at his feet. He walked to the sink and brushed off the snow. "It is my fault. I should have explained. Living matter operates by a slightly different set of rules. For all living things, there is always a beginning and an end. I am afraid that Walter and I are as much in this time as both you and Miss Wong. As you can see, my garment suffered no damage. As for me, I can only thank you for pulling me from the fire."

"But why did you do it if you knew you would be burned?" Albro asked.

"Thomas Crane saved my life and Walter's life. That is a long story, and when there is time, I will tell it to you. For that one act alone, we were beholden to whatever he asked of us. When we learned that he was searching for the *Jade Prince*, as were Walter and I, I knew that it was no coincident that we had met. We had been drawn together by the same force that brought us here. As I said before, you are that force. You are the *One*. I can no more disobey your requests than I can stop breathing. The same is true for Walter."

"So if I told you and your partner to go back from where you came from, you would do it?" Albro asked.

"I think that you will not ask that."

"You don't know me."

"Ah, but I do. And so does your bride to be. She knows that you will try to find the *Jade Prince*, and when you do, she will attempt to take it from you. And although we will try everything within our power to help you, we will fail. You will cry out for your mother to help you. In the end it will be up to you and you alone."

CHAPTER 24

ALBRO had thought it was going to be an easy matter to fall asleep. He had rolled into a lower bunk and had listened to each of the others as their breathing fell into slow, deep rhythms. After an hour of tossing back and forth, he had climbed out with his blankets and had huddled in a chair next to the stove. The fire had died and the room had begun to feel like a freezer. It was a small comfort he told himself, that sometime later in the day he would be back in Los Angeles with his beloved Monique. He had dismissed the rat man's comment out of hand. The idea that Monique could be involved in this was ludicrous. Nancy Wong, though, had stung him with her question about why Monique had taken so long to return his calls. The important thing was that she *had* returned his calls. She'd done more than that. She'd come looking for him. He'd soon be back to his own life and far away from Nancy Wong and her fantasies. This was going to make a great story for Roger: a stranger suddenly appearing and claiming to be his father; a couple of religious fanatics who looked to be escapees from a circus; a strong-willed, yet alluring oriental beauty tempting him to enter her web of deceit; time travel, an ancient artifact, the end of the world…. Roger would love it, but…

As much as he disbelieved everything they had told him, there was a part of him that wanted to believe it. It was like being seven years old and trying not to believe in Santa Clause. There was some part of the brain that refused to be rational. On top of that, the rat man had played his trump card, the one he'd held back until the end, and it had taken him completely by surprise. The rat man had implied that his mother was alive. Albro had always believed her to be dead, that she had died giving birth to him. What puzzled him was that there had never been a reason to believe so, but it had been as natural as believing in his father's existence. He'd tried to remember, tried to picture her, tried to reach back into that fathomless void. Once, he'd even gone so far as to participate in a rebirthing ceremony. He'd paid some big bucks to climb into an inflatable pool and splash around naked between the hairy legs of a fat woman and then get slapped on his backside. The stinging blow was supposed to light up long forgotten memory cells that had lain dormant since day one. His mother was supposed to appear in an aura of rarefied light supplied by a couple of 500 watt flood lamps. He'd seen green spots for days afterward, but not a glimmer of his mom.

After the rat man had mentioned his mother, he'd effectively dodged every question that Albro had put to him. If his mother was alive, where was she? The rat-man didn't know precisely. Had she married his father? The question had never come up. Did she have other children? That was entirely possible. Had he met her? Yes, he had, but only briefly, in the moment that she had passed him into the rat man's hands. etc., etc... So much for blind loyalty, Albro thought. The rat man would stick his hand in fire, but wouldn't give a straight answer. He said that she was dark haired with beautiful eyes. That was nice. There were probably only a few millions of women fitting that description. He had asked the rat man what he'd meant when he'd said that she had passed him into his hands. Had his father been there at that time? It had been the only way to save him, the rat man had said, and yes, his father had been present, but it was a story too long to tell. It would have to wait. They needed to rest. The rat man did have her name. It was Melody, and the name had struck Albro like a hammer blow between the eyes. He had literally staggered as the memory of the bartender's grotesque face came back to him. After that, the little rat man had said nothing more. And now, in dire need of sleep, but unable to stop his mind from thinking, he wondered why the name was stuck so firmly in his memory.

He looked down and saw the paperback book lying on the floor next to the hearth. Yes, that's where he had seen the name. He reached for the book and then fed a few branches into the fire to give him light. He opened the book and began to read.

At last I fell asleep and dreamed that I was with Monique, snuggling under a fluffy down comforter. It was like being under the dome of tent with soft, white light all around. I need to tell Monique something, but every time I try to speak, she presses her lips against mine, and twists her torso in such a way as to make me gasp for breath. She is astride me and has my shoulders pinned and the more I struggle to raise myself, the harder she pushes down upon me, her lips are welded to mine, her teeth grinding against mine, and her breath sucking the life out of me.

Albro woke with a gasp, flailing wildly against the tangle of blankets. A blinding white light stabbed him in the eyes, and he shut them tightly wishing for Monique's warm embrace and throaty laughter, but she had vanished. He sat up and shivered in the freezing air. The door to the cabin stood open. The light of dawn poured in along with a freezing gust of wind. Ice crystals floated in the air, dazzling his sleep swollen eyes. He pulled himself out of the chair, stiff and achy, and made his way to the door. Deep tracks led away and disappeared into the trees. In a moment of panic, he looked around the room for his bag. He found it beneath his chair he'd slept in. He dragged it forth and knelt to open it.

"No one's touched it, but count it if it makes you feel better."

Albro swung around. Nancy Wong was standing in the doorway brushing off snow from her leggings.

"I trust you," Albro said.

"Since when?" Nancy Wong asked without looking at him as she bent and adjusted the straps on her snowshoes.

"Look, about last night…"

"Don't say it. We've dug out the truck and we're going back to the city. I'll drop you at your hotel. I'm sure you'll want to freshen up before catching a flight home."

"What will you do then?"

"Do?"

303

"I mean you and Isaiah and Walter."

"I don't know. I haven't gotten that far yet. Come on, the break in the weather isn't going to last. If we're going to get out, we need to leave now."

"I'm in a position to help you. I could ask Martin Osborn Newton to find out who Thomas Crane really was."

Nancy Wong put her fist to her forehead. "You really are innocent, aren't you? Yes, ask him about Thomas Crane. And then ask your sweet Monique about him."

"What do you mean?"

"We haven't time for another argument. Besides, it's all in my imagination, remember? Come on, we're leaving."

"Did you make coffee?" Albro asked, but Nancy Wong had turned her back and pretended not to hear. What was the big hurry? He looked around. The place was a mess. Wasn't she going to tidy up a bit before leaving? He shrugged. It was fine by him to get back into town as soon as possible. He pocketed his phone and grabbed his bag.

Albro managed to follow Nancy Wong back to the truck without falling. The path had been packed solid by several trips while he'd slept. He stepped carefully trying to keep the snow out of his shoes. The air was very cold, making his nose hairs prickle. All the trees were heavily laden and the air sparkled. It was a picture perfect morning, but better enjoyed on a post-card, he thought. By the time he reached the road, a coating of frost had formed on his eyelashes and brows from his heavy breathing. The other two were standing off to the side of the Land Cruiser that was enshrouded in a cloud of vapor spewing out of truck's tail pipe.

"Wait with them," Nancy Wong said. "I might need you to push."

The trick was to get the big vehicle turned around and pointed downhill. Nancy Wong coaxed it forward and then backward, the tires alternately catching and then spinning until at last she had it turned. She stuck out her arm and motioned them to get in. The three of them started forward and then stopped.

"What's that sound, Izzy?" Walter asked. He stood very still with his head turned toward the slope that rose up from where the cabin stood, now hidden behind the trees. The morning had been remarkable for its quality of silence. The light fluffy snow had seemed to swallow up every sound. But now, there was an odd vibration in the air, like the distant buzzing of a swarm of angry wasps. And then closer there was the sudden Whup, Whup, Whup of helicopter blades. A high pitched sizzling split the sky overhead and a low, reverberating WHUMP shook the ground and a blossoming ball of flames rose above the treetops where the cabin stood. The black silhouette of the helicopter raced above the trees.

"Get in!" Nancy Wong shouted. She was standing on the running board with her face not turned toward the sky, but to the slope above them where six snowmobiles descended in wide, sweeping arcs.

She had the Land Cruiser rolling even before the three of them were inside. Albro looked through the windshield. The road, a smooth, uniform bed of white angled steeply downhill and appeared to end abruptly at a wall of trees where it turned sharply into a switchback

Nancy Wong gunned the engine and they began to pick up speed. The truck slewed wildly as they made the first turn. The trees offered a certain degree of protection from the deep snow, but they would be leaving them shortly and the snow would be deeper and more difficult to plow through, but worse than that, they would be completely exposed to anyone who cared to come at them from above. If she could keep her speed up, they might have a chance to get through the deeper drifts.

They shot from the trees and hit the first drift with an explosion of white crystals. They seem to be floating like a giant, lumbering bobsled. She managed to hit the second turn and then made a split-second decision. Instead of heading for the winding county road that would take them to the freeway, she turned onto an old logging road. It was steeper and the turns sharper, but it was a shorter route. Their only hope was to get to the main highway as quickly as possible.

The snow on the road was deep and the big truck groaned with the effort of plowing through it, but the road angled sharply and they began to pick up speed. The road had been cut into the slope of the mountain that faced the westerly oncoming winds. She knew there was a huge build up of snow on the slope above them, dumped there by the storm that had come through the night before and was held there in a fragile balance between gravity and friction. To their left, the slope dropped away steeply to the valley floor a thousand feet below. Nancy Wong made herself not look in that direction. She pressed the accelerator. There was a limit to the speed she could achieve with the hubs locked in four wheel drive. They seemed to be crawling along and at the same time going slightly airborne as they hit the deeper drifts. There was a billow of snow in their wake and she could see nothing but white in the mirrors.

"Where are they?" She shouted above the roar of the engine.

Isaiah, who had been peering through the back glass, shouted to her, "They are close behind us. I count six. The road is too narrow for them to pass." A spray of automatic gunfire shattered the glass and sent him diving for the floor.

"Are you hit?" Nancy Wong shouted.

"No. I am fine. But you must go faster!"

"I'm trying!"

"Look!" Albro shouted. "They're forcing us to stop."

The helicopter had come around to face them and hovered close to the ground. The wash from its blades sent clouds of snow into the air completely obscuring their view of the road. Nancy Wong had been over the road countless times and knew they were very close to a turn that would send them back into a steep hairpin turn in the opposite direction. The wall of rock that lay ahead would make a rather abrupt end to their downhill flight, but if they made the turn it could also make a big surprise for those behind them.

"Hang on!" She floored the accelerator and they flew into the white cloud. She spun the wheel to the left and felt the sickening sensation of the speeding truck continue in its set trajectory.

"Walter!" Nancy Wong cried.

Walter, who had been crouching in the rear with his arms outstretched and braced against the sides of the truck, lunged to the right rear corner. His shift of mass was enough to shove the vehicle into its turn. Albro got a brief glimpse of the dark rock wall and then they were

306

past it into clear, open air. The first explosion came quickly as the lead snowmobile slammed into the wall and its gas tank ruptured and ignited on the red hot engine, and then two more quickly followed.

The remaining three did not bother stopping, but closed on them. They surged up to within a few feet and Albro could see their masks and goggles and the guns slung over their shoulders. Ahead, the helicopter hovered high up and to their right and appeared to be watching them in the way that a bird of prey watches a mouse. Suddenly two bright streaks shot from under it and two distinct thuds echoed across the valley as the rockets exploded just below the heavy accumulation of snow at the top of the ridge.

"Fuck!" Nancy Wong uttered through clenched teeth.

At first nothing seemed to happen, except the three remaining snowmobiles had dropped back. And then they all heard the slow, deep-throated rumble. Ahead of them, above and to their left, it appeared that the entire mountainside was in motion.

Nancy Wong allowed herself one glance and then she shifted out of the low range of gears into the high range and floored the accelerator. The gears whined in protest, but the old Land Cruiser surged forward. If even the leading portion of the avalanche hit them it would crush them like a soda can. She had seen avalanches, had witnessed the deaths of fellow climbers, but always from a distance. Luck had always been on her side. Why? Had it simply been to bring her to this exact moment to die? Maybe that was just the way life was. Sooner, or later, your luck ran out and you died. And the surprising thing was, as the world sped past her in a blur of snow and trees and dazzling blue sky, she felt perfectly calm. If this was going to be end, then so be it. She had lived a good life.

Albro Swift, on the other hand, was far from calm. Somebody was actually trying to kill him! He had been on the brink of a new and wonderful life and now it was all about to be snatched away from him. He wasn't ready for it to end, especially like this. He hadn't scraped and fought and struggled through his entire life for this moment. No, there had to be more! A great deal more, if he had any say in the matter. But what if he didn't have a say? What if this had all been determined? What

307

if all this, as the rat man had asserted, had already happened? Did it mean that he was going to live through it? He glanced at Nancy Wong whose eyes were set in a wild Kamikaze stare as she drove them forward to their impending deaths. Albro braced himself against the steel rim of the dash, felt the vibration of the falling mountain, and closed his eyes.

Albro Swift heard an odd sound just before the wall of snow and ice and rocks and trees hit them. It was the sound of his own voice screaming louder than he could ever have imagined. And then his mind did a back flip and dropped like a stone into a bottomless well. Down, down, down he fell until he reached the lowest of lowest levels of consciousness and then fell even farther. He fell as far as one can fall and still be counted among the living.

CHAPTER 25

THE impact blew out the windows. Nancy Wong having sensed the inevitable, had waited until the last possible moment before spinning the wheel, sending them headlong over the embankment and straight down the mountainside, and they had ridden the roiling waves of snow and ice like rafters on a wild river. That is, until the undercarriage of the truck snagged on an outcropping of granite and they began to tumble end over end until finally coming to rest under several feet of snow and ice at the bottom of the ravine.

The helicopter had hovered above it all. From their vantage point high in the sky, its occupants had watched the tiny blue and white vehicle in its valiant attempt at escape, the incredible force of the avalanche tearing down the mountainside, and the resulting tranquility when the last bits and pieces of detritus came to rest. Satisfied that it would be late into the following summer before some hiker came upon a corner of the rusted Land Cruiser poking through the snow and the four bodies within, the occupants of the helicopter turned it west and disappeared between a notch in the distant peaks. Those on the snowmobiles scanned the scene with binoculars and when they too were satisfied that there were no survivors, returned to their injured companions and went back in the direction from which they had come. Except for the growing breeze in the treetops that signaled the coming of another storm, all was again quiet.

Albro Swift opens his eyes and looks up. The room is dimly lit, and he blinks and rubs his eyes in a jerky effort to get them to focus. It seems as if he is naked, but at least he is warm, and that is something to be thankful for. It had seemed for a long while as if he would never be warm again. He kicks his feet free from whatever is holding them down. Is it a blanket? After much struggling, he rolls over onto his stomach. He can raise his head just enough to get a look to his right and to his left, but his head is so heavy that he finally gives up and lies with his head on its side.

He feels so entirely weak and surmises that he must have been injured when the wall of snow and ice had hit them. He wonders where the others are. Perhaps, they had not survived. But all of that seems so far away. He tries to concentrate on what is before him in his sideways view of the world.

He can see a wall, and at right angle to it is curtain and beyond the curtain he can hear a murmur of voices. He must be in a hospital. He wonders what kind of injuries he has suffered in the crash. A pleasant, smoky fragrance fills the air. He looks toward the wall where he sees a glowing mound of coals in large brass cauldron and two candles. A dark form passes behind the curtain, but he can't make out who it is. And then there are more voices chanting in some foreign language and he is reminded of the Reverend C. Dobson Powel's congregation of holy-rollers and how they would speak in tongues when they'd been grabbed by the Holy Spirit. Has he been taken to a church?

Suddenly the curtain is pulled aside and he is surrounded by giant figures, their faces hidden in the dim light. They roll him onto his back and hold him down. Someone grasps his right arm. Don't they know it is broken? And then he is seeing the glowing iron that has been pulled from the coals. Holy Christ! They aren't going to do what he fears they are going to do, are they? He struggles to pull away, but it is no use. More hands hold his flailing limbs, and then the red hot iron is pressed against the inside of his forearm. The pain is excruciating. He screams a high-pitched, wailing cry.

Then he is in someone's arms and looking into the face of a beautiful woman. She is rubbing something cool and soothing on his arm and wrapping it in soft cloths and then he is being wrapped as if he were a baby. She holds him and looks down at him and her hair is as golden as *the sun and her lips full and soft and she kisses him and sooths him with a voice more lovely than the sound of doves cooing. She guides his face to her breast. He struggles until his mouth finds the knob of warm, firm flesh and the heat of her body fills his mouth. He doesn't care who might be watching. All he wants is to go on like this, sucking and listening to that luxuriant voice forever and ever, but his eyes grow heavy.*

He feels himself falling into a dream, and the lovely voice retreats down a long, dark tunnel. He begins to sense within the darkness, a deep and forbidding cold, a bone aching cold that holds him within its embrace and will steal his life if he doesn't escape from it. And yet, the more he struggles against it, the tighter it holds him. He feels a hand upon him and then a powerful release.

He opened his eyes and saw the face of the rat man bent over him. He coughed and sputtered and spit out a chunk of dirty snow. His body felt oddly dislocated, almost as if he were in one place and his mind was in another.

"Can you sit up?" the rat man asked him.

Albro rolled onto his hands and knees. "Am I alive?"

"Yes. By the grace of God, we all are. But we must move quickly. They may come looking for us."

"Who was that? I mean in the helicopter."

"That is something we'll need to discuss later. Miss Wong and Walter are attempting to retrieve some items from the vehicle and then we must make our way back to the main road."

There are times, when something becomes more remarkable for its absence than for its presence. Nancy Wong was the first to notice. She had tossed a parka to Albro and he caught it with both hands.

"Your cast," she said. "It's gone." She was still dazed from the crash. She had a deep cut over her left eye and she thought she might have a couple of fractured ribs. The pain was bearable if she took shallow breaths. Walter had taken a blow to the side of his head. His ear had swollen to the size of a catcher's mitt. He had bumps and bruises on his forehead and she noticed he was favoring his right leg. Isaiah's hair was matted with blood. He undoubtedly had suffered a concussion, but refused to let her have a look at it. They all needed medical attention except for Albro. He seemed to have come through the tumbling crash without so much as a scratch.

"Hey, you're right. It must have been shattered in the crash. He pulled up his sleeve. He expected his arm to be a discolored mass of bruises, but his arm looked perfectly normal. The rat man came closer and took his arm and turned it so the inside of the arm faced outward. Upon his skin was a long scar that had the look of two snakes twisted together, and ran the length of his forearm.

"How long have you known about this?" the rat man demanded.

"I've never seen it before. They must have done something at the hospital before they put the cast on.""No," said the rat man. "This is old. It is the mark of your birth. You've had this since you were an infant."

"I've never had a scar on my arm," Albro said.

"You were never meant to see it until now. And it is not a scar. A scar would have faded into obscurity by now."

"Then what is it?" Albro asked nervously. He ran his finger along the raised surface of the intertwining lines.

"It is a sign, and a warning," the rat man said.

"It is a sign of ownership, and a warning to all those who might dare step between the two of you."

"What are you talking about?" Albro demanded.

"Look at you, and look at us. Why were you not harmed in the crash?" The rat man paused, waiting for answer. When Albro didn't speak, he said, "She drew you near to her, didn't she?"

Albro had a sudden flash of memory of the first blast as the avalanche had swept upon them, of the truck tumbling through the air…, and then it was if he had been plucked away. The rat man was right. He didn't even have a bruise. Something had happened, but he couldn't quite remember what. He had been somewhere. He could remember shadows and voices, a face that lay just beyond his grasp, but nothing more. He flexed the muscles of his arm. How had it healed so quickly? Except for the weird scar there wasn't a mark. He suddenly had a nightmarish feeling that Sal and Jimmy and Hoppy had all been a bad dream, that everything had been a dream and he would wake up...where?

"In my mother's arms," he said out loud.

The rat man stared at Albro, but said nothing.

Albro looked at the sky. A line of dark clouds was advancing on them from the west. He looked down at his arm and then he looked at his three companions. "We have to hurry," he said.

CHAPTER 26

THE last light of day had long passed by the time they reached the Interstate. Snow was falling and they had spent the last hour stumbling through a tangle of fallen trees and waist-deep snow. The snowshoes had become useless and they had relied upon Walter's strength to break trail. He alternated between forging ahead and then returning to pull them through the deep drifts. It was a monumental task and even he had begun to fail by the time they had reached the main highway.

They huddled under the trees just off the shoulder watching for oncoming headlights. Nothing approached from either direction and Nancy Wong feared that the pass had been closed for the night, when a dim pair of yellowish lights cut through the falling snow from the east. She rose up and started forward.

"Wait," Albro cautioned her. "How do you know it's safe?"

"I don't but we can't wait. We're freezing."

Albro knew that she was right. The hours of exertion had left them soaked and exhausted. They had been still for only a few minutes and already he was shivering uncontrollably.

"Then let me go," he said. He'd been thinking about what had happened when the truck had tumbled down the mountain. If he did, in fact, have a charmed life, this was as good of a time as any to test it. He stumbled into the middle of the road and began waving his arms. The vehicle slowed and then came to a stop a few feet from him. He went to the driver's window. The driver was wearing a heavy parka and a bomber hat with the earflaps pulled down.

"Our car went off the road," Albro said. "Please, we need help."

Nick Lane tried speaking to the man, but his mind had TSTDed on him. TSTD was his own acronym for the phenomenon that occurred when his brain cells had temporarily overloaded on tetrahydrocannabinol. TSTD stood for 'ten second time delay'. He hadn't even known it was happening until a friend had pointed it out one day. It was as if one the major gears of the brain had become misaligned and he'd have to wait for a complete revolution for it to set things right. He'd timed the phenomenon down to the millisecond. He likened it to being on a spaceship ten light-seconds away from earth where there would be a ten second time delay between him and ground control. At one time, he'd found it amusing, but at the moment, he knew, it was no state to be in. Then again, it was beneficial because it always kept him from over reacting, which he tended to do when surprised.

He'd taken several deep hits just before leaving his compound in the hills east of the summit. The day had been cause for celebration. He had completed his first successful harvest and he was at last on his way to market. He'd chained all four tires of the jacked-up Suburban and bounced and jounced down the rutted, snow covered drive and then had turned onto the county road. He'd paused a moment at the onramp, watching the heavy curtains of snow dance and wave in the bright lights and straining to see if the state patrol were on watch. He was on alert, not that he had much to worry about. The Suburban was not too old, not too new, and he'd made damn sure that that it didn't have a missing tail light. Dope always gave him a slight edge of paranoia, but also a feeling of calm confidence. He'd reasoned it to be a kind of yin and yang state of mind. It was a precarious balance, but a balance nonetheless, which was an improvement over his previous life-style, which more often than not had been characterized by excessive indulgence in sex, drugs, tobacco, and alcohol. Except for a little weed now and then to attenuate his hyperactive nervous system, he'd been clean, sober, and celibate for nearly two years.

He'd observed only the occasional, intrepid trucker crawling along the nearly deserted freeway. That was good. The cops would be busy administering to the city folks who would be sitting cross-wise in the ditch with their flashers pulsing out SOS signals. He'd smiled to himself as he'd eased the Suburban down the onramp.

He'd switched off the headlights and switched on the yellow fog lamps which allowed him about forty feet of visibility. He'd driven under far worse conditions in Alaska. He'd slipped some Black Sabbath into the disc changer and had cranked up the volume. He'd let up on the gas just enough so that the chunk, chunk, chunk of the chain-wrapped tires kept beat with the music. In the back of the Suburban were two five gallon buckets packed solid with some of the sweetest bud he'd yet produced. The semi-truck container he'd buried on his property two summers ago was proving to be the best investment he'd ever made. Hell yes, it had cost him. Every penny he had saved up had gone into the project. The big steel container had been the least of it. The backhoe, the diesel generator, the lights, the entire hydroponic system had eaten up the entire war chest he'd accumulated during those two years rough-necking on the North Slope. He'd been down to eating beans and venison jerky during the last three months. But after two more harvests, he would recover the initial investment, and from then on he would only be out the cost of diesel and fertilizer. The math was simple: two harvests per year at 320 ounces per harvest, times $250 per ounce wholesale. He'd made careful inquiries and by luck had come across an old army buddy who had a burgeoning retail business and was anxious for everything he could supply. In five years, he'd turn sixty and be set for life. Maybe he would buy a little beach-front villa somewhere in the Caribbean. As much as he loved the snow, he dreamed of a place where he wouldn't have to worry about freezing his ass off every winter.

A flickering movement had caught his attention. At first, he'd thought it only a phantom created by the swirling snow and the wildly firing neurons along the crisscrossing pathways in the visual center of his dope infused brain. Luckily, he'd been creeping along. Otherwise, by the time the phantom had materialized into the shape of a man, he probably would have run him down. Obviously the man wasn't DEA. Those befuddled dickheads wouldn't be caught dead in a snowstorm. Could he be a bandit? That was a remote possibility, but one that was always there. Getting hijacked was more likely once he got close to his destination, but just as a precaution, he unlatched the sawed-off twelve gauge pump action shotgun with the pistol grip from beneath the dash and laid it in his lap. He cut the volume on the stereo and rolled to a stop. He let the window all the way down, and the sharp sting of the wind driven snow cleared his mind. If he had to use the sawed-off, he didn't want to be cramped. He might be stoned to the gills, but he wasn't careless. The man had said something about needing help. The man looked miserable. His parka was sodden and he was shivering in the below freezing temperature. Nick weighed the pros and cons of picking up a stranger while his mind went through its TSTD.

When the driver didn't answer, Albro felt a panic begin to rise. What if the man drove on? Just when he feared the worst, something clicked in the driver's expression and he spoke.

"What's up, partner?"

With a rush of relief Albro repeated, "Our car went off the road. We need a ride."

Hell if he didn't need a ride, Nick Lane thought. He knew all the signs of hypothermia. The man's teeth were chattering so hard he could hardly speak. He'd seen it enough times and had experienced it once or twice himself. At first, you were totally aware of the cold which seemed to be attacking you everywhere at once, and then gradually your extremities gave up the fight and went numb, and finally it was your mind that went numb. At that stage it actually became quite a pleasant sensation, rather like a heroin-induced high. Unfortunately, it was hard to pull the body out of it. He guessed that the shivering man had maybe twenty minutes left before he reached the point of no return. A question crossed his mind: what would he do if he had twenty minutes left to live? Would he worry about all the mistakes he had made, or would he think about all the things he'd yet to do, or would he be focused on how painful dying was? It was a topic he'd like to talk about. Living alone, he hadn't had a good conversation in a long time.

Nick Lane was gregarious by nature, and unaccustomed to living alone. He'd gone from a large family into the army where he'd put in his twenty years never rising above the level of corporal. Except for a stint in 'Nam, he'd always lived in barracks, had never cooked his own meals. After the army, he'd worked on oil rigs everywhere in the world. For another fifteen years he'd lived aboard the rigs while working, and shacked up with a woman when he wasn't.   He enjoyed company, especially the company of women.   He preferred either very young women or older, married women. He found both sets were eager for excitement, but eventually tired of cooking his meals and washing his clothes. He'd never rented an apartment, owned a home or ever had a savings account.   Now, he was a tax-paying land owner with money in the bank. Who would have thought that would ever happen?

He'd surprised himself that he'd actually possessed the self-discipline to keep his enterprise secret. Perhaps, more so, it was an unerring instinct for self-preservation, and though he often recited the old adage 'that no good deed goes unpunished', he had a profound belief in Karma. All in all, he'd had a remarkable success in getting his current enterprise off the ground. Failure could have stopped him cold at any number of points and yet, it had gone smoother than he could ever have imagined. Sure, it was a risk picking up strangers, but it might go a long way in keeping the Karmic ledger in balance, and besides, he was hungry for a little company. He eased his finger off the trigger and flicked the safety back into its place.

"I'm going to Seattle. Climb in."

When everyone was settled, with the two odd ones and the woman in the back and the man with the chattering teeth up front, he turned the heat on high and took a large pinch of the newly harvested bud from an open baggie which he'd positioned conveniently under the front seat and loaded it into the bowl of his pipe. The pipe, a long-stemmed affair fashioned from a curved section of copper tubing and attached to a rounded chunk of hand-carved human femur he'd picked up along a trail in a mountainous region of Laos back in '70, gave off a soft orange glow and a powerful stink as he touched his lighter to the resinous tendrils.

"It's going to be a slow trip," Nick Lane said as he turned around to face the others, and exhaled a cloud of smoke, "so we might as well enjoy ourselves."

Nancy Wong passed on the offer of the pipe, as did Walter and Isaiah.

"This is good shit," Nick Lane said, "one hundred percent organic." That wasn't true. He was using the same commercial fertilizers that corn growers used, but he'd been wondering if it might not be a good marketing strategy. He was a little disappointed when it failed to raise any interest in the three passengers.

"How about you, partner?" he asked offering the pipe to Albro.

Nancy Wong was about to object when she felt the cautionary pressure of Brother Isaiah's hand upon her arm, as if to convey, *this is all part of what has to be.*

Albro was neither a smoker nor was he practiced in the techniques of drafting the burning weed and every pull on the pipe sent a searing current of smoke down his throat into his lungs which he could hold only momentarily before he coughed it back out.

"Whoa, take it a little slower," Nick Lane advised, and he demonstrated by sucking on the pipe stem and making the embers of the burning dope glow softly.

Albro took back the pipe and tried again, and filled his lungs. He achieved only a marginal increase before coughing it all out. Nevertheless, the dope quickly took hold.

"That wasn't so hard, was it? I'm Nick." He stuck out his hand.

Albro had been staring at the dash lights and listening to the purr of the heater fan. He found that he had to jog himself to look at the driver. He had his hand sticking out. He'd said something. Albro had to think for a moment to remember that the man had given his name. After what seemed like a long interval, Albro said, "Albro. My name is Albro Swift."

"My pleasure," Nick Lane said grasping Albro hand in a firm shake. "Who are your friends?"

Albro turned. He could see the three of them huddle together in the back seat, Walters bulk on the left and Nancy on the right and the rat man in the middle. His thoughts seemed to be mired in something that had the consistency of molasses. Finally, he said, "Nancy Wong. Walter is the big one and Isaiah is the small one. The two of them are Mongi."

"Mongi. Far out," Nick Lane said. "Is that some kind of religious order? They look like monks. I always thought it would be cool to be a monk, you know, shave my head, meditate, chant, be one with the universe. Where you headed?"

Where were they headed? Albro had to think hard. His eyes had returned to the soft, green glow of the dash lights. For an instant the lights dissolved into the nighttime glow of a city seen from high up in an airplane. He blinked and they again became a display of numbers and symbols of gas pump, oil-can, thermometer... He stopped himself. The man had asked where they were going.

"Seattle," he said.

"Far out! That's where I'm headed. Let's roll." Nick Lane dropped the shifter into drive and they started rolling.

Albro felt the tires dig into the deep snow. The chains made the truck shake and the vibrations traveled through its frame, into the seat and up through Albro's spine. The driver turned up the volume on the stereo and the sound of the pounding beat of *Into the Void* blasted out of the speakers. Hot air blew into Albro's face.

He closed his eyes and leaned into the music. Someone pushed him and he felt his body spin slowly once, then twice and then he felt once more the sensation of being pulled out of himself and into another realm, and he is back in the dim nightclub and the throbbing music courses through his body like a pulsing current of electricity. A haze of bluish smoke wafts in front of his face. Tables are packed close, and women in tall heels and dark leotards are quartering the room like hunting dogs in a field. Men in dark jackets with their hair slicked back have their eyes focused on the stage where a dark-haired beauty sits, one leg pulled back, and the other leg outstretched, poised with the point of her high-heeled foot touching the black floor. Her dress rides low on her white shoulders and is split at the waist where it falls between her legs. Her cheekbones are high to the point of wanting to tear through her skin, but it is her eyes, which are slanted back with too wide of a space between them and glow in a color that is far too yellow to be anything close to human that catch Albro's attention and hold it unrelentingly.

She leans forward and reaches for the heel of her shoe, her long, slender fingers with their painted nails curl around it, and her dress slips from her shoulders as she pulls her foot to the seat of the stool. She casually lifts the front of her dress, and covers her breasts, and does not blink her yellow eyes as she looks out into the room. A blank look has come into her eyes, and a trickle of foamy blood begins to run from the corner of her wide mouth, and her eyes roll up and her head snaps back, and suddenly she is on the floor, sprawling in a spasm of flailing limbs.

Suddenly, Albro is back staring at the greenish glow of the dash lights.

"This is your stop, man." Nick Lane reached out and grasped his shoulder and shook him. "You awake?"

"Yeah, sure," Albro said. He got a momentary image of the dream he'd just had, of the woman having some sort of seizure. This was the second time he'd had that dream. Weird, he thought. He shook himself and rubbed his face. "I guess I fell asleep."

"Fell asleep? Fuck, man, you went out like a light. You slept the whole way."

"Where are we?" Albro looked through the windshield at the dark street.

"We're here, man. End of the road, partner," Nick Lane said.

Albro opened the door and stepped onto the street and swayed unsteadily on his feet. The dope had left a bad, cloying taste in his mouth, and his throat burned from the scorching smoke.

"Hey, don't forget this," Nick Lane shouted at him and tossed his bag out onto the sidewalk.

"Wait!" Albro called out as the Suburban started to pull away. "What about the others

Nick Lane leaned across the seat and spoke through the open window. "The woman said you were on your own. Sorry, partner." He sent the window up and drove away.

After all that, Albro thought, not so much as a good-bye. So, he was on his own. Fine by him, he thought. He picked up his bag and looked inside. Under his clothes was a neatly folded bundle of old news papers. Shit! They'd robbed him! He wondered when Nancy had made the switch. She must have done it while he'd been sleeping! He couldn't believe that he'd actually begun to trust her, to actually believe her crazy story. He turned the bag inside out. His clothes fluttered in the wind and the bundle of paper fell with a humiliating thud. He kicked the bundle and the newspaper scattered.

In a panic, he patted his pockets. They had taken his wallet and phone! He looked down the empty street. He could see a long row of brick buildings and in the distance the shadowy outline of high-rise office towers of the city center. It was odd for office towers not to be lighted. What time was it? There were no street lights either. The only light in the whole city seemed to coming from across the street. He could make out faint movements within. Maybe he could call a cab, and then he remembered that he was penniless. In that case, maybe he could borrow a phone and call Monique

He could just make out the sign above the door, the lettering outlined in dead neon glass: Terminal Bar and Grill. He shook his head. This was Nancy Wong's idea of a joke, no doubt

He crossed the street. Glass crunched under his shoes as he stepped onto the sidewalk. He tried the door, and found it locked. A waist high wall had once supported large windows that were now shattered and gaping. He leaned his face past the jagged edges of glass. Someone was in there. He pounded on the still intact glass door. He was feeling doubtful about finding someone with a phone, but maybe he could convince whoever was in there to give him a lift downtown. He could see a light on in the back. The man he'd seen had disappeared somewhere back there. He pounded *again. The man emerged, paused in the shadows, and then came to the door. The disfigured face that looked out at him jolted him like a roman candle exploding in his brain.*

He opened his eyes and gulped for air like a man who has been under water for a lung-bursting length of time. He whirled around. There was Nancy Wong slumped against Walter's huge, inert form. The rat-man, though, was wide awake, and his beady eyes stared back at him.

"Another dream," the rat-man said. "Now that it's started, they will continue."

Albro looked at the driver who had pulled his bomber cap low over his eyes and was hunched over the wheel peering into the near white-out ahead of them.

"Good shit, isn't it," he said, grinning.

"How long was I asleep?"

"Man, you haven't had time to take two breaths. Like I said, this is good shit."

"I thought…, I thought…," he tried to think of the dream, and the dream within the dream, but the dope was blurring the memory, pulling and stretching it like taffy. He stared ahead and saw ghostly shapes swirl in and out of existence as the snow engulfed them. After what seemed like a long interval, words popped into his mouth. "I was somewhere else."

"This shit will do that to you," Nick Lane said. "It's better than acid, I say. It's more natural. Want some jerky? I made it myself."

Albro pulled one of the shriveled brown sticks of meat from the bag that sat on the seat between them. It had a gamey, somewhat rancid smell to it. Maybe if he worked at chewing it, he could keep himself awake. The prospect made his stomach roil and he clamped his teeth until the feeling passed. He dropped the jerky back into the bag.

"Not hungry? Dope always makes me hungry." Nick Lane took a piece and chomped off a mouthful and chewed it thoughtfully. "You know, I almost didn't stop back there, but then I got this real strong feeling that if I didn't, something bad was going to happen. I mean not to

323

all of you, but to me. Maybe not tonight, maybe not tomorrow, but somewhere down the road, there it would be, just waiting for me like a ticking time bomb. I once spent a weekend in an ashram. The guru explained everything. It's like we're all connected by these threads that are almost invisible, but not quite. You have to look real close to see them. Most people go stumbling around totally unawares, breaking threads left and right. That's why their lives are so fucked up. They've lost connection to the world. They're drifting out of control.

"Believe it or not, that was me. I dropped out my third year of college, mechanical engineering. Big mistake. Uncle Sam grabbed my ass and sent me straight to 'Nam. I spent twenty years in the army. After that, I spent another fifteen bouncing from one place to another. Then I'm rough-necking on the 'Slope. I sign a two-year contract. It's like the fucking army all over again. I'm living in barracks and working around the clock. Everyone's into drugs, whores, booze. You name it, and you could have it, any diversion or perversion. I'm way too old for that shit, but I hang in there, and I'm almost through my contract when I meet this old dude, an Inuit. Some people still call them Eskimos. They're all over up there. Most live in Barrow, but some still live in villages scattered along the coast.

Work is slow on the well-heads, so the company's got me driving a truck. It's the same pay, and a whole lot easier than being outside in fucking subzero blizzards, so I'm happy to do it. It's dead of winter because that's when the ground's hard enough to drive on. Spring and summer it's nothing but fucking mush. In winter they can carve a road right out of solid ice. Anyway, I was hauling 80,000 pounds of drill casing three hundred miles south. By my watch, it's a little past midnight, but it could have been four in the afternoon. In winter, it's fucking dark all the time up there. The night's crystal clear and I've got the stereo cranked to the max, and I'm cold sober. No booze, no dope. Not that I couldn't have gotten anything I wanted. The 'Slope is a regular smorgasbord of drugs. They got random tests for everyone except the truck drivers. They made us pee in a cup every fucking day.

"I was maybe thirty miles out of Barrow when I see this dude just standing smack in the middle of the road. Lucky for him, they hang a whole extra rack of lights on those rigs. Otherwise I'd have run him down for sure. I get the rig stopped and he just stands there, staring into the headlights. I lay on the horn and he doesn't even bat an eye.

"I climb down from my rig and the air is somewhere around forty below. I know this because my eyeballs get that crackly feeling and my nose-hairs start freezing into little ice-picks. This little fucker is dressed in seal skins and he's got a spear in his hand. First and only Eskimo I ever saw with a spear. They all carry rifles. I shout in his face and get no fucking response. It's like he's in some sort of trance.

"Well, hell, I can't wait around for him to come out of it. I go around back of the truck to take a look to make certain it's safe to back up so I can swing around him. When I get back to the cab, there he is, sitting in the passenger seat. He's got his spear between his legs and he's barely tall enough to see over the dash, and he's looking straight ahead. He's got his hood pulled back and I see that his hair is just about as white as snow.

The fucking company's got a strict policy about passengers. Only company employees are allowed. Sometimes I'd have a passenger, someone needed at another drill site, but most times I drove alone. I knew there was a village a few klicks out from my destination and I figured that's where he's headed. Seeing how I'm well outside Barrow, I don't see any harm in giving the old man a ride.

"'Okay', I say, 'where to?' And he just stares straight ahead. 'Okay, dude,' I say, 'I hope you like heavy metal.' And off we go.

"After about an hour he starts to shouting and waving his spear, and I just about jump out of my skin. It's some native language, but the message it clear. He wants me to stop, and not waste any time doing it. Well, you just don't stop 80,000 pounds travelling at sixty miles an hour on a dime, especially when the road's made of ice. I check the GPS. We're twenty miles out on this frozen lake. Lakes actually make the best roadbeds because they're smooth and flat and solid to a depth of ten feet or more. Only this one isn't. By the time I get the rig stopped, there's maybe fifty feet of white roadway, and after that, nothing. There's just a

325

black expanse as far as the headlights go. Fuckin' A! It was like coming to the edge of the world!

"My heart feels like it's going to jump right out of my chest. Every now and then a truck goes into a lake, but that's in late spring, after the thaw gets underway, and some driver's got to make one last run, like maybe he's behind on his child support payments and the state's about to pull his license. But this is the middle of winter. The fucking temperature never gets above ten below.

"The dude opens his door and climbs down and trots out to the break. He dips his spear into the water, like maybe he's testing the depth. Then he turns and trots off into the night.

"I get on the two-way and send out the coordinates to any truckers who might be in the area, warning them of the break in the ice. No response. So, I call Barrow on the satellite phone. Again, no response. Fuck, man! Now I'm really starting to get spooked. The aurora will fuck with communications but the sky's quiet, just stars. They're cold and hard, like diamonds on black velvet.

"I say to myself, 'Nick, just stay cool, and look at your options. You can try to drive around the open water. Bad idea, Nick, because you don't know what's out there. You can sit tight and wait for another truck to come along. Another bad idea, Nick, because then you would have approximately twice the weight at nearly the same place. Or, you can try to get the rig turned around and go back the way you came.'

"And that's exactly what I do. I lay a necklace of flares across the roadway just in case anyone else comes that way. Then I get this urge to do something really crazy. I walk right out to the edge of the ice. The surface of the water is just like a fucking mirror. I look down, and I can see the stars as clearly as looking up. Suddenly I got this sensation that it's not an illusion, like I'm really standing at the edge of the world and if I take a step, I'll go spinning off into space. You know what? I almost did it. I mean, I had my foot up and ready to step off, when a voice inside my head said, 'Whoa, buddy, this ain't your time'. I'm telling, you, shit like that makes a man stop and think about his life. Know what I mean? Then and there, I decide I'm heading back to the lower forty-eight as soon as my contract is up, settle down, and maybe start a little business.

"So, I get in the truck and take it real slow until I know I'm off that frozen lake, at which point, I pull up and let my nerves calm down before driving back into Barrow. No shit, man.

The night supervisor is pissed as hell that I'm back. He's being a real dick and starts waving a paper cup in my face. I tell him to shove his paper cup up his ass. I'm done pissing in cups for him or anybody else. Next day, I get a call from the dispatcher's office saying they found something on the passenger seat and that it must be mine

Albro watched as the driver took his hands off the wheel long enough to reach into his shirt and pull out what looked to be a small gold coin strung on a leather cord. He lifted the looped cord over his head and handed it across to Albro, and turned on the dome light

"The old Inuit must have left it," Nick Lane said

It was about the size of a dime and had the heft of solid gold. It was as warm as flesh from having hung against the man's chest. Its lines had been smoothed by years of contact with skin and cloth, but the shape of the raised figure on its surface was unmistakable: a goat with pointed horns. On the reverse side were the same twisted strands as existed on the coin that hung around his neck. Albro ran his thumb across the twelve tiny marks that ran around the perimeter like the numbers on a watch. Albro glanced back over the seat at the rat man who had drawn up his hood, but whose eyes looked back into his own.

Cool, huh?" Nick Lane said. "It's kind of creepy how I came by it, but I wouldn't part with it for anything. It's my good luck charm, my mojo-maker.

Albro handed it back, and Nick Lane slipped it over his head and back into his shirt. It has to be pure coincidence, Albro told himself, but he was finding it hard to convince himself, because really, what were the odds...

He was beginning to accept that he was being forced to play a game for which he had no inkling of the rules, nor who his opponents might be. What were the stakes? Not only his life and the lives of Walter,

Isaiah and Nancy Wong, but according the rat man, the whole world was at stake. Somehow, the *Jade Prince* was going to bring about the destruction of the world? That couldn't be possible, could it? There had to be a rational explanation, but what was rationality other than an expression of probability?

Whether the *Jade Prince* was fact or fiction no longer seemed to matter. Why was this all linked him? That was the immediate question. He stared out the window, and thought about that as they came down out of the mountains, and the snow turned to rain and the darkness to shadows.

CHAPTER 27

"WHERE can I drop you?" Nick Lane asked. His meeting was scheduled for sometime after ten o'clock. He would hand over his two five gallon buckets for two of identical kind, only those would be filled with cash. Then he would go to the all night Pack 'n Save, load up on groceries and head back over the mountains.

Albro Swift, who had gone over any number of possible actions, had decided on one. If he was going to get to the bottom of this, he'd better start at the beginning. The face he'd seen in the dream was still with him. He said to the driver, "There's a small business district just south of the city called Georgetown. There's a place there called *The Terminal*. It's a bar and grill. I know it will be open. You could drop us there it it's not too far out of your way."

'Fuck all,' Nick Lane swore to himself. He glanced at the fellow next to him. That was exactly where his meeting was taking place! What were the fucking odds? An uncomfortable tension gripped his lower neck and settled between his shoulder blades. He reached up and felt for the gold coin around his neck. "Yeah, sure, not a problem," he said trying his best to sound unbothered by the notion that there was more to his four passenger than met the eye. "You know someone there who can help you out?" He was half-expecting, half-fearing that he would hear the name of his connection and was only somewhat relieved with the answer he got.

"Not a soul," Albro said, "except maybe a ghost."

It was Saturday night, and there was a good crowd. The space was long and narrow with the bar on one side, midway along the brick wall. In the front corner was a small stage where a Blues band was setting up. It wasn't exactly a place where you could slip in unobserved, but at least the lights were low, and it was Seattle, after all, where anyone could wear anything anywhere and not be noticed, a place where people seemed to go out of their way to avoid eye-contact with strangers and keep their focus centered on their own insular group. A table was open at the far end close to a green exit sign and adjacent to a narrow hallway. Back there, Albro knew, were the restrooms, a rear exit, and a phone booth. It was *the* phone booth, the one where he had been found. It was one of those you rarely saw anymore with the bi-fold door and a wooden bench seat and one of those ancient telephones in the shape of large rectangular black box. He knew, because he'd gone to look at it once, had closed the door and sat in the enclosed space that smelled strongly of cigarette smoke, hoping to feel some kind of connection to his past. He'd been disappointed. It was just an old phone booth. Albro took a deep breath and steered the ragged group toward an empty table.

Nick Lane had decided to drop his passengers at the front entrance, and had circled the block twice before pulling into the lot around back. There was really no reason, he told himself, to alter his plans. He would go to the bar, order a beer, and wait for his connection to arrive. Then he would finish his beer, exit out the back, drive to the warehouse next to the rail tracks and wait. Simple. He rolled his shoulders trying to dislodge the knotted muscles in the middle of his back. Relax; he told himself the exchange was going down as planned. Nevertheless, he unlatched the shotgun and slipped it into a slit he'd cut into his coat just for that purpose.

A waitress came to their table. She wore a tank top, short black skirt and work boots. A row of silver beads clung to her lower lip and her short blond hair stuck out in spikes. If she had any opinion of them, she didn't show it as she dropped a stack of menus on the table. "What can I get you to drink?"

"Bring us a pitcher of water," Albro answered. He saw a disappointed look in Walter's eyes. He added, "And a pitcher of beer."

"You got it. Anything to eat?"

They ordered sandwiches and a triple order of fish and chips for Walter. Nancy Wong's eyes kept darting toward the door.

After the waitress left, Albro said, "Relax Nancy, we're supposed to be buried under ten feet of snow and ice. No one is going to be looking for us."

"You don't know that."

"You're right, I don't. There's a lot I don't know. But I've had some time to think." He turned to the rat man. "This *Jade Prince* that everyone is so excited about, what do you think it's worth?"

"I knew it!" Nancy Wong whispered sharply. "All you're interested in is money. Besides, I thought you didn't believe it exists."

"What difference does it make if I believe in it or not, as long as someone else is convinced that I can somehow get my hands on it, and is willing to murder me and all of you to prevent me from doing so?"

"He has a point," Isaiah said quietly. "I cannot place a monetary value on it except to say that it is without doubt the most valuable object ever created."

"So, in other words, it's worth a bundle," Albro said. He asked, "A hundred million, two hundred million?"

"You could name any amount and it would not come close to its true value," the rat man answered.

"Good. That's what I wanted to know. So once we find it, the only problem will be unloading it."

"If you think for one moment I would risk my life just so you can make yourself rich, you're a worse human being than I ever imagined you to be!" Nancy Wong spit out each word.

"Settle down, Nancy. No one said anything about getting rich. At the moment, I'm more interested in staying alive. What good would it do to find your *Jade Prince* and be killed trying to hang on to it. We'll have to find a way to cut a deal."

"*She* will never '*cut a deal*' with you or anybody else," Isaiah said, his voice rising. Albro heard a note of anger in the rat man's voice that he hadn't heard before.

Albro let out an exasperated sigh, "Why do I get the feeling you're not telling me everything?"

"I am sorry," the rat man said. "I should not have spoken to you that way. It was disrespectful. Please forgive me."

Albro looked at his three companions. Walter sagged in his chair. The rat man had limped into the bar, and Nancy sat bent forward clutching her side. She had pulled her stocking cap low on her head to hide the cut at her temple. They were exhausted, he included. They couldn't go on much longer like this, and the last thing they needed was to start fighting with each other. "Look," he said, "if I had a dollar for every time someone yelled at me, I'd be a rich man. Don't worry, I forgive you, but you have to tell me everything."

"I promise you I will," said the rat man, "but not here."

"Okay, after we eat we'll find a safe place for the night. There's a motel not far from here. We can walk. We'll talk there. Agreed?"

"Agreed," said the rat man.

The waitress arrived with their food. Albro bit into his sandwich and looked up just as Nick Lane walked in and took a seat at the bar with his back to them. He looked across to the rat man who had also seen their Good Samaritan walk in.

Nancy Wong said, "I don't like the way this feels." She scanned the room nervously.

Albro noticed that the rat man had sent some sort of message to Walter who had paused in his steady intake of food and beer. He'd not bothered with the pint glass which was too small for his hands, and was drinking right from the pitcher. He'd finished the pitcher in a single, long draft. He'd looked up from his food just long enough to take in the man's back.

Albro set his eyes on Nancy Wong. "I think you know that this is the place where I was found," He said. "There's a phone booth down that hallway. Of course, I don't remember having been there. Why would I? I was only a few days old. But you know something more about this place than you're letting on. I can see it in your face. I can hear it in your voice. You're not good at playing dumb, Nancy."

Nancy Wong gave a furtive glance to the rat man whose eyes remained unreadable. After a long moment she said, "This place is a nexus. It's a place where threads from the future converge to a point. You were found here for that reason. Your father brought me here. He said that you would be drawn here. He didn't know when, but when the time came, you would not be able to avoid it. He did not tell me why, so don't ask."

"You don't know why, but you have an idea, don't you?"

"No! I don't know why. I only know a part of what's going to happen."

"Which part is that?"

Nancy Wong looked around at the crowd. "People are going to get hurt. Some of them will die."

"Crane arranged for something to happen?"

"No, it's not like that. Events have been set in motion that no one can stop."

"Right now? Tonight? Why didn't you say something?"

"You brought us here for a reason and now what happens, must happen," said the rat man. "Our fate is now in the hands of the Almighty God."

Albro was about to thank Bother Isaiah for his not so helpful insight, but stopped when his attention was caught by a commotion at the door.

Nick Lane had his beer halfway to his mouth when he saw the two men in ski masks out of the corner of his left eye. They had come through the front door in long powerful strides, and would have gone right past him had not the innocent individual who had had too much to drink risen to his feet and fallen into them. In an instant the man in the lead snapped

333

the drunk's neck and threw him aside, but the interruption had been just enough to throw him off balance so that when he pulled the gun from inside his coat and let off the first three rounds they smashed harmlessly into the soft brick a few inches above the heads of the group at the corner table. Nick Lane knew that hand guns are notoriously inaccurate unless the shooter is standing perfectly rigid and the target remains perfectly still. That was one reason he preferred a shotgun. One didn't have to worry so much about accuracy. Another reason was its shear stopping power. Lastly, was its ear splitting roar, the shock of which was almost as disabling as the blast itself.

He'd always prepared for this moment and so it was quite natural that he thought the two intruders were after him. The patrons barely had time to react to the first shots when he pulled the trigger of the sawed-off. The lead gunman jerked backwards like a puppet on strings. Nick Lane pumped another load into its chamber just as the second shooter fired a round that pierced his left eye, and all went black as his body spun around and hit the floor.

The place suddenly became a mass of screaming people scrambling for cover. Albro Swift looked up, half dazed from the explosions, into the mask of a gunman and a pistol pointed in his face, and then the gunman was flying across the room, and there was a great crash as he went through the front window.

It was all over in a matter of seconds. Walter had jumped up and charged the gunman before the first rounds had thudded into the wall above Albro's head, and then there had come the deafening roar of the shotgun, and then the crash of shattering glass as Walter had sent the second gunman flying into the street.

Then, they were running with Nancy in the lead, Isaiah behind her, Walter following with Nick Lane slung over his shoulder, and Albro bringing up the rear. But something stopped him, and he returned to the chaos of the room and knelt next to the inert form of the first gunman. He tried to not look at the bloody hole in the man's chest as he grasped the mask and pulled it off. The too far apart, yellowish eyes stared blankly at the ceiling, and the long line of the jaw protruded in a grimace of pain, baring a line of pointed teeth and fangs. Albro dropped the mask and sprinted for the others.

Walter had set Nick Lane on the bench in the phone booth, and they were huddled around him. In the distance came the wail of sirens.

"How is he?" Albro asked. He stared at the gaping hole where the man's eye had been and the creamy-white bone of his skull that hung by a flap of skin where the bullet had blown through the side of his head. He remembered the face in the dream and felt himself start to go dizzy. He clinched his teeth and squeezed his eyes tightly shut for a moment until his mind got a grip on the present.

"He's still breathing," Nancy Wong said.

"Find his keys," Albro said.

"We can't just leave him. He saved our lives." Her voice was getting that first hint of panic that could mean trouble for all of them.

Albro brushed her aside and began going through the man's pockets. At last, he found the keys, and then noticed the man's hand was clutched tightly. He pried open the fingers. In his palm lay the small gold coin. Why had Nick Lane removed his good luck charm? Was he supposed to take it? Was that why he'd been drawn here tonight? Albro looked into the dying man's vacant stare. Nick Lane wasn't going to need it any longer.

Albro stared at the coin and felt that he was being pulled back into the dream. He saw Nick Lane's drained face, the bloody rag tied around his head, the coin dangling from his limp hand. Then he heard someone shouting his name.

"What?" he asked annoyed that he was being pulled from the dream.

"We have to get out of here!" Nancy Wong shouted at him.

Albro looked at the coin again and then closed Nick Lane's hand around it. The man needed, Albro decided, as much mojo as he could get. He tossed the keys to Nancy. "Let's go."

"Where can we go?" Nancy Wong sounded frantic. There was screaming and shouting coming from the bar.

"Follow me," Albro said.

They ran out the rear entrance and found the Suburban angled in amongst the other cars in the small parking lot.

"Drive," he said to Nancy Wong.

"Where?" Nancy Wong asked. She got the big vehicle running and maneuvered it out of the tight parking space and onto the street.

"Just drive. Anywhere away from the sirens," he answered.

He needed time to think. There was slim chance amid the chaos that anyone had noticed them. Even Walter tossing the gunman would be a phantom memory. People in panic just didn't remember details, but he'd been left with an uneasy feeling that their escape had been observed. Two patrol cars passed them going in the opposite direction. Their blazing lights flashed across Nancy Wong's pale face.

"Would Auntie Lo take us in for the night?" Albro asked.

"It would be too dangerous for her. We might be followed."

"Have you seen anyone?"

"No, but it's likely."

Albro knew she was right. Someone was probably behind them right now. How had they found them so quickly? What had it taken, an hour? That gunman hadn't looked exactly human. He wished that he'd dragged the rat man back to have a look. He turned to Nancy Wong, "Where else can we go?"

Nancy Wong drove slowly, winding through the blocks of factories and pockets of residential sections that seemed cut off from other communities and struggling for survival. Satisfied that they were not being followed, she turned north and headed toward Chinatown. They were only minutes from the district that was defined by its old brick hotels and shops and restaurants. Its crowded and narrow streets had been her playground while growing up and it was always a comfort to enter its familiar enclaves and alleyways. But tonight something was not right. Ahead she could see an orange glow reflected in the low clouds approximately where the Hun Lo noodle factory was located. She sped up and cut down an alley that would bring them a few blocks to the north. They could walk from there, she decided. Her plan was to call one of her cousins and arrange for him to drive the Suburban out of the city, and wipe the interior thoroughly. The police would eventually find it and connect it to the man they'd left behind. By then they would be...where? She couldn't say.

She slowed as she approached the end of the alley, and eased out onto the street and was horrified by what she saw. Patrol cars blocked their path.

"Fuck!" She jammed the shifter in reverse.

"Wait!" Albro told her. "Look!"

Beyond the patrol cars, a phalanx of fire trucks were pulling to a halt at the base of one of the old brick buildings whose upper level was engulfed in flames.

"Auntie Lo!" Nancy Wong screamed.

Before Albro could react, she had thrown open her door and was running toward the flames. He chased her, ignoring the commands of the patrolmen who shouted through loudspeakers ordering them to stop. Albro could see flames shooting from all three levels now and huge clouds of smoke lit up by the flames. A full block away he could feel the heat. A muffled explosion sent a blast of superheated air into his face and a shower of sparks arced skyward and onto the tops of the surrounding buildings where the firemen were directing their hoses. He then saw Nancy, her face blackened by soot, struggling to be released from the grip of a fireman who was half dragging, half carrying her away from the burning building. He ran and got an arm around her.

"Hang on to her!" the fireman shouted at him.

"My aunt is in there!" she screamed at them and fought to be released.

"There's nothing we can do!" Albro shouted in her face and shook her hard. "We've got to get out of here!"

The walls of the structure began to sag inward as the upper levels started collapsing onto the ones below. The firemen were pulling back in a mad scramble when suddenly the aging façade fell in upon itself. Albro swung them around and forced their way through the tangle of hoses and equipment.

The Suburban sat empty with its doors open and was now blocked by emergency vehicles. Albro looked around for Walter and Isaiah. He held Nancy Wong tightly around her shoulders and steered her back into the alley. At the far end, he saw the shadowy figure of someone waving then forward. He hesitated, holding Nancy Wong close, feeling her sobs against his chest.

"Come this way," the figure called to them and then stepped into the light of a street lamp and Albro recognized the face of John Marlowe. As they approached, Albro saw the dark shape of a limousine parked at an angle to the alley. Marlowe motioned them toward the open door. Walter and the Isaiah were already in there. Marlowe shut the door and went around to the front and got in next to the driver who hit the accelerator. The tires on the big vehicle squealed and the car sped away from the inferno of blazing light and stench of burning timbers.

Marlowe turned and said, "Ah, Ms Wong, it is a pleasure to see you again. I had begun to worry that perhaps you had come to harm. No doubt, you have had your hands full during these past two days. Rest assured, neither your auntie, nor anyone else was in the building when they set fire to it."

"How could you know that?" Nancy Wong asked, still sobbing.

"I met with her yesterday, shortly after I spoke with Mr. Swift. I explained to her the danger she might be in. She agreed to warn the others."

"But where could she have gone? If she was in danger in her own home, she would be in danger anywhere in the city."

"That's correct. As you know, she has a sister in Kowloon, and although I won't rule out them tracking her there, she's really not the one they want. I saw her onto a plane last evening."

"I was so frightened when I saw the flames."

"Yes, I'm sure you were."

"But why?" Nancy Wong pleaded.

"Why, indeed," Marlowe said. "Either there was something they wanted destroyed, or they wanted to frighten all of you. Most likely it was both."

338

"Then who are they and what do they want?" Albro demanded.

Marlowe held up his hand and spoke softly to the driver who gave a quick nod and altered their course. Ahead of them Albro could see the lights of the airport. They were on a tangent that would bring them to a large hangar at the south end of the complex.

"As I said before, Mr. Swift, it's you they want and what you know. I said that before without being totally certain. Now I have no doubts."

"Then why try to kill me?"

"I think we can safely assume that there are those who are working at cross purposes to one another. Which, I'm sure you agree, places you in a vulnerable situation."

They came to a stop.

"I see that we have arrived," Marlowe said and turned to the driver. "Go ahead and pull the car into the hangar, we can leave it there."

Albro looked at the driver. "Charles?"

"Good evening, sir," Charles said glancing up into the rearview mirror.

"What are you doing here?" Albro asked.

"Long story, sir" Charles answered.

"Are you taking me to Monique and her father?"

"I'm afraid not, sir," the old chauffeur answered and drove the car through the open door of a gigantic hangar.

"I want some answers," Albro said to Marlowe.

"I'm sure that you do. There will be plenty of time for that," Marlowe said. "Now we must hurry. There is a plane waiting for us." Charles was out and opening up the doors. Marlowe motioned them out. Through the open hangar door, Albro could see a gigantic plane sitting on the tarmac. Lights flashed on its wingtips. An ear splitting whine filled the air. Rain had begun falling and the plane's snowy-white skin glistened in the powerful airport lights.

"Wait!" Albro said. "Where are we going?" His words were nearly drowned by the roar of the jet's engines.

Marlowe leaned in close to his ear, "Hong Kong, my dear boy. Chop, chop! We're due to lift off in five minutes."

CHAPTER 28

THE first thing Nick Lane did when he regained consciousness was to lean forward and vomit between his legs. The room was dark. Otherwise, he would have seen the mess of beer and gastric juices and the gray-brown chunks of reconstituted meat puddle between his work boots. He sat back. His head throbbed like a son-of-a-bitch! He lightly touched his wound and felt the pulpy remains of his left eyeball. A piece of his skull, he realized, was held by a flap of skin. He worked it like a door hinge. He closed it and held it there with his fingers, and tried to get up, but the slightest movement brought excruciating pain to his head. It was like the worst goddamned hangover magnified a thousand times. He slumped back down on the narrow bench and tried to make out exactly where he was. He had a vague memory of the bar erupting in gunfire and then all hell had broken lose. He'd fired off the shotgun and then everything had gone blank. He felt his stomach start to go queasy again and he gulped air to suppress another upchuck.

When his stomach settled again, he tried getting up to his feet. This time he succeeded, stumbling from the phone booth into the narrow hallway. The men's room was down there somewhere. He remembered seeing it when he'd come in through the back entrance. There would be a mirror in there. He needed to get a look at the damage to his head. Christ, it hurt! He felt his way until he came to a doorway and reached around the inside until he found the light switch and flipped it on. A dim bulb came on. In the blue-gray light he held himself against the sink and looked into the mirror.

His vision was assaulted by alternate waves of nausea and dizziness. His remaining eye didn't want to focus. It took him a moment of confusion to realize the mirror was coated in dust. He steadied himself and swiped the mirror with his sleeve. He calmly surveyed the damage. The bullet, probably a 9mm in a steel jacket, had entered the eye socket at a shallow angle, popped his eyeball like a nine-iron hitting and egg, and then had exited through the corner of his skull. Another degree or two on the angle and the bullet would have ricocheted around the interior of his skull thoroughly blending his brain tissue.

Blood still oozed from his eye socket and from the hole at his temple. He turned the faucet handles. All that came out was a sucking sound. "What the fuck," he muttered.

He looked at his face again. He raised the still intact eyelid and pushed the bloody tendrils that had once been the eyeball back where they belonged. He pulled out his handkerchief and tied it around his head, holding everything in place. He then made his way back into the main room of the bar. He tried more switches, but the only working light seemed to be the one in the bathroom. Yet, there was enough light coming in from the outside to see that something akin to a riot must have occurred. Tables and chairs were overturned. The mirror behind the bar, and the front windows were smashed. Oddly, the glass entry door was still intact. He went behind the bar hoping to find a bottle of liquor to use as a disinfectant on his wound, but the place looked as if it had been ransacked, although not recently. A pallor of dust covered everything.

A movement caught his eye. A figure was crossing the street. He retreated into the shadows and watched as the figure, a man, peered through the glass door. The man pounded on the door and started yelling.

Nick Lane stepped cautiously forward. He was going to need medical attention and help getting to a hospital. The man seemed more impatient than threatening. He stepped carefully around the detritus of the room and was about to reach for the door when the man jumped back and froze. In the half-light of the street he could see the surprised look of shock on the man's face. There was something familiar about him and then he remembered, but before he could react, the man turned and ran.

He fumbled with the door and finally got it open and rushed into the street. "Hey!" he shouted to the retreating figure. "Hey! It's me, Nick Lane!" But it was too late. The man was lost in the gloom of the night. He stood for a moment and then went back into the building. He would have to drive himself. He wasn't quite sure where the hospital was located, but he'd seen the signs from the freeway. He went through to the back of the building to the lot where he'd parked the Suburban. It was then, that his predicament began to register. The lot was empty save for the burned out and rusted hulks of two vehicles. His Suburban, along with the two five-gallon buckets of primo bud, was missing.

"Fuck me all to hell!" he said out loud. He could start walking, or wait until dawn. He decided the latter was the best option given the fact that the city seemed disturbingly dark and deserted. In fact, the only light seemed to be here in the men's restroom. He went back inside and began casting about for something to use as a pad, and finding nothing, finally resigned to balling up his coat for a pillow, lay down on the hard floor. At least it was warm, maybe even too warm. He had a distinct memory that it had been cold and snowy just a few hours ago, but he was suddenly too tired to puzzle that one out. He closed his good eye and fell asleep.

CHAPTER 29

NO sooner had the outer door of the aircraft closed than the plane began to taxi toward the far end of the runway. Marlowe ushered them to a large cabin near the center of the aircraft. Albro looked around. Padded chairs were clustered around low tables. Soft carpeting covered the floor and hidden sconces washed the ceiling and suffused the pastel greens and browns in a soft glow. The place was outfitted more like a cocktail lounge than an airliner.

"Please be seated. You will find safety belts tucked into the sides of the chairs," Marlowe informed them.

Albro was about to remind Marlowe of the questions he wanted answers to when a woman stepped in from the forward cabin and approached Marlowe.

"Elsa?" Albro asked. She smiled warmly at him and then put her mouth next to Marlowe's ear and spoke quietly.

Nancy Wong looked at Albro. "Do you know her?" She raised her chin toward the other woman.

"We met," Albro admitted, "very briefly."

She looked at Elsa, giving her tall, full figure a quick, once-over. She was conservatively dressed in dark slacks, white blouse buttoned at the neck and low-heeled shoes. A hint of subtle perfume drifted her way and Nancy suddenly became aware of her own rough appearance and the odor of her own dried sweat. She turned to face Albro, "I'm sure it was brief. I hear that she is very efficient."

"I see," Marlowe said softly to Elsa. He turned Albro and Nancy. "Elsa is our co-pilot, just one of her many talents." He paused to smile. "I presume you all know her, so we can dispense with introductions. You will have to excuse me for a time. I have some urgent communiqués to send. One doesn't land a plane this size unannounced. I will join you shortly. Charles will see to your needs."

The chauffeur had changed out of his dark uniform and now wore a white waiter's jacket with gold buttons. He asked that they all remain seated until they reached cruising altitude. He then bowed, excused himself, and disappeared into one of the forward compartments. The plane began to gather speed and lifted off smoothly into the blackness of the night.

Walter had his face pressed against the glass. "Look at the lights! Are we really flying?"

"Yes we are," answered Isaiah. He had flown in troop transports during the *Great Upheaval*. The memory of those metal airships smelling of fuel and fear was still very strong despite the intervening years. Of course, this was nothing like those previous flights with the ear splitting scream of the turbines, and the continual jerking up and down as the pilots attempted to evade enemy fire. This by comparison, was a floating palace. But the comparison did have one significant thing in common. Now, like then, he was on a journey of unknown destination, and once again, Marlow was in command.

He had been only mildly surprised when Marlowe had approached him and Walter as they stood watching the burning building. He had been expecting him, but still, seeing him materialize out of the shadows had been unsettling. What had it been, forty years since they had last seen each other? That had not been nearly enough years to forget their last meeting. Marlowe had addressed him by the name he had not used since joining the Order. It had cut him as a dull knife might have worked to penetrate the thick layer he'd built in defense of that older self. But penetrate it did, and he had turned to face the tall figure who had appeared out of nowhere illuminated by the flames and flashing lights like some demon pulled up from a hellish past. He would have preferred most anything to Marlowe's offer of assistance, but he had seen no other choice. Forces were closing in around them like a noose around a condemned man's neck. 'You need me now', Marlowe had said, 'just as I needed you then'.

Nor did it surprise him that Marlowe had become a very powerful man in this time, this place. He was one of those unique individuals who had the ability to convince others of the extraordinary opportunities he could provide and then to convince them to make the necessary sacrifices to achieve them. It would be in Marlowe's best interest to help them achieve their goals. And that was the dilemma. Marlowe always had his own interests at heart. Isaiah wondered if they had escaped one enemy's grasp only to find themselves caught between another's teeth.

A wave of intense fatigue swept over him. He leaned his head against the window and looked down into the rolling sea of clouds glowing in the light of a misshapen moon hanging in a starless sky. Far below was the western ocean and in contrast to his time, his own place, still full of life. This time was so full of life. How could they have lost so much? How could they have let it happen? The bitter irony was that few individuals in his time even knew to ask these questions. To them, the world was what it was and had always been so from the very beginning, and now, it had fallen to him to maintain that illusion.

His thoughts were interrupted by the man Albro Swift had called 'Charles'. Isaiah knew him by another name, and other skills. He wondered how many of Marlowe's loyal fighters had signed on with him. He felt the old anger rising in him liked a banked ember come back to life. He wondered absently if it would ever burn out entirely. God knows he had tried to smother it, drown it and bury its ashes in the pit of his subconscious. And yet, here it was, surging through his body like a resurrected demon.

"Regrettably, Mr. Marlowe has been delayed," Charles said. "We have reached cruising altitude which means you may now move about. We have a full complement of refreshments. In addition, there is a fully functional kitchen. Although the selection of meals is limited, I think you will find it accommodating to most tastes. Even the Mongi should find it acceptable." He said this last with a pointed look at Isaiah and Walter.

"This aircraft," he went on, "was specially built for Mr. Marlowe. The added fuel tanks give it a range of roughly fifteen thousand miles, which allows it to fly half-way around the world without refueling. If circumstances were to demand it, there is of course, the provision for mid-air refueling. There are six sleeping cabins, small, but the beds are comfortable. There are showers as well, if you care to freshen up. I can also see to your medical needs as I am a fully trained medic. Our transit time will be approximately thirteen hours. Now, what can I get for you?"

Albro stood up. "I don't know about the rest of you," he said, "but I could use a shower and shave." Actually he wanted most of all to get some answers from Nancy. He'd seen the looks exchanged between her and Marlowe. He was also curious to know how she knew Elsa, but didn't hold out much hope for getting any information on that issue. And there was Charles. He couldn't imagine Marlowe and Newton as co-conspirators. So what did that make Charles, Marlowe's spy?

"Ms. Wong?" Charles asked, "May I dress that wound for you?"

"Thanks," she said. "If you can give me a first-aid kit I can manage myself."

"Of course," Charles replied.

"I could use a shower too, but I don't have a change of clothes," she said.

"Mr. Marlowe has anticipated your needs. You will find a selection in cabin 2, and likewise for you, Mr. Swift in cabin 3. As for the Mongi, perhaps they would wish to observe the local custom and bathe as well."

"Thank you, Charles." Marlowe said as he entered the lounge area. "Please escort Ms. Wong and Mr. Swift to their cabins. I would like a word with our Mongi guests."

Albro Swift stood beneath the hot spray. He'd given up on the hope that this was all a dream. It was a nightmare. He looked at the scar on the inside of his arm. How the hell did that get there? And his arm, had it really been broken? There was proof, wasn't there, in the form of an x-ray sitting in a medical file at L.A. General? He ran his hands through his hair and felt shards of brick dust. That whole scene at the *Terminal* had been real, hadn't it? He remembered the gold coin in Nick Lane's hand. Why had he not taken it from the dying man? But the man hadn't died. He'd seen him alive. No, he had dreamed that, in that crazy dream within a dream, he reminded himself. But it was all there in the dream, the broken window, the chaotic state of the room, and Nick Lane with his eye shot out, and he'd dreamed it before any of it had happened, but it was somehow not right. In the dream the place had looked as if it had been abandoned for years. Everyone was missing, including the dead gunman whose face he'd seen, and could still see when he closed his eyes.

If Marlowe was to be believed, they were headed for Hong Kong. At least it was a familiar place, and he would be able to contact Monique and let her know that he was still alive. He needed to warn Martin that Krupp was somehow mixed up in all of this, and that Monique's life might be in danger. Had it been only five nights since Krupp had given him the private tour and made his pitch? He hadn't taken the old doctor seriously. He hadn't taken anything regarding the *Jade Prince* seriously, but everyone else sure as hell did. There were five, maybe six people dead and there had been two attempts on his life. He'd simply been trying to mind his own business. What kind of trouble would he invite if he took it seriously? Did he even have a choice in the matter? There were far too many questions and not enough answers.

He finished his shower and found that fresh clothes had been laid out for him on the bed. He dressed and then went to Nancy's cabin and knocked on the door. He heard Nancy give a curt, 'Yes', and he turned the latch and entered. She was in a white robe and standing before a small mirror, her hair still damp from the shower. A dark bruise discolored the lower edge of her jaw. She was attempting to close the wound on her temple with strips of tape.

She frowned at his reflection in the mirror. Without turning she said, "I'm busy."

"Let me help you," Albro said.

"I'm doing just fine, thank you," She said and tried once again to get the strips placed correctly.

"You can't see what you're doing," Albro said and closed the door behind him and stepped to the mirror. He reached to pull her hand away.

"Don't touch me," she said forcefully.

"Pipe down," Albro told her. "They'll think were up to something."

"That will never happen!"

"Hey, take it easy. I was only kidding. Now stop being so stubborn, and let me help you. You're still bleeding." He found a wash cloth and wiped away the blood and then pressed it to the wound.

"How does your head feel?"

"My ears are still ringing," she said grudgingly.

"What about your vision?"

"It goes blurry if I move too quickly."

"You probably suffered a concussion in the crash."

"I know that! I'm not stupid."

"You should let Charles examine you. He's a medic."

"I wouldn't let that beast close to me!"

Albro kept silent as he pulled away the wash cloth. He reached for the bottle of iodine that sat on the counter and found a swab. "This is going to sting," he said.

Nancy winced as he swabbed the brown liquid on the wound. Albro blew gently to cool the burning. "What do you know about Marlowe and Charles?" he asked as he reached for the steri-strips.

Nancy started to pull away. "Hold still," Albro said, "or you will start it bleeding again."

Reluctantly Nancy Wong held herself still. She said, "They were both soldiers. They committed unspeakable atrocities."

"Who told you this?"

"Your…" she began and then stopped. "Thomas Crane told me. Isaiah told me as well. And then I saw…" She stopped abruptly and Albro felt a shudder course through her body.

"You saw what?' Albro asked. He tilted her head so the light fell on the cut at her temple.

"I saw things no one should ever see. Bodies. Some of them were women and children."

"When and where was this?" Albro asked. He cut a square of gauze and folded under the edges.

"When and where it happened would not make any sense to you," Nancy said.

"But it does to you," Albro said. He cut two pieces of tape and stuck them to the gauze.

"Yes, because I was there."

"And still, you trust Marlowe?" Albro asked. He placed the square of gauze neatly over the wound and carefully pressed the tape against her skin.

"No, I don't trust Marlowe, but we need his help."

Albro said, "Marlowe gave me his card. On it was printed the word, '*Inquires*'. What does that mean?"

"He works for a branch of the Church whose job is to ask questions. Their techniques make the Spanish Inquisition look like a church social.

"What church are you talking about?"

"It is not just any church. It is *the* Church, the *only* Church. Think of CHURCH, all capital letters."

"He doesn't strike me as a religious fanatic."

"He's not. The branch of the Church he works for acts as a kind of liaison between the Church and the Purim government. He's cold and he's calculating, and he's not above putting his own interests first."

"Who are these Purim? The rat man mentioned them but he didn't provide much of an explanation."

"The long answer would take me hours to tell, and then I would only scratch the surface of the history of the Purim and the Mongi. The short answer is that the Purim live a life of modern luxury behind their walls. Their affluence comes by way of the Mongi whom they consider to be a lesser species and whom they have cruelly dominated for thousands of years."

"Oh," Albro said, "just when I thought you were starting to make sense, we're back in the land of make believe."

"Damn you!" Nancy Wong said harshly and started to pull away.

"Hang on," Albro said. "I'm almost done. Do you have a flashlight?"

"I saw a small one in that drawer. Why?"

"I want to see how your pupils respond. It's not fool-proof, but it's one way to assess the severity of your concussion."

"Oh, so now we're playing doctor?"

"Honestly, Nancy, I'm just trying to help you. I've learned a few things here and there about injuries, as I'm sure you have too." Albro said as he searched the drawers in the small vanity. He found the light and then flipped off the cabin lights. He cupped Nancy Wong's chin in his hand and then shone the light in one eye and then the other. He flipped the cabin lights back on. "I'm no expert, but you seem to respond normally to the light. Does your head ache? Are you experiencing any dizziness?"

"Yes, but it's better than before. The dizziness has passed."

"Good," Albro said, "Now open your robe and let me see your ribs."

"Thank you, Doctor, but I can manage that myself."

"Just trying to help," Albro said.

"Well, you could help a lot more if you would believe what I'm telling you about Marlowe."

"Believe me Nancy, I'm trying. But think about it from my point of view. Why should I believe anything you've told me?"

"Because if you don't, you're going to get us all killed. We're lucky to still be alive, but we can't depend on luck because sooner or later it's going to run out."

"All this stuff about people moving back and forth between the past and the future is just too bizarre."

"Then forget about it and concentrate on the here and now."

"Okay," Albro said. "How can Marlowe afford this airplane? Somebody must be paying for it. There are rules and regulations to follow. You don't just plunk down a half-billion dollars and fly one of these off the lot. Also, he and his cadre seem pretty damned comfortable. They don't act like your friends Isaiah and Walter. They're not refugees from the future. They act like they belong here. Marlowe told me that he knew Crane when they were students at Cambridge."

Nancy Wong looked at the ceiling and inhaled a deep breath before looking at Albro. "Thomas Crane," she said, "told me that Marlowe can pretty much do as he pleases. The Purim block all attempts at passage between our worlds, unless, of course, there is something of over-riding concern. That is why it is so dangerous to attempt passage. Marlowe has been given free reign. Can you imagine how simple it would be to accumulate wealth if you had a thorough understanding of the passage of history before it happened? Marlowe has used that knowledge to his distinct advantage. Furthermore, it will be almost impossible to gain any advantage over him. In many ways, he will be able to anticipate our every move."

Albro thought about the significance of that last statement. In some ways, it mirrored some of his experiences in life. Sometimes he knew exactly how things were going to turn out. He'd never had any explanation for the phenomenon. He'd never had any control over it. It just happened of its own accord. There was a randomness that he'd never understood. It was as if the messages were being fired at him, and because he was a moving target, only a few ever struck home. And then something occurred to him.

"You said, 'almost.'"

Nancy Wong shook her head trying to remember what she had just said, "Almost what?" she asked.

"You said, 'it will be almost impossible to gain any advantage over Marlowe'."

"Crane tried to explain it to me. He said there exists a very small uncertainty in the relationship between the past and the future. The connection is not absolute. He said the universe likes to leave a little room for improvisation. He claimed it was the universe's only chance at amusement."

"Then that's it," Albro said.

"That's what?" Nancy Wong asked.

"That's where we find our advantage. We'll find a way to make the universe laugh."

Nancy Wong sighed heavily. "Albro, don't do this. You have to take Marlowe seriously."

Someone knocked at the door. "Marlowe is ready to speak with you," Charles said.

"I'll be just a few minutes," Nancy called to him. She whispered to Albro, "You have to go."

Albro started to leave. "Wait," she said. "If anything happens to me, promise that you will listen to Isaiah."

He gave her a quizzical look. "Nothing's going to happen to you," he said.

"Promise me!"

"Okay, okay, I promise you." When he saw that she didn't believe him he added, "Scout's honor." He held up three fingers and placed his other hand over his heart and smiled at her.

"You were never a Boy Scout," she said meeting his gaze.

"It's not too late, is it?" he asked. When he joined the others, Nancy Wong was already there.

"Ah, Mr. Swift," Marlowe said, "We were just speaking of you."

The three of them, Marlowe, Isaiah and Nancy were seated in a group around a small table. Walter was nowhere to be seen. Evidently he'd been relieved of his body-guard duty for the time being and was probably parked in the kitchen, Albro thought. He took the empty chair next to Nancy.

"Would you care for something to drink, a bite to eat, perhaps?" Marlowe inquired politely. He seemed to relish playing the part of the magnanimous host, Albro thought.

"Coffee," Albro said.

"Charles," Marlowe called. "Bring us a plate of sandwiches and something for Colonel Rattam."

Albro saw the rat man stiffen, but he remained silent.

Marlowe turned to Albro, "A true Mongi does not eat meat, and a devout Mongi would rather starve to death than let flesh of any kind pass his lips. But perhaps our Mongi friends have told you that already."

"There has been little time for such explanations," said the rat man.

"Then I suggest that is where we start. I think Mr. Swift would appreciate an explanation of a good many things. Colonel Rattam, known to you as Brother Isaiah is a member of a religious sect known as the *Order*. Along with his companion Walter, they have come to us from another time. I realize, of course, that you are skeptical of this, and rightly so. We think of time as the ticking of a clock, which is a bit like trying to describe the surface of the earth by using a road map of your local township." Marlowe gave a sharp laugh and shook his head.

"Time, you see Mr. Swift, is really at the crux of everything, and it's a difficult thing to get one's mind around. It might help if you try to imagine time as a vast ocean, an infinite sphere enclosing an infinite volume, the surface of which defines our present reality. Imagine yourself in a ship upon that ocean sailing toward a horizon that recedes forever, a horizon you can never cross. Unbeknownst to you, there exists another realm that lies beneath you, a realm that holds all of existence. Every incident from the monumental explosion of stars to the single beat of an infant's heart is held there. It is a realm that no living creature can experience. It is a place where time ceases to have meaning, and yet, think of the possibilities if one were able to sink into it. The horizon of time would no longer be of issue. One could move freely from any point on the surface to any point in the whole of existence. That ability is the gift of the Mongi.

"Unfortunately, even among the Mongi, it is a rare gift. Millennia may pass with its secret locked within their genes and then suddenly, an awakening begins and the ability makes its presence known. A single individual surfaces and there occurs a calling forth to others with the same latent ability, and they begin to come together. The Mongi refer to this event as the 'Gathering'. It may be only a handful who have awakened to their amazing ability, or it may be a thousand; the greater the number, the greater their power.

"An awakening has been in progress for more than a century, growing in strength day by day, year by year and the Gathering will soon be complete. There are those whose aim is to use the power of the Gathering to achieve their own ends, that is, to unlock the secret of that power. One should consider that to move freely without any restriction anywhere in any *time*, is an ability that only God should possess.

"The *Jade Prince* might very well hold the key to that secret, but before I explain that, let me turn back to the Mongi. I am of your time, Mr. Swift, and yet I have had the privilege of living in other times as well. An experience, I'm sure, the good monk will accuse me of using to my personal advantage. Be that as it may. I'm sure he will also agree that it gives me a unique, and hopefully useful, perspective on our current situation.

"The Mongi were once the same as you and I. If you will allow me to once again return to the metaphor of our ship. Out there, ahead of us, there will come a time of great turmoil. Our course cannot be changed to avoid it. Believe me, it is a time that has already occurred for I have seen it with my own eyes. It is a time of great desperation. The earth has warmed considerably, which was begun by the profligate habits of the current seven billion inhabitants of this planet, and furthered by an increase of seven billion more in less than a hundred years. All of whom, I might add, wish to eat. Eventually the inevitable happens. Technology, as great as it may be, can no longer compensate for the ruined biosphere. A worldwide crop failure occurs. There is a brief recovery, and then there is another and another.

"I am not speaking of isolated failures around the world. I am speaking of the catastrophic failure of entire agricultural systems with world-wide consequences. Let me be brief with my description. Fourteen billion hungry mouths will very quickly consume every living creature within their grasp, and will eventually turn on each other.

"Imagine for a moment a world in which all living flesh is being consumed to feed one species. It is more than some individuals are willing to accept. A bold plan is conceived to save as many species as possible. You are probably thinking that cryogenics is the answer, a kind of genetic seed bank that future generations could open up and reconstitute like some kind of frozen fruit juice. Caught in technology's downward spiral such a scheme would have been doomed to failure. Besides, like any resource, a genetic bank would have been fought over to the last human standing.

"Instead, a way is found to hide the genetic material of a thousand key species where no one would find them in hopes that one day in the future, they could be retrieved. A method is discovered, in which a simple virus-like organism can hold within its shell not only its own simple genetic instructions, but that of another creature as well. Once it finds a host, an unknowing, unsuspecting human being, it will go about reproducing itself along with a perfect copy of the genetic secret held within its microscopic walls.

"It is hoped that within a few years the world, minus many billions of its human inhabitants, will recover. One individual aims to control the reintroduction of those species. It is a grand plan, one that not only has the heroic goal to save at least some semblance of the natural world, but also the god-like power to recreate it. Not only will that individual's power become immense, he will also be looked upon as a savior, and be recognized as perhaps the greatest human being the world has ever known. But nature itself is a player in all of this, a player who has been grossly underestimated.

"The years pass, and nature adamantly refuses to allow mankind even a brief respite from the punishment it had brought upon itself.

Civilization falters and then disintegrates. It will be several millennia before it rises again, this time with a very different face.

"You see, Nature had begun to work its way, patiently chipping away at the manmade edifice that held its creations within its prison of protoplasm. Eventually, nature found a way to break those walls and once again let those creatures of a past world see the light of day. Disturbing characteristics began to appear randomly among different races and ethnicities, and were thought to be birth defects. Often times, the infant was euthanized and the parents warned away from any further attempts to conceive. Governments attempt to control all reproductive matters, but it cannot control the sequence of events that had been set in motion by a past not only beyond their reach, but their understanding as well. Nature had its own designs upon the human race and the great division was already underway, and thus, the Mongi came into being.

"Millennia upon millennia will pass. Civilizations rise and fall. Each convinced beyond doubt that theirs is the pinnacle of all time. Knowledge is gained and lost and gained again in a cycle that seems doomed to forever repeat itself. The drama of life is very old on this planet and in absolute terms is very near its end. Yet, its last act will go on for hundreds of thousands of years.

"Granted, I cannot present to you the hard scientific proof of what I have just described, and even if I could, I have no doubt that Mongi scholars would dispute much of it. I am as much a prisoner of time as they are. But this fact remains: we are bound to their time as they are bound to ours, and we are slowly, but inexorably being pulled together. Think again of that ship. When one ship collides with another, there is the chance that one or both will sink and be lost forever in that vast ocean that lies below. The *Jade Prince* was sent here as a kind of lifeboat for those who survive that collision. Who created the Jade Prince? How has it come to exist in this time and space? The answers to those questions, and many others that have undoubtedly risen in your mind..." At this point Marlowe, for the first time, seemed to be at a loss for words. After a moment he shrugged his shoulders. "We may never know the answer to those questions," he concluded.

"That is true," spoke the rat man, "but only as far as it goes."

"There, you see," Marlowe said showing his palms the way a magician professes innocence to his audience, "Our learned Mongi, the esteemed Isaiah Rattam, former professor of ancient studies, former Colonel in the *Army of Liberation of the Great Revolution*, will now offer you his perspective, which I am sure you will find informative, and hopefully, not in total disagreement with my own."

Albro looked at Marlowe as he sat back. There was a look of expectation on the man's face as if he had just issued a challenge to the rat man, but his tone had conveyed quite another message: *'be careful of what you say, old boy.'*

Isaiah said, "Marlowe's explanation of how our race arose is plausible. As you can see, it supports the view that we are children not of God, but of man, and therefore we are somehow less than human. A great effort has taken place over the generations to sieve our genes from the Purim population in order to create a purity of form, and yet, it is the Mongi, the *homo animalis*, who have proven to be more resilient. We have withstood the purges, the genocides, the holocausts, the genetic manipulations that attempt to turn us into everything from slaving laborers, to cattle so *they* might have their flesh. The bitter irony is, although they would never admit it, our survival has meant the survival and prosperity of the Purim people. In our time, the world is nearing its end. That is why the Purim leaders have turned to the Mongi for help.

Yes, our worlds are bound together and there exists one pathway between them, a pathway jealously guarded by the Purim. That pathway is narrow and crossing it involves great risk. As those who awaken gather together, their combined strength will force new passages to open. It is conceivable that with enough power, an entire world could be brought through.

"Our world is crumbling. It has become like a piece of fruit left too long in the sun. The verdant lushness that you have here, has for us turned to dust. The oceans have become cauldrons for a salt-laden stew of poisonous slime. The rivers have gone dry and the lakes are empty bowls filled only with sand. It is only the deepest wells that continue to supply water, and they too have begun fail.

"The Prophets have long spoken of a time of deliverance in which the Mongi will be guided safely from one world into another. They speak of the Emissary who will arrive in our midst to announce the coming of the *'One who shows the way'*. We believe, Albro Swift, that your father was the Emissary. He came into our midst with news of the *Jade Prince*."

The rat man paused. He reached for the glass of water at his side. He looked at it sadly and then drank. "I'm sorry," he said. "It is still difficult for me to believe that something so precious in my time is so abundant in yours."

Albro, who had been struggling to keep everything straight in his mind said, "So, you think this *Jade Prince* is your Moses, so to speak, the one who's going to lead you to the promised-land."

"No," replied the rat man. "The *Jade Prince* is but a tool, a very powerful tool. In the wrong hands it could prove to be devastatingly powerful."

"Then who's your man, the captain of your lifeboat? It seems to me, that sooner or later he's the one we're going to have to deal with. Am I right?" He reached for another sandwich and took a bite"

The rat man sat silent. He looked first at Marlowe and then at Nancy Wong. They seemed to be daring each other to be the first to speak.

"Well?" Albro asked. "I need to know who were dealing with, or you'll have to find yourself another treasure hunter."

"Mr. Swift," said the rat man, "there are many who seek the *Jade Prince*, but there is only one who is destined to deliver us from our peril."

Albro slowed his chewing. There was something about the way that last statement made the skin of the back of neck tingle. "Are you suggesting that not only do I find this thing for you, you expect me to lead you and your people to the *Promised Land*?"

"At last you understand," the rat man said.

Albro looked from the rat man to Nancy Wong and then to Marlowe. He raised his hand. "Let's get something straight. Providing we can come to an agreement on what you're willing to pay and how to go about finding this thing, I'll play along, but that's as far as I go. After that, you're on your own."

"Ten million American dollars," Marlowe said, "has been deposited in your name with the Bank of Hong Kong. You can confirm that tomorrow. Whether or not you decide to find the *Jade Prince*, it is yours to do with as you please. Consider it compensation for the inconvenience you have suffered. In the short term, it should help you in buying some security for yourself, but I dare say it will not be enough to save you."

The figure of ten million dollars sat Albro back in his chair. He said, "Let's just say, for the sake of discussion, that I agree to look for the *Jade Prince*. What then?"

"Then we will help you in whatever way that we can," Marlowe said.

"And if I just happen to get lucky and actually find it, what's the prize?"

Marlowe furrowed his brow and looked gravely at Albro. "It is not a matter of winning a prize, Mr. Swift. It is a matter of saving lives, billions of them, your own included."

Albro sat very still. The three of them let Marlowe's last statement hang in the air like a cold fog. It was a bullshit story, but after what had transpired in the last sixty-odd hours, it was looking more and more like the genuine prize was to come out of this alive. There was a real temptation to believe that ten million dollars suggested there was some truth in all of this. Money always held an element of truth, and ten million was a lot of money. At least that part of it should be an easy thing to confirm.

"Okay," Albro said, "Where do we start?

CHAPTER 30

"THAT," said Marlowe, "is a very good question. By asking it I hope that you have agreed to join us."

"Don't let your hopes get too high," Albro answered. "At the moment, I don't see any other way to stay alive. That could change at any time."

"Fair enough," Marlowe said. "That at least gives us a starting point. The first order of business upon reaching Hong Kong will be to locate the map that Thomas Crane provided."

"Hang on," Albro said. "It's great that you think there's a map that's going to tell us where to find this thing, but I think you're putting the cart before the horse. I want to know exactly what we're looking for, and then maybe I'll understand the why of it. Only then will I have a chance of finding it." Albro paused, thinking. He said, "When you were a kid, did you ever play the game, *Blind Man's Bluff*? You know, where one kid is blindfolded and the others taunt him from just beyond reach. Curiously enough, it's believed to have originated in ancient China. The child who was 'It' was called *ling dai*. I'm the guy who's blindfolded. I'm *ling dai*.

"I know all about the legend, the myth, call it what you like, about the *Jade Prince*. You're saying there is some truth in that, but you're also saying it's some kind of bomb that could blow the hell out of everything. You all know who Krupp is, Newton's mad scientist? Of course you do, and you probably know that he showed me that holographic image. Is that what we're after, a six-foot stone statue? By the way, what would something like that weigh, three hundred, four hundred pounds? That's not something you're going to slip into your pocket and stroll away with. Or maybe, it's more like this?" Albro paused long enough to pull the small gold coin from under his shirt

A look of satisfaction eased the contours of Marlowe's brow. He asked, "Where did you get that?"

Albro had a sense that it was the kind of question someone asks when he already knows the answer. He dropped the gold coin back under his shirt. He felt like the fool who has given away his hand by prematurely playing his Ace. He had no choice now but to bluff his way ahead. "I'll tell you where that came from when you tell me what the *Jade Prince* really is."

"I wish that I could," Marlowe said. "I know something of what it can do. As I said before, I don't know what it is. I don't think anyone knows what it is. Even those who claim it as their own do not know what it is."

Marlowe gave a hard look to the rat man and seemed to wait for a rebuttal. The rat man only stared at him. Marlowe turned back to Albro. "Do you remember my telling you about the need to run an errand? I flew to London. I daresay I've been working my flight crew around the clock. As a matter of fact, they are sleeping right now. You needn't worry; this aircraft is a technological marvel. It is completely capable of flying itself and even landing itself if that were to become necessary.

"As I was saying, I went to the British Museum, that same place where Thomas Crane first stumbled on evidence of the *Jade Prince*, or so he said. I had a hunch that your father had been less than truthful with me regarding the discovery that he had made there. It did not take me long to verify my misgivings. Your father did not discover an artifact, the significance of which had been overlooked by others. Quite the contrary, he brought something *to* the museum and left it there, knowing full well that it would be the rare person who would recognize it, and realize its true significance."

362

Marlowe pressed a hidden button in the arm of his chair and spoke. "Charles, bring me the object."

A moment later, Charles entered carrying a small box. He set it on the table between them and retreated to the far end of the cabin where he stood watching. Marlowe took a pair of cotton gloves from his pocket. He removed the lid from the box, lifted out the object and held it in the palms of both hands.

Isaiah half rose out of his chair and then sat back down. "The Lamp of Arraam!" he said. "We were certain it had been destroyed."

Marlowe set it carefully on the table. The rat man's eyes followed every move of Marlowe's hands and then remained riveted to the object. It appeared to Albro to be nothing more than a simple oil lamp made of clay. Its only distinguishing feature was a double stranded-braid around its middle, very similar in design to the raised scar that now graced the inside of his forearm, and the design present on the gold coins. He reached out for the lamp.

"Don't," the rat man said before Albro could touch the object. "Please, you must not touch it with your bare skin."

"What's so special about it?" Albro asked.

"It is the *'lamp that lights the way'*," the rat man said.

"Yes," Marlowe said, "Tell Mr. Swift what makes it so special."

The rat man looked first at Marlowe, then at Albro. He said, "It is one of the most sacred objects of the one true religion."

"Go on, Brother Isaiah," Marlowe said, in a tone that one might use to encourage a shy student.

"Only the *Jade Prince* may touch the lamp."

"'*By its sacred light He shall find the Way and lead them from the hand of oppression,*'" Marlowe said with a theatrical tone of sincerity in his voice.

"It has thus been written," the rat man said solemnly. "Thomas Crane was in the temple when it was destroyed."

"Correction," Marlowe stated. "He was there moments before it was destroyed, and then he was gone."

"Wait a minute," Albro said. "Before you get into an argument over who did what, let's back up. The two of you are talking like the *Jade Prince* is a person. Not two minutes ago you told me that it is some kind of powerful tool. I can't shake the feeling that something's getting lost in translation here."

"Yes," said Marlowe. "You are correct. I know this must be confusing to you. Are you familiar with quantum theory, how an object such as an electron can both be a particle and an energy field? Have you ever wondered how an object, such as Ms Wong for instance, can be a living entity and yet be made up of inanimate particles, how she can be living and non-living at the same time?

"If one could look very closely at Ms Wong, one would see the cells which make up her tissue. If one looked closer still, one might see the chains of molecules which make up the walls of those cells. Look closer and you would discover the atoms that make up those molecules. Now, if you could delve even closer, you would see that the atoms are made of even smaller particles. Keep going and eventually Ms. Wong is nothing but a collection of seething energy fields held together by enormous forces. The curious thing is, no matter how closely one looks, one never finds the living part of her, yet it is there all the time.

"The *Jade Prince* is no different. It consists of inanimate particles held together by enormous forces and yet it is living. When Crane discovered the *Jade Prince*, all those years ago, it was deep underground, beneath the ruins of an ancient city. He found it embedded within a matrix of basalt with only a portion its face showing. Basalt is a volcanic rock of a particular crystalline structure. Those crystals, he explained to me, are like tiny clocks. Read the time on those clocks and you know the age of the rock. He found the age to be over three hundred million years. What he could see of the finely carved jade was enough to tell him that his was an extraordinary discovery, one that would shake mankind's vision of itself to its very roots.

"He could not proceed alone. He needed manpower, equipment, lab facilities. In addition he needed security. After all, this was Laos and in 1973 there was a war going on. To complicate matters, Crane was not an archeologist, but he had connections within the government. I told you he was involved with clandestine affairs. He put together a team, and with the assistance of the military, began excavating the site. There were conflicts from the beginning. Before long, he found that he had made something of a Faustian bargain. The military would allow him to be in charge, but they would keep the discovery to themselves. The relationship reached a breaking point when the military brought in a brilliant archeologist by the name of Heinrich Krupp, to assist Crane. Crane suspected, and rightly so, this new scientist was to be his replacement.

"Crane decided to announce the discovery in a public forum. It was at that gathering of physicists in Hong Kong that he planned to release the news. It was too late. Krupp suspected that Crane had discovered much about the *Jade Prince* that he had not revealed to his military partners. Krupp notified his superiors who prevented Crane from speaking at the forum. It was Martin Osborn Newton who informed Crane that he was finished with the project. You see, it was Newton who had been acting behind the scenes all along. It had been his intent from the very beginning to assume control of the project. He had no idea though, what Crane had already learned about the *Jade Prince*. Crane used that knowledge to destroy the excavation site. He disappeared from this world, and the *Jade Prince* was nowhere to be found. "Did he know what he was doing? I don't think so. If he had realized the events that he would set in motion, I don't believe he would have begun the excavation. He would have turned his back on the *Jade Prince* and left it sealed within its tomb.

"I believe that from the very beginning Crane thought the *Jade Prince* was meant to be found. He told me that he had a sense that it called to him from its stony grave, and that it would call to someone else and keep calling until it was released. The Mongi claim to hear its call, and they are not so naïve to believe that they are the only ones. As Brother Isaiah will attest, there are those who will stop at nothing to find it.

"That is why Thomas Crane formed a plan, of which we know only pieces and parts. It is a great tragedy that he is not sitting here with us. Did he know that he might die before he could once more find the *Jade Prince* before it was too late?   I think so, for he made a provision for that eventuality. Each one of us is a part of that plan, and you Mr. Swift, are at the center of it. You are that provision. Perhaps that is not fair. Perhaps it is not right to use someone's life as a means to one's own ends. I will not be the judge of that. Let the billions of people whose lives hang in the balance be the judge of that."

Albro sat very still trying to digest what Marlowe had just told him. He wished that Roger, who knew all about electrons and time warps, was here with him. And then, just as quickly, thanked his lucky stars that Roger wasn't.   He looked at the three of them: Nancy Wong, who couldn't hide the fear behind her oriental façade, the rat-man with his unfathomable eyes, and Marlowe with his look of aloof superiority. If he had his way, he would chuck the lot of them, big Wally included, although he had to admit that Walter had saved his life more than once already.

Albro looked at Marlowe. "You've left out one part."

"Yes," Marlowe admitted, "and I did so because I'm not sure that you're ready to hear it."

"Why don't you let me decide that," Albro said.

Marlowe looked at the other two and then cleared his throat. "Thomas Crane disappeared from this world, and reappeared in another. The way he described it to me, it was as if he had awakened from a dream. I'm sure you have noticed how the world is slightly different when you awaken than it was when you had fallen asleep. The clouds in the sky have rearranged themselves, the air smells different. You look in the mirror and notice that something has changed in your own face. You are aware of the changes, yet if you were to dwell on those things, you would very quickly become incapacitated. The mind has evolved in such a way as to make a leap of faith. It tells itself that all is just as it was the day before, ignores for the most part all of those little changes and gets on with the tasks of survival. Thomas Crane quickly focused on his new life, and it was not until later that he realized his old life had been only a shadow cast by this new life he found himself living."

CHAPTER 31

ALBRO lay in the narrow bed and stared up at the curved ceiling of the aircraft's skin. He reckoned they were somewhere over the broad reaches of the western Pacific Ocean, angling southward to Hong Kong. He listened to the muffled roar of the engines, and tried to make sense out of what was going on. Whichever way he looked it, he saw himself in the center of it, just like Marlowe said. Someone had put him there, had tied him so tight to this *Jade Prince*, whatever it was, he could literally feel the constraints. The only way to get lose was to find it, and even if he found it there was no guarantee they were going to let him go. The rat man kept insisting he was going to accompany him and Walter on some hare-brained liberation movement. Did they think he was a trained mercenary soldier? He'd never come close to joining the military. He'd never fired a gun, never wielded a bayonet. He had never even marched in a parade!

Plus, they had told him to stay away from Newton and Monique until this was over. For Christ sakes! He was engaged to be married! They had a date and everything! Monique was wearing a diamond the size of wren's egg. He hadn't bought it, of course, but did that matter? What was he supposed to say to her? 'Sorry, Sweetheart, but I have to save the world. Wait, make that two worlds! It shouldn't take more than a week or two. In the mean time keep the home-fires burning and put a candle in the window'.

If anybody could help them, it was Martin Osborne Newton. He had more resources at his disposal than most of the world governments combined. Who would even think of getting in his way? Martin could move heaven and earth if necessary. He'd tried to convince them of that, but to no avail. At last, he'd agreed to not contact Martin or Monique, and now he regretted having done so. How was he going to explain this to Monique? Would she call off the wedding? Would she accuse him of cheating on her? There had been that young thing from the hospital, and then Elsa. But those couplings had occurred while he'd been half asleep. They didn't even qualify as dalliances. He'd been in a vulnerable state! Real cheating involved planning, deliberation, *premeditation*! He was guilty of none of that. Women just seemed to fall his way, literally. Besides, fidelity came *after* marriage. Everybody knew that!

He needed to let her know that at least he was alive. He had told them that, but they had not relented. Nancy Wong had hammered him especially hard. It was clear that she was jealous of Monique, which made all of her arguments irrational, as far as he was concerned. Nevertheless, he had agreed. He was going to have to work with her, and he knew that if he gave her a sense of power now it would be easier to take it away from her later. When the time came for that he could point out to her how foolish she had been.

Still, with all that was in the mix, it was the concept of Monique trying to stop him from finding the Jade Prince that was the most troubling. The way they had described her she sounded like the Wicked Witch of the West, Snow White's evil step-mother and Lady Macbeth all rolled into one. She was remarkably intelligent, charming and incredibly beautiful. Only when it was too late would he discover that she was also deceiving, treacherous, vicious, and brutally self-serving. She would stop at nothing to get what she wanted. That wasn't the Monique that he had fallen in love with. He knew her in ways they did not.

He'd tried to defend her, and in so doing he had been drawn back to that dream he'd had when he'd passed out in the crash. It was as if his mind was trying to merge Monique with the woman in the dream. Freudians would have a heyday with that one, he thought. *'In every*

369

woman you encounter, you are searching for the mother who abandoned you.'

Monique had held him gently as had the unknown woman in the dream. He had suckled them both! Sure, his mouth did seem to aggressively seek out a woman's breast, like a starving infant in need of a good meal. But so what? He was willing to bet that he was not alone amidst thirty-something males in that behavior. So why did the idea now seem to feel uncomfortable?

Still, the revival of the memory had left him feeling bound even more tightly to Monique. She was the best thing that had ever happened to him, and yet they were telling him she was his greatest enemy.

"Why not let her have the *Jade Prince*, and save a lot of trouble?" he had asked.

The rat man had shuddered and had withdrawn into his own thoughts. Marlowe had said, "Yes, we could do that, and she might spare your life. She would kill the rest of us without a second thought, but she might let you live until you got in her way, or she simply tired of you."

"If she is such a bad girl, why do so many people love and admire her?" he had asked.

This time, Nancy Wong had responded. He'd been watching her grow ever more agitated until she was like a pot ready to boil over. She had finally lost her self control and had burst out, "You really don't see it do you. How she manipulates everyone, you included, with her beautiful body and her Hollywood smile! You're as blind as everyone else! I could tell you things about that woman that would make your heart stop!"

Marlowe had raised a hand before she could continue, but for one short moment Albro had seen something in Nancy Wong's eyes that he had not seen before. It had nothing to do with petty female jealousies and everything to do with stark, unvarnished fear.

Was he really supposed to believe everything they had told him? What else could he do? On the one hand, reality seemed to have taken a holiday, and on the other hand, people were getting killed. You couldn't get more real than that.

Still, his thoughts went back to Monique. Where was she? What was she doing? Was she thinking of him? He thought back to the first moment he had laid eyes on her. She had looked like an angel in that creamy white suit with her luxuriant hair flowing around her beautiful face. How lucky could a guy be? He'd been on the brink of disaster, and she had appeared like a rescuing angel, and all because of that jade dagger he'd been so desperate to retrieve. Had it just been luck, or had it been his destiny to meet her. He thought about what the rat man had said about the future making the past. Had that dagger pointed him in her direction, or had it prodded him? He thought about that until his eyes grew heavy.

As his eyes closed and he finally began to relax, his thoughts slowly backed him to the edge of consciousness. There his mind seemed to briefly pause, as if it had taken note of something vital, something he had previously missed. And then his mind tilted precipitously, dumping the entirety of his existence into the chasm of his subconscious. His life tumbled, shattered and came to rest in a pattern of profound clarity. And then in a painful realization, as if that jade dagger had pierced his heart, he saw Monique for who she was. But his subconscious chose not to rouse him, chose to not even place the truth in a dream that might be remembered, no matter how vaguely, upon awakening. Instead, his unconscious let the words of the Prophets rise like a resounding chorus, *'...and there is a time for angels and a time for rain; a time for sorrow and a time for pain; a time for fire and a time for lust; a time for dreams and a 'time for dust.'*

CHAPTER 32

MARLOWE had stood as the others left the lounge and went to their individual cabins. Always the polite host, Isaiah thought. Marlowe was always ready to put the comfort of his guests seemingly above his own. Always ready with the flattering words, the magnanimous gesture. Always ready to extend the offer of help. All of that was genuine, to be sure, but all at a cost. Marlowe never invested anything without an expectation of a generous return. That much soon became obvious to anyone pulled within his sphere of power. It was to be expected that Marlowe would have his own plans for the *Jade Prince*.

Marlowe turned and saw the look in the Mongi's face. "Well, comrade, here we are again, *brothers in arms*."

"I laid down my arms many years ago," Isaiah said, an undisguised note of contempt in his voice.

"Ah, yes. The great Colonel Rattam turned monk. The warrior lays down his sword and takes up the staff of righteousness. Have you found a better life among the Prophets?"

"I have found it to be a life free of treachery and betrayal."

"I would have thought the Prophets might have opened your eyes to the realities of existence. But you are as blind as ever. Treachery and betrayal exist at every level, even within the holiest confines of the Order. Surely, you know that better than anyone."

"If you are referring to the acquiescence of the Order to the demands of the Purim regime, I consider it an act of self-preservation, almost human in its utility. Martyrdom has its time and place."

"And is that why you have come to this place and time, to become a martyr to your cause?"

"I am here because I was called. As for my life, it is, as it has always been, in the hands of the Almighty."

"Spoken like a true believer!" Marlowe said smiling.

"That is something you will never understand."

"And yet, we are drawn together, you, the believer, and I, the infidel. You need me as much as I need you. Without my help, you won't even get close to the *Jade Prince*, and even if you managed by some miracle to do so, that young man whom you've put so much stock into will be entirely helpless to control it. Crane may have told you all he knew, but that wasn't enough was it? That's why he came back. Unfortunately, he failed."

"He was murdered," Isaiah said. And as yet, we do not know that he failed, he thought to himself.

"I offered my help, but he refused," Marlowe stated firmly, "I warned him, just as I am warning you."

"It was you who arranged his death," Isaiah challenged, rising out of his chair.

"If you mean that I was ineffectual in convincing him to take my help, then yes, I stand accused. But it was not I who tore his flesh to pieces. The assassin was a Mongi, your own kind, most likely one of the same group who attacked you earlier tonight."

Isaiah returned heavily to his seat. He had shamefully known the two gunmen to be Mongi. He had felt their murderous thoughts, had seen behind their masks. Yet, he was not ready to concede anything to Marlowe. He said, "You forget that I know you very well. Your offer to help Crane to retrieve the *Jade Prince*, I am certain, was not without a price."

"A price that he claimed was too high. He is dead and now that you you've had a taste of what you're up against, you might feel

373

differently regarding my offer of assistance. I thought that you might be more rational in your response."

Isaiah sighed, "What is it you want?"

"It is not what I want. I serve the wishes of the Church. And it is the Church's wish to get to the bottom of this mystery. I am only a humble investigator acting upon their behalf. Believe me Colonel; we are on the same side."

"There are no 'sides' in this affair. There is only existence," Isaiah retorted.

"Exactly," Marlowe said, "I could not have described the situation better. That is why our cooperation is of the utmost importance."

"Why should I cooperate with you?"

"Really, Colonel, you surprise me with your naiveté, or is it just plain stubbornness? Have you ever wondered why the Church tolerates the Order? Although you have sprung from the same roots, the Order seems to do everything in its power to disparage the Church, and yet the Church allows for your continued existence. Why do you think that is?"

"The Order follows the teachings of the one true God, and therefore we are protected by His Grace."

"Come now, Colonel, you know as well as I that the Church could wipe the Order clean from the earth, just as it has done countless other sects such as yours in the past."

"Only to have them sprout again," Isaiah said.

"Precisely," Marlowe said. "The Church has come to realize, in what I consider a perfectly pragmatic move, that the Order is an integral part of the Church itself. That is not to say the Church can sanction all that you profess. The Church has come to the realization that to eliminate the Order would be like you or I cutting off an arm or leg simply because we find it vexing in some way. The Church finds the Order far too useful."

Isaiah looked skeptically at Marlowe. He asked, "Do you expect me to believe the Church will support the Mongi people's desire to be free from Purim domination?"

"You are always too ready to mix politics with religion. What I've been entrusted to convey to you is a sense of assurance that if the *Jade*

Prince proves to be what we believe it to be, then the Church will allow the Order to benefit."

"But the Mongi people, how will they be allowed to benefit? The *Jade Prince* belongs to them!"

"Colonel, you know full well to allow the Mongi to possess the Jade Prince would lead them to destroy the Purim, and to the destruction of themselves in the process. So you see the Church is actually doing you a favor. After all, the struggles between the Mongi and the Purim are rather petty compared to the survival of entire worlds. But all of this talk of possession will be moot if we do not come to the point of this conversation. What are we going to do with Elijah? You may not know, but he no longer wishes to be called by that name. He now wishes to be known as the *Old Man*."

For all he wanted to confront Marlowe over the treatment of the Mongi by the Purim, Isaiah knew that he had to let it go for the time being. He had to face the facts of their situation. They could do little without Marlowe's help. They were strangers in a strange land with little or no resources, and to even consider going it alone against Elijah was a foolish waste of time. Elijah had been on their trail ever since they had come into this world.

Isaiah said absently, "I saw him burned at the stake, his bones ground into dust and scattered on the wind."

"Then I would say you under estimated the old boy," Marlowe said ruefully. "The last time I saw him, which wasn't all that long ago, he was looking alive and well. By the way, he told me to send you his regards. I do believe that he's looking forward to seeing you. I find that rather surprising, considering what the Order tried to do to him."

"How could he possibly be alive? I was there. I witnessed his death," Isaiah said.

"The people of this time have a very appropriate saying," Marlowe said. "*'Time heals all wounds'.* In this case, quite literally it seems. If you two meet, please try to restrain yourself. Your very existence depends upon his survival."

"What do you mean?"

"It is he who will save the life of Martin Osborne Newton."

"Other than his avaricious desire for power, what does Newton have to do with this?" Isaiah demanded, but the answer to his question began to form in his mind before the last word left his lips.

"It will be his vast enterprise that enables the transformation, the great division, as the Mongi like to refer to it, that changes the face of humanity. You see, all of this has been predetermined by what we must now think of as the future. In reality, you and I do not exist and will not exist if the Old Man does not live. That is what I tried to tell Thomas Crane, but he wouldn't listen. He was intent upon altering the future. That is why the Mongi assassins killed him."

"You cannot be certain that our existence depends upon Elijah. There are unnumbered pathways to our time."

"True. But change one and you run the risk of changing them all. I am afraid that we are in the uncomfortable position of making certain that Elijah comes to no harm."

"I cannot be partner to such evil. I must speak with the Council."

"Ah, and there is the irony. You, who have long disparaged the Council as a group of bickering cowards, are finally in a position to affect the lives of your people and you defer to the Council. The debate would require months. There is not time. You are their de facto representative. The decision rests with you."

"And if I say 'no' to your proposal?"

"Then you and your companions will lose whatever protection I can provide. Those who seek the *Jade Prince* will stop at nothing, and in their ignorance they will destroy this world and your almighty God only knows how many others."

"And you believe there is a way to control it?"

"At last we come to Albro Marshal Swift. And you needn't look so surprised. I have sources within the Council. I've known since the beginning that he holds the key. I take it he still does not realize that?"

"No."

"Good. We've waited a long time for this moment. We wouldn't want to spoil things by acting too soon." Marlowe looked down at the defeated countenance of the Mongi. "It's a shame that Crane could not bring himself to see beyond his own stubborn ideals. A world that is less than perfect is still better than no world at all. Wouldn't you agree?"

Isaiah wanted desperately to hold back his answer. Would it not be better, he thought, to stop all the suffering once and for all? But that would also mean ending all that was good, all that was beautiful, all that was hopeful, all that might yet be. He bowed his head as if to pray. "Yes," he replied.

"Can I take that to mean we have a deal?" Marlowe asked.

"Yes," Isaiah said in a voice that was barely audible.

"Good," Marlowe said. "I suggest you get some sleep while the opportunity still exists."

CHAPTER 33

ALBRO could see that Marlowe definitely had some influence with the authorities in Hong Kong. Once on the ground, the big jet avoided the terminal and was shunted to a smaller building with no windows that Albro suspected was used for high security. Only in this case, it was the lack of security that was striking. A single man met them inside the otherwise empty terminal.

"Mr. Chin will see you to the safe-house," Marlowe said. "We have already begun refueling. The less time I spend on the ground, the less chance there is of drawing attention. Officially, you are guests of the Chinese Government. Passports have been issued for you, complete with official stamp of entry. Mr. Chin has brought your travel visas. You now have the necessary documents to move about the country, but it is by no means a guarantee that you will be allowed to move freely. The documents will pass muster with low-level officials, but if you get into serious trouble, you will, in all likelihood, be detained. Try to be discreet."

Albro looked at the distinctly rodent features of Brother Isaiah, aka Colonel Ratham, aka Izzy, and the walrus-like figure of Walter, both of whom had been outfitted in tan slacks and sports coats and shirts with a tropical print. Albro rolled his eyes at the thought of discretion. If he'd had his way, he would have left the entire troupe on the plane and tackled the job himself. He'd listened as Marlowe had unveiled his plan to track down the *Jade Prince* using the sketchy information that Nancy Wong had supplied which had been given to her by Thomas Crane, his alleged father. None of it had felt right. Everything from the safe-house to the contacts to provide whatever transport might be needed had set off all kinds of alarm bells inside his head.

Marlowe's plan dictated that they locate the map which Crane had left somewhere in Hong Kong, follow its route which they were guessing led into Mainland China, and locate the *Jade Prince*. They would then call Marlowe on a satellite phone and he would fly in like the airborne cavalry, hopefully in something smaller than a jumbo jet, and pluck them to safety. It was simple and direct and guaranteed to get them all arrested, or maybe even killed. He had no intention of keeping to any of it except possibly the satellite phone. That might come in handy. In addition, Marlowe had given Albro and Nancy cell phones, but had warned them to use them only when absolutely necessary. Although their conversations would be secure, the signals could still be traced.

Chin ushered them to an elevator that took them down to a parking garage where a black Mercedes sedan idled. Marlowe had provisioned them with luggage filled with clothes and the essential toiletries of the average tourist. In their hats and dark glasses, Isaiah and Walter looked more like Miami Mafiosi than your average tourist, but at least they appeared passably human. The driver jumped out and loaded everything into the trunk and they all got in. The driver steered them into a tunnel. They avoided the main terminal and came out into emerging daylight onto the main highway that would take them away from the city center and into the surrounding hills.

When they were safely beyond the airport, Albro took out his own freshly charged phone, ignored the flashing message icon and punched in a local number. He spoke briefly and hung up.

"What are you doing?' Nancy asked him.

"Don't worry. I didn't call Monique. I said I wouldn't, and I won't," Albro answered.

"Then who did you call?"

"A friend," Albro answered. He'll help us with a slight change of plans."

"Why? I thought we'd all agreed on what to do."

E.D. HAYMAKER

"Relax, Nancy, I know what I'm doing." Albro tapped on Chin's shoulder and spoke to him. Chinn nodded and spoke to the driver. The driver made a maneuver that brought them around and pointed them back toward the city center.

The comfort of the luxury sedan temporarily sealed them off from the cacophony that was Hong Kong twenty-four hours a day. Not yet 6:00 a.m. and the highway was racing with heavy traffic. It was truly a city that never rested. Walter sat next to the window and was taking in the sights. As usual, the rat man remained impassive, sitting erect with his eyes straight ahead. Nancy Wong had a look of apprehension in her face. She winced whenever the sedan made a jerky motion.

"How are you feeling?" Albro asked.

"It's my ribs," she said. "I think I cracked a couple of them in the crash."

"I want you to see a doctor," Albro said.

"I don't need a doctor. I'll be fine in a few days."

"I thought you would say that. I've arranged for a doctor to see you."

"Where?"

"Like I said, a change of plans," Albro said. "That safe–house sounded to me like the perfect setup. We could be cornered and killed without the least interference."

"But Marlowe..."

"You told me yourself that you didn't trust him. I don't trust him either," Albro said. "I know a place much safer." He looked out the window. "You've been to Hong Kong before?"

"Of course," she said with an edge of irritation in her voice, as if he'd interrupted her thoughts. And then aware of how she had responded, softened with, "It was often a stopover on the way to Nepal, where I did a lot of climbing. I've never really explored the city."

"It's an amazing place. To realize that the entire western Pacific rotates around this city like a giant wheel on a hub helps to put it into perspective. And it's beautiful too. I'll show you around."

"There's no time for sightseeing."

380

"The city can be particularly beautiful at night. I'm sure Isaiah and Walter won't mind an evening in their room. They can catch up on their meditation and you and I can find a place for dinner. You can tell me all about climbing and then if you feel up for it, we'll go some place where there's music and dancing. Don't worry, I won't ask you to dance."

"You don't think I know how to dance?" she asked hotly.

"I was thinking of your broken ribs," Albro said.

Nancy was quiet for a moment. "Actually," she said, "I lost my taste for dancing a long time ago. As I recall, it happened soon after I agreed to attend a dance with you."

"C'mon, Nancy, I was eighteen years old, and I apologize a thousand times over for what happened. I should never have let your cousin put me up to that. You might not believe it, but I have learned to be a gentleman, and should have at least one chance to prove it to you, don't you think? Besides, that really wasn't dancing."

"What do you mean?"

"What we did back then was barely controlled flailing, hormones in high gear.

"And I suppose you're now some kind of *Fred Astaire*?"

"Not quite, but I think I can show a woman a good time. I've found that there's a little *Ginger Rogers* in all women. You should let yourself have some fun."

"Is that a challenge?"

Albro sighed. "Yes, if that's what it takes. Besides, what I've seen in the last two days leads me to believe that you secretly enjoy a challenge."

"I don't have anything to wear."

"Go shopping."

"That could get expensive. This is Hong Kong."

Albro reached into his pocket and pulled out the charge cards that Marlowe had given him. "Marlowe's treat," he said. "And if that's not enough, I'm now a multi-millionaire. You haven't forgotten that, have you?"

381

The driver slowed and eased the Mercedes into the large circular drive of the Hong Kong Hilton. Its sixty stories rose upward like a glass and steel monolith that proclaimed the presence of the rich and powerful.

"Where are we?" Nancy demanded.

"In the lap of luxury," Albro said. "Here, put these on, and whatever happens, don't take them off." He handed her a pair of dark glasses, and slipped a pair over his own eyes.

The Mercedes came to a stop. The sun was fully up now and heat and humidity hit them as soon as the doors opened. The last time they had breathed real air it had been fresh, cold and wet. This air was stale, hot and humid. Humanity swirled around them in a maelstrom of diesel exhaust and sweat. A swarm of smartly dressed hotel staff descended on the car. They opened doors, hefted bags and proffered outstretched hands as if they were all invalids in need of the utmost care, or celebrities of the highest order. Albro sincerely hoped the effect was of the latter. He noted several heads turn in their direction, and a crowd start to gather at the entrance. Good, that was just what he wanted. They were about to push their way through when the flashes started going off. Albro had begun to think that his friend Ernie Chan was going to fail him. It had been short notice, but Ernie prided himself on doing the impossible, no matter what the time frame. At a strategic moment, Albro let his dark glasses fall and turned with his best surprised look directly into the cameras. And then they were through the doors and into the expansive lobby.

"Are you totally insane?" Nancy Wong hissed in his ear.

A man in the hotel's uniform approached them. On the left side of his jacket was a gold emblem that read, *Ernest Chan, Concierge*. Nancy Wong said to him, "This is all a mistake. Bring back our bags. We'll be leaving right away."

"On the contrary, we have a suite of rooms all ready for you. Mr. Swift, how nice to see you again," Ernie Chan said, a broad smile spreading across his face.

"Thanks, Ernie. Good job on the reception." Albro slipped a fold of bills into Ernie's hand. "How about the doctor," Albro asked.

"She is on her way," Ernie said.

"Excellent. Could you arrange dinner and dancing for two?"

"I know the perfect place," Ernie assured Albro.

"Thanks. Ms. Wong may wish to go shopping later. She will need an escort."

"No problem."

"Good. I want to talk with you. There are a few things I'm going to need some help with."

"You have my number."

Albro looked around the lobby. People were still watching them, the Europeans attempting to hide their interest, the Asians staring blatantly, but everyone keeping a discreet distance. "I think we've aroused enough attention for the moment. Take us up to our suite."

Ernie Chan let them into their suite with a flourish of hand waving. "I think you will find the space most accommodating. There are three bedrooms, each with its own bath, an office through here, and a fully stocked bar." He crossed the large living area and opened the curtains as if he were announcing the opening act of a vaudeville show. "And the view! You cannot do better than this," he assured them.

"Very nice," Albro said.

"If there is anything you require, do not hesitate to call room service."

"We'll do that," Albro said.

No sooner had the concierge closed the door behind him, Nancy Wong erupted, "Have you taken total leave of your senses? I thought we had agreed to keep a low profile. We might have had a chance to remain undetected. Our pictures are going to be on the front page of whatever passes for a tabloid in this city. You might as well have painted targets on our backs! We had a plan, and you agreed to follow it." She held her hands in front of her body like two rigid walls, as if she could keep reality from escaping her grasp. It was a habit, Albro had noted, she displayed whenever it looked like she wasn't going to get her way.

"What can I say? I lied," Albro said calmly.

"I suppose you have a plan of your own."

383

"As a matter of fact, I don't," he admitted, "at least not yet."

"Then what are we going to do? My life is on the line. All of our lives are on the line, yours included."

"It will come to me, sweetheart, all in good time," Albro said and smiled.

"Don't treat me like a little girl!"

"Then stop acting like one. How long do you think we would have remained anonymous? One day? Two days? It's my guess that whoever's been trying to kill us knew of our whereabouts before we left the airport, maybe even before we landed. Our best chance at staying alive is to not give them a clear shot. For the time being, the more people we have around us, the better."

"He's right." The rat man who had been standing facing the window turned to them.

"It's about time you spoke up," Albro said. "I thought you were here to back me up."

"To guide and protect you," the rat man said.

"Same thing," Albro said.

"Not necessarily," the rat man replied to him. Then he said to Nancy Wong, "As I was saying, I think Mr. Swift is right. I have been considering our situation. For now, we are better off where we cannot be easily isolated, but we cannot delay for long our real purpose. It would be helpful to all of us, Mr. Swift, if you could explain to us why you have chosen to negate Marlowe's plan. Have you had a revelation?"

"A revelation?" Albro asked. "Do you mean some sort of vision?"

"Yes."

"I hadn't thought of it that way, but now that you've mentioned it, maybe so."

"Then please tell us," the rat man said.

"I can't. No yet. It's like it's still forming inside my head. I'm going out. There are a few things I need to do." Albro held up his hand. "I know what you're going to say about your mandate to protect me. You and Walter are staying here. You'll just have to trust me when I say I'll be far safer without you. In the meantime, a doctor will be here to have a look at Nancy. If you get bored, watch TV. If you get hungry, call room service. I'll be back by early evening. Nancy and I have a date. Before Nancy could protest he was out the door.

Albro spoke on the phone as he rode the elevator down. "Ernie."

"Yes?"

"Two things. First, I need a car and driver brought around to the rear entrance. Nothing flashy, but a dependable driver. Second, I need a set of evening clothes. Forty-two long. Thirty-six on the inseam, thirty-three on the waist. Eleven medium for the shoes. Got that?"

"Got it.

"Good. Any reaction yet to our arrival?"

"You bet. Everyone's asking why you're here without Ms Newton. Every newspaper and TV station is asking for an interview with you. What should I tell them?"

Albro hadn't progressed that far in his plan. He thought quickly and then asked, "Is that British reporter, the tall blonde, still around?"

"Sure. She's been trying to bribe me for information."

"Take the bribe and schedule me an interview for tomorrow morning."

"You got it."

"And one more thing, find Nit. Tell him I want a meeting."

Ernie was silent for a moment. He asked, "Are you sure about that?"

Albro felt the gold coin that hung around his neck and rested against his chest bones. Nit was someone he'd done business with in the past. Perhaps, the word 'business' was stretching the truth just a little. Nit was a smuggler who contracted out his services at a high price. The last time they had seen each other, Nit had been behind bars in a Myanmar prison with a murderous look in his eyes. Albro was hoping Nit could let bygones be bygones because there was no one else who could do what he needed done.

"As sure as I'm alive," he said to Ernie.

"Okay. Where and when?"

"Just get a number where he can be reached. I'll get back to him." If Nit was at sea, there was a good chance he'd have a satellite phone.

Albro rode the elevator down to the service level and got off. The wide, utilitarian corridors gave no hint of the opulence of the upper levels. He followed the exit signs to the loading dock. A nondescript sedan sat idling amongst the delivery trucks. He got in and told the driver he wanted to be taken to the central branch of the Bank of Hong Kong. He wanted to check on the ten million that Marlowe said was waiting for him. He had no doubt about Marlowe's assurance that the money would be there, but guys like Marlowe never let a dollar, let alone ten million of them, slip away without a very reliable string attached.

Albro looked around as they made their slow progress through the traffic filled streets. None of the dire predictions regarding the fate of the city when the communists took over had come to pass. If anything, the city was more robust. The Chinese from Beijing were like Chinese everywhere. They recognized a cash-cow when they saw one. And this one was not about to be sacrificed for some outdated Maoist ideals. Other than slightly tighter controls over the monetary policy, it was pretty much business as usual. If one knew the right person, most any business transaction could be made to happen. Mere ideology was no match for the allure and power of capitalism.

The bank was one of the glass and steel towers hardly distinguishable from the hundreds of others that had been anchored deeply into the bedrock of the island. Albro instructed the driver to wait and then entered and asked for the deposits manager. A man in a conservative blue suit greeted him with a short bow.

"How may I help you?" he asked politely.

"I want to check on a deposit in my name," Albro answered.

"Of course," the man replied and bowed his slightly in that odd oriental manner that was meant to convey that the man would do back flips if necessary to accommodate his needs, but Albro knew that it was an age old psychological ploy to put him at ease and cause him to lower his defenses. The man then asked, "May I see some identification?"

Albro handed him the passport which Marlowe had supplied. The manager examined the photo and handed it back. "Right this way, Mr. Swift."

The manager led him into a side office. "Please be seated. This should only take a moment."

Albro sat while the manager typed on a keyboard.

"Yes. A deposit was made four days ago in the amount of ten million dollars, U.S."

The figure did not even produce a reaction in the manager. That amount was hardly chump-change, but considering the billions that moved through the bank on a daily basis, ten million was barely more than they swept up off the floor at the end of the day.

"You're sure about the date?"

The manager looked at the screen again. "Yes," he answered, "December, 10."

Accounting for the fact that he was now west of the International Date Line that would make it five days ago, Albro reckoned. "Can you tell me where the transfer originated?"

"Yes, it came from a bank on Grand Bahama Island."

"And the account holder," Albro asked.

"I'm sorry sir, that information is confidential. Is there a problem? It appears that you have complete access to your funds. Do you wish to make a withdrawal?"

The prospect was tempting, to say the least. But then he considered Marlowe's warning. In addition, he had an uncomfortable feeling about it. Not from a moral point of view. It wouldn't have bothered him a bit if the money had been procured from the pension funds of impoverished widows. It was more from a sense of personal integrity. By either legal or not so legal methods, he'd always earned his own way. Someone had assumed well in advance that he could be bought. The ten million would be there if he needed it. In the mean time, he still had his poker winnings.

"I'm good for now," Albro told the manager, "but thanks."

Albro walked back through the lobby. There was nothing like knowing you had ten million in the bank to put a lift in your step.

The bank manager watched him leave and then went back to his office, closed the door and pushed the speed-dial button on his desk phone. He spoke briefly, listened, and then hung up.

Albro got in the waiting car and told the driver to take him to a sporting goods store. The driver found one in short order and pulled up in front, not bothering to search for a parking space and blithely ignored the blaring of horns behind him. Albro jumped out and hurried into the store. He bought a pair of powerful binoculars and got back in the car. The whole transaction had taken less than five minutes. He then directed the driver to take him up into the hills, telling the driver that he wanted to get a view of the city and the harbor. The driver wound up into the hills and brought him to a magnificent overlook

Albro got out and surveyed the expansive vista. Below him Hong Kong spread out and faded into the hazy obscurity of the thick air. The city was packed solid with human beings and still it continued to grow. Was this a vision of the future earth, when every city evolved into a bloated monster and then spilled over into every inhabitable niche? In the far distance he could make out the amorphous shape of the mainland. He looked in that direction for a long time. The *Jade Prince* was out there somewhere. He was feeling its pull. It was calling to him. Something had been calling to him his entire life. And now he knew that it was the *Jade Prince*. He couldn't quite put into words what made him so certain, but could feel it. He absently traced the lines of the scar on his forearm and felt an electric tingle move up and into his chest.

He got back into the car and directed the driver to continue farther up into the hills. The higher they went, the clearer the air became until at last they had escaped the worst of the city's stench and occasionally Albro would catch a drift of sub-tropical fragrance on the air. They came to a point where the road made an abrupt turn and a parting in the thick foliage gave a view across a ravine to a large, modernist mansion hung on the side of the hill. Albro instructed the driver to let him out and continue on until he found a place to park out of sight. He would meet him at this same spot in an hour. He watched the car pull ahead and round the next bend in the road, and then hanging the binoculars around his neck set off on a rudimentary trail that wound to the top of a narrow promontory that gave an unobstructed view of the mansion. He'd been in this exact spot a year earlier when he'd scouted the mansion before entering it and stealing the jade dagger. He found the spot where he had sat before and settled himself with his elbows in his knees to steady the binoculars.

The property was laid out in a series of terraces. The drive came in at the upper level where an entry stood that housed an elevator which descended to the main level. Two vehicles were parked there. An exterior stairway also ran around down the side of the hill to an open terrace with a low wall around it. He had come down those stairs on a dark night when the inhabitants were not at home. From that terrace, one would get a breath-taking view of the city and harbor. Large sets of plate glass doors opened onto the terrace. Below the terrace and almost hidden from view was a small structure where the housekeepers lived. The night he had entered, the whole place had been empty. Not a soul around, almost as if the place had been purposely abandoned. At the time, he had thanked his good fortune. Now, he was not so sure that it had been fortune at all.

The place was not empty now. Two guards patrolled the terrace. He spotted another strolling along the drive, and a fourth he caught relieving himself in the bushes at the corner of the servant's quarters. He saw movement behind the plate glass doors and focused his attention there. He'd been careful to time his observation so the sun would be positioned behind him so as not to reflect off the lenses of the binoculars. This gave him a clearer view and also prevented anyone from detecting his presence. After thirty minutes, his legs began to cramp and he stood and stretched and then settled back down.

Within a few minutes, one of the doors to the terrace opened and a man and a woman stepped out. Monique's beautiful face seemed to float just beyond his reach. He did not recognize the tall, elderly, man she was speaking to. Yet, there was an odd familiarity about him. His tanned face was deeply lined and white hair flowed down to his shoulders. He was dressed in a tropical weight suit. He seemed to be listening attentively to what Monique was saying to him. Suddenly he held up a gloved hand to silence her and he turned and looked directly in Albro's direction. The man's dark eyes seemed to look directly into his own. Albro lowered the binoculars immediately. He knew that it was impossible for anyone to spot him from that distance, but the look in the man's eyes had startled him. After a moment, he raised the binoculars.

Behind the glass he could discern the outline of another figure. The reflections on the glass prevented him from identifying who it was, but from the size and shape he had a pretty good idea that it was Newton. Suddenly a cloud passed before the sun killing the reflections on the glass and he could see Newton's face clearly. Something seemed to startle Newton and as he turned away, Albro saw another figure materialize in the shadows. Newton must have shouted because Monique and the silver-haired man rushed back into the house. Albro adjusted the focus on the binoculars and for a fleeting instance he saw the face of the figure in the shadows. He had seen that face before, but where? He peered into the binoculars until his eyes ached, but everyone had disappeared into the interior of the mansion. He scanned all of the windows, but saw no one. The security guards did not seem perturbed by anything that might be going on within.

Albro breathed slowly and regularly and watched the mansion until he heard the crunch of tires on gravel. He eased himself back into the bushes before rising and then retreated back down the hill to the waiting car.

CHAPTER 34

FRANK GIDDES prodded his toe amid the burned timbers. A few wisps of smoke still rose from a corner that was still hot, but the heavy, wet snow had done a good job of cooling the ashes. He looked up at the sky. Snow would be coming soon. He looked over at the two men standing next to the helicopter. They had started to accompany him toward the remains of the cabin and he'd ordered them to wait. They were standing with their arms crossed, watching him. They would report back to the Old Man, but right now he didn't care.

He'd wanted to see for himself what the Old Man had referred to as a 'precautionary action'. It hadn't taken long to discover that the girl had been working with Crane. That fact alone had been enough to warrant her elimination, but he had waited, the Old Man had explained to him. He had placed her under surveillance, and it had proved a fortuitous decision. They had spotted the other two individuals whom they might otherwise have missed. Seeing them together, had been a clear indication that they had to move quickly. Crane's son joined them and they had their opportunity to deal with all of them. The Old Man had even allowed himself a rare display of emotion and had smiled over their deaths.

"Fool!" Giddes uttered under his breath. They still didn't know who had killed Crane. The Old Man had questioned Newton personally and was satisfied of his innocence. Newton was a brute. As for shear intelligence, Giddes had never seen his equal, but he was a brute nonetheless and could be dealt with. Krupp had been dependable at one time, but that time was long past. His zealotry had taken him over the edge. Monique was the one who was going to give them trouble. He wondered how long the three of them would manage to hold their charade together. If the Old Man had been set on killing, he should have killed the three of them and saved him the trouble of having to do it later.

He kicked in disgust at the light covering of snow. Wet, black ashes peppered the blanket of pure white. He looked down and saw the corner of a book. He prodded it with the toe of his boot and bent down for it. He brushed off the snow and ashes and examined it. It was sodden, but it had survived the blaze undamaged. It was a small thing, but suddenly it gave him hope. He slipped it into his pocket, and signaled for the men to start up the chopper.

He ordered the pilot to take them to the site of the avalanche. His mind was methodical. They had traced Crane's movements and now had a rough outline of where he had been. There appeared to be no rhyme or reason to the sites he had visited. Their only thing in common seemed to be that each place had been a site where Chinese immigrants had labored, but their efforts to uncover what he'd been looking for had come to a dead end. He'd wanted to question the woman. When the Old Man had informed him that she was dead, he'd nearly lost his temper.

The voice of the pilot crackled in his head phones, "See that ridge? The whole thing came down and filled the ravine below us."

The pilot slowly turned giving them a panoramic view of the destructive force of the avalanche. Blocks of ice the size of houses had bulldozed a path down the side of the mountain taking out trees and dislodging boulders, filling the narrow confines of the ravine.

"Can you take us into the ravine?" Giddes asked the pilot.

"It's too narrow. I can hover above it. That's the best I can do.

Giddes nodded. He pulled a pair of compact binoculars from his parka. As the pilot hovered he scanned the scene below. He was about to conclude that no one could have survived such devastation when he spotted a small blue rectangle. He motioned the pilot to take them lower.

392

The pilot brought the helicopter down another hundred feet. Cold currents of air dropping off the slope buffeted them. The rock cliff was dangerously close. "I can't hold it here long," the pilot said.

Giddes maneuvered close to the window and looked down. A boulder had given way from higher up and had cut its way into the snow and ice. The blue that Giddes had seen from higher up now revealed itself as the door of the buried vehicle. He signaled the pilot to take them up.

Giddes spoke to the other man, "I want a team down there as soon as possible to check for bodies."

The man nodded and got on his radio.

A few hours later, Giddes got the news. The team had gone in and dug through to the vehicle. They had found it clogged with debris, but no bodies. They had searched the surrounding area with avalanche probes and had come up empty handed. It was not until the dog had arrived that they found the trail that led out of the ravine and into the forest. The searchers had been able to determine that more than one survivor had made it all the way to the Interstate highway. There the trail had ended.

It was with a certain sense of satisfaction that Giddes relayed this news to the Old Man.

"And you believe they are alive?" The Old Man asked Giddes. He had his back to Giddes with his hands at his sides and gazing out over the slate colored bay. Points of white marked the entrance to the bay where an incoming squall was stirring the waves. Rain ran in rivulets down the window. They were high enough to see the farthest reach of the bay and the distant green hills. Giddes could not help but think how different this world would become

"I believe all four of them made it out," Giddes answered

"Do you know where they are now?

Giddes did not answer the question. It was his way of telling the Old Man that he'd made a serious error. He would make him wait for the answer. He said, "There was an incident south of the city last night. It was a careless operation. There were witnesses. No one will believe them, because I got there in time to clean things up, but the locals are bound to start asking questions if this sort of thing continues."

Giddes saw the Old Man stiffen momentarily and then relax. "You think I was responsible for that?"

"You said the Mongi were cooperating."

"Yes, that is what I said," The Old Man said in a tone that cautioned Giddes to be careful not be become too impertinent. "But I do not have control over all the factions."

"Until we close off their access, they're going to be a problem," Giddes said.

"We have already begun that process. I am confident that we will find where they are coming through and stop them. Don't worry yourself with such mundane matters. You were about to answer my question."

"A witness at the incident remembered four individuals. They disappeared when the shooting started. Later in the night, a private aircraft lifted off with a flight plan that had them flying to Tokyo via Fairbanks. The plane did not arrive, but there was an unscheduled landing of a similar aircraft in Hong Kong at a time commensurate with a trans-Pacific flight. The plane remained on the ground only long enough to refuel."

"Where is it now?

"We are still attempting to trace it, but the plane is not what matters.

"Oh?" The Old Man turned to face him. "Then tell me, Mr. Giddes, what does matter.

"Four passengers were seen disembarking the plane. They did not pass through customs. Instead, they were driven into the city.

"Yes, I know," the Old Man said. "They are booked into the Hong Kong Hilton. Would you like their room numbers?

Giddes was caught off guard. He stood mute, looking at the smug expression on the Old Man's face

"You're surprised?" he asked the Old Man

"Yes. How did you know? I found this out only an hour ago.

"I met with Monique and Newton this morning," the Old Man said.

"But...," Giddes attempted to speak.

"But you are wondering how I could be six thousand miles away only hours ago and here now with you. My dear, Giddes, there are things you have never understood about me, nor do you need to. As I was saying, Monique and Newton and Krupp have been waiting for our little troupe since yesterday. You've been a good man, Giddes and I have appreciated your efforts over the years, but you must not let your sense of urgency overcome your sense of reason. Now is not the time to panic. You must keep a clear head. I have planned this very carefully, and my plan is almost complete."

CHAPTER 35

ALBRO got in the car and told the driver to take him to the market area near the northern edge of the harbor. By the time he got there, it was late afternoon. Their progress was slow and was finally halted by a snarl of cars, taxis, trucks and scooters. Albro paid the driver and got out. A thick cloud of bluish smoke hung in the heated air. He nearly choked on the fumes. Los Angeles with its bad air had nothing on the cities of the Far East. Yet there was something appealing about the seething mass of humanity all around him. There was an intensity here that excited him.

He threaded his way through the stopped traffic and got onto what passed for a sidewalk. Vendors, some with a small table, some with a carpet, some with only their arms and hands to display their goods crowded against one another. There appeared to be some kind of unofficial truce between them and the established storefronts. In a four square block area one could find anything one could possibly want. And if it wasn't here, you would find someone who would take you to it. He had visited this area many times and although it had been more than a year since he'd walked these streets, the occasional vendor recognized him and called out his name. You could find everything from a rare piece if Ming porcelain to Victorian era carved ivory. You could have the genuine article or an expert fake. He knew enough not to be swindled, or at least, he had thought so. But he was not interested in buying something today. He was looking for someone.

The antiques dealer he sought was located beyond the market area in the basement of an old tenement. He'd happened on it one day while searching for an individual whom he'd been told was in possession of an exquisite vase from the era of the Yuan dynasty. The vase had turned out to be a fake. It had been a good fake, but he had recognized it for what it was, and as such, there wasn't be much to be gained in the effort to resell it. He'd been about to return to his hotel when a cloudburst had sent him running for cover. He'd seen the descending stairway and the open door just as the big, fat raindrops had begun splattering the stone pavers of the narrow street.

The cramped space had been dimly lit by a single bulb hanging from the low ceiling and the air had had a strong, damp musty smell to it, overlaid by an even stronger scent of human habitation, of cooking oil, sweat and the faint, but unmistakable odor of sewage. The shop's inventory was laid out haphazardly on rickety tables and bowed shelves. He had seen at a glance that most of it was junk. Broken pots lay with half-rotted scrolls. Bits and pieces of bronze were mixed with fragments of carved stone. A gray pallor of dust had covered everything. As his eyes had adjusted to the gloom, he had noticed the back wall of the shop was taken up by a low cot piled with rags and a side table with a charcoal brazier upon which a battered tin pot sat with a wisp of steam curling from its spout.

He had started to reach for a small vase that was remarkably intact, but before he could lay a hand on it, a voice had startled him. The rags on the bed had materialized into a shrunken man in dirty black pajama pants and jacket who sat with his back against the back wall. The lower part of the pajama legs lay flaccid on the bed cover. Both of the man's legs appeared to have been severed above the knees. The man's hair was long and twisted, as was the mustache and thin beard that hung from his chin. His eyes had that milky whiteness of the blind. The visage had been so startling that Albro had backed hurriedly to the doorway. The shower had increased to a torrent and sounded like a battery of snare drums as it pounded the street turning it into a gray blur. A rivulet of water had begun to flow down the stairs and across to the center of the room where it disappeared into a crack in the floor.

"Welcome," the blind man had said. "I have been waiting a long time for you."

What had ensued had been a lively conversation regarding the trade in relics and antiquities. The man had not seemed so very old once he had begun speaking. Albro remembered thinking that he had sounded not only highly educated, but quite articulate in the subtle nuances of the double-speak employed by all those in the illicit trade of artifacts. The old trader had casually mentioned that he knew the whereabouts of a rare jade dagger, and how Albro might be able to acquire it.

What had the old trader asked in return for the information? Only that Albro return someday that they might again pass the afternoon in pleasant conversation. After parting from the shop, Albro had taken careful note of the streets as he had wound his way out of the labyrinth of old tenements back to the main thoroughfare. He had not thought that anything would come of what the old man had told him, but out of curiosity he'd done a reconnaissance, and after much careful planning, had removed the dagger from its resting place in a mansion high in the hills above the city.

He'd had a strong feeling when he'd felt the weight of the dagger in his hand that he would return to the old trader's shop, but not for the reason he now had for venturing down the narrow and twisting stone-paved corridor.

Albro stopped where the wide street suddenly narrowed before snaking its way into the shadows of the crumbling brick buildings. If anyone were going to jump him, this would be their chance. He took a deep breath and plunged forward. He soon left behind the cacophony of blowing horns and shouting voices and also the white-washed sunlight. One might expect it to be cooler, here in the shadows, but the heat and the closeness of the air only seemed to intensify the farther he went. There were no street signs to guide him and no sun to keep his bearings. He looked up past the metal fire escapes and wooden railings festooned with lines of laundry to small rectangles of sky.

398

He found it always a bit disorienting to come from temperate latitudes into the tropics. Even if one could see it, the sun never seemed to be in the right part of the sky. He studied the small piece of sky which had the dull white saturation of humidity so common here. It was then he caught a movement out of the corner of his eye. The figure had come around the corner he had just passed and had darted into a doorway. He had surprised the individual by pausing in the middle of the street. Albro shook his head. It was a clumsy, amateurish attempt at surveillance. He stuck his hands into his pocket and continued to the next corner. Once around it, he scanned the street quickly, found the spot he wanted and then dashed to its cover and waited until he heard the heavy footfalls pass. He quickly stepped out.

"Hey!" he called out. The hulking individual jumped and spun around. He was going to have to decide how to think of the beast, man/Mongi, since there seemed to be no getting away from him. Maybe it was best to simply think of him as 'Walter'. He had enough on his mind without trying to find a rung for him on the primate ladder.

"What are you doing here? Didn't I tell you to stay at the hotel?" Albro stepped closer.

"Yes, but..." Walter stammered.

"Where's Isaiah? Is he with you?" Albro looked up into Walter's face. The big man looked about to cry. He was back in his old robe, but he was also wearing the hat and dark glasses. Hell, it probably didn't matter anyway. A guy his size was going to attract attention no matter how he dressed.

"He went to the other place. I got worried about you."

"I told you that I would be fine. You don't have to worry about me."

"I'm sorry. Did I do a bad thing by following you?" Walter clasped his big hands together and looked down at his feet.

"No, no. You didn't do a bad thing. It's just that you don't exactly blend in," Albro said and then took a quick look around to see if they had been noticed.

"I wore my hat and dark glasses, just like you told me."

"Yeah, like it helps a lot. Anyway, you're here. What did you say about Izzy? He went somewhere?"

"He went to the other place."

"*What* other place?" Albro tried to be patient, but talking to Walter was like trying to talk to a four year old.

"He went to the other place. He went to our home."

Good, Albro thought. That was one less problem to deal with. "So what did he do, catch a plane back to the States?"

"No airplane. I loved the airplane. Can we fly again soon?"

"Yeah, Walter, real soon," Albro said. There were only three ways to leave Hong Kong, by air, by water, or the bridge over to Kowloon. "Did Izzy take a ship?"

"A ship?" Walter looked puzzled.

"You know, on the water," Albro said and put his hands together and made a wiggling motion.

"Oh, I know what you mean," Walter said and beamed a big, toothy smile.

"*Well*?" Albro asked. The whole conversation, if you could call it that, was getting nowhere fast.

"Nope, no ship," Walter answered and looked down at Albro expectantly as if he were waiting for his next guess.

Albro sighed. "Walter, just tell me what happened to Izzy and why he didn't take you with him."

"He went through the hole. The hole is small right now. I barely squeezed through to get here, but soon it will be big enough for all of us." He smiled again as if it were all so simple.

Albro shook his head. It was futile, Albro decided, to try to reason with him. The rat man must be up to something to leave the hotel. But what could it be? It didn't make any sense to send Walter back. He would no doubt get lost. Still, he didn't have a ready explanation as to how Walter had so easily tracked him.

"Did Nancy let the doctor have a look at her?"

"Miss Nancy left right after you."

"You can lead a horse to water..." Albro muttered to himself.

"What's a horse?" Walter asked.

"Never mind, Walter," Albro said. "It's just a saying to describe people who are too stubborn for their own good."

"Can I stay with you?" Walter asked.

"Okay pal, but you have to do what I tell you to do. Understood?"

"Don't you worry, Mr. Albro," Walter answered in a suddenly serious tone. He squared his sloping shoulders and stood erect.

Worry? Albro squeezed the point between his eyes. He was starting to get a headache. He said to Walter, "Stay behind me and keep a watch out for anyone who might be following." There were fewer people here than out in the market place, but they had already begun to attract a small crowd of onlookers. He reached up and pulled at Walter's elbow. "C'mon, let's go."

They hadn't gone far when Walter asked, "Do you like Miss Nancy?"

Albro thought it an odd question, but he assumed the big guy was just being chatty, and innocent in his own way. Even so, he had to think about his answer. At last, he said, "She's all right."

"Are you going to marry her?" Walter asked.

"Not on your life, pal," Albro said. "She's not my type. Besides, I'm engaged to marry someone else." This last statement literally made his heart skip a beat.

"I wish I could marry her," Walter said.

"Go for it, pal. I wish you all the luck in the world," Albro said. He would need it, too. Nancy Wong possessed all the classic attributes of a genuine ball-buster. He had no illusions about the evening ahead. There was not going to be any big seduction scene. Under other circumstances he would have relished the challenge. At the moment, there were more important things on his plate. Right now, he just wanted to get her away from the rat man so he could get some answers to some very important questions.

"Oh," Walter continued, "a Mongi could never marry one such as Miss Nancy. It would be a death sentence."

401

"You got that right," Albro said with a chuckle, and then got the feeling that Walter wasn't making a joke. "What do you mean?"

"The bad must never join with the good, because only bad will come of it." Walter said this in a sing-song sort of way that made it sound as if it had been drilled into him at an early age.

"The Purim always find them," Walter said in that matter of fact way of those who have witnessed terrible things multiple times. "If the Mongi is female, they will have their way with her and then mercifully cut her throat. If the Mongi is male, it is much worse. They also find his family and they are brought to the center of the malgreb where a fire is built. A malgreb is the place of the Mongi. It is as big as a city, but it is not a city. A city has beautiful buildings and fine houses. There is nothing beautiful in a malgreb. This place reminds me a little of a malgreb."

Walter paused and looked up at the decrepit brick buildings. He went on, "A fire is built and the family is forced to watch while their son or brother is burned alive. The screaming does not last long. Then the family must eat his flesh. Those who refuse will also die. It is the worst that can happen to a Mongi family. The Purim must do penance for having done what they have done. If there are children, the Purim take them. Sometimes the Purim take Mongi children for no reason, but I do not know what happens to them. Ask Izzy. I think he knows. I asked him once, but he refused to say. I saw something in his eyes that told me not to ask again. Where are we going, Mr. Albro?"

Albro was only half-listening to the gruesome story. It sounded like something out of the worst days of Apartheid, the Bosnian disaster, the Rwandan massacre and any of a dozen other human tragedies he could have brought to mind. It sounded like the Mongi had a tough life, but that was nothing he could do anything about. There were people all over the world who led tough lives. It wasn't his fault and it wasn't his responsibility to save them. If there was any of the ten million left after this was all over, maybe he could have a school built, or even a medical clinic. But he couldn't think about that now, he was having trouble remembering exactly how to get to the antiques seller.

"It's just a place I visited once. I know the way," Albro answered. They rounded a corner and the street split yet again. Albro hesitated and then started toward the right.

"Not that way, Mr. Albro," Walter said.

"What?" Albro asked.

"The place you want to go is this way," Walter said pointing to the left.

"How could you know that? Have you ever been here before?" Albro asked with a growing suspicion that good old Walter wasn't as innocent as he let on.

"No," Walter said. He looked around. "You're looking for the place where everything is very old."

Albro had to think about that for a moment. "How did you know that?" he asked.

"You want to ask something of the man who sits on the bed."

Albro looked at Walter. "How did you do that? It's like you just read my mind."

"You're not angry, are you Mr. Albro? Izzy told me not to do it, but sometimes I can't help myself."

Albro started to speak and then stopped. He looked up at Walter. "What am I thinking now?"

"You want to know if Izzy can read minds too."

"Well, can he?"

"Sure, all Mongi can, some better than others."

"And you, Walter, how good are you?"

"Izzy says I'm the best he's ever seen," Walter said and smiled broadly.

"Is that how you found me?"

"Sure. I just listened for your thoughts. I like the way you think. Most of it I don't understand. I just like the way it feels."

"That's how you know where the antiques seller is? You can hear his thoughts?"

"Yes, but I don't understand any of his thoughts. I can only feel them."

403

"You mean because he's thinking in a different language?"

"Oh, no, it's not words like we speak. It's just thoughts."

"But don't we think by forming our thoughts into words?"

"Yes!" Walter said, pleased that Albro understood.

"Okay, Walter," Albro said. He could see where the conversation was heading. "We'll talk more about this later." Talking with Walter was like asking for a headache. "You're certain we need to go this way?" he asked pointing to the left.

Walter nodded. They went another half block and sure enough there was the familiar stairway descending below the street.

"Wait here," Albro said.

Albro stepped into the gloom, and paused at the threshold to let his eyes adjust. The place looked as if nothing had been touched in his absence. If anything, the dust was even thicker. The overhead light was out and slightly blackened. Maybe the old trader had given up on the idea of attracting anyone into the dank, foul smelling shop. He approached the figure who still sat on the low platform. He looked as if he hadn't moved since his last visit.

"Ah, you have returned," the old man spoke and Albro felt the room suddenly grow cold. His skin tightened and he felt a tingling under his scalp. The old man's mouth had opened, but there had been no other movement, not even the slightest rise and fall of the old man's chest. The milky-white eyes stared straight and unblinking. "You have questions. Please sit."

Albro looked around. There was no chair. He lifted a box of moldy textiles, emptied the contents and placed it before the old man and sat. Seeing the nearly lifeless figure brought back a sharp memory of a time that he'd been hitchhiking northward from the Gulf of Mexico into the heartland of the country. He'd been somewhere along the border between Missouri and Kansas, penniless and days since he'd had anything more substantial than a candy bar, when he'd wandered into a county fair. The smells of the pies and cakes and roasting corn and cotton candy had made him dizzy and weak on his feet. There had been a small wooden booth with one of those figures made of cloth and wax and sticks enclosed in a glass case. A sign saying, 'Ask the Wizard', in ornate lettering hung above the case. He'd looked on as folks dropped in a nickel and the figure's eyes would pop open and a voice would come out like a scratchy 45 rpm record. It had given him the heebie-jeebies and he'd run out of there, but he'd dreamed about it for several nights afterward as he slept in open fields.

"You want to know about that dagger, don't you? Your father had left it here for safe keeping." The old man gave a high, cackling laugh. "You can't blame me for having sold it! After all, I told you where to find it. An old man must eat and have his tea." The grotesque figure grinned, showing his black gums and flapping tongue. He smacked his lips, and maybe it was Albro's imagination, but the blind eyes seemed to narrow. "There is something else that brought you here," the old man said, "a question that has troubled you all of your short life."

The old man inhaled deeply and then exhaled slowly. A tendril of oily black smoke snaked outward from the left nostril and floated into the space between them. Albro wanted to jerk away, but he felt mesmerized. The smoke poked tentatively at his face, and then, finding its mark, raced up his nose. Albro instantly broke out in a cold sweat, and his ears began to buzz as if a swarm of bees had suddenly hatched inside his head. He'd confirmed what he'd suspected, that his theft of the dagger had all been arranged. Wasn't that what he'd come for? He couldn't think straight with all that buzzing. He needed to get up, to run, but his legs wouldn't move.

The figure spoke in a low voice. "You want to know, don't you, why your mother and father abandoned you. You want to know why you were thrown out into the world like a naked piglet." The figure made an obscene squealing sound and erupted again in the terrible laughter. "Don't believe them when they tell you it was to save you."

Was there a look of sympathy in the blind eyes? Or, again, was it just his imagination. Albro turned and looked at the rectangle of light that formed the doorway. It seemed to have shrunk to a miniscule opening. Or, was it just so far away now?

"The answer is not out there," the voice said softly. "It's right here. But I am old with little time left." The old man wheezed and coughed weakly. "I have only strength left to whisper. Come close and I will tell you what you want most to know."

Albro turned back. The face had taken on a kind and gentle softness. He leaned forward, placing his hands on either side of the truncated legs and brought his ear close to the old man's mouth.

The old man whispered, "Come closer, I have but a few moments left."

Albro inched closer. He caught a whiff of the old man's fetid breath and nearly gagged. The bony hand that came up and patted him on the back felt oddly discomforting. He was not a little boy. He pushed backward, but the hand forced him back down. Then the other hand closed around his throat and began to tighten.

"Be still," whispered the old man. "I will take you to your father. You will be together. That is what you want, isn't it?"

The hand tightened further and Albro began to gasp. He pulled with all of his strength, but he was held too tightly. He flailed his arms and kicked his legs, but the grasp around his throat continued to tighten. His lungs began to burn like fire and his eyes bulged out of their sockets. The sounds of retching and gagging puzzled him until he realized the sounds were his own.

"Do you see your father's face yet? No? Then you will very soon," the hoarse whisper seemed to grind into his dying brain. A purple cloud with bright, spiky edges to it began to form, growing from a point until it all but obscured his vision and within it a face began to appear, but not just one face, it was a whole host of faces forming one after the other like a film running in reverse, speeding up faster and faster, spiraling crazily toward the very beginning of his life. And then, he was there, looking upward into a bright light, the shadowy face slowly coming into focus.

"Mr. Albro! Breathe!" pleaded Walter.

Albro gasped and pulled in a breath of air. He rolled out of Walter's arms onto his hands and knees and puked. A stream of black bile poured out of his mouth and hissed like a powerful acid as it puddled on the stone pavement. Albro gagged and coughed up the last of it and sat back.

"What happened?" he asked Walter who knelt next to him.

"It is a Black Djinnim. It is very powerful and very bad. It was inside the old man."

The way Walter said the word sounded a lot like the word genie. Albro asked, "What happened to the old man?"

"He is dead. He has been dead for many months. It was the thoughts of the Djinnim I felt. It tricked me."

The puddle seemed to quiver and collect itself at the mention of its name.

"That's it?" Albro asked pointing at the black ooze. "It's alive?"

"Yes," said Walter. "But it's not alive. Something that can not die cannot be alive. That is why it is so dangerous."

"C'mon, Walter, let's get away from it."

"We cannot leave it. Wait here. Do not let anyone near it."

Walter crossed the street and began digging through a garbage bin. He return with a small, brown bottle and set about prodding and coaxing the thick, black ooze with the end of a chopstick until it began streaming into the bottle. When it had completely removed itself from the pavement, Walter screwed the lid on tightly.

"There," he said and handed it Albro.

It was heavy for its size, like a bottle full of Mercury. "What am I supposed to do with it?"

"You are now its master."

"If it's all the same to you, I think I would feel safer it you carry it," Albro said, offering the bottle back to Walter, who shrugged nonchalantly, as if it were an everyday matter to carry around a genie in a bottle, and tucked it into the inner lining of his robe. "And by the way, thanks for saving my life."

"Oh, Mr. Albro, you are very welcome, but you should thank your father. It was he who taught me how to deal with a Djinnim."

"You knew my father?"

"Oh, yes. He saved my life and the lives of many others too."

407

Albro sat silent for a moment. "I think that I saw him, Walter, just before everything went black. Was that real or was that the genie?"

"Far be it for someone as humble as myself to know such things. I can only tell you what I saw with my own eyes. You were fading and then you came back. Was it your father who broke the power of the Black Djinnim and brought you from the place of darkness? I cannot say. What I can say Mr. Albro, is that you are truly very special and there are many who watch over you."

CHAPTER 36

ALBRO looked across the white linen table cloth to Nancy Wong. She wore a sleeveless sapphire blue satin gown that showed off the strength of her shoulder muscles. Albro could imagine her hanging from a cliff face for days if necessary. She wore a necklace of pearls and matching earrings. She had even applied a blush of make-up to her cheeks and a dark shade to the lids of her eyes. When the light was right, the bruising along the left side of her face was all but invisible. Wherever Ernie Chan had sent her, they'd done a very nice job. If she could just do something about the constant frown that creased her forehead, Albro thought, she would be very attractive. A bottle of expensive champagne rested in a silver bucket that sat on a small side table. They sat in a raised portion of the dining room next to windows that overlooked the harbor. Nancy Wong looked nervously around the room.

"Relax," Albro said, "We're safe."

"Why did you insist on coming here?"

"Ernie says the food is great and it's one of the few places in the city where there's a decent dance floor and orchestra. Besides, look at the view. What could be more romantic?"

"Stop it!"

"Stop what?"

"Don't think for a moment that I don't know what you're up to. It won't work with me, so don't bother."

A waiter filled two crystal flutes that sparkled like cut diamonds and backed away.

"Here's to letting bygones be bygones," Albro said and lifted his glass.

Nancy Wong hesitated a moment and then lifted hers.

After they sipped, Albro said, "You're the most beautiful woman here."

"No, I'm not," she said looking around trying to avoid his eyes. "But it's nice of you to say so." She tugged self-consciously at the top of her dress. The orchestra played soft music and she glanced quickly at the still empty dance floor. "I'm sorry, but I can't help thinking that we're wasting our time."

"Trust me," Albro said. "I have a feeling this might be the last time we'll have the opportunity to do something like this."

"You mean you've actually begun to think seriously about your impending marriage? You might not realize it, but there are certain behaviors a woman expects of her fiancé." She set the glass down too firmly and champagne sloshed onto the table cloth. She ignored it and went on, "When are you going to stop behaving like you're still seventeen years old? You're thirty-six!" She brought her hands up and gave the table two sharp karate chops for emphasis. "That scene at the hotel was bad enough. But this! What would you do if Ms. Newton walked in right now and found us together?"

A rosy color had risen into her cheeks. Albro thought it made a great counterpoint to her dark eyes.

"Take it easy, Nancy. Monique trusts me. I wouldn't be here if I didn't feel it was really necessary. After all, the fate of the world rests upon my shoulders. You said it yourself. I think Monique would understand, don't you?"

"It's impossible to reason with you!" Nancy Wong hit the table once more, this time hard enough to make the silverware jump. Several heads turned their way. Albro signaled the waiter who hurried over with a concerned look on his face.

"Is there something wrong?" the waiter asked.

410

"The lady doesn't care for the champagne. Could you bring us martinis instead?"

"This has nothing to do with the champagne!" Nancy Wong said to the waiter, her anger rising.

The waiter turned to Albro with an imploring look. "Do you prefer vodka or gin?" Albro asked Nancy.

Nancy Wong rose slightly out of her seat and was about to continue her line of attack when she noticed the heads that had turned in their direction. She felt the heat of her own face and knew that it was flushed. It was a characteristic that had plagued her in the courtroom to the point that she had given up on trial law. She sat back down and averted her gaze to a few couples who were venturing onto the dance floor.

"Gin," she said a little too loudly, and then paused to get her voice under control, "Sapphire, ice cold, no vermouth and no olive. Please," she added in a softened tone.

"I'll have the same," Albro said.

The waiter, greatly relieved, bowed and hurried away. Two servers came and cleared the champagne. The waiter returned shortly with their drinks. Albro sipped at the clear liquid and made a face.

"Is it too strong for you?" Nancy Wong asked, and took a long swallow from her glass. "Would you like me to call the waiter over ask for something else? Would a soft-drink suit you better?"

"No, this is fine. It's just that I've never been much of a drinker."

"Then my advice is to go easy. This stuff isn't for kids." She drained the glass. The waiter, who was watching nervously, hurried over. "Another," she told him.

"Yes madam," the waiter said and hurried off.

Albro raised his eyebrows.

"Don't look so surprised," Nancy said. "I'm not the school girl you once knew. I happen to have an extremely high tolerance for alcohol. I can out drink most men three times my size."

The waiter returned and set the fresh drink on the table. "Are you ready to order?" he asked.

After they ordered, Nancy asked, "While you were out did you happen to spend any time looking for the map?"

He wondered if he should tell Nancy what he'd seen on his excursion into the hills, and also about the incident with Walter. At first he'd thought the two events were directly related. Now he began to wonder. The fact was he hadn't the faintest idea as to where to begin looking for a map. Did they think he was some kind of mystic who could conjure something out of thin air? Or was he supposed to feel a tingle in the tip of his nose when he was getting close?

Albro said to Nancy, "I went to check on the money. It's all there, all ten million.

"So now you're rich," she said with obvious disdain in her voice. "I suppose you'll be leaving as soon as you can."

"I don't get it," Albro said, ignoring her remark. "Why would Marlowe bring us all the way here and then dangle a ten million dollar carrot in front of me?"

"He's serious about finding the *Jade Prince*."

"You're right. He's so serious that he's willing to pay what appears to be an exorbitant price, which makes me believe that it must be worth a lot more than that. I think we should consider our options."

"What options?"

"Other buyers, for one," Albro replied. "Look, I know this business. I've been in the illicit artifacts trade for years."

"You can't be serious! Marlowe said that we would be lucky to end up with our lives. Have you forgotten the Mongi? The *Jade Prince* belongs to them!"

"Do you really think Marlowe has any interest in the Mongi, whoever they are? You saw the way Izzy looked at him. There's no love lost there. And regarding, the Mongi, what makes you believe they're what they say they are?

"How else can you explain them?"

"C'mon, Nancy, they're right off the front page of the *National Inquirer*. I've heard that plastic surgeons can create any animal face a person wants."

"You're unbelievable!"

"No, Nancy, I'm looking for something believable in all of this. So, let's start with Marlowe. How much do you know about him?"

"I only know what Thomas Crane told me about him."

"And what was that?"

"That he was someone who could help us or hinder us, depending on how beneficial the outcome was for him."

"Marlowe seems to know you."

"We met one time. Your father introduced us and then asked me to leave them in private. I don't know what they discussed."

"When was that?"

"Three weeks ago."

"Where?"

Nancy Wong hesitated, looking down in her drink. "Here."

"You mean here, in Hong Kong?"

She looked up and her eyes were filled with tears. "Here, in this hotel. Marlowe had a room here. I sat in the bar while they talked. After Marlowe left, we ate dinner. Thomas Crane and I sat right here at this table."

And then the reality of her relationship with Thomas Crane, the man everyone claimed was his father, struck Albro with such a force and with such surprise, that he blurted out, "You were…"

"Don't say it, please," Nancy Wong said.

"He brought you here and you ate a nice meal and then you danced with him," Albro said and sat back in his chair somewhat dazed. He didn't know how he knew it, but he knew with a certainty that rang in his head like a church bell.

"Yes, that all happened."

"And more, later…" Albro uttered and then stopped. He had a sudden memory of Nancy Wong with her back to him and releasing the straps of her evening gown. He blinked hard and the whole room wavered for a moment as if he were looking through a fish bowl, and then snapped back into focus.

Nancy Wong looked down, and said, "Yes." She then looked up with a look of genuine fear in her eyes, and asked, "What's happening?"

"I don't know," Albro said. He thought for a moment. "How much do you remember from that night?"

"What do you mean?"

"I mean, how much do you remember? Did Crane order Champagne? Did you drink it? What kind of music did the band play? Look around you, do you recognize anyone?"

Nancy Wong scanned the room, a troubled look in her eyes. "I don't know. I wasn't paying any attention to the people or the music." She looked at Albro. "But, yes, Thomas ordered Champagne. He didn't know that I don't care for it. He asked the waiter to bring us drinks, just like you did."

Albro said, "Your dress, and your pearls, they're the same?"

"Yes. Earlier today I went back to the same shop. The salesperson brought them out. She said they would be perfect for me."

Albro looked at her. He asked, "What about our hotel?"

"It is the same suite of rooms. Albro, I want to leave. I can't sit here any longer, it's like I'm living my life all over again. I'm afraid." She started to rise out of her chair.

Albro felt as if a spike had just been driven through his brain. He winced and tried to gather his thoughts and then suddenly went rigid. Something had just occurred to him. In this seeming game of blind man's bluff his blind fold had started to slip.

"Sit down," he said. His mind was racing. There was something someone had said to him, but what was it? Then suddenly it came to him. It was something Krupp had said to him. He said to Nancy, "You're going to start telling me the truth."

"What?" Nancy Wong asked. The toughness in her face had started to crumble.

"Just what I said," Albro said quietly. "Sit down."

Nancy Wong lowered herself back into her seat. A look of apprehension tightened the corners of her mouth. Those around them had shifted their attention away from them to the music and the dancers who now filled the dance floor.

"How much of what you've told me before tonight is true?" Albro asked.

Nancy Wong looked at him and then away. In an injured voice she said, "All of it."

"How much have you left out?"

"Only what I've had to," she answered, and added quickly, "to protect you."

Albro snorted derisively. Everything was suddenly coming clear to him. "Thomas Crane isn't dead, is he?"

"He is!" Nancy Wong stated forcefully. Then she faltered, biting her lip. "No," she finally said, "he is not."

"And the *Jade Prince*, whatever it is, didn't go missing. Crane hid it."

"Yes, Thomas Crane hid it," she said, still unable to look at him.

"And you're not just a little familiar with Marlowe. In fact, you're working with him, aren't you?"

"I have to, otherwise they will kill Thomas."

"Where is Thomas Crane now?"

Nancy Wong stared at him. She said, "I can't tell you." She then buried her face in her hands and began to sob.

Albro Swift felt his anger rising and he might well have walked away and left it all hanging had there not been one more question that seemed to catch in his throat. He sat back and calmed himself by taking a deep breath. Nancy Wong was crying outright now, her face down and her hands in her lap. She suddenly looked like the shy and awkward little teenager he remembered.

Albro said, "A year ago, you and Crane were in Lhasa. What were you doing there?"

Nancy Wong looked at him questioningly. "How did you know that?"

"Krupp told me. He thought he saw a couple of ghosts, but it was you and Crane, wasn't it?"

"Yes, we were there. Thomas always knew that it was just a matter of time before they found the *Jade Prince*. He had to stop them."

"He killed a lot of people in the process."

"That was not his doing."

"You're telling me Krupp blew up the place?"

"Krupp is a fool. There was someone else involved."

"Who was it?" Albro asked.

"I overheard Thomas Crane and Marlowe talking. They were speaking of someone they referred to sometimes as Elijah and sometimes as the Old Man. Later, I asked Thomas who they were speaking of, and he told me there were things I was better off not knowing. I've questioned Isaiah and I've gotten the same response. I have this feeling that it is Elijah who has been trying to kill us. Although the more I think about it, the more I believe the intent has been to frighten us."

Or to maneuver us, Albro thought. "What else do you know about this Elijah?"

"Only that he is to be feared," Nancy Wong answered.

"Then I think it's time we have a talk with Brother Isaiah," Albro said and then paused. "Where is Crane now?" Albro asked again.

Nancy acted as if she were about to answer and then turned away and stared out the window.

"Look at me," Albro said to her. There was a cold edge to his voice. "Is Thomas Crane really my father?"

Nancy Wong said, "It is the only rational way for me to explain who you are!"

Albro was taken aback by what he'd just heard. "What are you saying?"

Nancy Wong clasped her hands to keep them from shaking. "I don't know how to tell you."

"Tell me what?" Albro asked trying his best to remain calm.

"I don't know how to tell you the truth about who you are," Nancy Wong said.

Are you saying that I am not Thomas Crane's son?"

Nancy Wong looked at Albro and shook her head. "We should not be here. We should not be having this conversation."

"What's that supposed to mean?"

"Thomas Crane would not do what the Purim asked him to do."

"What did they want from him, these Purim?"

"They wanted Crane to bring them the *Jade Prince*."

"Okay, so he refused. Did they kill him?"

"Yes, they sent assassins who found him and then killed him."

"A minute ago you said he was still alive."

"He is."

"Either he's alive or he isn't," Albro said, barely able to contain his frustration. "Either he's my father or he isn't. You're lying to me about something."

Nancy Wong struggled to meet his gaze. Her mouth trembled. "I'm not. I swear to you. I would never lie to you about that."

"You've lied about everything else."

"I have not!"

"Then you're withholding the truth. You're a lawyer, you know what that means."

"Don't mock me, please," she said and began sobbing.

"Then tell me what you know. All of it."

"I will, I will," she cried into her hands. "I'll tell you everything I know about your father. I will tell you who you really are. I will tell you everything…" Nancy Wong continued to sob for another minute and then took a deep breath. She dried her eyes with her napkin and looked at the black stains. "I must look terrible. Excuse me." She got up and headed off to the ladies lounge.

The band was in full swing and the dance floor was crowded. The band had switched to some fast Latin rhythms, but Albro was barely aware of anything around him. He swiped at the sweat that had sprung up on his brow. The room was hot. His thoughts were reeling from Nancy Wong's confession. Was this all just a bad dream? Maybe if he clicked his heels together three times he'd be back in his shabby Compton apartment. Either she was telling the truth, or she wasn't. Either the last six days had been real, or they hadn't. He felt like he'd missed a major signpost along the way, but where had it been? How could anyone keep track of everything that happened moment by moment? And when the moment was past, where exactly did it go, down into the depths of Marlowe's 'infinite sphere?'

What had Nancy Wong meant by saying she would tell him who he really was? He knew who he was. He was Albro Marshal Swift, but there seemed to be fragments of a past kicking around in memories that weren't his. He needed something more than fragments. He needed a whole picture. He pulled at his collar. Why was it so terribly hot? What had happened to the air-conditioning? He needed some cool, fresh air.

He looked out at the dancers. Were they spinning around the dance floor, or was he rotating around them? He stood up and steadied himself against the back of the chair. He had a profound feeling of drunkenness, but he had barely touched his drink. He blinked. The dancers had become a whirlpool of color. He could feel it tugging at him. He put his foot out and reeled slightly. He wasn't sure that he wanted to take a step. The chair seemed to offer a solid support. Out there, he thought, trying to focus on the dancers, he wasn't so sure. What choice did he have, though? *Choice*? The word seemed obsolete. He had no choice. He had to take the step. He looked down at his foot, hanging in the air like some kind of disembodied element from his imagination, and willed it to move, to meet the floor. It came down with an awkward flop. He released his grip from the chair, and caught the corner of the table. The whirling mass began to spin faster. A dark hole in its center opened and expanded outward, sucking in the band and the diners as they continued eating and drinking, the tables and chairs, the waiters all smiling and polite, the walls and windows until it was only he who was left, leaning precariously at its very edge. He willed his other foot to step and he pitched forward into the darkness.

CHAPTER 37

ALBRO hits the ground hard with his open hands. He rolls onto his back tearing the shoulder of his dinner jacket. The suddenness of the fall nearly knocks the wind out of him, and he lies staring up into a night sky. He is startled to see the rat man appear over him with his hand extended.

"Get up," he whispers. "You must not be seen out here."

"Izzy? What happened?" He looks around. "Where are we?"

"Hurry, we haven't much time." The little man grasps him by the lapels of his jacket.

"Okay, okay," Albro says as he gets to his feet. He looks around, feeling dazed, disoriented, but unsure why. They appear to be in a narrow alleyway. A dim, yellow light comes from a window above them. The air is hot with a dry and dusty feel to it

"Where are we going?

"Shush. Just come with me."   The rat man is already several paces ahead.

Albro brushes the red dust from his slacks and starts after him. He grimaces at the pain in his knee where he'd come down hard in the fall. He limps after the rat man who has disappeared around the corner of what looks to be a structure made of large, reddish-brown bricks. He rubs his temples. There is a ringing in his ears and a tingling under his scalp as if maybe he's received an electric shock. He remembers that Nancy Wong had gone to wash her face and then everything had started spinning. He

419

staggers to the corner and sees Izzy standing in the shadow of a doorway motioning for him to hurry.

They enter a room and the rat man closes the door behind them. The windows of the small room are shuttered and a table with two rough-hewn chairs sits against the wall. A lamp with a low flame rests on the table and its sputtering flame makes their shadows jump. A curtained doorway leads to another room. It all seems crazily familiar as if the fall has jarred lose some long, forgotten memory

"I've been here before," Albro says

"Yes, of course," the rat man says, as if his sudden realization should have come as no surprise. "Wait here," the rat man tells him. He parts the curtain and hurries through to the other room

He hears low voices in a language he doesn't recognize. The way the interchange goes back and forth, he thinks that they must be haggling, but over what, he hasn't the faintest idea. He sits in the chair. He knows that he should be pondering the absence of Nancy Wong and an entire dining room full of people, but instead his rational mind has skipped over that. It seems much more interested in the fact that he has been in this room once before. He reaches out and touches the mud coating on the wall. It is the same material that coated street, but here under the light of the oil lamp, the mud glows yellow to orange to nearly the color of blood where the light dies in the corners. The thought comes to him that he has endured something here, but for the life of him he can't remember what. The memory hovers just beyond the edge of his memory, tantalizingly close, like a dream fragment that needs a nudge to cause it to tumble back into consciousness

"Come here." The rat man has stuck his head through the curtain.

Albro rises, steps to the curtain and parts it tentatively with one hand. The fabric sends a shiver through his arm and down through his legs. He realizes that his skin has become hypersensitive, as if preparing for something..., for something that happened a long time ago. But what was it? He steps through the curtain. The room is larger than the other. The floor is smooth stone, polished, black. A single chair has been placed in the center and a steel cart like one might see in a medical facility stands next to it. On it is a tray filled with dozens of small vials each filled with a different color liquid, and next to that is an array of small needles and blades arranged very neatly upon a white cloth.

Next to Isaiah stands a woman. She is shorter than the rat man and stooped and wearing a garment of rough, grayish weave, that hangs to the floor. Her face has the unmistakable resemblance of a house cat. Her yellowish eyes stare at him.

"Do you know where you are?" Izzy asks him and looks closely into his face as if he is looking for signs of a long awaited change.

He feels an odd shift taking place inside not only his head, but his body as well. It is as if he is being divided, like a flowing river meeting an island of rock. And then with a roil of turbulence, he parts in two.

"Do you know where you are?" the rat man repeats.

His legs grow weak. A flash of memory overwhelms his thoughts for an instant and then it is gone. He suddenly becomes aware of another presence in the room. Against the far wall lies a figure upon a pallet of blankets, dressed in the same gray garment as the old woman, with the same feline features, but taller and younger. He recognizes her as the woman in the dream of the nightclub. She appears to be in a kind of restless sleep. Her limbs twitch and a slight whimpering comes from her lips. Her closed eyelids quiver and jump. On her face an oily sheen reflects the flame of the lamp.

"Do you know who she is, what she is doing?" asks Izzy.

"She's the singer from the nightclub," he answers. "I remember being there when she fainted. I carried her..." Albro Swift feels the river of his thoughts start to converge and the memory becomes a froth of confusion.

The old woman next to Isaiah speaks in the odd language. The rat man puts out a hand to silence her and continues to stare into his face. "Relax, Albro," he says gently, "just let your mind relax."

He kneels next to the pallet and takes the sleeping woman's hand in his own and he feels the tingling under his scalp intensify. The memory returns with startling clarity as if it had happened only seconds ago. And for a few moments there is more, so much more, days and weeks and

421

months, the memories racing at high speed. He drops her hand and the woman stirs and her eyelids flutter and the world rocks precariously back and forth, and he understands.

"She is dreaming," he says, turning to face the rat man. "This is all in her dream."

The old woman speaks again. This time there is agitation in her voice. The rat man says, "She tells me that you are now ready. We must not delay. The dream will not last through the night. Remove your coat and shirt and sit."

He does as instructed. He sits, straddling the chair with his arms over the back. The one side of his mind, the side that knows and understands how he has gotten to where he is, the side that knows what is about to happen looks at the tray of blades and needles and accepts what must be done. The other side, the side he imagines as his real self, the self that has been abducted by someone else's dream, looks on in horror, helpless to intervene.

"Drink this," the rat man says, offering him a small clay cup. "It will keep you conscious."

Albro drinks the bitter liquid. He looks at the sleeping woman. Her breathing is deep and regular. He feels the old woman's cold hands upon his back, palpating his bones and tracing his muscles. She speaks to Isaiah.

"Here," Isaiah says to him and holds out a thick piece of rope. "Put this between your teeth. It will keep you from biting off your tongue."

The old woman starts to work. Hours later, she lays down her tools and steps around to face him. His chin is resting on the top rail of the chair back. The lids to his eyes are open, but he sees only a glimmer of light. She grasped his hair and tilts his head back and speaks directly to him. It is the same guttural moans and tongue clicks he had heard before, but now it makes sense to him.

"Can you hear me?" she asks.

With a great effort, he brings his eyes to focus. The old woman's dress is spattered with what he assumes to be his own blood. He lets the rope drop from between his teeth. His jaws ache.

"Yes," he answers. His voice comes out in a dry croak.

"She will awaken soon. You must go. Brother Isaiah has already gone," she says.

He sits upright.   He doesn't see the rat man anywhere. The old woman helps him into his shirt and dinner jacket. His back burns as if it has been set on fire. His vision turns to black and he struggles not to faint.

"How do I go?" he manages to ask when the pain subsides. "Where do I go?" He looks to the doorway. His mind has returned to a single stream.

"Not through there, through her," the old woman says and points to the sleeping woman. "You must go to her and tell her what you want."

He stands. A gray light has begun to seep into the room from around the edges of the shutters. He looks down at the woman who still sleeps. Her skin has taken on a sickly pallor. He takes a step and nearly collapses. He steadies himself and then reaches for her hand. He can feel the grasp of her thoughts as she pulls him forward in a loving embrace. His thoughts press against hers like two lovers in the heat of passion, and he whispers what she must do, and he feels himself begin to fall.

CHAPTER 38

FRANK GIDDES closed the book and glanced out the window. The lights of the city obscured any indication that dawn was on its way, but he knew it must be. It was nearly six o'clock. He had not slept, but had sat dutifully reading the book, turning its pages that still smelled of smoke, until he had reached its end. If nothing else, Giddes had told himself, it would help to pass the time. To his surprise, the book had proved to be more than a simple diversion. On the contrary, it had been a revelation. It had brought him a valuable insight into the workings of Albro Swift's mind. The factual content of the book would soon no longer matter. Its portrayal of a future time was about to become a piece of pure fiction. There was no doubt in his mind about that. After all, the difference between fact and fiction was largely a function of who happen to hold the greatest power at a particular time. Very soon the greatest power of all would fall into his lap, and time would no longer matter. The book might even cease to exist; here one moment and gone the next. Or, perhaps it would continue to exist along with its entourage of characters in another universe entirely created in a backwash of cosmic foam. The universe was full of surprises, Giddes mused. What mattered most, though, was that he had heard the voice of the author, and hearing it had given him a strong sense of how Albro Swift was going to react as they closed in around him.

He had thought briefly of warning the Old Man. Had that impulse been a last twinge of loyalty? Loyalty to what or whom, he'd asked himself; a loyalty to his past ideals or to the Old Man? The Old Man would squash him like an annoying bug when the time came. As to his past ideals, did he feel loyalty to a world that didn't give a flying fuck about its own demise? No, there had never been any feelings like that, even in the old days. Giddes had never been one to harbor such sentimental ideals. He'd once had ambition, but that had been crushed a long time ago. He had come to feel that greatness lay ahead for others, not for himself, and he had soldiered on in obscurity. Now, the return of Thomas Crane had changed everything. He saw now that there was something in it for himself.

The Old Man had ordered him to stay where he was. He knew what that meant. He knew what it meant when the generals ordered the troops to stay in place while they retreated to safety. 'This is a war', the Old Man had said to him, as if he needed reminding. Only this war was not to be fought in the air, or on the oceans, or in the streets. This war was to be fought in the shadows of reality and in the interstices of time.

He did not resent being left behind. In fact, he was content to be where he was. He knew eventually the battle would come to him. He looked out the window again, down into the street and the row of red-brick buildings. Heavy fog made the scene materialize and then disappear. He glimpsed the yellow warning tape flapping in the wind, the shattered glass, and then it was gone. It was an apt illusion, he decided, for what was about to come. It was like having a front row seat to the main event. No, that was not the correct way to think of it. The *singular event* was how Crane had described it all those years ago. It would be the point where all things, and he had stressed *all things*, would come to focus.

CHAPTER 39

A waiter knelt next to Albro. He asked, "Are you all right, sir?"

Albro raised himself on one elbow and a burning pain ripped across the surface of his back. He caught the scream in his throat and groaned. He looked around. He appeared to have fallen on the last step of the low staircase that separated the dining area from the dance floor, and then he saw her striding toward him, her arm outstretched, a diamond studded bracelet dangling from her wrist and flashing like a warning light to any and all who might dare to get in her way.

"Albro!" she called out. And then she was there, bending over him, her soft hands on his face, her beautiful green eyes looking into his own.

"Monique?" he asked weakly. For a moment he thought that he might still be caught in that terrible dream, and then realized, as his mind cleared that Monique had not been a part of that dream and that this must be reality, or at least something close to it.

Monique whirled her attention around to the waiters who hovered close. "What happened?" she demanded.

The head waiter backed up a step as if having been pushed in the chest. He spluttered, "The gentleman slipped. I am so sorry. I am afraid the gentleman has had too much to drink."

"This man has been poisoned and I am holding you personally responsible!" Monique glared coldly at the head waiter who turned an ashen shade of yellow. "Where is the woman who was seated here?"

The head waiter looked around in a panic and then spoke rapidly to his underlings who dashed off toward the ladies lounge. "We will find her," he said to Monique.

"You will do more than that," Monique replied forcefully. "You will notify your security to cover all exits. No one is to leave this building until the police have arrived. Do you understand me?"

"Yes, yes, of course, I will do as you wish," the waiter said and hurriedly backed a few steps away. He pulled a phone from his pocket and spoke rapidly.

Monique turned back to Albro who had begun struggling to raise himself. "Keep still, darling, help is on the way."

"It's my back," he whispered hoarsely.

"I know, darling, I know. It must be excruciating."

"I think I twisted it when I fell."

"Oh, Albro, they've done something terrible to you."

No sooner had she said this than two medics pushing a gurney rushed into the dining room and positioned it next to Albro. They spread a sheet on the floor and rolled him face down onto it, and then lifted him onto the gurney and then he was rolling toward the elevators.

Albro could see a thick torso and hairy forearms. He tried to rise up in order to see where he was being taken. He felt a hand on his back and then a searing pain that snatched his breath away and made dark circles dance in front of his eyes. He felt the elevator begin its descent.

"Monique," he managed to say between gasps for breath. "Where is Nancy?"

"Don't worry, Albro," Monique said. "We're going to find her, and then we will find the others. We will punish them for what they have done to you."

"Monique, you don't understand. Nancy had nothing to do with this."

"Try not to speak, Albro. You are very, very ill. If an infection sets in you could die within hours. We're taking you to a hospital where you can get the care you need."

427

The elevator came to a slow halt and the doors slid open and then he was quickly wheeled through a maze of narrow corridors. He could hear the heavy breathing of the two medics and the steady click of Monique's heels on the hard surfaced floor. At last they came to an open door. Albro could feel the warm, moist air of the night brush past him as he was wheeled down an incline. Then he was lifted through the open doors of an ambulance. He felt his arms and legs being secured with straps.

"Monique, what's happening?" Albro asked.

He felt her fingers in his hair. "This is for your safety, Albro," he heard her say. And then he felt a sharp prick in the side of his neck and as the vehicle began to move, everything around him began to fade to gray and then slowly to black.

CHAPTER 40

NANCY WONG entered the ladies lounge and went straight to the sink and splashed water on her face. She held her hands against her face until she felt the sobs diminish and then she raised her eyes to the mirror. She looked at the worn, drawn, pale image and saw the mask of her future self, weakened by age and embittered by loneliness. She stared into her eyes and did not like what she saw. She looked like a woman whose life had run its course.

"How long do you think you can keep this up?" she asked out loud, and then scowled at herself. This was no time to start pining for what might have been. She could not let the self doubts locked away deep inside her out of their cages. She reached into her hand bag and applied two determined swipes of make-up to her cheeks. She thought about touching up her lipstick and then decided to hell with it. She had promised Albro the truth and when it came out, she wanted to look like herself. She slung her handbag over her shoulder and plunged back into the dining room.

The band had stopped and a low murmur came from the crowd. She took a few quick steps and then stopped cold. She saw a woman with flowing blonde hair crouched over Albro who lay sprawled on the floor. She was cradling the back of his head with one hand and with other, she was touching his face. The woman looked up, and turned her face to take in anyone behind her, as if she had sensed someone there, and then her view was blocked by a half-circle of waiters who rushed to them.

It had been little more than a glimpse, but Nancy Wong had seen enough to send a chill of fear and panic through her body. Monique Olivia Newton had the eyes of a lioness who warned that she had no intention of sharing the prey she had just brought down. And then two medics came out of the elevator pushing a gurney. Nancy turned away quickly and strode to the stairway exit. She descended two flights and then entered a hallway, found the elevator and rode it to the lobby. The grand entry was busy with people coming and going about their business. Nevertheless, she felt as if all eyes were upon her as she crossed the expansive lobby. She paused at the exit and glanced briefly around her in a vain attempt to give herself some reassurance that she was not being followed and then hurried outside and found a taxi.

She gave the driver the name of their hotel and ordered him to go. She drew a deep breath and sat back in the seat and tried to slow her heart, and forced herself to think. The question foremost in her mind was what had happened to Albro. Why had he been lying on the floor? And why was Monique Newton there with him? Had she panicked and left too soon? Should she have stayed and tried to find out where they were taking Albro? No, she'd had to get out of there so she could warn Isaiah and Walter.

Although she knew Isaiah would not pick up the phone, she dialed the hotel anyway and asked the receptionist to ring the room. There were certain things the Mongi refused to do, and using the telephone was one of them. After ten rings she cut the connection. How did she even know that Isaiah and Walter were still in their room? She didn't. She knew that she could very well be walking into a trap, but she would just have to take the chance and physically go there and find out.

When they arrived, she sat in the taxi and looked cautiously at the entrance. All seemed perfectly normal, but there were just too many people to judge whether or not it was safe. Any one of the dozens of people milling about could be waiting for her. Why had she let Albro put them in such a vulnerable position? As much as she distrusted Marlowe, they should have followed his plan. At least they would all still be together. She felt frozen, unsure as to what to do. She forced herself to study the scene. She knew there was a kind of safety in numbers. Dressed as she was, she should easily blend into the crowd, and the longer she waited in the taxi, the more likely it was that she would draw attention to herself. The driver turned to look at her, but before he could speak she thrust a handful of bills at him and was out of the taxi and walking into the hotel.

She glanced toward the reception desk and thought briefly of taking the stairs. Running thirty flights up would serve well to burn off the alcohol that still coursed through her body leaving what felt like a trail of toxic waste, but not in her stocking feet and definitely not in three inch heels. She kept her head down and went straight to the elevators where one of the cars stood open. She entered alone and punched the floor number. When the doors opened she held her breath and used the mirror in her compact to scan the floor. Empty. She let out her breath and went to the door, slipped the card key into its slot and entered. The room was dimly lit by a table lamp and at first she thought she was alone and then she saw the shadowed figure standing in front of the window.

"Isaiah," Nancy Wong said in a rush of words, "they've taken Albro. We were having dinner. I left for a few moments and when I returned I saw Monique Newton standing over him. He was on the floor. Something had happened to him. They took him away on a gurney. There was nothing I could do to stop them. We have to leave. They might be here any moment."

Isaiah uttered a barely audible, "Ah."

"Isaiah, we need to go," Nancy Wong said. "They will come for us."

Then Isaiah turned to her as if he had just become aware of her presence. His face came out of the shadow and Nancy Wong could see that it had become even more lined with fatigue. He said, "Yes, you are correct. They will not waste time. They have what they need and now they will come for the medallions."

"But what about Albro? We have to find him!" Nancy Wong pleaded.

431

"I am afraid there is little we can do," Isaiah said and turned back to the window. "In my time," he said, as if speaking to the night, "this city is a ruin. It was once the greatest of all cities. Structures made of diamonds and glass soared thousands of feet into the sky. All manner of machines flew through the air. The inhabitants are said to have had the skin of angels and spoke in the language of poets. In the center of the city a labyrinth of infinite complexity had been constructed and at its center had been placed the *Jade Prince* along with the twelve medallions, the emblems of the twelve states of Qi, the twelve dimensions, the three that are around us and the nine others that had remained hidden until they had been discovered by the great mathematicians of the time. As lines are attached to a spar, those twelve dimensions were anchored securely to the *Jade Prince*, and through them flowed unimaginable abundance. The city survived thus for ten thousand years."

Nancy Wong's mind was filled with the urgency to flee. "Isaiah, we don't have time for..."

"This is something you need to know," Isaiah said calmly, "in the event that I do not survive." He paused, and then continued. "The Holy Scriptures tell us how the people became complacent and then indifferent to their abundance. They grew to question its source. They wanted far more than mere abundance, they wanted knowledge. They lusted for it. They wanted to know only what God is allowed to know. They were not satisfied with His gifts. They became cruel and then savage. The abundance turned to scarcity. That which was fecund became fecal. A great battle engulfed the city, and so much blood flowed through the streets that the harbor turned red for weeks. The labyrinth was breached, and the medallions stolen. The city was destroyed, never to rise again."

"What happened to the *Jade Prince*?" Nancy Wong asked.

"The Holy Scriptures tell us it was God who destroyed the city, and that it was He who scattered the medallions, one to each continent and one to each ocean, buried in the deepest crevices, dropped into the lowest depths, and it was God who forced the *Jade Prince* into the *Dark Abyss*, that trackless, nameless oblivion where no living creature can venture."

"Why do we need to do this if it is going to result in death and destruction?" Nancy Wong asked.

"Implicit in your question is an assumption that we have a choice, that we can choose to go forward, or that we can turn our backs and resume lives that exist somewhere in our imaginations. Time may fold back on itself in layers more infinite than one finds in a hammered sword, but it will always move forward. The Gathering has begun and we cannot stop it. We are being swept along in a river that flows to a future that has already happened. We cannot change that."

"It is the lies I can't bear any longer," Nancy Wong said.

Isaiah turned to her. He said, "Then you must let them go."

She had come close to doing just that when circumstances had intervened. She wondered now if she would have been able to go through with it, to tell Albro everything she knew. But the chance had come and gone. She shuddered to think what might have transpired if she had been sitting at their table when Monique had arrived. Isaiah might be ready to give up, but she was not.

"Give me a few moments to change," she said to Isaiah. "Then we are leaving."

She went into the bathroom and stripped off her clothes, ignoring the pain of her cracked ribs. She examined the yellow and purple bruises under her left breast, decided there was nothing she could do about the injury. She ran cold water over her head to sharpen her concentration. She dressed in a tight fitting top which helped to relieve some of the pain around her ribs and lightweight slacks and running shoes.

She retrieved the gold medallion from its hiding place and placed it around her neck and let it drop inside her shirt. At least the little gold coin was one constant in her life, even if it were something she did not understand. Right now, she needed the comfort and the sense of security it always gave her, even though now she had a creeping fear of the price she would eventually have to pay for those benefits. The hell with it, she told herself. Either she could do this, or she couldn't. She gave her hair a final toss with a towel, shook it out and went into the common area.

Isaiah still stood at the window as if he had become rooted to the spot. A door to the side of them opened, and Walter came out of the room rubbing his eyes with one hand and dragging a blanket with the other. He looked like an overgrown child waking from a bad dream.

"Where is Mr. Albro?" he asked.

"What's wrong, Walter?" Nancy Wong asked and started toward him.

Isaiah put out a hand and stopped her. "Leave him."

Walter balled up the blanket and buried his face in it. He stumbled forward knocking over a lamp and bumping into the low table in front of the sofa. He moaned softly into the folds of the blanket.

"Walter, stop!" Isaiah said firmly. "Tell us what woke you."

Walter lowered the blanket and opened his bloodshot eyes. "I was sleeping. I was very tired so I went to sleep. It's a nice bed, but too small. I slept on the floor."

"Yes, Walter," Isaiah said patiently. "You were sleeping, but something woke you. You felt something."

"Yes," Walter said. "I was sleeping and dreaming that I was home." He paused and looked around. He then noticed Nancy Wong. "Hello, Miss Nancy."

She looked to Isaiah who nodded to her. She said, "Hello, Walter. Please, tell us what woke you."

Walter scratched his head. "I was walking down a street, in the dream, that is, and I heard Mr. Albro. The street was crowded with Mongi. I could feel Mr. Albro's thoughts, but I couldn't find him. Then..." Walter stopped.

"Then what happened, Walter? Try to remember," Isaiah said.

"Oh, I remember, alright. I always remember," Walter said.

"Walter," Nancy Wong said, "tell us."

"I felt Mr. Albro scream, and that's what woke me up. Where is Mr. Albro?"

Nancy Wong went to the room phone and called down to the front desk. "Let met speak with Ernie Chan."

"I am sorry, but Mr. Chan is not on duty," a voice told her.

"Then connect me to his cell. Now!"

"Please, hold," the voice said.

Nancy Wong cradled the phone against her ear. She said to Isaiah, "Get ready to leave."

"I'm sorry," the voice came back on. "Mr. Chan is not answering his cell. Would you like to leave a message?"

Nancy Wong slammed the phone down. She went to Walter and grasped him by both arms. "Walter, can you feel Albro's thoughts?"

"I can feel them a little. They come and they go."

"Can you find him?"

"I can try," Walter said.

"Okay, let's go." Nancy Wong grabbed her rucksack and headed for the door.

"What about Mr. Albro's things?" Walter asked. He held up Albro's battered overnight bag that still bulged with the bundles of cash.

"Bring it."

CHAPTER 41

BY the time Albro got to the part about Walter scraping the black ooze off the street, his voice had started to crack, but he couldn't stop talking. He was babbling like an idiot.

"He called it a genie, like in the Arabian nights!" he said. A slight slur had come into his speech. They had shot him with something to take away the pain, and then he'd started talking.

"A genie," Monique said, "are you sure?"

He heard Monique and felt her run her hand through his hair, but he couldn't see her. He was lying prone on his stomach, and his arms and legs seemed to be held by restraints. Not that he was uncomfortable and wanted to move. He felt like he was floating on a cloud. It was just that he couldn't see Monique, but that didn't stop him from babbling on.

"Look, if that thing really was from the future, then it could be anything. What do you think someone from two hundred years ago would have thought of something as common as television? It would be magic. Maybe the genie is some sort of nano machine that can change shape. Smoke one minute and solid the next."

"Yes, I suppose that could be true," she said.

Albro craned his neck around, but still he couldn't see her. He said, "I don't know what's true anymore. I've been having these visions. No, that's not right. It's more like out of body experiences. That's not right either. It's like my body is out of this experience and in another. No, that's not right. It's like time has pulled the rug out from under me. No, that's..." He stopped. Was he repeating himself?

Albro tried to gather his thoughts, but they all seemed frayed and tangled at the ends, like a rope becoming unraveled, but he plunged on anyway. He had an uncontrollable urge to get it right, first for Monique's sake, but more importantly for his own.

"It happened first when we were buried in the avalanche. The snow hit, and suddenly I was somewhere else. I mean literally someplace else. While the three of them were being churned like butter in a barrel, I was surrounded by chanting monks! I had the weirdest sensation that I was a newborn babe. I came back with this on my arm."

Albro tried to lift his arm, but the restraints held him firmly. Out of the corner of his eye he saw Monique's hand. She reached out and traced the shape of the odd design on his forearm with the painted nail of her index finger.

"You poor, poor baby," she said softly. "You've been through so much."

"And that's not the only time," Albro said. He was in a hurry to tell it all. He wanted to get it all out, hold nothing back from the woman he loved. "The second time, we were with this fellow who rescued us. Nick Lane was his name. We were freezing and he gave us a ride. I thought I had fallen asleep and was dreaming. I saw him hours after he was shot, and he recognized me. I saw it in his face. Later I saw him get shot, but then I wasn't dreaming.

"And then, tonight when I tried to take a step, I fell, but I didn't fall anywhere that you might think I would fall. I fell into another world. There was a room with a lamp and the rat man was there with an old woman who looked like a cat, and another woman who was sleeping and we were all in her dream. And then, and then..."

"Shush now, darling. Everything is going to be all right," Monique's soothing voice came to him.

Albro felt a sharp prick in his left buttock and a hot sensation flow through his body. "There's something waiting for me, Monique. It's close by. I can feel it."

"Yes, darling, we know. We're going to help you find it. But first you must sleep. You're tired."

"Oh, Monique, I want to sleep, but I keep having these dreams."

"Those dreams won't come back."

"Are you sure?"

"Yes, Albro, I am sure."

"Monique?"

"Yes, darling"

"Would you do something for me?"

"I would do anything for you, sweetheart." He voice was that of an angel, and not just one angel, but a chorus of angels.

"Would you sing to me?"

"I know a bedtime song. Would you like for me to sing it?"

"Yes, Monique."

"And now good night, your day is done.

Farewell to each and every one.

Good night, sleep tight, don't let the Mongi bite.

You'll see me in the afterlife.

Good night, my love. Good night, my love."

CHAPTER 42

THEY rode the elevator to the parking garage. It was now near 2 a.m. and people were still up and about. That was just what Nancy Wong was hoping for. When the elevator doors opened she pulled Isaiah and Walter into a secluded corner. She dropped her bag.

"Wait here," she said. She looked around for the security cameras and decided there was not much she could do about them, except try to move quickly. She turned back to the elevators and then stopped short and crouched between two parked cars. She waited, watching the elevator doors open and close until a lone young man approached, wavering slightly on his feet. She came up behind him, caught him around the neck with her forearm and dragged him backward. She applied steady pressure until he stopped struggling and then laid him between two cars. She made certain that he was still breathing and then searched his pockets, found the car key and pressed it. She heard a beep and walked toward the sound. She pressed the key again and saw the lights flash this time. It was a German sedan, small but sleek. Walter would be cramped, but there wasn't time to shop around. If they were lucky, whoever was monitoring the security cameras hadn't noticed that one of the hotel's guests had just been mugged. But their guest wouldn't be out for long and would soon raise the alarm.

She brought the car around and stopped it where she had left Isaiah and Walter. She beeped the horn and they got in. She drove slowly toward the exit. She stopped and scanned the area. Everything looked normal, no extra guards roaming around with drawn guns, and the attendant in the kiosk had his chair tilted back and was lazily smoking a cigarette. She drove up slowly, passed the attendant the card key from their room. He scanned the bar code and the gate went up. She pulled out on the street with the uneasy feeling that it had all been too easy, but she couldn't let that bother her. She had to keep her mind on her driving. She almost turned into oncoming traffic when she remembered that she was in Asia. Horns blared at her.

"Fucking Asians!" she muttered. Why did they insist on keeping with the British tradition of driving on the left? She got straightened out and entered the flow of traffic.

"Which way, Walter?" she asked.

Walter sat beside her, almost doubled over in the small space. He closed his eyes and pointed in the general direction of the harbor.

"There," he said.

That was the way it went for the next hour as they traced a rambling route across the city. Nancy would ask and Walter would gesture in one direction or another. At one point they had to back track due to a street closure, and once Nancy turned the wrong way onto a busy street. She had taken the first side street she had come to and had avoided any collisions. At last they came to a warehouse district. Nancy cruised slowly between the metal structures. Mercury vapor lights cast a pinkish glow that made every reflective surface shiny and every shadow impenetrable.

"Stop," Walter said. He paused and then said, "I think Mr. Albro is back there."

They had just passed a narrow alley. Nancy Wong eased the car back and then stopped. The alley was short, ending in metal-walled building with a single door.

"There," Walter said barely above a whisper, "behind that door."

"Are you sure?" Nancy asked.

"Yes, I'm sure. I can feel his thoughts. I think he's asleep."

"Who else is in there?" Nancy asked.

Walter closed his eyes. "One other," Walter said. "He's going to hurt Mr. Albro! I have to stop him!"

Walter burst out of the small car and ran toward the building.

Nancy Wong jumped out. "Walter, stop!" she cried after him. "You don't know who's in there!"

But there was no stopping Walter. He hit the metal door running with his full weight and it folded inward as if it were made of cardboard. Nancy and Isaiah ran after him. The smashed door lay on a polished linoleum floor that ran down a long corridor and angled to the right. Walter was nowhere to be seen, but they could hear a distant squealing, like a pig being slaughtered. Nancy sprinted down the hallway, her heart pounding in her ears, the awful sound growing louder until it abruptly stopped.

She skidded to a halt, confused by the sudden silence and by the rush of adrenaline that coursed through her blood. Isaiah came up silently behind her and she jumped at his touch. And then she heard a low, deep wailing that pulsed atavistic fear down her vertebrae into her leg muscles.

"This way," Nancy Wong said, and they moved forward quickly.

They found another door, this one hanging by one hinge, and entered what appeared to be a modern laboratory. The room was packed tight with machines that hummed and glowed and a strong chemical odor hung in the air. Nancy Wong went first threading her way amongst the machines and through a second door that opened into a larger room that was well lit. She recognized it immediately as an operating theater. Walter stood in the corner with his back to them. His massive shoulders heaved and with each breath the wailing issued forth.

Isaiah went up to him and laid a hand on his arm. At Walter's feet lay a contorted body. The man wore tinted goggles and his head was bent back at an unnatural angle. A trickle of blood dripped from the corner of his mouth. A scalpel was still clutched in the man's lifeless hand.

Nancy Wong stepped closer, afraid of what she was going to see and looked down at the misshapen figure. The man's head was turned one hundred eighty degrees from where it should be. She lifted the

441

goggles and stared into the lifeless eyes of Doctor Felix Krupp. She turned away quickly. The room was partitioned by a translucent curtain within which a bright light glowed. She ran to it and parted the fabric.

Albro lay on his stomach stripped to the waist. His arms and legs were strapped securely. Another strap held his head face down in a hollowed recess. Her hands and arms told her to release the straps and get Albro off the table, but her eyes held her back. Her mind literally froze with the image she was seeing painted on Albro's back. His skin had become a shimmering, undulating kaleidoscope of color that would suddenly snap into a recognizable image of forests and rivers and soaring peaks and then just as suddenly break into a thousand churning pieces and reappear as exotic birds, herds of animals stampeding across an open plain, and then the images would begin to writhe like a mass of coiling serpents. Faces appeared, dissolving from one visage into another. And then a dark cloud covered it all and within it a multitude of white flashes erupted, and then she saw herself, falling from a great height, smashing against icy ledges, as she tumbled into nothingness. And then there were only shreds and fragments, hurtling through space, but she could not turn away. The grotesque beauty of it, along with the dire wailing coming from Walter, began to tear her nerves apart.

Isaiah threw a sheet over Albro. "You must not look at it," he said to her.

Nancy Wong felt her mind rock back and forth as if something had been forcibly yanked away from it. Her eyes burned and began to water profusely. A foul taste coated her lips. She had a strong sense of smoke filling her nostrils, but there was no smoke, no fire. She wiped away the tears.

"What happened to him? Did Krupp do this?"

"No," Isaiah said as he began releasing the straps, "but he was about to do something far worse."

"What could be worse than this?" Nancy Wong asked.

"He was about to remove it."

"Remove his skin?" She had a sudden and awful memory of the scars on Thomas Crane's back. "But why?" she asked.

442

Isaiah asked her, "Don't you realize what is there on his back?"

The question stopped her with its sudden impact. She whispered, "The map!"

"Yes. Now help me get him up."

It was Albro who finally got Walter to calm down. After Nancy and Isaiah had him upright, he'd slowly come around. Whatever he'd been shot with had been intended to relax him. He'd been kept conscious for a reason, Isaiah had said. He'd been wobbly on his feet, but he'd been able to walk over to Walter and put his arms around him. That had broken whatever spell the big Mongi had fallen under and his wailings had stopped abruptly.

"Mr. Albro," Walter said. He seemed surprised to see him. "What are you doing here?"

"Long story, pal," Albro said. He looked down at Krupp. He supposed that he should feel something for the little bastard, but he was having a hard time even mustering a mild hatred. He had a bad feeling that there was more to come, and it was going to be far worse than this. He took Walter's arm and steered him away.

"Thanks for stopping him," he said. "We better get out of here."

"Wait," Nancy Wong said. "Krupp wasn't acting alone. You would never have come here with Krupp," she said accusingly.

Albro stopped and looked at her. He looked at the rat man. He could hear Walter's heavy breathing next to him. He tried to recall the events of the evening. He had only bits and pieces. Whatever drug they had given him had scrambled his memory. Even so, there were enough pieces to make a very disturbing picture.

"You're right, Nancy," he said. "But we'll talk about that later. They might be coming back."

"I doubt that is the case," Isaiah said. "They got what they wanted. But there are others we need to be concerned about."

They piled into the car with Walter squeezed into the rear with Isaiah, and Albro in the front with Nancy Wong behind the wheel.

"We can't go back to the hotel," Nancy said.

"Just drive. I need to think," Albro said.

443

Nancy switched on the headlights. "Look," she said, and flicked the lights on high beam.

Albro looked ahead of them. In the bright wash of light he could see a figure in stark relief against the darker background. Two more figures joined it from the shadows to either side. A low growl came from Walter. Albro felt the hair rise on the back of his neck and he heard the latch of the rear door click.

"No!" he said without taking his eyes from the trio. He said to Nancy Wong in an even voice, "Get us out of here."

Nancy Wong looked at Albro and then back at the three figures as they began to slowly advance toward them. She brushed the hair from her eyes. A silvery-pink slice of light caught the face of the leading figure. The yellow eyes held them and the line of the jaw opened to reveal two rows of yellowish teeth.

Nancy Wong's hand moved in an instinctively slow motion to the ignition switch. No sooner did the engine start to turn over, the three figures charged them as a wolf might charge a fleeing deer. The lead figure leapt and hit the windshield, shattering it into a spider's web of fractured glass. A claw-like hand burst through the glass and flailed blindly.

"Go!" Albro shouted.

The engine caught and Nancy Wong slammed the shifter into reverse and stomped the accelerator. The beastly figure clung to the hood and began ripping away chunks of the windshield. The roaring engine propelled them backward through the narrow street. Nancy Wong spun the wheel and hit the brakes hard. The careening car flung the creature off the hood and sent it rolling until it struck a building. Immediately it was on its feet. It signaled to its companions and together they leapt toward the car.

Nancy Wong didn't wait. She forced the car into gear and drove straight into the advancing creatures. The car hit them with a sickening crunch of metal against bone and kept going. She screeched around the next corner and blew through a red light.

Albro saw the speedometer approach the terminus of its arc and they were still picking up speed. Everything around them became a blur. Nancy Wong's eyes were fixed on the road and her body was rigid.

"It's okay," Albro said. "They're gone. You can slow down." He reached over and touched her arm. She flinched and let her foot slip from the accelerator. The car slowed and rolled to a stop.

Nancy Wong sat silent, breathing in short, ragged breaths until she could let go of the wheel. "What was that..., that thing?"

"It was Mongi," Isaiah answered.

"I thought you were the good guys," Albro said. He turned and faced the rat man.

"For some of us, *Mal* is a very appropriate word."

Albro said, "I saw something like it when we were in Seattle, when we were attacked. Nick Lane shot it. When I pulled off its mask I saw the face of a wolf. You knew then who they were."

"Not who they were, but yes, I knew what they were," the rat man admitted.

"Why didn't you warn us?"

"I did not know until now that they had followed us here."

"How many more like that one are there?"

"I cannot say. There may be just a few. There may be many. It all depends."

"On what?" Albro asked, trying to keep his voice under control.

"On how close we have become. It all depends upon how close our time has come to yours. All I can say with any certainty is that there will be others and they will find us."

"And when they do?"

"They are simple, but efficient creatures. The Purim created them for one purpose."

"What's that?"

"They kill."

Albro Swift looked out through the hole in the windshield, and listened to the smooth purr of the idling engine. The occasional car passed them. A faint siren wailed in the distance. Rain had begun falling

445

and it dripped onto the dash. He could smell the briny fragrance of the ocean, and closer, he could smell the sour odor of their fear. Impossible and bizarre as it all might seem, it was all real. It was no dream that he was suddenly going to wake from. Running back to Los Angeles was no longer in the cards. He thought of Roger, and hoped to God that they hadn't found him.

He dug through his pockets and found the card with Chang Wu's number printed on it. The card looked as though it had been through a washing machine, but the number was still legible. He thought of using one of the phones Marlowe had given them and then decided against it.

"Find us a phone," he said to Nancy.

CHAPTER 43

CHANG WU sat at a desk that appeared to have been carved from a solid block of black granite. The stone had been brought to a high polish and reflected the soft glow of the overhead lights. The four of them were seated before him in comfortable chairs. Chang Wu gave a barely perceptible nod to Nancy Wong and then looked intently at the two Mongi for several seconds.

Floor to ceiling windows looked down upon the lower skyscrapers and out to the dark expanse of the ocean to the left and the mainland to the right. It was not the sort of space that anyone with even a hint of vertigo would wish to pass the time.

Albro had just finished relating to Chang Wu an edited version of what had happened since their last meeting, including the events that had transpired that evening. He had sat alone with Chang Wu while the others had been held at gunpoint in an adjacent room. Chang Wu had moved only twice, a slight narrowing of the eyes when Albro had gotten to the part about the elaborate tattoo on his back, and a tightening of his lips at the mention of the creatures that had attacked them. After several minutes of silent contemplation, Wu had signaled for the others to be brought in.

Now, Albro sat waiting for a response while the seconds dragged into minutes. He was bone tired and he'd begun to fear that Chang Wu would dismiss them, or worse, feed them to the wolves for a few pieces of gold.

At long last he spoke, "You tell a very interesting story, Mr. Swift." He paused looking straight at Albro.   The two body guards stood unmoving in the shadows flanking the doorway.   "Now, *I* will tell *you* a story.

"When I was a boy I lived in a village in Yunnan province.   The Maoists were in charge and we were half-starved from their 'reforms'. Our previous prosperity had been the result of corrupt Western influences.   Our fields were burned, our businesses destroyed.   My parents were arrested and taken away to work as laborers.   My father's only crime was that he had been a successful merchant.   I would never see them again.   Our home was seized by the local Party boss.   My grandmother and I were assigned to a communal household.   One survived by whatever means one could.   Denouncing a neighbor could provide your family with a small bag of rice.

"There is talk of the war to the south.   Trucks are moving through our village night and day.   They carry supplies of food and weapons for the soldiers who are massing along the border with North Vietnam.   China has always been wary of their neighbor to the south and also of their Soviet comrades to the north.   The fact that the Soviets are supplying the North Vietnamese with arms makes Mao very nervous.   Plus there is talk that we will soon be fighting against the American invaders. Nevertheless, there is soon a thriving black market between China and North Vietnam.

I am only a boy, but I am old enough to know that there is money to be made and I go to work for a local Party official who is a thief and a smuggler.   I become friendly with the drivers and soon I am not even noticed because I am just a boy and it is an easy matter to learn the habits and needs of the guards who are more than willing to trade some of what is on the trucks for a hot meal, a little opium or perhaps a woman.   Before long, I am making the trip to Hanoi.   It is my first experience with a city and even though it is under constant threat of attack by the American B-52 bombers, I am taken in by its beauty and charms.   There is death and suffering all around, but for me, it is all a great adventure.

"The Americans are aware of the convoys and soon they are a target for the jets that fly from the great ships that sail in the Gulf of Tonkin and we are forced to travel at night and to seek cover on the jungle roads that wind through the mountains. One night we are attacked by ground troops who have lain in ambush waiting for us to pass. The truck I am riding in rolls onto a land mine. The explosion lifts the truck into the air. I am thrown free, but I have shrapnel in my leg. I lie in the mud and listen to the fight and then it is quiet. When daylight comes I can see tall soldiers dressed in camouflage with black paint on their faces. They look like devils that have come to take the souls of those who have died. It is my first encounter with the Americans. They have Laotians with them. They have the survivors seated on the ground. Many are injured. They are being questioned by the Laotians. After a while, I hear the crack of pistol shots. I wait until they have gone and I escape into the jungle.

"All I know is that I must be in Laos and somewhere near the China border. With each step I can feel the metal fragments in my leg. Soon, I am too weak to move on and I lie down to die.

"When I wake, I am in a bed in what looks to be a field hospital. My leg is bandaged. I am too weak to sit up, but I am alive. A woman enters and comes to my bedside. She is beautiful with black hair and dark eyes. She speaks in a language that I recognize as English, but of course, I cannot understand. She smiles and apologizes to me in my own language, and asks me how I feel.

"I say to her that I am thirsty, and she brings me a glass of water. She then tells me how Thomas Crane found me in the jungle and carried me there. She tells me that she is a doctor and she reaches into her pocket and holds up a piece of twisted metal that she removed from my leg.

"In a few days, I am strong enough to be up and moving about. I find that I am in a compound that has been erected in the middle of the jungle. I can see that it has recently been cleared and the area is large enough to allow helicopters to land. There are no roads. Several large tents are at the center of the clearing. Another area has a tall fence around it and there are guards with rifles. Behind the fence are the ruins of a temple. Naturally I am curious and I approach the fenced area and I ask the guards what is in the temple. They cannot understand what I am saying, but a man who has come up behind me does.

"He asks me if I feel up to a short walk. I say yes, and the guards let us pass. He introduces himself. He is Thomas Crane and the doctor, is his close friend. I learn later how he found me and how at first he thought I was dead. He was two days out, exploring the jungle and knew the only way to save me was to carry me back to the compound. But now, as we walk among the ruins, he tells me about the people who built them. I have had a little education so what he tells me is beyond belief, but I take an instant liking to him, which is a good thing, for although I am not a prisoner, my instincts tell me that I am not free to leave.

"It is the beginning of the monsoon season and I will be there until the beginning of the next. There is a great deal of activity during the year. I know that something of great importance has been discovered within the ruins, but it is a closely held secret. There are many helicopters in and out. Suddenly I am aware of a change. Thomas Crane and the doctor are placed under guard. A man in uniform has assumed command. There are more soldiers. There is a heightened sense of urgency.

"A helicopter arrives with several personnel. One among them is a man who is clearly in charge. He is tall and has an animal strength in the way he moves. There is also a beautiful woman. I have never seen a woman with golden hair and I think that she is the most beautiful woman that I have ever seen. I watch them enter the tent where Thomas Crane and the doctor are confined. I am still free to roam about. I understand now what saved me, what has saved me on several occasions throughout my life. It has been an odd ability to blend into the background, even now. You may think that I have no regard for the law. On the contrary, I have great regard and respect for the law, and like a chameleon I change to suit my surroundings. I have never wished to stand out. The ego is a dangerous liability if it is not disciplined." Chang Wu paused and stared coldly at Albro Swift.

"You must excuse me," Chang Wu continued. "I have not drawn these memories into my conscious mind for many years and they cause me to speak more than, perhaps, I should. As I was saying, no one notices that I listen outside the tent where Thomas Crane and the newly arrived strangers speak. During the past year I have learned enough language from the American soldiers to understand day to day conversation. Thomas Crane's voice is full of anger and accusation. The stranger responds in a voice that is cold and holds no compromise. In anger, Thomas Crane attacks the stranger. I hear screams from the doctor. The guards rush in and the two men are separated.

"When the stranger leaves the tent, I see that there is blood on his face. After that, there is no more talk between them.

"Now the work deep within the ruins becomes almost feverish. Large generators are brought in and the roar of their diesel engines becomes constant. They are working around the clock. I see very little of the stranger who seems to live inside the ruins. He is reported to never sleep and on the few occasions that I do see him his eyes are as cold and sharp as the point of a dagger.

"One day, the tall stranger leaves and when he returns he has brought with him an assistant who has the misshapen face of a dwarf. Together they disappear into the ruins.

"It has become my job to carry meals to Crane and the doctor. An armed guard accompanies me. The two of them must remain seated while I set down one tray and take away the empty dishes of their previous meal. I am not allowed to speak to them, but there are many ways to communicate. They have been given plastic utensils with which to eat over fear that Crane could turn a metal fork into a weapon. I notice that each time I retrieve the tray plates and cups, the utensils have been arranged in a certain pattern. The written form of the Chinese language is quite remarkable in its simplicity. Four lines can convey a surprising amount of information. It does not take long to spell out a message. They tell me that time is short and that I must help them get into the ruins.

451

"What can I do? I am only a boy and now there are a hundred armed soldiers plus dozens of others whose attention is focused on the ruins. But they have saved my life. It is my obligation to help them if I can. All I can do is watch and wait. Each time I see them, the look of desperation in their faces grows more intense.

"At last, an opportunity presents itself. I see the American commander and the tall stranger board a helicopter. I have no idea how long they will be gone, but I know that I must act. I have become friendly with many of the research staff as well as the soldiers. Many of the soldiers are young and like soldiers everywhere they miss their friends and families. I am like a little brother. They are always giving me candy and cigarettes. We play games together. They forget who I am. My true self becomes invisible.

"I slip into the infirmary and find the locked cabinet which holds the powerful drugs. Fortunately my early mentors had trained me to open locks. The hours before sunrise are a man's most vulnerable. Even the body accustomed to the routine of staying awake yearns for the chance to sleep. The guards welcome the coffee I bring to them.

"When they sleep, I go to Crane and wake him and tell him what I have done. We strip the guards of their uniforms and he and the doctor put them on. He tells me I must run as far and as fast as I can. Before we part, Thomas Crane gives me a small coin. It is dark and I cannot see it, but I can feel the outline of something on its surface. He tells me that I must never lose it and one day I will learn its purpose. I watch them enter the ruins. It is the last time I see them. I do as they have instructed me to do.

"It is not long before it happens. I have run perhaps three hundred yards. It is difficult running at night. I fall many times, but pick myself up and keep moving. Afterward, I wondered if they really knew what they were about to do, what exactly was going to happen. Many innocent people died. The two of them included. At least at the time that is what I thought. And I am certain others thought that as well.

"I am knocked down by the blast. I am far enough from the center of the explosion that I am not killed. As it is, with my face pressed against the earth, the whole world seems to be engulfed in a momentary blaze of light. And then it is past and except for the distant fires, the jungle is once more cast in darkness. I have severe burns on my back and legs. If I had looked directly at the light, I would have been blinded. It is several days before I regained my hearing, and then only partially. I find a river and follow it. Soon I begin to encounter villages. Eventually I find a refugee camp and a make-shift hospital. I am loaded onto a helicopter, but my ordeal is far from over.

"It was not until decades later, was I able to learn what Thomas Crane had discovered, and the fate that befell him and the doctor. Let me ask you something. If you had known only this room with its fine furniture and soft lights, if curtains hung before the windows, would you believe that anything exists beyond these four walls? The fact is you do know that something more exists, because you have experienced it. Most people are content to satisfy their needs as simply as possible, even to the extent of denying the possibility that something might exist beyond that which they have seen, that which they have experienced.

"Have you never felt the pull of the future, the inexorable pull that no matter how you twist and turn, leads you to an inevitable end? I have felt such a thing all of my life. To what end, you might ask, is a life such as mine, a life of luxury beyond the grasp of all but a minute fraction of the human race, meant to reach?

"Thomas Crane saved my life twice. First when he carried me from the jungle and a second time when he sent me running into the night. He knew all along that my life had become intertwined with his and that our separated lives would come together again in a distant world. That distant world is the one before us, the world of the here and now. Before he parted, he gave me that small coin. He described it as a souvenir from another place, another time. He said that it would protect me and bring me luck and good fortune. Do you believe in luck, Mr. Swift? We Chinese, I must admit, are a very superstitious people. I was just a boy and he knew my chances of survival were meager. I suspect that he wanted to give me a sense of hope."

453

Chang Wu slipped his hand into the inner pocket of his suit and removed a gold disk the size of a small coin and strung by a fine, silver thread, and held it so his guests could see it. His eyes narrowed to dark slits as he studied them.

"Are you familiar with Chinese astrology?" he asked them. "Of course, you are. Why else would you be here? Certainly you are not here of your own accord. You have been drawn by the Dragon, a symbol of the first trine."

The disk swung from his hand. It somehow seemed to magnify the dim light that fell upon it, or perhaps it was the pupils of the eyes who gazed upon it that had expanded in an effort to gather more of its essence. Time seemed to be momentarily suspended. The experience was similar to that of a very skilled magician who can lure his audience into surrendering, if only for a moment, their sense of disbelief in magic. But this was no bit of vaudeville trickery, Albro was certain of that. He had a sudden understanding that it was the disk itself who was the master and Chang Wu who was the loyal servant. Its sense of power displayed a palpable authority, even arrogance, in the self-assured control it had over Chang Wu, or anyone else who might attempt to own it.

"Of all my possessions," Chang Wu said, "this is the one that is the least in substance and quite possibly the greatest in value. But to refer to it as a possession, is, in the greater scheme of things, a momentary indulgence. Such a thing is never possessed. Rather, it possesses he holds it. I am right, am I not?"

Albro Swift, whose eyes had locked onto the dangling golden disk the moment he saw it, moved uncomfortably in his chair. It was as if the object were calling to him from across a great distance and down through eons of time, like the plaintive call of a lost lover.

"Thomas Crane told me to keep this safe for him. One day, he would come for it. Unfortunately, he died before I could fulfill my duty." He gathered the medallion and its silver thread and slipped it back into his pocket. "To let this fall into the wrong hands would be a mistake of unimaginable consequences."

Chang Wu stood and the guards came forward and stood next to him. "Take them to the ship and lock them below deck. Do not let them escape." Chang Wu dropped his head in a curt bow and turned his back on his four prisoners and walked quickly from the room.

"Wait!" Albro shouted at Chang Wu's back. He jumped out of his chair and started forward. The guard closest to him stuck out a broad hand. It stopped him in the same way a brick wall would have stopped him. In the guard's other hand was a black automatic.

The guard motioned with a flick of the pistol toward the door, never taking his eyes from Albro. "Go," he ordered.

CHAPTER 44

THE ship was an aged deep-sea container vessel scarred and rusted from long years of service plying the waters of the Pacific. It was a smaller version of the now gigantic ships that parted on a daily basis from every major port in the Far East in a vain attempt to fill the insatiable Western appetite for all the trinkets and accouterments of the modern age. It looked as if it had been used to the point of dereliction and then ostensibly sold for scrap. Most likely, Chang Wu had bribed some official in Panama to register the vessel and had managed to sidestep the insurance requirements for safety or operation in international waters. It was clear to Albro that the ship's destiny lay somewhere on a reef, or worse, at the bottom of the open ocean and the insurance pay-off to Chang Wu would far exceed the purchase price.

The ship was docked at the far end of the quay and was empty of cargo and riding high in the water. The guards herded them up a rickety gangway under a feeble light hanging from the deck rail. Sunrise was still an hour away and the dockyards were deserted. Winds heavy with warm moisture blew in from the ocean. A light burned in the wheel house, but Albro doubted that anyone bothered to stand watch on this hulk. Once on deck, the guards directed them through a hatch and two flights down a narrow companionway. They stopped at a metal door and the guards motioned them inside. There was the unmistakable sound of a steel bar dropping into place.

The rat man put his ear to the door and listened. "They have gone," he said.

A single dim bulb hung from the low ceiling. There were two bunks in the windowless room, a steel table, two chairs and two tall steel lockers. Behind a door was a toilet and small sink. A ventilator grill no larger than a man's head wafted in stale, oily smelling air.

"Very nice," Nancy Wong said. "I always wanted to take a cruise; leisurely days sunning in deck chairs, a good book, and cocktails at five, breathtaking sunsets, dining at the captain's table. Yes, Albro, it was a wonderful idea asking Chang Wu for help."

"Yeah, well, consider the alternative," Albro replied.

"It's not exactly difficult coming up with an alternative to this," Nancy Wong said.

"You weren't exactly a fountain of ideas as that thing was about to rip your head off. If I'm not mistaken, you were on the verge of panic, but maybe I was wrong. You were probably just gathering up your strength to take it on mano a mano."

"We're Chang Wu's prisoners. At this moment he's probably negotiating to sell us to the highest bidder," Nancy Wong said.

"At least we're alive, and I don't think Chang Wu has any intention of giving us up."

"What makes you so sure of that?"

A deep rumble came from somewhere in the bowels of the ship and set up a resonating vibration in the metal floor.

"Does that answer your question?" Albro asked.

"We're leaving?"

"You just said that you wanted to take a cruise."

"Where is he taking us?"

"With any luck, judging from the condition of this old bucket, it won't be to the bottom of the ocean."

Nancy Wong looked at him. "Have you seen what is on your back?"

"I had a glimpse of it."

"Do you know what it is?"

457

"Monique told me."

"That was very nice of her. Do you know what this means?"

"The wedding is off?"

"I swear, Albro, if we were not about to die, I would kill you!"

"I'm sorry," Albro said. "I guess I was a little infatuated with her. I wasn't thinking clearly."

"That," Nancy Wong said, "has got to be the greatest understatement of all time!"

"I said I was sorry."

"Knowing that makes me feel so much better! Does Chang Wu know that you have the map?"

"I had to show him. I don't know how, but he seemed to know about it."

"It was the Dragon who informed him," the rat man said. "You heard its voice, did you not?"

"I heard something," Albro answered. "I thought it was the wind against the windows."

"Yes, the wind," said the rat man. "The Dragon has called up the wind. There will be a storm. It is there, within the storm, that you will find the *Jade Prince*."

"How do you know that?" Albro asked.

"It is written, '*The winds shall rage and the seas become as mountains. Yet, the Sacred Light will shine forth from within and show Him the way.*'" the rat man said solemnly.

"Do you mean to say that it's on a ship somewhere out there in the ocean? Is that where Wu is taking us?"

"I cannot say. I can only tell you what the Scriptures have foretold," Isaiah said.

"I just don't see how this thing on my back, this map as you call it, is going to show us how to find something on the open ocean. We need coordinates, GPS, radar and someone who knows how to use all that stuff. I've just escaped being flayed alive for something totally useless."

"On the contrary, we are helpless without the map. We would be like the blind wandering in a world without light. The map will alert us to the dangers we will inevitably face. Take off your shirt. Walter, give me the Black Djinnim."

Albro lay face down on the steel table. Isaiah had switched off the feeble bulb, but they were not in darkness. A light with an acidic quality to it poured out from Albro's back. At first, Nancy Wong could only take short glimpses of the images on Albro's skin before her eyes burned to the point of near blindness. Gradually her eyes began to adjust and she could look for longer periods, but she was not at all sure of what she was seeing. If she held herself in one position she saw one thing, and if she shifted slightly she saw another, and if she moved too quickly the whole image broke into a jumble of disjointed fragments.

"My God!" she uttered when she could no longer hold her gaze upon it. "What is it?"

"It is the map," Isaiah said.

"But what is it a map of?" Nancy Wong asked.

"It is the map of all times and all places. It is what the *Jade Prince* sees when He looks upon the universe."

Isaiah took the bottle that held the Black Djinnim and opened it.

"What are you doing?" Nancy Wong stepped away, startled by the black form that had oozed up to the rim of the bottle, and like an articulated finger probed the air.

Albro rolled on his side and turned to look. "Hey, get that thing away from me. It tried to kill me."

"No," the rat man said. "If that had been the intent of the one who left it for you, you would now be with those who have passed into Paradise. Lie down, and hold still."

"Not until you tell me what you're going to do."

"The map must be kept from further prying eyes. The Black Djinnim can assume many forms. You are now its master. When you feel its touch, command it to become your skin."

"You're sure about this, Isaiah?' Nancy Wong asked.

Isaiah looked at her. "Did you not trust your Auntie Lo, and the physician she called to administer to Thomas Crane? Do you remember the black 'medicine' they applied to his wounds?"

"Auntie Lo gave this to you?"

"No, not to me, but she made certain that it would find Mr. Swift. Please, let me proceed. They may come for us at any time."

Albro took another look at the oozing form that had begun to move down the sides of the bottle. He remembered the sizzling sound it had made on the stone pavement. If he'd been asked about Auntie Lo earlier, he would have put her right up there with Mother Teresa as far as trustworthiness went. Now, thinking about having that thing on his skin, he wasn't so sure.

"Walter," Albro said.

"Yes, Mr. Albro?"

"If I start screaming, get that thing off of me. Okay?"

For the first time, Albro saw a look of uncertainty in his eyes. "I'll try," he said.

Albro turned on his stomach. Isaiah tipped the bottle and the Black Djinnim flowed out easily and pooled in the middle of Albro's back. Albro shuddered. The thing was ice cold, like it had just been pulled from the freezer. He felt it slowly spread across his back, gradually warming as it went.

"Now," the rat man said, "Tell it to become part of you."

Albro closed his eyes. How exactly was he supposed to talk to that thing? Instead of thinking about the Black Djinnim, he found himself thinking about a summer day during which he had gone for swim in a cool lake. When he'd come out of the water, he had seen a woman applying lotion to her long legs and her freckled arms. She had looked at him and smiled and he had offered to rub the lotion onto her back. He remembered that her hair was that rich auburn color that is incongruously called red, and her eyes were the color of the first leaves of spring. Later that evening, she had pressed herself against his back as if she had wanted to weld their two bodies together.

The others watched as the black form expanded amoeba like, slowly covering the ever changing scene beneath it. When it had reached the edges it seemed to ripple suddenly as if a light breeze had disturbed it and then it changed, and like a chameleon changing to match its background, there was nothing to see but Albro's skin.

"What's happening back there?" Albro asked. "Why is everybody so quiet?"

"It is complete," said the rat man. "You may get up."

Albro flexed his shoulders and stretched.

"How does it feel?" asked the rat man.

"Actually it's a little tight across the shoulders, but other than that, it seems to be a good fit."

It was then that Nancy Wong saw that something was terribly wrong. "Where is it?" she asked.

"Where's what?" Albro was fastening his shirt.

"Your medallion is not around your neck. Where is it?"

Albro's hand automatically went to his chest. It had not left its place ever since Anna Marshal had given it to him. He had no recollection of when or where it had gone missing. He couldn't understand why he had not missed it.

"You let Monique take it from you!" Nancy Wong said. "Not only did you provide her with the map, you gave her your medallion! How could you let that happen?"

"That would be very bad for us," the rat man said.

"Wait, Nancy," Albro said. He fingered the place where the medallion should be. "I should have been aware that it was gone. I would have felt something, unless it's not far away." He looked at the big Mongi who was standing with his arms slack and with an odd look on his face. "Walter?" Albro asked.

Walter hung his head and stood silent.

Albro got off the table and stepped to the big man. "Walter," he said, "Look at me."

Walter tried, but could not meet Albro's eyes. He said barely above a whisper. "I meant to give it back."

"You have it?" Albro asked.

"It fell from your neck when you coughed up the Black Djinnim. When you weren't looking, I put it in my pocket. I thought you would ask for it and when you didn't it got harder and harder to tell you about it."

"You should have given it to me, Walter, but I'm glad that you didn't. Can you give it to me now?"

With an agonizing combination of reluctance and shame, Walter lifted the delicate silver thread from his pocket and the small, gold disk that hung from it. The carved rabbit had an expression on its face that seemed to suggest it had been its idea all along. Walter handed it to Albro. "I'm sorry, Mr. Albro. I did something very bad."

"No, Walter," Albro said to him. "Actually, you did something very good. Without this, we'd be up shit creek without an oar."

Walter looked and him and then asked, "Where is shit creek, Mr. Albro?"

"Beats me, pal," Albro said and patted Walter on the shoulder. "All I know is that everybody says you don't want to go there."

Albro put the medallion around his neck, and the vessel shifted beneath their feet. The rumbling paused and then resumed more forcefully.

"What's happening?" Nancy Wong asked.

"It is the *Jade Prince*," Isaiah answered her. "Its strength is still weak, but it now has us in its grasp."

"It's just the ship being pulled away from the dock," Albro said. "We're getting underway."

The rat man said, "Did you not feel the force of the medallion Chang Wu held?"

"That medallion," Albro said, "had a dragon on one side and flames on the other."

"Yes. It is one of the twelve. It is no stronger than any of the others, but it will use the strength of he who holds it and thereby attempt to rule the others. You will need to control it, or it will control you."

"You make it sound as if it's in my pocket. I don't think Chang Wu has any interest in parting with it, and it looks as if he's putting as much distance between us and himself as he possibly can. Chang Wu has us, we don't have him."

"You will discover that is merely a matter of perception. Did you not see the tremor in his hand? How he fled from our presence? He cannot resist the will of the medallions for much longer, nor can we. They are now five and they grow in power."

"What can we do?" Nancy Wong asked. "We're prisoners locked in a cell."

Albro yawned and looked at Walter who had stretched out on the floor and was snoring softly. He seemed to have the best sense of any of them when it came to dealing with the futility of pondering one's fate.

"I think Walter has the answer to your question, Nancy," Albro said. "You two can have the bunks. I'm so tired I could sleep standing up if I had to. We all need some rest. There's no telling what they'll do with us."

Albro lay down on the metal floor. He could feel the thudding of the old diesels as well as the more rhythmic oscillations of the propeller as it struggled to push the massive bulk of the freighter through the water. He'd spent a few months earlier in his life working as a deck hand on a coastal freighter that plied the tepid waters between Darwin and Calcutta. There was little to romanticize about that life. The ship had been dirty, the food and water vile, and the tropical climate a see-saw of heat and humidity. Yet, he now felt a certain comfort in the vibrations that came up through the floor, or maybe his body was simply beyond the point of exhaustion and cared only for the opportunity to escape into sleep. He lay on his back with one hand on the small disk that rested on his chest. Was it vibrating as well? He'd felt its energy come alive when Walter had returned it to him. Now, there was something more. A nervous agitation flowed from the disk into his chest. He wondered if it was just him, or did the others feel it to? He had felt something different from the disk that Chang Wu had displayed. There was an aura of arrogance, a sense of self-assuredness, of power. At the time he had thought that it had come from Wu, but now he wondered if it had really come from the small coin that had dangled from Chang Wu's hand.

Chang Wu could help them, or he could stop them cold. Their fate seemed to lie in his hands. But where lay Chang Wu's fate? Did it, as the rat man asserted, lie within some superstitious belief in dragons? And the dragon, wasn't it just a symbol like the rabbit on his own coin, the tiger on Nancy's, the rat on Isaiah's and the ox on Walter's? The way the rat man spoke, the 'medallions', as he called them, were more than just symbols of a superstitious belief that one's fate was somehow fixed the moment one exited the womb and took a first breath of life-filling air. They were not symbols of a structure of beliefs. They were the structure itself, each a segment of a multi-dimensional existence that when dispersed led to destructive chaos, and when gathered together provided harmonic cohesion. The universe swung like the pendulum in an old fashioned Grandfather's clock between the two states of chaos and tranquility. This was the natural order of things and had been since the very beginning of it all, and thus, the Gathering of Mongi would happen as it always had, and in the process the medallions were being swept up like confetti left over from a real bender of a party by someone who knew their value and who was bent on hijacking the system, and in effect, grab hold of the pendulum and do with it as he pleased.

It sounded like a load of New-Age double speak to Albro. Could something out of Chinese folklore, fanciful images printed on placemats that distracted diners from their dingy surroundings while they waited for their egg-fu-yung, become transmuted by the millennia into what the rat man had described as an entirely changed world-order? The rat man kept saying it was the other way around. The changed world was already out there and it was pulling the past forward through time. Those other dimensions were out there waiting to be discovered and for better and for worse it would be the Chinese who were meant to find them and then lose them, and then find them again in a never ending cycle of destruction and renewal, in what to Albro sounded like a yin and yang struggle gone berserk.

Albro's body jerked in a spasmodic signal to his brain, telling it to shut off, that these mysteries would be answered in their own time, or perhaps, out of their own time. If what the rat man said were true, the answers would find him, as would the *Jade Prince*.

CHAPTER 45

A grating of metal against metal startles Albro awake. The door to the room swings lazily back and forth on its dry and rusted hinges squeaking like an out of tune cello. He watches it and then realizes the door itself is unmoving. It is the ship that is rolling in heavy seas. Waves are hitting the hull in resounding booms. Each time they strike, the ship shudders violently. He listens to the diesels. Their monotonous throb beat like a tired heart, but above the beat is a more ominous sound. He can hear the howling of the wind. The dangling light flickers each time a wave hits the ship.

He rises up on one elbow and looks around the room. The others are gone. He has no idea if it is morning or still night, but he feels rested. He looks at his watch. Eight o'clock. That had to make it early morning. He watches the second hand sweep around the dial and then recalls that the fake Rolex had stopped working months earlier. Now, it seems to be working just fine.

He gets up and sways, then steadies himself against the edge of the table. The bunks don't appear to have been slept in. He sticks his head out into the hallway. No one's in sight. He remembers how they had been taken somewhere amidships. The operational center of the ship is at the stern, but he is completely at a loss as to which direction that might be. Ordinarily he has a near perfect memory of place as well as a great sense of direction. Either all of his senses have gone haywire or he is on a different ship. It looks the same, but it doesn't feel the same. He turns to his left and heads down the corridor bracing himself along the wall against the roll of the ship.

He leans over the first companionway he comes to and shouts, "Hello! Anybody down there?"

Other than the throb of the engines and the general creaking of an old ship and the distant howl of the wind, there is only silence. He drops down another level. The sound of the engines becomes more prominent, but more puzzling, the howl of the wind is even stronger. If nothing else, he is certain to encounter someone in the engine compartment who can direct him topside. He walks to the end of the corridor and descends again to another narrow passageway and yet another iron stair way down. There is still no one to be seen. He grasps the handrail and descends again. With the two levels they had come down initially, he is now five levels below the main deck. This corridor leads in only one direction and ends at a door with a large wheel in its center.

He can hear the deep throated rumble of the engines behind the door. The howling of the wind is now so intense it is almost as if the storm were raging deep within the ship. He turns the wheel and then pulls on the door's lever handle. It is stuck. He grips it firmly and braces himself with one foot against the door's framework and pulls with all his strength. The door suddenly swings inward throwing Albro off balance and onto the floor. The howling of the wind abruptly ceases. A hand reaches through the opening and grasps him by the scruff of his shirt and pulls him through into the adjoining compartment.

It is a huge, open space, several levels high and is stiflingly hot. The roar of the diesel engines nearly deafens him. Albro pulls himself to a sitting position and looks up at the sweaty, grease smeared torso of a man who is stripped to the waist. The man steps back and wields a wrench as long as his arm. One wild eye stares at him; the other is covered by a black patch held in place by a strap that encircles his head. A small gold coin hangs from a silver thread around his neck.

"You!" the man shouts half in surprise, half in relief. He drops the wrench. It falls with a resounding clang which sets off the howling once again. He hurries forward and pulls Albro to his feet.

"Christ! Am I glad to see a familiar face!" he shouts above the din.

Albro looks at the man in stunned disbelief. It is Nick Lane. He tries to think, but the noise is splitting his head. They had left the man for dead, not even three days ago.

"Where are the others?" Albro shouts at the man.

"Others?" Nick Lane shouts out the question. "There are no others, unless you count them!"

Nick Lane points upward. The ceiling of the engine room is several stories tall and around the perimeter of the upper level are rows of barred cages. It is from inside these cages that the howling originates. Clinging to the steel bars is the same kind of creature that had attacked them earlier.

"They like the heat! Let them get cold and they complain even louder!" Nick Lane shouts in Albro's ear.

Albro looks up at the creatures. Their faces, an amalgam somewhere between a wolf and a tiger bulging beneath a human forehead, are pressed against the bars. Their bared fangs and long, curved claws glint in the harsh blue of the fluorescent lights. They wail like banshees on fire.

Nick Lane ignores the creatures. He turns and examines a row of gauges and dials at a console beside the gigantic engines. Satisfied, he grabs his shirt and shouts, "Everything's fine! Let's get out of here!"

He opens the door and motions Albro through. He leads Albro through a maze of passageways and up and down and then up again until Albro is totally confused. Albro still has not glimpsed the outside and has no idea if it is night or day. The waves are still pounding the ship and it shudders from stem to stern with each blow. At last, they come to the galley. A pot of coffee sits on a burner, and Nick Lane pours out two cups and sets them on a table with attached stools.

"I hope you like it black. Ran out of cream weeks ago," he says and sits heavily and leans forward with his elbows on the table.

Weeks, Albro thinks. How could that be? He sits facing Nick Lane and picks up his coffee. After sipping, he asks, "How long have you been on this ship?"

Without turning, Nick Lane jerks his thumb backward and says, "Feel free to count 'em. I gave up weeks ago. Oh, I still mark each day. Habit, I guess."

Albro looks at the wall behind Nick Lane. On it is a smaller version of the old style slate boards like they had in grade schools a long time ago. It looks to be two feet tall and three feet long. The cook probably used it to post the day's menu. It is nearly filled with hash marks organized neatly in groups of five. Albro shifts his gaze back to Nick Lane who is eyeing him suspiciously.

"The question is, partner, how long have you been on this ship?" Nick Lane asks. "The captain and crew abandoned ship not long after we left the coast. Said the old bucket was sinking and there was no more room in the life boat and since I was low man on the totem pole..." He pauses before going on. "I've been all over this ship and it's just been me and them." Nick Lane tips his head toward the engine room.

"We were brought aboard last night," Albro says. "At least I think it was last night. We all fell asleep. When I woke, they were gone. I went looking for them and that's when I found you.

"Do you mean the others who were with you before?"

"Yes, have you seen them?"

"Not since the night this happened." He answers and touches a finger to the black patch.

"We thought you were dying," Albro says and remembers vividly Nick Lane's lifeless form slumped against the walls of the phone booth.

"I thought I was dying," Nick Lane replies. "I couldn't make heads or tails of where I was or what had happened. But you know what? I remember seeing you. I mean, after I woke up. The place was all torn up. You came to the door, looked at me and then ran off like you'd seen a ghost."

A distant look comes into Nick Lane's remaining eye. He says, "Maybe I wasn't awake, or maybe I was in shock. Anyway, somehow I found my way to the docks. A medic fixed the empty socket and patched my skull back together. The captain figured I owed him medical expenses. He said they'd lost a crewman, and needed a cargo specialist. Zoo keeper is more like it. One voyage and he'd consider my debt squared. Oh, did I mention that by then we were already underway and no land in sight? He had me. I figured I'd jump ship at the first port. Only thing is, this ship ain't headed to port."

"Can't you steer it?" Albro asks. Another huge wave hits the ship and he has to grip the table edge to stay on the stool. He wonders how many more like that the ship can take before breaking apart.

Nick Lane shakes his head. "The controls have been jammed. As far as I can tell, we're traveling in a gigantic circle somewhere out in the middle of the Pacific Ocean. I keep the diesels turning over just enough to keep her from rolling too badly and to power the generators. I've got to keep the pumps running. This old bucket leaks like a sieve. There's a freezer full of food, mostly meat for those creatures down below. But sooner or later, we're going to run out of fuel. If there's a purpose to all this, I can't fathom it. If the captain wanted her sunk, why didn't he just scuttle her? The only explanation I've come up with is that at some point, someone will show up to claim the cargo. I thought maybe it was you coming for them."

Albro wonders what anyone would want with those beasts. He says to Nick Lane, "Chang Wu's men brought us aboard last night and locked us in a cabin."

"Chang Wu," Nick Lane said. "There's a name I didn't expect to here again."

"You know him?"

"I know of him. When I picked up you and your friends I was on my way to sell a shitload of prime bud. It was a damn shame to lose it. Anyway, my buyer was part of his organization. Far, far down the ladder, you have to understand. Still, it is interesting isn't it?"

"But putting us on this ship couldn't have happened if what you say is true," Albro asks.

Nick Lane looks at Albro. "Not unless they brought you out by helicopter and dropped you on deck."

Albro says, "The ship we boarded was tied up at the dock. We walked up the gangway. The ship set out later, but it was at the dock when we arrived."

"Did you see its name?" asks Nick Lane.

"The Sanshui," Albro answers.

"Not this ship," Nick Lane says. "This is the Jade Prince."

Albro started involuntarily. The Jade Prince? Is this it? Is this what he is supposed to find, a rusted ship with a cargo of fanged monsters? Or, is this just another sour joke taunting him forward in an unending series of puzzles.

"Can we go outside?" Albro asks.

"Trust me," Nick Lane says, taking a long drink from his mug. "You don't want to go out there."

"I want to get a look at the stern to confirm the name."

"The weather's shit. I'll take you to the wheelhouse. You can have a look. You might change your mind when you see those waves. Follow me."

They leave the galley and climb two flights of stairs. Large portholes of thick glass look out into darkness from three sides of the wheelhouse. Albro steps to one of them and shields his face from the interior light. His eyes take a moment to adjust to the night, and then he sees a ghostly scene of white-crested waves rising and falling all around them. Wind driven spray hits the glass and flows in horizontal rivulets. Waves crash over the bows sending a flood of foam and black water washing down the length of the deck to the base of the superstructure that houses the living quarters and the wheelhouse where it shoots sideways and gushes over the gunwales into the seething ocean.

"Still want to go out there?" Nick Lane asks.

"I'll pass, at least for now." Albro goes to the large, steel wheel that steers the ship and tries to move it. It refuses to budge.

"They completely disabled the gearbox that controls the rudder," Nick Lane informs him. "They literally smashed the gears. Even if I had a

471

clue as to how to repair it, there are no spare parts. Believe me; I've had plenty of time to look. We're on a steady course until the fuel runs out. At that point, we're fucked. When the pumps stop the ship starts filling up with water. It's only a matter of time before she sinks."

"What about the radio? A ship has to have a radio," Albro says hopefully.

"Yeah, there's a radio, or what's left of it," Nick Lane scowls. "Someone used an axe on it."

If only Roger were here, Albro thinks. Roger would be able to reassemble the pieces into a primitive transmitter, and send out a distress call to all ships in the area. Roger could do just about anything with almost nothing. What was Roger doing now? Would he ever see him again? He brought his mind back to the moment. "How much fuel is left?"

"Hard to say, a few days at best," Nick Lane answers.

"And after that, how long will the ship stay afloat?"

Nick Lane shrugs. "With no power, she'll start to wallow. In seas like this, it could only be a matter of minutes before a wave rolls her over. In calm water, it could be weeks, even months before she sinks."

"So, if someone is coming for the cargo, it has to happen soon, Albro said."

"Yeah, you're right. But I've got a feeling that whoever arrives isn't going to be interested in the two of us, leastwise me. You, I'm not so sure about. You still haven't explained how you got here."

A larger than average wave hits the ship and it lurches suddenly onto its side. They are on the highest deck above the water line, where the motion of the ship is greatly exaggerated. The wheelhouse swings in a wide arc and Albro hangs onto the wheel and waits for what seems an eternity as the ship slowly rolls back.

"I think I know," he replies to Nick Lane. "I think it has something to do with this." He pulls the gold coin from inside his shirt.

Nick Lane pats his chest. "You know," Nick Lane says, "I've had a lot of time to think while on this ship, and my mind keeps going back to that night and how the four of you showed up out of nowhere at just the

472

right place and just the right moment. And every time I think about it this little gold coin seems to…," Nick Lane pauses with his eye closed. He raises his hand to his lips and when he opens his eye he just stares into space without speaking.

Albro says, "I think they act as some sort of beacon. How or why, I don't know. But for some reason, our lives keep crossing paths, and we're being carried along by this ship to who knows where." He still wants to confirm the name of the vessel. A thought comes to him. "Ships always have a log book. Where would the captain keep it?"

"In his quarters, I suppose." Nick Lane says and scratches his head. "I don't know what you'll find. There was a fire in there. I think the captain tried to burn the ship's documents. We could have a look."

"Take me there," Albro says.

Nick Lane leads the way down one level where he first shows Albro the radio room and the smashed console and then proceeds down the corridor to an open door. He searches for the switch to an overhead light that illuminates a room of minimal comforts. There is a desk and a wardrobe and an open safe. A metal bed frame holds a mattress with a burned mess in the middle of it. The room stinks of charred cotton. It looks as if the captain had taken any papers of importance and piled them in the center of the bed and lit them. A discarded can of lighter fluid lies on the floor. The curtains around the porthole had caught and only a few charred remains still cling to the rod above the glass. A smudge of oily soot smears the wall behind the bed, but the paint has not blistered. The fire had not been all that hot. Scraps of half-burned pages form a ring around the central mound of ashes.

Albro starts digging through the remains until he finds what he is looking for. It is a large, thin, ledger-style book that had been opened and thrown in haste onto the flames. It had actually acted to smother the flames beneath it, and that which had been piled on top has only burned its leather binding. He pulls if free and blows flakes burned paper from the blackened volume. He takes it to the desk and opens it to the first page. On it is printed in bold, square letters: LOG OF THE MV JADE PRINCE.

473

A question suddenly occurs to Albro. He looks up at Nick Lane. "How many of those creatures are there?"

"Twelve," Nick Lane says.

"Are you certain?"

"I've been feeding them three times a day. Twelve chunks of meat for breakfast, twelve for lunch and twelve for dinner. I don't even bother to thaw it. They crunch it up like it was hard candy."

"They're all in separate cages?"

"Sure, otherwise they'd devour each other."

"Why do you think that?"

"You can look at them and see it in their eyes."

"Maybe I should."

"What?"

"Look at them."

The ship lurches and groans as it plows blindly through another gigantic wave. Albro hangs on while once again the ship rights. The storm gives no sign of abating. If anything, it is growing in intensity. A gray light has begun to seep through the clouds. A clock bolted to the wall shows twelve o'clock. He looks at his own watch which reads the same time. How could four hours have gone by? His sense of time has become totally scrambled. Surely, no more than an hour has passed since he had awakened.

Nick Lane looks at the clock. "It's lunch time. They'll be howling to beat the band. Come on, you can help."

Albro tucks the log inside his shirt and follows Nick Lane. The freezer is a cavernous compartment at one end of the galley.

"You'll need these," Nick Lane says and hands Albro a pair of thick gloves. A blast of frozen vapor envelopes them as he opens the door. He positions a heavy plastic garbage can in front of a wire bin and starts loading in chunks of frozen meat.

Albro reaches into the bin. He jumps back suddenly, releasing what he's grasped. It is the lower section of a forearm with the hand still attached. A wave of nausea sweeps through his body.

"What is this?" he gasps as a wave of nausea sweeps over him.

"Sorry. I forgot to warn you. I had the exact same reaction my first time. I nearly puked my guts out. I guess I've gotten used to it," Nick Lane says and continues to fill the container, the pieces clunking together like hardwood.

"But where did all this come from?" Albro asks, repulsed by the sight, yet unable to turn his eyes away.

"Dead people, I suppose," Nick Lane says matter-of-factly. "Not people like you and me, more like those two friends of yours. You know, the big one with the weird hands and the little one who looks like a rat."

Nick Lane bends over the bin and digs around. "Here, look at this," he says.

He holds up something the size of a grapefruit and tosses it to Albro who catches it in his gloved hands. It looks like a doll's head that had been torn from its torso.   It has a tangled strand of icy hair still clinging to one side of its head and its glassy eyes have the too far apart look of the Mongi. His hands fly apart and the head rolls to Nick Lane's feet. He deftly scoops it up and tosses it in with the rest of the pieces.

"That's enough," he says and drags the load out of the freezer. "You don't know how much I appreciate your help. It ain't easy getting this down the companionways. My back's been killing me. Grab a handle and let's go."

The two of them have worked up a sweat by the time they get down to the engine room.   The howling has changed to a kind of screeching and has grown steadily louder as they have approached, until it has become a raging wail beyond anything Albro could imagine coming from an animal.

"They can hear us coming," Nick Lane informs Albro, "and maybe even smell us too. It gets them real excited, that and the prospect of a meal. Don't get too close to the cages. They're real quick, faster than your eye can follow. And they're strong too. You get within grasping distance and they'll make a meal of you before you even realize it. Remember how I told you the Captain had lost a crewman? This was his job. I found out later the man hadn't been careful. Stand back and let me do the feeding."

Nick Lance swings open the door and they lift the heavy container into the compartment. The screeching suddenly ceases. The monotonous roar of the diesels seems almost soothing in the absence of the creature's cries. Albro looks up at the twelve pairs of eyes staring down at them. A cable and hook hang from an overhead winch. Nick Lane loops the cable through the handles of the garbage can and engages the motor. The container rises to the upper level. He pushes another button and it follows a track to a walkway where he lowers it down. Albro had fully expected the creatures' attention to follow their meal, but their eyes never leave him. They seem to be watching his every move. He fully intended to follow Nick Lane's advice and stay out of reach, but he follows Nick Lane up the ladder.

Albro keeps his distance. The memory of the previous night when a similar beast had tried to smash and tear its way into their car is vividly fresh in his mind. The creatures are naked, and he can see that all are male. A few of them start to make a ruckus until one of them turns, and with a growling hiss and silences them.

"Fucking hell," Nick Lane says, "I ain't seen that before."

"Do they speak to each other?" Albro asks.

"Do you mean in a language?" Nick Lane asks. "Not that I've ever heard. It's always howling and screeching just like you heard them."

"That one obviously has influence over the others," Albro says and moves a few steps closer.

"I wouldn't get any closer," Nick Lane advises.

"How do you feed them?"

"There's a trap door on top of the cages. It's way too small for them to get through. Still I have to be careful. One jumped and got an arm through and nearly grabbed my ankle. If it had, I wouldn't be standing here talking to you."

Nick Lane engages the winch and lifts the container of frozen body parts to the top of the first cage and then ascends a ladder to a catwalk that spans all twelve cages and begins dropping in the frozen body parts.

While the others immediately begin crunching their meal, the one who had silenced them ignores his food and continues to stare at Albro. It turns and tilts its head in that simian behavior that suggests a cognitive process is taking place. Its lips are pulled back from its over-sized teeth and it moves its jaws as if it were trying to mimic speech.

"Aaaaaaaaaa," comes out of its mouth in a kind of guttural pronouncement. "Aaaaaaaa," it voices again.

The other creatures are hunched over and completely focused on eating and pay no attention to the single individual who has his eyes on Albro. Nick Lane drops in the last chunk of frozen meat and comes down off the cages and stands next to Albro.

"It's trying to say something," Albro says.

"It's your imagination. They're animals, very dangerous animals. Come on, it's hotter than a mother-fucker in here," Nick Lane gestures toward the ladder.

"Aaaaaaaaaaaa," the creature sounds out.

Albro turns to face it. The creature is staring directly at him, its clawed fists wrapped around the bars, its yellow eyes alert with intelligence and the unmistakable look of recognition in them. Albro once again feels that odd sensation of his mind dividing.

"Craaaaaaaaaaaaane," the creature moans as if clearing its throat of mucus and then clearly and distinctly said, "Crane! Thomas Crane!"

This catches the attention of the others. They all stop eating and come to the front of their cages. One of them says, "Craaaane."

Another says the name, and then another and another until they are all chanting the name, louder and louder, "CRANE! CRANE! CRANE! CRANE!" Their voices resound like pounding hammers in the metallic walled space.

"Fucking Hell!" shouts Nick Lane. "Let's get out of here before they rip those cages apart!"

"Wait!" Albro whispers not taking his eyes off the creature in front of him. "Look, there's something in its hand. Albro steps closer.

"I wouldn't do that if I were you," Nick Lane cautions.

Albro advances another step. He is now within range should the creature decide to lunge at him through the bars. He can now feel the savage strength of the creatures. Why are they shouting that name? Do they think he has some knowledge of Thomas Crane? Is Crane the one who was supposed to come for them? The yellow eyes of the creatures are locked on his own. Nick Lane is pulling at him. He shakes Lane off and steps closer. He is now inches from the cage. He takes the coin from around his neck and thrusts his hand through the bars.

The chanting abruptly stops. One by one the creatures lower themselves to their hands and knees and place their foreheads on the floor of their cages, except for the one who stands before Albro. The creature stares at him and then opens his clawed fist. In the palm of its hand is a small gold coin. On its surface, Albro can just make out the raised highlights of a dog.

"Fucking hell," Nick Lane says in hoarse whisper.

Later, Nick Lane empties cans of beans into a pot. While it warms on the galley stove, Albro returns to the wheelhouse to peer out at the ocean. Night has descended upon them. He checks his watch. The hands are again straight up twelve o'clock. He isn't sure if time has passed or has stopped completely. He could accept a gray, overcast noon, but not the blackness of midnight. The strength of the storm seems to have eased. The ship is no longer rolling so violently. Maybe the storm has begun to abate, or maybe they have slipped into its eye. He stares into the night before he goes back to the galley.

The ordinarily voluble Nick Lane has become uncharacteristically quiet. He is obviously brooding over what had occurred down in the engine room. Not just about the creatures getting down on their hands and knees, but what had occurred afterward. Albro doesn't understand it himself. He'd gone right up to the cage of the one who had first spoken. The creature had remained motionless until it had opened its hand.

"What are you?" he had asked it.

The creature had looked back at him seemingly puzzled by the question. Then it had replied, "Mal."

Albro hadn't been sure that the creature had actually understood his question, so he'd asked, "Who are you?"

The creature had answered, "Grod."

"Who am I?" he'd asked it.

"Craaane," it had replied, drawing out the vowel.

"Thomas Crane?" he had asked.

"Crane," it had repeated.

Albro had seen that it had intelligence, but also that it had a limited vocabulary. He'd asked, "Are you Mongi?"

Albro saw the eyes flicker toward the chunk of meat still untouched in its cage. It had replied, "Mal."

"Okay, Grod," Albro had said, "does the name Chang Wu mean anything to you?"

There had been no response.

"How about Brother Isaiah?' he'd asked.

Again, there had been no response.

"Elijah?"

The creature's eyes had narrowed. "Elijah," it had repeated with a low growl.

"You know Elijah? " Albro had asked.

"Elijah," the creature had said again, and this time Albro had seen the bands of muscles tighten beneath the creature's skin.

"What about the Jade Prince?" he had asked.

The creature's eyes had glanced down at its open hand. A new look had come into the creature's face, a look Albro had not expected. It was a look of fear, a fear of something beyond its understanding. For a moment the creature had seemed to shrink within itself, and then it had closed its fist and had retreated into the corner of its cage. After that, Albro had been unable to get another response. In fact, all twelve had fallen into a disturbing silence.

Nick Lane spoons the last bite of beans into his mouth and pushes back his plate. Whatever it is he's been brooding over has finally bubbled to the surface. He says, "Remember my telling you that I'd been in 'Nam?"

Albro has a vague memory that Nick Lane had made a passing reference to Viet Nam in his rambling monolog as they had driven over the snowy pass and down into Seattle. He still can't grasp the fact that it occurred only two nights ago.

"Well," Nick Lane continues, "It wasn't 'Nam. That's what we were instructed to say. If we'd said otherwise we'd all been sent to prison for committing treason. What the fuck does it matter now? Let them come get me.

"I was in Laos on a super secret mission. It was actually just glorified guard duty. We were supposed to be protecting a group of scientists who had found something in some ruins up in the mountains close to the Chinese border. None of us was ever allowed in there, but I heard that the whole mountain was riddled with tunnels. But there were no Gooks up there. There were a few scattered villages of mountain people. The real war was to the south.

"So for me, it was a real cushy deployment: three decent meals a day and a tent to sleep in, and no one shooting at me. We were isolated, but believe me it was better than being on patrol and ending up getting my legs blown off by a land mine. Fuck man, some of the dudes who made it home barely had enough left of them to make living worthwhile.

"We had orders not to fraternize with the scientists. If they spoke to us, we were to have three responses: 'Yes sir,' 'No sir,' or 'Don't know, sir.' Anything more difficult than that was handled by our lieutenant. But that didn't keep us from trying to find out what was really going on.

"The lead scientist, everybody called him 'Doc', had a bad habit of wandering off by himself. That used to piss the hell out of the lieutenant, because if anything should happen to the dude, it would be the lieutenant's ass. If any of us saw Doc out and about, we were supposed to keep an eye on him. Not that it mattered much. If he was of a mind, he could lose an escort in a matter of seconds. The man knew how to move through the jungle like some sort of ghost. He'd be there one instant, right in front of you, and blink your eyes and he'd be gone. It happened to me more than once. It was spooky.

"But he always came back. Once, he was gone for two days. The lieutenant had us out combing the jungle looking for him. He walked right into camp carrying an injured boy who was hurt pretty bad in the leg. It

looked like shrapnel wounds that were going to gangrene. The camp doctor wasn't military. She was part of the Doc's research group. She was a Chinese national, which raised a lot of eyebrows considering how the Viet Cong wouldn't have lasted a week if Uncle Mao hadn't been shipping them rice by the truck loads, while his own people were starving. There was never any love lost between the Chinese and the Vietnamese, but that crazy bastard would do anything to stick a finger in Uncle Sam's eye. But I'm getting side tracked. All that's history and nobody gives a shit anyway.

"Like I was saying, the camp doctor was Chinese. She spoke perfect English, like she'd been educated in England. And she wasn't one of those bow-legged peasant girls. She was tall and slender, and carried herself with a kind of grace that you didn't see much in those days. She obviously had come from a life of privilege, but you could tell that she cared about her patients. She also cared about the Doc. She spent a lot of time in his tent. It was no secret that they were an item. Hell, we didn't know the Doc was married until later, when the shit hit the fan. Anyway, like I said, the boy was hurt bad, but she had him up and walking in less than a week.

"The lieutenant had strict orders not to allow anyone in camp who didn't have a security clearance. The boy would have to fly out when the next supply chopper arrived. He'd be taken to a refugee camp. Doc told the lieutenant that the boy was staying and that was that. The Doc got pretty much anything he wanted. But a few months later, all that changed.

All of a sudden, the Army was a whole lot more interested in the project. More troops were flown in, along with a hard-ass captain to command us. They mined the perimeter, fenced the main section of the compound and double fenced the tents that the Doc and the other scientists used. The official word from the captain is that we need to protect the scientists against an attack, but fuck man; even an idiot could see the real reason was to keep the Doc, or anyone else, from leaving. And the ruins, Christ! You would have thought from all the guards and razor wire they were storing nukes! Access was strictly forbidden to any *unauthorized personnel. No one but the scientists knew what was going on.*

"The Doc got mad as hell and ordered his staff to stop doing whatever it was they were doing down in the ruins. Next day, an entirely new crew was flown in, and the Doc's people were flown out, except for the Chinese doctor. The two of them were in the Doc's tent when another chopper arrived. I was on guard duty at the chopper pad and I saw it all. Two men got out. One of them was dressed in army fatigues, no insignias and had the look of a hardened soldier, the type who wouldn't waste time and resources on prisoners. He was definitely CIA, a genuine spook. He could have stamped it on his forehead and it wouldn't have been anymore fucking obvious.

"The other one...fuck man, just remembering him gives me the creeps. He had the build of a linebacker. Fucking size doesn't scare me. I've dropped plenty of big guys. They tend to be over confident and slow. I knew this guy wasn't like that. He had the look of, well, dominance. I'm not talking just physical power. He projected a mental dominance as well. I saw it in his eyes. Look into the eyes of your average dog and then into the eyes of a wolf and you'll know what I mean. You and I and most everybody else are dogs. This man was a fucking wolf. And the rest of his face added to the effect. It was the long and lean and locked in a half-smile that showed his predatory instincts. No one needed to tell me that this fucker was now in charge. I learned his name later. Newton. Dr. Martin Osborne Newton. I never learned the spook's name.

"But hang on, because there was one more passenger. Wolf-man turned back to the chopper and took the hand of a woman and helped her out. Her high heels made her nearly as tall as the man who had her hand, and she was dressed in a business outfit that was black and cut to show off her figure which was made to order if your intent was to drive a man to the brink of insanity. She was a fucking blonde bomb shell. The captain looked like he was about ready to squirt all over himself before he managed to choke out his few words of welcome. He finally got himself calmed down enough to lead them over to Doc's tent. The captain signaled for me to follow as some kind of armed escort. Doc was standing

482

there waiting for them. I could see by the way he was standing, with his feet apart, his knees slightly bent, his shoulders hunched, that he was ready for a fight. Newton greeted him with a broad smile and called him by his first name, like they're old buddies. The woman reached out her hand, but Doc ignored it. He didn't take his eyes off Newton. She let it hang there a long moment before letting it drop back to her side and then she said, 'That's hardly a way for a husband to greet his wife, especially after not seeing her for three months.' Right then, the Chinese doctor stepped out of the tent.

"Everything went real quiet and then Mrs. Thomas Crane said, 'This must be one of your colleagues, or is she something more? They usually are, aren't they Thomas? She's pretty, but that's not surprising.' She paused for effect. 'Thomas always had an eye for beautiful women.'

"She said that last bit to Newton, who'd dropped his smile, obviously pissed about the reference that Doc is the blonde's husband. She waited a moment, just long enough for the testosterone that was being pumped out, to saturate the air. And then she said, 'I've not come to negotiate, Thomas.'

"Hell's bells, I was thinking! She's the one who's in-fucking-charge! The two men were just some muscle that she'd brought along to kick ass, if it came to that.

"Finally, the Doc turned to her and said, 'you've disrupted my research. Until you return my staff, I have nothing to say to you.'

"'My dear, dear Thomas,' she said to him. 'You're as headstrong as ever. When I tell you what is about to happen, I think you will feel otherwise.'

"He said to her, 'whatever you're planning, I will not be a part of it. I'm closing down the project effective today.'

"She smiled sweetly at him, as if she was talking to a little boy. 'Don't be silly,' she said. 'You no longer have any authority to do anything, except perhaps, to entertain your oriental maiden.' This last was said with the same sweet voice, but her eyes had turned to ice.

"Nobody's prepared for what happened next. Doc took a step toward his wife, and raised his hand like he was going to slap her. Newton

483

stepped between them. Doc was no small man, but Newton had him outsized in every dimension. He grabbed Doc by the neck and lifted him off the ground. The Chinese doctor muffled a scream and Mrs. Thomas Crane just stood there with this appraising look on her face while the Doc's lights are starting to fade. The spook had his hands on his hips as if he had nothing better to do than watch a man suffocate. The captain finally took out his .45 and fired it into the air. Newton ignored the captain and looked casually over to the Doc's wife who gave the signal to let him go.

"It was a minute or two before Doc could stand, and when he did, he gave Newton a look that conveyed what just happened would never happen again. Then he turned to his wife and said through a cracked voice, 'you've said all that you need to say. Now get the hell out of here.' With that, he turned and went back into his tent. The Chinese doctor, whose face had gone pale, stood blocking the entrance to the tent. Mrs. Thomas Crane brushed past her like she was no more than a minor irritant. Newton and the spook followed her inside. I could see sweat beading on the captain's forehead. 'You,' he said to the doctor, 'come with me.' She hesitated and the captain said, 'Do I have to remind you that you're still under my command?' She dropped her head and allowed him to lead her away."

Nick Lane is about to continue when Albro stops him. Sweat has broken out on his forehead and he realizes that he has been gripping the sides of the table. He takes a breath and tries to force the tension out of his voice. "Crane's wife, did you hear anyone mention her name?"

"Hold on, I'm coming to that," Nick Lane replied. "Where was I? Oh yeah, so now, it was just me standing there with my M-16 resting across my chest. As usual, it was a mother-fucking hot day and I was hoping to hell, that the little powwow that was taking place inside was going to wrap up soon, because my mouth was as dry as a stone.

"The spook started in first. He was speaking low and I didn't catch it all, but it was pretty clear that he was giving Doc an ultimatum: either he follows the new game plan, or he's out of the game. Then Newton spoke. He made it sound like the project can't go forward without Doc's help. It was the bad cop, good cop routine, but the Doc wasn't fucking buying it. He said that he won't allow the project to proceed. What he doesn't realize is that the spook and Newton were holding the deck and they could deal the cards in whatever order pleased them. The meeting broke up and they all came out of the tent. Mrs. Crane stood with her hand resting on Newton's arm. The spook had an amused look on his face, but he'd pulled out his .45 and had it aimed at Doc's middle. Doc took a step toward them and the spook cocked the hammer on his gun. Doc looked at his wife and said, "Go to hell Laura. You won't need an escort. The Devil will welcome you with open arms."

Albro exhales forcefully. He'd been holding his breath, fully expecting to hear Monique's name, but she could not have been there. Newton, perhaps, but not Monique because that was over three decades ago! Even so, he feels his strength drain away and can only half-listen as Nick Lane continues his tale.

"The next day, Newton was back and he brought a little hunchback gnome of a fucker with him. They disappeared into the ruins. A week passed. Work in the ruins was going on twenty-four hours a day. A rumor went around that Newton didn't sleep. There was this overall sense of urgency. Something was going to happen soon, but none of us grunts knew what it was.

"In the mean time, Doc and the Chinese woman were under constant guard. No one went in or out of their tent except the Chinese boy who had somehow gotten himself attached to the mess detail. He brought their food and took away their empty plates.

"There was a buzz in the place that wasn't there before. They brought in a Chinook. That's a heavy-lift chopper. At first we all thought that they were getting ready to move personnel, maybe close the place down. But the big chopper just sat there, like they were waiting to move something big.

"Newton and the hunchback fly out in a Huey one afternoon. They had shuffled our guard assignments and that night I was out at the perimeter in a foxhole with a buddy. We saw the Chinese boy run past us and straight through our lines. 'Fuckin'-A!' My buddy shouted to me, 'He's going to blow himself to pieces!' I took off after him thinking that I *could catch the little fucker before he crosses the area that'd been mined. The lights of the compound were at my back and the jungle in front of me was as black as the bottom of a well. I caught my foot on a vine and I took a tumble into a shallow ravine. That was a lucky fall, because just then whole sky lit up for a couple of seconds, like it was the middle of the day, and there was a tremendous whoosh of super-heated air. At first I thought that I had tripped a land mine and I wasn't yet feeling the pain of having the lower half of my body blown away.*

"After a few minutes, I realized that I was okay. I climbed back to our position and discovered that my buddy was gone. It was dark, but I could just make out that something weird had happened. The ground was bare. I mean swept clean! No rocks, no plants, nothing. I made my way to where I thought the compound should be, but there was nothing there. No tents, no equipment, no people."

Nick Lane pauses and stares down at his splayed hands. "It was like the earth had been scraped as clean as this table. I totally freaked. I thought maybe I was dead and I was in some kind of purgatory. They found me the next morning curled up in a ball in the middle of that barren space babbling like an idiot. They shot me full of something to get me to calm down. I remember looking up into the face of the spook. He kept asking me what happened to the Doc and his girlfriend. He didn't seem to give a shit about anyone else. There were over three hundred people there and I was the only one left. I could only tell him about chasing the Chinese boy and falling."

Nick Lane looks straight at Albro, "That creature thinks you're Crane, doesn't it? You do look a lot like him. That was over thirty-five years ago. I suppose my memory could be playing tricks on me, but I don't think so. His Chinese girlfriend was pregnant. I remember that clearly. You look to be just about the right age. You could be their child, but that raises some difficult questions."

Albro pulls himself out of his malaise and struggles to concentrate on what Nick Lane is saying.

Nick Lane raises his hand and starts by grasping his little finger and continues to count out the questions. "First, if Dr. Crane and the doctor weren't vaporized in the blast, what happened to them? Second, if they survived, did anyone else? Third, if you're really their child, why don't you look even a bit Chinese? Fourth, how did you get on this ship? And fifth, why the fuck am I caught in the middle of all this?"

Albro, who has been listening to Nick Lane's story, has been slowly forming some of the same questions, plus a few more, in his own mind. Why had the creature looked at him with such recognition? And what was that bowing all about? The response had seemed filial, as if Crane might have been their master and they were his slaves. He'd had the sensation that he could have stepped inside the cage, and the creature would not have harmed him. And why had they cowered when he had mentioned the Jade Prince. Is the Jade Prince somewhere on the ship? Is the ship the Jade Prince? Can the one called Grod tell him anything more? And why, most importantly, does that creature have that gold coin?

And Nick Lane's story has raised another important question in Albro's mind. Has Martin Osborne Newton known all along that he, Albro Marshal Swift, just might be Thomas Crane's son? Has he been in Newton's sights from the very beginning, and Monique has just been a sparkling lure to grab his attention?

Right now, though, they have to either find a way to get control of the ship, or find a way to get off. The seas have calmed considerably. At least, that is something he is grateful for. He is about to rise from his seat when a terrible screeching sound of metal against metal echoes throughout the ship.

Nick Lane jumps up from his seat, and runs to the wheelhouse. When Albro catches up with him, he finds Nick Lane standing at a window staring outside.

"It looks like we have company," Nick Lane says, "whether we want them or not."

Albro presses his face against the glass. Bright floodlights from another ship illuminate the deck of their own. The other vessel has backed off and holds its position in the wallowing seas. He sees a flurry of activity as inflatable boats are lowered onto the black water and black-clad men scramble into them. In a few minutes he sees the same men climbing over *the rail below and hears their pounding footsteps on the companionway leading up to where he and Nick Lane stand.*

Nick Lane reaches into a drawer and pulls out a large, black automatic. He cocks a bullet into the chamber and then stuffs it into his pants. What happens next seems to unfold in adrenalin-charged slow motion. The two individuals who enter are carrying weapons. Nick Lane pulls his gun out and might have shot them, but he hesitates as a third individual enters. He wears heavy storm gear and his face is mostly hidden by a watch cap. Suddenly the man charges forward. The lead gunman reaches out to stop him, but manages to grab only his hat. Albro stares at the man's face, stunned by who he sees. Water streams down the man's face and his long, white hair is plastered against his head. He is clutching his side and his mouth is twisted in a grimace of pain and his wild eyes are scanning the room. The overhead lights flicker. The man lunges forward and Nick Lane swings the big automatic in the intruders' direction. Albro is standing to Nick Lane's blind side. Puzzled, Nick Lane swivels his body and turns to look momentarily at Albro, and then back at the man who has now stopped and has flung out his outstretched hands.

"Don't shoot!" the man shouts.

Albro's legs threaten to turn to jelly. He can see Nick Lane's finger begin to tighten on the trigger. The lights flicker again and then go out. The diesels have finally run out of fuel. The ship lurches as it loses power. The room is suddenly cast in total darkness.

"Don't shoot!" Albro shouts, but it is too late. Orange fire erupts from Nick Lane's pistol and a deafening blast fills the small space as the gunmen return fire. Albro has a brief sense of being hit in his midsection and his chest collapses like a deflated balloon. He feels himself falling, falling, like a leaf spiraling down from a great height, and he hears the wind crying out like a chorus of voices in an agony of grief before he hits the metal deck.

CHAPTER 46

ALBRO SWIFT awoke gasping for breath. He felt as if a giant was sitting on his chest. The bulb hanging from the ceiling was surrounded by red and black blobs. He was going to faint if he didn't get some air inside of him. It was just like the time when he'd been nine years old and lost his grasp while climbing a large maple and he'd fallen square onto his back and had the wind knocked out of him. He'd seen someone in the distance watching him and he'd completely forgotten that he was twenty feet up. Who had it been that he'd seen? He'd completely forgotten about the incident. Having the ground come at him so suddenly and snatching his breath away had left him totally disoriented, but now the memory was coming back to him. The watcher had been a man, standing just beyond the point where recognition might have been possible, as if the watcher had known precisely where that point was. But now, he could remember the man had silver hair. That's what had grabbed his attention. The sun had reflected off the man's silver hair. He could see him now, as the bulb above slowly began to fade.

"Roll him over," someone ordered. Was that Nancy Wong? He felt hands on his body and then he was over and being pulled to his hands and knees. He felt a stinging blow to the middle of his back and suddenly air rushed into his lungs. He breathed deeply until his vision cleared. "Albro, look at me!" Nancy Wong said at him. She was squatting in front of him with her hands on his shoulders. "Are you all right?"

He tried to stand, but wobbled back to a sitting position. "Sorry. I feel a little dizzy. What happened?"

"You were dreaming. You woke the rest of us. You were shouting 'Don't shoot', and then you couldn't breathe."

"Yeah, I remember," Albro said feeling dazed by the memory. "Only it wasn't a dream. Walter, help me up, please."

Walter reached his hands under Albro's armpits and raised him to his feet. The scorched, leather bound volume fell out of his shirt.

"There, see that?" Albro said. "That's proof I wasn't dreaming."

"What is this?" The rat man picked up the book and set it on the table. He opened it to the first page. The binding made a sound like the crackling of dry leaves. The rat man's eyes widened and he lifted his hands from the page. "Where did you find this?" he asked, his voice a mixture of surprise and reverence.

"I was on a ship," Albro said. "Not this ship, but another one. That's the captain's log. I found it in his room. Someone had tried to burn it along with other documents."

"That is not what this is!" the rat man exclaimed. He stared down at the book, visibly shaken.

Albro stepped to the table and looked down at the book. The page was covered in a script that had the curling and flowing lines of a Cyrillic-style script. Intricate designs in red, black and gold embellished the margins. He reached for the book to examine it, but the rat man caught his hand.

"Please, do not touch it. It is sacred. It is the holiest of Holies," the rat man said. "I never thought that I would lay eyes upon it again."

"Wait a minute," Albro contested. "That's the captain's log. There were other documents, but they were mostly burned."

"What is it?" Nancy Wong asked. She came close, but did not reach out for the book.

"It is the Book of Araam. Even to speak its name is a sacrilege, and I shall not say it again. In it is the story of our people. It is our alpha and our omega, our beginning and our end. It was thought to have been lost when the Great Temple was destroyed. First the Lamp of Araam, now this, blessed are we who have witnessed these miracles."

The rat man gently closed the book and then turned to Albro and looked at him as if seeing him for the first time. "You say you were on a ship. What was the name of that ship?"

"The *Jade Prince*," Albro said.

A look of relief eased the tension in the rat man's eyes. "The map has shown you the way," he said.

Albro asked, "The *Jade Prince* is a ship?"

"The *Jade Prince* may take many forms depending upon its intent. You must tell us what happened."

"What do you mean, its intent," Albro asked. "I thought..."

Nancy Wong interrupted, "Albro, please, just tell us what happened."

Albro rubbed his face. The room had grown stuffy. What he'd really like right now was a breath of fresh air. He could hear the low throb of the engines. They were still underway. He looked at his watch. Once again, the hands were frozen. He had a sudden recollection of the clock in the captain's quarters, right down to the name on the faceplate and the shape of the bolts that held it to the wall.

"How long have we been asleep?" he asked.

"Only two hours," Nancy Wong answered him.

He had been several hours, maybe even a full day, on the other ship. He felt like he was being batted back and forth like a ball in some kind of weird game of temporal ping-pong. What had the rat man meant? The *Jade Prince* had found him? Had he seen the *Jade Prince* and hadn't recognized it for what it was? He stared at the book that lay on the table. How had he mistaken it for a ship's log? The memories of being on that other ship sparked and arced in his mind and threatened to sputter out. He squeezed his eyes shut and locked onto the half-blind visage of Nick Lane until his recollections settled into a coherent picture.

"I woke up, and all of you were gone," he began, and told them the dream. It hadn't really been a dream, but that was the only way to describe it. He dredged up every detail he could remember. When he

491

told them about the creatures in the cages and about the one who called himself Grod, and the coin the creature held in its clawed hand, the rat man stopped him and made him try to recall every little nuance about the scene. When he got to the part just before Nick Lane fired the gun, he hesitated.

"Who was it?" the rat man asked him. "Who did you see?"

"I couldn't believe what I was seeing," Albro said. "When Nick Lane looked at me, I knew that he couldn't believe it either. And then the voice, that was the clincher. I don't think Nick Lane meant to shoot, but then the lights went out, and the ship rolled. He lost his balance and the gun went off."

"The rat man said, "But you recognized who it was, didn't you?"

"It was a dream," Albro said.

"From a dream you brought back The Book of Araam?"

"That's what I've been trying to understand. How could I bring back something from a dream that wasn't even in the dream?"

"That mark on your arm, the map on your back, and now The Book of Araam, none of them has come from a dream."

"If not from dreams, then where have they come from?" Albro asked.

"They have all come from the life you have already lived," the rat man said excitedly. "You are at the center of the *Twelve*. The *Jade Prince* will..."

"Stop," Nancy Wong said. "Please Isaiah, let him finish."

Albro took a deep breath. He said, "I saw him. I saw myself. I saw another version of me, only I seemed older. I was dressed differently, but it was me. I saw myself enter the wheelhouse of that ship. My other self knew that I was there, but he was looking straight at Nick Lane, because he knew that something terrible was about to happen. And if all of that wasn't weird enough, for an instant I felt as if I existed in two places at the same time. I actually felt that I was inside the mind of my other self and my other self was inside my mind. I know that doesn't make sense, but that's as close as I can come to describing what happened. Then the lights went out and I got the wind knocked out of me and I woke up here."

Nancy Wong crossed her arms and gave Isaiah a stern look, as if to say, 'Not now'. Thomas Crane had told her this would happen. The medallion Albro had around his neck would cause him to experience profound dislocations in time and space and that he would have to learn to master it. If not, Albro could pull them all into the same vast and intricate loops of time into which he had fallen. But, Nancy thought, if Albro could learn to use the medallion, he might be able to, if not get them off this ship, then at least he might get them out of this locked room.

She paced the tiny room thinking. Thomas Crane had not been able to tell her much about the medallions except that each possessed powers of their own, and the medallion chose where and when to release those powers, not the wearer. So far, hers had done nothing more than adorn her neck like a piece of dime-store jewelry. Thomas Crane had told her that any one of the medallions might call out to the others. She had indeed heard the voice of the dragon that Wu had dangled before them, but for her, it had not been the sound of the wind, rather it had been the sound of a beating heart.

"Albro, I want you to try something," she said. "I want you to close your eyes and think of yourself as standing just on the other side of the door."

"What?" Albro asked.

The rat man did not look at him. He said to Nancy Wong, "What you're proposing is very dangerous. Even those who are quite practiced run a very grave risk."

"We should have tried this sooner. It's happening to him anyway."

"Yes, for the woman who sleeps to direct him is one thing, but it is quite another for him to attempt it himself."

"He needs to learn to control it. We have tried to control our own, and we have all failed. You say he is at the center of the *Twelve*. We are four in strength. We can help him, can't we? It's time we start acting in unison."

493

"If we do that," Isaiah said, "the others will sense it. They will feel what we are doing. It will make it easier for them to find us."

"And for us to find them," Nancy Wong said. "You said, yourself, that at some point all twelve medallions must come together."

"But only at their predestined moment. To force their union could destroy everything."

Albro, who had been considering Nancy's proposal in light of the powerful mind trips he'd been experiencing said, "What the heck, either I can do it, or I can't. Where's the harm in trying?"

"You could easily end up out in the ocean for one thing. For another, it is conceivable that you could pull all of us with you," the rat man said.

"This might be our only advantage," Albro said. "We don't know what Chang Wu has in store for us. We can just sit here, or we can act." Albro paused to think. "The medallions that you and Walter have, you never told me how you came by them."

Brother Isaiah turned, as if looking for advice, to Walter who had slumped onto his haunches with his back to the wall. Walter, who always seemed to have his mind elsewhere, had actually been following the conversation closely. He said, "I think you should tell him, Izzy. I know that someday I will have to pay for what I did."

The rat man closed his eyes for a long moment and then opened them. He said, "We could never have found you without the medallions. They had been kept within the Order for thousands of years. The Bishops knew that their lives, the Order, the existence of the entire world, depended upon giving them up, but they would never have entrusted them to Walter and me. We had to take them by force. Two of our members died."

"I killed them," Walter said, "and I must pay for my crime."

"I take full responsibility," the rat mans said. "The Council will not punish you, Walter. They will punish me."

"You are kind to say that, Izzy, but you know that is not true. *'He, who takes a life, shall forfeit his own.'* It is written. When I am called, I am prepared to leave this life."

494

"This Council," Albro said. "Is that who's been after us? Is your Order trying to get back their medallions?"

"No, the Council would never condone such a thing. Although they could not bring themselves to act, they knew this is what had to be done. I'm sure they now regret their indecision."

"Then who do you think it is?"

"Our history is long and convoluted, an intertwining of stories passed down through the ages. At one time, the stories tell, the Order watched over all twelve medallions, but they were lost in the *Great Upheaval*, a devastating war that changed the face of the earth. Three medallions were recovered in the years after. You have heard me speak of Elijah. At one time, he was the most revered of our prophets. How he became the most reviled is a long, long story. It was Elijah who foretold the beginning of the *Gathering*. He had an extraordinary ability to see beyond the edge of time. He saw another great war in which the Mongi triumph over the Purim. The Holy Scriptures warn that if the Mongi should ever take up arms again they will be destroyed. *'The Mongi shall be as straw in a fire, and their ashes scattered into nothingness.'* Elijah began to preach against the teachings of the Holy Scriptures. He garnered a following who challenged the authority of the Council of Elders. He became so emboldened that he staged an attack upon the Temple of Araam. His small army reached the inner sanctum where they found the three medallions of the Mongi. Elijah was later captured at the cost of many lives. Elijah's two sons were killed. He swore that their deaths would be avenged.

"Two of the medallions were recovered. The third was never found. Elijah was burned at the stake. I watched him die, yet Marlowe informed me that he lives. I believe that it is Elijah, who is attempting to stop us."

"If you saw him die, how can he come back to life?'

"When I saw Elijah burn, I witnessed his existence at one place, in one time. The medallions encompass all time. Within their realm, there is no beginning, no end. There exists a complete freedom to be at any point in time and therefore any place. As to 'where' and any 'when' Elijah may exist I cannot say. But I fear that he is near. He does not possess all of the medallions, and so his abilities are limited. But his knowledge is deep and his desire is great."

"Do you mean to say that there is probably more than one Elijah out there?"

"Yes, but there will only be one Elijah at any one time and place."

"Well," said Albro, "that's a relief. I'd hate to be surrounded." He thought for a moment. "We have four medallions. Can the same thing happen to us? Can we exist in more than one place and one time?"

"You saw for yourself what can happen. But two individuals cannot exist for long in the same moment."

"What about the other medallions? Chang Wu has one. Counting the one that you're assuming your old friend Elijah has, plus our four that makes six. If I really wasn't dreaming you can add to it the one Nick Lane has and that creature, Grod. That makes eight. Where are the other four?"

"The woman who sleeps, possess one. It has been passed from one individual to another in her family, for generations. Only a few know of its existence. That is how she is able to pull you to her. Where are the other three? Marlowe has one. Although I have not seen it, I have heard its voice. I assume that Martin and his daughter have one each."

"How are we going to find them?"

"They will find us. Prophesy states that once the Gathering has begun nothing can stop it."

"What happens then, when all twelve are, as you say, 'gathered'?"

"The *Jade Prince* awakens."

"And all hell breaks loose."

"Unless we find a way to prevent it," the rat man said.

"Right," Albro agreed, but he was unsure of what, exactly, he was agreeing to. "So what do I do to move through walls?" he asked.

The rat man had them sit on the floor with Albro in the center. The ship had recently begun a long, gentle roll. Albro guessed that they must now be in the open ocean. Even if he could get them out of the room, what were they going to do?   What chance did they have to overpower the crew and take over the ship? One step at a time, he told himself.

"Okay, now what?" Albro asked.

"We gather our hands and concentrate on you. You concentrate on simply being outside the door. If we sense you going too far, we'll try to pull you back."

In the previous mind trips it had seemed as if he'd simply closed his eyes and suddenly he was somewhere else, but he'd not been expecting anything. It had always been a spontaneous event that seemed to control itself. He now sat with his legs drawn up against his chest and with his head resting on his knees. He closed his eyes and imagined himself in the same position on the other side of the door. He could feel the vibration of the ship and hear the breathing of his companions. He was hungry, and his head itched. He needed a shower. He realized that it was difficult to think of one thing and one thing only. Stray thoughts kept buzzing through his mind like pesky flies. He opened his eyes. He was still in the room.

He closed his eyes and tried again. Only this time, he thought about a card game in which he'd lost a great deal of money and it had remained a sore point on his pride to not know why. In his memory he examined the faces of each player looking for the tell-tale shift of the eyes, the subtle change of breathing, the all but unnoticeable tensing of muscles. And then he saw it, as obvious as a billboard in the middle of a living room. The realization startled him and he opened his eyes.

He was sitting in the hallway outside the room in which he had just been moments ago. He nearly fainted from the sudden sense of dislocation.   When he'd opened his eyes there had been a sudden deceleration, like being on one of those amusement rides that jerks you back and forth and threatens to snap your neck. Bile crept up in his throat and his mouth tasted like creosote. He swallowed hard and took a deep breath before standing. He put his ear to the door and listened. He could hear voices. He tapped lightly.

"Albro, are you all right?" It was Nancy Wong.

497

"I'm fine," he said. The nausea had begun to pass and he felt almost giddy.

"Can you open the door?" she called to him. He could hear a note of exasperation in her voice. In his excitement he had forgotten that they were prisoners. He lifted the metal bar and opened the door.

"You did it! You actually did it!" Nancy Wong exclaimed. She was smiling, almost laughing.

"Amazing, huh?" Albro said.

Walter said, "I saw you disappear. One instant you were there and then you were gone. Just like a magic trick." He grinned broadly. "Can you do it again, Mr. Albro?"

"Later. Right now, we're going to find out who's driving the ship and where we're headed."

The four of them ran down the narrow hallway to the companionway leading up. Albro took the steps slowly, stopping at the top to peek down the next corridor. Empty. He signaled the others to follow and found the next stairway up. They emerged into a wider corridor with a porthole. Albro looked outside. He could see a portion of the deck and clear, blue sky. The ship was eerily similar to the one he'd been on with Nick Lane. He had the uncanny feeling that if he turned to the left he would find the galley, and to the right would be the companionway that led to the wheelhouse.

He'd been acting as if he had some sort of plan, but nothing could be farther from the truth. He'd simply had a compulsion to move. He stopped and considered what the rat man had said about the medallions' ability to find each other. Was he being pulled toward one right now?

"Do you feel anything?" he asked the others. They shook their heads. He closed his eyes and slowly turned in a circle. When he felt the pull most strongly, he stopped. "Up there," he said and pointed at an angle toward the low ceiling. "Come on."

He led them down the corridor and up to the next level. He strode down the corridor. The feeling was very strong now, and without stopping swung open the first door he came to.

The room was cool and well lighted. A thick red carpet covered the floor and walnut paneling covered the walls. A long, dark table set with plates and silverware and glasses sat in the middle of the room. Four ornately carved arm chairs had been placed two on a side. A fifth chair had been placed at the head of the table and in it sat Chang Wu.

"Ah, Mr. Albro Swift," Chang Wu said and motioned him forward with his hand. "Please, enter. Bring your companions with you. As you can see, I have arranged for us to breakfast together. You have proved me correct. I never really doubted your abilities, only your awareness of them. Come. Please be seated."

Albro stepped into the room and a man dressed in a waiter's outfit entered pushing a cart piled high with tin pots and began placing them on the table.

Chang Wu said, "I trust that you all like Dim Sum. My chef does a most excellent job."

The server began pulling off lids and fragrant steam rose from the pots and filled the room. Chang Wu was smiling, obviously pleased with his assessment and sense of timing. The food looked delicious. Albro's stomach groaned and his mouth began to water. He wanted to eat, but he wanted to get something clear first.

Albro said to Chang Wu, "You locked us in the hold as a kind of test?"

"Yes, and also for your own protection," Chang Wu answered. "There appears to be a world-wide hunt for you. Agents of the Chinese government searched the ship before allowing it to depart. What gave them the idea that I was involved, I am not at all certain. I could have earned a very large sum by surrendering you to the authorities."

"There's a reward for my arrest?"

"Twenty million dollars," Chan Wu shook his head in mock amazement. "That seems to be the going rate these days for the apprehension of a world-renown terrorist."

"Terrorist? But I haven't done anything!"

"Then they must consider your very existence an act of terrorism." Chang Wu smiled. He was obviously enjoying himself.

"Where are you taking us?"

"In three days, this ship will arrive in Shanghai. There, it will take on a cargo of fish meal and other supplies. The fish meal is not important to us. It is the supplies that most interests us. In another six days it will arrive at the port city of Lushunkou. You may know it as Port Arthur. It is a city with a fascinating history.

Nancy Wong asked, "Why are you taking us there?"

"We are seeking the *Jade Prince*. It is from there, that we will begin our journey into the northern desert to the lost city of Lal, which thanks to the resourcefulness of Mr. Swift, is no longer lost."

"The map," Albro said.

"A most amazing thing!" Chang Wu exclaimed. "My good friend Martin Osborne Newton informs me that the images originate from your own DNA. He explained to me how rapidly shifting proteins in your skin create the incredible array of images. He is the world's foremost geneticist, you know. He was able to view the images, analyze them and solve the puzzle that has vexed us for so many years. He and his beautiful daughter will arrive at the site by helicopter. Martin thought it best to get started as soon as possible. We will follow with our load of supplies. Excuse me, I did not mean to delay our meal." He motioned with his hands at the array of dishes. "Please, eat."

Albro felt his mouth turn to sawdust. "What are you going to do with us?" he asked.

Chang Wu hesitated then reached for one of the steaming morsels with extended chopsticks, plucked it deftly from its pot, popped it into his mouth and chewed thoughtfully, savoring the rich flavors as a connoisseur might savor a fine wine. When he had swallowed he said, "Let us enjoy this food. Afterward, we will talk of such things."

Albro tried to eat, but each time he swallowed the food seemed to catch in his throat. Every now and then Nancy would glare at him. Otherwise she kept her face down and picked at the food. Isaiah sat with his hands folded in his lap and his eyes half closed. Albro had not seen him consume more than a few bites of food in the past three days. He wondered how long he could go on without eating. Walter ate enough to satisfy all of them. The tin pots that had been spread around the table had gradually accumulated at his end.

As they ate, Chang Wu continued the story that he had begun the night before. He told them how he had made his way to Saigon where he had survived by entering the seemingly carnival world that satisfied the pleasures and desires of the young American soldiers.

Chang Wu said, "I began by running errands for a pimp, but before long I had discovered the incredible demand for opiates. Its allure was far stronger than sex, for it offered a means of escape from the horrors of war. I was quite young, but I was able to easily grasp the fundamentals of supply and demand and the concept of profit margins. I began my organization by first recruiting street boys much like myself, refugees forced into the city after their villages had been burned and their mothers raped and their fathers shot. Sometimes it was the Viet Cong who did such things. Sometimes it was the South Vietnamese army. Sometimes it was the Americans. The result was the same. I established supply chains and distribution networks and created a good business all before the age of sixteen.

"The end of the war was only a minor setback. I bought my way aboard an overloaded ferry and escaped into the open waters of the South China Sea. The boat had been built to cross the Mekong River, and was never intended to face the powers of the open ocean. After just two days, the engine failed. After a week, we had run out of water. Among the one hundred and fifty or so refugees was a young Chinese business man from Hong Kong who had been stranded in Saigon at the fall of the regime. The man was ill with dysentery, as we all were. As those on board died, we threw them overboard to the sharks that followed the boat as if drifted in the ocean. The man had a British passport. Opportunities present themselves, it seems, when we least expect them. One day the young man was amongst us and the next day he was gone. Those who were left were too ill to even notice his absence. When we were rescued no one questioned my new identity."

An awkward silence ensued in which they finished the meal. The server continued to bring pots until Wu laid his chopsticks aside. The server then brought out two large pots of tea and poured it into delicate porcelain cups.

Chang Wu pulled the medallion from around his neck and laid it on the table in front of him. "It is curious, is it not, the twists and turns that define the path of one's life. Yet all of our paths lead, in the end, to the same great abyss we call death. This medallion, like the ones the four of you possess, has directed my life in such a way as to bring me to this place and this moment. Thomas Crane told me that a time would come when I must give it up, if not in life, then in death, as did all those who possessed it in the past, and that I would know when the time had come to do so."

Chang Wu looked at his watch. "We should now be well beyond the two hundred mile territorial limit. As long as we remain on the high seas, no government authority has the legal right to search this vessel without the permission of the captain. In the unfortunate circumstance that you have been traced to this vessel, I do not believe that international law would stop those who wish to apprehend you. For that to happen would be a tragedy." He lifted the medallion and placed it over his head, and snapped his fingers.

The two gunmen who had escorted them on board the night before entered, each holding an automatic. Chang Wu said, "In the interest of all of you, I must ask you to hand over your medallions."

Walter was on his feet in an instant. The gunman closest to Nancy Wong grabbed her by the hair and placed the pistol next to her temple.

"Walter!" Albro shouted, "Stop." Walter froze where he stood, his shoulders hunched and a look of blackest hatred distorting his face.

"As I said, Mr. Swift, in the interest of all of you..." Chang Wu said calmly and left the statement unfinished.

Albro lifted the medallion from around his neck and tossed it to the table in front of Chang Wu. He looked at the others. "Give them to him."

Isaiah removed his medallion, as did Walter. They passed them to Albro who weighed them in his hand and then placed them next to his.

502

"Thank you, "Chang Wu said. He turned to the gunman holding Nancy Wong. "Release her," he ordered.

Nancy Wong glared at Chang Wu and then yanked the medallion snapping the silver chain and tossed it with the others.

Chang Wu looked at them coldly. "Return them to the hold," he said to the gunmen.

"Wait!" cried Nancy Wong. "You claimed to owe Thomas Crane an obligation for saving your life. This is how you repay him?"

"Indeed. Cooperate, and I will see that the four of you live. Resist me, and you will fall into the Great Abyss."

CHAPTER 47

"I really thought for a moment that Chang Wu was going to help us," Albro said.

They were locked in the room once again. Albro sat on one of the bunks and Nancy Wong was pacing furiously, her hands curled into fists and her jaw clinched.

"Don't you worry, Mr. Albro, I'm sure you will think of something," offered Walter. He was sitting at the table fumbling with the deck of cards that Albro had given him. The size of his hands and the webbing between the fingers made it almost impossible for him to handle the cards. Albro had tried to teach him how to play solitaire, but for some reason, Walter could not grasp the concept of hierarchy amongst the cards. Nevertheless, he seemed content to lay the cards out in patterns that made sense to him.

"That's all we need, isn't it!" Nancy Wong exclaimed. She paused pacing long enough to shake her fists at the low ceiling. "For *Mr. Albro* to come up with another great idea."

"Wait a minute," Albro said. "It was your idea for me to walk through walls."

"Yes, but whose idea was it to surrender ourselves to a scheming and ruthless criminal?" Nancy Wong threw a look at Albro that made him flinch. She then resumed her pacing.

"What chance would we have out on the streets with a twenty million dollar bounty on our heads?"

504

"It's you not us, that has the bounty on his head."

"I thought we were all for one, and one for all," Albro said.

"That's my point. When are you going to start thinking about the rest of us?"

"Chang Wu can't help himself. It's that gold disk that's making him do this, Albro said."

"Oh, so now you're feeling sorry for the bastard."

"He promised to let us live."

"And you believe him?"

"Oddly enough, I do. I have an unerring sense of when people are lying to me."

"Is that a fact? Well you can add to it an unerring sense of arrogant stupidity, along with an unerring sense of chauvinism, an unerring sense of selfishness, an unerring sense of, of..." Nancy Wong stopped. Her face was flushed and she was breathing hard,

"Finished?" Albro asked. "As I was about to say, I've had some time to think and things are beginning to make sense to me. I found the *Jade Prince*. It's not an ancient artifact endowed with magical powers. I haven't believed that from the very beginning, nor have you. It's a ship, and it's floating out there in some other dimension with a cargo of twelve beasts you wouldn't want in your worst nightmare. You've known that all along, only you couldn't get to it. You told me as much last night. You were about to tell me more, but you couldn't bring yourself to do it."

Albro looked into Nancy Wong's eyes until she turned away. Then he continued, "Does the number twelve ring a bell? You say there are twelve medallions. Those creatures knew Thomas Crane. They thought *I* was Thomas Crane. Whoever put them on that ship knew that I would find them. There has to be some connection between those beasts, Thomas Crane, and the twelve medallions." Albro stopped. His mind was running too fast.

"Let me ask you this, Nancy" he said. "When did Thomas Crane tell you about what he had found in those ruins?"

"Not long after he came to me," Nancy Wong said. "Why are you asking that?"

"Because it wasn't the *Jade Prince* that he found," Albro said.

Nancy Wong said, "He told me he found a statue carved out of jade."

"And that statue," Albro said, "looked a lot like those creatures on that ship I was on. I think that carved statue had been placed in the ruins for a reason. Looking at Krupp's hologram was enough to make my hair stand on end. I think it was a warning to anyone who found it, to stop, get the hell out of there and don't look back. But that jade statue fit everything Crane knew about the ancient legend. It was an incredible find. Once word got out, there was no turning back. Look what it did to Krupp. He wanted it so badly I think it drove him insane.

"If Crane had been working alone, maybe he could have walked away from it. I think he tried, but they wouldn't let him. Crane was no archeologist. He was a physicist. He understood the forces that create stars and atom bombs. He found something there that must have frightened him to his very soul. From what I gather, he didn't trust Marlowe and he sure as hell didn't want Newton interfering. Whatever he found, he had to keep Newton and company from taking it.

"Crane must have had some understanding of what he was doing. Even so, he took a terrible risk. He didn't blow up the world, only a small piece of it. But I doubt that he knew what was going to happen."

Albro looked at Isaiah. "This high-tech tattoo that's on my back, is that what Crane discovered?"

Isaiah said, "It was not what he discovered, but rather, a result of that discovery."

"Crane told you what happened," Albro said.

"Part of it," the rat man said. "Within the ruins, Thomas Crane found a single medallion. It allowed him to open another dimension. He stepped into that dimension and discovered the locations of the remaining nine sacred dimensions. Together with the three dimensions that we live within, they make up the twelve lines of force that hold the universe together. The medallions are mere representations of those dimensions. Unless one knows how to open a dimension, they have no value. Without you, they are little more than trinkets. You are the key to open the doors to those dimensions. You hold the twelve lines of force in your body, but you cannot hold them for much longer."

"Well, that's good news," Albro said. "The idea of having that black genie on me gives me the creeps."

"No, that is not good news," Isaiah said. "If you do not return to the *Jade Prince* soon, the dimensions will start to separate. They will pull your body to pieces, and as they further separate, all that we think of as existence will be pulled apart as well."

Albro had the unsettling image of twelve sticks of dynamite strapped around his midsection. "Not good," Albro said.

"No," the rat man said, "that is not good. You *must* return to that ship."

"What's going to happen if and when I make it back on board?"

"You know part of what happens, you were there. More importantly, when the *Jade Prince* reaches the exact center of the storm you must be there. That is all I know."

"And if I don't make it in time?"

"Then you will not make it all."

The rat man came close and looked up into Albro's face. "What do you remember of that day?"

Albro looked down at the little rat-faced man. His question seemed to have come out of the blue. What was he asking? What day was he referring to? But then he knew what the rat man was asking him. It was the day of the disaster, the day all hell had broken loose in that jungle compound, and for an instant, he remembered it clearly.

Albro said, "Crane gave that single medallion to the Chinese boy who later became Chang Wu. How did he know...?" Albro stopped abruptly. He had a distinct memory of the gold disk. On it had been the image of a dragon. He could see the boy's eyes as he handed it to him. It had been raining and the clouds were touching the tops of the hills. He could smell the hot, sweetly rotten fragrance of the jungle. He saw the puzzled look in the boy's eyes. The rat man's voice broke into his thoughts

"He knew because he had seen the boy's life as if he had experienced every moment of it himself. He knew that your paths would cross."

Albro said, "Crane escaped whatever destroyed the ruins."

"Yes," Isaiah said. "The woman who dreams drew him to her."

"The same woman I saw," Albro said, and the memory of her lean, muscular body came to him. He saw her hair blowing away from her face, a blue sky and dry, jagged peaks behind her. "She took him into the mountains."

"Yes, and that is where he found me and Walter."

"He placed his foot upon your throat," Albro said. He looked down at his foot and saw the rat man's frightened face.

"If he had not I would have cried out," Isaiah said.

"And they would have killed Walter first, and then you and I...," Albro felt stunned by what he had just said, because it was not simply words, it was a memory as vivid and fresh as if he just lived through it. "I..." Albro began and he could say no more. A bright light bloomed inside his brain and his legs gave way, and Walter caught him just before he crumpled, and laid him gently on the floor.

"What's happened to him?" Nancy Wong asked.

"He has begun to remember," Isaiah said, and looked at her with cold eyes. "You know what that is like."

Nancy Wong looked down at Albro and then brought a cloth soaked in tepid water and laid it across his forehead. His eyelids fluttered and his eyeballs jittered beneath the lids.

"He is asleep," Isaiah said, "dreaming of another life. When he awakes he will be changed. He may not wish to let us know that, but he will be changed. We must be prepared for that."

Nancy Wong looked down at Albro. "Will he remember everything about Thomas Crane?"

"Perhaps, I cannot say. The lady who dreams may keep some memories for herself."

"What will he remember about Thomas Crane and me? Will he remember all that we did together?"

"If he does, you must accept that. You must also accept that he is not Thomas Crane. I know that this has been extremely difficult for you, and even though he looks exactly like Thomas Crane and will have many of his memories, perhaps all of his memories, he is still Albro Swift and you must treat him as so."

Nancy Wong sighed and placed her hand against Albro's cheek. "How long will he sleep?"

"Minutes, hours, who can say? Where his mind has gone, time has no meaning. We will have to be patient. You should try to get some more sleep."

"You are the one who should sleep. How many days has it been since you have slept?"

"I have rested. Now, I will read this book." He lifted the large leather volume and lowered himself to the floor carefully cradling the heavy book in his arms.

CHAPTER 48

"I'M not Thomas Crane's son," Albro croaked. He sat up, wide awake. He had slept, truly slept. It had been a welcome break from the cosmic pin-ball machine that had been bouncing him around for the past four days, five days. That is, if he didn't count the minutes within seconds, the hours within the minutes, the days within the hours. He glanced down at his broken watch. The second hand was counting off the seconds as reliable as any genuine Rolex. Did that mean he'd awakened to someone else's idea of reality? He thought about what he'd just said. Where had that conclusion come from? Had his tired brain been churning through the data while he'd slept, like some old Univac that had been posed a puzzler by its white-coated minders? He ran his hands through his sweaty hair. The room was hot and he was thirsty. He swung down from the bunk and went to the rust stained sink. There was no cup, so he placed his mouth under the sink tap and drank the warm, rusty, foul tasting water and then splashed more on his face. He looked at Nancy Wong. "You've known that all along, haven't you?"

"We had to tell you something," Nancy Wong said. "We knew that you had searched for your mother and father."

Albro looked to the rat man. "You knew that I would begin to remember. Why didn't you tell me?"

"You would not have believed me if I had. You had to come to the realization yourself," the rat man answered.

"What, a realization that I would remember things about Thomas Crane, a man I never knew?" He looked to Nancy Wong and she turned away.

"You are Thomas Crane, and you are not," the rat man said.

"What's that supposed to mean?

"You are Albro Marshal Swift. The Black Djinnim is providing you with Thomas Crane's memories," the rat man said.

"All of his memories?" Albro asked.

"That will be up to you," the rat man replied. "As I said before, you must learn to control the Black Djinnim."

Albro wondered how exactly he was supposed to learn to control something that he couldn't see, feel, or was even aware of. It was like asking him to control a virus that had entered his body. He only knew that the black, sometimes oozy, sometimes smoky, endogenous mass was now a part of him and was not only hiding that other entity, the tattoo that had been cut into his back, but was force–feeding him Thomas Crane's memories. For the moment, though, he had to table those concerns. He said to the rat man, "But you're telling me that I am becoming Thomas Crane? How…"

"Albro, we were not there when it began!" Nancy Wong interjected. "If we had been, maybe we could have fixed it and avoided the mess were in."

"Take it easy, Nancy. I know this must be hard for you, but stop and think for a moment how it must be for me. One minute I'm trying to figure out how my father could have appeared after an absence of thirty five years and the next minute I'm recalling names, faces, experiences I've never known. It's not exactly an easy thing to understand."

"I'm sorry," she said. "It was one thing to see Thomas Crane every time I looked at you. Now…"

"It's all right," Albro said. "It's somehow reassuring to know how much you loved him." He turned to Isaiah. "It's not like one side of my brain belongs to me and the other side to Thomas Crane. It's more like I have all of these memories I shouldn't have and none of the context to put them in." Albro looked at Nancy Wong and the obvious came to him

511

in another sudden flood of memories. He saw the tents, the fences topped with razor wire. He could feel the moist warmth of the jungle, the cool, shadowy tunnels where Crane had conducted the excavations. He said, "While I was on that ship, the *Jade Prince*, Nick Lane told me that Thomas Crane was in love with the camp doctor, a Chinese woman. He told me that she was pregnant."

"Yes," Nancy Wong said. "He was devastated when she died. He tried, but he could not save both her and the child."

"Your mother…" Albro uttered and the memories began to surge in Albro's mind and he cut them off. He hurriedly changed the subject. "I met your grandfather once. He read my fortune." Albro looked at his palm as if were the hand of another man that somehow had become attached to his own arm.

"Yes," Nancy Wong said. "He was my mother's father. I was raised by him and my Auntie Lo. She is my grandfather's sister."

Albro felt himself being pulled into a disjointed past where none of the pieces seemed to fit anymore. "Nancy," he said, "I always thought that you were younger than I am by at least three years."

"I am. Don't you remember? I was the gawky freshman and you were the handsome senior."

"Yes, I do remember, but that's not my point. You had not yet been born when Crane destroyed the ruins, which means you were conceived in the past but were born in some other place and time."

"I don't know how to explain my life."

"Are you…?" Albro started to ask.

"Am I half-Caucasian? Is that what you were about to ask?"

"I never saw it before," Albro said.

"There is a great deal of physical variation amongst Chinese. Europeans mixed with the Chinese, particularly in eastern China. To answer your question directly, yes, I am half-Caucasian, but my Chinese half seems to dominate. That happens. I always had a sense that something lay beneath my Oriental features. I had my DNA analyzed, and then I knew what I had always suspected. Not that it mattered. In the end, most people see what they want to see, including you."

"And that tells you what? That I didn't want to recognize you as Thomas Crane's daughter, my half-sister?"

"Now you understand what I've been going through. I didn't know until Thomas Crane told me. Presumably we share half of our DNA, but it takes more than the sharing of genetic material to be true siblings."

"Tell me about it," Albro said.

"Look, I'm sorry I lied to you," Nancy Wong said.

"Then how do you expect me to believe that you are who you say you are, and I am who you say I am?"

"Albro, do you remember me telling you how Thomas Crane and I traveled to Idaho and what happened there. The Chinese laborer whom we sought and found and then returned to his own time was my great-great grandfather. If Thomas Crane had not been my father, that Chinese laborer would not have survived his ordeal and would not have had the child who became my great-grandfather. If I had not been born, none of my ancestors would have been born. My mother would never have existed.

"Albro, I came into this world the same way as you. An old man brought me to Auntie Lo. His name was Swift. He found me in that phone booth in the Terminal Tavern. His wife told him that I had to be taken to China Town. My uncles were lawyers. They knew how to falsify documents to make it appear that I had come from an orphanage in China. The Chinese are very good at keeping family secrets. I don't think my grandfather understood, but I know that he had a strong sense of what had happened to my parents. His palm reading wasn't just a parlor trick. I think he was able to feel his way along the force lines. I think that he was able to see how the future makes the past."

Albro looked at her. He said, "When I left our hotel in Hong Kong, I hired a driver to take me into the hills above the city. I saw a man and a woman. The man seemed familiar, as if I had seen him in an old family photo album. But why would I think that? I never had a family. I could have sworn the man looked directly at me, but he couldn't possibly have seen me. I was across a ravine, a thousand feet away, hidden under the trees. The woman was Monique Olivia Newton. Who was the man wearing the gloves?"

Isaiah said, "That had to have been Elijah."

"I saw another man behind the glass," Albro said. "At the time I thought it was Newton. Who, Nancy, was that man?"

"Thomas Crane," the rat man answered for her.

Albro glance at the rat man. He sensed there was a great deal more the rat man could tell him. Not least of which was how Crane could be in Hong Kong if his body lay in a Seattle morgue? And then, the reason for the meeting came to him. Was the Black Djinnim speaking to him? Albro said, "Crane threatened Monique."

"Yes," Nancy Wong said. "He told her that you would kill her if she did not stop."

"He said that *I* would kill Monique?" Albro asked.

"Yes," Nancy Wong answered.

"Is Thomas Crane still there?"

"No," Nancy Wong said. "That was two years ago. He's now beyond their reach."

"That was yesterday," Albro said.

"*Your* yesterday," Isaiah said.

"What do you mean, *my yesterday*?" Albro demanded.

"I don't know how you could have witnessed that meeting. I only know that Thomas Crane wanted you to be there," Nancy Wong said.

"Will he come back?" Albro asked.

"Albro, he is dead! He will never come back! You have to try to understand that!" Nancy Wong pleaded.

"Will I see him in some other time?" Albro asked. He turned to the rat man and said, "You said my yesterday happened two years ago. Will that happen again?"

"I cannot say," the rat man replied.

"Nancy?" Albro asked.

"Albro, I don't know! I don't know! There is so much none of us knows!" Nancy Wong shouted.

Albro stepped close to Nancy Wong and put his hand under her chin and gently raised her eyes to his own. "Look at me now, Nancy, and tell me who you see."

Nancy Wong looked up. Her lower lip trembled and then tears began to flow from her eyes.

"Albro Marshal Swift," she said.

"And when you look in the mirror, who do you see?"

"I see myself!"

"And when Monique Olivia Newton looks in the mirror, who does she see?"

"Please, Albro, don't do this to me. It's tearing me apart!"

"What happened to my mother?" Albro asked. When neither of them answered, Albro went to his battered overnight bag and dug past the bundles of cash until he found the photo he had found amid the destruction of Nancy Wong's office. He handed it to her. "I found this in your office. Look at the two faces in the upper window. I thought it was a picture of me with a woman I've never met. I was never in that building until I went there looking for you. Turn it over. There's a date, and a note. It says *'Lee, Ho and Wong Law Office June, 1942'*. That's Crane and your mother looking out from that window, isn't it?"

Nancy Wong held the photo, her hand trembling. "Yes, that is your father, but not my mother. She would not be born for another two years. The woman is Auntie Lo."

"How can that be? Where did you get it?"

"It was in some things Auntie Lo gave to me, things that had belonged to my mother."

"How could Crane be there in 1942? He looks to be in his mid-twenties. He should have been a child."

"I don't know the answers to your questions," Nancy Wong said.

Albro again held up the photograph. "Was Crane really there in 1942?"

"Only in a very strict sense," the rat man said.

515

"In the same *'strict sense'* that I am Thomas Crane?" Albro asked, his voice rising. He was getting tired of the run around. Every question, every answer seemed to be herding him back to his starting point.

"No. Something occurred that caused Thomas Crane's existence to become divided," the rat man said.

That *'something'*, Albro considered, was that the minute chance, that slice of unpredictability built into the workings of the universe that Thomas Crane had told Nancy about that had come into play? "Divided how many times?" Albro asked.

"We believe," Isaiah said, "that any or none of those who disappeared from the ruins may exist in one, or all nine of the hidden dimensions. There is no way of knowing."

"Like cats," Albro said.

"I do not understand," the rat man said.

"Cats are supposed to have nine lives, although I think they're only allowed to live one life at a time. It sounds like Thomas Crane and who knows how many others, are living all nine at the same time. But you're saying that I am not part of that."

"No, you are not. You are very special," the rat man said.

Albro remembered Nick Lane telling him how Crane's wife had come to tell him what she was going to do, and he suddenly realized that it had nothing to do with excavations at the ruins, but everything to do with Martin Osborne Newton. A stabbing pain struck Albro between the eyes as a dark cloud rippled through his mind. The Black Djinnim had squirted out memories like a squid expelling ink. His knees grew weak and he reached out for the back of a chair to steady himself. He looked down at his forearm and the scar of twisted strands. "What happened to Laura Crane after the disaster at the ruins?" he managed to ask.

"She disappeared," Nancy Wong said. "She was not seen again until a few years ago when she appeared in a movie."

"She's been posing as Newton's daughter," Albro said.

"Yes," Nancy Wong answered.

"She should be much older," Albro said.

"She is," the rat man said.

Albro looked at the rat man. He said, "She's one of you, isn't she. I don't mean Mongi. She's one of the others. She's one of the Purim." There was something more to all this, but he just couldn't see it. It was like trying to recognize a familiar figure shrouded in fog. He could see the outlines, but he couldn't make out the details. He said, "Crane was in love with her until he found that out."

Albro waited for the rat man to confirm or deny what he had just said. Isaiah hesitated and then said, "She did not reveal her true self until much later."

"Until after she met Newton," Albro said, as the memory came to him.

"She needed Martin Osborne Newton," the rat man said.

"Yes," Albro said, but he could not remember why. "Does Marlowe know all of this?"

"Yes, of course," the rat man said.

"Who else knows?"

"Elijah has known ever since he first held one of the medallions."

Albro said to Nancy Wong, "That mansion, where I found the jade dagger, belongs to Newton, doesn't it?"

"Yes," she said. "Thomas was his prisoner." Nancy Wong saw the baffled look in Albro's eyes. She went on, "He appeared in Hong Kong more than two years ago. He had no one else to turn to for help. Thomas thought Newton might have changed in the intervening years and at first it seemed that he had, that he was willing to help him. He believed that there was a chance to bring back all of the others who had been lost in the disaster. Thomas felt deeply responsible for their lives. He did not know that Monique was with Newton. He assumed her to be dead. But she was alive and was calling herself Monique Olivia Newton. She saw a greater opportunity, one in which she might control access to the nine hidden dimensions. Thomas escaped, but they later found him."

Albro began, "Yesterday...," He paused to correct himself, "*My yesterday*, which was *two years ago*, there was a Thomas Crane in Hong Kong, and today, a day that we are all sharing, there's another Thomas Crane in a Seattle morgue." And there was also his self to consider.

517

Where did he fall in the line-up? A man's voice just off stage was saying to him 'Would the real Thomas Crane please stand up'! Albro stifled a laugh and glanced reflexively into the corner, but no one was there. "How many other versions have made an appearance?"

"There is no way of knowing," Isaiah said. "You described someone who came aboard the *Jade Prince* while you were there. That could have been Thomas Crane."

Albro thought about that for a moment. When exactly had he been there and whom had he seen? Whose voice had shouted out to Nick Lane? And then the memory of waking up in an old pickup on a Colorado mountain pass came to him. Had that been Thomas Crane behind the wheel? And what about the old card-sharp there in Baja who had taken him and Roger in tow and had taught him how to really play the game of poker. Had that white haired geezer been another Thomas Crane? It could all be true, but what were the odds...?

"What about Monique," Albro asked, "how many versions of Laura Crane are roaming around?"

"Only the one that we know of," Nancy Wong answered.

Albro let out a laugh that sounded slightly hysterical. He said, "It just occurred to me that if we all got together we could field two softball teams. Walter could stand in for the dead Thomas Crane. What do you think Walter, ever played softball? It's a great way to spend a summer afternoon."

"Albro," Nancy Wong said, "this is nothing to joke about."

"But it's damned hard to take seriously, don't you think?"

"This is serious. Pull yourself together."

Another wave of memories struck Albro and he staggered. When his thoughts cleared he said, "Laura Crane was pregnant. What happened to the child?" He stood, half in shock. He realized that he had almost said *the monster*. That was what she had come to tell Thomas Crane. He could see her standing there in the tent, the tight lines of her dress giving only the merest hint of what lay beneath. He could feel the suffocating heat and humidity. He could see Martin's wolf-like face, the parting of the man's lips into an arrogant smile, the yellowish teeth.

"He is safe," Isaiah said, "at least for now; the woman who sleeps watches over him."

"Do you mean the woman I keep seeing in my dreams?" Albro asked.

"Yes," the rat man said.

"I want to see him," Albro said. He heard his own voice, but it was a voice he didn't recognize. He imagined it to be Thomas Crane's voice.

"You have seen him," Isaiah said. "You need only remember."

"But he was still in her womb," Albro said as the memory came to him, vivid with the naked body of Laura Crane, the body of Monique Olivia Newton.

Nancy Wong said, "Thomas found you, but he could not keep you safe. He had to send you away."

"Laura, Monique, Laura, Monique...she had a son she could not keep," Albro muttered in sing-song.

"Albro," Nancy Wong said, "you may look like Thomas Crane, but you are who you have always been."

"You keep saying that."

"Because it's the truth," Nancy Wong said.

Albro closed his eyes tightly. Spikes of light danced green and yellow and red then white and then, out of their prismatic image, came the mouth of Laura Crane and the words she spoke all of those years ago. He opened his eyes. "It was Martin's doing," Albro said. "He was a genius, and it was his way of getting back at Crane."

"You were the first, and it was just the beginning," Nancy Wong said.

CHAPTER 49

"HE called me a monster," Albro said.

"His anger was directed at them, not you," Nancy Wong said.

"Martin Osborne Newton created me. Laura Crane gave birth to me. Monique..." Albro faltered. He could not take it all in.

"Yes," Nancy Wong said quietly. "We tried to find you. When we did find you, it was too late. I'm sorry."

"She knew," Albro said. "From the moment she saw me, she knew."

"When we found out, there was nothing we could do but discourage you from seeing her," Nancy Wong said.

Albro let his gaze fall to the welded plates of the steel floor. In the paint-chipped, rusted patterns he saw the outlines of city streets and buildings and parklands all enclosed within a vast, dark wall. He looked at the scar on his arm. He looked at the rat man. "Where was I born?" he asked.

"You were born in the City of ...," the rat man began to reply, but before he could finish, Albro completed the statement.

"Angels," Albro said. "You took me from Laura Crane."

"To the woman who sleeps," the rat man said. "She sent you away."

"That must have been a thumb in Newton's eye. Is this what my whole life has been about, a jealous rivalry between two geniuses?" Albro asked.

"Thomas Crane wanted to save you. He wanted you as far from the struggles between the Mongi and the Purim as was possible," Nancy Wong said.

"And Laura Crane," Albro said.

"Yes," Nancy Wong said, "and Laura Crane."

"But she found me," Albro said.

"It was only a matter of time," the rat man said. "Without you, she, nor anyone else, can release the *Jade Prince*."

"Thomas Crane discovered how to release the *Jade Prince*," Albro said. "And I am Thomas Crane. The *Jade Prince* is a ship, a battered old freighter! *How can a ship be released*? *Released from what*?"

"From the dimension that confines it," the rat man said.

"The gold coins, the medallions..." Albro uttered, suddenly understanding why he had to return to the MV JADE PRINCE.

"Yes," the rat man said. "Once they have all twelve medallions, there will be no stopping them. You are the final key that will release the *Jade Prince*. You are Thomas Crane in the only way that matters to them."

"What matters to Monique...," Albro said and stopped abruptly. He suddenly didn't care what mattered most to her because a more important question had crowded into his thoughts. She had given birth to him, but she was not his mother. She had made love to him, had agreed to marry him. He had no mother and he had no father. He had no lover. Still, there was suddenly a question that he needed the answer to. "Who is she?" he asked.

The rat man went to the corner of the small room and lifted a bundle wrapped in a dirty towel. He brought it and laid it carefully on the table. Albro saw that it was the book he'd brought back, the log of the MV JADE PRINCE, which as it turned out, was not a log book at all, but a book full of unreadable text. According to the rat man, it was the sacred book of the Mongi.

"Clear all else from your thoughts and then form your question in your mind and exhale gently over the book," the rat man said.

Albro had an uncomfortable feeling of what was about to happen. That thing that resided inside him was going to once again make its appearance. He thought of how tape worms could be coaxed out of someone's stomach by first starving him, and then wafting the vapors of a rich soup into his open mouth, enticing the tape worm inch by inch up its victim's throat. He put that thought out of his mind, and then gradually all the others until only the one thought remained. He exhaled as the rat man had instructed. Dark tendrils appeared as before only this time it remained as an amorphous form and seemed to seep between the pages of the leather bound volume.

"Open it," the rat man said.

Albro turned the cover. What had been unreadable before was now filled with stately, engraved lettering, no longer Cyrillic, and utterly meaningless, but as plainly printed as Reverend Powell's old Nine Pounder. The red and black embellishments with gold leaf accents that decorated the margins were still there, but now he saw lavish gardens overflowing with vines and flowers.

'IN THE BEGINNING...' began the first line. Instinctively, as if old Reverend C. Dobson Powell were instructing him from a far off past, he turned the pages until he came to the section where he knew that he would find the answer to his question.

Albro read and then he closed the book. He looked at the rat man who seemed to be studying him closely. "She was your Messiah," Albro said.

"A false Messiah," the rat man said. "Yet many still believe."

"Elijah foretold her coming," Albro said.

"Yes," the rat man agreed.

"He also foretold that she would...," Albro had to stop for a moment to recall the exact verse that he had read. "...that *'She would bear a child, not from the seed of man. From a drop of blood a child shall grow within her womb...'.*"

"'*...and through his suffering the People shall find their way'.*" The rat man said. "You are that child. You are the One."

That was what the rat man had told him that first night, there in Nancy Wong's cabin, and he had not understood. Did he understand any better now? He looked at the rat man. He said, "I need to see her."

"No," Nancy Wong said. Albro could hear the fear in her voice.

"Not Monique," Albro said to her. "I need to see the woman who sleeps.

"You have already seen her," Isaiah said. "She is the one who dances in your mind. She is one who pulls you into her dreams."

"Still," Albro said, "I need to see her. They are coming for her, and they will take the medallion that she wears. I need to warn her. Send me to her."

"That, I cannot do. When she is ready for you, she will pull you to her. She is well hidden. I do not think that even with the medallions they possess they have the power to open the dimension in which she exists."

"*The Terminal Tavern*,' Albro said. His mind was running too fast. He couldn't keep up with his own thoughts. No, they were not his thoughts. They were Thomas Crane's thoughts. "That's where I can reach her. That place, that back corner, the wooden bench inside the phone booth is the end point, the anchor, the terminus of that line of force, the vibrating line of energy that binds this world to hers." Albro gasped for air as his mind filled with the exquisite beauty of the mathematical formulae that defined, explained, it all in detail so fine that....

"Yes," Nancy said, interrupting his thoughts. "Thomas told me that place is an anchor point for one of the nine hidden dimensions."

Albro turned to the rat man. "Is that where you and Walter arrived?"

"Yes."

"Is that where you're catching the bus home?"

"There once were eleven anchor points," Isaiah said. "That is the last remaining. Elijah destroyed the others."

"*The Twelve Dimensions*," Albro said, his eyes glowing, as the radiating spokes of a great wheel slowly turned inside his mind."

"Elijah intends to destroy it," Isaiah said. "When he does so, he will be free to change the future, and he will remake not just this world, but the entire universe, in Her image."

"Cut the arcane speech, Izzy. Just tell me plainly what that means," Albro said suddenly himself again. Where had Crane's thoughts gone?

"In simple language, it means that this world as it exists now will become unrecognizable. It may even cease to exist altogether."

"I realize that now," Albro said, and he knew this thought was a remnant of Thomas Crane's intellect exerting its influence. His own mind could almost grasp what was going on, but each time he got close, understanding seemed to slip away, and every time the rat man spoke, he felt as if he already had known what he was told. A mental image of the ancient Yin and Yang symbol came to him and he had the sensation that one side of his brain was chasing the other.

Nancy Wong said, "It's impossible to change the future, no matter how hard you try to change the past."

"Providing the twelve sacred dimensions are securely anchored to the past," Isaiah said. "Cut them loose and..." He let his voice trail off. He dropped his face and was silent for a long moment. Then he said, "Thomas Crane opened one of the nine sacred dimensions. He did not realize what would happen."

"Three hundred lives vanished," Albro said.

"It was an act of desperation," Isaiah said. "He did not know that Elijah had been waiting for that opportunity."

"And Nancy and I were left in a phone booth," Albro said. "And Monique..."

"The balance between lives cannot be comprehended," the rat man said.

"How can our lives balance three hundred?" Albro asked.

"You may come to understand that very soon. The Thomas Crane whom I knew was not aware of the life you lived, but your life undoubtedly influenced him on some level."

"He wasn't going to allow Monique.., Laura..., whoever she is..., was...," Albro stumbled over the words like a blind man running an obstacle course. He remembered what Nick Lane and Chang Wu had told him. He could see Laura Crane standing next to Newton, the two of them

524

telling him that he was helpless to do anything. No, it wasn't him they speaking to. It was Crane, but he could remember it clearly. He could recall the conversation, if you wanted to call it that. It was more like a shouting match, each of them throwing everything that had at each other until he'd had enough, and he'd slammed his fist into Newton's face. No, goddamn it, he hadn't been there. It was Crane! He suddenly realized he was hot. No, he was roasting. Sweat poured off his brow and into his eyes. He swiped it away.

"It wasn't advice Newton was giving him," the rat man said. "It was an ultimatum. Crane had found a way to open a new dimension and he appeared in our time," the rat man said.

"The sleeping woman," Albro said. He had a profound memory of holding her in his arms as she slept.

"Yes. She gathered him into her dream."

Like a butterfly caught in a net, Albro thought. "There was a child...," Albro said and looked at Nancy Wong. He tried to concentrate, but the memory was fleeting. He tried to draw it back, but it would not come.

"What happened to Nancy's mother?" He felt a stabbing pain in his heart as her image filled his memory. He is running with an infant tucked against his chest.

The rat man shrugged. "The sleeping woman never found her."

Albro took a deep breath and tried to clear his mind of Thomas Crane's memories if only for a moment. He asked, "Did he know? I mean, does he know anything about me?"

"You are why he had to return to this time."

"But why me?"

"You started to say it earlier, but you stopped. Try to remember."

Albro started to protest. Every time he let Thomas Crane's memories crowd into his mind he felt himself slipping away. What if he didn't come back? Who would he become? But did he have any choice? He couldn't summon up Crane's memories. He couldn't force himself to forget. The thoughts in his mind seemed to come and go by whims of their own making. He tried to think back to what he had said. He had

525

said something about a child, but what child, Laura Crane's child? No, there was another child. He closed his eyes and suddenly he saw the naked body of Nancy Wong's mother pulling him to her. No, not pulling him, but pulling Thomas Crane to her, into her. He opened his eyes, and looked at Nancy Wong. He said, "I held you."

"Yes," said Isaiah, "You saved the child, your child. If you did not, Elijah would have taken her."

"He took her mother," Albro said, "I couldn't stop him."

"You needed to save the child," the rat man said.

Albro reached out his hand and steadied himself against the table. His mind wanted to jump off a cliff. It wanted to soar if only for a few seconds, but he sensed the plummeting fall and the abrupt end that awaited him. He remembered the small shape of the child's hand, the knowing look in the dark eyes. Albro forcibly pulled himself back to the present. He remembered the night he entered the mansion. "The jade dagger," Albro said.

"Yes," Nancy Wong said. "Thomas knew that you would find it, and that is how we found you. He had a sense of what was going on in your mind."

"That was the lure. You were going to reel me in like a big flopping fish from your ocean of time. What happened?"

"You happened, Albro," Nancy said.

"What do you mean?"

"You changed everything. Everything you've done in your life has changed everything."

Isaiah said, "When Thomas Crane returned to the ruins, he did not find the medallions. They were gone; stolen, dispersed in the geologic strata, he had no way of knowing. In their place he found something far different, something he never imagined that he would find there. You know what he found."

Yes, he knew. He felt it the moment old Krupp had switched on his laser light show. "He found the *Jade Prince*."

"Yes," the rat man said.

"But he couldn't have, because Crane had made up all of that. It was just a cover to keep the military in the dark long enough to understand what he'd actually found."

"And yet it became reality," Isaiah said. "As Ms Wong said, your life changed everything."

"The medallions, they exist," Albro said. "I had one. The three of you had one each. Chang Wu showed us the medallion he wears around his neck."

"Yes, they have existed from time before time, and because of you, the *Jade Prince* exists," Isaiah said.

Albro closed his eyes and tried to take it all in. He kept getting fleeting memories from Thomas Crane's life. He had to keep them pushed back for now. He wanted to tell Nancy and Isaiah what was happening inside his head, but he had to be himself right now. He had one more question that needed answering if he were to not drown in his own panicky thoughts.

"Nancy, I have a memory of you with Thomas Crane. I can see how you look at him. I see you touch his face." Nancy Wong lowered her eyes. Albro saw her shoulders sag. "You still have not told me the truth," he said to her. "He is the Thomas Crane who came to you. He is the Thomas Crane you wanted to love, but he wouldn't let you." He watched Nancy Wong's face break and the sobs came in convulsive waves. No one moved until it was over. When at last she took a deep breath and wiped her eyes, Albro said. "I'm going to ask you a question and I need to know the truth. I have the uncanny feeling that you know what I am going to ask."

Nancy Wong nodded and gave a grim smile. "Yes, I know. And although you already know the answer, I will tell you the truth."

"That man who came to Auntie Lo's house looking for you, that man who had been tortured and had lost so much blood he barely had the strength to speak you, that man who lay dying on the wet brick in a narrow alley, who was he?"

Nancy Wong looked at him and bit her lip and forced back the tears. "That man was you, Albro. You," she said and paused, lowering her head. "I'm so sorry," she whispered. "I wanted to tell you, but I could not find a way." She put her back to the wall and slumped to the floor and buried her face in her hands.

Albro closed his eyes and clasped his hands around the back of neck. He felt jarred, shaken, as if his world had begun to wobble like a top slowly winding down. He tried desperately to conjure up his past, to find some solid remnant that he could plant his life on. What had been the point of any of it? Was he nothing more than a spare part waiting to be plucked from its shelf when the need arose? He opened his eyes and looked down at his expensive Italian loafers. The hand sewn seams had begun to split and unravel. They began to recede from him and he was struck by an intense feeling of vertigo. He clamped his eyes shut and felt the steel deck heave under him. He felt for the bunk and pulled himself into it and curled his body into a tight ball. He'd been stamped for general delivery and then shipped by cosmic express down the threads of time to the terminus of a hard wooden bench, the *Terminal Tavern*, the end of the line, the boundary between past and the future.

All of those years he had drifted about, holding onto the fantasy that one day he would find his real parents and have a real family and do all of the things that a real family does, were nothing more than a fix, a necessary patch on a torn bit of reality. A wispy memory of the old man and the old woman who had first cared for him materialized in his mind like smoke behind a mirror. He thought of Roger and the other boys at the juvenile centers he'd bounced in and out of. He remembered old Reverend Powell and his dough-faced wife, and then Ruth and Jackie and their closed caskets. He thought of Monique and the life that was supposed to be unfolding for him. It seemed like months since the big party. In a matter of five days, his whole life had been turned upside down and inside out, sliced and diced and thrown like confetti into the wind.

"Albro," Nancy Wong said, "sit up."

"Go away," he said, and pulled the thin blanket over his head.

Nancy Wong yanked the blanket away. "You can feel sorry for yourself later. Right now, we have to think of a way to get out of here. Listen."

Albro listened. The engines had sped up. He could hear it as well as feel it in the vibration of the ship.

"What do you think is happening?" she asked.

"They have found us," the rat man said.

"I don't suppose the Chinese have sent their navy out to rescue us," Albro said.

"No," said the rat man.   "It is Elijah. He has come for the medallions."

"Chang Wu's men are armed," Nancy Wong said.

"The will be overpowered," Isaiah said.

"What about us?" Albro asked.

"Elijah is not interested in us. He is only interested in medallions and you," the rat man said.

Albro stood. Nancy Wong was right. They had to do something, but what? His first impulse was to find a weapon, but what, a chair, to protect them against guns? What was the use in even thinking about resisting? He was about to fall into another round of despair when the cards that Walter had laid out caught his eye. He stepped to the table and examined the pattern that Walter had quietly created. Walter had placed the four aces at the points of the compass and connecting them to form a circle were their accompanying kings and jacks, for a total of twelve cards. Inside the circle he'd arranged the four queens, each at the matching ace. In the center, he'd placed the joker. Walter performed a crude shuffle of the remaining cards and turned up a four of diamonds and placed it on the queen of clubs.

Curious now, Albro asked, "Why did you do that?"

"She's the Queen of the Earth. If I give her water, it will distract her for a time," Walter said and turned another card. The nine of clubs came up. He placed it on the queen of hearts. "She's the Queen of Blood. That card is a present to her from the King of the Earth. He is planning a great battle and wants her on his side."

529

Walter turned another card, and placed the three of hearts on the queen of diamonds. "She is the Queen of the Wind. Her three children have died and she mourns their deaths." He sat back and studied the cards and then turned up one more, and laid the ten of spades on the queen of the same suit. "She is the Queen of Fire, the most powerful of the four queens. She will do whatever she can to rule the others. She demanded that card. It will give her great strength.

"How do you know where to place the cards? What are the rules?" Albro asked.

"Rules?" Walter responded with a puzzled look on his face.

"Sure. A game has to have rules. Otherwise, how would you decide where to play the cards?"

Walter looked at Albro then looked at the cards and scratched his head. "Oh, I see what you mean. The only rule is that I play the cards where they want to be played."

"They tell you?" Albro asked.

"Oh, yes. Don't the cards talk to you, Mr. Albro?"

The question caught Albro by surprise. He had to think about that. Did the cards actually talk to him in a language other than probability? Didn't cards sometimes call to him from the deck? He could imagine that, sure, but in the end it was still a matter of how aware he was of the probabilities, conscious or not. But what of all those times in which he had defied the probabilities and had drawn the exact card that he had needed? That was luck. But what exactly was luck? He'd wondered about that a lot, and had never been able to come up with a rational explanation. Maybe there wasn't one. Maybe it was just a matter of listening to the cards.

Albro looked down at the pattern of cards. Walter had continued turning up cards and placing them in what seemed a purely random way, and had yet to place any cards on the joker. He asked, "Who's that in the middle?"

"That one," Walter said as he tapped the joker lightly with the tip of his finger. "He's the *Prince of Time*. The queen who takes him wins the game and lives forever. Right now, all he can think about is how to escape, but as you can see, he is trapped."

"Sounds familiar," Albro said. "Wish him good luck from me."

"There is no luck in this game, Mr. Albro. The *Prince of Time* never escapes. One of the queens always takes him."

Albro looked at the cards. Walter had begun moving them around. A few he'd turned face down. The king of diamonds was missing. So was the jack of clubs. He had the disturbing feeling that they were dead. He looked at the queen of spades. What had Walter called her, the Queen of Fire? She now occupied the twelve-o'clock position in the circle. Had the look in her eyes changed? He sensed that she had a plan to take the Prince, and it involved the death of the Queen of the Earth. How did he know that? She was looking straight at him and telling him so! He could hear her voice coming from somewhere in the middle part of his forehead. He felt a ripple of movement across his shoulders and down through his loins.

Albro shook himself and tried to tear his gaze from the game. He was supposed to be thinking of a plan to get them out of the fix he'd gotten them into, but the Queen of Fire was commanding him to play. She was refusing to allow that 'black buffoon', as she called Walter, to continue. He looked to Walter, who indeed seemed to be perplexed over what to do next. He was about to reach for the remaining cards in Walter's hand when a resounding boom echoed through the ship causing it to shudder violently. Albro fell onto the table and scattered the cards. The Queen of Fire screamed at him in contempt and disgust. The light went out and the room was cast in absolute blackness.

"The engines have stopped," said the rat man.

From somewhere beyond the bulkhead they could hear a barrel that had come lose rolling and banging as the ship rocked back and forth on the deep swells of the open ocean. The ventilation had also died and the stagnant air in the small room began to grow hot.

"What are the crew members doing?" Nancy Wong asked.

"They are surrendering," Isaiah said.

"To whom?" Nancy Wong demanded, but there was no strength in her voice. Fear had drained away the last of her courage.

"Elijah," Isaiah answered. "His men will kill the crew first. Then he will question Chang Wu."

"How do you know they'll do that?" Albro asked.

"I fought in wars for many years. We took prisoners only when necessary and we kept them only for as long as they were useful."

They heard a hesitant rumble and then the steady beat of the engines. The light came on, a feeble orange glow at first and then it slowly brightened.

"They have secured the engine room," Isaiah said. "It won't be long now."

And then true to the rat man's words, they heard footsteps advancing toward them. Metal clanged against metal and the door swung open. Two men wearing sleek black outfits and carrying compact automatic rifles held at waist level stepped into the room. A third man entered holding a pistol in his hand.

Albro recognized him immediately. "Alexi!"

Alexi Ruslonov smiled a tight, lipless smile. "We meet again," he said and glanced at the table with the playing cards askew. "I see you have been practicing. I would enjoy a game, but I fear you have nothing to lose but your life and the lives of your friends. Come with me."

Ruslonov turned to the others and looked them over with cold, unemotional eyes. "The rest of you will remain here."

"No," Albro said. "We all go."

Ruslonov pointed toward Nancy Wong, Isaiah and Walter, and spoke to the gunmen while keeping his eyes on Albro. "Shoot them."

"NO!" Albro shouted and quickly stepped between the gunmen and his three companions. He'd seen the gunmen's trigger fingers begin to tighten. His heart was pounding wildly. "I'll come with you."

"If you think that you can save them, you are wrong. They may come to regret that you did not allow them a quick and merciful death." Ruslonov shrugged his shoulders. "This way then," he said calmly to Albro and motioned with his hand toward the door.

Albro reached for his overnight bag.

"Leave it," Ruslonov ordered. To the gunmen he said, "If the others move, kill them."

Ruslonov went through the door, followed by Albro and then the two gunmen. Ruslonov secured the door and then said to Albro, "After you."

They made their way back to the dining salon. Albro managed a glimpse through a porthole at a smaller gray vessel with a gun turret on its bow not far off the port side of the ship and behind it, a distant line of solid black clouds.

Ruslonov opened the salon door and motioned Albro inside. The first thing he saw was Chang Wu slumped in the corner. His dark eyes were half open and between them was a dark hole that dripped blood onto his fine white shirt and silk jacket. The man in the chef's outfit lay next to him.

Albro turned. At the head of the table sat a trim white haired man with chopsticks poised over a plate of food. He was dressed in the same dark uniform that the others wore except that he wore a pair of tight fitting gloves. He stared intently at Albro for a moment, his dark, piercing eyes taking him in from head to toe. He finished what he had in his mouth and then dabbed his lips with a white napkin. "Mr. Swift, please excuse me. I was just enjoying a wonderful preparation of abalone. A man as busy as I rarely has the opportunity for such exquisite dining. Chang Wu had an excellent chef in his employ. A pity he got in the way. We could have put him to good use. Our cook hasn't a tenth of the talent that man had. Won't you join me? There's more than enough."

"Thanks. I already ate," Albro replied. "Who are you?"

"My name is Elijah," he paused. "Excuse me for staring, but I'm quite impressed. It appears that Newton did an excellent job. Although, I have been informed there are some interesting imperfections." He let that last statement hang in the air for a moment, and then abruptly changed the subject. "You won't mind if I continue eating? I must confess that you and your cohorts have kept me busy. Please sit down.

You would like a cup of tea, perhaps?" He motioned for Ruslonov to pour tea.

The man said, "You know, you're very lucky we found you. We're over a hundred miles south of the position Chang Wu assured me he would be. That's what I get, I suppose, for dealing with the likes of him. I find that deceit makes more work for everyone, and more often than not, ends in tragedy. Wouldn't you agree, Mr. Swift?"

"Honesty's the best policy," Albro spat out. "That's always been my motto," He added flippantly.

"I was hoping that you would agree. Your father would have profited from that same policy. I hope that you don't mind that I refer to Thomas Crane as your father. It's a technicality, I know, but one I think we can overlook. But, perhaps, I am being presumptuous. I'm assuming that the good friar, Isaiah, has informed you of your parentage." He paused, lowering his gaze and looking at Albro in an inquisitive manner.

"Yeah, Isaiah told me everything."

"Everything?" The man laughed. "The Isaiah I know is a Mongi who, how does one say, 'plays his cards very close to his chest'.

"It's *vest*, not 'chest,'" Albro said.

"Ah, so it is," Elijah agreed and smiled. "I've never been able to keep your colloquialisms straight. My point was that I doubt very much Isaiah has told you everything."

"He told me the part about you being burned at the stake."

"Ah, one of my better performances, I must admit. For some unknown reason the Council of Elders got it into their heads that I was intent upon destroying their precious beliefs. They thought a little torturing would bring me around to their point of view. In reality, torture does little other than demean the perpetrator, and provides little in the way of reliable information or cooperation, and wastes valuable time."

"So that's why you killed Chang Wu?"

Elijah laid the chopsticks neatly across the plate and sat back. "Chang Wu reacted poorly to our arrival. He pulled a gun and was about to shoot me. It's there, at his side, if you care to examine it.

Furthermore, I had nothing to do with Thomas Crane's death. I had great respect for him. Ah, you think that you saw Thomas Crane recently."

Albro was stunned and surprised. He'd been thinking that very thought. Elijah had read his mind as easily as the label on a soup can. Albro said, trying to keep his voice level, "Thomas Crane is not dead. I saw him in Hong Kong."

"Are you certain of that?"

"Yes. I also saw you. I had this funny feeling, as if I had seen you someplace before."

"That was more than two years ago. I recall that I had the sense that someone was watching us. That was you, of course. It seems like only yesterday that we were all together," He added wistfully and then smiled at his own joke. "You really don't believe everything that Ms. Wong and Isaiah have told you, do you?"

"Why shouldn't I?"

"I ask you that, because this affair is a good deal more complex than you know. Later, I will explain it to you. Chang Wu's change of plans, I'm sorry to say, has cost us valuable time. There is a storm approaching and will be upon us within the hour. My ship has the speed to outrun it, this one does not."

Albro jumped to his feet. "What about the others? We can't leave them."

"They have served their purpose. Countless lives have been lost and countless more, I am certain, will be sacrificed before we find the *Jade Prince*. Now, we must be going."

Albro said, "You can't get to the *Jade Prince* without my help. Unless you bring them, I won't help you."

"You are right, Mr. Swift, I do need your help, but you will provide it regardless of whether your three friends live or die. Far greater things are a stake than three insignificant lives."

Elijah motioned to the two gunmen. They grabbed Albro by the arms and held him tightly. Alexi Ruslonov approached holding a needle and syringe. He jammed the needle into Albro's neck and pushed the plunger. In seconds, the world turned into a haze of shifting colors and shapes. He legs began moving, his feet slapping the deck. Like a marionette dangling from strings, he half-walked, half-floated outside and then down a ladder into the bottom of a rubber boat. He looked up at a swirl of dark clouds and felt the boat beneath him plunging up and down in the swells, and then he was being hauled upward and half-carried along narrow corridors to a bunk and rolled into it. He felt another prick of a needle, and a momentary warmth pass through his body before everything went black.

CHAPTER 50

NANCY WONG jumped from the bunk where she had been sitting, and slammed her fist on the table causing the cards to leap. "They can't have just left us here!"

An hour had passed since the men dressed in black had taken away Albro. Walter had reshuffled the cards and had begun another game to pass the time. He patiently moved the cards back into position.

"Oh, I'm sorry, Walter," Nancy Wong said.

"That's alright, Miss Nancy," Walter said calmly.

The engines had continued to beat at a steady rate, but the ship had begun to rise and plunge in a seesaw motion, and at each plunge they heard and felt an ominous booming as waves crashed over the bow.

"They can, and they would," replied Isaiah, who then added, "To make matters worse, we are heading into a storm."

"Do you think they are still on board?" Nancy Wong asked.

"If for some reason they have yet to find the medallions, then yes they are still on board."

"And if they found them?"

"Then Chang Wu and the crew are most certainly dead, and Elijah and his men have abandoned the ship."

"We have to find a way to get out of here," Nancy Wong said.

"I believe we have explored every option," Isaiah said.

Nancy Wong wracked her brain for a solution. They had tried breaking down the door, but even Walter's great strength was no match for the heavy steel. The ventilation shaft was not large enough for the Isaiah, the smallest of them, to even fit his head through. They had examined every square inch of the floor, walls and ceiling looking for a lose panel. The toilet and sink offered no hope. They were in a steel-walled room that had obviously been constructed as a cell with only one way in and one way out. Yet, Albro had found another way. He had moved through the wall as if it didn't exist. Then, they'd had had their medallions. Now, they had nothing. She groaned out loud.

"Don't worry, Miss Nancy," Walter said without looking up from the cards. "Mr. Albro will think of something. He hasn't forgotten us."

"Oh, Walter, he's probably happy to be rid of us. He'll run back to Monique. I know he will."

At the mention of Monique, Walter looked up and met Isaiah's eyes. Neither said anything, but Nancy saw the look that passed between them.

"What?" Nancy Wong asked.

Walter pretended not to hear her. He shifted a card and then studied the table. Brother Isaiah looked at her but said nothing. If either of them had spoken, and they could have said anything, she would have let it go. But there was something about silence that always made her suspicious. She said to Isaiah, "You know something about her, don't you." She waited for one of them to respond and when neither of them spoke, she asked, "What is it you don't want to tell me?"

Isaiah continued to look at her, but something had changed in his eyes. Where there had been a look of stubborn optimism, there was now a look of fearful uncertainty. She had seen that look before in the eyes of climbing partners when she was about to be told some very bad news. But climbing was all about knowledge and skill and making the right decision at the right moment and using one's endurance and strength to face the challenges that the mountain threw at you. So, whatever the bad news might be, you worked the problem as a team. She sensed that there was much about the two Mongi that she didn't know. For one thing, Walter was not the bumbling innocent that he feigned to be and Brother Isaiah, aka Colonel Ratham, had a past antithetical to his present calling.

"Izzy," she said, "talk to me. We'll never get out of here if we don't work together."

Isaiah shuffled to the bed and hugged the leather bound volume that Albro had brought back. A look of tired sadness came into Isaiah's eyes, and his bony shoulders slumped. In a matter of seconds he seemed to have taken on a lifetime of years. At that moment Nancy Wong realized that he was much older than she had assumed. The past few days had been hard on all of them, but the days had been more than cruel and punishing to the old Mongi, they had taken something from him that would not return.

Isaiah sat with his eyes half closed, lost in his thoughts and far distant memories. He felt the ship rise and fall as it attempted to ride the ever increasing swells. They were, he knew, doomed. Without a crew to steer the ship into the waves, it would break apart and go down. His own death did not trouble him. He should have died long ago along with so many others who were much braver than himself. What he regretted most...no, what shamed him most was that he would die knowing that he had failed his people. Elijah would use the twelve medallions to release the Jade Prince and seal the fate of the Mongi, and the fate of the Earth. Nancy Wong had helped them in every way she could while attempting to save the lives of Thomas Crane, Walter and himself, and Albro Swift. Now she was about to lose her life in a cause that she did not understand. It was the least he could do to tell her that which she was about to die for. He sat upright.

"There is something that you must understand. When your father, Thomas Crane, entered into our world, it was not because of something he had planned, nor was it by accident. He was destined to find the nine sacred dimensions, and by his discovery he fulfilled prophesy, a prophesy foretelling the start of the Gathering. Our past became his future. And now, our three lives have become a great weight upon the balance of time.

"The Mongi had waited countless millennia. In truth, I did not know what the Gathering would bring. I have looked into this book, I have read many of its passages, and I fear for the Earth and its people. It is the book of Araam, and it is not. It has somehow been changed. By what or by whom, I cannot say. Perhaps, its tumble through the canyons of time has corrupted the text, and in its passage forward it will once again become restored to the book I have known it to be. Or, in its passage forward it will destroy all which has been.

"The existence of the Mongi is now coupled to the existence of Thomas Crane. These two worlds are now held fast. Any incident in one, no matter how slight, will be felt in the other, as long as that connection exists. I think you know what that means, Miss Wong. You have not wanted to think about it, but I see it in your face, in the shadow of fear that resides in your eyes.

"The Book of Araam foretells the One, the One whose purpose it is to bring life to a dying world and to seal the gates of time. He is the One who was conceived without father and without mother. He is the One whose death occurred before his birth, and has lived in innocence of what has befallen him.

"The body of a man lies mutilated and cold; a man whom this world believes to be Thomas Crane. Yet, Thomas Crane lives and breathes. If that is so, who is the man who lies dead?

"I do not blame you for not telling him everything. I could not tell him. Should a man have knowledge of the moment of his death? Who is to say? Death comes for us all eventually. For Albro Swift death has already come, and it has come in the form of a beautiful woman. From what I know of the young man, I think that he would prefer it that way. Time may be convoluted, but it is still of one piece. There is nothing we can do for him, or ourselves."

CHAPTER 51

ALBRO SWIFT opened his eyes, and tried to decide if he was in one of those weird dream worlds, or if he was in the real world. He reached for the medallion around his neck, and then remembered that he'd handed it over to Chang Wu. Chang Wu had not so readily acquiesced, and now was dead. He sat up and looked around. There was no sleeping lady to be seen. That was a point in favor of reality. He felt a bit woozy, but he did have a memory of Alexi coming at him with a needle and syringe. That should count for another point on the reality side of the ledger. He remembered how they'd dropped him into the rubber boat and then had lifted him onto another ship. After that, he drew a blank.

He was in a well appointed stateroom sitting on a full sized bed and a thick carpet covered the floor. Floor to ceiling mirrors enclosed the closets. An open door revealed a bathroom. Louvered blinds covered the windows. Except for the lower than normal ceiling and the motion of the ship, he might have guessed that he was in a hotel room.

He eased himself off the bed and the room went all wonkers for a few seconds. The residue of drugs they had given him still lingered in his body causing his vision to take a moment to catch up with his movements. He held himself still and waited for everything to stop jittering around.

Someone had removed his shoes. He still wore the shirt and slacks that Marlowe had supplied on the plane. They were stiff with grime and dried sweat. He saw his ruined loafers at the foot of the bed.

On a chair someone had placed a stack of clean clothes along with a new pair of rubber soled shoes. He looked around for his overnight bag full of cash and remembered that Alexi had ordered him to leave it. Then he remembered that Alexi had also ordered Nancy, Isaiah and Walter to remain in the room. He remembered how Alexi had secured the door. What had happened to them? Then he remembered that Elijah had left them on Chang Wu's freighter. Or worse, had Elijah dealt with them in the same way that he had dealt with Chang Wu and the ship's crew? Elijah had mentioned an approaching storm, and he'd been in a hurry. Chances were, he hadn't taken the time to kill them outright. Had he left them to the mercy of the storm? Without a crew, the ship could go down. And if not, how long before they were discovered by a passing vessel? Would it be days, weeks? He had to think of some way to help them, but what could he do? Even if he managed somehow to send out an emergency SOS, he had no idea of their position. Then he remembered that he'd moved through a wall, a solid steel wall. Could he do it again? Again, he reached to touch the medallion around his neck, but it was gone. He cursed himself. Elijah had it now, along with the others. But did he need to have it? He'd gotten through all kinds of scrapes in his life before Anna Marshal had handed it to him. Besides, it had to be on the ship. Maybe having it nearby was good enough. He closed the bathroom door.

Albro sat on the edge of the bed and tried to remember exactly how he had done it. There had been no magic words or incantations. He'd simply created a vision in his mind of another place and then he'd been there. But there had been something more. *The woman who sleeps* had been there, like a shadow cast by his thoughts. He closed his eyes and searched for her. He ran down that long dark corridor of memories, tearing open doors and slamming them shut until suddenly she was there lying on her side, her face hidden under the curve of her arm, her hair spread out like a tangled mass of seaweed washed across a dirty blanket. He reached out and touched her and concentrated on seeing himself in the adjoining room. He waited for the slight push and dropping sensation that he'd experienced before, but it didn't come. Her image faded as a fog of uncontrollable thoughts crowded into his mind. She was gone. He opened his eyes. He was still on the bed. He tried again, without her this time, willing himself to float like a ghost and move effortlessly through the wall into the other room. He opened his eyes and saw that he hadn't moved an inch.

Frustrated, he jumped off the bed and took only one step before he sensed that something wasn't quite right. He looked around the room. The blinds still swayed to the motion of the ship, the stack of neatly folded clothes still rested on the chair. He glanced toward the bathroom and his eyes came back to the foot of the bed. His old loafers were missing! He quickly opened the bathroom door. His shoes rested on the toilet seat.

He heard footsteps and a rattle of keys outside the door. He grabbed the shoes and went back into the bedroom. He closed his eyes and suddenly she was with him. He could sense her thinking of the small, cell like room in which he'd last seen Nancy and Izzy and Walter. He saw himself there with them. He saw the bed, the table, the single bulb dangling from the ceiling.

The door opened. He opened his eyes and saw Alexi Ruslonov looking at him. He purposely avoided looking to where he had placed his shoes. He said, "Hello, Alexi."

"What are you doing?" Ruslonov asked and looked around suspiciously.

"Meditating. I always meditate after I wake up. I find it brightens my outlook upon the day. You should try it. It might improve your concentration."

"My concentration is fine. The Old Man wishes to see you. I suggest you take time to bathe. As you see, a change of clothes has been provided for you. When you are finished, use the intercom." He pointed to the speaker and switch next to the door. He glanced once more around the room, a puzzled look on his face, and then backed out and closed the door.

The shoes were gone. He hoped that somehow they had made it across miles of ocean and were resting on the floor of the room where

Nancy, Izzy and Walter were imprisoned. A pair of worn Italian hand-sewns wouldn't exactly do them a lot of good, but maybe it would at least let them know that he was alive and working on a way to rescue them.

He went into the small bathroom and looked in the mirror. A four day growth of beard covered his face and his hair was matted with salt. He turned on the shower and stripped off his clothes. He took his time, luxuriating under the hot water. He decided to forgo shaving and dressed in the clothes provided. It was the same uniform worn by Elijah's men: black trousers, black tunic and black shoes. Everything fit perfectly and he had to admit, as he took one last glance in the mirror, that he looked rather dashing. He pushed the intercom button.

Within a few moments, a crewman unlocked the door. "Follow me," he said to Albro.

The crewman led him outside. The air was fresh and cold. Bright shafts of sunlight came through broken clouds and a stiff breeze cut the tops of the waves into crescents of white foam. To the east he could see a wall of black clouds. The ship was moving fast. Judging from the wake, he'd guess at least thirty knots. If he'd been out for twenty-four hours they could have traveled over seven hundred miles. He followed the crewman forward and up a flight of stairs to the bridge where he opened a door and stood waiting for Albro to enter. He saw Elijah standing with binoculars raised to his eyes gazing toward the line of dark clouds.

"Ah, Mr. Swift, I trust you rested well," Elijah spoke without looking at him.

"How long was I out?" Albro asked.

Elijah lowered the glasses and turned to Albro. He said, "Twenty-six hours to be exact. You must be famished. I'm afraid that dinner is hours away. I will have some breakfast brought to you." He paused, spoke to a crewman, and then turned back to Albro. "What do you think of my ship? She's a beauty, isn't she? A gift from a grateful sheik for whom I'd done a favor. Originally built for the French navy, she's very seaworthy, and very fast. The sheik found little use for a naval vessel, but it suits my needs perfectly. I had it refitted, of course. No need to be Spartan when one can be comfortable."

"What have you done with the others?" Albro asked.

"I'm sorry to have to tell you that it was not possible to bring then on board. We barely made it ourselves. The storm was upon us and it was entirely too dangerous to attempt another trip to the freighter. I fear that it will not have survived the storm. Lucky for us, we were able to outrun the worst of it. Believe me, I feel your loss. Many have sacrificed their lives to bring us this far and they will not be forgotten." Elijah creased his brow in a look that was genuinely solemn.

"Where are the medallions?" Albro asked. He had no illusion that Elijah was going to tell him where they were, let alone, give them back to him, but he wanted to see what his face might tell him. Just the mention of the medallions instantly changed the look in his eyes from grieving solemnity to one of aloofness and cunning vengeance, and then that too disappeared.

Elijah smiled an avuncular smile. "That's one less thing for you to worry about. They are in a safe place and will remain there until they are needed."

"When and where will that be?" Albro asked.

"All in good time, my boy. All in good time." Elijah paused as if a new idea had suddenly occurred to him. "I want to show you something. Come with me."

Elijah led him through a door into a plush office space, similar to what one might find in the executive suite of an office tower except that it was on a much smaller scale. A highly polished mahogany table sat in the middle of the room with six black leather swivel chairs that were bolted to the floor. A panel screen filled one entire wall and on it was displayed a grid of longitude and latitude, and a myriad of tiny green lights flashed like a swarm of fireflies. Near the center a single red light glowed.

Elijah said, "The green lights are the positions of commercial vessels within a thousand mile radius. The red light is us. Now watch this." He pressed a spot on the table top. The green lights disappeared and yellow ones lit up, much fewer in number. "These are military vessels, including submarines. Fantastic, wouldn't you say? And here, watch this." He pressed more places on the table top. He was like a

545

proud parent showing off the talents of a precocious child. Blue lights appeared. "Aircraft. Utterly fantastic!" He gazed at the screen. "Now, if you wanted to indentify one of those lights," he paused while he moved a cursor across the screen until he found a target. A window opened on the spot and identified the aircraft as a commercial airliner bound for Honolulu.

"Do the Chinese and Americans know that you can do that?" Albro asked.

"I maintain close ties with several governments. I do certain favors for them and in return, I gain access to information that otherwise might be impossible to obtain. Officially, I don't exist. And that provides me with a remarkable freedom of movement. But enough about me."

The screen went blank. A knock came at the door and a steward entered carrying a silver tray loaded with covered dishes.

Elijah said to the steward, "Thank you. Set it there." He pointed to where Albro sat. The steward nodded and left the room. "Please, eat," he said.

Albro lifted the largest of the silver covers. Steam rose from a golden omelet. There was also a tray of toast, a bowl of fresh fruit, and a tall glass of milk. His stomach growled. He was starving, but he hesitated, thinking of his companions locked in the hold of the *Sanshui*. "If it's any consolation to you, your friends did exactly as they said they would. They all knew, Nancy Wong included, that they were not likely to survive this ordeal. There was nothing you could do to save them." Elijah said.

"You sent them to their deaths." Albro said.

Elijah brought his hands together and touched the tips of his gloved fingers to his lips and looked gravely at Albro as if he were a doctor about to impart some sobering news to his patient. "You understand so little."

"I understand enough to know that Isaiah, Walter and Nancy Wong do not need to die. I also know that you need all twelve medallions. I've made a rough accounting and I'm guessing that you're still short, and that's a problem because you're running out of time. I know where you can find one more. If you send out an emergency distress call to all ships in the area to search for the *Sanshui*, I will tell you where you can find it."

"There is no guarantee that your friends will be found."

"I realize that, but how else can I help them?"

Elijah tilted his head to the low ceiling while he contemplated Albro's offer. "Alright," he said, "the medallion first, then I will do as you request."

"No, you make the call first, or no deal. Even if I were to attempt to bluff you, what do you have to lose? There is no way that they can interfere with your plans."

Elijah gave Albro a long, hard look and then pressed a spot on the table top, and waited until a voice answered. He said, "Send out a distress call giving the last known position of the freighter, *Sanshui*. Make it appear as if the call originates from the *Sanshui* and make certain the call cannot be traced to us." He looked up at Albro. "There, I have done what you asked."

"Thanks," he said. "Can that screen give us a satellite image of the weather patterns?"

"Of course," Elijah said. He pressed the table top and immediately an image of the western Pacific came into view. In the center of the screen, a vast swirl of clouds spun like a whirlpool. It looked as benign as a lovely white rose opening on a warm summer day, but Albro knew that at the base of those clouds terrible winds were lifting the sea into mountainous waves.

Albro stepped to the screen and pointed to the center of the mass of clouds. "There," he said, "is your medallion." He then told Elijah everything about Nick Lane, about how Nick Lane had rescued them. He told him how Nick Lane had acquired the medallion and how he had taken a bullet through his skull. He then told about being on board the ship with Nick Lane. He told Elijah about the twelve caged monsters, except he left out how the one beast had spoken to him and how they had all chanted Crane's name, nor did he mention what the beast had held in its hand.

Elijah stared at the screen. His right hand slowly crept to the middle of his chest where it spread it fingers and moved in lazy concentric circles. The man seemed entranced by the swirling storm, and then Albro realized it was not the storm that had hijacked his attention, it was the prospect of getting his hands on another medallion. His eyes were drawn to Elijah's hand and he realized that the man had not locked them in his treasure vault, or some other inaccessible place. He had them around his neck. Albro could feel their pull, their power. He could take them now, they were telling him. He gripped the fork in his right hand and prepared himself to lunge the few feet that separated them and plunge the fork into Elijah's throat.

"You were nearly correct in your rough accounting," Elijah said without turning. "I now possess six of the medallions. Two more are in the possession of Martin Osborne Newton and his beautiful Monique, with whom I am told you are quite familiar. I will be joining them soon. With the one you have told me about, that makes nine. It is far more than I ever hoped for. Marlowe will provide a tenth. The lady who sleeps is unaware of the men who approach her door. They will bring another. Before he died, Thomas Crane told me where I would find the remaining medallion, and that will make twelve. A great circle will have closed and at the center of that circle we will place the *Jade Prince.*"

Elijah turned abruptly and bore his gaze down on Albro. Albro felt a sudden and excruciating pain in the hand that held the fork. He dropped it immediately and it clattered on the table top.

Elijah said, "I understand your thoughts, but you cannot harm me. Use that fork for what it was intended, and eat your meal. You are going to need your strength." Elijah strode from the cabin.

CHAPTER 52

ALBRO nervously paced the short distance from one wall where he would stop, turn sharply, and return to the opposite where he would begin again.   By any standard of ship board accommodations the room was luxurious, but to him, it felt like a cell. After he had finished his meal, Alexi had marched him back at gun point and locked the door. The ship had changed course and in the face of the oncoming winds, the vessel rose and fell in ever increasing arcs. They were heading directly into the storm in search of the MV *Jade Prince*, or whatever was the true name of that ghost ship. There was surprisingly little doubt in his mind that that they would find it, and when they did, Elijah would send his men on board and order them to kill Nick Lane, and retrieve another medallion.   And what about the medallion held by the creature named, Grod? Elijah had hinted that he knew of that one as well. But did he? Albro had a hunch that old Elijah was bluffing.

Albro racked his brain trying to recall every scrap of detail of the time he'd spent on board that ship, particularly the moments leading up to when the lights went out and the wheelhouse had erupted in an exchange of gunfire. Had he really seen what he thought he'd seen? He stopped suddenly and stared at his reflection in a mirror that hung above an ornate chest. He tried to imagine his own visage aged into a mask of deep lines, and a mane of white hair falling down to his shoulders. Had he really seen himself returning from a time far in the future, or was it he who had intruded upon the other man's time and space? And now, was he looping back around like an errant satellite caught in the gravitational grip of a larger body. The previous encounter had been a near miss. Would this encounter end in a direct hit?

What was he thinking? Hadn't it all been a dream? He gripped the sides of the dresser and leaned in closer until all he could see were his own eyes. Who was he looking at? Who had he been all of his life, and who was he becoming? Was there a constant, an unchanging soul, hidden in there somewhere, and if so, did it have an existence separate from the reality of flesh and bone? Did it romp freely among different realities dragging its fleshly counterpart along with it like a reluctant accomplice? Albro shuttered his eyes, dropped his head and let his shoulders sag. He would surrender, if only he knew what, or whom he could surrender to. He feels the ship shudder as it takes a wave on its bow.

He looks up, the mirror has disappeared and he is looking through a window of broken glass. Sand is blowing and a hot wind scorches his eyes. He blinks away tears, clears his vision, and sees a line of figures crossing a distant sand dune. At first, he is alarmed, thinking that the figures have spotted him, but they keep moving and soon disappear. He breathes a sigh of relief and turns to look at two individuals, a woman and an infant child, huddled in the shadowed corner of the room. He feels his heart nearly cleave, half in love, half in horror at the thought of what he will need to do. He knows that the individuals he has seen disappear will not be gone long. They will skirt the abandoned village and then circle back and begin a house to house search. At most, they will have an hour. He looks at the woman. She is beautiful, skin as white as marble. He remembers how, when they had first lain together, he could not resist passing his hands over her breasts, and belly and legs, and how he had stared into the depths of her yellow eyes. He turns away knowing that she can read his thoughts. They cannot save themselves, but they can save the child. Isaiah will be with them in a minute or two. Isaiah has the means to take only the child. After that, they will be captured. There is only one other alternative. He looks down at the heavy automatic thrust into his belt. It holds two bullets.

The turning of the lock startled him and the vision was suddenly replaced with his own grave reflection. Alexi came through the door. Water dripped from his face. His cool and arrogant countenance had disappeared. His eyes now held the look of uncertainty and in incipient fear. He said, "The Old Man is ready for you now."

"Thanks Alexi, but I think I'll just relax in my cabin," Albro said.

"Were you thinking this was going to be a pleasure cruise? Come with me." Alexi clamped a hand on Albro's arm.

Albro shook him off. "You look worried, Alexi. I've never known you to look worried. What's the matter?"

Alexi wiped back the sodden strands of hair that had fallen into his eyes and said evenly, "Yes, I am worried and if you really want to why, you'll come with me."

Albro was taken aback by Alexi's response; he'd never expected to hear Alexi Ruslonov admit such a thing. "If you know what's good for you, Alexi, you'll commandeer the ship and turn it around."

"That's impossible. You know that as well as I. We're all in this too deep, you included. Are you coming with me, or do I have to go for help?"

"I don't suppose you'd like to settle the issue by cutting cards," Albro said.

"Very funny," Alexi answered.

Alexi led Albro to the bridge. Elijah stood facing the thick, reinforced windows. Rain lashed the glass, smearing the view. Albro could discern an island of dark mountains, half hidden by a wall of dark clouds that roiled in shades of purple and black. Bolts of lightning fractured the clouds causing them to glow from within. And then Albro realized that what he was not looking at an island. It was a shear wall rising out of the ocean. He could see huge breakers smashing into it and spray flying high into the air.

"What is it?" Albro asked.

"That is your storm," Elijah said without turning.

"That has to be an island," Albro said, but as he said it, he knew that he was wrong.

551

"No," Elijah said. "Satellite imagery shows a storm of enormous magnitude and GPS confirms our position. "What we see is quite amazing. It is water in a dynamic flux, changing from liquid to solid to vapor. What you are looking at is ice is of such density that it does not reflect light and our radar cannot penetrate it."

"Then I must be wrong about the medallion," Albro said. "I must have been dreaming."

"No, you were not dreaming. It is in there, I can feel it." Elijah turned to face Albro. He had brought his gloved hand to his chest. His eyes seemed to glow with an unearthly radiance. "We have been cruising around the storm's perimeter for an hour. There has been no break. We could circle the entire storm and I'm sure that we would find the same thing. Someone has gone to a great deal of trouble to protect that medallion."

"Who could make something like that?" Albro asked.

"There are forces at work here that are beyond your comprehension," Elijah said.

"Then I guess you're out of luck," Albro said.

"Ah, fortunately for your sake, I am not," Elijah said. "You know, I tried once to have you killed. When I failed, I realized that I had misread the role that you were to play in finding the *Jade Prince*." Elijah paused, letting his eyes rest on Albro's face. "You're thinking of the incident in the snow, aren't you? Rest assured that was not my doing. When I learned about it, I found it very amusing that Marlowe would go to such ends to convince you to play along, but play along you did, to the benefit of all of us. You see, he and I have been in somewhat of a contest. Fortunately, the odds tipped in my favor when you escaped from my men.

"Forgive me, please," Elijah said. "I have confused you. I am referring to the time in the desert where you had fled with your lover and bastard child. You do remember that, don't you?"

Albro felt a lurch in his consciousness as when an elevator drops to another level.

Men are shouting for him to surrender. He places the barrel of the gun against the temple of the woman with yellow eyes.

"Was it luck that I found you here, in this far off time and place?" Elijah asked in a tone more rhetorical than challenging.

Albro looked at Elijah and his mind came alive with the full memory of that time.

It is dark and they have been running with bullets whizzing around them when she falls.

Albro heard Elijah's voice like an incongruous voiceover to the drama that is taking place as the memory unfolds in his mind.

"That is a very difficult question to answer," Elijah continued. "What is luck exactly? Is it that tiny percentage of uncertainty that exists in an otherwise predictable universe? Or is it simply a chimera conjured up by your subconscious in order to find hope in your hopelessly pitiful life? Or is it your soul's last grasp for salvation, a salvation that seems to forever recede into the future? Luck, hope, salvation, they all lie behind that wall out there and you are going to show me the way inside."

"I am?" Albro asked feeling dazed and confused. The roll of the ship added to his unbalanced state as he teetered between the memory and the reality of Elijah's voice.

"Our fates have been conjoined from the very beginning," Elijah said. "You feel that don't you?"

"I know what I remember and I feel what I know," Albro whispered.

"Good, that is very good," Elijah said. "And what is it you hope that knowledge will bring?"

"I hope," Albro began. He felt the floor lift as a wave passed under the ship. His knees flexed slightly absorbing the energy of the heaving ocean beneath him. "I hope," Albro said, "that in the end I will find the *Jade Prince*."

Elijah chuckled and shook his head, "*'Hope springs eternal in the human breast'*. Is that how the saying goes?"

"*'Man never is, but always to be blest'*. Alexander Pope," Albro said completing the quote, the words coming from somewhere deep within his store of memories.

"I am very curious. Does hope lend you the strength to survive, to persevere in the face of overwhelming odds? Or is it the yearning for God's blessing that drives man forever forward? How do you propose that something as evanescent as hope will guide you to the *Jade Prince*? There is only one way to find the *Jade Prince*."

Elijah clapped his hands. Two men grasped Albro by the wrists. They bent him over a metal table and tied his wrists to the legs. Albro felt another rope going around his waist and then tighten. He could move his legs, but his torso was immobilized.

"What are you doing?" Albro shouted. His mind had popped back to the very clear and dire present.

"Cut away his shirt," Elijah ordered.

Albro felt the cold edge of a blade run down his back and then the stripping away of his shirt. Elijah stood before him. Albro watched as Elijah worked the gloves from his hands. But instead of skin, Albro saw gray overlapping scales and instead of fingers he saw bony claws each ending in a curved, razor like talon.

Elijah said, "You did not know that I am Mongi. Ordinarily one born with such a severe abnormality would have been destroyed at birth, but these talons were taken to be a sign that I was the Chosen One, he who would one day lead the Mongi people. Others disagreed and they tried to kill me. Your friend Isaiah even tried to consume my body with fire. But as you can see, the flames never touched me. My fate lay on a different path from those who wished to destroy me.

"And now, that path has brought you to me. You are hiding something from me. If you do not show me, I will be forced to find it myself." He ran one of the talons lightly down the side of Albro's face.

Pain pierced Albro's skull, and a tiny river of blood appeared where the talon had touched him. He felt Elijah's thoughts enter his mind. "The image on my back," Albro uttered through clenched teeth. "You want to see the image on my back." Suddenly he knew why it had been put there. "It will show you where you can enter the wall."

"Yes," Elijah said. "Show it to me," he said softly and I will make the pain go away.

554

"Isaiah covered it with the Black Djinnim," Albro groaned. Pain raced through his skull like a fire running through dry grass. He could hear the pop and crackle of his teeth grinding together.

"Release it!" Elijah commanded.

"It's a part of me. I don't know how to make it not part of me," Albro heaved up the words and then struggled for breath.

"Then I will have to remove it physically," Elijah said.

Elijah moved beyond Albro's sight. He craned his neck around to see where Elijah had gone and then he felt an intense burning sensation across the top of his shoulders. His whole body convulsed in pain.

"Wait!" Albro pleaded breathlessly. "Let me try." He tried to focus his mind on the oozing, seething image of the thing that Walter had scooped into the bottle and that Isaiah later had released onto his back. He let everything else fall away from his consciousness until all he was aware of was his naked skin. Nothing happened for what seemed like ages of time and then he began to feel a prickling and then suddenly a myriad of tiny feet were crawling across his flesh like a seething, churning mass of ants. And then a trickling sensation ran up his neck and through his hair, probed his ears and then circled the side of his face until it found his nose at which point it became a torrent. He hiccupped loudly and the torrent filled his lungs. He coughed and gagged until the crawling sensation died away. At last he was able to take a ragged breath. An aura of ghostly blue light played at the corners of his vision. "Is it gone?" he croaked.

"Not gone," Elijah said. "Your intimate companion has simply relocated itself." He felt Elijah's claws touch his head and the pain flowed away.

"What do you see?" Albro had to force the words out of his mouth. He felt a terrible weight inside his chest, a presence that allowed little room for air.

"A most amazing sight," Elijah answered. "It is a shame that you cannot see it. But then, it was never meant for your eyes. Shall I describe it for you?"

"If it's not too much trouble for you," Albro said.

"It's no trouble at all." Elijah's voice was almost giddy with excitement. "Lower the lights," he commanded.

The room became dimmer which served to intensify the simmering glow. Albro could see that two crew members had donned dark glasses. Gradually the weight inside his chest eased. He had a sense that the Black Djinnim was changing itself from a foreign object into an element of his own body.

Elijah spoke, "Imagine if you will a window into the entirety of existence, all that has existed and all that ever will exist. Some might call it the *Eye of God*, all seeing, all knowing."

"And I was hoping for a sexy tattoo," Albro said.

"You make light of something that is beyond your comprehension. Let me demonstrate something for you. Let us say that I wish to see your beginning. I reach into the light and there you are in your mother's arms with your father standing next to her."

Albro felt an odd stirring in the flesh of his back. Was that a result of Elijah's claw reaching into him? Ripples of light flickered in his peripheral vision like a shadowy dance of puppet figures. He yearned to see what Elijah saw. He struggled to turn his head. If only he had the neck joints of an owl, or better yet, a poltergeist's ability to twist body parts into unimaginable shapes.

"You need not struggle," Elijah said gently. "I don't recommend it, but if you really want to see, you need only close your eyes."

Albro squeezed his eyes shut and for the briefest of moments he saw the woman with yellow eyes with a child swaddled in white silk sleeping in her folded arms, and the man, his face turned away, looking into the shadows at the unmistakable form and face of Isaiah. And then the image was snatched away.

"Wait!" Albro shouted. "I want to see more."

"I'm sure you do, but we have more important things to attend to. We must find our way through that wall."

"I won't help you," Albro said. "I said that I would show you where you could find the medallion. I didn't say that I would help you steal it."

"I see," Elijah said. His voice had gone cold. "Perhaps, you need some inducement." He dug a talon into Albro's armpit and pulled downward across his ribs, opening an inch deep wound that poured blood. Elijah said, "You were inside there. You told me so. If you were there once, you can go there again."

Albro writhed in pain. His side felt as if a searing brand had been thrust against his ribs. He gasped for breath. "That was different. I had my medallion, and I was alone," Albro said, each word a spasm of pain. His vision nearly faded to black. He could not mention that he had his doubts about the medallion's power. It wasn't some token that he could drop into a cosmic turnstile and hop onto the wormhole express to another space and time. Something else had happened. He had felt *her* presence. *She* had pulled him through. The sleeping lady, the woman with the yellow eyes, the exotic dancer, the mother of his.... He had almost thought, *child*, before catching himself. He tried to bring into his mind's eye her image, but he had a sinking feeling that the game was not played by those rules. She was the one who did the conjuring. She was the one who had sent those visions. "You can't expect me take a ship and entire crew."

"You are correct," Elijah said. "I don't expect that. All you need show me is the portal, the gateway, the crack that allowed you passage. Search your memory and leave the rest to me."

"I don't know what to look for, and if I did, I wouldn't recognize it." Albro sensed a growing puddle forming between his torso and the table.

"You underestimate your resourcefulness, my young friend. Perhaps you should call upon your yellow-eyed lady, or should I say, mother."

"What are you talking about?" Albro asked, in a panic. Was Elijah deliberately trying to confuse him? What did he know about the woman with the yellow eyes? What did he mean by referring to her as his mother? He had seen her holding the child, had watched as she had handed the infant to the rat man. Elijah had it wrong. Nevertheless, he felt himself reaching out to her.

557

He chokes as a swirl of dust penetrates the cloth covering around his face. Through its loose weave he can see shifting light and shadow. He can feel her arms around him. He can hear the rhythm of her breath, the beating of her heart. He can sense her conscious effort to not run. Above and beyond his tight enclosure, a cacophony of sound assaults them from every side. And then suddenly all is still. The sun has gone away and they are in deep shadow. The cloth falls from his eyes and he looks up at a rising wall of dark stone. He sees her hands unfold like the white wings of a dove from the sleeves of her garment and reach into a crevice of the stone wall where they flutter briefly, and then along invisible seams, the stones part and they are through.

Albro rolled his eyes. Sweat dripped from his brow and flowed into his eyes and down his cheeks like tears. He saw Elijah standing over him, his clawed hands crossed at his chest. Albro raised his head and said, "Take us closer to the wall. There is a crevice. Reach into it." He could say no more. He rested his head on the table and half-closed his eyes.

"There," Elijah said gently. "That wasn't so difficult, was it?" He laid his claw on Albro's head, and withdrew the pain. He then spoke to the man at the ship's controls, "Bring us as close to the wall as you dare."

The helmsman brought the ship in close to the wall. Its featureless surface rose out of the sea straight as a plum-line until it disappeared into the clouds. Wind driven waves smashed into its unyielding surface and shot hundreds of feet into the air before falling back as curtains of spray.

"That's as close as I can bring her," the helmsman stated. "Any closer and we risk being crushed."

"Hold us steady," Elijah ordered, but he was not looking at the unnatural spectacle before them. He had his eyes on Albro's back. There he studied the wall, but in a setting as incongruous as one could imagine. Instead of raging waves and slashing rain, it was a scene of bright sunlight and sand-strewn cobbles. His eyes scanned the polished stone looking for the anomaly in its uniformly featureless surface. He saw nothing until a small cloud drifted before the sun, and in its ensuing shadow he saw a crevice that was only a hair's breadth in width until he touched it, and then realized it was only a play of light and shadow that made it appear so small. He reached his hand into to it and felt the shape of a wheel. He grasped it with both of his clawed hands and began to turn it.

"There!" the helmsman shouted. All eyes save for Elijah's turned to scan the wall. A jagged crack was slowly opening. Great slabs of the black ice were cleaving off and falling into the ocean as if an invisible wedge were being driven up from below.

Elijah gave a final twist on the wheel and withdrew his hands from inside Albro's back. "Take us in," he commanded. He turned to the man at his side and said, "Carry him to his quarters and dress his wound."

Albro lay on his side, dimly aware of the two men who worked on him. He could feel the slight prick of the needle each time the medic poked it through his flesh and pulled the thread tight. He had vomited the meal he had eaten earlier. His throat was raw and burning and his mouth tasted sour.

"Water," he managed to whisper.

"In a moment," the medic said. "I'm nearly finished sewing you up."

"Bad?" Albro asked.

"You lost some blood," the medic answered. "You'll live, at least until the Old Man is finished with you."

Albro felt the medic give a final tug on the thread as he closed the last stitch. He heard the tearing of tape, felt the wound being covered with gauze.

"Sit up," the medic ordered.

Albro pushed himself into a sitting position. The room threatened to spin, but he caught it and held it still. The medic thrust a paper cup and some pills at him. "Take these," he said. "They'll help with the pain. Then the medic and his companion left the room. Albro heard the lock click into place. He drank the water and tossed the pills at the sink. He was going to need his wits about him. He thought briefly about Nancy and Isaiah and Walter and then dismissed them from his mind. There was nothing he could do for them now. They were on their own.

He eased off the bed and pressed his face to the port hole. The ship had gone from daylight to night. Ghostly outlines of whitecaps covered the sea and the wind grated against the metal superstructure of the ship as if it were seeking a handhold to rip it apart. No matter how brutal the conditions became, he knew that they would find the *Jade Prince* and attempt to board her. That was insane under these conditions, but then he remembered how the wind had died and the seas had calmed just before they had been boarded. The *Jade Prince* had entered the eye of the storm. The *Jade Prince* was out there with Nick Lane and his live cargo. Albro wandered, if he too, were on board. But that was crazy! That was then, and this was now! He was here with a sewn-up gash in his side and his back glowing like freakish video screen! Everything was different. But was it? Was this a facet he could not see until now? Was this *now*, a part of the whole that he could not have seen *then*? Albro's thoughts reeled in confused circles until he collapsed back on the bed. There was nothing he could do but wait, and he drifted away into a dreamless sleep.

Hours later, Albro was jolted awake by the screeching of metal against metal. The ship abruptly shifted direction and tossed him to the floor. He had lost all reckoning of time. Rain still lashed the ship and he could still hear the wind, but the storm was no longer the raging maelstrom they had sailed into earlier. The wound in his side had stiffened and he groaned as he struggled onto his feet. He went to the small window. It was still night. Perhaps this place had never known the light of day, and never would. A search light played across the waves and then found the stern of another ship. In bold letters he could read its name, MV JADE PRINCE. He could see its prop lazily turning as a wave heaved the vessel and tipped it into a trough. All but the top most section of the superstructure disappeared momentarily, and then the entire ship, whole and gigantic rose up and crested another wave.

Albro made the decision then that he was going on board, but not dressed as one of Elijah's men. He remembered Nick Lane's huge pistol and he wanted no mistake about who Nick Lane thought he might be. He found the clothes that he had been wearing earlier and changed into them. He caught a glimpse of himself in the mirror and stopped cold. His hair had gone white, and hung down to his shoulders. Age lines cut deep creases on both sides of his mouth and his brow was furrowed like a plowed field. He put a hand to his face and felt the leathery skin. He backed away from the mirror, aghast at what he saw. He could hear footsteps running on deck and Alexi shouting orders outside his door. He had no time to contemplate the image in the mirror. Quickly he opened the wardrobe and found a watch cap which he pulled over head and tucked up the long strands of hair. He reached for the foul weather jacket that hung there and got into it just as the door swung open and Alexi entered.

"You're coming with us, hurry!" Alexi ordered.

Alexi took him by the arm and pulled him forward. Albro kept his face down and averted and let himself be pulled through the door. A small army of men with guns slung over their shoulders had gathered amidships and were clambering over the rail and down a rope net to a waiting inflatable that rose and fell violently on the large swells. He spotted Elijah standing complacently at the bow as composed as a wood figurehead.

Alexi shouted into his ear, "You'll have to jump the last few feet! Wait until the craft rises!" And then he was being shoved forward. He gripped the rope and swung himself over and immediately felt the stitches tearing at his flesh and blood began to ooze down his side. He reached the bottom of the ladder and watched the inflatable rise and fall. Alexi shouted at him to jump, but his hands refused to release their grip. Then he was propelled downward as Alexi's boot landed between his shoulder blades, and he landed in the bottom of the boat. Hands gripped him and pulled him into a sitting position. The motors roared and they were riding the swells to the *Jade Prince*.

The much larger vessel loomed above them as they pulled alongside at her mid-ships. The stern was much lower, but Albro reckoned the turning prop made it much too dangerous to attempt boarding her there. Two men fired grappling hooks which caught on the rail. Four men ascended the slender ropes and together they hauled up a climbing net. The remaining men ascended. First among them was Elijah who climbed with surprising speed for an old man.

When all had gone Alexi prodded Albro with the nose of a pistol. "Go," he said.

By the time Albro reached the top, his breath was coming in short gasps, the pain in his side stabbing him with each intake of air. He clamped his arm down on the wound and hunched forward. Alexi grasped him by the shoulder, "This way," he ordered. The men had assembled where the deck met the superstructure. Alexi pushed Albro forward.

"You will lead us to the medallion," Elijah said.

Albro looked at Elijah whose silver hair blew away from his face in the warm wind. Albro shuddered. His knees felt weak. Was this fear, he wondered, or was it terror? He remembered with the clarity of just awakening from a nightmare the scene that was about to replay itself in the ship's wheelhouse. The explosion of Nick Lane's gun still rang in his ears. Had anything changed in the intervening hours, and if so would he recognize it for what it was in the chaos that was about to erupt? Then another question fed into his panic. Had any time even passed in this place? Had he made a mistake in telling Elijah about the existence of the remaining medallion? Had he made a deal with the Devil in order to save his companions? Albro suddenly felt the need to pray. He looked at Elijah and thought he saw the devilish countenance of the Reverend C. Dobson Powel, and the thought of prayer repulsed him.

"You two go first," Elijah ordered and pointed to two men. They unslung their automatic rifles. "You will go next," he said to Albro. "I want two men directly behind him. If he attempts to break ranks, shoot him. Do not hesitate for any reason. Remember, the man up there has a weapon. When we enter the wheelhouse, he will fire it. You must let him fire his weapon. Do you understand that?" Elijah paused to let that sink in. Then he said, "After he has fired his weapon, kill him. Let's go."

They began climbing the stairs. It did not take them long to reach the door to the wheel house. A yellow-green light glowed in its round glass. With every step, Albro had tried to think of something that would change the outcome of what was about to happen. In a few seconds, he would see his own, startled face, and shout for Nick Lane to not shoot. At that point, the throbbing diesels would drink their last sip of fuel and die, and the ship would be plunged into darkness, and the gun would go off. What would happen after that, he did not know.

Albro's heart pounded in his ears as he watched in seeming slow motion as the lead soldier swung open the door and then they were moving into the wheelhouse and then everything happened in a flash. He saw a shadowy figure standing at Nick Lane's side. He lunged forward in total disregard to the orders given to Elijah's men. He sensed a hand reach out for him, but it caught only his knit cap and he felt his long, white hair unfurl, not like a white flag of surrender, but as a plea to Nick Lane not fire his weapon.

Albro shouted, "DON'T SHOOT!" But it was to no avail. He saw Nick Lane draw the pistol from his belt and raise it with both hands, his finger wrapped around the trigger and then the shudder of the dying engines and suddenly the millisecond of absolute darkness before Nick Lane's gun exploded, a flare of bright orange flame cleaving the darkness and then the fusillade of bullets cutting to pieces everything in their path.

Albro threw himself to the deck and lay flat until the firing ceased. Someone produced a light and shone it around the room. He saw Nick Lane slumped against the opposite wall where the impact of the bullets had thrown him. Albro rushed to him, ignoring the commands to remain where he was. Blood poured out of Nick Lane's chest. As Albro knelt next to him, Nick Lane opened his one good eye and stared into Albro's face. His lips moved, and a trickle of blood ran down his chin. He took a ragged breath and coughed out blood. Albro leaned close and said, "I'm sorry."

Nick Lane managed to shake his head. "Nothing you could do," he whispered. "There's something you need to know..." He squeezed his eye shut in a spasm of pain and then drew another breath, "...about those creatures." Nick Lane coughed more blood. " I...I..." Nick Lane struggled to speak. He coughed blood as he tried to breathe.

"You what," Albro pleaded desperately. He could see Elijah approaching.

"I turned them loose," Nick Lane sighed with his last breath. Albro shook him, but he was already dead. His eye stared blankly into Albro's face.

"Stand up," Elijah said.

Before he stood, Albro closed Nick Lane's eye. "He's dead," he said.

"Yes, I can see that. Back away," Elijah ordered.

Albro straightened and turned to face Elijah. Someone had switched on the emergency lights. In the dim, hellish glow, he saw the shock of surprise in Elijah's face as a momentary tremor of uncertainty rippled across his features and disappeared as quickly as it came. Elijah turned to Nick Lane's body and reached down and lifted the medallion from around the dead man's neck. As he raised it to his face, a drop of blood dripped from its shiny surface. Albro thought he saw the boar grin in satisfaction that it would at last be joining its companions. Elijah slipped it around his neck and tucked it inside his tunic. An almost beatific smile spread across his otherwise devilish face. "*The Gathering* is nearly complete."

"You're still short," Albro said.

"The final medallions are not far away," Elijah said.

"Do you really believe that Monique will give them to you?" Albro asked.

"My dear boy, you have it all wrong. This has been *Her* game all along. I will be delivering these seven to her. Marlowe is already there. That makes ten, a nice round number and more than enough to complete the task. At this point, the two remaining medallions are superfluous."

"I don't believe you," Albro said.

"Believe what you like," Elijah said, "but you were caught in *Her* web long before you can even remember, or perhaps you will remember now that you have grown old. Tell me Albro Swift, how does it feel to appear and disappear in and out of time? It must be terribly confusing. Right now you are probably thinking that you will have one more chance to save yourself; that the layers of time and space will be reshuffled like a deck of playing cards and you will live to play another round. When you realize what awaits you out there in the darkness, you will know that you have placed your final bet and you have lost."

"The *Jade Prince* is a prisoner of this storm," Albro said. "You cannot release it from its grasp."

"You are correct," Elijah said. "Unless one holds all twelve medallions one could not hope to release the *Jade Prince*.

"Then you are as imprisoned as the *Jade Prince*," Albro said.

"That's where you have not understood your fate Albro Marshal Swift, or perhaps, I should call you Thomas Crane. You are the One who was chosen to release the *Jade Prince*, and you will do that for me. That yellow eyed witch thought she could remake you, and she came very close to succeeding. Is it the fate of all sons to become like their fathers? You have tried your best to keep me from releasing the *Jade Prince*, but like your father, you have failed. I needed you to play out this little drama, but I need you no longer. You will remain aboard this vessel with your twelve monsters."

Elijah moved to the window and looked out. "Let me tell you what lies out there at the center of this storm. There is a swirl of darkness, ever growing, ever expanding, and swallowing everything down its throat into nothingness so complete as to defy all rational thought. You would call it the beginning of the end. I call it the beginning of a new existence. The new cannot begin without the destruction of the old. The future cannot be free to fulfill its destiny if the past is within its reach. But I need not explain that to you. When you have released the *Jade Prince* from this world I will hunt down your Mongi mistress and your bastard child and I will personally pluck out their yellow eyes before I kill them both."

Albro lunged at Elijah and caught him by the throat. Even with blood leaking from his side he still had strength in his hands that he had never known, but the struggle did not last long. Elijah dug the talons of his claws into Albro's hands. Albro screamed as blood spurted from pierced veins and arteries. He released his grip, and a dozen hands pulled him backwards. A look of rage burned in the old man's eyes. He turned to his men. "Tie him to the cross arm of the mast!" he ordered. "In the last few moments of his life I want him to look upon the eternal darkness that awaits his soul. Hurry, we've no time to waste!"

Elijah's men dragged Albro from the wheelhouse and down to the main deck. The wind had returned and the ship, without the stabilizing thrust of its diesels, had begun to pitch and roll violently. They hoisted Albro fifty feet above the deck where two men lashed his outstretched arms to the opposing steel spars. His torso sagged, tearing the stitches from the wound in his side. Blood poured from his body and mixed with the rain and salty spray. He swayed in wide, wild arcs as the ship surrendered itself to the fury of the waves. Albro glimpsed Elijah standing alone at the rail looking up at him, and then he was gone.

Lightning crackled and the sky opened in a stinging deluge. The wind tore at his breath and he gasped for air. The rain came with such force he felt that he was slowly drowning. Was this a foretaste of what was to come when the ship finally rolled onto its side and he was plunged into the sea? No, he would not drown. The impact would certainly kill him, crushing him in an instant. He would have no chance to consciously inhale that last liquid breath.

Why had his life come to this? How had he come to inhabit the body of another man? The wind screamed at him through the rigging in a chorus of unknown tongues. He screamed back at them. "Who am I?" Although the words were snatched away even before they left his mouth, they reverberated in the hollow, empty and lonely recesses of his mind.

A massive wave struck the ship. He heard the screech and low the groan of tearing metal. He felt the agony of the old vessel vibrate through his spine and out through his arms. He thought of the poor, dumb creatures trapped somewhere in the ship. Did they have any sense that death was only minutes away? If he could help them, it would be to a purpose he did not know. Had Crane put them on this ship? If he had truly become Thomas Crane why could he not even answer that simplest of questions? He was not Crane. He could not be Crane. He was Albro Marshal Swift! He willed the ropes that held him to unravel, but nothing happened. He strained, pulling with all his strength until he cried out in a spasm of pain-filled defeat.

Lightning exploded searing his eyes into blindness. The ship yawed in a great gyrating turn, falling backward into a deep trough. His vision slowly returned and overhead he saw a mountainous crest begin to break. He opened his mouth to scream one last time. No sound emerged. Instead he saw what looked to be a black cloud of flies emerge and disappear into the night. The Black Djinnim had escaped to save itself. Albro laughed hysterically at this last bit of irony as a million tons of water fell onto the ship, pushing it down, down until only he remained above the surface. The ship wallowed beneath him, and then as if gathering the last of its strength, slowly rose above the surface. Albro looked down. In the nearly constant flashes of lightning he could see that the deck had been swept clean of its cranes and winches. If he could have turned, he would have seen that much of the superstructure had been torn away.

A wave gathered the crippled vessel like a giant hand and lifted it caringly, gently as one might lift an injured bird. The wave rose and at its extreme height Albro saw what Elijah had wanted him to see. There, beyond the battered bow of the ship, the ocean foamed and boiled in a churning whirlpool whose center held a velvety blackness, a seeming refuge from the terrible storm. Albro knew that in that darkness lay his ending, an ending so complete as to have little meaning in the conventional sense. It would be an ending that stripped away even his beginning, an ending that would erase every aspect of his life, every act, and every thought. Even his soul would be reduced to its elemental spark and then snuffed out, forgotten, never to be resurrected, an empty memory of an unformed thought.

The ship began to slide slowly down. Albro looked upon the emptiness that lay before him. Wind whipped the tears that flowed from his eyes. He thought of the lady who slept. Did she, in her dream, know what was about to happen to him? Was she trapped in the same nightmare? The ship lurched sharply as it was caught by the leading edge of the widening gyre. The wind howled in ear splitting oscillations, and suddenly he realized that it was not the wind, but the cry of voices spewing out of the black void. The ship canted sharply onto its side and

Albro closed his eyes and let the voices wash over him, anointing him in pure vibrations of agony and lament, of joy and laughter, of pain and fear. He felt the ship begin to break apart beneath him, the rending of steel blending seamlessly into the chorus that filled every crevice in his mind. He opened his eyes and looked up. The wind had torn a rent in the clouds and a lone star appeared.

As Albro's body began to disintegrate, he locked the star in his memory as if he were a traveler in need of a landmark to find his way home. But he knew there would be no way home. He had been forsaken by his mother and father, separated from each and every one of his friends and companions, beyond reach of the lady who slept. Had he merely imagined her? Had it all been a dream? Did the *Jade Prince* truly exist? He watched as the star stretched into an infinite curve of dimming red light. He could no longer feel his body and he knew that his mind was going. He offered up one last, whispering thought, a questioning plea to any part of the universe that might still be listening, *"Why, father, did you abandon me?"*

THE END

Made in the USA
San Bernardino, CA
11 March 2019